A
McBAIN
Omnibus

Ed McBain, who is also known
as the novelist Evan Hunter,
lives in Norwalk, Connecticut.

A
McBAIN
Omnibus

DOLL

FUZZ

DOWNTOWN

Mandarin

A Mandarin Paperback

A MCBAIN OMNIBUS

Doll first published in Great Britain 1966
by Hamish Hamilton Ltd
Published by Mandarin Paperbacks 1991

Fuzz first published in Great Britain 1968
by Hamish Hamilton Ltd
Published by Mandarin Paperbacks 1991

Downtown first published in Great Britain 1989
by William Heinemann Ltd
Published by Mandarin Paperbacks 1990

First published in this omnibus edition 1992
by Mandarin Paperbacks
an imprint of Reed Consumer Books Limited
Michelin House, 81 Fulham Road, London SW3 6RB
and Auckland, Melbourne, Singapore and Toronto

Doll copyright © Evan Hunter 1965
Fuzz copyright © Doubleday & Co. Inc. 1968
Downtown copyright © 1989 by HUI Corporation
This omnibus edition copyright © 1992 by HUI Corporation

A CIP catalogue record for this title
is available from the British Library
ISBN 0 7493 1401 X

Phototypeset by Intype, London
Printed and bound in Great Britain
by Cox & Wyman Ltd, Reading, Berks.

DOLL

A novel of the 87th precinct

*this, too, is for
Dodie and Ray Crane*

The city in these pages is imaginary.
The people, the places are all fictitious.
Only the police routine is based on
established investigatory technique.

1

The child Anna sat on the floor close to the wall and played with her doll, talking to it, listening. She could hear the voices raised in anger coming from her mother's bedroom through the thin separating wall, but she busied herself with the doll and tried not to be frightened. The man in her mother's bedroom was shouting now. She tried not to hear what he was saying. She brought the doll close to her face and kissed its plastic cheek, and then talked to it again, and listened.

In the bedroom next door, her mother was being murdered.

Her mother was called Tinka, a chic and lacquered label concocted by blending her given name, Tina, with her middle name, Karin. Tinka was normally a beautiful woman, no question about it. She'd have been a beautiful woman even if her name were Beulah. Or Bertha. Or perhaps even Brunhilde. The Tinka tag only enhanced her natural good looks, adding an essential gloss, a necessary polish, an air of mystery and adventure.

Tinka Sachs was a fashion model.

She was, no question about it, a very beautiful woman. She possessed a finely sculptured face that was perfectly suited to the demands of her profession, a wide forehead, high pronounced cheekbones, a generous mouth, a patrician nose, slanted green eyes flecked with chips of amber; oh, she was normally a beauty, no question about it. Her body was a model's body, lithe and loose and gently angled, with long slender legs, narrow hips, and a tiny bosom. She walked with

7

a model's insinuating glide, pelvis tilted, crotch cleaving the air, head erect. She laughed with a model's merry shower of musical syllables, painted lips drawing back over capped teeth, amber eyes glowing. She sat with a model's carelessly draped ease, posing even in her own living room, invariably choosing the wall or sofa that best offset her clothes, or her long blonde hair, or her mysterious green eyes flecked with chips of amber; oh, she was normally a beauty.

She was not so beautiful at the moment.

She was not so beautiful because the man who followed her around the room shouting obscenities at her, the man who stalked her from wall to wall and boxed her into the narrow passage circumscribed by the king-sized bed and the marble-top dresser opposite, the man who closed in on her oblivious to her murmuring, her pleading, her sobbing, the man was grasping a kitchen knife with which he had been slashing her repeatedly for the past three minutes.

The obscenities spilled from the man's mouth in a steady unbroken torrent, the anger having reached a pitch that was unvaried now, neither rising or falling in volume or intensity. The knife blade swung in a short, tight arc, back and forth, its rhythm as unvaried as that of the words that poured from the man's mouth. Obscenities and blade, like partners in an evil copulation, moved together in perfect rhythm and pitch, enveloping Tinka in alternating splashes of blood and spittle. She kept murmuring the man's name pleadingly, again and again, as the blade ripped into her flesh. But the glittering arc was relentless. The razor-sharp blade, the monotonous flow of obscenities, inexorably forced her bleeding and torn into the far corner of the room, where the back of her head collided with an original Chagall, tilting it slightly askew, the knife moving in again in its brief terrifying arc, the blade slicing parallel bleeding ditches across her small breasts and moving lower across the flat abdomen, her peignoir tearing again with a clinging silky blood-sotted sound as the knife blade plunged deeper with each step closer he took. She said his name once more, she shouted his name, and then she murmured the word "Please", and then she fell back against the wall again, knocking the Chagall from its hook so that a riot of framed color dropped heavily over her shoulder, falling in a lopsided angle past the long blonde hair, and the open red gashes across her throat and naked chest, the tattered blue peignoir, the natural brown of her exposed pubic hair, the blue satin slippers. She fell gasping for breath, spitting blood, headlong over the painting, her forehead colliding with the wide oaken frame, her blonde hair covering the Chagall reds and yellows and violets with a fine misty golden haze, the knife slash across her throat pouring blood onto the canvas, setting her hair afloat in a pool of red that finally overspilled the oaken frame and ran onto the carpet.

Next door, the child Anna clung fiercely to her doll.

She said a reassuring word to it, and then listened in terror as she heard footfalls in the hall outside her closed bedroom door. She kept listening breathlessly until she heard the front door to the apartment open and then close again.

She was still sitting in the bedroom, clutching her doll, when the superintendent came up the next morning to change a faucet washer Mrs Sachs had complained about the day before.

April is the fourth month of the year.

It is important to know that – if you are a cop, you can sometimes get a little confused.

More often than not, your confusion will be compounded of one part exhaustion, one part tedium, and one part disgust. The exhaustion is an ever present condition and one to which you have become slowly accustomed over the years. You know that the department does not recognize Saturdays, Sundays, or legal holidays, and so you are even prepared to work on Christmas morning if you have to, especially if someone intent on committing mischief is inconsiderate enough to plan it for that day – witness General George Washington and the unsuspecting Hessians, those drunks. You know that a detective's work schedule does not revolve around a fixed day, and so you have learned to adjust to your odd waking hours and your shorter sleeping time, but you have never been able to adjust to the nagging feeling of exhaustion that is the result of too much crime and too few hours, too few men to pit against it. You are sometimes a drag at home with your wife and children, but that is only because you are tired, boy what a life, all work and no play, wow.

The tedium is another thing again, but it also helps to generate confusion. Crime is the most exciting sport in the world, right? Sure, ask anybody. Then how come it can be so boring when you're a working cop who is typing reports in triplicate and legging it all over the city talking to old ladies in flowered house dresses in apartments smelling of death? How can the routine of detection become something as prescribed as the ritual of a bullfight, never changing, so that even a gun duel in a nighttime alley can assume familiar dimensions and be regarded with the same feeling of ennui that accompanies a routine request to the B.C.I.? The boredom is confusing as hell. It clasps hands with the exhaustion and makes you wonder whether this is January or Friday.

The disgust comes into it only if you are a human being. Some cops aren't. But if you are a human being, you are sometimes appalled by what your fellow human beings are capable of doing. You can understand lying because you practice it in a watered-down form as a daily method of smoothing the way, helping the machinery of mankind to function more easily without getting fouled by too much truth-stuff. You can understand stealing because when you were a kid you sometimes swiped pencils from the public school supply closet, and once a toy airplane from the five and ten. You can even understand murder because there is a dark and secret place in your own heart where you have hated deeply enough to kill. You can understand all these things, but you are nonetheless disgusted when they are piled upon you in profusion, when you are constantly confronted with liars, thieves, and slaughterers, when all human decency seems in a state of suspension for the eight or twelve or thirty-six hours you are in the squadroom or out answering a squeal. Perhaps you could accept an occasional corpse – death is only a part of life, isn't it? It is corpse heaped upon corpse that leads to disgust and further leads to confusion. If you can no longer tell one corpse from another, if you can no longer distinguish one open bleeding head from the next, then how is April any different from October?

It was April.

The torn and lovely woman lay in profile across the bloody

face of the Chagall painting. The lab technicians were dusting for latent prints, vacuuming for hairs and traces of fiber, carefully wrapping for transportation the knife found in the corridor just outside the bedroom door, the dead girl's pocket book, which seemed to contain everything but money.

Detective Steve Carella made his notes and then walked out of the room and down the hall to where the little girl sat in a very big chair, her feet not touching the floor, her doll sleeping across her lap. The little girl's name was Anna Sachs – one of the patrolmen had told him the moment Carella arrived. The doll seemed almost as big as she did.

"Hello," he said to her, and felt the old confusion once again, the exhaustion because he had not been home since Thursday morning, the tedium because he was embarking on another round of routine questioning, and the disgust because the person he was about to question was only a little girl and her mother was dead and mutilated in the room next door. He tried to smile. He was not very good at it. The little girl said nothing. She looked up at him out of very big eyes. Her lashes were long and brown, her mouth drawn in stoic silence beneath a nose she had inherited from her mother. Unblinkingly, she watched him. Unblinkingly, she said nothing

"Your name is Anna, isn't it?" Carella said.

The child nodded.

"Do you know what my name is?"

"No."

"Steve."

The child nodded again.

"I have a little girl about your age," Carella said. "She's a twin. How old *are* you, Anna?"

"Five."

"That's just how old my daughter is."

"Mmm," Anna said. She paused a moment, and then asked, "Is Mommy killed?"

"Yes," Carella said. "Yes, honey, she is."

"I was afraid to go in and look."

"It's better you didn't."

"She got killed last night, didn't she?" Anna asked.

"Yes."

There was a silence in the room. Outside, Carella could

hear the muted sounds of a conversation between the police photographer and the m.e. An April fly buzzed against the bedroom window. He looked into the child's upturned face.

"Were you here last night?" he asked.

"Um-huh."

"Where?"

"Here. Right here in my room." She stroked the doll's cheek, and then looked up at Carella and asked, "What's a twin?"

"When two babies are born at the same time."

"Oh."

She continued looking up at him, her eyes tearless, wide, and certain in the small white face. At last she said, "The man did it."

"What man?" Carella asked.

"The one who was with her."

"Who?"

"Mommy. The man who was with her in her room."

"Who was the man?"

"I don't know."

"Did you see him?"

"No. I was here playing with Chatterbox when he came in."

"Is Chatterbox a friend of yours?"

"Chatterbox is my *dolly*," the child said, and she held up the doll and giggled, and Carella wanted to scoop her into his arms, hold her close, tell her there was no such thing as sharpened steel and sudden death.

"When was this, honey?" he asked. "Do you know what time it was?"

"I don't know," she said, and shrugged. "I only know how to tell twelve o'clock and seven o'clock, that's all."

"Well . . . was it dark?"

"Yes, it was after supper."

"This man came in after supper, is that right?"

"Yes."

"Did your mother know this man?"

"Oh, yes," Anna said. "She was laughing and everything when he first came in."

"Then what happened?"

"I don't know," Anna shrugged again. "I was here playing."

12

There was another silence.

The first tears welled into her eyes suddenly, leaving the rest of the face untouched; there was no trembling of lip, no crumbling of features, the tears simply overspilled her eyes and ran down her cheeks. She sat as still as a stone, crying soundlessly while Carella stood before her helplessly, a hulking man who suddenly felt weak and ineffective before this silent torrent of grief.

He gave her his handkerchief.

She took it wordlessly and blew her nose, but she did not dry her eyes. Then she handed it back to him and said, "Thank you," with the tears still running down her face endlessly, sitting stunned with her small hands folded over the doll's chest.

"He was hitting her," she said. "I could hear her crying, but I was afraid to go in. So I . . . I made believe I didn't hear. And then . . . then I *really* didn't hear. I just kept talking with Chatterbox, that was all. That way I couldn't hear what he was doing to her in the other room."

"All right, honey," Carella said. He motioned to the patrolman standing in the doorway. When the patrolman joined him, he whispered, "Is her father around? Has he been notified?"

"Gee, I don't know," the patrolman said. He turned and shouted, "Anybody know if the husband's been contacted?"

A Homicide cop standing with one of the lab technicians looked up from his notebook and said, "He's in Arizona. They been divorced for three years now."

Lieutenant Peter Byrnes was normally a patient and understanding man, but there were times lately when Bert Kling gave him a severe pain in the ass. And whereas Byrnes, being patient and understanding, could appreciate the reasons for Kling's behaviour, this in no way made Kling any nicer to have around the office. The way Byrnes figured it, psychology was certainly an important factor in police work because it helped you to recognize that there were no longer any villains in the world, there were only disturbed people. Psychology substituted understanding for condemnation. It was a very nice tool to possess, psychology was, until a cheap thief kicked you in the groin one night. It then become somewhat difficult to imagine the thief as a put-upon soul who'd had a shabby childhood. In much the same way, though Byrnes completely understood the trauma that was responsible for Kling's current behavior, he was finding it more and more difficult to accept Kling as anything but a cop who was going to hell with himself.

"I want to transfer him out," he told Carella that morning.

"Why?"

"Because he's disrupting the whole damn squadroom that's why," Byrnes said. He did not enjoy discussing this, nor would he normally have asked for consultation on any firm decision he had made. His decision, however, was anything but final, that was the damn thing about it. He liked Kling, and yet he no longer liked him. He thought he could be a good cop, but he was turning into a bad one. "I've got enough bad cops around here," he said aloud.

"Bert isn't a bad cop," Carella said. He stood before Byrnes's cluttered desk in the corner office and listened to the sounds of early spring on the street outside the building, and he thought of the five-year-old girl named Anna Sachs who had taken his handkerchief while the tears streamed down her face.

"He's a surly shit," Byrnes said. "Okay, I know what happened to him, but people have died before, Steve, people have been killed before. And if you're a man you grow up to it, you don't act as if everybody's responsible for it. We didn't have anything to do with his girl friend's death, that's the plain and simple truth, and I personally am sick and tired of being blamed for it."

"He's not blaming you for it, Pete. He's not blaming any of us."

"He's blaming the *world*, and that's worse. This morning, he had a big argument with Meyer just because Meyer picked up the phone on his desk. I mean, the goddamn phone was ringing, so instead of crossing the room to his own desk, Meyer picked up the closest phone, which was on Kling's desk, so Kling starts a row. Now you can't have that kind of attitude in a squadroom where men are working together, you can't have it, Steve. I'm going to ask for his transfer."

"That'd be the worst thing that could happen to him."

"It'd be the best thing for the squad."

"I don't think so."

14

"Nobody's asking your advice," Byrnes said flatly.

"Then why the hell did you call me in here?"

"You see what I mean?" Byrnes said. He rose from his desk abruptly and began pacing the floor near the meshed-grill windows. He was a compact man and he moved with an economy that belied the enormous energy in his powerful body. Short for a detective, muscular, with a bullet-shaped head and small blue eyes set in a face seamed with wrinkles, he paced briskly behind his desk and shouted, "You see the trouble he's causing? Even you and I can't sit down and have a sensible discussion about him without starting to yell. That's *just* what I mean, that's *just* why I want him out of here."

"You don't throw away a good watch because it's running a little slow," Carella said.

"Don't give me any goddamn similes," Byrnes said. "I'm running a squadroom here, not a clock shop."

"Metaphors," Carella corrected.

"What*ever*," Byrnes said. "I'm going to call the Chief tomorrow and ask him to transfer Kling out. That's it."

"Where?"

"What do you mean *where*? What do I care where? Out of here, that's all."

"But *where*? To another squadroom with a bunch of strange guys, so he can get on *their* nerves even more than he does ours? So he can—"

"Oh, so you admit it."

"That Bert gets on my nerves? Sure, he does."

"And the situation isn't improving, Steve, you know that too. It gets worse every day. Look, what the hell am I wasting my breath for? He goes, and that's it." Byrnes gave a brief emphatic nod, and then sat heavily in his chair again, glaring up at Carella with an almost childish challenge on his face.

Carella sighed. He had been on duty for close to fifty hours now, and he was tired. He had checked in at eight-forty-five Thursday morning, and had been out all that day gathering information for the backlog of cases that had been piling up all through the month of March. He had caught six hours' sleep on a cot in the locker room that night, and then been called out at seven on Friday morning by the fire department, who suspected arson in a three-alarm blaze they'd answered on the

South Side. He had come back to the squadroom at noon to find four telephone messages on his desk. By the time he had returned all the calls – one from an assistant m.e. who took a full hour to explain the toxicological analysis of a poison they had found in the stomach contents of a beagle, the seventh such dog similarly poisoned in the past week – the clock on the wall read one-thirty. Carella sent down for a pastrami on rye, a container of milk, and a side of French fries. Before the order arrived, he had to leave the squadroom to answer a burglary squeal on North Eleventh. He did not come back until five-thirty, at which time he turned the phone over to a complaining Kling and went down to the locker room to try to sleep again. At eleven o'clock Friday night, the entire squad, working in flying wedges of three detectives to a team, culminated a two-month period of surveillance by raiding twenty-six known numbers banks in the area, a sanitation project that was not finished until five on Saturday morning. At eight-thirty a.m., Carella answered the Sachs squeal and questioned a crying little girl. It was now ten-thirty a.m., and he was tired, and he wanted to go home, and he didn't want to argue in favor of a man who had become everything the lieutenant said he was, he was just too damn weary. But earlier this morning he had looked down at the body of a woman he had not known at all, had seen her ripped and lacerated flesh, and had felt a pain bordering on nausea. Now – weary, bedraggled, unwilling to argue – he could remember the mutilated beauty of Tinka Sachs, and he felt something of what Bert Kling must have known in that Culver Avenue bookshop not four years ago when he'd held the bullet-torn body of Claire Townsend in his arms.

"Let him work with me," he said.

"What do you mean?"

"On the Sachs case. I've been teaming with Meyer lately. Give me Bert instead."

"What's the matter, don't you like Meyer?"

"I *love* Meyer, I'm tired, I want to go home to bed, will you please let me have Bert on this case?"

"What'll that accomplish?"

"I don't know."

"I don't approve of shock therapy," Byrnes said. "This

16

Sachs woman was brutally murdered. All you'll do is remind Bert—"

"Therapy, my ass," Carella said. "I want to be with him. I want to talk to him. I want to let him know he's still got some people on this goddamn squad who think he's a decent human being worth saving. Now, Pete, I *really* am very tired and I don't want to argue this any further, I mean it. If you want to send Bert to another squad, that's your business, you're the boss here, I'm not going to argue with you, that's all. I mean it. Now just make up your mind, okay?"

"Take him," Byrnes said.

"Thank you," Carella answered. He went to the door. "Good night," he said, and walked out.

2

Sometimes a case starts like sevens coming out.

The Sachs case started just that way on Monday morning when Steve Carella and Bert Kling arrived at the apartment building on Stafford Place to question the elevator operator.

The elevator operator was close to seventy years old, but he was still in remarkable good health, standing straight and tall, almost as tall as Carella and of the same general build. He had only one eye, however – he was called Cyclops by the superintendent of the building and by just about everyone else he knew – and it was this single fact that seemed to make him a somewhat less than reliable witness. He had lost his eye, he explained, in World War I. It had been bayoneted out of his head by an advancing German in the Ardennes Forest. Cyclops – who up to that time had been called Ernest – had backed away from the blade before it had a chance to pass completely through his eye and into his brain, and then had carefully and passionlessly shot the German three times in the chest, killing him. He did not realize his eye was gone until he got back to the aid station. Until then, he thought the bayonet had only gashed his brow and caused a flow of blood that made it difficult to see. He was proud of his missing eye, and proud of the nickname Cyclops. Cyclops had been a giant, and although Ernest Messner was only six feet tall, he had lost his eye for democracy, which is as good a cause as any for which to lose an eye. He was also very proud of his remaining eye, which he claimed was capable of twenty/twenty vision. His remaining eye was a clear penetrating blue, as sharp as the mind lurking somewhere behind it. He listened intelligently to everything the two detectives asked him, and then he said, "Sure, I took him up myself."

"You took a man up to Mrs Sachs's apartment Friday night?" Carella asked.

"That's right."

"What time was this?"

Cyclops thought for a moment. He wore a black patch over his empty socket, and he might have looked a little like an aging Hathaway Shirt man in an elevator uniform, except that he was bald. "Must have been nine or nine-thirty, around then."

"Did you take the man *down*, too?"

"Nope."

"What time did you go off?"

"I didn't leave the building until eight o'clock in the morning."

"You work from when to when, Mr Messner?"

"We've got three shifts in the building," Cyclops explained. "The morning shift is eight a.m. to four p.m. The afternoon shift is four p.m. to midnight. And the graveyard shift is midnight to eight a.m."

"Which shift is yours?" Kling asked.

"The graveyard shift. You just caught me, in fact. I'll be relieved here in ten minutes."

"If you work at midnight, what were you doing here at nine p.m. Monday?"

"Fellow who has the shift before mine went home sick. The super called me about eight o'clock, asked if I could come in early. I did him the favor. That was a long night, believe me."

"It was an even longer night for Tinka Sachs," Kling said.

"Yeah. Well, anyway, I took that fellow up at nine, nine-thirty, and he still hadn't come down by the time I was relieved,"

"At eight in the morning," Carella said.

"That's right."

"Is that usual?" Kling asked.

"What do you mean?"

"Did Tinka Sachs usually have men coming here who went

19

up to her apartment at nine, nine-thirty and weren't down by eight the next morning?"

Cyclops blinked with his single eye. "I don't like to talk about the dead," he said.

"We're here precisely so you *can* talk about the dead," Kling answered. "And about the living who visited the dead. I asked you a simple question, and I'd appreciate a simple answer. Was Tinka Sachs in the habit of entertaining men all night long?"

Cyclops blinked again. "Take it easy, young fellow," he said. "You'll scare me right back into my elevator."

Carella chose to laugh at this point, breaking the tension. Cyclops smiled in appreciation.

"You understand, don't you?" he said to Carella. "What Mrs Sachs did up there in her apartment was *her* business, not anyone else's."

"Of course," Carella said. "I guess my partner was just wondering why you weren't suspicious. About taking a man up who didn't come down again. That's all."

"Oh," Cyclops thought for a moment. Then he said, "Well, I didn't give it a second thought."

"Then it *was* usual, is that right?" Kling asked.

"I'm not saying it was usual, and I'm not saying it wasn't. I'm saying if a woman over twenty-one wants to have a man in her apartment, it's not for me to say how long he should stay, all day or all night, it doesn't matter to me, sonny. You got that?"

"I've got it," Kling said flatly.

"And I don't give a damn what they do up there, all day or all night, that's their business if they're old enough to vote. You got that, too?"

"I've got it," Kling said.

"Fine," Cyclops answered, and he nodded.

"Actually," Carella said, "the man didn't *have* to take the elevator down, did he? He could have gone up to the roof, and crossed over to the next building."

"Sure," Cyclops said. "I'm only saying that neither me nor anybody else working in this building has the right to wonder about what anybody's doing up there or how long they're taking to do it, or whether they choose to leave the building by the front door or the roof or the steps leading to the basement or even by jumping out the window, it's none of our business. You close that door, you're private. That's my notion."

"That's a good notion," Carella said.

"Thank you."

"You're welcome."

"What'd the man look like?" Kling asked. "Do you remember?"

"Yes, I remember," Cyclops said. He glanced at Kling coldly, and then turned to Carella. "Have you got a pencil and some paper?"

"Yes," Carella said. He took a notebook and a slender gold pen from his inside jacket pocket. "Go ahead."

"He was a tall man, maybe six-two or six-three. He was blond. His hair was very straight, the kind of hair Sonny Tufts has, do you know him?"

"Sonny *Tufts*?" Carella said.

"That's right, the movie star, him. This fellow didn't look at all like him, but is hair was the same sort of straight blond hair."

"What color were his eyes?" Kling asked.

"Didn't see them. He was wearing sunglasses."

"At night?"

"Lots of people wear sunglasses at night nowadays," Cyclops said.

"That's true," Carella said.

"Like masks," Cyclops added.

"Yes."

"He was wearing sunglasses, and also he had a very deep tan, as if he'd just come back from down south someplace. He had on a light grey raincoat; it was drizzling a little Friday night, do you recall?"

"Yes, that's right," Carella said. "Was he carrying an umbrella?"

"No umbrella."

"Did you notice any of his clothing under the raincoat?"

"His suit was a dark grey, charcoal grey, I could tell that by his trousers. He was wearing a white shirt – it showed up here, in the opening of the coat – and a black tie."

"What color were his shoes?"

"Black."

"Did you notice any scars or other marks on his face or hands?"

"No."

"Was he wearing any rings?"

"A gold ring with a green stone on the pinky of his right hand – no, wait a minute, it was his left hand."

"Any other jewelry you might have noticed? Cuff links, tie clasp?"

"No, I didn't see any."

"Was he wearing a hat?"

"No hat."

"Was he clean-shaven?"

"What do you mean?"

"Did he have a beard or a mustache?" Kling said.

"No. He was clean-shaven."

"How old would you say he was?"

"Late thirties, early forties."

"What about his build? Heavy, medium, or slight?"

"He was a big man. He wasn't fat, but he was a big man, muscular. I guess I'd have to say he was heavy. He had very big hands. I noticed the ring on his pinky looked very small for his hand. He was heavy, I'd say, yes, very definitely."

"Was he carrying anything? Briefcase, suitcase, attaché—"

"Nothing."

"Did he speak to you?"

"He just gave me the floor number, that's all. Nine, he said. That was all."

"What sort of voice did he have? Deep, medium, high?"

"Deep."

"Did you notice any accent or regional dialect?"

"He only said one word. He sounded like anybody else in the city."

"I'm going to say that word several ways," Carella said. "Would you tell me which way sounded most like him?"

"Sure, go ahead."

"Ny-un," Carella said.

"Nope."

"Noin."

"Nope."

"Nahn."

"Nope."

"Nan."

"Nope."

"Nine."

"That's it. Straight out. No decorations."

"Okay, good," Carella said. "You got anything else, Bert?"

"Nothing else," Kling said.

"You're a very observant man," Carella said to Cyclops.

"All I do every day is look at the people I take up and down," Cyclops answered. He shrugged. "It makes the job a little more interesting."

"We appreciate everything you've told us," Carella said. "Thank you."

"Don't mention it."

Outside the building, Kling said, "The snotty old bastard."

"He gave us a lot," Carella said mildly.

"Yeah."

"We've really got a good description now."

"*Too* good, if you ask me."

"What do you mean?"

"The guy has one eye in his head, and one foot in the grave. So he reels off details even a trained observer would have missed. He might have been making up the whole thing, just to prove he's not a worthless old man."

"Nobody's worthless," Carella said mildly. "Old or otherwise."

"The humanitarian school of criminal detection," Kling said.

"What's wrong with humanity?"

"Nothing. It was a human being who slashed Tinka Sachs to ribbons, wasn't it?" Kling asked.

And to this, Carella had no answer.

A good modeling agency serves as a great deal more than a booking office for the girls it represents. It provides an answering service for the busy young girl about town, a baby-sitting service for the working mother, a guidance-and-counseling service for the man-beleaguered model, a *pied-à-terre* for the harried and hurried between-sittings beauty.

Art and Leslie Cutler ran a good modeling agency. They ran it with the precision of a computer and the understanding of an analyst. Their offices were smart and walnut-paneled, a suite of three rooms on Carrington Avenue, near the bridge leading to Calm's Point. The address of the agency was announced over a doorway leading to a flight of carpeted steps. The address plate resembled a Parisian street sign, white enameled on a blue field, 21 Carrington, with the blue-carpeted steps beyond leading to the second story of the building. At the top of the stairs there was a second blue-and-white enameled sign, Paris again, except that this one was lettered in lowercase and it read, the cutlers.

Carella and Kling climbed the steps to the second floor, observed the chic nameplate without any noticeable show of appreciation, and walked into a small carpeted entrance foyer in which stood a white desk starkly fashionable against the walnut walls, nothing else. A girl sat behind the desk. She was astonishingly beautiful, exactly the sort of receptionist one would expect in a modeling agency; if she was only the receptionist, my God, what did the *models* look like?

"Yes, gentlemen, may I help you?" she asked. Her voice was Vassar out of finishing school out of country day. She wore eyeglasses with exaggerated black frames that did nothing whatever to hide the dazzling brilliance of her big blue eyes. Her makeup was subdued and wickedly innocent, a touch of pale pink on her lips, a blush of rose at her cheeks, the frames of her spectacles serving as a liner for her eyes. Her hair was black and her smile was sunshine. Carella answered with a sunshine smile of his own, the one he usually reserved for movie queens he met at the governor's mansion.

"We're from the police," he said. "I'm Detective Carella; this is my partner, Detective Kling."

"Yes?" the girl said. She seemed completely surprised to have policemen in her reception room.

"We'd like to talk to either Mr or Mrs Cutler," Kling said. "Are they in?"

"Yes, but what is this in reference to?" the girl asked.

"It's in reference to the murder of Tinka Sachs," Kling said.

"Oh," the girl said. "Oh, yes." She reached for a button on the executive phone panel, hesitated, shrugged, looked up at them with radiant blue-eyed innocence, and said, "I suppose you have identification and all that."

Carella showed her his shield. The girl looked expectantly

at Kling. Kling sighed, reached into his pocket, and opened his wallet to where his shield was pinned to the leather.

"We never get detectives up here," the girl said in explanation, and pressed the button on the panel.

"Yes?" a voice said.

"Mr Cutler, there are two detectives to see you, a Mr King and a Mr Coppola."

"Kling and Carella," Carella corrected.

"Kling and Capella," the girl said.

Carella let it go.

"Ask them to come right in," Cutler said.

"Yes, sir." The girl clicked off and looked up at the detectives. "Won't you go in. please? Through the bull pen and straight back."

"Through the what?"

"The bull pen. Oh, that's the main office, you'll see it. It's right inside the door there." The telephone rang. The girl gestured vaguely toward what looked like a solid walnut wall, and then picked up the receiver. "The Cutlers," she said. "One moment, please." She pressed a button and then said, "Mrs Cutler, it's Alex Jamison on five-seven, do you want to take it?" She nodded, listened for a moment, and then replaced the receiver. Carella and Kling had just located the walnut knob on the walnut door hidden in the walnut wall. Carella smiled sheepishly at the girl (blue eyes blinked back radiantly) and opened the door.

The bull pen, as the girl had promised, was just behind the reception room. It was a large open area with the same basic walnut-and-white decor, broken by the color of the drapes and the upholstery fabric on two huge couches against the left-hand window wall. The windows were draped in diaphanous saffron nylon, and the couches were done in a complementary brown, the fabric nubby and coarse in contrast to the nylon. Three girls sat on the couches, their long legs crossed. All of them were reading *Vogue*. One of them had her head inside a portable hair dryer. None of them looked up as the men came into the room. On the right-hand side of the room, a fourth woman sat behind a long white Formica counter, a phone to her ear, busily scribbling on a pad as she listened. The woman was in her early forties, with the unmistakable bones of an ex-model.

She glanced up briefly as Carella and Kling hesitated inside the doorway, and then went back to her jottings, ignoring them.

There were three huge charts affixed to the wall behind her, Each chart was divided into two-by-two squares, somewhat like a colorless checkerboard. Running down the extreme left-hand side of each chart was a column of small photographs. Running across the top of each chart was a listing for every working hour of the day. The charts were covered with plexiglass panels, and a black crayon pencil hung on a cord to the right of each one. Alongside the photographs, crayoned onto the charts in the appropriate time slots, was a record and a reminder of any model's sittings for the week, readable at a glance. To the right of the charts, and accessible through an opening in the counter, there was a cubbyhole arrangement of mailboxes, each separate slot marked with similar small photographs.

The wall bearing the door through which Carella and Kling had entered was covered with eight-by-ten black-and-white photos of every model the agency represented, some seventy-five in all. The photos bore no identifying names. A waist-high runner carried black crayon pencils spaced at intervals along the length of the wall. A wide white band under each photograph, plexiglass-covered, served as the writing area for telephone messages. A model entering the room could, in turn, check her eight-by-ten photo for any calls, her photo-marked mailbox for any letters, and her photo-marked slot on one of the three charts for her next assignment. Looking into the room, you somehow got the vague impression that photography played a major part in the business of this agency. You also had the disquieting feeling that you had seen all of these faces a hundred times before, staring down at you from bill-boards and up at you from magazine covers. Putting an identifying name under any single one of them would have been akin to labeling the Taj Mahal or the Empire State Building. The only naked wall was the one facing them as they entered, and it – like the reception-room wall – seemed to be made of solid walnut, with nary a door in sight.

"I think I see a knob," Carella whispered, and they started across the room toward the far wall. The woman behind the counter glanced up as they passed, and then pulled the phone abruptly from her ear with a "Just a second, Alex," and said to the two detectives, "Yes, may I help you?"

"We're looking for Mr Cutler's office," Carella said.

"Yes?" she said.

"Yes, we're detectives. We're investigating the murder of Tinka Sachs."

"Oh. Straight ahead," the woman said. "I'm Leslie Cutler. I'll join you as soon as I'm off the phone."

"Thank you," Carella said. He walked to the walnut wall, Kling following close behind him, and knocked on what he supposed was the door.

"Come in," a man's voice said.

Art Cutler was a man in his forties with straight blond hair like Sonny Tufts, and with at least six feet four inches of muscle and bone that stood revealed in a dark blue suit as he rose behind his desk, smiling, and extended his hand.

"Come in, gentlemen," he said. His voice was deep. He kept his hand extended while Carella and Kling crossed to the desk, and then he shook hands with each in turn, his grip firm and strong. "Sit down, won't you?" he said, and indicated a pair of Saarinen chairs, one at each corner of his desk. "You're here about Tinka," he said dolefully.

"Yes," Carella said.

"Terrible thing. A maniac must have done it, don't you think?"

"I don't know," Carella said.

"Well, it *must* have been, don't you think?" he said to Kling.

"I don't know," Kling said.

"That's why we're here, Mr Cutler," Carella explained. "To find out what we can about the girl. We're assuming that an agent would know a great deal about the people he repre – "

"Yes, that's true," Cutler interrupted, "and especially in Tinka's case."

"Why especially in her case?"

"Well, we'd handled her career almost from the very beginning."

"How long would that be, Mr Cutler?"

"Oh, at least ten years. She was only nineteen when we took her on, and she was . . . well, let me see, she was thirty in February, no, it'd be almost *eleven* years, that's right."

"February what?" Kling asked.

"February third," Cutler replied. "She'd done a little modeling on the coast before she signed with us, but nothing very impressive. We got her into all the important magazines, *Vogue, Harper's, Mademoiselle*, well, you name them. Do you know what Tinka Sachs was earning?"

"No, what?" Kling said.

"Sixty dollars an hour. Multiply that by an eight – or ten – hour day, an average of six days a week, and you've got somewhere in the vicinity of a hundred and fifty thousand dollars a year." Cutler paused. "That's a lot of money. That's more than the president of the United States earns."

"With none of the headaches," Kling said.

"Mr Cutler," Carella said, "when did you last see Tinka Sachs alive?"

"Late Friday afternoon," Cutler said.

"Can you give us the circumstances?"

"Well, she had a sitting at five, and she stopped in around seven to pick up her mail and to see if there had been any calls. That's all."

"Had there?" Kling asked.

"Had there what?"

"Been any calls?"

"I'm sure I don't remember. The receptionist usually posts all calls shortly after they're received. You may have seen our photo wall—"

"Yes," Kling said.

"Well, our receptionist takes care of that. If you want me to check with her, she may have a record, though I doubt it. Once a call is crayoned onto the wall—"

"What about mail?"

"I don't know if she had any or . . . wait a minute, yes, I think she did pick some up. I remember she was leafing through some envelopes when I came out of my office to chat with her."

"What time did she leave here?" Carella asked.

"About seven-fifteen."

"For another sitting?"

"No, she was heading home. She has a daughter, you know. A five-year-old."

"Yes, I know," Carella said.

"Well, she was going home," Cutler said.

"Do you know where she lives?" Kling asked.

"Yes."

"Where?"

"Stafford Place."

"Have you ever been there?"

"Yes, of course."

"How long do you suppose it would take to get from this office to her apartment?"

"No more than fifteen minutes."

"Then Tinka would have been home by seven-thirty . . . *if* she went directly home."

"Yes, I suppose so."

"Did she say she was going directly home?"

"Yes. No, she said she wanted to pick up some cake, and *then* she was going home."

"Cake?"

"Yes. There's a shop up the street that's exceptionally good. Many of our mannequins buy cakes and pastry there."

"Did she say she was expecting someone later on in the evening?" Kling asked.

"No, she didn't say what her plans were."

"Would your receptionist know if any of those telephone messages related to her plans for the evening?"

"I don't know, we can ask her."

"Yes, we'd like to," Carella said.

"What were *your* plans for last Friday night, Mr Cutler?" Kling asked.

"*My* plans?"

"Yes."

"What do you mean?"

"What time did *you* leave the office?"

"Why would you possibly want to know *that*?" Cutler asked.

"You were the last person to see her alive," Kling said.

"No, her *murderer* was the last person to see her alive," Cutler corrected. "And if I can believe what I read in the newspapers, her *daughter* was the *next*-to-last person to see her alive. So I really can't understand how Tinka's visit to the agency or *my* plans for the evening are in any way germane, or even related, to her death."

"Perhaps they're not, Mr Cutler," Carella said, "but I'm sure you realize we're obliged to investigate every possibility."

Cutler frowned, including Carella in whatever hostility he had originally reserved for Kling. He hesitated a moment and then grudgingly said, "My wife and I joined some friends for dinner at *Les Trois Chats*." He paused and added caustically, "That's a French restaurant."

"What time was that?" Kling asked.

"Eight o'clock."

"Where were you at nine?"

"Still having dinner."

"And at nine-thirty?"

Cutler sighed and said, "We didn't leave the restaurant until a little after ten."

"And then what did you do?"

"Really, is this necessary?" Cutler said, and scowled at the detectives. Neither of them answered. He sighed again and said, "We walked along Hall Avenue for a while, and then my wife and I left our friends and took a cab home."

The door opened.

Leslie Cutler breezed into the office, saw the expression on her husband's face, weighed the silence that greeted her entrance, and immediately said, "What is it?"

"Tell them where we went when we left here Friday night," Cutler said. "The gentlemen are intent on playing cops and robbers."

"You're joking," Leslie said, and realized at once that they were not. "We went to dinner with some friends," she said quickly. "Marge and Daniel Ronet – she's one of our mannequins. Why?"

"What time did you leave the restaurant, Mrs Cutler?"

"At ten."

"Was your husband with you all that time?"

"Yes, of course he was." She turned to Cutler and said, "Are they allowed to do this? Shouldn't we call Eddie?"

"Who's Eddie?" Kling said.

"Our lawyer."

"You won't need a lawyer."

"Are you a new detective?" Cutler asked Kling suddenly.

"What's that supposed to mean?"

"It's supposed to mean your interviewing technique leaves something to be desired."

"Oh? In what respect? What do you find lacking in my approach, Mr Cutler?"

"Subtlety, to coin a word."

"That's very funny," Kling said.

"I'm glad it amuses you."

"Would it amuse you to know that the elevator operator at 791 Stafford Place gave us an excellent description of the man he took up to Tinka's apartment on the night she was killed? And would it amuse you further to know that the description fits you to a tee? How does *that* hit your funny bone, Mr Cutler?"

"I was nowhere near Tinka's apartment last Friday night."

"Apparently not. I know you won't mind our contacting the friends you had dinner with, though – just to check."

"The receptionist will give you their number," Cutler said coldly.

"Thank you."

Cutler looked at his watch. "I have a lunch date," he said. "If you gentlemen are finished with your—"

"I wanted to ask your receptionist about those telephone messages," Carella said. "And I'd also appreciate any information you can give me about Tinka's friends and acquaintances."

"My wife will have to help you with that." Cutler glanced sourly at Kling and said, "I'm not planning to leave town. Isn't that what you always warn a suspect not to do?"

"Yes, don't leave town," Kling said.

"Bert," Carella said casually, "I think you'd better get back to the squad. Grossman promised to call with a lab report sometime this afternoon. One of us ought to be there to take it."

"Sure," Kling said. He went to the door and opened it. "My partner's a little more subtle than I am," he said, and left.

Carella, with his work cut out for him, gave a brief sigh, and said, "Could we talk to your receptionist now, Mrs Cutler?"

3

When Carella left the agency at two o'clock that Monday afternoon, he was in possession of little more than he'd had when he first climbed those blue-carpeted steps. The receptionist, radiating wide-eyed helpfulness, could not remember any of the phone messages that had been left for Tinka Sachs on the day of her death. She knew they were all personal calls, and she remembered that some of them were from men, but she could not recall any of the men's names. Neither could she remember the names of the women callers – yes, some of them were women, she said, but she didn't know exactly how many – nor could she remember why *any* of the callers were trying to contact Tinka.

Carella thanked her for her help, and then sat down with Leslie Cutler – who was still fuming over Kling's treatment of her husband – and tried to compile a list of men Tinka knew. He drew another blank here because Leslie informed him at once that Tinka, unlike most of the agency's mannequins (the word "mannequin" was beginning to rankle a little) kept her private affairs to herself, never allowing a date to pick her up at the agency, and never discussing the men in her life, not even with any of the other mannequins (in fact, the word was beginning to rankle a lot). Carella thought at first that Leslie was suppressing information because of the jackass manner in which Kling had conducted the earlier interview. But as he questioned her more completely, he came to believe that she really knew nothing at all about Tinka's personal matters. Even

32

on the few occasions when she and her husband had been invited to Tinka's home, it had been for a simple dinner for three, with no one else in attendance, and with the child Anna asleep in her own room. Comparatively charmed to pieces by Carella's patience after Kling's earlier display, Leslie offered him her agency flyer on Tinka, the composite that went to all photographers, advertising agency art directors, and prospective clients. He took it, thanked her, and left.

Sitting over a cup of coffee and a hamburger now, in a luncheonette two blocks from the squadroom, Carella took the composite out of its manila envelope and remembered again the way Tinka Sachs had looked the last time he'd seen her. The composite was an eight-by-ten black-and-white presentation consisting of a larger sheet folded in half to form two pages, each printed front and back with photographs of Tinka in various poses.

Carella studied the composite from first page to last:

TINKA SACHS

SIZE 10-12
HEIGHT (S/F) 5'8"
BUST 34
WAIST 23
HIPS 34
HAIR BLONDE
EYES GREEN
SHOE 7-½AA
GLOVE 7
HAT 22

The Cutlers
21 CARRINGTON ST.

The only thing the composite told him was that Tinka posed fully clothed, modeling neither lingerie nor swimwear, a fact he considered interesting, but hardly pertinent. He put the composite into the manila envelope, finished his coffee, and went back to the squadroom.

Kling was waiting and angry.

"What was the idea, Steve?" he asked immediately.

"Here's a composite on Tinka Sachs," Carella said. "We might as well add it to our file."

"Never mind the composite. how about answering my question?"

"I'd rather not. Did Grossman call?"

"Yes. The only prints they've found in the room so far are the dead girl's. They haven't yet examined the knife, or her pocket book. Don't try to get me off this, Steve. I'm goddamn good and sore."

"Bert, I don't want to get into an argument with you. Let's drop it, okay?"

"No."

"We're going to be working on this case together for what may turn out to be a long time. I don't want to start by—"

"Yes, that's right, and I don't like being ordered back to the squadroom just because someone doesn't like my line of questioning."

"Nobody ordered you back to the squadroom."

"Steve, you outrank me, and you told me to come back, and that was *ordering* me back. I want to know why."

"Because you were behaving like a jerk, okay?"

"I don't think so."

"Then maybe you ought to step back and take an objective look at yourself."

"Damnit, it was *you* who said the old man's identification seemed reliable! Okay, so we walk into that office and we're face to face with the man who'd just been *described* to us! What'd you expect me to do? Serve him a cup of tea?"

"No, I expected you to accuse him—"

"Nobody accused him of anything!"

"—of murder and take him right up here to book him," Carella said sarcastically. "*That's* what I expected."

"I asked perfectly reasonable questions!"

"You asked questions that were snotty and surly and hostile and amateurish. You treated him like a criminal from go, when you had no reason to. You immediately put him on the defensive instead of disarming him. If I were in his place, I'd have lied to you just out of spite. You made an enemy instead of a friend out of someone who might have been able to help us. That means if I need any further information about Tinka's professional life, I'll have to beg it from a man who now has good reason to hate the police."

"He fit our description! Anyone would have asked—"

"Why the hell couldn't you ask in a civil manner? And *then* check on those friends he said he was with, and *then* get tough if you had something to work with? What did you accomplish your way? Not a goddamn thing. Okay, you asked me, so I'm telling you. I had work to do up there, and I couldn't afford to waste more time while you threw mud at the walls. *That's* why I sent you back here. Okay? Good. Did you check Cutler's alibi?"

"Yes."

"*Was* he with those people?"

"Yes."

"And *did* they leave the restaurant at ten and walk around for a while?"

"Yes."

"Then Cutler couldn't have been the man Cyclops took up in his elevator."

"Unless Cyclops got the time wrong."

"That's a possibility, and I suggest we check it. But the checking should have been done *before* you started hurling accusations around."

"I didn't accuse anybody of anything!"

"Your entire approach did! Who the hell do you think you are, a Gestapo agent? You can't go marching into a man's office with nothing but an idea and start—"

"I was doing my best!" Kling said. "If that's not good enough, you can go to hell."

"It's not good enough," Carella said, "and I don't plan to go to hell, either."

"I'm asking Pete to take me off this," Kling said.

"He won't."

"Why not?"

"Because I outrank you, like you said, and *I* want you on it."

"Then don't ever try that again, I'm warning you. You embarrass me in front of a civilian again and—"

"If you had any sense, you'd have been embarrassed long before I asked you to go."

"Listen, Carella—"

"Oh, it's *Carella* now, huh?"

"I don't have to take any crap from you, just remember that. I don't care what your badge says. Just remember I don't have to take any crap from you."

"Or from anybody."

"Or from anybody, right."

"I'll remember."

"See that you do," Kling said, and he walked through the gate in the slatted railings and out of the squadroom

Carella clenched his fists, unclenched them again, and then slapped one open hand against the top of his desk.

Detective Meyer Meyer came out of the men's room in the corridor, zipping up his fly. He glanced to his left toward the iron-runged steps and cocked his head, listening to the angry clatter of Kling's descending footfalls. When he came into the squadroom, Carella was leaning over, straight-armed, on his desk. A dead, cold expression was on his face.

"What was all the noise about?" Meyer asked.

"Nothing," Carella said. He was seething with anger, and the word came out as thin as a razor blade.

"Kling again?" Meyer asked.

"Kling again."

"Boy," Meyer said, and shook his head, and said nothing more.

On his way home late that afternoon, Carella stopped at the Sachs apartment, showed his shield to the patrolman still stationed outside her door, and then went into the apartment to search for anything that might give him a line on the men Tinka Sachs had known – correspondence, a memo pad, an address book, anything. The apartment was empty and still.

The child Anna Sachs had been taken to the Children's Shelter on Saturday and then released into the custody of Harvey Sadler – who was Tinka's lawyer – to await the arrival of the little girl's father from Arizona. Carella walked through the corridor past Anna's room, the same route the murderer must have taken, glanced in through the open door at the rows of dolls lined up in the bookcase, and then went past the room and into Tinka's spacious bedroom. The bed had been stripped, the blood-stained sheets and blanket sent to the police laboratory. There had been blood stains on the drapes as well, and these too had been taken down and shipped off to Grossman. The windows were bare now, overlooking the rooftops below, the boats moving slowly on the River Dix. Dusk was coming fast, a reminder that it was still only April. Carella flicked on the lights and walked around the chalked outline of Tinka's body on the thick green carpet, the blood soaked into it and dried to an ugly brown. He went to an oval table serving as a desk on the wall opposite the bed, sat in the pedestal chair before it, and began rummaging through the papers scattered over its top. The disorder told him that detectives from Homicide had already been through all this and had found nothing they felt worthy of calling to his attention. He sighed and picked up an envelope with an airmail border, turned it over to look at the flap, and saw that it had come from Dennis Sachs – Tinka's ex-husband – in Rainfield, Arizona. Carella took the letter from the envelope, unfolded it, and began reading:

Tuesday, April 6

My darling Tinka —

Here I am in the middle of the desert, writing by the light of a flickering Kerosene lamp, and listening to the howl of the wind outside my tent. The others are all asleep already. I have never felt farther away from the city — or from you.

I become more impatient with Oliver's project every day of the week, but perhaps that's because I know what you are trying to do, and everything seems insignificant beside your monumental struggle. Who cares whether or not the Hohokam traversed this desert on their way from Old Mexico? Who cares whether we uncover any of their lodges here? All I know is that I miss you enormously, and respect you, and pray for you. My only hope is that your ordeal will soon be ended, and we can go back to the way it was in the beginning; before the nightmare began, before our love was shattered.

I will call East again on Saturday. All my love to Anna...

... and to you.

Dennis

Carella refolded the letter and put it back into the envelope. He had just learned that Dennis Sachs was out in the desert on some sort of project involving the Hohokam, whoever the hell they were, and that apparently he was still carrying the torch for his ex-wife. But beyond that Carella also learned that Tinka had been going through what Dennis called a "monumental struggle" and "ordeal". What ordeal? Carella wondered. What struggle? And what exactly was the "nightmare" Dennis mentioned later in his letter? Or was the nightmare the struggle itself, the ordeal, and not something that predated it? Dennis Sachs had been phoned in Arizona this morning by the authorities at the Children's Shelter, and was presumably already on his way East. Whether he yet realized it or not, he would have a great many questions to answer when he arrived.

Carella put the letter in his jacket pocket and began leafing through the other correspondence on his desk. There were bills from the electric company, the telephone company, most of the city's department stores, the Diners' Club, and many of the local merchants. There was a letter from a woman who had done house cleaning for Tinka and who was writing to say she could no longer work for her because she and her family were moving back to Jamaica, B.W.I. There was a letter from the editor of one of the fashion magazines, outlining her plans for shooting the new Paris line with Tinka and several other mannequins that summer, and asking whether she would be available or not. Carella read these cursorily, putting them into a small neat pile at one edge of the oval table, and then found Tinka's address book.

There were a great many names, addresses, and telephone numbers in the small red leather book. Some of the people listed were men. Carella studied each name carefully, going through the book several times. Most of the names were run-of-the-mill Georges and Franks and Charlies, while others were a bit more rare like Clyde and Adrian, and still others were pretty exotic like Rion and Dink and Fritz. None of them rang a bell. Carella closed the book, put it into his jacket pocket and went through the remainder of the papers on the desk. The only other item of interest was a partially completed poem in Tinka's handwriting.

When I think of what I am
And of what I might have been,
I tremble.
I fear the night.
Throughout the day,
I push from dragons conjured in the dark
Why will they not

He folded the poem carefully and put it into his jacket pocket together with the address book. Then he rose, walked to the door, took a last look into the room, and snapped out the light. He went down the corridor toward the front door. The last pale light of day glanced through Anna's window into her room, glowing feebly on the faces of her dolls lined up in rows on the bookcase shelves. He went into the room and gently lifted one of the dolls from the top shelf, replaced it, and then recognized another doll as the one Anna had been holding in her lap on Saturday when he'd talked to her. He lifted the doll from the shelf.

The patrolman outside the apartment was startled to see a grown detective rushing by him with a doll under his arm. Carella got into the elevator, hurriedly found what he wanted in Tinka's address book, and debated whether he should call the squad to tell where he was headed, possibly get Kling to assist him with the arrest. He suddenly remembered that Kling had left the squadroom early. His anger boiled to the surface again. The *hell* with him, he thought, and came out into the street at a trot, running for his car. His thoughts came in a disorderly jumble, one following the next, the brutality of it, the goddamn stalking animal brutality of it, should I try making the collar alone, God that poor kid listening to her mother's murder, maybe I ought to go back to the office first, get Meyer to assist, but suppose my man is getting ready to cut out, why doesn't Kling shape up. Oh God, slashed again and again. He started the car. The child's doll was on the seat beside him. He looked again at the name and address in Tinka's book. Well? he thought. Which? Get help or go it alone?

He stepped on the accelerator.

There was an excitement pounding inside him now, coupled with the anger, a high anticipatory clamor that drowned out whatever note of caution whispered automatically in his mind. It did not usually happen this way, there were usually weeks or months of drudgery. The surprise of his windfall, the idea of a sudden culmination to a chase barely begun, unleashed a wild energy inside him, forced his foot onto the gas pedal more firmly. His hands were tight on the wheel. He drove with a recklessness that would have brought a summons to a civilian, weaving in and out of traffic, hitting the horn and the brakes, his hands and his feet a part of the machine that hurtled steadily downtown toward the address listed in Tinka's book.

He parked the car, and came out onto the sidewalk, leaving the doll on the front seat. He studied the name plates in the entrance hallway – yes, this was it. He pushed a bell button at random, turned the knob on the locked inside door when the answering buzz sounded. Swiftly he began climbing the steps to the third floor. On the second-floor landing, he drew his service revolver, a .38 Smith and Wesson Police Model 10. The gun had a two-inch barrel that made it virtually impossible to snag on clothing when drawn. It weighed only two ounces and was six and seven-eighths of an inch long, with a blue finish and a checked walnut Magna stock with the familiar S&W monogram. It was capable of firing six shots without reloading.

He reached the third floor and started down the hallway. The mailbox had told him the apartment number was 34. He found it at the end of the hall, and put his ear to the door, listening. He could hear the muted voices of a man and a woman inside the apartment. Kick it in, he thought. You've got enough for an arrest. Kick in the door, and go in shooting if necessary – he's your man. He backed away from the door. He braced himself against the corridor wall opposite the door, lifted his right leg high, pulling back the knee, and then stepped forward and simultaneously unleashed a piston kick, aiming for the lock high on the door.

The wood splintered, the lock ripped from the jamb, the door shot inward. He followed the opening door into the room, the gun leveled in his right hand. He saw only a big beautiful dark-haired woman sitting on a couch facing the door, her legs crossed, a look of startled surprise on her face. But he had heard a man from outside. Where – ?

He turned suddenly. He had abruptly realized that the apartment fanned out on both sides of the entrance door, and that the man could easily be to his right or his left, beyond his field of vision. He turned naturally to the right because he was right-handed, because the gun was in his right hand, and made the mistake that could have cost him his life.

The man was on his left.

Carella heard the sound of his approach too late, reversed his direction, caught a single glimpse of straight blond hair like Sonny Tufts, and then felt something hard and heavy smashing into his face.

4

There was no furniture in the small room, save for a wooden chair to the right of the door. There were two windows on the wall facing the door, and these were covered with drawn green shades. The room was perhaps twelve feet wide by fifteen long, with a radiator in the center of one of the fifteen-foot walls.

Carella blinked his eyes and stared into the semidarkness.

There were nighttime noises outside the windows, and he could see the intermittent flash of neon around the edges of the drawn shades. He wondered what time it was. He started to raise his left hand for a look at his watch, and discovered that it was handcuffed to the radiator. The handcuffs were his own. Whoever had closed the cuff onto his wrist had done so quickly and viciously; the metal was biting sharply into his flesh. The other cuff was clasped shut around the radiator leg. His watch was gone, and he seemed to have been stripped as well of his service revolver, his billet, his cartridges, his wallet and loose change, and even his shoes and socks. The side of his face hurt like hell. He lifted his right hand in exploration and found that his cheek and temple were crusted with dried blood. He looked down again at the radiator leg around which the second cuff was looped. Then he moved to the right of the radiator and looked behind it to see how it was fastened to the wall. If the fittings were loose—

He heard a key being inserted into the door lock. It suddenly occurred to him that he was still alive, and the knowledge filled him with a sense of impending dread rather than elation. *Why* was he still alive? And was someone opening the door right this minute in order to remedy that oversight?

The key turned.

The overhead light snapped on.

A big brunette girl came into the room. She was the same girl who had been sitting on the couch when he'd bravely kicked in the front door. She was carrying a tray in her hands, and he caught the aroma of coffee the moment she entered the room, that and the overriding scent of the heavy perfume the girl was wearing.

"Hello," she said.

"Hello," he answered.

"Have a nice sleep?"

"Lovely."

She was very big, much bigger than she had seemed seated on the couch. She had the bones and body of a showgirl, five feet eight or nine inches tall, with firm full breasts threatening a low-cut peasant blouse, solid thighs sheathed in a tight black skirt that ended just above her knees. Her legs were long and very white, shaped like a dancer's with full calves and slender ankles. She was wearing black slippers, and she closed the door behind her and came into the room silently, the slippers whispering across the floor.

She moved slowly, almost as though she were sleepwalking. There was a current of sensuality about her, emphasized by her dreamlike motion. She seemed to possess an acute awareness of her lush body, and this in turn seemed coupled with the knowledge that whatever she might be – housewife or whore, slattern or saint – men would try to do things to that body, and succeed, repeatedly and without mercy. She was a victim, and she moved with the cautious tread of someone who had been beaten before and now expects attack from any quarter. Her caution, her awareness, the ripeness of her body, the certain knowledge that it was available, the curious look of inevitability the girl wore, all invited further abuses, encouraged fantasies, drew dark imaginings from hidden corners of the mind. Rinsed raven-black hair framed the girl's face. It was a face hard with knowledge. Smoky Cleopatra makeup shaded her eyes and lashes, hiding the deeper-toned flesh there. Her nose had been fixed once, a long time ago, but it was beginning to fall out of shape so that it looked now as if someone had broken it, and this too added to the victim's look she wore. Her mouth was brightly painted, a whore's mouth, a doll's mouth. It had said every word ever invented. It had done everything a mouth was ever forced to do.

"I brought you some coffee," she said.

Her voice was almost a whisper. He watched her as she came closer. He had the feeling that she could kill a man as readily as kiss him, and he wondered again why he was still alive.

He noticed for the first time that there was a gun now, on the tray, alongside the coffee pot. The girl lifted the gun, and pointed it at his belly, still holding the tray with one hand.

"Back," she said.

"Why?"

"Don't fuck around with me," she said. "Do what I tell you to do when I tell you to do it."

Carella moved back as far as his cuffed wrist would allow him. The girl crouched, the tight skirt riding up over her thighs, and pushed the tray toward the radiator. Her face was dead serious. The gun was a super .38-caliber Llama automatic. The girl held it steady in her right hand. The thumb safety on the left side of the gun had been thrown. The automatic was ready for firing.

The girl rose and backed away toward the chair near the entrance door, the gun still trained on him. She sat, lowered the gun, and said, "Go ahead."

Carella poured coffee from the pot into the single mug on the tray. He took a swallow. The coffee was hot and strong.

"How is it?" the girl asked.

"Fine."

"I made it myself."

"Thank you."

"I'll bring you a wet towel later," she said. "So you can wipe off that blood. It looks terrible."

"It doesn't feel so hot, either," Carella said.

"Well, who invited you?" the girl asked. She seemed about to smile, and then changed her mind.

"No one, that's true." He took another sip of coffee. The girl watched him steadily.

"Steve Carella," she said. "Is that it?"

"That's right. What's *your* name?"

He asked the question quickly and naturally, but the girl did not step into the trap.

"Detective second/grade," she said. "87th Squad." She paused. "Where's that?"

"Across from the park."

"What park?"

"Grover Park."

"Oh, yeah," she said. "That's a nice park. That's the nicest park in this whole damn city."

"Yes," Carella said.

"I saved your life, you know," the girl said conversationally.

"Did you?"

"Yeah. *He* wanted to kill you."

"I'm surprised he didn't."

"Cheer up, maybe he will."

"When?"

"You in a hurry?"

"Not Particularly."

The room went silent. Carella took another swallow of coffee. The girl kept staring at him. Outside, he could hear the sounds of traffic.

"What time is it?" he asked.

"About nine. Why? You got a date?"

"I'm wondering how long it'll be before I'm missed, that's all," Carella said, and watched the girl.

"Don't try to scare me," she said. "Nothing scares me."

"I wasn't trying to scare you."

The girl scratched her leg idly, and then said, "There're some questions I have to ask you."

"I'm not sure I'll answer them."

"You will," she said. There was something cold and deadly in her voice. "I can guarantee that. Sooner or later, you will."

"Then it'll have to be later."

"You're not being smart, mister."

"I'm being very smart."

"How?"

"I figure I'm alive only because you don't know the answers."

"Maybe you're alive because I *want* you to be alive," the girl said.

50

"Why?"

"I've never had anything like you before," she said, and for the first time since she'd come into the room, she smiled. The smile was frightening. He could feel the flesh at the back of his neck beginning to crawl. He wet his lips and looked at her, and she returned his gaze steadily, the tiny evil smile lingering on her lips. "I'm life or death to you," she said. "If I tell him to kill you, he will."

"Not until you know all the answers," Carella said.

"Oh, we'll get the answers. We'll have plenty of time to get the answers." The smile dropped from her face. She put one hand inside her blouse and idly scratched her breast, and then looked at him again, and said, "How'd you get here?"

"I took the subway."

"That's a lie," the girl said. There was no rancor in her voice. She accused him matter-of-factly, and then said, "Your car was downstairs. The registration was in the glove compartment. There was also a sign on the sun visor, something about a law officer on a duty call."

"All right, I drove here," Carella said.

"Are you married?"

"Yes."

"Do you have any children?"

"Two."

"Girls?"

"A girl and a boy."

"Then that's who the doll is for," the girl said.

"What doll?"

"The one that was in the car. On the front seat of the car."

"Yes," Carella lied. "It's for my daughter. Tomorrow's her birthday."

"He brought it upstairs. It's outside in the living room." The girl paused. "Would you like to give your daughter that doll?"

"Yes."

"Would you like to see her again?"

"Yes."

"Then answer whatever I ask you, without any more lies about the subway or anything."

"What's my guarantee?"

"Of what?"

"That I'll stay alive."

"*I'm* your guarantee."

"Why should I trust you?"

"You have to trust me," the girl said. "You're mine." And again she smiled, and again he could feel the hairs stiffening at the back of his neck.

She got out of the chair. She scratched her belly, and then moved toward him, that same slow and cautious movement, as though she expected someone to strike her and was bracing herself for the blow.

"I haven't got much time," she said. "He'll be back soon."

"Then what?"

The girl shrugged. "Who knows you're here?" she asked suddenly.

Carella did not answer.

"How'd you get to us?"

Again, he did not answer.

"Did somebody see him leaving Tinka's apartment?"

Carella did not answer.

"How did you know where to come?"

Carella shook his head.

"Did someone identify him? How did you trace him?"

Carella kept watching her. She was standing three feet away from him now, too far to reach, the Llama dangling loosely in her right hand. She raised the gun.

"Do you want me to shoot you?" she asked conversationally.

"No."

"I'll aim for your balls, would you like that?"

"No."

"Then answer my questions."

"You're not going to kill me," Carella said. He did not take his eyes from the girl's face. The gun was pointed at his groin now, but he did not look at her finger curled inside the trigger guard.

The girl took a step closer. Carella crouched near the radiator, unable to get to his feet, his left hand manacled close to the floor. "I'll enjoy this," the girl promised, and struck him suddenly with the butt of the heavy gun, turning the butt up swiftly as her hand lashed out. He felt the numbing shock of

52

metal against bone as the automatic caught him on the jaw and his head jerked back.

"You like?" the girl asked.

He said nothing.

"You *no* like, huh, baby?" She paused. "How'd you find us?"

Again, he did not answer. She moved past him swiftly, so that he could not turn in time to stop the blow that came from behind him, could not kick out at her as he had planned to do the next time she approached. The butt caught him on the ear, and he felt the cartilage tearing as the metal rasped downward. He whirled toward her angrily, grasping at her with his right arm as he turned, but she danced out of his reach and around to the front of him again, and again hit him with the automatic, cutting him over the left eye this time. He felt the blood start down his face from the open gash.

"What do you say?" she asked.

"I say go to hell," Carella said, and the girl swung the gun again. He thought he was ready for her this time. But she was only feinting, and he grabbed out at empty air as she moved swiftly to his right and out of reach. The manacled hand threw him off balance. He fell forward, reaching for support with his free hand, the handcuff biting sharply into his other wrist. The gun butt caught him again just as his hand touched the floor. He felt it colliding with the base of his skull, a two-pound-six-and-a-half-ounce weapon swung with all the force of the girl's substantial body behind it. The pain shot clear to the top of his head. He blinked his eyes against the sudden dizziness. Hold on, he told himself, hold on, and was suddenly nauseous. The vomit came up into his throat, and he brought his right hand to his mouth just as the girl hit him again. He fell back dizzily against the radiator. He blinked up at the girl. Her lips were pulled back taut over her teeth, she was breathing harshly, the gun hand went back again, he was too weak to turn his head aside. He tried to raise his right arm, but it fell limply into his lap.

"Who saw him?" the girl asked.

"No," he mumbled.

"I'm going to break your nose," she said. Her voice sounded very far away. He tried to hold the floor for support, but he

53

wasn't sure where the floor was any more. The room was spinning. He looked up at the girl and saw her spinning face and breasts, smelled the heavy cloying perfume and saw the gun in her hand. "I'm going to break your nose, mister."

"No."

"Yes," she said.

"No."

He did not see the gun this time. He felt only the excruciating pain of bones splintering. His head rocked back with the blow, colliding with the cast-iron ribs of the radiator. The pain brought him back to raging consciousness. He lifted his right hand to his nose, and the girl hit him again, at the base of the skull again, and again he felt sensibility slipping away from him. He smiled stupidly. She would not let him die, and she would not let him live. She would not allow him to become unconscious, and she would not allow him to regain enough strength to defend himself.

"I'm going to knock out all of your teeth," the girl said.

He shook his head.

"Who told you where to find us? Was it the elevator operator? Was it that one-eyed bastard?"

He did not answer.

"Do you want to lose all your teeth?"

"No."

"Then tell me."

"No."

"You have to tell me," she said. "You *belong* to me."

"No," he said.

There was a silence. He knew the gun was coming again. He tried to raise his hand to his mouth, to protect his teeth, but there was no strength in his arm. He sat with his left wrist caught in the fierce biting grip of the handcuff, swollen, throbbing, with blood pouring down his face and from his nose, his nose a throbbing mass of splintered bone, and waited for the girl to knock out his teeth as she had promised, helpless to stop her.

He felt her lips upon him.

She kissed him fiercely and with her mouth open, her tongue searching his lips and his teeth. Then she pulled away from

54

him, and he heard her whisper, "In the morning, they'll find you dead."

He lost consciousness again.

On Tuesday morning, they found the automobile at the bottom of a steep cliff some fifty miles across the River Harb, in a sparsely populated area of the adjoining state. Most of the paint had been burned away by what must have been an intensely hot fire, but it was still possible to tell that the car was a green 1961 Pontiac sedan bearing the license plate RI 7–3461.

The body on the front seat of the car had been incinerated. They knew by what remained of the lower portions that the body had once been a man, but the face and torso had been cooked beyond recognition, the hair and clothing gone, the skin black and charred, the arms drawn up into the typical pugilistic attitude caused by post-mortem contracture of the burned muscles, the fingers hooked like claws. A gold wedding band was on the third finger of the skeletal left hand. The fire had eaten away the skin and charred the remaining bones and turned the gold of the ring to a dull black. A .38 Smith & Wesson was caught in the exposed springs of the front seat, together with the metal parts that remained of what once had been a holster.

All of the man's teeth were missing from his mouth.

In the cinders of what they supposed had been his wallet, they found a detective's shield with the identifying number 714–5632.

A call to headquarters across the river informed the investigating police that the shield belonged to a detective second/grade named Stephen Louis Carella.

5

Teddy Carella sat in the silence of her living room and watched the lips of Detective Lieutenant Peter Byrnes as he told her that her husband was dead. The scream welled up into her throat, she could feel the muscles there contracting until she thought she would strangle. She brought her hand to her mouth, her eyes closed tight so that she would no longer have to watch the words that formed on the lieutenant's lips, no longer have to see the words that confirmed what she had known was true since the night before when her husband had failed to come home for dinner.

She would not scream, but a thousand screams echoed inside her head. She felt faint. She almost swayed out of the chair, and then she looked up into the lieutenant's face as she felt his supporting arm around her shoulders. She nodded. She tried to smile up at him sympathetically, tried to let him know she realized this was an unpleasant task for him. But the tears were streaming down her face and she wished only that her husband were there to comfort her, and then abruptly she realized that her husband would never be there to comfort her again, the realization circling back upon itself, the silent screams ricocheting inside her.

The lieutenant was talking again.

She watched his lips. She sat stiff and silent in the chair, her hands clasped tightly in her lap, and wondered where the children were, how would she tell the children, and saw the lieutenant's lips as he said his men would do everything possible to uncover the facts of her husband's death. In the meantime, Teddy, if there's anything I can do, anything I can do personally I mean, I think you know how much Steve meant to me, to all of us, if there's anything Harriet or I can do to help in any way, Teddy, I don't have to tell you we'll do anything we can, anything.

She nodded.

There's a possibility this was just an accident, Teddy, though we doubt it, we think he was, we don't think it was an accident, why would he be across the river in the next state, fifty miles from here?

She nodded again. Her vision was blurred by the tears. She could barely see his lips as he spoke.

Teddy, I loved that boy. I would rather have a bullet in my heart than be here in this room today with this, with this information. I'm sorry. Teddy I am sorry.

She sat in the chair as still as a stone.

Detective Meyer Meyer left the squadroom at two p.m. and walked across the street and past the low stone wall leading into the park. It was a fine April day, the sky a clear blue, the sun shining overhead, the birds chirping in the newly leaved trees.

He walked deep into the park, and he found an empty bench and sat upon it, crossing his legs, one arm stretched out across the top of the bench, the other hanging loose in his lap. There were young boys and girls holding hands and whispering nonsense, there were children chasing each other and laughing, there were nannies wheeling baby carriages, there were old men reading books as they walked, there was the sound of a city hovering on the air.

There was life.

Meyer Meyer sat on the bench and quietly wept for his friend.

Detective Cotton Hawes went to a movie.

The movie was a western. There was a cattle drive in it, thousands of animals thundering across the screen, men sweating and shouting, horses rearing, bullwhips cracking. There was also an attack on a wagon train, Indians circling, arrows and spears whistling through the air, guns answering, men screaming. There was a fight in a saloon, too, chairs and bottles flying, tables collapsing, women running for cover with their skirts pulled high, fists connecting. Altogether, there was noise and color and loud music and plenty of action.

When the end titles flashed onto the screen, Hawes rose and walked up the aisle and out into the street.

Dusk was coming.

The city was hushed.

He had not been able to forget that Steve Carella was dead.

Andy Parker, who had hated Steve Carella's guts when he was alive, went to bed with a girl that night. The girl was a prostitute, and he got into her bed and her body by threatening to arrest her if she didn't come across. The girl had been hooking in the neighborhood for little more than a week. The other working hustlers had taken her aside and pointed out all the Vice Squad bulls and also all the local plainclothes fuzz so that she wouldn't make the mistake of propositioning one of them. But Parker had been on sick leave for two weeks with pharyngitis and had not been included in the girl's original briefing by her colleagues. She had approached what looked like a sloppy drunk in a bar on Ainsley, and before the bartender could catch her eye to warn her, she had given him the familiar "Wanna have some fun, baby?" line and then had compounded the error by telling Parker it would cost him a fin for a single roll in the hay or twenty-five bucks for all night. Parker had accepted the girl's proposition, and had left the bar with her while the owner of the place frantically signaled his warning. The girl didn't know why the hell he was waving his arms at her. She knew only that she had a John who said he wanted to spend the night with her. She didn't know the John's last name was Law.

She took Parker to a rented room on Culver. Parker was very drunk – he had begun drinking at twelve noon when word of Carella's death reached the squadroom – but he was not drunk enough to forget that he could not arrest this girl until she exposed her "privates". He waited until she took off her clothes, and then he showed her his shield and said she could take her choice, a possible three years in the jug, or a pleasant hour or two with a very nice fellow. The girl, who had met very nice fellows like Parker before, all of whom had been Vice Squad cops looking for fleshy handouts, figured this was only a part of her normal overhead, nodded briefly, and spread out on the bed for him.

Parker was very very drunk.

To the girl's great surprise, he seemed more interested in talking than in making love, as the euphemism goes.

"What's the sense of it all, would you tell me?" he said, but he did not wait for an answer. "Son of a bitch like Carella gets cooked in a car by some son of a bitch, what's the sense of it? You know what I see every day of the week, you know what we *all* of us see every day of the week, how do you expect us to stay human, would you tell me? Son of a bitch gets cooked like that, doing his job is all, how do you expect us to stay human? What am I doing here with you, a two-bit whore, is that something for me to be doing? I'm a nice fellow. Don't you know I'm a nice fellow?"

"Sure, you're a nice fellow," the girl said, bored.

"Garbage every day," Parker said. "Filth and garbage, I have the stink in my nose when I go home at night. You know where I live? I live in a garden apartment in Majesta. I've got three and a half rooms, a nice little kitchen, you know, a nice apartment. I've got a hi-fi set and also I belong to the Classics Club. I've got all those books by the big writers, the important writers. I haven't got much time to read them, but I got them all there on a shelf, you should see the books I've got. There are nice people living in that apartment building, not like here, not like what you find in this crumby precinct, how old are you anyway, what are you nineteen, twenty?"

"I'm twenty-one," the girl said.

"Sure, look at you, the shit of the city."

"Listen, mister—"

"Shut up, shut up, who the hell's asking you? I'm *paid* to deal with it, all the shit that gets washed into the sewers, that's my job. My neighbors in the building know I'm a detective, they respect me, they look up to me. They don't know that all

I do is handle shit all day long until I can't stand the stink of it any more. The kids riding their bikes in the courtyard, they all say, 'Good morning, Detective Parker.' That's me, a detective. They watch television, you see. I'm one of the good guys. I carry a gun. I'm brave. So look what happens to that son of a bitch Carella. What's the sense?"

"I don't know what you're talking about," the girl said.

"What's the sense, what's the sense?" Parker said. "People, boy, I could tell you about people. You wouldn't believe what I could tell you about people."

"I've been around a little myself," the girl said drily.

"You can't blame me," he said suddenly.

"What?"

"You can't blame me. It's not my fault."

"Sure. Look, mister, I'm a working girl. You want some of this, or not? Because if you—"

"Shut up, you goddam whore, don't tell me what to do."

"Nobody's—"

"I can pull you in and make your life miserable, you little slut. I've got the power of life and death over you, don't forget it."

"Not quite," the girl said with dignity.

"Not quite, not quite, don't give me any of that crap."

"You're drunk," the girl said. "I don't even think you can—"

"Never mind what I am, I'm not drunk." He shook his head. "All right, I'm drunk, what the hell do you care what I am? You think I care what *you* are? You're *nothing* to me, you're *less* than nothing to me."

"Then what are you doing here?"

"Shut up," he said. He paused. "The kids all yell good morning at me," he said.

He was silent for a long time. His eyes were closed. The girl thought he had fallen asleep. She started to get off the bed, and he caught her arm and pulled her down roughly beside him.

"Stay where you are."

"Okay," she said. "But look, you think we could get this over with? I mean it, mister, I've got a long night ahead of me. I got expenses to meet."

60

"Filth," Parker said. "Filth and garbage."

"Okay, already, filth and garbage, do you want it or not?"

"He was a good cop," Parker said suddenly.

"What?"

"He was a good cop," he said again, and rolled over quickly and put his head into the pillow.

6

At seven-thirty Wednesday morning, the day after the burned wreckage was found in the adjoining state, Bert Kling went back to the apartment building on Stafford Place, hoping to talk again to Ernest Cyclops Messner. The lobby was deserted when he entered the building.

If he had felt alone the day that Claire Townsend was murdered, if he had felt alone the day he held her in his arms in a bookshop demolished by gunfire, suddenly bereft in a world gone cold and senselessly cruel, he now felt something curiously similar and yet enormously different.

Steve Carella was dead.

The last words he had said to the man who had been his friend were angry words. He could not take them back now, he could not call upon a dead man, he could not offer apologies to a corpse. On Monday, he had left the squadroom earlier than he should have, in anger, and sometime that night Carella had met his death. And now there was a new grief within him, a new feeling of helplessness, but it was coupled with an overriding desire to set things right again – for Carella, for Claire, he did not really know. He knew he could not reasonably blame himself for what had happened, but neither could he stop blaming himself. He had to talk to Cyclops again. Perhaps there was something further the man could tell him. Perhaps Carella had contacted him again that Monday night, and uncovered new information that had sent him rushing out to investigate alone.

The elevator doors opened. The operator was not Cyclops.

"I'm looking for Mr Messner," Kling told the man. "I'm from the police."

"He's not here," the man said.

"He told us he has the graveyard shift."

"Yeah, well, he's not here."

"It's only seven-thirty," Kling said.

"I know what time it is."

"Well, where is he, can you tell me that?"

"He lives someplace here in the city," the man said, "but I don't know where."

"Thank you," Kling said, and left the building.

It was still too early in the morning for the rush of white-collar workers to subways and buses. The only people in the streets were factory workers hurrying to punch an eight-a.m. timeclock; the only vehicles were delivery trucks and an occasional passenger car. Kling walked swiftly, looking for a telephone booth. It was going to be another beautiful day; the city had been blessed with lovely weather for the past week now. He saw an open drugstore on the next corner, a telephone plaque fastened to the brick wall outside. He went into the store and headed for the directories at the rear.

Ernest Cyclops Messner lived at 1117 Gainesborough Avenue in Riverhead, not far from the County Court Building. The shadow of the elevated-train structure fell over the building, and the frequent rumble of trains pulling in and out of the station shattered the silence of the street. But it was a good low-to-middle-income residential area, and Messner's building was the newest on the block. Kling climbed the low flat entrance steps, went into the lobby, and found a listing for E. Messner. He rang the bell under the mailbox, but there was no answering buzz. He tried another bell. A buzz sounded, releasing the lock mechanism on the inner lobby door. He pushed open the door, and began climbing to the seventh floor. It was a little after eight a.m., and the building still seemed asleep.

He was somewhat winded by the time he reached the seventh floor. He paused on the landing for a moment, and then walked into the corridor, looking for apartment 7A. He found it just off the stairwell, and rang the bell.

There was no answer.

He rang the bell again.

He was about to ring it a third time when the door to the apartment alongside opened and a young girl rushed out, looking at her wrist watch and almost colliding with Kling.

"Oh, hi," she said, surprised. "Excuse me."

"That's all right." He reached for the bell again. The girl had gone past him and was starting down the steps. She turned suddenly.

"Are you looking for Mr Messner?" she asked.

"Yes, I am."

"He isn't home."

"How do you know?"

"Well, he doesn't get home until about nine," she said. "He works nights, you know."

"Does he live here alone?"

"Yes, he does. His wife died a few years back. He's lived here a long time, I know him from when I was a little girl." She looked at her watch again. "Listen, I'm going to be late. Who *are* you anyway?"

"I'm from the police," Kling said.

"Oh, hi." The girl smiled. "I'm Marjorie Gorman."

"Would you know where I can reach him, Marjorie?"

"Did you try his building? He works in a fancy apartment house on—"

"Yes, I just came from there."

"Wasn't he there?"

"No."

"That's funny," Marjorie said. "Although, come to think of it, we didn't hear him last night, either."

"What do you mean?"

"The television. The walls are very thin, you know. When he's home, we can hear the television going."

"Yes, but he works nights."

"I mean before he leaves. He doesn't go to work until eleven o'clock. He starts at midnight, you know."

"Yes, I know."

"Well, that's what I meant. Listen. I really do have to hurry. If you want to talk, you'll have to walk me to the station."

"Okay," Kling said, and they started down the steps. "Are you sure you didn't hear the television going last night?"

"I'm positive."

"Does he usually have it on?"

"Oh, *constantly*," Marjorie said. "He lives alone, you know, the poor old man. He's got to do *some*thing with his time."

"Yes, I suppose so."

"Why did you want to see him?"

She spoke with a pronounced Riverhead accent that somehow marred her clean good looks. She was a tall girl, perhaps nineteen years old, wearing a dark-grey suit and a white blouse, her auburn hair brushed back behind her ears, the lobes decorated with tiny pearl earrings.

"There are some things I want to ask him," Kling said.

"About the Tinka Sachs murder?"

"Yes."

"He was telling me about that just recently."

"When was that?"

"Oh, I don't know. Let me think." They walked out of the lobby and into the street. Marjorie had long legs, and she walked very swiftly. Kling, in fact, was having trouble keeping up with her. "What's today, anyway?"

"Wednesday," Kling said.

"Wednesday, mmm, boy where does the week go? It must have been Monday. That's right. When I got home from the movies Monday night, he was downstairs putting out his garbage. So we talked awhile. He said he was expecting a detective."

"A detective? Who?"

"What do you mean?"

"Did he say *which* detective he was expecting? Did he mention a name?"

"No, I don't think so. He said he'd talked to some detectives just that morning – that was Monday, right? – and that he'd got a call a few minutes ago saying another detective was coming up to see him."

"Did he say that exactly? That *another* detective was coming up to see him? A *different* detective?"

"Oh. I don't know if he said just that. I mean, it could have been one of the detectives he'd talked to that morning. I really don't know for sure."

"Does the name Carella mean anything to you?"

"No." Marjorie paused. "Should it?"

"Did Mr Messner use that name when he was talking about the detective who was coming to see him?"

"No, I don't think so. He only said he'd had a call from a detective, that was all. He seemed very proud. He told me they probably wanted him to describe the man again, the one he saw going up to her apartment. The dead girl's. Brrrr, it gives you the creeps, doesn't it?"

"Yes," Kling said. "It does."

They were approaching the elevated station now. They paused at the bottom of the steps.

"This was Monday afternoon, you say?"

"No. Monday night. Monday *night*, I said."

"What time Monday night?"

"About ten-thirty, I guess. I told you, I was coming home from the movies."

"Let me get this straight," Kling said. "At ten-thirty Monday night, Mr Messner was putting out his garbage, and he told you he had just received a call from a detective who was on his way over? Is that it?"

"That's it." Marjorie frowned. "It *was* kind of late, wasn't it?" I mean, to be making a business visit. Or do you people work that late?"

"Well, yes, but . . ." Kling shook his head.

"Listen, I really have to go," Marjorie said. "I'd like to talk to you, but—"

"I'd appreciate a few more minutes of your time, if you can—"

"Yes, but my boss—"

"I'll call him later and explain."

"Yeah, you don't *know* him," Marjorie said, and rolled her eyes.

"Can you just tell me whether Mr Messner mentioned anything about this detective the next time you saw him. I mean, *after* the detective was there."

"Well, I haven't seen him since Monday night."

"You didn't see him at *all* yesterday?"

"Nope. Well, I usually miss him in the morning, you know, because I'm gone before he gets home. But sometimes I drop in at night, just to say hello, or he'll come in for something, you know, like that. And I told you about the television. We just didn't hear it. My mother commented about it, as a matter of fact. She said Cyclops was probably – that's what we call him, Cyclops, everybody does, he doesn't mind – she said Cyclops was probably out on the town."

"Does he often go out on the town?"

"Well, I don't think so – but who knows? Maybe he felt like having himself a good time, you know? Listen, I really have to –"

"All right, I won't keep you. Thank you very much, Marjorie. If you'll tell me where you work, I'll be happy to–"

"Oh, the hell with him. I'll tell him what happened, and he can take it or leave it. I'm thinking of quitting, anyway."

"Well, thank you again."

"Don't mention it," Marjorie said, and went up the steps to the platform.

Kling thought for a moment, and then searched in his pocket for a dime. He went into the cafeteria on the corner, found a phone booth, and identified himself to the operator, telling her he wanted the listing for the lobby phone in Tinka's building on Stafford Place. She gave him the number, and he dialed it. A man answered the phone. Kling said, "I'd like to talk to the superintendent, please."

"This is the super."

"This is Detective Kling of the 87th Squad," Kling said. "I'm investigating—"

"Who?" the superintendent said.

"Detective Kling. Who's this I'm speaking to?"

"I'm the super of the building. Emmanuel Farber. Manny. Did you say this was a detective?"

"That's right."

"Boy, when are you guys going to give us some rest here?"

"What do you mean?"

"Don't you have nothing to do but call up here?"

"I haven't called you before, Mr Farber."

"No, not you, never mind. This phone's been going like sixty."

"Who called you?"

"Detectives, never mind."

"Who? Which detectives?"

"The other night."

"When?"

"Monday. Monday night."

"A detective called you Monday night?"

"Yeah, wanted to know where he could reach Cyclops. That's one of our elevator operators."

"Did you tell him?"

"Sure, I did."

"Who was he? Did he give you his name?"

"Yeah, some Italian fellow."

Kling went silent for a moment.

"Would the name have been Carella?" he asked.

"That's right."

"Carella?"

"Yep, that's the one."

"What time did he call?"

"Oh, I don't know. Sometime in the evening."

"And he said his name was Carella?"

"That's right, Detective Carella, that's what he said. Why? You know him?"

"Yes," Kling said. "I know him."

"Well you ask him. He'll tell you."

"What time in the evening did he call? Was it early or late?"

"What do you mean by early or late?" Farber asked.

"Was it before dinner?"

"No. Oh no, it was after dinner. About ten o'clock, I suppose. Maybe a little later."

"And what did he say to you?"

"He wanted Cyclops' address, said he had some questions to ask him."

"About what?"

"About the murder."

"He said that specifically? He said, 'I have some questions to ask Cyclops about the murder?' "

"About the Tinka Sachs murder, is what he actually said."

"He said, 'This is Detective Carella, I want to know—' "

"That's right, this is Detective Carella—"

" '—I want to know Cyclops Messner's address because I have some questions to ask him about the Tinka Sachs murder.' "

"No, that's not it exactly."

"What's wrong with it?" Kling asked.

"He didn't say the name."

"You just said he *did* say the name. The Tinka Sachs murder. You said—"

"Yes, that's right. That's not what I mean."

"Look, what – ?"

"He didn't say Cyclops' name."

"I don't understand you."

"All he said was he wanted the address of the one-eyed elevator operator because he had some questions to ask him about the Tinka Sachs murder. That's what he said."

"He referred to him as the one-eyed elevator operator?"

"That's right."

"You mean he didn't know the name?"

"Well, I don't know about that. He didn't know how to *spell* it, though, that's for sure."

"Excuse me," the telephone operator said. "Five cents for the next five minutes, please."

"Hold on," Kling said. He reached into his pocket, and found only two quarters. He put one into the coin slot.

"Was that twenty-five cents you deposited, sir?" the operator asked.

"That's right."

"If you'll let me have your name and address, sir, we'll—"

"No, forget it."

"—send you a refund in stamps."

"No, that's all right, operator, thank you. Just give me as much time as the quarter'll buy, okay?"

"Very well, sir."

"Hello?" Kling said. "Mr Farber?"

"I'm still here," Farber said.

"What makes you think this detective couldn't spell Cyclops' name?"

"Well, I gave him the address, you see, and I was about to

hang up when he asked me about the spelling. He wanted to know the correct spelling of the name."

"And what did you say?"

"I said it was Messner, M-E-S-S-N-E-R, Ernest Messner, and I repeated the address for him again, 1117 Gainesborough Avenue in Riverhead."

"And then what?"

"He said thank you very much and hung up."

"Sir, was it your impression that he did not know Cyclops' name until you gave it to him?"

"Well, I couldn't say that for sure. All he wanted was the correct spelling."

"Yes, but he asked for the address of the one-eyed elevator operator, isn't what what you said?"

"That's right."

"If he knew the name, why didn't he use it?"

"You got me. What's *your* name?" the superintendent asked.

"Kling. Detective Bert Kling."

"Mine's Farber, Emmnauel Farber, Manny."

"Yes, I know. You told me."

"Oh. Okay."

There was a long silence on the line.

"Was that all, Detective Kling?" Farber said at last. "I've got to get these lobby floors waxed and I'm—"

"Just a few more questions," Kling said.

"Well, okay, but could we—?"

"Cyclops had his usual midnight-to-eight-a.m. shift Monday night, is that right?"

"That's right, but—"

"When he came to work, did he mention anything about having seen a detective?"

"He *didn't*," Farber said.

"He didn't mention a detective at all? He didn't say—"

"No, he didn't come to work."

"What?"

"He didn't come to work Monday nor yesterday, either," Farber said. "I had to get another man to take his place."

"Did you try to reach him?"

"I waited until twelve-thirty, with the man he was supposed to relieve taking a fit, and finally I called his apartment, three times in fact, and there was no answer. So I phoned one of the other men. Had to run the elevator myself until the man got here. That must've been about two in the morning."

"Did Cyclops contact you at all any time yesterday?"

"Nope. You think he'd call, wouldn't you?"

"Did he contact you today?"

"Nope."

"But you're expecting him to report to work tonight, aren't you?"

"Well, he's due at midnight, but I don't know. I hope he shows up."

"Yes, I hope so, too," Kling said. "Thank you very much, Mr Farber. You've been very helpful."

"Sure thing," Farber said, and hung up.

Kling sat in the phone booth for several moments, trying to piece together what he had just learned. Someone had called Farber on Monday night at about ten, identifying himself as Detective Carella, and asking for the address of the one-eyed elevator operator. Carella knew the man was named Ernest Messner and nicknamed Cyclops. He would not have referred to him as the one-eyed elevator operator. But more important than that, he would never have called the superintendent at all. Knowing the man's name, allegedly desiring his address, he would have done exactly what Kling had done this morning. He would have consulted the telephone directories and found a listing for Ernest Messner in the Riverhead book, as simple as that, as routine as that. No, the man who had called Farber was not Carella. But he had known Carella's name, and had made good use of it.

At ten-thirty Monday night, Marjorie Gorman had met Cyclops in front of the building and he had told her he was expecting a visit from a detective. That could only mean that "Detective Carella" had already called Cyclops and told him he would stop by. And now, Cyclops was missing, had indeed been missing since Monday night.

Kling came out of the phone booth, and began walking back toward the building on Gainesborough Avenue.

The landlady of the building did not have a key to Mr Messner's apartment. Mr Messner had his own lock on the door, she said, the same as any of the other tenants in the building, and she certainly did not have a key to Mr Messner's lock, nor to the locks of any of the other tenants. Moreover, she would *not* grant Kling permission to try his skeleton key on the door, and she warned him that if he forced entry into Mr Messner's apartment, she would sue the city. Kling informed her that if she cooperated, she would save him the trouble of going all the way downtown for a search warrant, and she said she didn't *care* about his going all the way downtown, suppose Mr Messner came back and learned she had let the police in there while he was away, *who'd* get the lawsuit then, would he mind telling her?

Kling said he would go downtown for the warrant.

Go ahead then, the landlady told him.

It took an hour to get downtown, twenty minutes to obtain the warrant, and another hour to get back to Riverhead again. His skeleton key would not open Cyclops' door, so he kicked it in.

The apartment was empty.

7

Dennis Sachs seemed to be about forty years old. He was tall and deeply tanned, with massive shoulders and an athlete's easy stance. He opened the door of his room at the Hotel Capistan, and said, "Detective Kling? Come in, won't you?"

"Thank you," Kling said. He studied Sachs's face. The eyes were blue, with deep ridges radiating from the edges, starkly white against the bronzed skin. He had a large nose, an almost feminine mouth, a cleft chin. He needed a shave. His hair was brown.

The little girl, Anna, was sitting on a couch at the far end of the large living room. She had a doll across her lap, and she was watching television when Kling came in. She glanced up at him briefly, and then turned her attention back to the screen. A give-away program was in progress, the m.c. unveiling a huge motor launch to the delighted shrieks of the studio audience. The couch was upholstered in a lush green fabric against which the child's blonde hair shone lustrously. The place was oppressively over-furnished, undoubtedly part of a suite, with two doors leading from the living room to the adjoining bedrooms. A small cooking alcove was tucked discreetly into a corner near the entrance door, a screen drawn across it. The dominant colors of the suite were pale yellows and deep greens, the rugs were thick, the furniture was exquisitely carved. Kling suddenly wondered how much all this was costing Sachs per day, and then tried to remember where he'd picked up the notion that archaeologists were poverty-stricken.

"Sit down," Sachs said. "Can I get you a drink?"

"I'm on duty," Kling said.

"Oh, sorry. Something soft then? A Coke? Seven-Up? I think we've got some in the refrigerator."

"Thank you, no," Kling said.

The men sat. From his wing chair, Kling could see through the large windows and out over the park to where the sky-scrapers lined the city. The sky behind the buildings was a vibrant blue. Sachs sat facing him, limned with the light flowing through the windows.

"The people at the Children's Shelter told me you got to the city late Monday, Mr Sachs. May I ask where in Arizona you were?"

"Well, part of the time I was in the desert, and the rest of the time I was staying in a little town called Rainfield, have you ever heard of it?"

"No."

"Yes. Well, I'm not surprised," Sachs said. "It's on the edge of the desert. Just a single hotel, a depot, a general store, and that's it."

"What were you doing in the desert?"

"We're on a dig, I thought you knew that. I'm part of an archaeological team headed by Dr Oliver Tarsmith. We're trying to trace the route of the Hohokam in Arizona."

"The Hohokam?"

"Yes, that's a Pima Indian word meaning 'those who have vanished.' The Hohokam were a tribe once living in Arizona, haven't you ever heard of them?"

"No, I'm afraid I haven't."

"Yes, well. In any case, they seem to have had their origins in Old Mexico. In fact, archaeologists like myself have found copper bells and other objects that definitely link the Hohokam to the Old Mexican civilization. And, of course, we've excavated ball courts – an especially large one at Snaketown – that are definitely Mexican or Mayan in origin. At one site, we found a rubber ball buried in a jar, and it's our belief that it must have been traded through tribes all the way from southern Mexico. That's where the wild rubber grows, you know."

"No, I didn't know that."

"Yes, well. The point is that we archaeologists don't know

what route the Hohokam traveled from Mexico to Arizona and then to Snaketown. Dr Tarsmith's theory is that their point of entry was the desert just outside Rainfield. We are now excavating for archaeological evidence to support this theory."

"I see. That sounds like interesting work."

Sachs shrugged.

"Isn't it?"

"I suppose so."

"You don't sound very enthusiastic."

"Well, we haven't had too much luck so far. We've been out there for close to a year, and we've uncovered only the flimsiest sort of evidence, and . . . well, frankly, it's getting a bit tedious. We spend four days a week out on the desert, you see, and then come back into Rainfield late Thursday night. There's nothing much in Rainfield, and the nearest big town is a hundred miles from there. It can get pretty monotonous."

"Why only *four* days in the desert?"

"Instead of five, do you mean? We usually spend Fridays making out our reports. There's a lot of paperwork involved, and it's easier to do at the hotel."

"When did you learn of your wife's death, Mr Sachs?"

"Monday morning."

"You had not been informed up to that time?"

"Well, as it turned out, a telegram was waiting for me in Rainfield. I guess it was delivered to the hotel on Saturday, but I wasn't there to take it."

"Where were you?"

"In Phoenix."

"What were you doing there?"

"Drinking, seeing some shows. You can get very sick of Rainfield, you know."

"Did anyone go with you?"

"No."

"How did you get to Phoenix?"

"By train."

"Where did you stay in Phoenix?"

"At the Royal Sands."

"From when to when?"

"Well, I left Rainfield late Thursday night. I asked Oliver – Dr Tarsmith – if he thought he'd need me on Friday, and he said he wouldn't. I guess he realized I was stretched a little thin. He's a very perceptive man that way."

"I see. In effect, then, he gave you Friday off."

"That's right."

"No reports to write?"

"I took those with me to Phoenix. It's only a matter of organizing one's notes, typing them up, and so on."

"Did you manage to get them done in Phoenix?"

"Yes, I did."

"Now, Let me understand this, Mr Sachs . . ."

"Yes?"

"You left Rainfield sometime late Thursday night . . ."

"Yes, I caught the last train out."

"What time did you arrive in Phoenix?"

"Sometime after midnight. I had called ahead to the Sands for a reservation."

"I see. When did you leave Phoenix?"

"Mr Kling," Sachs said suddenly, "are you just making small talk, or is there some reason for your wanting to know all this?"

"I was simply curious, Mr Sachs. I knew Homicide had sent a wire off to you, and I was wondering why you didn't receive it until Monday morning."

"Oh. Well, I just explained that. I didn't get back to Rainfield until then."

"You left Phoenix Monday morning?"

"Yes. I caught a train at about six a.m. I didn't want to miss the jeep." Sachs paused. "The expedition's jeep. We usually head out to the desert pretty early, to get some heavy work in before the sun gets too hot."

"I see. But when you got back to the hotel, you found the telegram."

"That's right."

"What did you do then?"

"I immediately called the airport in Phoenix to find out what flights I could get back here."

"And what did they tell you?"

"There was a TWA flight leaving at eight in the morning, which would get here at four-twenty in the afternoon – there's a two-hour difference, you know."

"Yes, I know that. Is that the flight you took?"

"No, I didn't. It was close to six-thirty when I called the airport. I might have been able to make it to Phoenix in time, but it would have been a very tight squeeze, and I'd have had to borrow a car. The trains out of Rainfield aren't that frequent, you see."

"So what *did* you do?"

"Well, I caught American's eight-thirty flight, instead. Not a through flight; we made a stop at Chicago. I didn't get here until almost five o'clock that night."

"That was Monday night?"

"Yes, that's right."

"When did you pick up your daughter?"

"Yesterday morning. Today is Wednesday, isn't it?"

"Yes."

"You lose track of time when you fly cross-country," Sachs said.

"I suppose you do."

The television m.c. was giving away a fourteen-cubic-foot refrigerator with a big, big one-hundred-and-sixty-pound freezer. The studio audience was applauding. Anna sat with her eyes fastened to the screen.

"Mr Sachs, I wonder if we could talk about your wife."

"Yes, please."

"The child . . ."

"I think she's absorbed in the program. He glanced at her, and then said, "Would you prefer we discussed it in one of the other rooms?"

"I thought that might be better, yes," Kling said.

"Yes, you're right. Of course," Sachs said. He rose and led Kling toward the larger bedroom. His valise, partially unpacked, was open on the stand alongside the bed. "I'm afraid everything's a mess," he said. "It's been hurry up, hurry up from the moment I arrived."

"I can imagine," Kling said. He sat in an easy chair near the bed. Sachs sat on the edge of the bed and leaned over intently, waiting for him to begin. "Mr Sachs, how long had you and your wife been divorced?"

"Three years. And we separated a year before that."

"The child is how old?"

"Anna? She's five."

"Is there another child?"

"No."

"The way you said 'Anna,' I thought—"

"No, there's only the one child. Anna. That's all."

"As I understand it, then, you and your wife separated the year after she was born."

"That's right, yes. Actually, it was fourteen months. She was fourteen months old when we separated."

"Why was that, Mr Sachs?"

"Why was what?"

"Why did you separate?"

"Well, you know." Sachs shrugged.

"No, I don't."

"Well, that's personal. I'm afraid."

The room was very silent. Kling could hear the m.c. in the living room leading the audience in a round of applause for one of the contestants.

"I can understand that divorce is a personal matter, Mr Sachs, but—"

"Yes, it is."

"Yes, I understand that."

"I'd rather not discuss it, Mr Kling. Really, I'd rather not. I don't see how it would help you in solving . . . in solving my wife's murder. Really."

"I'm afraid *I'll* have to decide what would help us, Mr Sachs."

"We had a personal problem, let's leave it at that."

"What sort of a personal problem?"

"I'd rather not say. We simply couldn't live together any longer, that's all."

"Was there another man involved?"

"Certainly not!"

"Forgive me, but I think you can see how another man might be important in a murder case."

"I'm sorry. Yes. Of course. Yes, it would be important. But it wasn't anything like that. There was no one else involved. There was simply a . . . a personal problem between the two of us and we . . . we couldn't find a way to resolve it, so . . . so we thought it best to split up. That's all there was to it."

"What was the personal problem?"

"Nothing that would interest you."

"Try me."

"My wife is dead," Sachs said.

"I know that."

"Any problem she might have had is certainly—"

"Oh, it was *her* problem then, is that right? Not yours?"

"It was *our* problem," Sachs said. "Mr Kling, I'm not going to answer any other questions along these lines. If you insist that I do, you'll have to arrest me, and I'll get a lawyer, and we'll see about it. In the meantime, I'll just have to refuse to co-operate if that's the tack you're going to follow. I'm sorry."

"All right, Mr Sachs, perhaps you can tell me whether or not you mutually agreed to the divorce."

"Yes, we did."

"Whose idea was it? Yours or hers?"

"Mine."

"Why?"

"I can't answer that."

"You know, of course, that adultery is the only grounds for divorce in this state."

"Yes, I know that. There was no adultery involved. Tinka went to Nevada for the divorce."

"Did you go with her?"

"No. She knew people in Nevada. She's from the West Coast originally. She was born in Los Angeles."

"Did she take the child with her?"

"No. Anna stayed here with me while she was gone."

"Have you kept in touch since the divorce, Mr Sachs?"

"Yes."

"How?"

"Well, I see Anna, you know. We share the child. We agreed to that before the divorce. Stuck out in Arizona there, I didn't have much chance to see her this past year. But usually, I see quite a bit of her. And I talk to Tinka on the phone, I *used* to talk to her on the phone, and I also wrote to her. We kept in touch, yes."

"Would you have described your relationship as a friendly one?"

"I loved her," Sachs said flatly.

"I see."

Again, the room was silent. Sachs turned his head away.

"Do you have any idea who might have killed her?" Kling asked.

"No."

"None whatever?"

"None whatever."

"When did you communicate with her last?"

"We wrote to each other almost every week."

"Did she mention anything that was troubling her?"

"No."

"Did she mention any of her friends who might have had reason to . . . ?"

"No."

"When did you write to her last?"

"Last week sometime."

"Would you remember exactly when?"

"I think it was . . . the fifth or the sixth, I'm not sure."

"Did you send the letter by air?"

"Yes."

"Then it should have arrived here before her death."

"Yes, I imagine it would have."

"Did she usually save your letters?"

"I don't know. Why?"

"We couldn't find any of them in the apartment."

"Then I guess she didn't save them."

"Did *you* save *her* letters?"

"Yes."

"Mr Sachs, would you know one of your wife's friends who answers this description: six feet two or three inches tall, heavily built, in his late thirties or early forties, with straight blond hair and—'

"I don't know who Tinka saw after we were divorced. We led separate lives."

"But you still loved her."

"Yes."

"Then why did you divorce her?" Kling asked again, and Sachs did not answer. "Mr Sachs, this may be very important to us . . ."

"It isn't."

"Was your wife a dyke?"

"No."

"Are you homosexual?"

"No."

"Mr Sachs, *whatever* it was, believe me, it won't be something new to us. Believe me, Mr Sachs, and please trust me."

"I'm sorry. It's none of your business. It has nothing to do with anything but Tinka and me."

"Okay," Kling said.

"I'm sorry."

"Think about it. I know you're upset at the moment, but—"

"There's nothing to think about. There are some things I will never discuss with anyone, Mr Kling. I'm sorry, but I owe at least that much to Tinka's memory."

"I understand," Kling said, and rose. "Thank you for your time. I'll leave my card, in case you remember anything that might be helpful to us."

"All right," Sachs said.

"When will you be going back to Arizona?"

"I'm not sure. There's so much to be arranged. Tinka's lawyer advised me to stay for a while, at least to the end of the month, until the estate can be settled, and plans made for Anna . . . there's so much to do."

"*Is* there an estate?" Kling asked.

"Yes."

"A sizable one?"

"I wouldn't imagine so."

"I see." Kling paused, seemed about to say something, and then abruptly extended his hand. "Thank you again, Mr Sachs," he said. "I'll be in touch with you."

Sachs saw him to the door. Anna, her doll in her lap, was still watching television when he went out.

At the squadroom, Kling sat down with a pencil and pad, and then made a call to the airport, requesting a list of all scheduled flights to and from Phoenix, Arizona. It took him twenty minutes to get all the information, and another ten minutes to type it up in chronological order. He pulled the single sheet from his machine and studied it:

EASTBOUND:

Frequency	Airline & Flt.	Departing Phoenix	Arriving Here	Stops		
Exc. Sat.	American #946	12:25 AM	10:45 AM	(Tucson	12:57 AM-	1:35 AM
				(Chicago	6:35 AM-	8:00 AM
Daily	American # 98	7:25 AM	5:28 PM	(Tucson	7:57 AM-	8:25 AM
				(El Paso	9:10 AM-	9:40 AM
				(Dallas	12:00 PM-	12:30 PM
Daily	TWA #146	8:00 AM	4:20 PM	Chicago	12:58 PM-	1:30 PM
Daily	American # 68	8:30 AM	4:53 PM	Chicago	1:27 PM-	2:00 PM
Daily	American # 66	2:00 PM	10:23 PM	Chicago	6:57 PM-	7:30 PM

WESTBOUND:

Frequency	Airline & Flt.	Departing Here	Arriving Phoenix	Stops		
Exc. Sun.	American #965	8:00 AM	11:05 AM	Chicago	9:12 AM-	9:55 AM
Daily	TWA #147	8:30 AM	11:25 AM	Chicago	9:31 AM-	10:15 AM
Daily	American #981	4:00 PM	6:55 PM	Chicago	5:12 PM-	5:45 PM
Daily	TWA #143	4:30 PM	7:40 PM	Chicago	5:41 PM-	6:30 PM
Daily	American # 67	6:00 PM	10:10 PM	(Chicago	7:12 PM-	7:45 PM
				(Tucson	9:08 PM-	9:40 PM

It seemed entirely possible to him that Dennis Sachs could have taken either the twelve twenty-five flight from Phoenix late Thursday night, or any one of three flights early Friday morning, and still have been here in the city in time to arrive at Tinka's apartment by nine or nine-thirty p.m. He could certainly have killed his wife and caught an early flight back the next morning. Or any one of four flights on Sunday, all of which – because of the time difference – would have put him back in Phoenix that same night and in Rainfield by Monday to pick up the telegram waiting there for him. It was a possibility – remote, but a possibility nonetheless. The brown hair, of course, was a problem. Cyclops had said the man's hair was blond. But a commercial dye or bleach—

One thing at a time, Kling thought. Wearily, he pulled the telephone directory to him and began a methodical check of the two air lines flying to Phoenix. He told them he wanted to know if a man named Dennis Sachs, or any man with the initials D.S., had flown here from Phoenix last Thursday night or Friday morning, and whether or not he had made the return flight any time during the weekend. The airlines were helpful and patient. They checked their flight lists, Something we don't ordinarily do, sir, is this a case involving a missing person? No, Kling said, this is a case involving a murder. Oh, well in that case, sir, but we don't ordinarily do this, sir, even for the police, our flight lists you see . . . Yes, well I appreciate your help, Kling said.

Neither of the airlines had any record of either a Dennis Sachs or a D.S. taking a trip from or to Phoenix at any time before Monday, April 12th. American Airlines had him listed as a passenger on Flight 68, which had left Phoenix at eight-thirty a.m. Monday morning, and had arrived here at four-fifty-three p.m. that afternoon. American reported that Mr Sachs had not as yet booked return passage.

Kling thanked American and hung up. There was still the possibility that Sachs had flown here and back before Monday, using an assumed name. But there was no way of checking that – and the only man who could make any sort of a positive identification had been missing since Monday night.

The meeting took place in Lieutenant Byrnes's office at five o'clock that afternoon. There were five detectives present in addition to Byrnes himself. Miscolo had brought in coffee for most of the men, but they sipped at it only distractedly, listening intently to Byrnes as he conducted the most unorthodox interrogation any of them had ever attended.

"We're here to talk about Monday afternoon," Byrnes said. His tone was matter-of-fact, his face expressed no emotion. "I have the duty chart for Monday, April twelfth, and it shows Kling, Meyer and Carella on from eight to four, with Meyer catching. The relieving team is listed as Hawes, Willis and Brown, with Brown catching. Is that the way it was?"

The men nodded.

"What time did you get here, Cotton?"

Hawes, leaning against the lieutenant's filing cabinet, the only one of the detectives drinking tea, looked up and said, "It must've been about five."

"Was Steve still here?"

"No."

"What about you, Hal?"

"I got here a little early, Pete," Willis said. "I had some calls to make."

"What time?"

"Four-thirty."

"Was Steve still here?"

"Yes."

"Did you talk to him?"

"Yes."

"What about?"

"He said he was going to a movie with Teddy that night."

"Anything else?"

"That was about it."

"I talked to him, too, Pete," Brown said. He was the only Negro cop in the room. He was sitting in the wooden chair to the right of Byrnes's desk, a coffee container clasped in his huge hands.

"What'd he say to you, Art?"

"He told me he had to make a stop on the way home."

"Did he say where?"

"No."

"All right, now let's get this straight. Of the relieving team, only two of you saw him, and he said nothing about where he might have been headed. Is that right?"

"That's right," Willis said.

"Were you in the office when he left, Meyer?"

"Yes. I was making out a report."

"Did he say anything to you?"

"He said good night, and he made some joke about bucking for a promotion, you know, because I was hanging around after I'd been relieved."

"What else?"

"Nothing."

"Did he say anything to you at any time during the afternoon? About where he might be going later on?"

"Nothing."

"How about you, Kling?"

"No, he didn't say anything to me, either."

"Were you here when he left?"

"No."

"Where were you?"

"I was on my way home."

"What time did you leave?"

"About three o'clock."

"Why so early?"

There was a silence in the room.

"Why so early?" Byrnes said again.

"We had a fight."

"What about?"

"A personal matter."

"The man is dead," Byrnes said flatly. "There are no personal matters any more."

"He sent me back to the office because he didn't like the way I was behaving during an interview. I got sore." Kling paused. "That's what we argued about."

"So you left here at three o'clock?"

"Yes."

"Even though you were supposed to be working with Carella on the Tinka Sachs case, is that right?"

"Yes."

"Did you know where he was going when he left here?"

"No, sir."

"Did he mention anything about wanting to question anyone, or about wanting to see anyone again?"

"Only the elevator operator. He thought it would be a good idea to check him again."

"What for?"

"To verify a time he'd given us."

"Do you think that's where he went?"

"I don't know, sir."

"Have you talked to this elevator operator?"

"No, sir, I can't locate him."

"He's been missing since Monday night," Meyer said. "According to Bert's report, he was expecting a visit from a man who said he was Carella."

"Is that right?" Byrnes asked.

"Yes," Kling said. "But I don't think it *was* Carella."

"Why not?"

"It's all in my report, sir."

"You've read this, Meyer?"

"Yes."

"What's your impression?"

"I agree with Bert."

Byrnes moved away from his desk. He walked to the window and stood with his hands clasped behind his back, looking at the street below. "He found something, that's for sure," he said, almost to himself. "He found *something* or *somebody*, and he was killed for it." He turned abruptly. "And not a single goddamn one of you knows where he was going. Not even the man who was allegedly working this case with him." He walked back to his desk. "Kling, you stay. The rest of you can leave."

The men shuffled out of the room. Kling stood uncomfortably before the lieutenant's desk. The lieutenant sat in his swivel chair, and turned it so that he was not looking directly at Kling. Kling did not know where he was looking. His eyes seemed unfocused.

"I guess you know that Steve Carella was a good friend of mine," Byrnes said.

"Yes, sir."

"A good friend," Byrnes repeated. He paused for a moment, still looking off somewhere past Kling, his eyes unfocused, and then said, "Why'd you let him go out alone, Kling?"

"I told you, sir. We had an argument."

"So you left here at three o'clock, when you knew goddamn well you weren't going to be relieved until four-forty-five. Now what the hell do you call that, Kling?"

Kling did not answer.

"I'm kicking you off this goddamn squad," Byrnes said. "I should have done it long ago. I'm asking for your transfer, now get the hell out of here."

Kling turned and started for the door.

"No, wait a minute," Byrnes said. He turned directly to Kling now, and there was a terrible look on his face, as though he wanted to cry, but the tears were being checked by intense anger.

"I guess you know, Kling, that I don't have the power to suspend you, I guess you know that. The power rests with the commissioner and his deputies, and they're civilians. But a man can be suspended if he's violated the rules and regulations or if he's committed a crime. The way I look at it, Kling, you've done *both* those things. You violated the rules and regulations by leaving this squadroom and heading home when you were supposed to be on duty, and you committed a crime by allowing Carella to go out there alone and get killed."

"Lieutenant, I—"

"If I could personally take away your gun and your shield, I'd do it, Kling, believe me. Unfortunately, I can't. But I'm going to call the Chief of Detectives the minute you leave this office. I'm going to tell him I'd like you suspended pending a complete investigation, and I'm going to ask that he recommend that to the commissioner. I'm going to *get* that suspension, Kling, if I have to go to the mayor for it. I'll get departmental charges filed, and a departmental trial, and I'll get you dismissed from the force. I'm *promising* you. Now get the hell out of my sight."

Kling walked to the door silently, opened it, and stepped into the squadroom. He sat at his desk silently for several moments, staring into space. He heard the buzzer sound on Meyer's phone, heard Meyer lifting the instrument to his ear. "Yeah?" Meyer said. "Yeah, Pete. Right. Okay, I'll tell him." He heard Meyer putting the phone back onto its cradle. Meyer rose and came to his desk. "That was the lieutenant," he said. "He wants me to take over the Tinka Sachs case."

8

The message went out on the teletype at a little before ten Thursday morning:

MISSING PERSON WANTED FOR QUESTIONING CONNECTION HOMICIDE XXX ERNEST MESSNER ALIAS CYCLOPS MESSNER XXX WHITE MALE AGE 68 XXX HEIGHT 6 FEET XXX WEIGHT 170 LBS XXX COMPLETELY BALD XXX EYES BLUE LEFT EYE MISSING AND COVERED BY PATCH XXXXX LAST SEEN VICINITY 1117 GAINESBOROUGH AVENUE RIVERHEAD MONDAY APRIL 12 TEN THIRTY PM EST XXX CONTACT MISPERBUR OR DET/2G MEYER MEYER EIGHT SEVEN SQUAD XXXXXXXXX

A copy of the teletype was pulled off the squadroom machine by Detective Meyer Meyer who wondered why it had been necessary for the detective at the Missing Persons Bureau to insert the word "completely" before the word "bald". Meyer, who was bald himself, suspected that the description was redundant, over-emphatic, and undoubtedly derogatory. It was his understanding that a bald person had no hair. None. Count them. None. Why, then, had the composer of this bulletin (Meyer visualized him as a bushy-headed man with thick black eyebrows, a black mustache and a full beard) insisted on inserting the word "completely", if not to point a deriding finger at all hairless men everywhere? Indignantly, Meyer went to the squadroom dictionary, searched through balas, balata, Balaton, Balboa, balbriggan, and came to:

bald (bôld) adj. **1**. lacking hair on some part of the scalp: *a bald head or person*. **2**. destitute of some natural growth or covering: *a bald mountain*. **3**. bare; plain; unadorned: *a bald prose style*. **4**. open; undisguised: *a bald lie*. **5**. *Zool*. having white on the head: *bald eagle*.

Meyer closed the book, reluctantly admitting that whereas it was impossible to be a little pregnant, it was not equally impossible to be a little bald. The composer of the bulletin, bushy-haired bastard that he was, had been right in describing Cyclops as "completely bald". If ever Meyer turned up missing one day, they would describe him in exactly the same way. In the meantime, his trip to the dictionary had not been a total loss. He would hereafter look upon himself as a person who lacked hair on his scalp, a person destitute of some natural growth, bare, plain and unadorned, open and undisguised, having white on the head. Hereafter, he would be known zoologically as The Bald Eagle – Nemesis of All Evil, Protector of the Innocent, Scourge of the Underworld!

"Beware The Bald Eagle!" he said aloud, and Arthur Brown looked up from his desk in puzzlement. Happily, the telephone rang at that moment. Meyer picked it up and said, "87th Squad."

"This is Sam Grossman at the lab. Who'm I talking to?"

"You're talking to The Bald Eagle," Meyer said.

"Yeah?"

"Yeah."

"Well, this is The Hairy Ape," Grossman said. "What's with you? Spring fever?"

"Sure, it's such a beautiful day out," Meyer said, looking through the window at the rain.

"Is Kling there? I've got something for him on this Tinka Sachs case."

"I'm handling that one now," Meyer said.

"Oh? Okay. You feel like doing a little work, or were you planning to fly up to your aerie?"

"Up *your* aeire, Mac," Meyer said, and burst out laughing.

"Oh boy, I see I picked the wrong time to call," Grossman said. "Okay. Okay. When you've got a minute later, give me a ring, Okay? I'll—"

"The Bald Eagle *never* has a minute later," Meyer said. "What've you got for me?"

"This kitchen knife. The murder weapon. According to the tag, it was found just outside her bedroom door, guy probably dropped it on his way out."

"Okay, what about it?"

"Not much. Only it matches a few other knives in the girl's kitchen, so it's reasonable to assume it belonged to her. What I'm saying is the killer didn't go up there with his own knife, if that's of any use to you."

"He took the knife from a bunch of other knives in the kitchen, is that it?"

"No, I don't think so. I think the knife was in the bedroom."

"What would a knife be doing in the bedroom?"

"I think the girl used it to slice some lemons."

"Yeah?"

"Yeah. There was a pitcher of tea on the dresser. Two lemons, sliced in half, were floating in it. We found lemon-juice stains on the tray, as well as faint scratches left by the knife. We figure she carried the tea, the lemons, and the knife into the bedroom on that tray. Then she sliced the lemons and squeezed them into the tea."

"Well, that seems like guesswork to me," Meyer said.

"Not at all. Paul Blaney is doing the medical examination. He says he's found citric-acid stains on the girl's left hand, the hand she'd have held the lemons with while slicing with the right. We've checked, Meyer. She was right-handed."

"Okay, so she was drinking tea before she got killed," Meyer said.

"That's right. The glass was on the night table near her bed, covered with her prints."

"Whose prints were covering the knife?"

"Nobody's," Grossman said. "Or I should say *everybody's*. A whole mess of them, all smeared."

"What about her pocketbook? Kling's report said—"

"Same thing, not a good print on it anywhere. There was no

money in it, you know. My guess is that the person who killed her also robbed her."

"Mmm, yeah," Meyer said. "Is that all?"

"That's all. Disappointing, huh?"

"I hoped you might come up with something more."

"I'm sorry."

"Sure."

Grossman was silent for a moment. Then he said, "Meyer?"

"Yeah?"

"You think Carella's death is linked to this one?"

"I don't know," Meyer said.

"I liked that fellow," Grossman said, and hung up.

Harvey Sadler was Tinka Sachs's lawyer and the senior partner in the firm of Sadler, McIntyre and Brooks, with offices uptown on Fisher Street. Meyer arrived there at ten minutes to noon, and discovered that Sadler was just about to leave for the Y.M.C.A. Meyer told him he was there to find out whether or not Tinka Sachs had left a will, and Sadler said she had indeed. In fact, they could talk about it on the way to the Y, if Meyer wanted to join him. Meyer said he wanted to, and the two men went downstairs to catch a cab.

Sadler was forty-five years old, with a powerful build and craggy features. He told Meyer he had played offensive back for Dartmouth in 1940, just before he was drafted into the army. He kept in shape nowadays, he said, by playing handball at the Y two afternoons a week, Mondays and Thursdays. At least, he *tried* to keep in shape. Even handball twice a week could not completely compensate for the fact that he sat behind a desk eight hours a day.

Meyer immediately suspected a deliberate barb. He had become oversensitive about his weight several weeks back when he discovered what his fourteen-year-old son Alan meant by the nickname "Old Crisco". A bit of off-duty detective work uncovered the information that "Old Crisco" was merely high school jargon for "Old Fat-in-the-Can", a disrespectful term of affection if ever he'd heard one. He would have clobbered the boy, naturally, just to show who was boss, had not his wife Sarah agreed with the little vontz. You *are* getting fat, she told

Meyer; you should begin exercising at the police gym. Meyer, whose boyhood had consisted of a series of taunts and jibes from Gentiles in his neighborhood, never expected to be put down by vipers in his own bosom. He looked narrowly at Sadler now, a soldier in the enemy camp, and suddenly wondered if he was becoming a paranoid Jew. Worse yet, an *obese* paranoid Jew.

His reservations about Sadler and also about himself vanished the moment they entered the locker room of the Y.M.C.A., which smelled exactly like the locker room of the Y.M.H.A. Convinced that nothing in the world could eliminate suspicion and prejudice as effectively as the aroma of a men's locker room, swept by a joyous wave of camaraderie, Meyer leaned against the lockers while Sadler changed into his handball shorts, and listened to the details of Tinka's will.

"She leaves everything to her ex-husband," Sadler said. "That's the way she wanted it."

"Nothing to her daughter?"

"Only if Dennis predeceased Tinka. In that case, a trust was set up for the child."

"Did Dennis know this?" Meyer asked.

"I have no idea."

"Was a copy of the will sent to him?"

"Not by me."

"How many copies did you send to Tinka?"

"Two. The original was kept in our office safe."

"Did she *request* two copies?"

"No. But it's our general policy to send two copies of any will to the testator. Most people like to keep one at home for easy reference, and the other in a safe deposit box. At least, that's been our experience."

"We went over Tinka's apartment pretty thoroughly, Mr Sadler. We didn't find a copy of any will."

"Then perhaps she *did* send one to her ex-husband. That wouldn't have been at all unusual."

"Why not?"

"Well, they're on very good terms, you know. And, after all, he *is* the only real beneficiary. I imagine Tinka would have wanted him to know."

"Mmm," Meyer said. "How large an estate is it?"

"Well, there's the painting."

"What do you mean?"

"The Chagall."

"I still don't understand."

"The Chagall painting. Tinka bought it many years ago, when she first began earning top money as a model. I suppose it's worth somewhere around fifty thousand dollars today."

"That's a sizable amount."

"Yes," Sadler said. He was in his shorts now, and he was putting on his black gloves and exhibiting signs of wanting to get out on the court. Meyer ignored the signs.

"What about the rest of the estate?" he asked.

"That's it," Sadler said.

"That's what?"

"The Chagall painting *is* the estate, or at least the substance of it. The rest consists of household furnishings, some pieces of jewelry, clothing, personal effects – none of them worth very much."

"Let me get this straight, Mr Sadler. It's my understanding that Tinka Sachs was earning somewhere in the vicinity of a hundred and fifty thousand dollars a year. Are you telling me that all she owned of value at her death was a Chagall painting valued at fifty thousand dollars?"

"That's right."

"How do you explain that?"

"I don't know. I wasn't Tinka's financial adviser. I was only her lawyer."

"As her lawyer, did you ask her to define her estate when she asked you to draw this will?"

"I did."

"How did she define it?"

"Essentially as I did a moment ago."

"When was this, Mr Sadler?"

"The will is dated March twenty-fourth."

"March twenty-fourth? You mean just last month?"

"That's right."

"Was there any specific reason for her wanting a will drawn at that time?"

"I have no idea."

"I mean, was she worried about her health or anything?"

"She seemed in good health."

"Did she seem frightened about anything? Did she seem to possess a foreknowledge of what was going to happen?"

"No, she did not. She seemed very tense, but not frightened."

"Why was she tense?"

"I don't know."

"Did you ask her about it?"

"No, I did not. She came to me to have a will drawn. I drew it."

"Had you ever done any legal work for her prior to the will?"

"Yes. Tinka once owned a house in Mavis County. I handled the papers when she sold it."

"When was that?"

"Last October."

"How much did she get for the sale of the house?"

"Forty-two thousand, five hundred dollars."

"Was there an existing mortgage?"

"Yes. Fifteen thousand dollars went to pay it off. The remainder went to Tinka."

"Twenty . . ." Meyer hesitated, calculating. "Twenty-seven thousand, five hundred dollars went to Tinka, is that right?"

"Yes."

"In cash?"

"Yes."

"Where is it, Mr Sadler?"

"I asked her that when we were preparing the will. I was concerned about estate taxes, you know, and about who would inherit the money she had realized on the sale of the house. But she told me she had used it for personal needs."

"She had spent it?"

"Yes." Sadler paused. "Mr Meyer, I only play here two afternoons a week, and I'm very jealous of my time. I was hoping . . ."

"I won't be much longer, please bear with me. I'm only trying to find out what Tinka did with all this money that came her way. According to you, she didn't have a penny of it when she died."

"I'm only reporting what she told me. I listed her assets as she defined them for me."

"Could I see a copy of the will, Mr Sadler?"

"Certainly. But it's in my safe at the office, and I won't be going back there today. If you'd like to come by in the morning . . ."

"I'd hoped to get a look at it before—"

"I assure you that I've faithfully reported everything in the will. As I told you, I was only her lawyer, not her financial adviser."

"Did she *have* a financial adviser?"

"I don't know."

"Mr Sadler, did you handle Tinka's divorce for her?"

"No. I began representing her only last year, when she sold the house. I didn't know her before then, and I don't know who handled the divorce."

"One last question," Meyer said. "Is anyone else mentioned as a beneficiary in Tinka's will, other than Dennis or Anna Sachs?"

"They are the only beneficiaries," Sadler said. "And Anna only if her father predeceased Tinka."

"Thank you," Meyer said.

Back at the squadroom, Meyer checked over the typewritten list of all the personal belongings found in Tinka's apartment. There was no listing for either a will or a bankbook, but someone from Homicide had noted that a key to a safety deposit box had been found among the items on Tinka's workdesk. Meyer called Homicide to ask about the key, and they told him it had been turned over to the Office of the Clerk, and he could pick it up there if he was interested and if he was willing to sign a receipt for it. Meyer was indeed interested, so he went all the way downtown to the Office of the Clerk, where he searched through Tinka's effects, finding a tiny red snap-envelope with the safety deposit box key in it. The name of the bank was printed on the face of the miniature envelope. Meyer signed out the key and then – since he was in the vicinity of the various court buildings, anyway – obtained a court order authorizing him to open the safety deposit box. In the company of a court official, he went uptown again by subway and then ran through a pouring rain, courtesy of the vernal equinox, to the First Northern National Bank on the corner of Phillips and Third, a few blocks from where Tinka had lived.

A bank clerk removed the metal box from a tier of similar boxes, asked Meyer if he wished to examine the contents in private, and then led him and the court official to a small room containing a desk, a chair, and a chained ballpoint pen. Meyer opened the box.

There were two documents in the box. The first was a letter from an art dealer, giving appraisal of the Chagall painting. The letter stated simply that the painting had been examined, that it was undoubtedly a genuine Chagall, and that it could be sold at current market prices for anywhere between forty-five and fifty thousand dollars.

The second document was Tinka's will. It was stapled inside lawyer's blueback, the firm name Sadler, McIntyre and Brooks printed on the bottom of the binder, together with the address, 80 Fisher Street. Typewritten and centered on the page was the legend LAST WILL AND TESTAMENT OF TINKA SACHS. Meyer opened the will and began reading:

LAST WILL AND TESTAMENT
of
TINKA SACHS

I, Tinka Sachs, a resident of this city, county, and state, hereby revoke all wills and codicils by me at any time heretofore made and do hereby make, publish and declare this as and for my Last Will and Testament.

FIRST: I give, devise and bequeath to my former husband, DENNIS R. SACHS, if he shall survive me, and, if he shall not survive me, to my trustee, hereinafter named, all of my property and all of my household and personal effects including without limitation, clothing, furniture and furnishings, books, jewelry, art objects, and paintings.

SECOND: If my former husband Dennis shall not survive me, I give, devise and bequeath my said estate to my Trustee hereinafter named, IN TRUST NEVERTHELESS, for the following uses and purposes:

(1) My Trustee shall hold, invest and re-invest the principal of said trust and shall collect the income therefrom until my daughter, ANNA SACHS, shall attain the age of twenty-one (21) years, or sooner die.

(2) My Trustee shall, from time to time; distribute to my daughter ANNA before she has attained the age of twenty-one (21) so much of the net income (and the net income of any year not so distributed shall be accumulated and

shall, after the end of such year, be deemed principal for purposes of this trust) and so much of the principal of this trust as my Trustee may in his sole and unreviewable discretion determine for any purposes deemed advisable or convenient by said Trustee, provided, however, that no principal or income in excess of an aggregate amount of Five Thousand Dollars ($5,000) in any one year shall be used for the support of the child unless the death of the child's father, DENNIS R. SÁCHS, shall have left her financially unable to support herself. The decision of my Trustee with respect to the dates of distribution and the sums to be distributed shall be final.

(3) If my daughter, ANNA, shall die before attaining the age of twenty-one (21) years, my Trustee shall pay over the then principal of the trust fund and any accumulated income to the issue of my daughter, ANNA, then living, in equal shares, and if there be no such issue then to those persons who would inherit from me had I died intestate immediately after the death of ANNA.

THIRD: I nominate, constitute and appoint my former husband, DENNIS R. SACHS, Executor of this my Last Will and Testament. If my said former husband shall predecease me or shall fail to qualify or cease to act as Executor, then I appoint my agent and friend, ARTHUR G. CUTLER, in his place as successor or substitute executor and, if my former husband shall predecease me,

as TRUSTEE of the trust created hereby. If my said friend and agent shall fail to qualify or cease to act as Executor or Trustee, then I appoint his wife, LESLIE CUTLER, in his place as successor or substitute executor and/or trustee, as the case may be. Unless otherwise provided by law, no bond or other security shall be required to permit any Executor or Trustee to qualify or act in any jurisdiction.

The rest of the will was boilerplate. Meyer scanned it quickly, and then turned to the last page where Tinka had signed her name below the words "IN WITNESS WHEREOF, I sign, seal, publish and declare this as my Last Will and Testament" and where, below that, Harvey Sadler, William McIntyre and Nelson Brooks had signed as attesting witnesses. The will was dated March twenty-fourth.

The only thing Sadler had forgotten to mention – or perhaps Meyer hadn't asked him about it – was that Art Cutler had been named trustee in the event of Dennis Sachs's death.

Meyer wondered if it meant anything.

And then he calculated how much money Tinka had earned in eleven years at a hundred and fifty thousand dollars a year, and wondered again why her only possession of any real value was the Chagall painting she had drenched with blood on the night of her death.

Something stank.

9

He had checked and rechecked his own findings against the
laboratory's reports on the burned wreckage, and at first only
one thing seemed clear to Paul Blaney. Wherever Steve Carella
had been burned to death, it had not been inside that automobile. The condition of the corpse was unspeakably horrible;
it made Blaney queasy just to look at it. In his years as medical
examiner, Blaney had worked on cases of thermic trauma rang-
ing from the simplest burns to cases of serious and fatal
exposure to flame, light, and electric energy – but these were
the worst fourth-degree burns he had ever seen. The body had
undoubtedly been cooked for hours: The face was unrecogniz-
able, all of the features gone, the skin black and tight, the single
remaining cornea opaque, the teeth undoubtedly loosened and
then lost in the fire; the skin on the torso was brittle and split;
the hair had been burned away, the flesh completely gone in
many places, showing dark red-brown skeletal muscles and
charred brittle bones. Blaney's internal examination revealed
pale, cooked involuntary muscles, dull and shrunken viscera.
Had the body been reduced to its present condition inside that
car, the fire would have had to rage for hours. The lab's report
indicated that the automobile, ignited by an explosion of gasoline, had burned with extreme intensity, but only briefly. It was
Blaney's contention that the body had been burned elsewhere,
and then put into the automobile to simulate death there by
explosion and subsequent fire.

Blaney was not paid to speculate on criminal motivation, but he wondered now why someone had gone to all this trouble, especially when the car fire would undoubtedly have been hot enough to eliminate adequately and forever any intended victim. Being a methodical man, he continued to probe. His careful and prolonged investigation had nothing to do with the fact that the body belonged to a policeman, or even to a policeman he had known. The corpse on the table was not to him a person called Steve Carella; it was instead a pathological puzzle.

He did not solve that puzzle until late Friday afternoon.

Bert Kling was alone in the squadroom when the telephone rang. He lifted the receiver.

"Detective Kling, 87th Squad," he said.

"Bert, this is Paul Blaney."

"Hello, Paul, how are you?"

"Fine, thanks. Who's handling the Carella case?"

"Meyer's in charge. Why?"

"Can I talk to him?"

"Not here right now."

"I think this is important," Blaney said. "Do you know where I can reach him?"

"I'm sorry, I don't know where he is."

"If I give it to you, will you make sure he get it sometime tonight?"

"Sure," Kling said.

"I've been doing the autopsy," Blaney said. "I'm sorry I couldn't get back to you people sooner, but a lot of things were bothering me about this, and I wanted to be careful. I didn't want to make any statements that might put you on the wrong track, do you follow?"

"Yes, sure," Kling said.

"Well, if you're ready, I'd like to trace this for you step by step. And I'd like to say at the onset that I'm absolutely convinced of what I'm about to say. I mean, I know how important this is, and I wouldn't dare commit myself on guesswork alone – not in a case of this nature."

"I've got a pencil," Kling said. "Go ahead."

"To begin with, the comparative conditions of vehicle and

cadaver indicated to me that the body had been incinerated elsewhere for a prolonged period of time, and only later removed to the automobile where it was found. I now have further evidence from the lab to support this theory. I sent them some recovered fragments of foreign materials that were embedded in the burned flesh. The fragments proved to be tiny pieces of *wood* charcoal. It seems certain now that the body was consumed in a wood fire, and not a gasoline fire such as would have occurred in the automobile. It's my opinion that the victim was thrust head first into a fireplace."

"What makes you think so?"

"The upper half of the body was severely burned, whereas most of the pelvic region and all of the lower extremities are virtually untouched. I think the upper half of the body was pushed into the fireplace and kept there for many hours, possibly throughout the night. Moreover, I think the man was murdered *before* he was thrown into the fire."

"Before?"

"Yes, I examined the air passages for possible inhaled soot, and the blood for carboxyhemoglobin. The presence of either would have indicated that the victim was alive during the fire. I found neither."

"Then how *was* he killed?" Kling asked.

"That would involve guesswork," Blaney said. "There's evidence of extradural hemorrhage, and there are also several fractures of the skull vault. But these may only be postmortem fractures resulting from charring, and I wouldn't feel safe in saying the victim was murdered by a blow to the head. Let's simply say he was dead before he was incinerated, and leave it at that."

"Then why was he thrown into the fire?" Kling asked.

"To obliterate the body beyond recognition."

"Go on."

"The teeth, as you know, were missing from the head, making dental identification impossible. At first I thought the fire had loosened them, but upon further examination, I found bone fragments in the upper gum. I now firmly believe that the teeth were knocked out of the mouth before the body was incinerated, and I believe this was done to further prevent identification."

"What are you saying, Blaney?"

"May I go on? I don't want any confusion about this later."

"Please," Kling said.

"There was no hair on the burned torso. Chest hair, underarm hair and even the upper region of pubic hair had been singed away by the fire. Neither was there any hair on the scalp, which would have been both reasonable and obvious had the body been thrust into a fireplace head first, as I surmise it was. But upon examination, I was able to find surviving hair roots in the sub-cutaneous fat below the dermis on the torso and arms, even though the shaft and epithelial sheath had been destroyed. In other words, though the fire had consumed whatever hair had once existed on the torso and arms, there was nonetheless evidence that hair *had been growing there*. I could find no such evidence on the victim's scalp."

"What do you mean?"

"I mean that the man who was found in that automobile was bald to begin with."

"What?"

"Yes, nor was this particularly surprising. The atrophied internal viscera, the distended aorta of the heart, the abundant fatty marrow, large medullary cavities, and dense compact osseous tissue all indicated a person well on in years. Moreover, it was my initial belief that only one eye had survived the extreme heat – the right eye – and that it had been rendered opaque whereas the left eye had been entirely consumed by the flames. I have now carefully examined that left socket and it is my conclusion that there had not been an eye in it for many many years. The optic nerve and tract simply do not exist, and there is scar tissue present which indicates removal of the eye long before—"

"Cyclops!" Kling said. "Oh my God, it's Cyclops!"

"Whoever it is," Blaney said, "it is *not* Steve Carella."

He lay naked on the floor near the radiator.

He could hear rain lashing against the window panes, but the room was warm and he felt no discomfort. Yesterday, the girl had loosened the handcuff a bit, so that it no longer was clamped so tightly on his wrist. His nose was still swollen, but

103

the throbbing pain was gone now, and the girl had washed his cuts and promised to shave him as soon as they were healed.

He was hungry.

He knew that the girl would come with food the moment it grew dark; she always did. There was one meal a day, always at dusk, and the girl brought it to him on a tray and then watched him while he ate, talking to him. Two days ago, she had showed him the newspapers, and he had read them with a peculiar feeling of unreality. The picture in the newspapers had been taken when he was still a patrolman. He looked very young and very innocent. The headline said he was dead.

He listened for the sound of her heels now. He could hear nothing in the other room; the apartment was silent. He wondered if she had gone, and felt a momentary pang. He glanced again at the waning light around the edges of the window shades. The rain drummed steadily against the glass. There was the sound of traffic below, tires hushed on rainswept streets. In the room, the gloom of dusk spread into the corners. Neon suddenly blinked against the drawn shades. He waited, listening, but there was no sound.

He must have dozed again. He was awakened by the sound of the key being inserted in the door lock. He sat upright, his left hand extended behind him and manacled to the radiator, and watched as the girl came into the room. She was wearing a short silk dressing gown belted tightly at the waist. The gown was a bright red, and she wore black high-heeled pumps that added several inches to her height. She closed the door behind her, and put the tray down just inside the door.

"Hello, doll," she whispered.

She did not turn on the overhead light. She went to one of the windows instead and raised the shade. Green neon rainsnakes slithered along the glass pane. The floor was washed with melting green, and then the neon blinked out and the room was dark again. He could hear the girl's breathing. The sign outside flashed again. The girl stood near the window in the red gown, the green neon behind her limning her long legs. The sign went out.

"Are you hungry, doll?" she whispered, and walked to him swiftly and kissed him on the cheek. She laughed deep in her throat, then moved away from him and went to the door. The

Llama rested on the tray alongside the coffeepot. A sandwich was on a paper plate to the right of the gun.

"Do I still need this?" she asked, hefting the gun and pointing it at him.

Carella did not answer.

"I guess not," the girl said, and laughed again, that same low throaty laugh that was somehow not at all mirthful.

"Why am I alive?" he said. He was very hungry, and he could smell the coffee deep and strong in his nostrils, but he had learned not to ask for his food. He had asked for it last night, and the girl had deliberately postponed feeding him, talking to him for more than an hour before she reluctantly brought the tray to him.

"You're not alive," the girl said. "You're dead. I showed you the papers, didn't I? You're dead."

"Why didn't you really kill me?"

"You're too valuable."

"How do you figure that?"

"You know who killed Tinka."

"Then you're better off with me dead."

"No." The girl shook her head. "No, doll. We want to know how you found out."

"What difference does it make?"

"Oh, a lot of difference," the girl said. "He's very concerned about it, really he is. He's getting very impatient. He figures he made a mistake someplace, you see, and he wants to know what it was. Because if *you* found out, chances are somebody else will sooner or later. Unless you tell us what it was, you see. Then we can make sure nobody else finds out. Ever."

"There's nothing to tell you."

"There's plenty to tell," the girl said. She smiled. "You'll tell us. Are you hungry?"

"Yes."

"Tch," the girl said.

"Who was that in the burned car?"

"The elevator operator. Messner." The girl smiled again. "It was my idea. Two birds with one stone."

"What do you mean?"

"Well, I thought it would be a good idea to get rid of Messner just in case he was the one who led you to us. Insurance. And

I also figured that if everybody thought you were dead, that'd give us more time to work on you."

"If Messner was my source, why do you have to work on me?"

"Well, there are a lot of unanswered questions," the girl said. "Gee, that coffee smells good, doesn't it?"

"Yes," Carella said.

"Are you cold?"

"No."

"I can get you a blanket if you're cold."

"I'm fine, thanks."

"I thought, with the rain, you might be a little chilly."

"No."

"You look good naked," the girl said.

"Thank you."

"I'll feed you, don't worry," she said.

"I know you will."

"But about those questions, they're really bothering him, you know. He's liable to get bugged completely and just decide the hell with the whole thing. I mean, I like having you and all, but I don't know if I'll be able to control him much longer. If you don't cooperate, I mean."

"Messner was my source," Carella said. "He gave me the description."

"Then it's a good thing we killed him, isn't it?"

"I suppose so."

"Of course, that still doesn't answer those questions I was talking about."

"What questions?"

"For example, how did you get the name? Messner may have given you a description, but where did you get the name? Or the address, for that matter?"

"They were in Tinka's address book. Both the name *and* the address."

"Was the description there, too?"

"I don't know what you mean."

"You know what I mean, doll. Unless Tinka had a *description* in that book of hers, how could you match a name to what Messner had told you?" Carella was silent. The girl smiled again. "I'm *sure* she didn't have descriptions of people in her address book, did she?"

"No."

"Good, I'm glad you're telling the truth. Because we found the address book in your pocket the night you came busting in here, and we know damn well there're no descriptions of people in it. You hungry?"

"Yes, I'm very hungry," Carella said.

"I'll feed you, don't worry," she said again. She paused. "How'd you know the name and address?"

"Just luck. I was checking each and every name in the book. A process of elimination, that's all."

"That's another lie," the girl said. "I wish you wouldn't lie to me." She lifted the gun from the tray. She held the gun loosely in one hand, picked up the tray with the other, and then said, "Back off."

Carella moved as far back as the handcuff would allow. The girl walked to him, crouched, and put the tray on the floor.

"I'm not wearing anything under this robe," she said.

"I can see that."

"I thought you could," the girl said, grinning, and then rose swiftly and backed toward the door. She sat in the chair and crossed her legs, the short robe riding up on her thighs. "Go ahead," she said, and indicated the tray with a wave of the gun.

Carella poured himself a cup of coffee. He took a quick swallow, and then picked up the sandwich and bit into it.

"Good?" the girl asked, watching.

"Yes."

"I made it myself, You have to admit I take good care of you."

"Sure," Carella said.

"I'm going to take even better care of you," she said. "Why'd you lie to me? Do you think it's nice to lie to me?"

"I didn't lie."

"You said you reached us by luck, a process of elimination. That means you didn't know who or what to expect when you got here, right? You were just looking for someone in Tinka's book who would fit Messner's description."

"That's right."

"Then why'd you kick the door in? Why'd you have a gun in your hand? See what I mean? You knew who he was *before* you got here. You knew he was the one. How?"

"I told you. It was just luck."

"Ahh, gee, I wish you wouldn't lie. Are you finished there?"

"Not yet."

"Let me know when."

"All right."

"I have things to do."

"All right."

"To *you*," the girl said.

Carella chewed on the sandwich. He washed it down with a gulp of coffee. He did not look at the girl. She was jiggling her foot now, the gun hand resting in her lap.

"Are you afraid?" she asked.

"Of what?"

"Of what I might do to you."

"No. Should I be?"

"I might break your nose all over again, who knows?"

"That's true, you might."

"Or I might even keep my promise to knock out all your teeth." The girl smiled. "*That* was my idea, too, you know, knocking out Messner's teeth. You people can make identifications from dental charts, can't you?"

"Yes."

"That's what I thought. That's what I told him. *He* thought it was a good idea, too."

"You're just *full* of good ideas."

"Yeah, I have a lot of good ideas," the girl said. "You're not scared, huh?"

"No."

"I would be, if I were you. Really, I would be."

"The worst you can do is kill me," Carella said. "And since I'm already dead, what difference will it make?"

"I like a man with a sense of humor," the girl said, but she did not smile. "I can do worse than kill you."

"What can you do?"

"I can corrupt you."

"I'm incorruptible," Carella said, and smiled.

"Nobody's incorruptible," she said. "I'm going to make you *beg* to tell us what you know. Really. I'm warning you."

"I've told you everything I know."

"Uh-uh," the girl said, shaking her head. "Are you finished there?"

"Yes."

"Shove the tray away from you."

Carella slid the tray across the floor. The girl went to it, stooped again, and picked it up. She walked back to the chair and sat. She crossed her legs. She began jiggling her foot.

"What's your wife's name?" she asked.

"Teddy."

"That's a nice name. But you'll soon forget it soon enough."

"I don't think so," Carella said evenly.

"You'll forget her name, and you'll forget her, too."

He shook his head.

"I promise," the girl said. "In a week's time, you won't even remember your *own* name."

The room was silent. The girl sat quite still except for the jiggling of her foot. The green neon splashed the floor, and then blinked out. There were seconds of darkness, and then the light came on again. She was standing now. She had left the gun on the seat of the chair and moved to the center of the room. The neon went out. When it flashed on again, she had moved closer to where he was manacled to the radiator.

"What would you like me to do to you?" she asked.

"Nothing."

"What would you like to do to me?"

"Nothing," he said.

"No?" she smiled. "Look, doll."

She loosened the sash at her waist. The robe parted over her breasts and naked belly. Neon washed the length of her body with green, and then blinked off. In the intermittent flashes, he saw the girl moving – as though in a silent movie – toward the light switch near the door, the open robe flapping loose around her. She snapped on the overhead light, and then walked slowly back to the center of the room and stood under the bulb. She held the front of her robe open, the long pale white sheath of her body exposed, the red silk covering her

109

back and her arms, her fingernails tipped with red as glowing as the silk.

"What do you think?" she asked. Carella did not answer. "You want some of it?"

"No," he said.

"You're lying."

"I'm telling you the absolute truth," he said.

"I could make you forget her in a minute," the girl said. "I know things you never dreamed of. You want it?"

"No."

"Just try and get it," she said, and closed the robe and tightened the sash around her waist. "I don't like it when you lie to me."

"I'm not lying."

"You're naked, mister, don't tell *me* you're not lying." She burst out laughing and walked to the door, opening it, and then turned to face him again. Her voice was very low, her face serious. "Listen to me, doll," she said. "You are *mine*, do you understand that? I can do whatever I want with you, don't your forget it. I'm promising you right here and now that in a week's time you'll be crawling on your hands and knees to me, you'll be licking my feet, you'll be *begging* for the opportunity to tell me what you know. And once you tell me, I'm going to throw you away, doll, I'm going to throw you broken and cracked in the gutter, doll, and you're going to wish, believe me, you are just going to *wish* it was you they found dead in that car, believe me." She paused. "Think about it," she said, and turned out the light and went out of the room.

He heard the key turning in the lock.

He was suddenly very frightened.

10

The car håd been found at the bottom of a steep embankment off Route 407. The road was winding and narrow, a rarely used branch connecting the towns of Middlebarth and York, both of which were serviced by wider, straighter highways. 407 was an oiled road, potholed and frost-heaved, used almost entirely by teen-agers searching for a nighttime necking spot. The shoulders were muddy and soft, except for one place where the road widened and ran into the approach to what had once been a gravel pit. It was at the bottom of this pit that the burned vehicle and its more seriously burned passenger had been discovered.

There was only one house on Route 407, five and a half miles from the gravel pit. The house was built of native stone and timber, a rustic affair with a screened back porch overlooking a lake reportedly containing bass. The house was surrounded by white birch and flowering forsythia. Two dogwoods flanked the entrance driveway, their buds ready to burst. The rain had stopped but a fine mist hung over the lake, visible from the turn in the driveway. A huge oak dripped clinging raindrops onto the ground. The countryside was still. The falling drops clattered noisily.

Detectives Hal Willis and Arthur Brown parked the car at the top of the driveway, and walked past the dripping oak to the front door of the house. The door was painted green with a huge brass doorknob centered in its lower panel and a brass knocker centered in the top panel. A locked padlock still hung in a hinge hasp and staple fastened to the door. But the hasp staple had been pried loose of the jamb, and there were deep gouges in the wood where a heavy tool had been used for the job. Willis opened the door, and they went into the house.

There was the smell of contained woodsmoke, and the stench of something else. Brown's face contorted. Gagging, he pulled a handkerchief from his back pocket and covered his nose and mouth. Willis had backed away toward the door again, turning his face to the outside air. Brown took a quick look at the large stone fireplace at the far end of the room, and then caught Willis by the elbow and led him outside.

"Any question in your mind?" Willis asked.

"None," Brown said. "That's the smell of burned flesh."

"We got any masks in the car?"

"I don't know. Let's check the trunk."

They walked back to the car. Willis took the keys from the ignition and leisurely unlocked the trunk. Brown began searching.

"Everything in here but the kitchen sink," he said. "What the hell's this thing?"

"That's mine," Willis said.

"Well, what is it?"

"It's a hat, what do you think it is?"

"It doesn't look like any hat I've ever seen," Brown said.

"I wore it on a plant couple of weeks ago."

"What were you supposed to be?"

"A foreman."

"Of what?"

"A chicken market."

"That's *some* hat, man," Brown said, and chuckled.

"That's a good hat," Willis said. "Don't make fun of my hat. All the ladies who came in to buy chickens said it was a darling hat."

"Oh, no question," Brown said. "It's a cunning hat."

"Any masks in there?"

"Here's *one*. That's all I see."

"The canister with it?"

"Yeah, it's all here."

"Who's going in?" Willis said.

"I'll take it," Brown said.

"Sure, and then I'll have the N.A.A.C.P. down on my head."

"We'll just have to chance that," Brown said, returning Willis' smile. "We'll just have to chance it, Hal." He pulled the mask out of its carrier, found the small tin of antidim compound, scooped some onto the provided cloth, and wiped it onto the eyepieces. He seated the facepiece on his chin, moved the canister and head harness into place with an upward, backward sweep of his hands, and then smoothed the edges of the mask around his face.

"Is it fogging?" Willis said.

"No, it's okay."

Brown closed the outlet valve with two fingers and exhaled, clearing the mask. "Okay," he said, and began walking toward the house. He was a huge man, six feet four inches tall and weighing two hundred and twenty pounds, with enormous shoulders and chest, long arms, big hands. His skin was very dark, almost black, his hair was kinky and cut close to his scalp, his nostrils were large, his lips were thick. He looked like a Negro, which is what he was, take him or leave him. He did not at all resemble the white man's pretty concept of what a Negro *should* look like, the image touted in a new wave of magazine and television ads. He looked like himself. His wife Caroline liked the way he looked, and his daughter Connie liked the way he looked, and – more important – *he* liked the way he looked, although he didn't look so great at the moment with a mask covering his face and hoses running to the canister resting at the back of his neck. He walked into the house and paused just inside the door. There were parallel marks on the floor, beginning at the jamb and running vertically across the room. He stopped to look at the marks more closely. They were black and evenly spaced, and he recognized them immediately as scuff marks. He rose and followed the marks to the fireplace, where they ended. He did not touch anything in or near the open mouth of the hearth; he would leave that for the lab boys. But he was convinced now that a man wearing shoes, if nothing else, had been dragged across the room from the door to the fireplace. According to what they'd learned yesterday, Ernest Messner had been incinerated in a wood-burning fire. Well, there had certainly been a wood-burning fire in this room, and the stink he and Willis had encountered when entering was sure as hell the stink of burned human flesh. And now there were heel marks leading from the door to the fireplace. Circumstantially, Brown needed nothing more.

The only question was whether the person cooked in this particular fireplace was Ernest Messner or somebody else.

He couldn't answer that one, and anyway his eyepieces were beginning to fog. He went outside, took off the mask, and suggested to Willis that they drive into either Middlebarth or York to talk to some real estate agents about who owned the house with the smelly fireplace.

Elaine Hinds was a small, compact redhead with blue eyes and long fingernails. Her preferences ran to small men, and she was charmed to distraction by Hal Willis, who was the shortest detective on the squad. She sat in a swivel chair behind her desk in the office of Hinds Real Estate in Middlebarth, and crossed her legs, and smiled, and accepted Willis's match to her cigarette, and graciously murmured, "Thank you," and then tried to remember what question he had just asked her. She uncrossed her legs, crossed them again, and then said, "Yes, the house on 407."

"Yes, do you know who owns it?" Willis asked. He was not unaware of the effect he seemed to be having on Miss Elaine Hinds, and he suspected he would never hear the end of it from Brown. But he was also a little puzzled. He had for many years been the victim of what he called the Mutt and Jeff phenomenon, a curious psychological and physiological reversal that made him irresistibly attractive to very big girls. He had never dated a girl who was shorter than five-nine in heels. One of his girl friends was five-eleven in her stockinged feet, and she was hopelessly in love with him. So he could not now understand why tiny little Elaine Hinds seemed so interested in a man who was only five feet eight inches tall, with the slight build of a dancer and the hands of a Black Jack dealer. He had, of course, served with the Marines and was an expert at judo, but Miss Hinds had no way of knowing that he was a giant among men, capable of breaking a man's back by the mere flick of an eyeball – well, almost. What then had caused

114

her immediate attraction? Being a conscientious cop, he sincerely hoped it would not impede the progress of the investigation. In the meantime, he couldn't help noticing that she had very good legs and that she kept crossing and uncrossing them like an undecided virgin.

"The people who own that house," she said, uncrossing her legs, "are Mr and Mrs Jerome Brandt, would you like some coffee or something? I have some going in the other room."

"No, thank you," Willis said. "How long have—"

"Mr Brown?"

"No, thank you."

"How long have the Brandts been living there?"

"Well, they haven't. Not really."

"I don't think I understand," Willis said.

Elaine Hinds crossed her legs, and leaned close to Willis, as though about to reveal something terribly intimate. "They bought it to use as a summer place," she said. "Mavis County is a marvelous resort area, you know, with many lakes and streams and with the ocean not too far from any point in the county. We're supposed to have less rainfall per annum than—"

"When did they buy it, Miss Hinds?"

"Last year. I expect they'll open the house after Memorial Day, but it's been closed all winter."

"Which explains the broken hasp on the front door," Brown said.

"Has it been broken?" Elaine said. "Oh, dear," and she uncrossed her legs.

"Miss Hinds, would you say that many people in the area knew the house was empty?"

"Yes, I'd say it was common knowledge, do you enjoy police work?"

"Yes, I do," Willis said.

"It must be terribly exciting."

"Sometimes the suspense is unbearable," Brown said.

"I'll just *bet* it is," Elaine said.

"It's my understanding," Willis said, glancing sharply at Brown, "that 407 is a pretty isolated road, and hardly ever used. Is that correct?"

"Oh, yes," Elaine said. "Route 126 is a much better connection between Middlebarth and York, and of course the new highway runs past both towns. As a matter of fact, most people in the area *avoid* 407. It's not a very good road, have you been on it?"

"Yes. Then, actually, anyone living around here would have known the house was empty, and would also have known the road going by it wasn't traveled too often. Would you say that?"

"Oh, yes, Mr Willis, I definitely *would* say that," Elaine said.

Willis looked a little startled. He glanced at Brown, and then cleared his throat. "Miss Hinds, what sort of people are the Brandts? Do you know them?"

"Yes, I sold the house to them. Jerry's an executive at IBM."

"And his wife?"

"Maxine's a woman of about fifty, three or four years younger than Jerry. A lovely person."

"Respectable people, would you say?"

"Oh, yes, *entirely* respectable," Elaine said. "My goodness, of *course* they are."

"Would you know if either of them were up here Monday night?"

"I don't know. I imagine they would have called if they were coming. I keep the keys to the house here in the office, you see. I have to arrange for maintenance, and it's necessary—"

"But they didn't call to say they were coming up?"

"No, they didn't." Elaine paused. "Does this have anything to do with the auto wreck on 407?"

"Yes, Miss Hinds, it does."

"Well, how could Jerry or Maxine be even *remotely* connected with that?"

"You don't think they could?"

"Of course not. I haven't seen them for quite some time now, but we did work closely together when I was handling the deal for them last October. Believe me, you couldn't find a sweeter couple. That's unusual, especially with people who have their kind of money."

"Are they wealthy, would you say?"

"The house cost forty-two thousand five hundred dollars. They paid for it in cash."

"Who'd they buy it from?" Willis asked.

"Well, you probably wouldn't know her, but I'll bet your wife would."

"I'm not married," Willis said.

"Oh? *Aren't* you?"

"Who'd they buy it from?" Brown asked.

"A fashion model named Tinka Sachs. Do you know her?"

If they had lacked, before this, proof positive that the man in the wrecked automobile was really Ernest Messner, they now possessed the single piece of information that tied together the series of happenings and eliminated the possibility of reasonable chance or coincidence:

1) Tinka Sachs had been murdered in an apartment on Stafford Place on Friday, April ninth.

2) Ernest Messner was the elevator operator on duty there the night of her murder.

3) Ernest Messner had taken a man up to her apartment and had later given a good description of him.

4) Ernest Messner had vanished on Monday night, April twelfth.

5) An incinerated body was found the next day in a wrecked auto on Route 407, the connecting road between Middlebarth and York, in Mavis County.

6) The medical examiner had stated his belief that the body in the automobile had been incinerated in a wood fire elsewhere and only later placed in the automobile.

7) There was only one house on Route 407, five and a half miles from where the wrecked auto was found in the gravel pit.

8) There had been a recent wood fire in the fireplace of that house, and the premises smelled of burned flesh. There were also heel marks on the floor, indicating that someone had been dragged to the fireplace.

9) The house had once been owned by Tinka Sachs, and was sold only last October to its new owners.

It was now reasonable to assume that Tinka's murderer knew he had been identified, and had moved with frightening dispatch to remove the man who'd seen him. It was also reasonable to assume that Tinka's murderer knew of the empty house in Mavis County and had transported Messner's body there for the sole purpose of incinerating it beyond recognition, the further implication being that the murderer had known Tinka at least as far back as last October when she'd still owned the house. There were still a few unanswered questions, of course, but they were small things and nothing that would trouble any hard-working police force anywhere. The cops of the 87th wondered, for example, who had killed Tinka Sachs, and who had killed Ernest Messner, and who had taken Carella's shield and gun from him and wrecked his auto, and whether Carella was still alive, and where?

It's the small things in life that can get you down.

Those airline schedules kept bothering Kling.

He knew he had been taken off the case, but he could not stop thinking about those airline schedules, or the possibility that Dennis Sachs had flown from Phoenix and back sometime between Thursday night and Monday morning. From his apartment that night, he called Information and asked for the name and number of the hotel in Rainfield, Arizona. The local operator connected him with Phoenix Information, who said the only hotel listing they had in Rainfield was for the Major Powell on Main Street, was this the hotel Kling wanted? Kling said it was, and they asked if they should place the call. He knew that if he was eventually suspended, he would lose his gun, his shield and his salary until the case was decided, so he asked the operator how much the call would cost, and she said it would cost two dollars and ten cents for the first three minutes, and sixty-five cents for each additional minute. Kling told her to go ahead and place the call, station to station.

The man who answered the phone identified himself as Walter Blount, manager of the hotel.

"This is Detective Bert Kling," Kling said. "We've had a murder here, and I'd like to ask you some questions, if I may. I'm calling long distance."

"Go right ahead, Mr Kling," Blount said.

"To begin with, do you know Dennis Sachs?"

"Yes, I do. He's a guest here, part of Dr Tarsmith's expedition."

"Were you on duty a week ago last Thursday night, April eighth?"

"I'm on duty *all* the time," Blount said.

"Do you know what time Mr Sachs came in from the desert?"

"Well, I couldn't rightly say. They usually come in at about seven, eight o'clock, something like that."

"Would you say they came in at about that time on April eighth?"

"I would say so, yes."

"Did you see Mr Sachs leaving the hotel at any time that night?"

"Yes, he left, oh, ten-thirty or so, walked over to the railroad station."

"Was he carrying a suitcase?"

"He was."

"Did he mention where he was going?"

"The Royal Sands in Phoenix, I'd reckon. He asked us to make a reservation for him there, so I guess that's where he was going, don't you think?"

"Did you make the reservation for him personally, Mr Blount?"

"Yes, sir, I did. Single with a bath, Thursday night to Sunday morning. The rates—"

"What time did Mr Sachs return on Monday morning?"

"About six a.m. Had a telegram waiting for him here, his wife got killed. Well, I guess you know that, I guess that's what this is all about. He called the airport right away, and then got back on the train for Phoenix, hardly unpacked at all."

"Mr Blount, Dennis Sachs told me that he spoke to his ex-wife on the telephone at least once a week. Would you know if that was true?"

"Oh, sure, he was always calling back east."

"How often, would you say?"

"At least once a week, that's right. Even more than that, I'd say."

"How much more?"

"Well . . . in the past two months or so, he'd call her three, maybe four times a week, something like that. He spent a hell

119

of a lot of time making calls back east, ran up a pretty big phone bill here."

"Calling his wife, you mean."

"Well, not only her."

"Who else?"

"I don't know who the other party was."

"But he *did* make calls to other numbers here in the city?"

"Well, *one* other number."

"Would you happen to know that number offhand, Mr Blount?"

"No, but I've got a record of it on our bills. It's not his wife's number because I've got that one memorized by heart, he's called it regular ever since he first came here a year ago. This other one is new to me."

"When did he start calling it?"

"Back in February, I reckon."

"How often?"

"Once a week, usually."

"May I have the number, please?"

"Sure, just let me look it up for you."

Kling waited. The line crackled. His hand on the receiver was sweating.

"Hello?" Blount said.

"Hello?"

"The number is SE – I think that stands for Sequoia – SE 3–1402."

"Thank you," Kling said.

"Not at all," Blount answered.

Kling hung up, waited patiently for a moment with his hand on the receiver, lifted it again, heard the dial tone, and instantly dialed SE 3–1402. The phone rang insistently. He counted each separate ring, four, five, six, and suddenly there was an answering voice.

"Dr Levi's wire," the woman said.

"This is Detective Kling of the 87th Squad here in the city," Kling said. "Is this an answering service?"

"Yes, sir, it is."

"Whose phone did you say this was?"

"Dr Levi's."

"And the first name?"

120

"Jason."

"Do you know where I can reach him?"

"I'm sorry, sir, he's away for the weekend. He won't be back until Monday morning." The woman paused. "Is this in respect to a police matter, or are you calling for a medical appointment?"

"A police matter," Kling said.

"Well, the doctor's office hours begin at ten Monday morning. If you'd care to call him then, I'm sure—"

"What's his home number?" Kling asked.

"Calling him there won't help you. He really is away for the weekend."

"Do you know where?"

"No, I'm sorry."

"Well, let me have his number, anyway," Kling said.

"I'm not supposed to give out the doctor's home number. I'll try it for you, if you like. If the doctor's there – which I know he isn't – I'll ask him to call you back. May I have your number, please?"

"Yes, it's Roxbury 2, that's RO2, 7641."

"Thank you."

"Will you please call me in any event, to let me know if you reached him or not?"

"Yes, sir, I will."

"Thank you."

"What did you say your name was?"

"Kling, Detective Bert Kling."

"Yes, sir, thank you," she said, and hung up.

Kling waited by the phone.

In five minutes' time, the woman called back. She said she had tried the doctor's home number and – as she'd known would be the case all along – there was no answer. She gave him the doctor's office schedule and told him he could try again on Monday, and then she hung up.

It was going to be a long weekend.

Teddy Carella sat in the living room alone for a long while after Lieutenant Byrnes left, her hands folded in her lap, staring into the shadows of the room and hearing nothing but the murmur of her own thoughts.

We now know, the lieutenant had said, that the man we found in the automobile definitely wasn't Steve. He's a man named Ernest Messner, and there is no question about it, Teddy, so I want you to know that. But I also want you to know this doesn't mean Steve is still alive. We just don't know anything about that yet, although we're working on it. The only thing it *does* indicate is that at least he's not for certain dead.

The lieutenant paused. She watched his face. He looked back at her curiously, wanting to be sure she understood everything he had told her. She nodded.

I knew this yesterday, the lieutenant said, but I wasn't sure, and I didn't want to raise your hopes until I had checked it out thoroughly. The medical examiner's office gave this top priority, Teddy. They still haven't finished the autopsy on the Sachs case because, well, you know, when we thought this was Steve, well, we put a lot of pressure on them. Anyway, it isn't. It isn't Steve, I mean. We've got Paul Blaney's word for that, and he's an excellent man, and we've also got the corroboration – what? Corroboration, did you get it? the corroboration of the chief medical examiner as well. So now I'm sure, so I'm telling you. And about the other, we're working on it, as you know, and as soon as we've got anything, I'll tell you that, too. So that's about all, Teddy. We're doing our best.

She had thanked him and offered him coffee, which he refused politely, he was expected home, he had to run, he hoped she would forgive him. She had shown him to the door, and then walked past the playroom, where Fanny was watching television, and then past the room where the twins were sound asleep and then into the living room. She turned out the lights and went to sit near the old piano Carella had bought in a secondhand store downtown, paying sixteen dollars for it and arranging to have it delivered by a furniture man in the precinct. He had always wanted to play the piano, he told her, and was going to start lessons – you're never too old to learn, right, sweetheart?

The lieutenant's news soared within her, but she was fearful of it, suspicious: was it only a temporary gift that would be taken back? Should she tell the children, and then risk another reversal and a second revelation that their father was dead? "What does that mean?" April had asked. "Does dead mean he's never coming back?" And Mark had turned to his sister and angrily shouted, "Shut up, you stupid dope!" and had run to his room where his mother could not see his tears.

They deserved hope.

They had the right to know there was hope.

She rose and went into the kitchen and scribbled a note on the telephone pad, and then tore off the sheet of paper and carried it out to Fanny. Fanny looked up when she approached, expecting more bad news, the lieutenant brought nothing but bad news nowadays. Teddy handed her the sheet of paper, and Fanny looked at it:

Wake the children.
Tell them their father
may still be alive.

Fanny looked up quickly.

"Thank God," she whispered, and rushed out of the room.

11

The patrolman came up to the squadroom on Monday morning, and waited outside the slatted rail divider until Meyer signaled him in. Then he opened the gate and walked over to Meyer's desk.

"I don't think you know me," he said. "I'm Patrolman Angieri."

"I think I've seen you around," Meyer said.

"I feel funny bringing this up because maybe you already know it. My wife said I should tell you, anyway."

"What is it?"

"I only been here at this precinct for six months, this is my first precinct, I'm a new cop."

"Um-huh," Meyer said.

"If you already know this, just skip it, okay? My wife says maybe you don't know it, and maybe it's important."

"Well, what is it?" Meyer asked patiently.

"Carella."

"What about Carella?"

"Like I told you, I'm new in the precinct, and I don't know all the detectives by name, but I recognized him later from his picture in the paper, though it was a picture from when he was a patrolman. Anyway, it was him."

"What do you mean? I don't think I'm with you, Angieri."

"Carrying the doll," Angieri said.

"I still don't get you."

"I was on duty in the hall, you know? Outside the apartment. I'm talking about the Tinka Sachs murder."

Meyer leaned forward suddenly. "Yeah, go ahead," he said.

"Well, he come up there last Monday night, it must've been five-thirty, six o'clock, and he flashed the tin, and went inside the apartment. When he came out, he was in a hell of a hurry, and he was carrying a doll."

"Are you telling me Carella was at the Sachs apartment last Monday night?"

"That's right."

"Are you sure?"

"Positive." Angieri paused. "You *didn't* know this, huh? My wife was right." He paused again. "She's *always* right."

"What did you say about a doll?"

"A doll, you know? Like kids play with? Girls? A big doll. With blonde hair, you know? A *doll*."

"Carella came out of the apartment carrying a child's doll?"

"That's right."

"Last Monday night?"

"That's right."

"Did he say anything to you?"

"Nothing."

"A doll," Meyer said, puzzled.

It was nine a.m. when Meyer arrived at the Sachs apartment on Stafford Place. He spoke briefly to the superintendent of the building, a man named Manny Farber, and then took the elevator up to the fourth floor. There was no longer a patrolman on duty in the hallway. He went down the corridor and let himself into the apartment, using Tinka's own key, which had been lent to the investigating precinct by the Office of the Clerk.

The apartment was still.

He could tell at once that death had been here. There are different silences in an empty apartment, and if you are a working policeman, you do not scoff at poetic fallacy. An apartment vacated for the summer has a silence unlike one that is empty only for the day, with its occupants expected back that night. And an apartment that has known the touch of

125

death possesses a silence unique and readily identifiable to anyone who has ever stared down at a corpse. Meyer knew the silence of death, and understood it, though he could not have told you what accounted for it. The disconnected humless electrical appliances; the unused, undripping water taps; the unringing telephone; the stopped unticking clocks; the sealed windows shutting out all street noises; these were all a part of it, but they only contributed to the whole and were not its sum and substance. The real silence was something only felt, and had nothing to do with the absence of sound. It touched something deep within him the moment he stepped through the door. It seemed to be carried on the air itself, a shuddering reminder that death had passed this way, and that some of its frightening grandeur was still locked inside these rooms. He paused with his hand on the doorknob, and then sighed and closed the door behind him and went into the apartment.

Sunlight glanced through closed windows, dust beams silently hovered on the unmoving air. He walked softly, as though reluctant to stir whatever ghostly remnants still were here. When he passed the child's room, he looked through the open door and saw the dolls lined up in the bookcase beneath the windows, row upon row of dolls, each dressed differently, each staring back at him with unblinking glass eyes, pink cheeks glowing, mute red mouths frozen on the edge of articulation, painted lips parted over even plastic teeth, nylon hair in black, and red, and blonde, and the palest silver.

He was starting into the room when he heard a key turning in the front door.

The sound startled him. It cracked into the silent apartment like a crash of thunder. He heard the tumblers falling, the sudden click of the knob being turned. He moved into the child's room just as the front door opened. His eyes swept the room – bookcases, bed, closet, toy chest. He could hear heavy footsteps in the corridor, approaching the room. He threw open the closet door, drew his gun. The footsteps were closer. He eased the door toward him, leaving it open just a crack. Holding his breath, he waited in the darkness.

The man who came into the room was perhaps six feet two inches tall, with massive shoulders and a narrow waist. He paused just inside the doorway, as though sensing the presence of another person, seemed almost to be sniffing the air for a telltale scent. Then, visibly shrugging away his own correct intuition, he dismissed the idea and went quickly to the bookcases. He stopped in front of them and began lifting dolls from the shelves, seemingly at random, bundling them into his arms. He gathered up seven or eight of them, rose, turned toward the door, and was on his way out when Meyer kicked open the closet door.

The man turned, startled, his eyes opening wide. Foolishly, he clung to the dolls in his arms, first looking at Meyer's face, and then at the Colt .38 in Meyer's hand, and then up at Meyer's face again.

"Who are you?" he asked.

"Good question," Meyer said. "Put those dolls down, hurry up, on the bed there."

"What . . . ?"

"Do as I say, mister!"

The man walked to the bed. He wet his lips, looked at Meyer, frowned, and then dropped the dolls.

"Get over against the wall," Meyer said.

"Listen, what the hell . . . ?"

"Spread your legs, bend over, lean against the wall with your palms flat. Hurry up!"

"All right, take it easy." The man leaned against the wall. Meyer quickly and carefully frisked him – chest, pockets, waist, the insides of his legs. Then he backed away from the man and said, "Turn around, keep your hands up."

The man turned, his hands high. He wet his lips again, and again looked at the gun in Meyer's hand.

"What are you doing here?" Meyer asked.

"What are *you* doing here?"

"I'm a police officer. Answer my—"

"Oh. Oh, okay," the man said.

"What's okay about it?"

"I'm Dennis Sachs."

"Who?"

"Dennis—"

"Tinka's husband?"

"Well, her ex-husband."

"Where's your wallet?"

"Right here in my—"

"Don't reach for it! Bend over against that wall again, go ahead."

The man did as Meyer ordered. Meyer felt for the wallet and found it in his right hip pocket. He opened it to the driver's license. The name on the license was Dennis Robert Sachs. Meyer handed it back to him.

"All right, put your hands down. What are you doing here?"

"My daughter wanted some of her dolls," Sachs said. "I came back to get them."

"How'd you get in?"

"I have a key. I used to live here, you know."

"It was my understanding you and your wife were divorced."

"That's right."

"And you still have a key?"

"Yes."

"Did she know this?"

"Yes, of course."

"And that's all you wanted here, huh? Just the dolls."

"Yes."

"Any doll in particular?"

"No."

"Your daughter didn't specify any particular doll?"

"No, she simply said she'd like some of her dolls, and she asked if I'd come get them for her."

"How about *your* preference?"

"*My* preference?"

"Yes. Did *you* have any particular doll in mind?"

"Me?"

"That's right, Mr Sachs. You."

"No. What do you mean? Are you talking about *dolls*?"

"That's right, that's what I'm talking about."

"Well, what would I want with any *specific* doll?"

"That's what *I'd* like to know."

"I don't think I understand you."

"Then forget it."

Sachs frowned and glanced at the dolls on the bed. He hesitated, then shrugged and said, "Well, is it all right to take them?"

"I'm afraid not."

128

"Why not? They belong to my daughter."

"We want to look them over, Mr Sachs."

"For what?"

"I don't know for what. For *anything*."

Sachs looked at the dolls again, and then he turned to Meyer and stared at him silently. "I guess you know this has been a pretty bewildering conversation," he said at last.

"Yeah, well, that's the way mysteries are," Meyer answered. "I've got work to do, Mr Sachs. If you have no further business here, I'd appreciate it if you left."

Sachs nodded and said nothing. He looked at the dolls once again, and then walked out of the room, and down the corridor, and out of the apartment. Meyer waited, listening. The moment he heard the door close behind Sachs, he sprinted down the corridor, stopped just inside the door, counted swiftly to ten, and then eased the door open no more than an inch. Peering out into the hallway, he could see Sachs waiting for the elevator. He looked angry as hell. When the elevator did not arrive, he pushed at the button repeatedly and then began pacing. He glanced once at Tinka's supposedly closed door, and then turned back to the elevator again. When it finally arrived, he said to the operator, "What took you so long?" and stepped into the car.

Meyer came out of the apartment immediately, closed the door behind him, and ran for the service steps. He took the steps down at a gallop, pausing only for an instant at the fire door leading to the lobby, and then opening the door a crack. He could see the elevator operator standing near the building's entrance, his arms folded across his chest. Meyer came out into the lobby quickly, glanced back once at the open elevator doors, and then ran past the elevator and into the street. He spotted Sachs turning the corner up the block, and broke into a run after him. He paused again before turning the corner. When he sidled around it, he saw Sachs getting into a taxi. There was no time for Meyer to go to his own parked car. He hailed another cab and said to the driver, just like a cop, "Follow that taxi," sourly reminding himself that he would have to turn in a chit for the fare, even though he knew Petty Cash would probably never reimburse him. The taxi driver turned for a quick look at Meyer, just to see who was pulling all this cloak and dagger nonsense, and then silently began following Sachs's cab.

"You a cop?" he asked at last.

"Yeah," Meyer said.

"Who's that up ahead?"

"The Boston Strangler," Meyer said.

"Yeah?"

"Would I kid you?"

"You going to pay for this ride, or is it like taking apples from a pushcart?"

"I'm going to pay for it," Meyer said. "Just don't lose him, okay?"

It was almost ten o'clock, and the streets were thronged with traffic. The lead taxi moved steadily uptown and then crosstown, with Meyer's driver skillfully following. The city was a bedlam of noise – honking horns, grinding gears, squealing tires, shouting drivers and pedestrians. Meyer leaned forward and kept his eye on the taxi ahead, oblivious to the sounds around him.

"He's pulling up, I think," the driver said.

"Good. Stop about six car lengths behind him." The taxi meter read eighty-five cents. Meyer took a dollar bill from his wallet, and handed it to the driver the moment he pulled over to the curb. Sachs had already gotten out of his cab and was walking into an apartment building in the middle of the block.

"Is this all the city tips?" the driver asked. "Fifteen cents on an eighty-five-cent ride?"

"The city, my ass," Meyer said, and leaped out of the cab. He ran up the street, and came into the building's entrance alcove just as the inner glass door closed behind Sachs. Meyer swung back his left arm and swiftly ran his hand over every bell in the row on the wall. Then, while waiting for an answering buzz, he put his face close to the glass door, shaded his eyes against the reflective glare, and peered inside. Sachs was nowhere in sight; the elevators were apparently around a corner of the lobby. A half-dozen answering buzzes sounded at once, releasing the lock mechanism on the door. Meyer pushed it open, and ran into the lobby. The floor indicator over the single elevator was moving, three, four, five – and stopped. Meyer nodded and walked out to the entrance alcove again, bending to look at the bells there. There were six apartments on the fifth floor. He was studying the names under the bells when a voice behind him said, "I think you're looking for Dr Jason Levi."

Meyer looked up, startled.

The man standing behind him was Bert Kling.

Dr Jason Levi's private office was painted an antiseptic white, and the only decoration on its walls was a large, easily readable calendar. His desk was functional and unadorned, made of grey steel, its top cluttered with medical journals and books, X-ray photographs, pharmaceutical samples, tongue depressors, prescription pads. There was a no-nonsense look about the doctor as well, the plain face topped with leonine white hair, the thick-lensed spectacles, the large cleaving nose, the thin-lipped mouth. He sat behind his desk and looked first at the detectives and then at Dennis Sachs, and waited for someone to speak.

"We want to know what you're doing here, Mr Sachs," Meyer said.

"I'm a patient," Sachs said.

"Is that true, Dr Levi?"

Levi hesitated. Then he shook his massive head. "No," he said. "That is not true."

"Shall we start again?" Meyer asked.

"I have nothing to say," Sachs answered.

"Why'd you find it necessary to call Dr Levi from Arizona once a week?" Kling asked.

"Who said I did?"

"Mr Walter Blount, manager of the Major Powell Hotel in Rainfield."

"He was lying."

"Why would he lie?"

"I don't *know* why," Sachs said. "Go ask *him*."

"No, we'll do it the easy way," Kling said. "Dr Levi, *did* Mr Sachs call you from Arizona once a week?"

"Yes," Levi said.

"We seem to have a slight difference of opinion here," Meyer said.

"Why'd he call you?" Kling asked.

"Don't answer that, Doctor!"

"Dennis, what are we trying to hide? She's dead."

"You're a doctor, you don't have to tell them anything. You're like a priest. They can't force you to—"

"Dennis, she is dead."

"Did your calls have something to do with your wife?" Sachs asked.

"No," Sachs said.

"Yes," Levi said.

"Was *Tinka* your patient, Doctor, is that it?"

"Yes."

"Dr Levi, I *forbid* you to tell these men anything more about—"

"She was my patient," Levi said. "I began treating her at the beginning of the year."

"In January?"

"Yes. January fifth. More than three months ago."

"Doctor, I swear on my dead wife that if you go ahead with this, I'm going to ask the A.M.A. to—"

"Nonsense!" Levi said fiercely. "Your wife is dead! If we can help them find her killer—"

"You're not helping them with anything! All you're doing is dragging her memory through the muck of a criminal investigation."

"Mr Sachs," Meyer said, "whether you know it or not, her memory is already in the muck of a criminal investigation."

"Why did she come to you, Doctor?" Kling asked. "What was wrong with her?"

"She said she had made a New Year's resolution, said she had decided once and for all to seek medical assistance. It was quite pathetic, really. She was so helpless, and so beautiful, and so alone."

"I *couldn't* stay with her any longer!" Sachs said. "I'm not made of iron! I couldn't handle it. That's why we got the divorce. It wasn't my fault, what happened to her."

"No one is blaming you for anything," Levi said. "Her illness went back a long time, long before she met you."

"What was this illness, Doctor?" Meyer asked.

"Don't tell them!"

"Dennis, I *have* to—"

"You *don't* have to! Leave it the way it is. Let her live in everyone's memory as a beautiful exciting woman instead of—"

Dennis cut himself off.

"Instead of what?" Meyer asked.

The room went silent.

"Instead of what?" he said again.

Levi sighed and shook his head.

"Instead of a drug addict."

12

In the silence of the squadroom later that day, they read Dr Jason Levi's casebook

The patient's name is Tina Karin Sachs. She is divorced, has a daughter aged five. She lives in the city and leads an active professional life, which is one of the reasons she was reluctant to seek assistance before now. She stated, however, that she had made a New Year's resolution, and that she is determined to break the habit. She has been a narcotics user since the time she was seventeen, and is now addicted to heroin.

I explained to her that the methods of withdrawal which I had thus far found most satisfactory were those employing either morphine or methadone, both of which had proved to be adequate substitutes for whatever drugs or combinations of drugs my patients had previously been using. I told her, too, that I personally preferred the morphine method.

She asked if there would be much pain involved. Apparently she had once tried cold-turkey withdrawal and had found the attempt too painful to bear. I told her that she would experience withdrawal symptoms – nausea, vomiting, diarrhea, lacrimation, dilation of pupils, rhinorrhea, yawning, gooseflesh, sneezing, sweating – with either method. With morphine, the withdrawal would be more severe, but she could expect relative comfort after a week or so. With methadone, the withdrawal would be easier, but she might still feel somewhat tremulous for a long as a month afterward.

She said she wanted to think it over, and would call me when she had decided.

I had not expected to see or hear from Tinka Sachs again, but she arrived here today and asked my receptionist if I could spare ten minutes. I said I could, and she was shown into my private office, where we talked for more than forty-five minutes.

She said she had not yet decided what she should do, and wanted to discuss it further with me. She is, as she had previously explained, a fashion model. She receives top fees for her modeling and was now afraid that treatment might entail either pain or sickness which would cause her to lose employment, thereby endangering her career. I told her that her addiction to heroin had made her virtually careerless anyway, since she was spending much of her income on the purchase of drugs. She did not particularly enjoy this observation, and quickly rejoindered that she thoroughly relished all the fringe benefits of modeling – the fame, the recognition, and so on. I asked her if she really enjoyed anything but heroin, or really thought of anything but heroin, and she became greatly agitated and seemed about to leave the office.

Instead, she told me that I didn't know what it was like, and she hoped I understood she had been using narcotics since she was seventeen, when she'd first tried marijuana at a beach party in Malibu. She had continued smoking marijuana for almost a year, never tempted to try any of "the real shit" until a photographer offered her a sniff of heroin shortly after she'd begun modeling. He also tried to rape her afterwards, a side effect that nearly caused her to abandon her beginning career as a model. Her near-rape, however, did not dissuade her from using marijuana or from sniffing heroin every now and then, until someone warned her that inhaling the drug could damage her nose. Since her nose was part of her face, and her face was part of what she hoped would become her fortune, she promptly stopped the sniffing process.

The first time she tried injecting the drug was with a confirmed addict, male, in a North Hollywood apartment. Unfortunately, the police broke in on them, and they were both arrested. She was nineteen years old at the time, and was luckily released with a suspended sentence. She came to this city the following month, determined never to fool with drugs again, hoping to put three thousand miles between herself and her former acquaintances. But she discovered, almost immediately upon arrival, that the drug was as readily obtainable here as it was in Los Angeles. Moreover, she began her association with the Cutler Agency several weeks after she got here, and found herself in possession of more money than she would ever need to support both herself *and* a narcotics habit. She began injecting the drug under her skin, into the soft tissue of her body. Shortly afterwards, she abandoned the subcutaneous route and began shooting heroin directly into her veins. She has been using it intravenously ever since, has for all intents and purposes been hopelessly hooked since she first began skin-popping. How, then, could I expect to cure her? How could she wake up each morning without knowing that a supply of narcotics was available, in fact accessible? I explained that hers was the common fear of all addicts about to undergo treatment, a reassurance she accepted without noticeable enthusiasm.

I'll think about it, she said again, and again left. I frankly do not believe she will ever return again.

January 20

Tinka Sachs began treatment today

She has chosen the morphine method (even though she understands the symptoms will be more severe) because she does not want to endanger her career by a prolonged withdrawal, a curious concern for someone who has been endangering her career ever since it started. I had previously explained that I wanted to hospitalize her for several months, but she flatly refused hospitalization of any kind, and stated that the deal was off if that was part of the treatment. I told her that I could not guarantee lasting results unless she allowed me to hospitalize her, but she said we would have to hope for the best because she wasn't going to admit herself to any damn hospital. I finally extracted from her an agreement to stay at home under a nurse's care at least during the first several days of withdrawal, when the symptoms would be most severe. I warned her against making any illegal purchases and against associating with any known addicts or pushers. Our schedule is a rigid one. To start, she will receive ¼ grain of morphine four times daily – twenty minutes before each meal. The doses will be administered hypodermically, and the morphine will be dissolved in thiamine hydrocholoride.

It is my hope that withdrawal will be complete within two weeks.

January 21

I have prescribed Thorazine for Tinka's nausea, and belladonna and pectin for her diarrhea. The symptoms are severe. She could not sleep at all last night. I have instructed the nurse staying at her apartment to administer three grains of Nembutal tonight before Tinka retires, with further instructions to repeat 1½ grains if she does not sleep through the night.

Tinka has taken excellent care of her body, a factor on our side. She is quite beautiful and I have no doubt she is a superior model, though I am at a loss to explain how photographers can have missed her obvious addiction. How did she keep from "nodding" before the cameras? She has scrupulously avoided marking either her lower legs or her arms, but the insides of her thighs (she told me she does not model either lingerie or bathing suits) are covered with hit marks.

Morphine continues at ¼ grain four times daily.

January 22

I have reduced the morphine injections to ¼ grain twice daily, alternating with ⅛ grain twice daily. Symptoms are still severe. She has cancelled all of her sittings, telling the agency she is menstruating and suffering cramps, a complaint they have apparently heard from their models before. She shows no desire to eat. I have begun prescribing vitamins.

January 23

The symptoms are abating. We are now administering ⅛ grain four times daily.

January 24

Treatment continuing with ⅛ grain four times daily. The nurse will be discharged tomorrow, and Tinka will begin coming to my office for her injections, a procedure I am heartily against. But it is either that or losing her entirely, and I must go along.

January 25

Started one grain codeine twice daily, alternating with ⅛ grain morphine twice daily. Tinka came to my office at eight-thirty, before breakfast, for her first injection. She came again at twelve-thirty, and at six-thirty. I administered the last injection at her home at eleven-thirty. She seems exceptionally restless, and I have prescribed ½ grain of phenobarbital daily to combat this.

January 26

Tinka Sachs did not come to the office today. I called her apartment several times, but no one answered the telephone. I did not dare call the modeling agency lest they suspect she is undergoing treatment. At three o'clock, I spoke to her daughter's governess. She had just picked the child up at the play-school she attends. She said she did not know where Mrs Sachs was, and suggested that I try the agency. I called again at midnight. Tinka was still not home. The governess said I had awakened her. Apparently, she saw nothing unusual about her employer's absence. The working arrangement calls for her to meet the child after school and to spend as much time with her as is necessary. She said that Mrs Sachs is often gone the entire night, in which case she is supposed to take the child to school in the morning, and then call for her again at two-thirty. Mrs Sachs was once gone for three days, she said.

I am worried.

Tinka returned to the office again today, apologizing profusely, and explaining that she had been called out of town on an assignment, they were shooting some new tweed fashions and wanted a woodland background. I accused her of lying, and she finally admitted that she had not been out of town at all, but had instead spent the past week in the apartment of a friend from California. After further questioning, she conceded that her California friend is a drug addict, is in fact the man with whom she was arrested when she was nineteen years old. He arrived in the city last September, with very little money, and no place to live. She staked him for a while, and allowed him to live in her Mavis County house until she sold it in October. She then helped him to find an apartment on South Fourth, and she still sees him occasionally.

It was obvious that she had begun taking heroin again.

She expressed remorse, and said that she is more than ever determined to break the habit. When I asked if her friend expects to remain in the city, she said that he does, but that he has a companion with him, and no longer needs any old acquaintance to help him pursue his course of addiction.

I extracted a promise from Tinka that she would never see this man again, nor try to contact him.

We begin treatment again tomorrow morning. This time I insisted that a nurse remain with her for at least two weeks.

We will be starting from scratch.

We have made excellent progress in the past five days. The morphine injections have been reduced to ⅛ grain four times daily, and tomorrow we begin alternating with codeine.

Tinka talked about her relationship with her husband for the first time today, in connection with her resolve to break the habit. He is, apparently, an archaeologist working with an expedition somewhere in Arizona. She is in frequent touch with him, and in fact called him yesterday to say she had begun treatment and was hopeful of a cure. It is her desire, she said, to begin a new life with him once the withdrawal is complete. She knows he still loves her, knows that had it not been for her habit they would never have parted.

She said he did not learn of her addiction until almost a year after the child was born. This was all the more remarkable since the baby – fed during pregnancy by the bloodstream of her mother, metabolically dependent on heroin – was quite naturally an addict herself from the moment she was born. Dennis, and the family pediatrician as well, assumed she was a colicky baby, crying half the night through, vomiting, constantly fretting. Only Tinka knew that the infant was experiencing all the symptoms of cold-turkey withdrawal. She was tempted more than once to give the child a secret fix, but she refrained from doing so, and the baby survived the torment of force withdrawal only to face the subsequent storm of separation and divorce.

Tinka was able to explain the hypodermic needle Dennis found a month later by saying she was allergic to certain dyes in the nylon dresses she was modeling and that her doctor had prescribed an antihistamine in an attempt to reduce the allergic reaction. But she could not explain the large sums of money that seemed to be vanishing from their joint bank account, nor could she explain his ultimate discovery of three glassine bags of a white powder secreted at the back of her dresser drawer. She finally confessed that she was a drug addict, that she had been a drug addict for close to seven years and saw nothing wrong with it so long as she was capable of supporting the habit. He goddamn well knew she was earning most of the money in this household, anyway, so what the fuck did he want from her?

He cracked her across the face and told her they would go to see a doctor in the morning.

In the morning, Tinka was gone.

She did not return to the apartment until three weeks later, disheveled and bedraggled, at which time she told Dennis she had been on a party with three coloured musicians from a club downtown, all of them addicts. She could not remember what they had done together. Dennis had meanwhile consulted a doctor, and he told Tinka that drug addiction was by no means incurable, that there were ways of treating it, that success was almost certain if the patient – Don't make me laugh, Tinka said. I'm hooked through the bag and back, and what's more I like it, now what the hell do you think about that? Get off my back, you're worse than the monkey!

He asked for the divorce six months later.

During that time, he tried desperately to reach this person he had taken for a wife, this stranger, who was nonetheless the mother of his child, this driven animal whose entire life seemed bounded by the need for heroin. Their expenses were overwhelming. She could not let her career vanish because without her career she could hardly afford the enormous amounts of heroin she required. So she dressed the part of the famous model, and lived in a lavishly appointed apartment, and rode around town in hired limousines, and ate at the best restaurants, and was seen at all the important functions – while within her the clamour for heroin raged unabated. She worked slavishly, part of her income going toward maintaining the legend that was a necessary adjunct of her profession, the remainder going toward the purchase of drugs for herself and her friends.

There were always friends.

She would vanish for weeks at a time, lured by a keening song she alone heard, compelled to seek other addicts, craving the approval of people like herself, the comradeship of the dream society, the anonymity of the shooting gallery where scars were not stigmata and addiction was not a curse.

He would have left her sooner but the child presented a serious problem. He knew he could not trust Anna alone with her mother, but how could he take her with him on archaeological expeditions around the world? He realized that if Tinka's addiction were allowed to enter the divorce proceedings, he would be granted immediate custody of the child. But Tinka's career would automatically be ruined, and who knew what later untold hurt the attendant publicity could bring to Anna? He promised Tinka that he would not introduce the matter of her addiction if she would allow him to hire a responsible governess for the child. Tinka readily agreed. Except for her occasional binges, she considered herself to be a devoted and exemplary mother. If a governess would make Dennis happy and keep this sordid matter of addiction out of the proceedings, she was more than willing to go along with the idea. The arrangements were made.

Dennis, presumably in love with his wife, presumably concerned about his daughter's welfare, was nonetheless content to abandon one to eternal drug addiction, and the other to the vagaries and unpredictabilities of living with a confirmed junkie. Tinka, for her part, was glad to see him leave. He had become a puritanical goad, and she wondered why she'd ever married him in the first place. She supposed it had had something to do with the romantic notion of one day kicking the habit and starting a new life.

Which is what you're doing now, I told her.

Yes, she said, and her eyes were shining.

February 12

Tinka is no longer dependent on morphine, and we have reduced the codeine intake to one grain twice daily, alternating with ½ grain twice daily.

140

February 13

I received a long-distance call from Dennis Sachs today. He simply wanted to know how his wife was coming along and said that if I didn't mind he would call once a week – it would have to be either Friday or Saturday since he'd be in the desert the rest of the time – to check on her progress. I told him the prognosis was excellent, and I expressed the hope that withdrawal would be complete by the twentieth of the month.

February 14

Have reduced the codeine to ½ grain twice daily, and have introduced thiamine twice daily.

February 15

Last night, Tinka slipped out of the apartment while her nurse was dozing. She has not returned, and I do not know where she is.

February 20

Have been unable to locate Tinka.

March 1

Have called the apartment repeatedly. The governess continues to care for Anna – but there has been no word from Tinka.

March 8

In desperation, I called the Cutler Agency today to ask if they have any knowledge of Tinka's whereabouts. They asked me to identify myself, and I said I was a doctor treating her for a skin allergy (Tinka's own lie!). They said she had gone to the Virgin Islands on a modeling assignment and would not be back until the twentieth of March. I thanked them and hung up.

March 22

Tinka came back to my office today.

The assignment had come up suddenly, she said, and she had taken it, forgetting to tell me about it.

I told her I thought she was lying.

All right, she said. She had seized upon the opportunity as a way to get away from me and the treatment. She did not know why, but she had suddenly been filled with panic. She knew that in several days, a week at most, she would be off even the thiamine – and then what would there be? How could she possibly get through a day without a shot of *something*?

Art Cutler had called and proposed the St Thomas assignment, and the idea of sun and sand had appealed to her immensely. By coincidence, her friend from California called that same night, and when she told him where she was going he said that he'd pack a bag and meet her down there.

I asked her exactly what her connection is with this "friend from California," who now seems responsible for two lapses in her treatment. What lapse? she asked, and then swore she had not touched anything while she was away. This friend was simply *that*, a good friend.

But you told me he is an addict, I said.

Yes, he's an addict, she answered. But he didn't even *suggest* drugs while we were away. As a matter of fact, I think I've kicked it completely. That's really the only reason I came here, to tell you that it's not necessary to continue treatment any longer. I haven't had anything, heroin or morphine or *anything*, all the while I was away. I'm cured.

You're lying, I said.

All right, she said. If I wanted the truth, it was her California friend who'd kept her out of prison those many years ago. He had told the arresting officers that he was a pusher, a noble and dangerous admission to make, and that he had forced a shot on Tinka. She had got off with the suspended sentence while he'd gone to prison; so naturally she was indebted to him. Besides, she saw no reason why she shouldn't spend some time with him on a modeling assignment, instead of running around with a lot of faggot designers and photographers, not to mention the Lesbian editor of the magazine. Who the hell did I think I was, her keeper?

I asked if this "friend from California" had suddenly struck it rich.

What do you mean? she said.

Well, isn't it true that he was in need of money and a place to stay when he first came to the city?

Yes, that's true.

Then how can he afford to support a drug habit and also manage to take a vacation in the Virgin Islands? I asked.

She admitted that she paid for the trip. If the man had saved her from a prison sentence, what was so wrong about paying his fare and his hotel bill?

I would not let it go.

Finally, she told me the complete story. She had been sending him money over the years, not because he asked her for it, but simply because she felt she owed something to him. His lie had enabled her to come here and start a new life. The least she could do was send him a little money every now and then. Yes, she had been supporting him ever since he arrived here. Yes, yes, it was she who'd invited him along on the trip; there had been no coincidental phone call from him that night. Moreover, she had not only paid for *his* plane fare and hotel bill, but also for that of his companion, whom she described as "an extremely lovely young woman".

And no heroin all that while, right?

Tears, anger, defense.

Yes, there had been heroin! There had been enough heroin to sink the island, and she had paid for every drop of it. There had been heroin morning, noon, and night. It was amazing that she had been able to face the cameras at all, she had blamed her drowsiness on the sun. That needle had been stuck in her thigh constantly, like a glittering glass cock! Yes, there had been heroin, and she had loved every minute of it! What the hell did I want from her?

I want to cure you, I said.

March 23

She accused me today of trying to kill her. She said that I had been trying to kill her since the first day we met, that I know she is not strong enough to withstand the pains of withdrawal, and that the treatment will eventually result in her death.

Her lawyer has been preparing a will, she said, and she would sign it tomorrow. She would begin treatment after that, but she knew it would lead to her ultimate death.

I told her she was talking nonsense.

March 24

Tinka signed her will today.

She brought me a fragment of a poem she wrote last night:

> *When I think of what I am*
> *And of what I might have been,*
> *I tremble.*
> *I fear the night.*
> *Throughout the day,*
> *I rush from dragons conjured in the dark.*
> *Why will they not*

I asked her why she hadn't finished the poem. She said she couldn't finish it until she knew the outcome herself. What outcome do you want? I asked her.

I want to be cured, she said.

You *will* be cured, I told her.

143

We began treatment once more.

Dennis Sachs called from Arizona again to inquire about his wife. I told him she had suffered a relapse but that she had begun treatment anew, and that we were hoping for complete withdrawal by April 15th at the very latest. He asked if there was anything he could do for Tinka. I told him that the only person who could do anything for Tinka was Tinka.

Treatment continues.
¼ grain morphine twice daily.
⅛ grain morphine twice daily.

⅛ grain morphine four times daily.
Prognosis good.

⅛ grain morphine twice daily.
One grain codeine twice daily.

Tinka confessed today that she has begun buying heroin on the sly, smuggling it in, and has been taking it whenever the nurse isn't watching. I flew into a rage. She shouted "April Fool!" and began laughing.
I think there is a chance this time.

One grain codeine four times daily.

One grain codeine twice daily.
½ grain codeine twice daily.

½ grain codeine four times daily.

½ grain codeine twice daily, thiamine twice daily.

April 6

Thiamine four times daily. Nurse was discharged today.

April 7

Thiamine three times daily.
We are going to make it!

April 8

Thiamine twice daily.

April 9

She told me today that she is certain the habit is almost kicked. This is my feeling as well. The weaning from hypodermics is virtually complete. There is only the promise of a new and rewarding life ahead.

That was where the doctor's casebook ended because that was when Tinka Sachs was murdered.

Meyer glanced up to see if Kling had finished the page. Kling nodded, and Meyer closed the book.

"He took two lives from her," Meyer said. "The one she was ending, and the one she was beginning."

That afternoon Paul Blaney earned his salary for the second time in four days. He called to say he had completed the post-mortem examination of Tinka Sachs and had discovered a multitude of scars on both upper front thighs. It seemed positive that the scars had been caused by repeated intravenous injections, and it was Blaney's opinion that the dead girl had been a drug addict.

13

She had handcuffed both hands behind his back during one of his periods of unconsciousness, and then had used a leather belt to lash his feet together. He lay naked on the floor now and waited for her arrival, trying to tell himself he did not need her, and knowing that he needed her desperately.

It was very warm in the room, but he was shivering. His skin was beginning to itch but he could not scratch himself because his hands were manacled behind his back. He could smell his own body odors – he had not been bathed or shaved in three days – but he did not care about his smell or his beard, he only cared that she was not here yet, what was keeping her?

He lay in the darkness and tried not to count the minutes.

The girl was naked when she came into the room. She did not put on the light. There was the familiar tray in her hands, but it did not carry food any more. The Llama was on the left-hand side of the tray. Alongside the gun were a small cardboard box, a book of matches, a spoon with its handle bent back toward the bowl, and a glassine envelope.

"Hello, doll," she said. "Did you miss me?"

Carella did not answer.

"Have you been waiting for me?" the girl asked. "What's the matter, don't you feel like talking?" She laughed her mirthless laugh. "Don't worry, baby," she said. "I'm going to fix you."

She put the tray down on the chair near the door, and then walked to him.

146

"I think I'll play with you awhile," she said. "Would you like me to play with you?"

Carella did not answer.

"Well, if you're not even going to talk to me, I guess I'll just have to leave. After all, I know when I'm not—"

"No, don't go," Carella said.

"Do you want me to stay?"

"Yes."

"Say it."

"I want you to stay."

"That's better. What would you like, baby? Would you like me to play with you a little?"

"No."

"Don't you like being played with?"

"No."

"What do you like, baby?"

He did not answer.

"Well, you have to tell me," she said, "or I just won't give it to you."

"I don't know," he said.

"You don't know what you like?"

"Yes."

"Do you like the way I look without any clothes on?"

"Yes, you look all right."

"But that doesn't interest you, does it?"

"No."

"What *does* interest you?"

Again, he did not answer.

"Well, you *must* know what interests you. Don't you know?"

"No, I don't know."

"Tch," the girl said, and rose and began walking toward the door.

"Where are you going?" he asked quickly.

"Just to put some water in the spoon, doll," she said soothingly. "Don't worry. I'll be back."

She took the spoon from the tray and walked out of the room, leaving the door open. He could hear the water tap running in the kitchen. Hurry up, he thought, and then thought. No, I don't need you, leave me alone, goddamn you, leave me alone!

"Here I am," she said. She took the tray off the seat of the chair and then sat and picked up the glassine envelope. She emptied its contents into the spoon, and then struck a match and held it under the blackened bowl. "Got to cook it up," she said. "Got to cook it up for my baby. You getting itchy for it, baby? Don't worry, I'll take care of you. What's your wife's name?"

"Teddy," he said.

"Oh my," she said, "you still remember. That's a shame." She blew out the match. She opened the small box on the tray, and removed the hypodermic syringe and needle from it. She affixed the needle to the syringe, and depressed the plunger to squeeze any air out of the cylindrical glass tube. From the same cardboard box, which was the original container in which the syringe had been marketed, she took a piece of absorbent cotton, which she placed over the milky white liquid in the bowl of the spoon. Using the cotton as a filter, knowing that even the tiniest piece of solid matter would clog the tiny opening in the hypodermic needle, she drew the liquid up into the syringe, and then smiled and said, "There we are, all ready for my doll."

"I don't want it," Carella said suddenly.

"Oh, honey, please don't lie to me," she said calmly. "I *know* you want it, what's your wife's name?"

"Teddy."

"Teddy, tch, tch, well, well," she said. From the cardboard box, she took a loop of string, and then walked to Carella and put the syringe on the floor beside him. She looped the piece of string around his arm, just above the elbow joint.

"What's your wife's name?" she asked.

"Teddy."

"You want, this doll?"

"No."

"Oooh, it's very good," she said. "We had some this afternoon, it was very good stuff. Aren't you just aching all over for it, what's your wife's name?"

"Teddy."

"Has she got tits like mine?"

Carella did not answer.

"Oh, but that doesn't interest you, does it? All that interests you is what's right here in this syringe, isn't that right?"

"No."

"This is a very high-class shooting gallery, baby. No eye-droppers here, oh no. Everything veddy veddy high-tone. Though I don't know how we're going to keep ourselves in junk now that little Sweetass is gone. He shouldn't have killed her, he really shouldn't have."

"Then why did he?"

"I'll ask the questions, doll. Do you remember your wife's name?"

"Yes."

"What is it?"

"Teddy."

"Then I guess I'll go. I can make good use of this myself." She picked up the syringe. "Shall I go?"

"Do what you want to do."

"If I leave this room," the girl said, "I won't come back until tomorrow morning. That'll be a long long night, baby. You think you can last the night without a fix?" She paused. "Do you want this or not?"

"Leave me alone," he said.

"No. No, no, we can't leave you alone. In a little while, baby, you are going to tell us everything you know, you are going to tell us exactly how you found us, you are going to tell us because if you don't we'll leave you here to drown in your own vomit. Now what's your wife's name?"

"Teddy."

"No."

"Yes. Her name is Teddy."

"How can I give you this if your memory's so good?"

"Then don't give it to me."

"Okay," the girl said, and walked toward the door. "Good-night, doll. I'll see you in the morning."

"Wait."

"Yes?" The girl turned. There was no expression on her face.

"You forgot your tourniquet," Carella said.

"So I did," the girl answered. She walked back to him and removed the string from his arm. "Play it cool," she said. "Go

149

ahead. See how far you get by playing it cool. Tomorrow morning you'll be rolling all over the floor when I come in." She kissed him swiftly on the mouth. She sighed deeply. "Ahh," she said, "why do you force me to be mean to you?"

She went back to the door and busied herself with putting the string and cotton back into the box, straightening the book of matches and the spoon, aligning the syringe with the other items.

"Well, good night," she said, and walked out of the room, locking the door behind her.

Detective Sergeant Tony Kreisler of the Los Angeles Police Department did not return Meyer's call until nine o'clock that Monday night, which meant it was six o'clock on the Coast.

"You've had me busy all day long," Kreisler said. "It's tough to dig in the files for these ancient ones."

"Did you come up with anything?" Meyer asked.

"I'll tell you the truth, if this hadn't been a homicide you're working on, I'd have given up long ago, said the hell with it."

"What've you got for me?" Meyer asked patiently.

"This goes back twelve, thirteen years. You really think there's a connection?"

"It's all we've got to go on," Meyer said. "We figured it was worth a chance."

"Besides, the city paid for the long-distance call, right?" Kreisler said, and began laughing.

"That's right," Meyer said, and bided his time, and hoped that *Kreisler's* city was paying for *his* call, too.

"Well, anyway," Kreisler said, when his laughter had subsided, "you were right about that arrest. We picked them up on a violation of Section 11500 of the Health and Safety Code. The girl's name wasn't Sachs then, we've got her listed as Tina Karin Grady, you suppose that's the same party?"

"Probably her maiden name," Meyer said.

"That's what I figure. They were holed up in an apartment in North Hollywood with more than twenty-five caps of H, something better than an eighth of an ounce, not that it makes any difference out here. Out here, there's no minimum quantity constituting a violation. Any amount that can be analyzed as a narcotic is admissible in court. It's different with you guys, I know that."

"That's right," Meyer said.

"Anyway, the guy was a mainliner, hit marks all over his arms. The Grady girl looked like a sweet young meat, it was tough to figure what she was doing with a creep like him. She claimed she didn't know he was an addict, claimed he'd invited her up to the apartment, got her drunk, and then forced a shot on her. There were no previous marks on her body, just that one hit mark in the crook of her el—"

"Wait a minute," Meyer said.

"Yeah, what's the matter?"

"The *girl* claimed he'd forced the shot on her?"

"That's right. Said he got her drunk."

"It wasn't the *man* who alibied her?"

"What do you mean?"

"Did the man claim he was a pusher and that he'd forced a fix on the girl?"

Kreisler began laughing again. "Just catch a junkie who's willing to take a fall as a pusher. Are you kidding?"

"The girl told her doctor that the man alibied her."

"Absolute lie," Kreisler said. "*She* was the one who did all the talking, convinced the judge she was innocent, got off with a suspended sentence."

"And the man?"

"Convicted, served his time at Soledad, minimum of two, maximum of ten."

"Then *that's* why she kept sending him money. Not because she was indebted to him, but only because she felt guilty as hell."

"She deserved a break," Kreisler said. "What the hell, she was a nineteen-year-old kid. How do you know? Maybe he *did* force a blast on her."

"I doubt it. She'd been sniffing the stuff and using pot since she was seventeen."

"Yeah, well, we didn't know that."

"What was the man's name?" Meyer asked.

"Fritz Schmidt."

"Fritz? Is that a nickname?"

"No, that's his square handle. Fritz Schmidt."

151

"What's the last you've got on him?"

"He was paroled in four. Parole Office gave him a clean bill of health, haven't had any trouble from him since."

"Do you know if he's still in California?"

"Couldn't tell you."

"Okay, thanks a lot," Meyer said.

"Don't mention it," Kreisler said, and hung up.

There were no listings for Fritz Schmidt in any of the city's telephone directories. But according to Dr Levi's casebook Tinka's "friend from California" had only arrived here in September. Hardly expecting any positive results, Meyer dialed the Information operator, identified himself as a working detective, and asked if she had anything for a Mr Fritz Schmidt in her new listings.

Two minutes later, Meyer and Kling clipped on their holsters and left the squadroom.

The girl came back into the room at nine-twenty-five. She was fully clothed. The Llama was in her right hand. She closed the door gently behind her, but did not bother to switch on the overhead light. She watched Carella silently for several moments, the neon blinking around the edges of the drawn shade across the room. Then she said, "You're shivering, baby."

Carella did not answer.

"How tall are you?" she asked.

"Six-two."

"We'll get some clothes to fit you."

"Why the sudden concern?" Carella asked. He was sweating profusely, and shivering at the same time, wanting to tear his hands free of the cuffs, wanting to kick out with his lashed feet, helpless to do either, feeling desperately ill and knowing the only thing that would cure him.

"No concern at all, baby," she said. "We're dressing you because we've got to take you away from here."

"Where are you taking me?"

"Away."

"Where?"

"Don't worry," she said. "We'll give you a nice big fix first."

He felt suddenly exhilarated. He tried to keep the joy from showing on his face, tried not to smile, hoping against hope that she wasn't just teasing him again. He lay shivering on the floor, and the girl laughed and said, "My, it's rough when a little jolt is overdue isn't it?"

Carella said nothing.

"Do you know what an overdose of heroin is?" she asked suddenly.

The shivering stopped for just a moment, and then began again more violently. Her words seemed to echo in the room, do you know what an overdose of heroin is, overdose, heroin, do you, do you?

"Do you?" the girl persisted.

"Yes."

"It won't hurt you," she said. "It'll *kill* you, but it won't hurt you." She laughed again. "Think of it, baby. How many addicts would you say there are in this city? Twenty thousand, twenty-one thousand, what's your guess?"

"I don't know," Carella said.

"Let's make it twenty thousand, okay? I like round numbers. Twenty thousand junkies out there, all hustling around and wondering where their next shot is coming from, and here we are about to give you a fix that'd take care of seven or eight of them for a week. How about that? That's real generosity, baby."

"Thanks," Carella said. "What do you think," he started, and stopped because his teeth were chattering. He waited. He took a deep breath and tried again. "What do you think you'll . . . you'll accomplish by killing me?"

"Silence," the girl said.

"How?"

"You're the only one in the world who knows who we are or where we are. Once you're dead, silence."

"No."

"Ah, *yes*, baby."

"I'm telling you no. They'll find you."

"Uh-uh."

"Yes."

"How?"

"The same way I did."

"Uh-uh. Impossible."

"If *I* uncovered your mistake—"

"There *was* no mistake, baby." The girl paused. "There was only a little girl playing with her doll."

The room was silent.

"We've got the doll, honey. We found it in your car, remember? It's a very nice doll. Very expensive, I'll bet."

"It's a present for my daughter," Carella said. "I told you—"

"You weren't going to give your daughter a *used* doll for a present, were you? No, honey." The girl smiled. "I happened to look under the doll's dress a few minutes ago. Baby, it's all over for you, believe me." She turned and opened the door. "Fritz," she yelled to the other room, "come in here and give me a hand."

The mailbox downstairs told them Fritz Schmidt was in apartment 34. They took the steps up two at a time, drawing their revolvers when they were on the third floor, and then scanning the numerals on each door as they moved down the corridor. Meyer put his ear to the door at the end of the hall. He could hear nothing. He moved away from the door, and then nodded to Kling. Kling stepped back several feet, bracing himself, his legs widespread. There was no wall opposite the end door, nothing to use as a launching support for a flat-footed kick at the latch. Meyer used Kling's body as the support he needed, raising his knee high as Kling shoved him out and forward. Meyer's foot connected. The lock sprang and the door swung wide. He followed it into the apartment, gun in hand, Kling not three feet behind him. They fanned out the moment they were inside the room. Kling to the right, Meyer to the left.

A man came running out of the room to the right of the large living room. He was a tall man with straight blond hair and huge shoulders. He looked at the detectives and then thrust one hand inside his jacket and down toward his belt. Neither Meyer not Kling waited to find out what he was reaching for. They opened fire simultaneously. The bullets caught the man in his enormous chest and flung him back against the wall,

154

which he clung to for just a moment before falling headlong to the floor. A second person appeared in the doorway. The second person was a girl, and she was very big, and she held a pistol in her right hand. A look of panic was riding her face, but it was curiously coupled with a fixed smile, as though she'd been expecting them all along and was ready for them, was in fact welcoming their arrival.

"Watch it, she's loaded!" Meyer yelled, but the girl swung around swiftly, pointing the gun into the other room instead, aiming it at the floor. In the split second it took her to turn and extend her arm, Kling saw the man lying trussed near the radiator. The man was turned away from the door, but Kling knew instinctively it was Carella.

He fired automatically and without hesitation, the first time he had ever shot a human being in the back, placing the shot high between the girl's shoulders. The Llama in her hand went off at almost the same instant, but the impact of Kling's slug sent her falling halfway across the room, her own bullet going wild. She struggled to rise as Kling ran into the room. She turned the gun on Carella again, but Kling's foot struck her extended hand, kicking the gun up as the second shot exploded. The girl would not let go. Her fingers were still tight around the stock of the gun. She swung it back a third time and shouted, "Let me *kill* him, you bastard!" and tightened her finger on the trigger.

Kling fired again.

His bullet entered her forehead just above the right eye. The Llama went off as she fell backward, the bullet spanging against the metal of the radiator and then ricocheting across the room and tearing through the drawn window shade and shattering the glass behind it.

Meyer was at his side.

"Easy," he said.

Kling had not cried since that time almost four years ago when Claire was killed, but he stood in the center of the neon-washed room now with the dead and bleeding girl against the wall and Carella naked and shivering near the radiator, and he allowed the hand holding the pistol to drop limply to his side, and then he began sobbing, deep bitter sobs that racked his body.

Meyer put his arm around Kling's shoulders.

"Easy," he said again. "It's all over."

"The doll," Carella whispered. "Get the doll."

14

The doll measured thirty inches from the top of her blonde head to the bottoms of her black patent-leather shoes. She wore white bobby sox, a ruffled white voile dress with a white nylon underslip, a black velveteen bodice, and a ruffled lace bib and collar. What appeared at first to be a simulated gold brooch was centred just below the collar.

The doll's trade name was Chatterbox.

There were two D-size flashlight batteries and one 9-volt transistor battery in a recess in the doll's plastic belly. The recess was covered with a flesh-colored plastic top that was kept in place by a simple plastic twist-lock. Immediately above the battery box, there was a flesh-colored, open plastic grid that concealed the miniature electronic device in the doll's chest. It was this device after which the doll had been named by its creators. The device was a tiny recorder.

The brooch below the doll's collar was a knob that activated the recording mechanism. To record, a child simply turned the decorative knob counterclockwise, waited for a single beep signal, and began talking until the beep sounded again, at which time the knob has to be turned once more to its center position. In order to play back what had just been recorded, the child had only to turn the knob clockwise. The recorded message would continue to play back over and over again until the knob was once more returned to the center position.

When the detectives turned brooch-knob clockwise, they heard three recorded voices. One of them belonged to Anna Sachs. It was clear and distinct because the doll had been in Anna's lap when she'd recorded her message on the night of her mother's murder. The message was one of reassurance. She kept saying over and over again to the doll lying across her lap "Don't be frightened, Chatterbox, please don't be frightened. It's nothing, Chatterbox, don't be frightened," over and over again.

The second voice was less distinct because it had been recorded through the thin wall separating the child's bedroom from her mother's. Subsequent tests by the police laboratory showed the recording mechanism to be extremely sensitive for a device of its size, capable of picking up shouted words at a distance of twenty-five feet. Even so, the second voice would not have been picked up at all had Anna not been sitting very close to the thin dividing wall. And, of course, especially toward the end, the words next door had been screamed.

From beep to beep, the recording lasted only a minute and a half. Throughout the length of the recording, Anna talked reassuringly to her doll. "Don't be frightened, Chatterbox, please don't be frightened. It's nothing, Chatterbox, don't be frightened." Behind the child's voice, a running counterpoint of horror, was the voice of Tinka Sachs, her mother. Her words were almost inaudible at first. They presented only a vague murmur of faraway terror, the sound of someone repeatedly moaning, the pitiable rise and fall of a voice imploring – but all without words because the sound had been muffled by the wall between the rooms. And then, as Tinka became more and more desperate, as her killer followed her unmercifully around the room with a knife blade, her voice became louder, the words became more distinct. "Don't! Please don't!" always behind the child's soothing voice in the foreground. "Don't be frightened, Chatterbox, please don't be frightened," and her mother shrieking, "Don't! Please don't! Please," the voices intermingling, "I'm bleeding, please, it's nothing, Chatterbox, don't be frightened, Fritz stop, please, Fritz, stop, stop, oh please, it's nothing, Chatterbox, don't be frightened."

The third voice sounded like a man's. It was nothing more than a rumble on the recording. Only once did a word come through clearly, and that was the word·"Slut!" interspersed between the child's reassurances to her doll, and Tinka's weakening cries for mercy.

In the end, Tinka shouted the man's name once again, "Fritz!" and then her voice seemed to fade. The next word she uttered could have been a muted "please", but it was indistinct and drowned out by Anna's "Don't cry, Chatterbox, try not to cry."

The detectives listened to the doll in silence, and then watched while the ambulance attendants carried Carella out on one stretcher and the still-breathing Schmidt out on another.

"The girl's dead," the medical examiner said.

"I know," Meyer answered.

"Who shot her?" one of the Homicide cops asked.

"I did," Kling answered.

"I'll need the circumstances."

"Stay with him," Meyer said to Kling. "I'll get to the hospital. Maybe that son of a bitch wants to make a statement before he dies."

I didn't intend to kill her.

She was happy as hell when I came in, laughing and joking because she thought she was off the junk at last.

I told her she was crazy, she would never kick it.

I had not had a shot since three o'clock that afternoon, I was going out of my head. I told her I wanted money for a fix, and she said she couldn't give me money any more, she said she wanted nothing more to do with me or Pat, that's the name of the girl I'm living with. She had no right to hold out on me like that, not when I was so sick. She could see I was ready to climb the walls, so she sat there sipping her goddamn iced <u>tea</u>, and telling me she was not going to keep me supplied any more, she was not going to spend half her income keeping me in shit. I told her she owed it to me. I spent four years in Soledad

159

because of her, the little bitch, she owed it to
me! She told me to leave her alone. She told
me to get out and leave her alone. She said she
was finished with me and my kind. She said she
had kicked it, did I understand, she had kicked
it!

Am I going to die?

I

I picked

I picked the knife up from the tray.

I didn't intend to kill her, it was just I
needed a fix, couldn't she see that? For
Christ's sake, the times we used to have
together. I stabbed her, I don't know how many
times.

Am I going to die?

The painting fell off the wall, I remember
that.

I took all the bills out of her pocketbook
on the dresser, there was forty dollars in tens.

I ran out of the bedroom and dropped the knife
someplace in the hall, I guess, I don't even
remember. I realized I couldn't take the
elevator down, that much I knew, so I went up to
the roof and crossed over to the next building
and got down to the street that way. I bought
twenty caps with the forty dollars. Pat and me
got very high afterwards, very high.

I didn't know Tina's kid was in the
apartment until tonight, when Pat accidentally
tipped to that goddamn talking doll.

If I'd known she was there, I might have
killed her, too. I don't know.

160

Fritz Schmidt never got to sign his dictated confession because he died seven minutes after the police stenographer began typing it.

The lieutenant stood by while the two Homicide cops questioned Kling. They had advised him not to make a statement before Byrnes arrived, and now that he was here they went about their routine task with dispatch. Kling could not seem to stop crying. The two Homicide cops were plainly embarrassed as they questioned him, a grown man, a cop no less, crying that way. Byrnes watched Kling's face, and said nothing.

The two Homicide cops were called Carpenter and Calhoun. They looked very much alike. Byrnes had never met any Homicide cops who did not look exactly alike. He supposed it was a trademark of their unique speciality. Watching them, he found it difficult to remember who was Carpenter and who was Calhoun. Even their voices sounded alike.

"Let's start with your name, rank, and shield number," Carpenter said.

"Bertram Kling, detective/third, 74579."

"Squad?" Calhoun said.

"The Eight-Seven." He was still sobbing. The tears rolled down his face endlessly.

"Technically, you just commited a homicide, Kling."

"It's excusable homicide," Calhoun said.

"Justifiable," Carpenter corrected.

"Excusable," Calhoun repeated. "Penal Law 1054."

"Wrong," Carpenter said. "Justifiable, P.L. 1055. Homicide is justifiable when committed by a public officer in arresting a person who has committed a felony and is fleeing from justice. *Justi*fiable."

"Was the broad committing a felony?" Calhoun asked.

"Yes," Kling said. He nodded. He tried to wipe the tears from his eyes. "Yes. Yes, she was." The tears would not stop.

"Explain it."

"She was . . . she was ready to shoot Carella. She was trying to kill him."

"Did you fire a warning shot?"

"No. Her back was turned to me and she was . . . she was

161

leveling the gun at Carella, so I fired the minute I came into the room. I caught her between the shoulders, I think. With my first shot."

"Then what?"

Kling wiped the back of his hand across his eyes. "Then she . . . she started to fire again, and I kicked out at her hand, and the slug went wild. When she . . . when she got ready to fire the third time, I . . . I . . ."

"You killed her," Carpenter said flatly.

"Justifiable," Calhoun said.

"Absolutely," Carpenter agreed.

"I said so all along," Calhoun said.

"She'd already committed a felony by abducting a police officer, what the hell. And then she fired two shots at him. If that ain't a felony, I'll eat all the law books in this crumby state."

"You got nothing to worry about."

"Except the Grand Jury. This has to go to the Grand Jury, Kling, same as if you were an ordinary citizen."

"You still got nothing to worry about," Calhoun said.

"She was going to kill him," Kling said blankly. His tears suddenly stopped. He stared at the two Homicide cops as though seeing them for the first time. "Not again," he said. "I couldn't let it happen again."

Neither Carpenter nor Calhoun knew what the hell Kling was talking about. Byrnes knew, but he didn't particularly feel like explaining. He simply went to Kling and said, "Forget those departmental charges I mentioned. Go home and get some rest."

The two Homicide cops didn't know what the hell *Byrnes* was talking about, either. They looked at each other, shrugged, and chalked it all up to the eccentricities of the 87th.

"Well," Carpenter said. "I guess that's that."

"I guess that's that," Calhoun said. Then, because Kling seemed to have finally gotten control of himself, he ventured a small joke. "Stay out of jail, huh?" he said.

Neither Byrnes nor Kling even smiled.

Calhoun and Carpenter cleared their throats and walked out without saying good night.

She sat in the darkness of the hospital room and watched her sedated husband, waiting for him to open his eyes, barely able to believe that he was alive, praying now that he would be well again soon.

The doctors had promised to begin treatment at once. They had explained to her that it was difficult to fix the length of time necessary for anyone to become an addict, primarily because heroin procured illegally varied in its degree of adulteration. But Carella had told them he'd received his first injection sometime late Friday night, which meant he had been on the drug for slightly more than three days. In their opinion, a person psychologically prepared for addiction would undoubtedly become a habitual user in that short a time, if he was using pure heroin of normal strength. But they were working on the assumption that Carella had never used drugs before and had been injected only with narcotics acquired illegally and therefore greatly adulterated. If this was the case, anywhere between two and three weeks would have been necessary to transform him into a confirmed addict. At any rate, they would begin withdrawal (if so strong a word was applicable at all) immediately, and they had no doubt that the cure (and again they apologized for using so strong a word) would be permanent. They had explained that there was none of the addict's usual psychological dependence evident in Carella's case, and then had gone on at great length about personality disturbances, and tolerance levels, and physical dependence – and then one of the doctors suddenly and quietly asked whether or not Carella had ever expressed a prior interest in experimenting with drugs.

Teddy had emphatically shaken her head.

Well, fine then, they said. We're sure everything will work out fine. We're confident of that, Mrs Carella. As for his nose, we'll have to make a more thorough examination in the morning. We don't know when he sustained the injury, you see, or whether or not the broken bones have already knitted. In any case, we should be able to reset it, though it may involve an operation. Please be assured we'll do everything in our power. Would you like to see him now?

She sat in the darkness.

When at last he opened his eyes, he seemed surprised to see her. He smiled and then said, "Teddy."

She returned the smile. She touched his face tentatively.

"Teddy," he said again, and then – because the room was dark and because she could not see his mouth too clearly – he said something which she was sure she misunderstood.

"That's your name," he said. "I didn't forget."

FUZZ

A novel of the 87th precinct

This is for my father-in law,
Harry Melnick,
who inspired *The Heckler*,
and who must therefore take
at least partial blame for this one

The city in these pages is imaginary.
The people, the places are all fictitious.
Only the police routine is based on
established investigatory technique.

1

Oh boy, what a week.

Fourteen muggings, three rapes, a knifing on Culver Avenue, thirty-six assorted burglaries, and the squadroom was being painted.

Not that the squadroom didn't *need* painting.

Detective Meyer Meyer would have been the first man to admit that the squadroom definitely needed painting. It merely seemed idiotic for the city to decide to paint it now, at the beginning of March, when everything outside was rotten and cold and miserable and dreary, and when you had to keep the windows shut tight because you never could get enough damn heat up in the radiators, and as a result had the stink of turpentine in your nostrils all day long, not to mention two painters underfoot and overhead, both of whom never would have made it in the Sistine Chapel.

"Excuse me," one of the painters said, "could you move that thing?"

"What thing?" Meyer said.

"That thing."

"*That* thing," Meyer said, almost blowing his cool, "happens to be our Lousy File. *That* thing happens to contain information on known criminals and trouble-makers in the precinct, and *that* thing happens to be invaluable to the hard-working detectives of this squad."

"Big deal," the painter said.

"Won't he move it?" the other painter asked.

"You move it," Meyer said. "You're the painters, *you* move it."

"We're not supposed to move nothing," the first painter said.

"We're only supposed to paint," the second painter said.

"I'm not supposed to move things, either," Meyer said. "I'm supposed to detect."

"OK, so don't move it," the first painter said, "it'll get all full of green paint."

"Put a dropcloth on it," Meyer said.

"We got our dropcloths over there on those desks there," the second painter said, "that's all the dropcloths we got."

"Why is it I always get involved with vaudeville acts?" Meyer asked.

"Huh?" the first painter said.

"He's being wise," the second painter said.

"All I know is I don't plan to move that filing cabinet," Meyer said. "In fact, I don't plan to move *anything*. You're screwing up the whole damn squadroom, we won't be able to find anything around here for a week after you're gone."

"We do a thorough job," the first painter said.

"Besides, we didn't ask to come," the second painter said. "You think we got nothing better to do than shmear around up here? You think this is an interesting job or something? This is a *boring* job, if you want to know.'

"It is, huh?" Meyer said.

"Yeah, it's boring," the second painter said.

"It's boring, that's right," the first painter agreed.

"Everything apple green, you think that's interesting? The ceiling apple green, the walls apple green, the stairs apple green, that's some interesting job, all right."

"We had a job last week at the outdoor markets down on Council Street, *that* was an interesting job."

"That was the most interesting job we ever had," the second painter said. "Every stall was a different pastel colour, you know those stalls they got? Well, every one of them was a different pastel colour, *that* was a *good* job."

"*This* is a *crappy* job," the first painter said.

"It's boring and it's crappy," the second painter agreed.

"I'm still not moving that cabinet," Meyer said, and the

telephone rang. "87th Squad, Detective Meyer," he said into the receiver.

"Is this Meyer Meyer in person?" the voice on the other end asked.

"Who's this?" Meyer asked.

"First please tell me if I'm speaking to Meyer Meyer himself?"

"This is Meyer Meyer himself."

"Oh God, I think I may faint dead away."

"Listen, who . . ."

"This is Sam Grossman."

"Hello, Sam, what's . . ."

"I can't tell you how thrilled I am to be talking to such a famous person," Grossman said.

"Yeah?"

"Yeah."

"OK, what is it? I don't get it."

"You mean you don't know?"

"No, I don't know. What is it I'm supposed to know?" Meyer asked.

"I'm sure you'll find out," Grossman said.

"There's nothing I hate worse than a mystery," Meyer said, "so why don't you just tell me what you're talking about and save me a lot of trouble?"

"Ah-ha," Grossman said.

"You I need today," Meyer said, and sighed.

"Actually, I'm calling about a man's sports jacket, size thirty-eight, colour red-and-blue plaid, label Tom's Town and Country, analysis of suspect stain on left front flap requested. Know anything about it?"

"I requested the test," Meyer said.

"You got a pencil handy?"

"Shoot."

"Blood negative, semen negative. Seems to be an ordinary kitchen stain, grease or oil. You want us to break it down?"

"No, that won't be necessary."

"This belong to a rape suspect?"

"We've had three dozen rape suspects in here this week. We also have two painters."

"I beg your pardon?"

"Forget it. Is that all?"

"That's all. It certainly was a pleasure talking to you, Mr Meyer Meyer, you have no idea how thrilled I am."

"Listen, what the hell . . . ?" Meyer started, but Grossman hung up. Meyer held the receiver in his hand a moment longer, looking at it peculiarly, and then put it back on to the cradle. He noticed that there were several spatters of apple green paint on the black plastic. "Goddam slobs," he muttered under his breath, and one of the painters said, "What?"

"Nothing."

"I thought you said something."

"Listen, what department are you guys from, anyway?" Meyer asked.

"Public Works," the first painter said.

"Maintenance and Repair," the second painter said.

"Whyn't you come paint this damn place last summer, instead of now when all the windows are closed?"

"Why? What's the matter?"

"It stinks in here, that's what's the matter," Meyer said.

"It stunk in here even before we got here," the first painter said, which was perhaps true. Meyer sniffed disdainfully, turned his back on the two men, and tried to locate the filing cabinet containing last week's DD reports, which cabinet seemed to have vanished from sight.

If there was one thing (and there were *many* things) Meyer could not abide, it was chaos. The squadroom was in a state of utter, complete, and total chaos. Stepladders, dropcloths, newspapers, closed paint cans, open paint cans, used paint brushes, clean paint brushes, cans of turpentine and cans of thinner, mixing sticks, colour samples (all in various lovely shades of apple green), rollers, rolling trays, rolls of masking tape, coveralls, stained rags were strewn, thrown, draped, scattered, leaning against, lying upon, spread over and balanced precariously on desks, cabinets, floors, walls, water coolers, window-sills, and anything inanimate. (Yesterday, the painters had almost thrown a dropcloth over the inert form of Detective Andy Parker who was, as usual, asleep in the swivel chair behind his desk, his feet propped up on an open drawer). Meyer stood in the midst of this disorder like the monument to patience he most certainly was, a sturdy man with china blue eyes and a bald head, speckled now (he didn't even realize it) with apple green paint. There was a pained look on his round face, his shoulders slumped with fatigue, he seemed disoriented and discombobulated, and he didn't know where the hell anything *was*! Chaos, he thought, and the telephone rang again.

He was standing closest to Carella's desk, so he groped around under the dropcloth for the ringing telephone, came away with a wide apple green stain on his jacket sleeve, and bounded across the room to the phone on his own desk. Swearing, he lifted the receiver.

"87th Squad, Detective Meyer," he said.

"Parks Commissioner Cowper will be shot to death tomorrow night unless I receive five thousand dollars before noon," a man's voice said. "More later."

"What?" Meyer said.

The line went dead.

He looked at his watch. It was 4.15 PM.

At four-thirty that afternoon, when Detective Steve Carella got to the squadroom, Lieutenant Byrnes asked him to come into his office for a moment. He was sitting behind his desk in the two-windowed room, puffing on a cigar and looking very much like a boss (which he was) in his grey pin-striped suit, a shade darker than his close-cropped hair, a black-and-gold silk rep tie on his white shirt (tiny spatter of apple green on one cuff), college ring with maroon stone on his right ring finger, wedding band on his left. He asked Carella if he wanted a cup of coffee, and Carella said yes, and Byrnes buzzed Miscolo in the Clerical Office and asked him to bring in another cup of coffee, and then asked Meyer to fill Carella in on the telephone call. It took Meyer approximately ten seconds to repeat the content of the conversation.

"Is that it?" Carella asked.

"That's it."

"Mmm."

"What do you think, Steve?" Byrnes asked.

Carella was sitting on the edge of Byrnes' scarred desk, a tall slender man who looked like a vagrant at the moment because as soon as it got dark he would take to the streets,

11

find himself an alley or a doorway and lie there reeking of wine and hoping somebody would set fire to him. Two weeks ago, a *real* vagrant had been set ablaze by some fun-loving youngsters, and last week another bum had supplied fuel for a second bonfire, a fatal one this time. So Carella had been spending his nights lying in assorted doorways simulating drunkenness and wishing for arson. He had not shaved for three days. There was a bristly stubble on his jaw, the same colour as his brown hair, but growing sparsely and patchily and giving his face a somewhat incomplete look, as though it had been hastily sketched by an inexpert artist. His eyes were brown (he liked to think of them as penetrating), but they appeared old and faded now through association with the scraggly beard and the layers of unadulterated dirt he had allowed to collect on his forehead and his cheeks. What appeared to be a healing cut ran across the bridge of his nose, collodion and vegetable dye skilfully applied to resemble congealing blood and pus and corruption. He also looked as if he had lice. He made Byrnes a little itchy. He made everybody in the room a little itchy. He blew his nose before answering the lieutenant's question, and the handkerchief he took from the back pocket of his greasy pants looked as if it had been fished from a nearby sewer. He blew his nose fluidly (There's such a thing as carrying an impersonation *too* far, Meyer thought), replaced the handkerchief in his trouser pocket, and then said, "He ask to talk to anyone in particular?"

"Nope, just began talking the minute I said who I was."

"Could be a crank," Carella said.

"Could be."

"Why *us*?" Byrnes said.

It was a good question. Assuming the man was *not* a crank, and assuming he *did* plan to kill the commissioner of parks unless he got his five thousand dollars by noon tomorrow, why call the Eight-Seven? There were a great many squadrooms in this fair city, none of which (it was safe to assume) were in the midst of being painted that first week in March, all of which contained detectives every bit as hard-working and determined as the stalwart fellows who gathered together now to sip their afternoon beverages and while away the deepening hours, all of whom doubtless knew the commissioner of parks as inti-

12

mately as did these very minions of the law – so why the Eight-Seven?

A good question. Like most good questions, it was not immediately answered. Miscolo came in with a cup of coffee, asked Carella when he planned to take a bath, and then went back to his clerical duties. Carella picked up the coffee cup in a filth-encrusted hand, brought it to his cracked and peeling lips, sipped at it, and then said, "We ever have anything to do with Cowper?"

"How do you mean?"

"I don't know. Any special assignments, anything like that?"

"Not to my recollection," Byrnes said. "Only thing I can think of is when he spoke at that PBA thing, but every cop in the city was invited to that one."

"It must be a crank," Carella said.

"Could be," Meyer said again.

"Did he sound like a kid?" Carella asked.

"No, he sounded like a grown man."

"Did he say when he'd call again?"

"No. All he said was 'More later'."

"Did he say when or where you were supposed to deliver the money?"

"Nope."

"Maybe he expects us to take up a collection," Carella said.

"Five grand is only five hundred and fifty dollars less than I make in a year," Meyer said.

"Sure, but he's undoubtedly heard how generous the bulls of the 87th are."

"I admit he sounds like a crank," Meyer said. "Only one thing bothers me about what he said."

"What's that?"

"Shot to death. I don't like that, Steve. Those words scare me."

"Yeah. Well," Carella said, "why don't we see if he calls again, OK? Who's relieving?"

"Kling and Hawes should be in around five."

"Who's on the team?" Byrnes asked.

"Willis and Brown. They're relieving on post."

"Which case?"

"Those car snatches. They're planted on Culver and Second."

"You think it's a crank, Meyer?"

"It could be. We'll have to see."

"Should we call Cowper?"

"What for?" Carella said. "This may turn out to be nothing. No sense alarming him."

"OK," Byrnes said. He looked at his watch, rose, walked to the hat rack in the corner, and put on his overcoat. "I promised Harriet I'd take her shopping, the stores are open late tonight. I should be home around nine if anybody wants to reach me. Who'll be catching?"

"Kling."

"Tell him I'll be home around nine, will you?"

"Right."

"I hope it's a crank," Byrnes said, and went out of the office.

Carella sat on the edge of the desk, sipping his coffee. He looked very tired. "How does it feel to be famous?" he asked Meyer.

"What do you mean?"

Carella looked up. "Oh, I guess you don't know yet."

"Don't know *what* yet?"

"About the book."

"What book?"

"Somebody wrote a book."

"So?"

"It's called *Meyer Meyer*."

"What?"

"Yeah. *Meyer Meyer*. It was reviewed in today's paper."

"Who? What do you mean? Meyer *Meyer*, you mean?"

"It got a nice review."

"Meyer Meyer?" Meyer said. "That's *my* name."

"Sure."

"He can't do that!"

"She. A woman."

"Who?"

"Her name's Helen Hudson."

"She can't do that!"

"She's already done it."

"Well, she *can't*. I'm a *person*, you can't go naming some character after a *person*." He frowned and then looked at Carella suspiciously. "Are you putting me on?"

"Nope, God's honest truth."

"Is this guy supposed to be a cop?"

"No, I think he's a teacher."

"A *teacher*, Jesus Christ!"

"At a university."

"She can't do that!" Meyer said again. "Is he bald?"

"I don't know. He's short and plump, the review said."

"Short and plump! She can't use my name for a short plump person. I'll sue her."

"So sue her," Carella said.

"You think I won't? Who published that goddamn book?"

"Dutton."

"OK!" Meyer said, and took a pad from his jacket pocket. He wrote swiftly on a clean white page, slammed the pad shut, dropped it to the floor as he was putting it back into his pocket, swore, stooped to pick it up, and then looked at Carella plaintively and said, "After all, *I* was here first.'

The second call came at ten minutes to eleven that night. It was taken by Detective Bert Kling, who was catching, and who had been briefed on the earlier call before Meyer left the squadroom.

"87th Squad," he said, "Kling here."

"You've undoubtedly decided by now that I'm a crank," the man's voice said. "I'm not."

"Who is this?" Kling asked, and motioned across the room for Hawes to pick up the extension.

"I was quite serious about what I promised," the man said. "Parks Commissioner Cowper will be shot to death some time tomorrow night unless I receive five thousand dollars by noon. This is how I want it. Have you got a pencil?"

"Mister, why'd you pick on *us*?" Kling asked.

"For sentimental reasons," the man said, and Kling could have sworn he was smiling on the other end of the line. "Pencil ready?"

"Where do you expect us to get five thousand dollars?"

"Entirely your problem," the man said. "*My* problem is

15

killing Cowper if you fail to deliver. Do you want this information?"

"Go ahead," Kling said, and glanced across the room to where Hawes sat hunched over the other phone. Hawes nodded.

"I want the money in singles, need I mention they must be unmarked?"

"Mister, do you know what extortion is?" Kling asked suddenly.

"I know what it is," the man said. "Don't try keeping me on the line. I plan to hang up long before you can effect a trace."

"Do you know the penalty for extortion?" Kling asked, and the man hung up.

"*Son* of a bitch," Kling said.

"He'll call back. We'll be ready next time," Hawes said.

"We can't trace it through automatic equipment, anyway."

"We can try."

"*What'd* he say?"

"He said 'sentimental reasons'."

"That's what I thought he said. What's that supposed to mean?"

"Search me," Hawes said, and went back to his desk, where he had spread a paper towel over the dropcloth, and where he had been drinking tea from a cardboard container and eating a cheese Danish before the telephone call interrupted him.

He was a huge man, six feet two inches tall and weighing two hundred pounds, some ten pounds more than was comfortable for him. He had blue eyes, and a square jaw with a cleft chin. His hair was red, except for a streak over his left temple where he had once been knifed and where the hair had curiously grown in white after the wound healed. He had a straight unbroken nose, and a good mouth with a wide lower lip. Sipping his tea, munching his Danish, he looked like a burly Captain Ahab who had somehow been trapped in a civil service job. A gun butt protruded from the holster under his coat as he leaned over the paper towel and allowed the Danish crumbs to fall on to it. The gun was a big one, as befitted the size of the man, a Smith & Wesson .357 Magnum, weighing forty-four and a half ounces, and capable of putting a hole the size of a baseball on your head if you happened to cross the path of Cotton Hawes on a night when the moon was full. He was biting into the Danish when the telephone rang again.

"87th Squad, Kling here."

"The penalty for extortion," the man said, "is imprisonment not exceeding fifteen years. Any other questions?"

"Listen . . ." Kling started.

"*You* listen," the man said. "I want five thousand dollars in unmarked singles. I want them put into a metal lunch pail, and I want the pail taken to the third bench on the Clinton Street footpath into Grover Park. More later," he said, and hung up.

"We're going to play Fits and Starts, I see," Kling said to Hawes.

"Yeah. Shall we call Pete?"

"Let's wait till we have the whole picture," Kling said, and sighed and tried to get back to typing up his report. The phone did not ring again until eleven-twenty. When he lifted the receiver, he recognized the man's voice at once.

"To repeat," the man said, "I want the lunch pail taken to the third bench on the Clinton Street footpath into Grover Park. If the bench is watched, if your man is not alone, the pail will not be picked up, and the commissioner will be killed."

"You want five grand left on a park bench?" Kling asked.

"You've got it," the man said, and hung up.

"You think that's all of it?" Kling asked Hawes.

"I don't know," Hawes said. He looked up at the wall clock. "Let's give him till midnight. If we don't get another call by then, we'll ring Pete."

"OK," Kling said.

He began typing again. He typed hunched over the machine, using a six-finger system that was uniquely his own, typing rapidly and with a great many mistakes, overscoring or erasing as the whim struck him, detesting the paperwork that went into police work, wondering why anyone would want a metal pail left on a park bench where any passing stranger might pick it up, cursing the decrepit machine provided by the city, and then wondering how anyone could have the unmitigated gall to demand five thousand dollars *not* to commit a murder. He frowned as he worked, and because he was the youngest detective on the squad, with a face comparatively unravaged by the pressures of his chosen profession, the only wrinkle in evidence was the one caused by the frown, a deep cutting ridge across his smooth forehead. He was a blond man, six feet tall, with hazel eyes and an open countenance. He wore a yellow sleeveless pullover, and his brown sports jacket was draped over the back of his chair. The Colt .38 Detective's Special he usually wore clipped to his belt was in its holster in the top drawer of his desk.

He took seven calls in the next half-hour, but none of them was from the man who had threatened to kill Cowper. He was finishing his report, a routine listing of the persons interrogated in a mugging on Ainsley Avenue, when the telephone rang again. He reached for the receiver automatically. Automatically, Hawes lifted the extension.

"Last call tonight," the man said. "I want the money before noon tomorrow. There are more than one of us, so don't attempt to arrest the man who picks it up or the commissioner will be killed. If the lunch pail is empty, or if it contains paper scraps or phoney bills or marked bills, or if for any reason or by any circumstance the money is not on that bench before noon tomorrow, the plan to kill the commissioner will go into effect. If you have any questions, ask them now."

"You don't really expect us to hand you five thousand dollars on a silver platter, do you?"

"No, in a lunch pail," the man said, and again Kling had the impression he was smiling.

"I'll have to discuss this with the lieutenant," Kling said.

"Yes, and he'll doubtless have to discuss it with the parks commissioner," the man said.

"Is there any way we can reach you?" Kling asked, taking a wild gamble, thinking the man might hastily and automatically reveal his home number or his address.

"You'll have to speak louder," the man said. "I'm a little hard of hearing."

"I said is there any way . . ."

And the man hung up.

The bitch city can intimidate you sometimes by her size alone, but when she works in tandem with the weather she can make you wish you were dead. Cotton Hawes wished he was dead on that Tuesday, March 5th. The temperature as recorded at the Grover Park Lane at 7 AM that morning was twelve degrees above zero, and by 9 AM – when he started on to the Clinton Street footpath – it had risen only two degrees to stand at a frigid fourteen above. A strong harsh wind was blowing off the River Harb to the north, racing untrammelled through the narrow north-south corridor leading directly to the path. His red hair whipped fitfully about his hatless head, the tails of his overcoat were flat against the backs of his legs. He was wearing gloves and carrying a black lunch pail in his left hand. The third button of his overcoat, waist high, was open, and the butt of his Magnum rested just behind the gaping flap, ready for a quick right-handed, spring-assisted draw.

The lunch pail was empty.

They had awakened Lieutenant Byrnes at five minutes to twelve the night before, and advised him of their subsequent conversations with the man they now referred to as The Screwball. The lieutenant had mumbled a series of grunts into the telephone and then said, "I'll be right down," and then asked what time it was. They told him it was almost midnight. He grunted again, and hung up. When he got to the squadroom, they filled him in more completely, and it was decided to call the parks commissioner to appraise him of the threat against his life, and to discuss any possible action with him. The parks commissioner looked at his bedside clock the moment the phone rang and immediately informed Lieutenant Byrnes that it was half past midnight, wasn't this something that could wait until morning?

Byrnes cleared his throat and said, "Well, someone says he's going to shoot you."

The parks commissioner cleared his throat and said, "Well, why didn't you say so?"

The situation was ridiculous.

The parks commissioner had never heard of a more ridiculous situation, why this man had to be an absolute maniac to assume anyone would pay him five thousand dollars on the strength of a few phone calls. Byrnes agreed that the situation was ridiculous, but that none the less a great many crimes in this city were committed daily by misguided or unprincipled

19

people, some of whom were doubtless screwballs, but sanity was not a prerequisite for the successful perpetration of a criminal act.

The situation was unthinkable.

The parks commissioner had never heard of a more unthinkable situation, he couldn't even understand why they were bothering him with what were obviously the rantings of some kind of lunatic. Why didn't they simply forget the entire matter?

"Well, Byrnes said, "I hate to behave like a television cop, sir, I would really *rather* forget the entire thing, as you suggest, but the possibility exists that there *is* a plan to murder you, and in all good conscience I cannot ignore that possibility, not without discussing it first with you."

"Well, you've discussed it with me," the parks commissioner said, "and I say forget it."

"Sir," Byrnes said, "we would like to try to apprehend the man who picks up the lunch pail, and we would also like to supply you with police protection tomorrow night. Had you planned on leaving the house tomorrow night?"

The parks commissioner said that Byrnes could do whatever he thought fit in the matter of apprehending the man who picked up the lunch pail, but that he did indeed plan on going out tomorrow night, was in fact invited by the mayor to attend a performance of Beethoven's *Eroica* given by the Philharmonic at the city's recently opened music and theatre complex near Remington Circle, and he did not want or need police protection.

Byrnes said, "Well, sir, let's see what results we have with the lunch pail, we'll get back to you."

"Yes, get back to me," the parks commissioner said, "but not in the middle of the night again, OK?" and hung up.

At 5 AM on Tuesday morning, while it was still dark, Detectives Hal Willis and Arthur Brown drank two fortifying cups of coffee in the silence of the squadroom, donned foul-weather gear requisitioned from an Emergency Squad truck, clipped on their holsters, and went out on to the arctic tundra to begin a lonely surveillance of the third bench on the Clinton Street footpath into Grover Park. Since most of the park's paths meandered from north to south and naturally had entrances on either end they thought at first there might be some confusion concerning the Clinton Street footpath. But a look at the map on the precinct wall showed that there was only one entrance to this particular path, which began on Grover Avenue, adjacent to the park, and then wound through the park to end at the band shell near the lake. Willis and Brown planted themselves on a shelf of rock overlooking the suspect third bench, shielded from the path by a stand of naked elms. It was very cold. They did not expect action, of course, until Hawes dropped the lunch pail where specified, but they could hardly take up posts after the events, and so it had been Byrnes' brilliant idea to send them out before anyone watching the bench might observe them. They did windmill exercises with their arms, they stamped their feet, they continuously pressed the palms of their hands against portions of their faces that seemed to be going, the telltale whiteness of frostbite appearing suddenly and frighteningly in the bleak early morning hours. Neither of the two men had ever been so cold in his life.

Cotton Hawes was almost, but not quite, as cold when he entered the park at 9 AM that morning. He passed two people on his way to the bench. One of them was an old man in a black overcoat, walking swiftly towards the subway kiosk on Grover Avenue. The other was a girl wearing a mink coat over a long pink nylon nightgown that flapped dizzily about her ankles, walking a white poodle wearing a red wool vest. She smiled at Hawes as he went by with his lunch pail.

The third bench was deserted.

Hawes took a quick look around and then glanced up and out of the park to the row of apartment buildings on Grover Avenue. A thousand windows reflected the early morning sun. Behind any one of these windows, there might have been a man with a pair of binoculars and a clear unobstructed view of the bench. He put the lunch pail on one end of the bench, moved it to the other end, shrugged, and relocated it in the exact centre of the bench. He took another look around, feeling really pretty stupid, and then walked out of the park and back to the office. Detective Bert Kling was sitting at his desk, monitoring the walkie-talkie operated by Hal Willis in the park.

"How you doing down there?" Kling asked.

"We're freezing our asses off," Willis replied.

"Any action yet?"

"You think anybody's crazy enough to be out in this weather?" Willis said.

"Cheer up," Kling said, "I hear the boss is sending you both to Jamaica when this is over."

"Fat Chance Department," Willis said. "Hold it!"

There was silence in the squadroom. Hawes and Kling waited. At last, Willis' voice erupted from the speaker on Kling's box.

"Just a kid," Willis said. "Stopped at the bench, looked over the lunch pail, and then left it right where it was."

"Stay with it," Kling said.

"We have to stay with it," Brown's voice cut in. "We're frozen solid to this goddamn rock."

There were people in the park now.

They ventured into the bitch city tentatively, warned by radio and television forecasters, further cautioned by the visual evidence of thermometers outside apartment windows, and the sound of the wind whipping beneath the eaves of old buildings, and the touch of the frigid blast that attacked any exploratory hand thrust outdoors for just an instant before a window slammed quickly shut again. They dressed with no regard to the dictates of fashion, the men wearing ear muffs and bulky mufflers, the women bundled into layers of sweaters and fur-lined boots, wearing woollen scarves to protect their heads and ears, rushing at a quick trot through the park, barely glancing at the bench or the black lunch pail sitting in the centre of it. In a city notorious for its indifference, the citizens were more obviously withdrawn now, hurrying past each other without so much as eyes meeting, insulating themselves, becoming tight private cocoons that defied the cold. Speech might have made them more vulnerable, opening the mouth might have released the heat they had been storing up inside, commiseration would never help to diminish the wind that tried to cut them down in the streets, the sabre-slash wind that blew in off the river and sent newspapers wildly soaring into the air, fedoras wheeling into the gutter. Speech was a precious commodity that cold March day.

In the park, Willis and Brown silently watched the bench.

The painters were in a garrulous mood.

"What have you got going, a stakeout?" the first painter asked.

"Is that what the walkie-talkie's for?" the second painter asked.

"Is there gonna be a bank holdup?"

"Is that why you're listening to that thing?"

"Shut up," Kling said encouragingly.

The painters were on their ladders, slopping apple green paint over everything in sight.

"We painted the DA's office once," the first painter said.

"They were questioning this kid who stabbed his mother forty-seven times."

"Forty-*seven* times."

"In the belly, the head, the breasts, every place."

"With an ice-pick."

"He was guilty as sin."

"He said he did it to save her from the Martians."

"A regular bedbug."

"Forty-*seven* times."

"How could that save her from the Martians?" the second painter asked.

"Maybe Martians don't like ladies with ice-pick holes in them," the first painter said, and burst out laughing. The second painter guffawed with him. Together, they perched on their ladders, helpless with laughter, limply holding brushes that dripped paint on the newspapers spread on the squadroom floor.

The man entered the park at 10 AM.

He was perhaps twenty-seven years old, with a narrow cold-pinched face, his lips drawn tight against the wind, his eyes watering. He wore a beige car coat, the collar pulled up against the back of his neck, buttoned tight around a green wool muffler at his throat. His hands were in the slash pockets of the coat. He wore brown corduroy trousers, the wale cut diagonally, and brown high-topped workman's shoes. He came on to the Clinton Street footpath swiftly, without looking either to the right or the left, walked immediately and directly to the third bench on the path, picked up the lunch pail, tucked it under his arm, put his naked hand back into his coat pocket, wheeled abruptly, and was starting out of the park again, when a voice behind him said, "Hold it right there, Mac."

He turned to see a tall burly Negro wearing what looked like a blue astronaut's suit. The Negro was holding a big pistol in his right hand. His left hand held a wallet which fell open to reveal a gold and blue shield.

"Police officer," the Negro said. "We want to talk to you."

2

Miranda-Escobedo sounds like a Mexican bullfighter.

It is not.

It is the police shorthand for two separate Supreme Court decisions. These decisions, together, lay down the ground rules for the interrogation of suspects, and cops find them a supreme pain in the ass. There is not one working cop in the United States who thinks Miranda-Escobedo is a good idea. They are all fine Americans, these cops, and are all very concerned with the rights of the individual in a free society, but they do not like Miranda-Escobedo because they feel it makes their job more difficult. Their job is crime prevention.

Since the cops of the 87th had taken a suspect into custody and intended to question him, Miranda-Escobedo immediately came into play. Captain Frick, who was in charge of the entire precinct, had issued a bulletin to his men shortly after the Supreme Court decision in 1966, a flyer printed on green paper and advising every cop in the precinct, uniformed and plain-clothes, on the proper interrogation of criminal suspects. Most of the precinct's uniformed cops carried the flyer clipped inside their notebooks, where it was handy for reference whenever they needed it.

The detectives, on the other hand, normally questioned more people than their uniformed colleagues, and had committed the rules to memory. They used them now with easy familiarity, while continuing to look upon them with great distaste.

"In keeping with the Supreme Court decision in *Miranda v.*

25

Arizona," Hal Willis said, "we're required to advise you of your rights, and that's what I'm doing now. First, you have the right to remain silent if you choose, do you understand that?"

"I do."

"Do you also understand that you need not answer any police questions?"

"I do."

"And do you also understand that if you *do* answer questions, your answers may be used as evidence against you?"

"Yes, I understand."

"I must also inform you that you have the right to consult with an attorney before or during police questioning, do you understand that?"

"I understand."

"And if you decide to exercise that right but do not have the funds with which to hire counsel, you are entitled to have a lawyer appointed without cost, to consult with him before or during the questioning. Is that also clear?"

"Yes."

"You understand all of your rights as I have just explained them to you?"

"I do."

"Are you willing to answer questions without the presence of an attorney?"

"Gee, I don't know," the suspect said. "Should I?"

Willis and Brown looked at each other. They had thus far played Miranda-Escobedo by the book, warning the suspect of his privilege against self-incrimination, and warning him of his right to counsel. They had done so in explicit language, and not by merely making references to the Fifth Amendment. They had also made certain that the suspect understood his rights before asking him whether or not he wished to waive them. The green flyer issued by Captain Frick had warned that it was not sufficient for an officer simply to give warnings and then proceed with an interrogation. It was necessary for the prisoner to *say* he understood, and that he was willing to answer questions without counsel. Only then would the court find that he had waived his constitutional rights.

In addition, however, the flyer had warned all police officers to exercise great care in avoiding language which could later be used by defence attorneys to charge that the officer had "threatened, tricked, or cajoled" the defendant into waiving. The officer was specifically cautioned against advising the suspect not to bother with a lawyer, or even implying that he'd be better off without a lawyer. He was, in short, supposed to inform the defendant of his privilege against self-incrimination and his right to counsel, period. Both Willis and Brown knew that they could not answer the suspect's question. If either of the two had advised him to answer questions without an attorney present, any confession they thereafter took would be inadmissible in court. If, on the other hand, they advised him *not* to answer questions, or advised him to consult with an attorney, their chances of getting a confession would be substantially lessened.

So Willis said, "I've explained your rights, and it would be improper for me to give you any advice. The decision is yours."

"Gee, I don't know," the man said.

"Well, think it over," Willis said.

The young man thought it over. Neither Willis nor Brown said a word. They knew that if their suspect refused to answer questions, that was it, the questioning would have to stop then and there. They also knew that if he began answering questions and suddenly decided he didn't want to go on with the interrogation, they would have to stop immediately, no matter what language he used to express his wishes – "I claim my rights," or "I don't want to say nothing else," or "I demand a mouthpiece."

So they waited.

"I got nothing to hide," the young man said at last.

"Are you willing to answer questions without the presence of an attorney?" Willis asked again.

"I am."

"What's your name?" Willis asked.

"Anthony La Bresca."

"Where do you live, Anthony?"

"In Riverhead."

"Where in Riverhead, Anthony?" Brown said.

Both detectives had automatically fallen into the first-name basis of interrogation that violated only human dignity and not human rights, having nothing whatever to do with Miranda-

Escobedo, but having everything in the world to do with the psychological unsettling of a prisoner. Call a man by his first name without allowing him the return courtesy and:

(*a*) you immediately make him a subordinate; and
(*b*) you instantly rob the familiarity of any friendly connotation, charging its use with menace instead.

"Where in Riverhead, Anthony?" Willis said.
"1812 Johnson."
"Live alone?"
"No, with my mother."
"Father dead?"
"They're separated."
"How old are you, Anthony?"
"Twenty-six."
"What do you do for a living?"
"I'm unemployed at the moment."
"What do you normally do?"
"I'm a construction worker."
"When's the last time you worked?"
"I was laid off last month."
"Why?"
"We completed the job."
"Haven't worked since?"
"I've been looking for work."
"But didn't have any luck, right?"
"That's right."
"Tell us about the lunch pail."
"What about it?"
"Well, what's *in* it, first of all?"
"Lunch, I guess," La Bresca said.
"Lunch, huh?"
"Isn't that what's usually in lunch pails?"
"We're asking *you*, Anthony."
"Yeah, lunch," La Bresca said.
"Did you call this squadroom yesterday?" Brown asked.
"No."
"How'd you know where that lunch pail would be?"
"I was told it would be there."

"Who told you?"

"This guy I met."

"What guy?"

"At the employment agency."

"Go on," Willis said, "let's hear it."

"I was waiting on line outside this employment agency on Ainsley, they handle a lot of construction jobs, you know, and that's where I got my last job from, so that's where I went back today. And this guy is standing on line with me, all of a sudden he snaps his fingers and says, 'Jesus, I left my lunch in the park.' So I didn't say nothing, so he looks at me and says, 'How do you like that, I left my lunch on a park bench.' So I said that's a shame, and all, I sympathized with him, you know. What the hell, poor guy left his lunch on a park bench."

"So then what?"

"So he tells me he would run back into the park to get it, except he has a bum leg. So he asks me if I'd go get it for him."

"So naturally you said yes," Brown said. "A strange guy asks you to walk all the way from Ainsley Avenue over to Grover and into the park to pick up his lunch pail, so naturally you said yes."

"No, naturally I said no," La Bresca said.

"Then what were you doing in the park?"

"Well, we got to talking a little, and he explained how he got his leg hurt in World War II fighting against the Germans, picked up shrapnel from a mortar explosion, he had a pretty rough deal, you know?"

"So naturally you decided to go for the lunch pail after all."

"No, naturally I still didn't decide to do nothing."

"So how *did* you finally end up in the park?"

"That's what I've been trying to tell you."

"You took pity on this man, right? Because he had a bum leg, and because it was so cold outside, right?" Willis said.

"Well, yes, and no."

"You didn't want him to have to walk all the way to the park, right?" Brown said.

"Well, yes and no. I mean, the guy was a stranger, why the hell should I care if he walked to the park or not?"

"Look, Anthony," Willis said, beginning to lose his temper,

and trying to control himself, reminding himself that it was exceptionally difficult to interrogate suspects these days of Miranda-Escobedo when a man could simply refuse to answer at any given moment, Sorry, boys, no more questions, must shut your dear little flatfoot mouths or run the risk of blowing your case. "Look, Anthony," he said more gently, "we're only trying to find out how *you* happened to walk to the park and go directly to the third bench to pick up that lunch pail."

"I know," La Bresca said.

"You met a disabled war veteran, right?"

"Right."

"And he told you he left his lunch pail in the park."

"Well, he didn't say lunch *pail* at first. He just said *lunch*."

"When did he say lunch *pail*?"

"After he gave me the five bucks."

"Oh, he offered you five dollars to go get his lunch pail, is that it?"

"He didn't *offer* it to me, he *handed* it to me."

"He handed you five bucks and said, 'Would you go get my lunch pail for me?' "

"That's right. And he told me it would be on the third bench in the park, on the Clinton Street footpath. Which is right where it was."

"What were you supposed to do with this lunch pail after you got it?"

"Bring it back to him. He was holding my place in line."

"Mm-huh," Brown said.

"What's so important about that lunch pail, anyway?" La Bresca asked.

"Nothing," Willis said. "Tell us about this man. What did he look like?"

"Ordinary-looking guy."

"How old would you say he was?"

"Middle thirties, thirty-five, something like that."

"Tall, short, or average?"

"Tall. About six feet, I would say, give or take."

"What about his build? Heavy, medium, or slight?"

"He was built nice. Good shoulders."

"Heavy?"

"Husky, I would say. A good build."

"What colour was his hair?"

"Blond."

"Was he wearing a moustache or a beard?"

"No."

"What colour were his eyes, did you notice?"

"Blue."

"Did you notice any scars or identifying marks?"

"No."

"Tattoos?"

"No."

"What sort of voice did he have?"

"Average voice. Not too deep. Just average. A good voice."

"Any accent or regional dialect?"

"No."

"What was he wearing?"

"Brown overcoat, brown gloves."

"Suit?"

"I couldn't see what he had on under the coat. I mean, he was wearing pants, naturally, but I didn't notice what colour they were, and I couldn't tell you whether they were part of a suit or whether . . ."

"Fine, was he wearing a hat?"

"No hat."

"Glasses?"

"No glasses."

"Anything else you might have noticed about him?"

"Yeah," La Bresca said.

"What?"

"He was wearing a hearing aid."

The employment agency was on the corner of Ainsley Avenue and Clinton Street, five blocks north of the entrance to the park's Clinton Street footpath. On the off-chance that the man wearing the hearing aid would still be waiting for La Bresca's return, they checked out a sedan and drove over from the station house. La Bresca sat in the back of the car, willing and eager to identify the man if he was still there.

There was a line of men stretching halfway around the corner of Clinton, burly men in work clothes and caps, hands thrust into coat pockets, faces white with cold, feet moving incessantly as they shuffled and jigged and tried to keep warm.

"You'd think they were giving away dollar bills up there," La Bresca said. "Actually, they charge you a whole week's pay. They got good jobs, though. The last one they got me paid real good, and it lasted eight months."

"Do you see your man anywhere on that line?" Brown asked.

"I can't tell from here. Can we get out?"

"Yeah, sure," Brown said.

They parked the car at the kerb. Willis, who had been driving, got out first. He was small and light, with the easy grace of a dancer and the steady cold gaze of a blackjack dealer. He kept slapping his gloved hands together as he waited for Brown. Brown came out of the car like a rhinoceros, pushing his huge body through the door frame, slamming the door behind him, and then pulling his gloves on over big-knuckled hands.

"Did you throw the visor?" Willis asked.

"No. We'll only be a minute here."

"You'd better throw it. Goddamn eager beavers'll give us a ticket sure as hell."

Brown grunted and went back into the car.

"Boy, it's cold out here," La Bresca said.

"Yeah," Willis said.

In the car, Brown lowered the sun visor. A hand-lettered cardboard sign was fastened to the visor with rubber bands. It read:

POLICE DEPARTMENT VEHICLE

The car door slammed again. Brown came over and nodded, and together they began walking towards the line of men standing on the sidewalk. Both detectives unbuttoned their overcoats.

"Do you see him?" Brown asked La Bresca.

"Not yet," La Bresca said.

They walked the length of the line slowly.

"Well?" Brown asked.

"No," La Bresca said. "He ain't here."

"Let's take a look upstairs," Willis suggested.

The line of job seekers continued up a flight of rickety

wooden steps to a dingy second-floor office. The lettering on a frosted glass door read

MERIDIAN EMPLOYMENT AGENCY
Jobs Our Speciality

"See him?" Willis asked.

"No," La Bresca said.

"Wait here," Willis said, and the two detectives moved away from him, towards the other end of the corridor.

"What do you think?" Brown asked.

"What can we hold him on?"

"Nothing."

"So *that's* what I think."

"Is he worth a tail?"

"It depends on how serious the loot thinks this is."

"Why don't you ask him?"

"I think I will. Hold the fort."

Brown went back to La Bresca. Willis found a pay phone around the bend in the corridor, and dialled the squadroom. The lieutenant listened carefully to everything he had to report, and then said, "How do you read him?"

"I think he's telling the truth."

"You think there really *was* some guy with a hearing aid?"

"Yes."

"Then why'd he leave before La Bresca got back with the pail?"

"I don't know, Pete. I just don't make La Bresca for a thief."

"Where'd you say he lived?"

"1812 Johnson. In Riverhead."

"What precinct would that be?"

"I don't know."

"I'll check it out and give them a ring. Maybe they can spare a man for a tail. Christ knows we can't."

"So shall we turn La Bresca loose?"

"Yeah, come on back here. Give him a little scare first, though, just in case."

"Right," Willis said, and hung up, and went back to where La Bresca and Brown were waiting.

"OK, Anthony," Willis said, "you can go."

"Go? Who's *going* any place? I got to get back on that line again. I'm trying to get a job here."

"And remember, Anthony, if anything happens, we know where to find you."

"What do you mean? What's gonna happen?"

"Just remember."

"Sure," La Bresca said. He paused and then said, "Listen, you want to do me a favour?"

"What's that?"

"Get me up to the front of the line there."

"How can we do that?"

"Well, you're cops, ain't you?" La Bresca asked, and Willis and Brown looked at each other.

When they got back to the squadroom, they learned that Lieutenant Byrnes had called the 115th in Riverhead and had been informed they could not spare a man for the surveillance of Anthony La Bresca. Nobody seemed terribly surprised.

That night, as Parks Commissioner Cowper came down the broad white marble steps outside Philharmonic Hall, his wife clinging to his left arm, swathed in mink and wearing a diaphanous white scarf on her head, the commissioner himself resplendent in black tie and dinner jacket, the mayor and his wife four steps ahead, the sky virtually starless, a bitter brittle dryness to the air, that night as the parks commissioner came down the steps of Philharmonic Hall with the huge two-storey-high windows behind him casting warm yellow light on to the windswept steps and pavement, that night as the commissioner lifted his left foot preparatory to placing it on the step below, laughing at something his wife said in his ear, his laughter billowing out of his mouth in puffs of visible vapour that whipped away on the wind like comic strip balloons, that night as he tugged on his right-hand glove with his already gloved left hand, that night two shots cracked into the plaza, shattering the wintry stillness, and the commissioner's laugh stopped, the commissioner's hand stopped, the commissioner's foot stopped, and he tumbled headlong down the steps, blood pouring from his forehead and his cheek, and his wife screamed, and the mayor turned to see what was the matter, and an enterprising photographer on the sidewalk caught the toppling commissioner on film for posterity.

He was dead long before his body rolled to a stop on the wide white bottom step.

3

Concetta Esposita La Bresca had been taught only to dislike and distrust all Negroes. Her brothers, on the other hand, had been taught to dismember them if possible. They had learned their respective lessons in a sprawling slum ghetto affectionately and sarcastically dubbed Paradiso by its largely Italian population. Concetta, as a growing child in this dubious garden spot, had watched her brothers and other neighbourhood boys bash in a good many Negro skulls when she was still just a *piccola ragazza*. The mayhem did not disturb her. Concetta figured if you were stupid enough to be born a Negro, and were further stupid enough to come wandering into Paradiso, why then you deserved to have your fool black head split wide open every now and then.

Concetta had left Paradiso at the age of nineteen, when the local iceman, a fellow *Napolitano* named Carmine La Bresca moved his business to Riverhead and asked the youngest of the Esposito girls to marry him. She readily accepted because he was a handsome fellow with deep brown eyes and curly black hair, and because he had a thriving business of which he was the sole owner. She also accepted because she was pregnant at the time.

Her son was born seven months later, and he was now twenty-seven years old, and living alone with Concetta in the second-floor apartment of a two-family house on Johnson Street. Carmine La Bresca had gone back to Pozzuoli, fifteen miles outside Naples, a month after Anthony was born. The last Concetta heard of him was a rumour that he had been killed during World War II, but, knowing her husband, she suspected he was king of the icemen somewhere in Italy, still fooling around with young girls and getting them pregnant in the icehouse, as was her own cruel misfortune.

Concetta Esposita La Bresca still disliked and distrusted all Negroes, and she was rather startled – to say the least – to find one on her doorstep at 12.01 AM on a starless, moonless night.

"What is it?" she shouted. "Go away."

"Police officer," Brown said, and flashed the tin, and it was then that Concetta noticed the other man standing with the Negro, a white man, short, with a narrow face and piercing brown eyes, *madonna mia*, it looked as if he was giving her the *malocchio*.

"What do you want, go away," she said in a rush, and lowered the shade on the glass-panelled rear door of her apartment. The door was at the top of a rickety flight of wooden steps (Willis had almost tripped and broken his neck on the third one from the top) overlooking a back yard in which there was a tar-paper-covered tree. (Doubtless a fig tree, Brown remarked on their way up the steps.) A clothes-line stiff with undergarments stretched from the tiny back porch outside the glass-panelled door to a pole set diagonally at the other end of the yard. The wind whistled around the porch and did its best to blow Willis off and down into the grape arbour covering the outside patio below. He knocked on the door again and shouted, "Police officers, you'd better open up, lady."

"*Sta zitto!*" Concetta said, and unlocked the door. "You want to wake the whole neighbour? *Ma che vergogna!*"

"Is it all right to come in, lady?" Willis asked.

"Come in, come in," Concetta said, and stepped back into the small kitchen, allowing Willis and then Brown to pass her.

"So what you want two o'clock in the morning?" Concetta said, and closed the door against the wind. The kitchen was narrow, the stove, sink, and refrigerator lined up against one wall, an enamel-topped table on the opposite wall. A metal cabinet, its door open to reveal an array of breakfast cereals and canned foods, was on the right-angled wall, alongside a radiator. There was a mirror over the sink and a porcelain dog on top of the refrigerator. Hanging on the wall over the radiator was a picture of Jesus Christ. A light bulb with a pull chain and a large glass globe hung in the centre of the kitchen. The faucet was dripping. An electric clock over the range hummed a steady counterpoint.

"It's only midnight," Brown said. "Not two o'clock."

There was an edge to his voice that had not been there on the long ride up to Riverhead, and Willis could only attribute it to the presence of Mrs La Bresca, if indeed that was who the lady was. He wondered for perhaps the hundredth time what radar Brown possessed that enabled him to pinpoint unerringly any bigot within a radius of a thousand yards. The woman was staring at both men with equal animosity, it seemed to Willis, her long black hair pinned into a bun at the back of her head, her brown eyes slitted and defiant. She was wearing a man's bathrobe over her nightgown, and he saw now that she was barefoot.

"Are you Mrs La Bresca?" Willis asked.

"I am Concetta La Bresca, who wants to know?" she said.

"Detectives Willis and Brown of the 87th Squad," Willis said. "Where's your son?"

"He's asleep," Concetta said, and because she was born in Naples and raised in Paradiso, immediately assumed it was necessary to provide him with an alibi. "He was here with me all night," she said, "you got the wrong man."

"You want to wake him up, Mrs La Bresca?" Brown said.

"What for?"

"We'd like to talk to him."

"What for?"

"Ma'am, we can take him into custody, if that's what you'd like," Brown said, "but it might be easier all around if we just asked him a few simple questions right here and now. You want to go fetch him, ma'am?"

"I'm up," La Bresca's voice said from the other room.

"You want to come out here, please, Mr La Bresca?" Willis said.

"Just a second," La Bresca said.

"He was here all night," Concetta said, but Brown's hand drifted none the less towards the revolver holstered at his waist, just in case La Bresca had been out pumping two bullets into the commissioner's head instead. He was a while coming. When he finally opened the door and walked into the kitchen, he was carrying nothing more lethal in his hand than the sash of his bathrobe, which he knotted about his waist. His hair was tousled, and his eyes were bleary.

"What now?" he asked.

Since this was a field investigation, and since La Bresca couldn't conceivably be considered "in custody", neither Willis nor Brown felt it necessary to advise him of his rights. Instead, Willis immediately said, "Where were you tonight at eleven thirty?"

"Right here," La Bresca said.

"Doing what?"

"Sleeping."

"What time'd you go to bed?"

"About ten."

"You always hit the sack so early?"

"I do when I gotta get up early."

"You getting up early tomorrow?"

"Six AM," La Bresca said.

"Why?"

"To get to work."

"We thought you were unemployed."

"I got a job this afternoon, right after you guys left me."

"What kind of a job?"

"Construction work. I'm a labourer."

"Meridian get you the job?"

"That's right."

"Who with?"

"Erhard Engineering."

"In Riverhead?"

"No, Isola."

"What time'd you get home tonight?" Brown asked.

"I left Meridian, it musta been about one o'clock, I guess. I went up the pool hall on South Leary and shot a few games with the boys. Then I came home here, it musta been about five or six o'clock."

"What'd you do then?"

"He ate," Concetta said.

"Then what?"

"I watched a little TV, and got into bed," La Bresca said.

"Can anybody besides your mother verify that story?"

"Nobody was here, if that's what you mean."

"You get any phone calls during the night?"

"No."

"Just your word then, right?"

"And *mine*," Concetta said.

"Listen, I don't know what you guys want from me," La Bresca said, "but I'm telling you the truth, I mean it. What's going on, anyway?"

"Did you happen to catch the news on television?"

"No, I musta fell asleep before the news went on. Why? What happened?"

"I go in his room and turn off the light at ten thirty," Concetta said.

"I wish you guys would believe me," La Bresca said. "Whatever it is you've got in mind, I didn't have nothing to do with it."

"I believe you," Willis said. "How about you, Artie?"

"I believe him, too," Brown said.

"But we have to ask questions," Willis said, "you understand?"

"Sure, I understand," La Bresca said, "but I mean, it's the middle of the night, you know? I gotta get up tomorrow morning."

"Why don't you tell us about the man with the hearing aid again," Willis suggested gently.

They spent at least another fifteen minutes questioning La Bresca and at the end of that time decided they'd either have to pull him in and charge him with something, or else forget him for the time being. The man who'd called the squadroom had said, "There are more than one of us," and this information had been passed from Kling to the other detectives on the squad, and it was only this nagging knowledge that kept them there questioning La Bresca long after they should have stopped. A cop can usually tell whether he's on to real meat or not, and La Bresca did not seem like a thief. Willis had told the lieutenant just that only this afternoon, and his opinion hadn't changed in the intervening hours. But if there *was* a gang involved in the commissioner's murder, wasn't it possible that La Bresca was one of them? A lowly cog in the organization, perhaps, the gopher, the slob who was sent to pick up things, the expendable man who ran the risk of being caught by the police if anything went wrong? In which case, La Bresca was lying.

Well, if he was lying, he did it like an expert, staring out of his baby blues and melting both those hardhearted cops with tales of the job he was anxious to start tomorrow morning, which is why he'd gone to bed so early and all, got to get a full eight hours' sleep, growing mind in a growing body, red-blooded second-generation American, and all that crap. Which raised yet another possibility. If he *was* lying – and so far they hadn't been able to trip him up, hadn't been able to budge him from his description of the mystery man he'd met outside Meridian, hadn't been able to find a single discrepancy between the story he'd told that afternoon and the one he was telling now – but if he *was* lying, then wasn't it possible the caller and La Bresca were one and the same person? *Not* a gang at all, that being a figment of his own imagination, a tiny falsehood designed to lead the police into believing this was a well-organized group instead of a single ambitious hood trying to make a killing. And if La Bresca and the caller were one and the same, then La Bresca and the man who'd murdered the commissioner were also one and the same. In which case, it would be proper to take the little liar home and book him for murder. Sure, and then try to find something that would stick, *anything* that would stick, they'd be laughed out of court right at the preliminary hearing.

Some nights you can't make a nickel.

So after fifteen minutes of some very fancy footwork designed to befuddle and unsettle La Bresca, with Brown utilizing his very special logically persistent method of questioning while Willis sniped and jabbed around the edges, they knew nothing more than they had known that afternoon. The only difference was that now the commissioner was dead. So they thanked Mrs La Bresca for the use of the hall, and they shook hands with her son and apologized for having pulled him out of bed, and they wished him luck at his new job, and then they both said goodnight again and went out of the house and heard Mrs La Bresca locking the kitchen door behind them, and went down the rickety wooden steps, and down the potholed driveway, and across the street to where they had parked the police sedan.

Then Willis started the car, and turned on the heater, and both men talked earnestly and softly for several moments and decided to ask the lieutenant for permission to bug La Bresca's phone in the morning.

Then they went home.

It was cold and dark in the alley where Steve Carella lay on his side huddled in a tattered overcoat. The late February snow had been shovelled and banked against one brick alley wall, soiled now with the city's grime, a thin layer of soot crusted on to its surface. Carella was wearing two pairs of thermal underwear and a quilted vest. In addition, a hand warmer was tucked into one pocket of the vest, providing a good steady heat inside the threadbare overcoat. But he was cold.

The banked snow opposite him only made him colder. He did not like snow. Oh yes, he could remember owning his own sled as a boy, and he could remember belly-whopping with joyous abandon, but the memory seemed like a totally fabricated one in view of his present very real aversion to snow. Snow was cold and wet. If you were a private citizen, you had to shovel it, and if you were a Department of Sanitation worker, you had to truck it over to the River Dix to get rid of it. Snow was a pain in the arse.

This entire stakeout was a pain in the arse.

But it was also very amusing.

It was the amusing part of it that kept Carella lying in a cold dark alley on a night that wasn't fit for man or beast. (Of course, he had also been *ordered* to lie in a cold dark alley by the lieutenant for whom he worked, nice fellow name of Peter Byrnes, *he* should come lie in a cold dark alley some night.) The amusing part of this particular stakeout was that Carella wasn't planted in a bank hoping to prevent a multimillion dollar robbery, nor was he planted in a candy store some place, hoping to crack an international ring of narcotics peddlers, nor was he even hidden in the bathroom of a spinster lady's apartment, hoping to catch a mad rapist. He was lying in a cold dark alley, and the amusing part was that two vagrants had been set on fire. That wasn't so amusing, the part about being set on fire. That was pretty serious. The amusing part was that the victims had been vagrants. Ever since Carella could remember, the police had been waging an unremitting war against this city's vagrants, arresting them, jailing them, releasing them, arresting them again, on and on *ad infinitum*. So now the police had been presented with two benefactors who were generously attempting to rid the streets of any and all bums by setting them aflame, and what did the police do? The police promptly dispatched a valuable man to a cold dark alley to lie on his side facing a dirty snowbank while hoping to catch the very fellows who were in charge of incinerating bums. It did not make sense. It was amusing.

A lot of things about police work were amusing.

It was certainly funnier to be lying here freezing than to be at home in bed with a warm and loving woman; oh God, that was so amusing it made Carella want to weep. He thought of Teddy alone in bed, black hair spilling all over the pillow, half-smile on her mouth, nylon gown pulled back over curving hip, God, I could freeze to death right here in this goddamn alley, he thought, and my own wife won't learn about it till morning. My own passionate wife! She'll read about it in the papers! She'll see my name on page four! She'll—

There were footsteps at the other end of the alley.

He felt himself tensing. Beneath the overcoat, his naked hand moved away from the warmer and dropped swiftly to the cold steel butt of his service revolver. He eased the gun out of its holster, lay hunched on his side with the gun ready, and waited as the footsteps came closer.

"Here's one," a voice said.

It was a young voice.

"Yeah," another voice answered.

Carella waited. His eyes were closed, he lay huddled in the far corner of the alley, simulating sleep, his finger curled inside the trigger guard now, a hair's-breadth away from the trigger itself.

Somebody kicked him.

"Wake up!" a voice said.

He moved swiftly, but not swiftly enough. He was shoving himself off the floor of the alley, yanking the revolver into firing position, when the liquid splashed on to the front of his coat.

"Have a drink!" one of the boys shouted, and Carella saw a match flare into life, and suddenly he was in flames.

His reaction sequence was curious in that his sense of smell supplied the first signal, the unmistakable aroma of petrol fumes rising from the front of his coat, and then the flaring match, shocking in itself, providing a brilliant tiny explosion of light in the nearly black alley, more shocking in combination with the smell of petrol. Warning slammed with physical force into his temples, streaked in a jagged electric path to the back of his skull, and suddenly there were flames. There was no shock coupled with the fire that leaped up towards his face from the front of his coat. There was only terror.

Steve Carella reacted in much the same way Cro-Magnon must have reacted the first time he ventured too close to a raging fire and discovered that the flames can cook people as well as sabre-toothed tigers. He dropped his weapon, he covered his face, he whirled abruptly, instinctively rushing for the soot-crusted snowbank across the alley, forgetting his attackers, only vaguely aware that they were running, laughing, out of the alley and into the night, thinking only in a jagged broken pattern fire run burn fire out fire fire and hurling himself full length on to the snow. His hands were cupped tightly to his face, he could feel the flames chewing angrily at the backs of them, could smell the terrifying stench of burning hair and flesh, and then heard the sizzle of fire in contact with the snow, felt the cold and comforting snow, was suddenly enveloped in a white cloud of steam that rose from the beautiful snow, rolled from shoulder to shoulder in the glorious marvellous soothing beneficial white and magnificent snow, and found tears in his eyes, and thought nothing, and lay with his face pressed to the snow for a long while, breathing heavily, and still thinking nothing.

He got up at last and painfully retrieved his discarded revolver and walked slowly to the mouth of the alley and looked at his hands in the light of the street lamp. He caught his breath, and then went to the call box on the next corner. He told Sergeant Murchison at the desk that the fire bugs had hit, and that his hands had been burned and he would need a meat wagon to get him over to the hospital. Murchison said, "Are you all right?" and Carella looked at his hands again, and said, "Yes, I'm all right, Dave."

4

Detective Bert Kling was in love, but nobody else was.

The mayor was not in love, he was furious. The mayor called the police commissioner in high dudgeon and wanted to know what kind of goddamn city this was when a man of the calibre of Parks Commissioner Cowper could be gunned down on the steps of the Philharmonic Hall, what the hell kind of a city was this, anyway?

"Well, sir," the police commissioner started, but the mayor said, "Perhaps you can tell me why adequate police protection was not provided for Commissioner Cowper when his wife informs me this morning that the police *knew* a threat had been made on his life, perhaps you can tell me that," the mayor shouted into the phone.

"Well, sir," the police commissioner started, but the mayor said, "Or perhaps you can tell me why you still haven't located the apartment from which those shots were fired, when the autopsy has already revealed the angle of entrance and your ballistics people have come up with a probable trajectory, perhaps you can tell me that."

"Well, sir," the police commissioner started, but the mayor said, "Get me some results, do you want this city to become a laughing-stock?"

The police commissioner certainly didn't want the city to become a laughing-stock, so he said, "Yes, sir, I'll do the best I can," and the mayor said, "You had better," and hung up.

There was no love lost between the mayor and the police

commissioner that morning. So the police commissioner asked his secretary, a tall wan blond man who appeared consumptive and who claimed his constant hacking cough was caused by smoking three packs of cigarettes a day in a job that was enough to drive anyone utterly mad, the police commissioner asked his secretary to find out what the mayor had meant by a threat on the parks commissioner's life, and report back to him immediately. The tall wan blonde secretary got to work at once, asking around here and there, and discovering that the 87th Precinct had indeed logged several telephone calls from a mysterious stranger who had threatened to kill the parks commissioner unless five thousand dollars was delivered to him by noon yesterday. When the police commissioner received this information, he said, "Oh, *yeah*?" and immediately dialled Frederick 7–8024 and asked to talk to Detective-Lieutenant Peter Byrnes.

Detective-Lieutenant Peter Byrnes had enough headaches that morning, what with Carella in the hospital with second-degree burns on the backs of both hands, and the painters having moved from the squadroom into his own private office, where they were slopping up everything in sight and telling jokes on their ladders. Byrnes was not over fond of the police commissioner to begin with, the commissioner being a fellow who had been imported from a neighbouring city when the new administration took over, a city which, in Byrnes' opinion, had an even larger crime rate than this one. Nor was the new commissioner terribly fond of Lieutenant Byrnes, because Byrnes was the sort of garrulous Irishman who shot off his mouth at Police Benevolent Association and Emerald Society functions, letting anyone within earshot know what he thought of the mayor's recent whiz-kid appointee. So there was hardly any sweetness and light oozing over the telephone wires that morning between the commissioner's office at Headquarters downtown on High Street, and Byrnes' paint-spattered corner office on the second floor of the grimy station house on Grover Avenue.

"What's this all about, Byrnes?" the commissioner asked.

"Well, sir," Byrnes said, remembering that the *former* commissioner used to call him Pete, "we received several threatening telephone calls from an unidentified man yesterday, which telephone calls I discussed personally with Parks Commissioner Cowper."

"What did you do about those calls, Byrnes?"

"We placed the drop site under surveillance, and apprehended the man who made the pick-up."

"So what happened?"

"We questioned him and released him."

"Why?"

"Insufficient evidence. He was also interrogated after the parks commissioner's murder last night. We did not have ample grounds for an arrest. The man is still free, but a telephone tap went into effect this morning, and we're ready to move in if we monitor anything incriminating."

"Why wasn't the commissioner given police protection?"

"I offered it, sir, and it was refused."

"Why wasn't your suspect put under surveillance *before* a crime was committed?"

"I couldn't spare any men, sir, and when I contacted the 115th in Riverhead, where the suspect resides, I was told they could not spare any men either. Besides, as I told you, the commissioner did not *want* protection. He felt we were dealing with a crackpot, sir, and I must tell you that was our opinion here, too. Until, of course, recent events proved otherwise."

"Why hasn't that apartment been found yet?"

"What apartment, sir?"

"The apartment from which the two shots were fired that killed Parks Commissioner Cowper."

"Sir, the crime was not committed in our precinct. Philharmonic Hall, sir, is in the 53rd Precinct and, as I'm sure the commissioner realizes, a homicide is investigated by the detectives assigned to the squad in the precinct in which the homicide was committed."

"Don't give me any of that bullshit, Byrnes," the police commissioner said.

"That is the way we do it in this city, sir," Byrnes said.

"This is your case," the commissioner answered. "You got that, Byrnes?"

"If you say so, sir."

"I say so. Get some men over to the area, and find that goddamn apartment."

"Yes, sir."

"And report back to me."

"Yes, sir," Byrnes said, and hung up.

"Getting a little static, huh?" the first painter said.

"Getting your arse chewed out, huh?" the second painter said.

Both men were on their ladders, grinning and dripping apple green paint on the floor.

"Get the hell out of this office!" Byrnes shouted.

"We ain't finished yet," the first painter said.

"We don't leave till we finish," the second painter said.

"That's our orders," the first painter said.

"We don't work for the Police Department, you know."

"We work for the Department of Public Works."

"Maintenance and Repair."

"And we don't quit a job till we finish it."

"Stop dripping paint all over my goddamn floor!" Byrnes shouted, and stormed out of the office. "Hawes!" he shouted. "Kling! Willis! Brown! Where the hell *is* everybody?" he shouted.

Meyer came out of the men's room, zipping up his fly. "What's up, Skipper?" he said.

"Where were you?"

"Taking a leak. Why, what's up?"

"Get somebody over to the area!" Byrnes shouted.

"What area?"

"Where the goddamn commissioner got shot!"

"Okay, sure," Meyer said. "But why? That's not our case."

"It is now."

"Oh?"

"Who's catching?"

"I am."

"Where's Kling?"

"Day off."

"Where's Brown?"

"On that wire tap."

"And Willis?"

"He went to the hospital to see Steve."

"And Hawes?"

"He went down for some Danish."

"What the hell am I running here, a resort in the mountains?"

"No, sir. We . . ."

"Send Hawes over there! Send him over the minute he gets back. Get on the phone to Ballistics. Find out what they've got. Call the ME's office and get that autopsy report. Get cracking, Meyer!"

"Yes, *sir*!" Meyer snapped, and went immediately to the telephone.

"This goddamn racket drives me crazy," Byrnes said, and started to storm back into his office, remembered that the jolly green painters were in there slopping around, and stormed into the Clerical Office instead.

"Get these files in order!" he shouted. "What the hell do you do in here all day, Miscolo, make coffee?"

"Sir?" Miscolo said, because that's exactly what he was doing at the moment.

Bert Kling was in love.

It was not a good time of the year to be in love. It is better to be in love when flowers are blooming and balmy breezes are wafting in off the river, and strange animals come up to lick your hand. There's only one good thing about being in love in March, and that's that it's better to be in love in March than not to be in love at all, as the wise man once remarked.

Bert Kling was madly in love.

He was madly in love with a girl who was twenty-three years old, full-breasted and wide-hipped, her blonde hair long and trailing midway down her back or sometimes curled into a honey conch shell at the back of her head, her eyes a cornflower blue, a tall girl who came just level with his chin when she was wearing heels. He was madly in love with a scholarly girl who was studying at night for her master's degree in psychology, while working during the day conducting interviews for a firm downtown on Shepherd Street; a serious girl who hoped to go on for her PhD, and then pass the state boards, and then practise psychology; a nutty girl who was capable of sending to the squadroom a six-foot high heart cut out of plywood and painted red and lettered in yellow with the words Cynthia Forrest Loves Detective 3rd/Grade Bertram Kling, So Is That A Crime?, as she had done on St Valentine's Day just last month (and which Kling had still not heard the end of from all his comical colleagues); an emotional girl who could burst into tears at the sight of a blind man playing an accordion on The Stem, to whom she gave a five-dollar bill, merely put the bill silently into the cup, soundlessly, it did not even make a rustle, and turned away to weep into Kling's shoulder; a passionate girl who clung to him fiercely in the night and who woke him sometimes at six in the morning to say, "Hey, Cop, I have to go to work in a few hours, are you interested?" to which Kling invariably answered, "No, I am not interested in sex and things like that," and then kissed her until she was dizzy and afterwards sat across from her at the kitchen table in her apartment, staring at her, marvelling at her beauty and once caused her to blush when he said, "There's a woman who sells *pidaguas* on Mason Avenue, her name is Iluminada, she was born in Puerto Rico. Your name should be Illuminada, Cindy. You fill the room with light."

Boy, was he in love.

But, it being March, and the streets still banked high with February snow, and the winds howling, and the wolves growling and chasing civilians in troikas who cracked whips and huddled in bear rugs, it being a bitter cold winter which seemed to have started in September and showed no signs of abating till next August, when possibly, but just possibly, all the snow might melt and the flowers would bloom – it being that kind of a treacherous winter, what better to do than discuss police work? What better to do than rush along the frozen street on Cindy's lunch hour with her hand clutched tightly in the crook of his arm and the wind whipping around them and drowning out Kling's voice as he tried to tell her of the mysterious circumstances surrounding the death of Parks Commissioner Cowper.

"Yes, it *sounds* very mysterious," Cindy said, and brought her hand out of her pocket in an attempt to keep the wind from tearing her kerchief from her head. "Listen, Bert," she said, "I'm really very tired of winter, aren't you tired of it?"

"Yeah," Kling said. "Listen, Cindy, you know who I hope this isn't?"

"Hope who isn't?" she said.

"The guy who made the calls. The guy who killed the commissioner. You know who I hope we're not up against?"

"*Who*?" Cindy said.

"The deaf man," he said.

"What?" she said.

"He was a guy we went up against a few years back, it must have been maybe seven, eight years ago. He tore this whole damn city apart trying to rob a bank. He was the smartest crook we ever came up against."

"*Who*?" Cindy said.

"The deaf man," Kling said again.

"Yes, but what's his name?"

"We don't know his name. We never caught him. He jumped in the river and we thought he drowned, but maybe he's back now. Like Frankenstein."

"Like Frankenstein's monster, you mean," Cindy said.

"Yeah, like him. Remember he was supposed to have died in that fire, but he didn't."

"I remember."

"That was a scary picture," Kling said.

"I wet my pants when I saw it," Cindy said. "And that was on television."

"You wet your pants on *television*?" Kling said. "In front of forty million *people*?"

"No, I saw *Frankenstein* on television," Cindy said, and grinned and poked him.

"The deaf man," Kling said. "I hope it's not him."

It was the first time any man on the squad had voiced the possibility that the commissioner's murderer was the man who had given them so much trouble so many years ago. The thought was somewhat numbing. Bert Kling was a young man, and not a particularly philosophical one, but he intuitively understood that the deaf man (who had once signed a note L. Sordo, very comical, El Sordo meaning 'The Deaf One' in Spanish) was capable of manipulating odds with computer accuracy, of spreading confusion and fear, of juggling permutations and combinations in a manner calculated to upset the strict and somewhat bureaucratic efficiency of a police precinct, making law enforcers behave like bumbling Keystone cops in a yellowing ancient film, knew instinctively and with certainty that if the commissioner's murderer was indeed the deaf man, they had not heard the end of all this. And because the very thought of what the deaf man might and *could* do was too staggering to contemplate, Kling involuntarily shuddered, and he knew it was not from the cold.

"I hope it isn't him," he said, and his words were carried away on the wind.

"Kiss me," Cindy said suddenly, "and then buy me a hot chocolate, you cheapskate."

The boy who came into the muster room that Wednesday afternoon was about twelve years old.

He was wearing his older brother's hand-me-down ski parka which was blue and three sizes too large for him. He had pulled the hood of the parka up over his head, and had tightened the drawstrings around his neck, but the hood was still too big, and it kept falling off. He kept trying to pull it back over his head as he came into the station house carrying an envelope in the same hand with which he wiped his runny nose. He was wearing high-topped sneakers with the authority of all slum kids who wear sneakers winter and summer, all year round, despite the warnings of paediatrists. He walked to the muster desk with a sneaker-inspired bounce, tried to adjust the parka hood again, wiped his dripping nose again, and then looked up at Sergeant Murchison and said, "You the desk sergeant?"

"I'm the desk sergeant," Murchison answered without looking up from the absentee slips he was filling out from that morning's muster sheet. It was 2.10 PM, and in an hour and thirty-five minutes the afternoon shift of uniformed cops would be coming in, and there'd be a new roll call to take, and new absentee slips to fill out, a regular rat race, he should have become a fireman or a postman.

"I'm supposed to give you this," the kid said, and reached up to hand Murchison the sealed envelope.

"Thanks," Murchison said, and accepted the envelope

53

without looking at the kid, and then suddenly raised his head and said, "Hold it just a second."

"Why, what's the matter?"

"Just hold it right there a second," Murchison said, and opened the envelope. He unfolded the single sheet of white paper that had been neatly folded in three equal parts, and he read what was on the sheet, and then he looked down at the kid again and said, "Where'd you get this?"

"Outside."

"Where?"

"A guy gave it to me."

"What guy?"

"A tall guy outside."

"Outside where?"

"Near the park there. Across the street."

"Gave you this?"

"Yeah."

"What'd he say?"

"Said I should bring it in here and give it to the desk sergeant."

"You know the guy?"

"No, he gave me five bucks to bring it over here."

"What'd he look like?"

"A tall guy with blond hair. He had a thing in his ear."

"What kind of a thing?"

"Like he was deaf," the kid said, and wiped his hand across his nose again.

Deputy

Mayor

SCANLON

GOES

NEXT

!

That was what the note read.

So they studied the note, being careful not to get any more fingerprints on it than Sergeant Murchison had already put there, and then they stood around a runny-nosed twelve-year-old kid wearing a blue ski parka three sizes too large for him, and fired questions at him as though they had captured Jack the Ripper over from London for the weekend.

They got nothing from the kid except perhaps his cold.

He repeated essentially what he had told Sergeant Murchison, that a tall blond guy wearing a thing in his ear (A hearing aid, you mean, kid?) yeah, a thing in his ear, had stopped him across the street from the police station and offered him five bucks to carry an envelope in to the desk sergeant. The kid couldn't see nothing wrong with bringing an envelope into the police station, so he done it, and that was all, he didn't even

55

know who the guy with the thing in his ear was (You mean a hearing aid, kid?) yeah, a thing in his ear, he didn't know who he was, never even seen him around the neighbourhood or nothing, so could he go home now because he had to make a stop at Linda's Boutique to pick up some dresses for his sister who did sewing at home for Mrs Montana? (He was wearing a hearing aid, huh kid?) Yeah, a thing in his ear, the kid said.

So they let the kid go at two thirty without even offering him an ice-cream cone or some gumdrops, and then they sat around the squadroom handling the suspect note with a pair of tweezers and decided to send it over to Lieutenant Sam Grossman at the police lab, in the hope that he could lift some latent prints that did not belong to Sergeant Murchison.

None of them mentioned the deaf man.

Nobody likes to talk about ghosts.

Or even *think* about them.

"Hello, Bernice," Meyer said into the telephone, "is your boss around? Yeah, sure, I'll wait."

Patiently, he tapped a pencil on his desk and waited. In a moment, a bright perky voice materialized on the line.

"Assistant District Attorney Raoul Chabrier," the voice insisted.

"Hello, Rollie, this is Meyer Meyer up here at the 87th," Meyer said. "How's every little thing down there on Chelsea Street?"

"Oh, pretty good, pretty good," Chabrier said, "what have you got for us, a little homicide up there perhaps?"

"No, nothing like that, Rollie," Meyer said.

"A little axe murder perhaps?" Chabrier said.

"No, as a matter of fact, this is something personal," Meyer said.

"Oh-*ho*!" Chabrier said.

"Yeah. Listen, Rollie, what can you do if somebody uses your name?"

"What do you mean?" Chabrier said.

"In a book."

"Oh-*ho*!" Chabrier said. "Did somebody use your name in a book?"

"Yes."

"In a book about the workings of the police department?"

"No."

"Were you mentioned specifically?"

"No. Well, yes *and* no. What do you mean?"

"Did the book specifically mention Detective 3rd/Grade Meyer . . ."

"Detective *2nd*/Grade," Meyer corrected.

"It specifically mentioned Detective 2nd/Grade Meyer Meyer of the . . ."

"No."

"It *didn't* mention you?"

"No. Not that way."

"I thought you said somebody used your name."

"Well, they did. She did."

"Meyer, I'm a busy man," Chabrier said. "I've got a case load here that would fell a brewer's horse, now would you please tell me what's on your mind?"

"A novel," Meyer said. "It's a novel named *Meyer Meyer*."

"That is the title of the novel?" Chabrier asked.

"Yes. Can I sue?"

"I am a criminal lawyer," Chabrier said.

"Yes, but . . ."

"I am not familiar with the law of literary property."

"Yes, but . . ."

"Is it a good book?"

"I don't know," Meyer said. "You see," he said, "I'm a *person*, and this book is about some college professor or something, and he's a short plump fellow . . ."

"I'll have to read it," Chabrier said.

"Will you call me after you've read it?"

"What for?"

"To advise me."

"On what?"

"On whether I can sue or not."

"I'll have to read the law," Chabrier said. "Do I owe you a favour, Meyer?"

"You owe me *six* of them," Meyer said somewhat heatedly, "as for example the several times I could have got you out of bed at three o'clock in the morning when we had real meat here in the squadroom and at great risk to myself I held the suspect until the following morning so you could get your beauty sleep on nights when you had the duty. Now, Rollie, I'm asking a very tiny favour, I don't want to go to the expense of getting some fancy copyright lawyer or whatever the hell, I just want to know whether I can sue somebody who used my name that's on record in the Department of Health on a birth certificate, can I sue this person who uses my name as the title of a novel, and for a *character* in a novel, when here I am a real *person*, for Christ's sake!"

"OK, don't get excited," Chabrier said.

"Who's excited?" Meyer said.

"I'll read the law and call you back."

"When?"

"Sometime."

"Maybe if we get somebody in the squadroom sometime when you've got the duty, I'll fly in the face of Miranda-Escobedo again and hold off till morning so you can peacefully snore the night . . ."

"OK, OK, I'll get back to you tomorrow." Chabrier paused. "Don't you want to know what *time* tomorrow?"

"What time tomorrow?" Meyer asked.

The landlady had arthritis, and she hated winter, and she didn't like cops too well, either. She immediately told Cotton Hawes that there had been other policeman prowling around ever since that big mucky-muck got shot last night, why couldn't they leave a lady alone? Hawes, who had been treated to similar diatribes from every landlady and superintendent along the street, patiently explained that he was only doing his job, and said he knew she would want to cooperate in bringing a murderer to justice. The landlady said the city was rotten and corrupt, and as far as she was concerned they could shoot *all* those damn big mucky-mucks, and she wouldn't lose no sleep over any of them.

Hawes had thus far visited four buildings in a row of identical slum tenements facing the glittering glass and concrete structure that was the city's new Philharmonic Hall. The building, a triumph of design (the acoustics weren't so hot, but what the hell) could be clearly seen from any one of the tenements, the wide marble steps across the avenue offering an unrestricted view of anyone who happened to be standing on them, or coming down them, or going up them. The man who had plunked two rifle slugs into Cowper's head could have done so from *any* of these buildings. The only reason the police department was interested in the exact source of the shots was that the killer may have left some evidence behind him. Evidence is always nice to have in a murder case.

The first thing Hawes asked the landlady was whether she had rented an apartment or a room recently to a tall blond man wearing a hearing aid.

"Yes," the landlady said.

That was a good start. Hawes was an experienced detective, and he recognized immediately that the landlady's affirmative reply was a terribly good start.

"Who?" he asked immediately. "Would you know his name?"

"Yes."

"What's his name?"

"Orecchio. Mort Orrecchio."

Hawes took out his pad and began writing. "Orecchio," he said, "Mort. Would you happen to know whether it was Morton or Mortimer or exactly what?"

"Just Mort," the landlady said. "Mort Orecchio. He was Eye-talian."

"How do you know?"

"Anything ending in O is Eye-talian."

"You think so? How about Shapiro?" Hawes suggested.

"What are you, a wise guy?" the landlady said.

"This fellow Orecchio, which apartment did you rent him?"

"A *room*, not an apartment," the landlady said. "Third floor front."

"Facing Philharmonic?"

"Yeah."

"Could I see the room?"

"Sure, why not? I got nothing else to do but show cops rooms."

They began climbing. The hallway was cold and the air shaft windows were rimed with frost. There was the commingled smell of garbage and urine on the stairs, a nice clean old lady this landlady. She kept complaining about her arthritis all the way up to the third floor, telling Hawes the cortisone didn't help her none, all them big mucky-muck doctors making promises that didn't help her pain at all. She stopped outside a door with the brass numerals 31 on it, and fished into the pocket of her apron for a key. Down the hall, a door opened a crack and then closed again.

"Who's that?" Hawes asked.

"Who's who?" the landlady said.

"Down the hall there. The door that just opened and closed."

"Musta been Polly," the landlady said, and unlocked the door at 31.

The room was small and cheerless. A three-quarter bed was against the wall opposite the door, covered with a white chenille bedspread. A framed print was over the bed. It showed a logging mill and a river and a sheepdog looking up at something in the sky. A standing floor lamp was on the right of the bed. The shade was yellow and soiled. A stain, either whisky or vomit, was on the corner of the bedspread where it was pulled up over the pillows. Opposite the bed, there was a single dresser with a mirror over it. The dresser had cigarette burns all the way around its top. The mirror was spotted and peeling. The sink alongside the dresser had a big rust ring near the drain.

"How long was he living here?" Hawes asked.

"Took the room three days ago."

"Did he pay by cheque or cash?"

"Cash. In advance. Paid for the full week. I only rent by the week, I don't like none of these one-night stands."

"Naturally not," Hawes said.

"I know what you're thinking. You're thinking it ain't such a fancy place, I shouldn't be so fussy. Well, it may not be fancy," the landlady said, "but it's clean."

"Yes, I can see that."

"I mean it ain't got no *bugs*, mister."

Hawes nodded and went to the window. The shade was torn and missing its pull cord. He grabbed the lower edge in his gloved hand, raised the shade and looked across the street.

"You hear any shots last night?"

"No."

He looked down at the floor. There were no spent cartridge cases anywhere in sight.

"Who else lives on this floor?"

"Polly down the hall, that's all."

"Polly who?"

"Malloy."

"Mind if I look through the dresser and the closet?"

"Go right ahead. I got all the time in the world. The way I spend my day is I conduct guided tours through the building."

Hawes went to the dresser and opened each of the drawers. They were all empty, except for a cockroach nestling in the corner of the bottom drawer.

"You missed one," Hawes said, and closed the drawer.

"Huh?" the landlady said.

Hawes went to the closet and opened it. There were seven wire hangers on the clothes bar. The closet was empty. He was about to close the door when something on the floor caught his eye. He stooped for a closer look, took a pen light from his pocket, and turned it on. The object on the floor was a dime.

"If that's money," the landlady said, "it belongs to me."

"Here," Hawes said, and handed her the dime. He did so knowing full well that even if the coin *had* belonged to the occupant of the room, it was as impossible to get latent prints from money as it was to get re-imbursed by the city for petrol used in one's private car on police business.

"Is there a john in here?" he asked.

"Down the hall. Lock the door behind you."

"I only wanted to know if there was another room, that's all."

"It's clean, if that's what you're worrying about."

"I'm sure it's spotless," Hawes said. He took another look around. "So this is it, huh?"

"This is it."

"I'll be sending a man over to dust that sill," Hawes said.

"Why?" the landlady said. "It's clean."

"I mean for fingerprints."

"Oh." The landlady stared at him. "You think that big mucky-muck was shot from this room?"

"It's possible," Hawes said.

"Will that mean trouble for me?"

"Not unless you shot him," Hawes said, and smiled.

"You got some sense of humour," the landlady said.

They went out of the apartment. The landlady locked the door behind her. "Will that be all?" she asked, "or did you want to see anything else?"

"I want to talk to the woman down the hall," Hawes said, "but I won't need you for that. Thank you very much, you were very helpful."

"It breaks the monotony," the landlady said, and he believed her.

"Thank you again," he said, and watched her as she went down the steps. He walked to the door marked 32 and knocked. There was no answer. He knocked again and said, "Miss Malloy?"

The door opened a crack.

"Who is it?" a voice said.

"Police officer. May I talk to you?"

"What about?"

"About Mr Orecchio."

"I don't know any Mr Orecchio," the voice said.

"Miss Malloy . . ."

"It's *Mrs* Malloy, and I don't know any Mr Orecchio."

"Could you open the door, ma'am?"

"I don't want any trouble."

"I won't . . ."

"I know a man got shot last night, I don't want any trouble."

"Did you hear the shots, Miss Malloy?"

"*Mrs* Malloy."

"Did you?"

"No."

"Would you happen to know if Mr Orecchio was in last night?"

"I don't know who Mr Orecchio is."

"The man in 31."

"I don't know him."

"Ma'am, could you please open the door?"

"I don't want to."

"Ma'am, I can come back with a warrant, but it'd be a lot easier . . ."

"Don't get me into trouble," she said. "I'll open the door, but please don't get me into trouble."

Polly Malloy was wearing a pale green cotton wrapper. The wrapper had short sleeves. Hawes saw the hit marks on her arms the moment she opened the door, and the hit marks explained a great deal about the woman who was Polly Malloy. She was perhaps twenty-six years old, with a slender youthful body and a face that would have been pretty if it were not so clearly stamped with knowledge. The green eyes were intelligent and alert, the mouth vulnerable. She worried her lip and held the wrapper closed about her naked body, and her fingers were long and slender, and the hit marks on her arms shouted all there was to shout.

"I'm not holding," she said.

"I didn't ask."

"You can look around if you like."

"I'm not interested," Hawes said.

"Come in," she said.

He went into the apartment. She closed and locked the door behind him.

"I don't want trouble," she said. "I've had enough trouble."

"I won't give you any. I only want to know about the man down the hall."

"I know somebody got shot. Please don't get me involved in it."

They sat opposite each other, she on the bed, he on a straight backed chair facing her. Something shimmered on the air between them, something as palpable as the tenement stink of garbage and piss surrounding them. They sat in easy informality, comfortably aware of each other's trade, Cotton Hawes detective, Polly Malloy addict. And perhaps they knew each other better than a great many people ever get to know each other. Perhaps Hawes had been inside too many shooting galleries not to understand what it was like to be this girl, perhaps he had arrested too many hookers who were screwing for the couple of bucks they needed for a bag of shit, perhaps he had watched the agonized writhings of too many cold turkey kickers, perhaps his knowledge of this junkie or any junkie was as intimate as a pusher's, perhaps he had seen too much and knew too much. And perhaps the girl had been collared too many times, had protested too many times that she was clean, had thrown too many decks of heroin under bar stools or down sewers at the approach of a cop, had been in too many different squadrooms and handled by too many different bulls, been offered the Lexington choice by too many different magistrates, perhaps her knowledge of the law as it applied to narcotics addicts was as intimate as any assistant district attorney's, perhaps she too had seen too much and knew too much. Their mutual knowledge was electric, it generated a heat lightning of its own, ascertaining the curious symbiosis of lawbreaker and enforcer, affirming the interlocking subtlety of crime and punishment. There was a secret bond in that room, an affinity – almost an empathy. They could talk to each other without any bullshit. They were like spent lovers whispering on the same pillow.

"Did you know Orecchio?" Hawes asked.

"Will you keep me clean?"

"Unless you had something to do with it?"

"Nothing."

"You've got my word."

"A cop?" she asked, and smiled wanly.

"You've got my word, if you want it."

"I need it, it looks like."

"You need it, honey."

"I knew him."

"How?"

"I met him the night he moved in."

"When was that?"

"Two, three nights ago."

"Where'd you meet?"

"I was hung up real bad, I needed a fix. I just got out of Caramoor, *that* sweet hole, a week ago. I haven't had time to get really connected yet."

"What were you in for?"

"Oh, hooking."

"How old are you, Polly?"

"Nineteen. I look older, huh?"

"Yes, you look older."

"I got married when I was sixteen. To another junkie like myself. Some prize."

"What's he doing now?"

"Time at Castleview."

"For what?"

Polly shrugged. "He started pushing."

"OK, what about Orecchio next door?"

"I asked him for a loan."

"When was this?"

"Day before yesterday."

"Did he give it to you?"

"I didn't actually ask him for a loan. I offered to turn a trick for him. He was right next door, you see, and I was pretty sick, I swear to God I don't think I coulda made it to the street."

"Did he accept?"

"He gave me ten bucks. He didn't take nothing from me for it."

"Sounds like a nice fellow."

Polly shrugged.

"Not a nice fellow?" Hawes asked.

"Let's say not my type," Polly said.

"Mm-huh."

"Let's say a son of a bitch," Polly said.

"What happened?"

"He came in here last night."

"When? What time?"

"Musta been about nine-thirty."

"After the symphony started," Hawes said.

"Huh?"

"Nothing, I was just thinking out loud. Go on."

"He said he had something nice for me. He said if I came into his room, he would give me something nice."

"Did you go?"

"First I asked what it was. He said it was something I wanted more than anything else in the world."

"But did you go into his room?"

"Yes."

"Did you see anything out of the ordinary?"

"Like what?"

"Like a high-powered rifle with a telescopic sight."

"No, nothing like that."

"All right, what was this 'something nice' he promised you?"

"Hoss."

"He had heroin for you?"

"Yes."

"And that's why he asked you to come into his room? For the heroin?"

"That's what he said."

"He didn't attempt to sell it to you, did he?"

"No. But . . ."

"Yes?"

"He made me beg for it."

"What do you mean?"

"He showed it to me, and he let me taste it to prove that it was real stuff, and then he refused to give it to me unless I . . . begged for it."

"I see."

"He . . . teased me for . . . I guess for . . . for almost two hours. He kept looking at his watch and making me . . . do things."

"What kind of things?"

"Stupid things. He asked me to sing for him. He made me sing 'White Christmas', that was supposed to be a big joke, you see, because the shit is white and he knew how bad I needed a fix, so he made me sing 'White Christmas' over and over again, I musta sung it for him six or seven times. And all the while he kept looking at his watch."

"Go ahead."

"Then he . . . he asked me to strip, but . . . I mean, not just take off my clothes, but . . . you know, do a strip for him. And I did it. And he began . . . he began making fun of me, of the way I looked, of my body. I . . . he made me stand naked in front of him, and he just went on and on about how stupid and pathetic I looked, and he kept asking me if I really wanted the heroin, and then looked at his watch again, it was about eleven o'clock by then, I kept saying Yes, I want it, please let me have it, so he asked me to dance for him, he asked me to do the waltz, and then he asked me to do the shag, I didn't know what the hell he was talking about, I never even heard of the shag, have you ever heard of the shag?"

"Yes, I've heard of it," Hawes said.

"So I did all that for him, I would have done anything for him, and finally he told me to get on my knees and explain to him why I felt I really needed the bag of heroin. He said he expected me to talk for five minutes on the subject of the addict's need for narcotics, and he looked at his watch and began timing me, and I talked. I was shaking by this time, I had the chills, I needed a shot more than . . ." Polly closed her eyes. "I began crying. I talked and I cried, and at last he looked at his watch and said, 'Your five minutes are up. Here's your poison, now get the hell out of here.' And he threw the bag to me."

"What time was this?"

"It musta been about ten minutes after eleven. I don't have a watch, I hocked it long ago, but you can see the big electric numbers on top of the Mutual Building from my room, and when I was shooting up later it was eleven fifteen, so this musta been about ten after or thereabouts.'

"And he kept looking at his watch all through this, huh?"

"Yes. As if he had a date or something."

"He did," Hawes said.

"Huh?"

"He had a date to shoot a man from his window. He was just amusing himself until the concert broke. A nice fellow, Mr Orecchio."

"I got to say one thing for him," Polly said.

"What's that?"

"It was good stuff." A wistful look came on to her face and into her eyes. "It was some of the best stuff I've had in years. I wouldn't have heard a *cannon* if it went off next door."

Hawes made a routine check of all the city's telephone directories, found no listing of an Orecchio – Mort, Morton, or Mortimer – and then called the Bureau of Criminal Identification at four o'clock that afternoon. The BCI, fully automated, called back within ten minutes to report that they had nothing on the suspect. Hawes then sent a teletype to the FBI in Washington, asking them to check their voluminous files for any known criminal named Orecchio, Mort or Mortimer or Morton. He was sitting at his desk in the paint-smelling squadroom when Patrolman Richard Genero came up to ask whether he had to go to court with Kling on the collar they had made jointly and together the week before. Genero had been walking his beat all afternoon, and he was very cold, so he hung around long after Hawes had answered his question, hoping he would be offered a cup of coffee. His eye happened to fall on the name Hawes had scribbled on to his desk pad when calling the BCI, so Genero decided to make a quip.

"Another Italian suspect, I see," he said.

"How do you know?" Hawes asked.

"Anything ending in O is Italian," Genero said.

"How about Munro?" Hawes asked.

"What are you, a wise guy?" Genero said, and grinned. He looked at the scribbled name again, and then said, "I got to admit *this* guy has a very funny name for an Italian."

"Funny how?" Hawes asked.

"Ear," Genero said.

"What?"

"Ear. That's what Orecchio means in Italian. Ear."

Which when coupled with Mort, of course, could mean nothing more or less than Dead Ear.

Hawes tore the page from the pad, crumpled it into a ball, and threw it at the wastebasket, missing.

"I said something?" Genero asked, knowing he'd never get his cup of coffee now.

5

The boy who delivered the note was eight years old, and he had instructions to give it to the desk sergeant. He stood in the squadroom now surrounded by cops who looked seven feet tall, all of them standing around him in a circle while he looked up with saucer-wide blue eyes and wished he was dead.

"Who gave you this note?" one of the cops asked.

"A man in the park."

"Did he pay you to bring it here?"

"Yeah. Yes. Yeah."

"How much?"

"Five dollars."

"What did he look like?"

"He had yellow hair."

"Was he tall?"

"Oh, yeah."

"Was he wearing a hearing aid?"

"Yeah. A *what*?"

"A thing in his ear."

"Oh, yeah," the kid said.

Everybody tiptoed around the note very carefully, as though it might explode at any moment. Everybody handled the note with tweezers or white cotton gloves. Everybody agreed it should be sent at once to the police lab. Everybody read it at least twice. Everybody studied it and examined it. Even some patrolmen from downstairs came up to have a look at it. It was a very important document. It demanded at least an hour of valuable police time before it was finally encased in a celluloid folder and sent downtown in a manilla envelope.

Everybody decided that what this note meant was that the deaf man (who they now reluctantly admitted was once again in their midst) wanted fifty thousand dollars in lieu of killing the deputy mayor exactly as he had killed the parks commissioner. Since fifty thousand dollars was considerably more than the previous demand for five thousand dollars, the cops of the 87th were quite rightfully incensed by the demand. Moreover, the audacity of this criminal somewhere out there was something beyond the ken of their experience. For all its resemblance to a kidnapping, with its subsequent demand for ransom, this case was *not* a kidnapping. No one had been abducted, there was nothing to ransom. No, this was very definitely extortion, and yet the extortion cases they'd dealt with over the years had been textbook cases involving a 'wrongful use of force or fear' in an attempt to obtain 'property from another'. The key word was 'another'. 'Another' was invariably the person against whom mayhem had been threatened. In this case, though, their extortionist didn't seem to care *who* paid the money so long as someone did. *Any*one. Now how were you supposed to deal with a maniac like that?

"He's a maniac," Lieutenant Byrnes said. "Where the hell does he expect us to get fifty thousand dollars?"

Steve Carella, who had been released from the hospital that afternoon and who somewhat resembled a boxer about to put on gloves, what with assorted bandages taped around his hands, said, "Maybe he expects the deputy mayor to pay it."

"Then why the hell didn't he *ask* the deputy mayor?'

"We're his intermediaries," Carella said. "He assumes his demand will carry more weight if it comes from law enforcement officers."

Byrnes looked at Carella.

"Sure," Carella said. "Also, he's getting even with us. He's sore because we fouled up his bank-robbing scheme eight years ago. This is his way of getting back."

"He's a maniac," Byrnes insisted.

"No, he's a very smart cookie," Carella said. "He knocked off Cowper after a measly demand for five thousand dollars. Now that we know he can do it, he's asking ten times the price not to shoot the deputy mayor."

"Where does it say 'shoot'?" Hawes asked.

"Hmmm?"

"He didn't say anything about *shooting* Scanlon. The note yesterday just said 'Deputy Mayor Scanlon Goes Next.' "

"That's right," Carella said. "He can poison him or bludgeon him or stab him or . . ."

"Please," Byrnes said.

"Let's call Scanlon," Carella suggested. "Maybe he's got fifty grand lying around he doesn't know what to do with."

They called Deputy Mayor Scanlon and advised him of the threat upon his life, but Deputy Mayor Scanlon did not have fifty grand lying around he didn't know what to do with. Ten minutes later, the phone on Byrnes' desk rang. It was the police commissioner.

"All right, Byrnes," the commissioner said sweetly, "what's this latest horseshit?"

"Sir," Byrnes said, "we have had two notes from the man we suspect killed Parks Commissioner Cowper, and they constitute a threat upon the life of Deputy Mayor Scanlon."

"What are you doing about it?" the commissioner asked.

"Sir," Byrnes said, "we have already sent both notes to the police laboratory for analysis. Also, sir, we have located the room from which the shots were fired last night, and we have reason to believe we are dealing with a criminal known to this precinct."

"Who?"

"We don't know."

"I thought you said he was known . . ."

"Yes, sir, we've dealt with him before, but to our knowledge, sir, he is unknown."

"How much money does he want this time?"

"Fifty thousand dollars, sir."

"When is Scanlon supposed to be killed?"

"We don't know, sir."

"When does this man want his money?"

"We don't know, sir."

"Where are you supposed to deliver it?"

"We don't know, sir."

"What the hell *do* you know, Byrnes?"

"I know, sir, that we are doing our best to cope with an unprecedented situation, and that we are ready to put our entire squad at the deputy mayor's disposal, if and when he asks for protection. Moreover, sir, I'm sure I can persuade Captain Frick who, as you may know, commands this entire precinct . . ."

"What do you mean, *as* I may know, Byrnes?"

"That is the way we do it in this city, sir."

"That is the way they do it in *most* cities, Byrnes."

"Yes, sir, of course. In any case, I'm sure I can persuade him to release some uniformed officers from their regular duties, or perhaps to call in some off-duty officers, if the commissioner feels that's necessary.

"I feel it's necessary to protect the life of the deputy mayor."

"Yes, of course, sir, we all feel that," Byrnes said.

"What's the matter, Byrnes, don't you like me?" the commissioner asked.

"I try to keep personal feelings out of my work, sir," Byrnes said. "This is a tough case. I don't know about you, but I've never come up against anything like it before. I've got a good team here, and we're doing our best. More than that, we can't do."

"Byrnes," the commissioner said, "you may *have* to do more."

"Sir . . ." Byrnes started, but the commissioner had hung up.

Arthur Brown sat in the basement of Junior High School 106, with a pair of earphones on his head and his right hand on the start button of a tape recorder. The telephone at the La Bresca house diagonally across the street from the school had just rung for the thirty-second time that day, and as he waited for Concetta La Bresca to lift the receiver (as she had done on thirty-one previous occasions) he activated the recorder and sighed in anticipation of what was to come.

It was very clever of the police to have planted a bug in the La Bresca apartment, that bug having been installed by a plainclothes cop from the lab. who identified himself as a telephone repairman, did his dirty work in the La Bresca living-room, and then strung his overhead wires from the roof of the La Bresca house to the telephone pole outside, and from there to a pole on the school sidewalk, and from there to the roof of the school building, and down the side wall, and into a basement window, and across the basement floor to a tiny room containing stacked textbooks and the school's old sixteen-millimetre sound projector, where he had set up Arthur Brown's monitoring station.

It was also very clever of the police to have assigned Arthur Brown to this eavesdropping plant because Brown was an experienced cop who had conducted wiretaps before and who was capable of separating the salient from the specious in any given telephone conversation.

There was only one trouble.

Arthur Brown did not understand Italian, and Concetta La Bresca spoke to her friends exclusively in Italian. For all Brown knew, they might have plotted anything from abortion to safe cracking thirty-one times that day, and for all he knew were about to plot it yet another time. He had used up two full reels of tape because he hadn't understood a word that was said, and he wanted each conversation recorded so that someone – probably Carella – could later translate them.

"Hello," a voice said in English.

Brown almost fell off his stool. He sat erect, adjusted the headset, adjusted the volume on the tape recorder, and began listening.

"Tony?" a second voice asked.

"Yeah, who's this?" The first voice belonged to La Bresca. Apparently he had just returned home from work. The second voice . . .

"This is Dom."

"Who?"

"Dominick."

"Oh, hi, Dom, how's it going?"

"Great."

"What's up, Dom?"

"Oh, nothing," Dom said. "I was just wondering how you was, that's all."

There was silence on the line. Brown tilted his head and brought his hand up to cover one of the earphones.

"I'm fine," La Bresca said at last.

"Good, good," Dom said.

Again, there was silence.

"Well, if that was all you wanted," La Bresca said, "I guess . . ."

"Actually, Tony, I was wondering . . ."

"Yeah?"

"I was wondering if you could lend me a couple of bills till I get myself organized here."

"Organized doing what?" La Bresca asked.

"Well, I took a big loss on that fight two weeks ago, you know, and I still ain't organized."

"You never been organized in your life," La Bresca said.

"That ain't true, Tony."

"OK, it ain't true. What *is* true I ain't got a couple of bills to lend you."

"Well, I heard different," Dom said.

"Yeah? What'd you hear?"

"The rumble is you're coming into some very big loot real soon."

"Yeah? Where'd you hear *that* shit?"

"Oh, I listen around here and there, I'm always on the earie."

"Well, this time the rumble is wrong."

"I was thinking maybe just a few C-notes to tide me over for the next week or so. Till I get organized."

"Dom, I ain't seen a C-note since Hector was a pup."

"Tony . . ."

There was a slight hesitation, only long enough to carry the unmistakable weight of warning. Brown caught the suddenly ominous note and listened expectantly for Dom's next words.

"I *know*," Dom said.

There was another silence on the line. Brown waited. He could hear one of the men breathing heavily.

"*What* do you know?" La Bresca asked.

"About the caper."

"*What* caper?"

"Tony, don't let me say it on the phone, huh? You never know who's listening these days."

"What the hell are you trying to do?" La Bresca asked. "Shake me down?"

"No, I'm trying to borrow a couple of hundred is all. Until I get organized. I'd hate like hell to see all your planning go down the drain, Tony. I'd really hate to see that happen."

"You blow the whistle, pal, and we'll know just who done it."

"Tony, if *I* found out about the caper, there's lots of other guys also know about it. It's all over the street. You're lucky the fuzz aren't on to you already."

"The cops don't even know I exist," La Bresca said. "I never took a fall for nothing in my life."

"What you took a fall for and what you done are two different things, right, Tony?"

"Don't bug me, Dom. You screw this up . . ."

"I ain't screwing nothing up. I'm asking for a loan of two hundred bucks, now yes or no, Tony, I'm getting impatient here in this goddamn phone booth. Yes or no?"

"You're a son of a bitch," La Bresca said.

"Does that mean yes?"

"Where do we meet?" La Bresca asked.

Lying in the alleyway that night with his bandaged hands encased in woollen gloves, Carella thought less often of the two punks who had burned him, and also burned him up, than he did about the deaf man.

As he lay in his tattered rags and mildewed shoes, he was the very model of a modern major derelict, hair matted, face streaked, breath stinking of cheap wine. But beneath that torn and threadbare coat, Carella's gloved right hand held a .38 Detective's Special. The right index finger of the glove had been cut away to the knuckle, allowing Carella to squeeze the finger itself inside the trigger guard. He was ready to shoot, and this time he would not allow himself to be cold-cocked. Or even pan-broiled.

But whereas his eyes were squinted in simulated drunken slumber while alertly he watched the alley mouth and listened for tandem footsteps, his thoughts were on the deaf man. He did not like thinking about the deaf man because he could remember with painful clarity the shotgun blast fired at him eight years ago, the excruciating pain in his shoulder, the numbness of his arm and hand, and then the repeated smashing of the shotgun's stock against his face until he fell senseless to the floor. He did not like thinking about how close he had come to death at the hands of the deaf man. Nor did he enjoy thinking of a criminal adversary who was really quite smarter than any of the detectives on the 87th Squad, a schemer, a planner, a brilliant bastard who juggled life and death with the dexterity and emotional sang-froid of a mathematician. The deaf man – somewhere out there – was a machine, and Carella was terrified of things that whirred with computer precision, logical but unreasoning, infallible and aloof, cold and deadly. He dreaded the thought of going up against him once again, and yet he knew this stakeout was small potatoes, two punks itching to get caught, two punks who *would* be caught because they assumed all their intended victims were defenceless and did not realize that one of them could be a detective with his finger curled around the trigger of a deadly weapon. And once they were caught, he would move from the periphery of the deaf man case into the very nucleus of the case itself. And perhaps, once again, come face to face with the tall blond man who wore the hearing aid.

He thought it oddly coincidental and perfectly ironic that the person he loved most in the world was a woman named Teddy Carella, who happened to be his wife, and who also happened to be a deaf mute, whereas the person who frightened him most as a cop and as a man was also deaf, or at least purported to be so, advertised it blatantly – or was this only another subterfuge, a part of the overall scheme? The terrifying thing about the deaf man was his confident assumption that he was dealing with a bunch of nincompoops. Perhaps he was. That was *another* terrifying thing about him. He moved with such certainty that his assumptions took on all the aspects of cold fact. If he said that all flatfoots were fools, then by God that's exactly what they must be – better pay the man whatever he wants before he kills off every high-ranking official in the city. If he could outrageously outline a murder scheme and then execute it before the startled eyes of the city's finest, how could he possibly be stopped from committing the *next* murder, or the one after that, or the one after that?

Carella did not enjoy feeling like a fool.

There were times when he did not necessarily enjoy police work (like right now, freezing his arse off in an alley) but there were never times when he lacked respect for what he did. The concept of law enforcement was simple and clear in his mind. The good guys against the bad guys. He was one of the good guys. And whereas the bad guys in this day and age won often enough to make virtue seem terribly unfashionable sometimes, Carella none the less felt that killing people (for example) was not a very nice thing. Nor was breaking into someone's dwelling-place in the night-time over considerate. Nor was pushing dope quite thoughtful. Nor were mugging, or forging, or kidnapping, or pimping (or spitting on the sidewalk, for that

77

matter) civilized acts designed to uplift the spirit or delight the soul.

He was a cop.

Which meant that he was stuck with all the various images encouraged by countless television shows and motion pictures: the dim-witted public servant being outsmarted by the tough private eye; the overzealous jerk inadvertently blocking the attempts of the intelligent young advertising executive in distress; the insensitive dolt blindly encouraging the young to become adult criminals. Well, what're you gonna do? You got an image, you got one. (He wondered how many television writers were lying in an alley tonight waiting for two hoods to attack.) The damn thing about the deaf man, though, was that he made all these stereotypes seem true. Once he appeared on the scene, every cop on the squad *did* appear dim-witted and bumbling and inefficient.

And if a man could do that merely by making a few phone calls or sending a few notes, what would happen if—

Carella tensed.

The detective assigned to the surveillance of Anthony La Bresca was Bert Kling, whom he had never seen before. Brown's call to the squadroom had advised the lieutenant that La Bresca had admitted he was involved in a forthcoming caper, and this was reason enough to put a tail on him. So Kling took to the sub-zero streets, leaving the warmth and generosity of Cindy's apartment, and drove out to Riverhead, where he waited across the street from La Bresca's house, hoping to pick up his man the moment he left to meet Dominick. Brown had informed the lieutenant that the pair had arranged a meeting for ten o'clock that night, and it was now 9.07 by Kling's luminous dial, so he figured he had got here good and early, just in time to freeze solid.

La Bresca came down the driveway on the right of the stucco house at ten minutes to ten. Kling stepped into the shadows behind his parked car. La Bresca began walking east, towards the elevated train structure two blocks away. Just my luck, Kling thought, he hasn't got a car. He gave him a lead of half a block, and then began following him. A sharp wind was blowing west off the wide avenue ahead. Kling was forced to lift his face to its direct blast every so often because he didn't want to lose sight of La Bresca, and he cursed for perhaps the fifty-seventh time that winter the injustice of weather designed to plague a man who worked outdoors. Not that he worked outdoors all of the time. Part of the time, he worked at a desk typing up reports in triplicate or calling victims or witnesses. But *much* of the time (it was fair to say much of the time) he worked outdoors, legging it here and there all over this fair city, asking questions and compiling answers and this was the worst son of a bitch winter he had ever lived through in his life. I hope you're going some place nice and warm, La Bresca, he thought. I hope you're going to meet your friend at a Turkish bath or some place.

Ahead, La Bresca was climbing the steps to the elevated platform. He glanced back at Kling only once, and Kling immediately ducked his head, and then quickened his pace. He did not want to reach the platform to discover that La Bresca had already boarded a train and disappeared.

He need not have worried. La Bresca was waiting for him near the change booth.

"You following me?" he asked.

"What?" Kling said.

"I *said* are you following me?" La Bresca asked.

The choices open to Kling in that moment were severely limited. He could say, "What are you out of your mind, why would I be following you, you're so handsome or something?" Or he could say, "Yes, I'm following you, I'm a police officer, here's my shield and my ID card," those were the open choices. Either way, the tail was blown.

"You looking for a rap in the mouth?" Kling said.

"What?" La Bresca said, startled.

"I said what are you, some kind of paranoid nut?" Kling said, which wasn't what he had said at all. La Bresca didn't seem to notice the discrepancy. He stared at Kling in honest surprise, and then started to mumble something, which Kling cut short with a glowering, menacing, thoroughly frightening look. Mumbling to himself, Kling went up the steps to the uptown side of the platform. The station stop was dark and deserted and windswept. He stood on the platform with his coat-tails flapping about him, and waited until La Bresca came up the steps on the downtown side. La Bresca's train pulled in not three minutes later, and he boarded it. The train rattled out of the station. Kling went downstairs again and found a telephone booth. When Willis picked up the phone at the squadroom, Kling said, "This is Bert. La Bresca made me a couple of blocks from his house. You'd better get somebody else on him."

"How long you been a cop?" Willis asked.

"It happens to the best of us," Kling said. "Where'd Brown say they were meeting?"

"A bar on Crawford."

"Well, he boarded a downtown train just a few minutes ago, you've got time to plant somebody there before he arrives."

"Yeah, I'll get O'Brien over there right away."

"What do you want me to do, come back to the office or what?"

"How the hell did you manage to get spotted?"

"Just lucky, I guess," Kling said.

It was one of those nights.

They came into the alley swiftly, moving directly towards Carella, both of them boys of about seventeen or eighteen, both of them brawny, one of them carrying a large tin can, the label gone from it, the can catching light from the street lamp, glinting in the alleyway as they approached, that's the can of petrol, Carella thought.

He started to draw his gun and for the first time ever in the history of his career as a cop, it snagged.

It snagged somewhere inside his coat. It was supposed to be a gun designed for negligible bulk, it was not supposed to catch on your goddamn clothing, the two-inch barrel was not supposed to snag when you pulled it, here we go, he thought, the Keystone cops, and leaped to his feet. He could not get the damn gun loose, it was tangled in the wool of his slipover sweater, the yarn pulling and unravelling, he knew the can of petrol would be thrown into his face in the next moment, he knew a match or a lighter would flare into life, this time they'd be able to smell burning flesh away the hell back at the squadroom. Instinctively, he brought his left hand down as straight and as rigid as a steel pipe, slammed it down on to the forearm of the boy with the can, hitting it hard enough to shatter bone, hearing the scream that erupted from the boy's mouth as he dropped the can, and then feeling the intense pain that rocketed into his head and almost burst from his own lips as his burned and bandaged hand reacted. This is great, he thought, I have no hands, they're going to beat the shit out of me, which turned out to be a fairly good prediction because that's exactly what they did.

There was no danger from the petrol now, small consolation, at least they couldn't set fire to him. But his hands were useless, and his gun was snagged somewhere inside there on his sweater – he tried ripping the tangled yarn free, ten seconds, twenty seconds, a millennium – and his attackers realized instantly that they had themselves a pigeon, so they all jumped on him, all forty guys in the alley, and then it was too late. They were very good street fighters, these boys. They had learned all about punching to the Adam's apple, they had learned all about flanking operations, one circling around to his left and the other coming up behind him to clout him on the back of the head with the neatest rabbit's punch he had ever taken, oh, they were nice fighters, these boys, he wondered whether the coffin would be metal or wood. While he was wondering this, one of the boys who had learned how to fight in some clean friendly slum, kicked him in the groin, which can hurt. Carella doubled over, and the other clean fighter behind him delivered a second rabbit punch, rabbit punches doubtless being his speciality, while the lad up front connected with a good hard-swinging uppercut that almost tore off his head. So now he was down on the alley floor, the alley covered with refuse and grime and not a little of his own blood, so they decided to stomp him, which is of course what you must necessarily do when your opponent falls down, you kick him in the head and the shoulders and the chest and everywhere you can manage to kick him. If he's a live one, he'll squirm around and try to grab your feet, but if you happen to be lucky enough to get a pigeon who was burned only recently, why you can have an absolute field day kicking him at will because his hands are too tender to grab at *anything*, no less feet. That's why guns were invented,

Carella thought, so that if you happen to have second-degree burns on your hands you don't have to use them too much, all you have to do is squeeze a trigger, it's a shame the gun snagged. It's a shame, too, that Teddy's going to be collecting a widow's dole tomorrow morning, he thought, but these guys are going to kill me unless I do something pretty fast. The trouble is I'm a bumbling goddamn cop, the deaf man is right. The kicks landed now with increasing strength and accuracy, nothing encourages a stomper more than an inert and increasingly more vulnerable victim. I'm certainly glad the petrol, he thought, and a kick exploded against his left eye. He thought at once he would lose the eye, he saw only a blinding flash of yellow, he rolled away, feeling dizzy and nauseous, a boot collided with his rib, he thought he felt it crack, another kick landed on the kneecap of his left leg, he tried to get up, his hands, 'You fucking fuzz,' one of the boys said, Fuzz, he thought, and was suddenly sick, and another kick crashed into the back of his skull and sent him falling face forward into his own vomit.

He lost consciousness.

He might have been dead, for all he knew.

It was one of those nights.

Bob O'Brien got a flat tyre on the way to the Erin Bar & Grill on Crawford Avenue, where Tony La Bresca was to meet the man named Dom.

By the time he changed his flat, his hands were numb, his temper was short, the time was 10.32, and the bar was still a ten-minute drive away. On the off-chance that La Bresca and his fair-weather friend would still be there, O'Brien drove downtown, arriving at the bar at ten minutes to eleven. Not only were both gone already, but the bartender said to O'Brien the moment he bellied up, "Care for something to drink, Officer?"

It was one of those nights.

6

On Friday morning, March 8th, Detective-Lieutenant Sam
Grossman of the Police Laboratory called the squadroom and
asked to talk to Cotton Hawes. He was informed that Hawes,
together with several other detectives on the squad, had gone
to Buena Vista Hospital to visit Steve Carella. The man answering the telephone was Patrolman Genero, who was holding the
fort until one of them returned.

"Well, do *you* want this information or what?" Grossman
asked.

"Sir, I'm just supposed to record any calls till they get back,"
Genero said.

"I'm going to be tied up later," Grossman said, "why don't
I just give this to you?"

"All right, sir," Genero said, and picked up his pencil. He
felt very much like a detective. Besides, he was grateful not to
be outside on another miserable day like this one. "Shoot," he
said, and quickly added, "Sir."

"It's on these notes I received."

"Yes, sir, what notes?"

" 'Deputy Mayor Scanlon goes next'," Grossman quoted,
"and 'Look! A whole new', et cetera."

"Yes, sir," Genero said, not knowing what Grossman was
talking about.

"The paper is Whiteside Bond, available at any stationery
store in the city. The messages were clipped from national

magazines and metropolitan dailies. The adhesive is rubber cement."

"Yes, sir," Genero said, writing frantically.

"Negative on latent prints. We got a whole mess of smeared stuff, but nothing we could run a make on."

"Yes, sir."

"In short," Grossman said, "you know what you can do with these notes."

"What's that, sir?" Genero asked.

"We only run the tests," Grossman said. "*You* guys are supposed to come up with the answers."

Genero beamed. He had been included in the phrase, "You guys' and felt himself to be a part of the élite. "Well, thanks a lot," he said, "we'll get to work on it up here."

"Right," Grossman said. "You want these notes back?"

"No harm having them."

"I'll send them over," Grossman said, and hung up.

Very interesting, Genero thought, replacing the receiver on its cradle. If he had owned a deerstalker hat, he would have put it on in that moment.

"Where's the john?" one of the painters asked.

"Why?" Genero said.

"We have to paint it."

"Try not to slop up the urinals," Genero said.

"We're Harvard men," the painter said. "We never slop up the urinals."

The other painter laughed.

The third note arrived at eleven o'clock that morning.

It was delivered by a high school drop-out who walked directly past the muster desk and up to the squadroom where Patrolman Genero was evolving an elaborate mystery surrounding the rubber cement that had been used as an adhesive.

"What's everybody on vacation?" the kid asked. He was seventeen years old, his face sprinkled with acne. He felt very much at home in the squadroom because he had once been a member of a street gang called The Terrible Ten, composed of eleven young men who had joined together to combat the Puerto Rican influx into their turf. The gang had disbanded just before Christmas, not because the Puerto Ricans had managed to demolish them, but only because seven of the eleven called The Terrible Ten had finally succumbed to an enemy common to Puerto Rican and white Anglo-Saxon alike: narcotics. Five of the seven were hooked, two were dead. Of the remaining three, one was in prison for a gun violation, another had got married because he'd knocked up a little Irish girl, and the last was carrying an envelope into a detective squadroom, and feeling comfortable enough there to make a quip to a uniformed cop.

"What do you want?" Genero asked.

"I was supposed to give this to the desk sergeant, but there's nobody at the desk. You want to take it?"

"What is it?"

"Search me," the kid said. "Guy stopped me on the street and give me five bucks to deliver it."

"Sit down," Genero said. He took the envelope from the kid and debated opening it, and then realized he had got his fingerprints all over it. He dropped it on the desk. In the toilet down the hall, the painters were singing. Genero was only supposed to answer the phone and take down messages. He looked at the envelope again, severely tempted. "I said sit down," he told the kid.

"What for?"

"You're going to wait here until one of the detectives gets back, that's what for."

"Up yours, fuzz," the kid said, and turned to go.

Genero drew his service revolver. "Hey," he said, and the boy glanced over his shoulder into the somewhat large bore of a .38 Police Special.

"I'm hip to Miranda-Escobedo," the kid said, but he sat down none the less.

"Good, that makes two of us," Genero said.

Cops don't like other cops to get it. It makes them nervous. It makes them feel they are in a profession that is not precisely white collar, despite the paperwork involved. It makes them feel that at any moment someone might hit them or kick them or even shoot them. It makes them feel unloved.

The two young sportsmen who had unloved Carella so magnificently had broken three of his ribs and his nose. They had also given him such a headache, due to concussion caused by a few well-placed kicks in the medulla oblongata. He had gained consciousness shortly after being admitted to the hospital and he was conscious now, of course, but he didn't look good, and he didn't feel good, and he didn't feel much like talking. So he sat with Teddy beside the bed, holding her hand and breathing shallowly because the broken ribs hurt like hell. The detectives did most of the talking, but there was a cheerlessness in their banter. They were suddenly face to face with violence of a most personal sort, not the violence they dealt with every working day of their lives, not an emotionless confrontation with broken mutilated strangers, but instead a glimpse at a friend and colleague who lay in battered pain on a hospital bed while his wife held his hand and tried to smile at their feeble jokes. The four detectives left the hospital at twelve noon. Brown and Willis walked ahead of Hawes and Kling, who trailed behind them silently.

"Man, they got him good," Brown said.

The seventeen-year-old drop-out was beginning to scream Miranda-Escobedo, quoting rights like a lawyer. Genero kept telling him to shut up, but he had never really understood the Supreme Court decision too well, despite the flyers issued to every cop in the precinct, and he was afraid now that the kid knew something he didn't know. He was overjoyed to hear the ring of footsteps on the recently painted iron-runged steps leading to the squadroom. Willis and Brown came into view on the landing first. Kling and Hawes were behind them. Genero could have kissed them all.

"These the bulls?" the drop-out asked, and Genero said, "Shut up."

"What's up?" Brown asked.

"Tell your friend here about Miranda-Escobedo," the kid said.

"Who're you?" Brown asked.

"He delivered an envelope," Genero said.

"Here we go," Hawes said.

"What's your name, kid?"

"Give me some advice on my rights," the kid said.

"Tell me your name, or I'll kick your arse in," Brown said. "How do you like *that* advice?" He had just witnessed what a pair of young hoods had done to Carella, and he was in no mood to take nonsense from a snotnose.

"My name is Michael McFadden, and I won't answer no questions without a lawyer here," the kid said.

"Can you afford a lawyer?" Brown asked.

"No."

"Get him a lawyer, Hal," Brown said, bluffing.

"Hey, wait a minute, what is this?" McFadden asked.

"You want a lawyer, we'll get you a lawyer," Brown said.

"What do I need a lawyer for? All I done was deliver an envelope."

"*I* don't know why you need a lawyer," Brown said. "*You're* the one who said you wanted one. Hal, call the DA's office, get this suspect here a lawyer."

"Suspect?" McFadden said. "*Suspect*? What the hell did *I* do?"

"I don't know, kid," Brown said, "and I can't find out because you won't let me ask any questions without a lawyer here. You getting him that lawyer, Hal?"

Willis, who had lifted the phone receiver and was listening to nothing more vital than a dial tone, said, "Tie-line's busy, Art."

"OK, I guess we'll just have to wait then. Make yourself comfortable, kid, we'll get a lawyer up here for you as soon as we can."

"Look, what the hell," McFadden said, "I don't need no lawyer."

"You said you wanted one."

"Yeah, but, I mean, like if this is nothing serious . . ."

"We just wanted to ask you some questions about that envelope, that's all."

"Why? What's in it?"

"Let's open the envelope and show the kid what's in it, shall we do that?" Brown said.

"All I done was deliver it," McFadden said.

"Well, let's see what's inside it, shall we?" Brown said. He folded his handkerchief over the envelope, slit it open with a letter opener, and then used a tweezer to yank out the folded note.

"Here, use these," Kling said, and took a pair of white cotton gloves from the top drawer of his desk. Brown put on the gloves, held his hands widespread alongside his face, and grinned.

"Whuffo does a chicken cross de road, Mistuh Bones?" he said, and burst out laughing. The other cops all laughed with him. Encouraged, McFadden laughed too. Brown glowered at him, and the laugh died in his throat. Gingerly, Brown unfolded the note and spread it flat on the desk top.

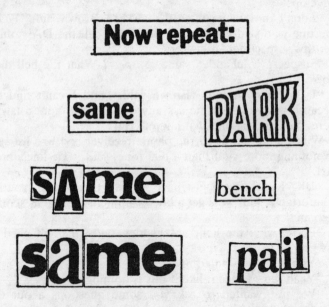

before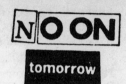

OR ELSE

sAme ASSASSINS

"What's that supposed to mean?" McFadden asked.

"You tell us," Brown said.

"Beats me."

"Who gave you this note?"

"A tall blond guy wearing a hearing aid."

"You know him?"

"Never saw him before in my life."

"He just came up to you and handed you the envelope, huh?"

"No, he came up and offered me a fin to take it in here."

"Why'd you accept?"

"Is there something wrong with bringing a note in a police station?"

"Only if it's an extortion note," Brown said.

"What's extortion?" McFadden asked.

"You belong to The Terrible Ten, don't you?" Kling asked suddenly.

"The club broke up," McFadden said.

"But you *used* to belong."

"Yeah, how do you know?" McFadden asked, a trace of pride in his voice.

"We know every punk in this precinct," Willis said. "You finished with him, Artie?"

"I'm finished with him."

"Goodbye, McFadden."

"What's extortion?" McFadden asked again.

"Goodbye," Willis said again.

The detective assigned to tailing Anthony La Bresca was Meyer Meyer. He was picked for the job because detectives aren't supposed to be bald, and it was reasoned that La Bresca, already gun shy, would never tip to him. It was further reasoned that if La Bresca was really involved in a contemplated caper, it might be best not to follow him from his job to wherever he was going, but instead to be waiting for him there when he arrived. This presented the problem of second-guessing where he might be going, but it was recalled by one or another of the detectives that La Bresca had mentioned frequently a pool hall on south Leary, and so this was where Meyer stationed himself at four o'clock that afternoon.

He was wearing baggy corduroy trousers, a brown leather jacket, and a brown watch cap. He looked like a longshoreman or something. Actually, he didn't know what he looked like, he just hoped he didn't look like a cop. He had a matchstick in his mouth. He figured that was a nice touch, the matchstick. Also because criminal types have an uncanny way of knowing when somebody is heeled, he was not carrying a gun. The only weapon on his person was a longshoreman's hook tucked into the waistband of his trousers. If anyone asked him about the hook, he would say he needed it on the job, thereby establishing his line of work at the same time. He hoped he would not have to use the hook.

He wandered into the pool hall, which was on the second floor of a dingy brick building, said "Hi," to the man sitting behind the entrance booth, and then said, "You got any open tables?"

"Pool or billiards?" the man said. He was chewing on a matchstick, too.

"Pool," Meyer said.

"Take Number Four," the man said, and turned to switch on the table lights from the panel behind him. "You new around here?" he asked, his back to Meyer.

"Yeah, I'm new around here," Meyer said.

"We don't dig hustlers," the man said.

"I'm no hustler," Meyer answered.

"Just make sure you ain't."

Meyer shrugged and walked over to the lighted table. There were seven other men in the pool hall, all of them congregated around a table near the windows, where four of them were playing and the other three were kibitzing. Meyer unobtrusively took a cue from the rack, set up the balls, and began shooting. He was a lousy player. He kept mentally calling shots and missing. Every now and then he glanced at the door. He was playing for perhaps ten minutes when one of the men from the other table sauntered over.

"Hi," the man said. He was a burly man wearing a sports jacket over a woollen sports shirt. Tufts of black hair showed above the open throat of the shirt. His eyes were a deep brown, and he wore a black moustache that seemed to have leaped from his chest on to the space below his nose. The hair on his head was black too. He looked tough and he looked menacing, and Meyer immediately made him for the local cheese.

"You play here before?" the man asked.

"Nope," Meyer said without looking up from the table.

"I'm Tino."

"Hello, Tino," Meyer said, and shot.

"You missed," Tino said.

"That's right, I did."

"You a hustler?" Tino said.

"Nope."

"We break hustlers' arms and throw them down the stairs," Tino said.

"The arms or the whole hustler?" Meyer asked.

"I got no sense of humour," Tino said.

"Me, neither. Buzz off, you're ruining my game."

"Don't try to take nobody, mister," Tino said. "This's a friendly neighbourhood pool hall."

"Yeah, you sure make it sound very friendly," Meyer said.

"It's just we don't like hustlers."

"I got your message three times already," Meyer said. "Eight ball in the side." He shot and missed.

"Where'd you learn to shoot pool?" Tino said.

"My father taught me."

"Was he as lousy as you?"

Meyer didn't answer.

"What's that in your belt there?"

"That's a hook," Meyer said.

"What's it for?"

"I use it," Meyer said.

"You work on the docks?"

"That's right."

"Where?"

"On the docks," Meyer said.

"Yeah, *where* on the docks?"

"Look, friend," Meyer said, and put down the pool cue and stared at Tino.

"Yeah?"

"What's it your business where I work?"

"I like to know who comes in here."

"Why? You own the joint?"

"My brother does."

"OK," Meyer said. "My name's Stu Levine, I'm working the Leary Street docks right now, unloading the SS *Agda* out of Sweden. I live downtown on Ridgeway, and I happened to notice there was a pool hall here, so I decided to come in and run off a few racks before heading home. You think that'll satisfy your brother, or do you want to see my birth certificate?"

"You Jewish?" Tino asked.

"Funny I don't look it, right?"

"No, you *do* look it."

"So?"

"So nothing. We get some Jewish guys from around the corner in here every now and then."

"I'm glad to hear it. Is it OK to shoot now?"

"You want company?"

"How do I know *you're* not a hustler?"

"We'll play for time, how's that?"

"You'll win," Meyer said.

"So what? It's better than playing alone, ain't it?"

"I came up here to shoot a few balls and enjoy myself," Meyer said. "Why should I play with somebody better than me? I'll get stuck with the time, and you'll be doing all the shooting."

"You could consider it a lesson."

"I don't need lessons."

"You need lessons, believe me," Tino said. "The way you shoot pool, it's a disgrace."

"If I need lessons, I'll get Minnesota Fats."

"There ain't no real person named Minnesota Fats," Tino said, "he was just a guy they made up," which reminded Meyer that someone had named a fictitious character after him, and which further reminded him that he had not yet heard from Rollie Chabrier down at the DA's office.

"Looks like I'll never get to shoot, anyway," he said, "if you're gonna stand here and gab all day."

"OK?" Tino said.

"Go ahead, take a cue," Meyer said, and sighed. He felt he had handled the encounter very well. He had not seemed too anxious to be friendly, and yet he had succeeded in promoting a game with one of the pool hall regulars. When La Bresca walked in, if indeed he ever did, he would find Tino playing with his good old buddy Stu Levine from the Leary Street docks. Very good, Meyer thought, they ought to up me a grade tomorrow morning.

"First off, you hold your cue wrong," Tino said. "Here's how you got to hold it if you expect to sink anything."

"Like this?" Meyer said, trying to imitate the grip.

"You got arthritis or something?" Tino asked, and burst out laughing at his own joke, proving to Meyer's satisfaction that he really did not have a sense of humour.

Tino was demonstrating the proper English to put on the cue ball in order to have it veer to the left after contact, and Meyer was alternately watching the clock and the door when La Bresca walked in some twenty minutes later. Meyer recognized him at once from the description he'd been given, but turned away immediately, not wanting to seem at all interested, and listened to Tino's explanation, and then listened to the meagre joke Tino offered, something about the reason it's called English is because if you hit an Englishman in the balls with a stick, they'll turn white just like the cue ball on the table, get it? Tino laughed, and Meyer laughed with him, and that was what

La Bresca saw as he approached the table, Tino and his good old buddy from the Leary Street docks, laughing it up and shooting a friendly game of pool in the friendly neighbourhood pool hall.

"Hi, Tino," La Bresca said.

"Hi, Tony."

"How's it going?"

"So-so. This here is Stu Levine."

"Glad to meet you," La Bresca said.

"Same here," Meyer said, and extended his hand.

"This here is Tony La Bresca. He shoots a good game."

"Nobody shoots as good as you," La Bresca said.

"Stu here shoots the way Angie used to. You remember Angie who was crippled? That's the way Stu here shoots."

"Yeah, I remember Angie," La Bresca said, and both men burst out laughing. Meyer laughed with them, what the hell.

"Stu's father taught him," Tino said.

"Yeah? Who taught his father?" La Bresca said, and both men burst out laughing again.

"I hear you got yourself a job," Tino said.

"That's right."

"You just getting through?"

"Yeah, I thought I'd shoot a game or two before supper. You see Calooch around?"

"Yeah, he's over there by the windows."

"Thought maybe I'd shoot a game with him."

"Why'nt you join us right here?" Tino said.

"Thanks," La Bresca said, "but I promised Calooch I'd shoot a game with him. Anyway, you're too much of a shark."

"A shark, you hear that, Stu?" Tino said. "He thinks I'm a shark."

"Well, I'll see you," La Bresca said, and walked over to the window table. A tall thin man in a striped shirt was bent over the table, angling for a shot. La Bresca waited until he had run off three or four balls, and then they both went up to the front booth. The lights suddenly came on over a table across the hall. La Bresca and the man named Calooch went to the table, took sticks down, racked up the balls, and began playing.

"Who's Calooch?" Meyer asked Tino.

"Oh, that's Pete Calucci," Tino said.

"Friend of Tony's?"

"Oh, yeah, they know each other a long time."

Calooch and La Bresca were doing a lot of talking. They weren't doing too much playing, but they sure were talking a lot. They talked, and then one of them took a shot, and then they talked some more, and after a while the other one took a shot, and it went like that for almost an hour. At the end of the hour, both men put up their sticks, and shook hands. Calooch went back to the window table, and La Bresca went up front to settle for the time. Meyer looked up at the clock and said, "Wow, look at that, already six o'clock, I better get home, my wife'll murder me."

"Well, Stu, I enjoyed playing with you," Tino said. "Stop in again sometime."

"Yeah, maybe I will," Meyer said.

The street outside was caught in the pale grey grasp of dusk, empty, silent except for the keening of the wind, bitterly cold, forbidding. Anthony La Bresca walked with his hands in the pockets of his beige car coat, the collar raised, the green muffler wound about his neck and flapping in the fierce wind. Meyer stayed far behind him, mindful of Kling's embarrassing encounter the night before and determined not to have the same thing happen to an old experienced workhorse like himself. The cold weather and the resultant empty streets did not help him very much. It was comparatively simple to tail a man on a crowded street, but when there are only two people left alive in the world, the one up front might suddenly turn at the sound of a footfall or a tail-of-the-eye glimpse of something or someone behind him. So Meyer kept his distance and utilized every doorway he could find, ducking in and out of the street, grateful for the frantic activity that helped ward off the cold, convinced he would not be spotted, but mindful of the alternate risk he was running: if La Bresca turned a corner suddenly, or entered a building unexpectedly, Meyer could very well lose him.

The girl was waiting in a Buick.

The car was black, Meyer made the year and make at once, but he could not read the licence plate because the car was too far away, parked at the kerb some two blocks up the street.

The engine was running. The exhaust threw grey plumes of carbon monoxide into the grey and empty street. La Bresca stopped at the car, and Meyer ducked into the closest doorway, the windowed alcove of a pawnshop. Surrounded by saxophones and typewriters, cameras and tennis rackets, fishing rods and loving cups, Meyer looked diagonally through the joined and angled windows of the shop and squinted his eyes in an attempt to read the licence plate of the Buick. He could not make out the numbers. The girl had blonde hair, it fell loose to the base of her neck, she leaned over on the front seat to open the door for La Bresca.

La Bresca got into the car and slammed the door behind him.

Meyer came out of the doorway just as the big black Buick gunned away from the kerb.

He still could not read the licence plate.

7

Nobody likes to work on Saturday.

There's something obscene about it, it goes against the human grain. Saturday is the day before the day of rest, a good time to stomp on all those pressures that have been building Monday to Friday. Given a nice blustery rotten March day with the promise of snow in the air and the city standing expectantly monolithic, stoic, and solemn, given such a peach of a Saturday, how nice to be able to start a cannel coal fire in the fireplace of your three-room apartment and smoke yourself out of the joint. Or, lacking a fireplace, what better way to utilize Saturday than by pouring yourself a stiff hooker of bourbon and curling up with a blonde or a book, spending your time with *War and Peace* or *Whore and Piece*, didn't Shakespeare invent some of his best puns on Saturday, drunk with a wench in his first best bed?

Saturday is a quiet day. It can drive you to distraction with its prospects of leisure time, it can force you to pick at the coverlet wondering what to do with all your sudden freedom, it can send you wandering through the rooms in search of occupation while moodily contemplating the knowledge that the loneliest night of the week is fast approaching.

Nobody likes to work on Saturday because nobody else is working on Saturday.

Except cops.

Grind, grind, grind, work, work, work, driven by a sense of public-mindedness and dedication to humanity, law enforcement officers are forever at the ready, alert of mind, swift of body, noble of purpose.

Andy Parker was asleep in the swivel chair behind his desk.

"Where is everybody?" one of the painters said.

"What?" Parker said. "Huh?" Parker said, and sat bolt upright, and glared at the painter and then washed his huge hand over his face and said, "What the hell's the matter with you, scaring a man that way?"

"We're leaving," the first painter said.

"We're finished," the second painter said.

"We already got all our gear loaded on the truck, and we wanted to say goodbye to everybody."

"So where is everybody?"

"There's a meeting in the lieutenant's office," Parker said.

"We'll just pop in and say goodbye," the first painter said.

"I wouldn't advise that," Parker said.

"Why not?"

"They're discussing homicide. It's not wise to pop in on people when they're discussing homicide."

"Not even to say goodbye?"

"You can say goodbye to *me*," Parker said.

"It wouldn't be the same thing," the first painter said.

"So then hang around and say goodbye when they come out. They should be finished before twelve. In fact, they *got* to be finished before twelve."

"Yeah, but *we're* finished *now*," the second painter said.

"Can't you find a few things you missed?" Parker suggested. "Like, for example, you didn't paint the typewriters, or the bottle on the water cooler, or our guns. How come you missed our guns? You got green all over everything else in the goddamn place."

"You should be grateful," the first painter said. "Some people won't work on Saturday *at all*, even at time and a half."

So both painters left in high dudgeon, and Parker went back to sleep in the swivel chair behind his desk.

"I don't know what kind of a squad I'm running here," Lieutenant Byrnes said, "when two experienced detectives can blow a surveillance, one by getting made first crack out of the box, and the other by losing his man; that's a pretty good batting average for two experienced detectives."

"I was told the suspect didn't have a car," Meyer said. "I was told he had taken a train the night before."

"That's right, he did," Kling said.

"I had no way of knowing a woman would be waiting for him in a car," Meyer said.

"So you lost him," Byrnes said, "which might have been all right if the man had gone home last night. But O'Brien was stationed outside the La Bresca house in Riverhead, and the man never showed, which means we don't know where he is today, now do we? We don't know where a prime suspect is on the day the deputy mayor is supposed to get killed."

"No, sir," Meyer said, "we don't know where La Bresca is."

"Because *you* lost him."

"I guess so, sir."

"Well, how would you revise that statement, Meyer?"

"I wouldn't, sir. I lost him."

"Yes, very good, I'll put you in for a commendation."

"Thank you, sir."

"Don't get flip, Meyer."

"I'm sorry, sir."

"This isn't a goddamn joke here, I don't want Scanlon to wind up with two holes in his head the way Cowper did."

"No, sir, neither do I."

"OK, then learn for Christ's sake how to tail a person, will you?"

"Yes, sir."

"Now what about this other man you say La Bresca spent time with in conversation, what was his name?"

"Calucci, sir. Peter Calucci."

"Did you check him out?"

"Yes, sir, last night before I went home. Here's the stuff we got from the BCI."

Meyer placed a manilla envelope on Byrne's desk, and then stepped back to join the other detectives ranged in a military line before the desk. None of the men were smiling. The lieutenant was in a lousy mood, and somebody was supposed to come up with fifty thousand dollars before noon, and the possibility existed that the deputy mayor would soon be dispatched to that big City Hall in the sky, so nobody was smiling. The lieutenant reached into the envelope and pulled out a photocopy of a fingerprint card, glanced at it cursorily, and then pulled out a photocopy of Calucci's police record.

Byrnes read the sheet, and then said, "When did he get out?"

"He was a bad apple. He applied for parole after serving a third of the sentence, was denied, and applied every year after that. He finally made it in seven."

Byrnes looked at the sheet again.

"What's he been doing?" Byrnes asked.

"Construction work."

"That how he met La Bresca?"

"Calucci's parole officer reports that his last job was with Abco Construction, and a call to the company listed La Bresca as having worked there at the same time."

"I forget, does this La Bresca have a record?"

"No, sir."

"Has Calucci been clean since he got out?"

"According to his parole officer, yes, sir."

"Now who's this person 'Dom' who called La Bresca Thursday night?"

"We have no idea, sir."

"Because La Bresca tipped to your tailing him, isn't that right, Kling?"

"Yes, sir, that's right, sir."

"Is Brown still on that phone tap?"

"Yes, sir."

"Have you tried any of our stoolies?"

"No, sir, not yet."

"Well, when the hell do you propose to get moving? We're supposed to deliver fifty thousand dollars by twelve o'clock. It's now a quarter after ten, when the hell . . ."

"Sir, we've been trying to get a line on Calucci. His parole officer gave us an address, and we sent a man over, but his landlady says he hasn't been there since early yesterday morning."

"Of course not!" Byrnes shouted. "The two of them are probably shacked up with that blonde woman, whoever the hell *she* was, planning how to murder Scanlon when we fail to

100

IDENTIFICATION BUREAU

NAME ___ Peter Vincent Calucci ___

IDENTIFICATION JACKET NUMBER ___ P 421904 ___

ALIAS ___ "Calooch"   "Cooch"   "Kook" ___

___ **COLOR** ___ White ___

RESIDENCE ___ 336 South 91st Street, Isola ___

DATE OF BIRTH ___ October 2, 1938 ___ **AGE** 22 ___

BIRTHPLACE ___ Isola ___

HEIGHT 5'9" ___ **WEIGHT** 156 ___ **HAIR** Brown ___ **EYES** Brown ___

COMPLEXION Swarthy ___ **OCCUPATION** Construction worker ___

SCARS AND TATTOOS ___ Appendectomy scar, no tattoos. ___

ARRESTED BY: ___ Patrolman Henry Butler ___

DETECTIVE DIVISION NUMBER: ___ 63-R1-1605-1960 ___

DATE OF ARREST 3/14/60 ___ **PLACE** 812 North 65 St., Isola ___

CHARGE ___ Robbery ___

BRIEF DETAILS OF CRIME ___ Calucci entered gasoline station at 812 North 65 Street at or about midnight, threatened to shoot attendant if he did not open safe. Attendant said he did not know combination, Calucci cocked revolver and was about to fire when patrolman Butler of 63rd Precinct came upon scene and apprehended him.

PREVIOUS RECORD ___ None ___

INDICTED ___ Criminal Courts, March 15, 1960. ___

FINAL CHARGE ___ Robbery in first degree, Penal Law 2125 ___

DISPOSITION ___ Pleaded guilty 7/8/60, sentenced to ten years at Castleview Prison.

deliver the payoff money. Get Danny Gimp or Fats Donner, find out if they know a fellow named Dom who dropped a bundle on a big fight two weeks ago. Who the hell was fighting two weeks ago, anyway? Was that the champion fight?"

"Yes, sir."

"All right, get cracking. Does anybody use Gimp besides Carella?"

"No, sir."

"Who uses Donner?"

"I do, sir."

"Then get to him right away, Willis."

"If he's not in Florida, sir. He usually goes south in the winter."

"Goddamn stool pigeons go south," Byrnes grumbled, "and we're stuck here with a bunch of maniacs trying to kill people. All right, go on, Willis, get moving."

"Yes, sir," Willis said, and left the office.

"Now what about this other possibility, this deaf man thing? Jesus Christ, I hope it's not him. I hope this is La Bresca and Calucci and the blonde bimbo who drove him clear out of sight last night, Meyer . . ."

"Yes, sir . . ."

". . . and not that deaf bastard again. I've talked to the commissioner on this, and I've also talked to the deputy mayor *and* the mayor, and we're agreed that paying the fifty thousand dollars is out of the question. We're to try apprehending who-ever picks up that lunch pail and see if we can't get a lead this time. And we're to provide protection for Scanlon and that's all for now. So I want you two to arrange the drop, and saturation coverage of that bench, and I want a suspect brought in here today, and I want him questioned till he's blue in the face, have a lawyer ready and waiting for him in case he screams Miranda-Escobedo, I want a *lead* today, have you got that?"

"Yes, sir," Meyer said.

"Yes, sir," Kling said.

"You think you can set up the drop and cover without fouling it up like you fouled up the surveillance?"

"Yes, sir, we can handle it."

"All right, then get going, and bring me some meat on this goddamn case."

"Yes, sir," Kling and Meyer said together, and then went out of the office.

"Now what's this about a junkie being in that room with the killer?" Byrnes asked Hawes.

"That's right, sir."

"Well, what's your idea, Cotton?"

"My idea is he got her in there to make sure she'd be stoned when he started shooting, that's my idea, sir."

"That's the stupidest idea I've ever heard in my life," Byrnes said. "Get the hell out of here, go help Meyer and Kling, go call the hospital, find out how Carella's doing, go set up another plant for those two punks who beat him up, go do *something*, for Christ's sake!"

"Yes, sir," Hawes said, and went out into the squadroom.

Andy Parker, awakened by the grumbling of the other men, washed his hand over his face, blew his nose, and then said, "The painters said to tell you goodbye."

"Good riddance," Meyer said.

"Also, you got a call from the DA's office."

"Who from?"

"Rollie Chabrier."

"When was this?"

"Half-hour ago, I guess."

"Why didn't you put it through?"

"While you were in there with the loot? No, sir."

"I've been waiting for this call," Meyer said, and immediately dialled Chabrier's number.

"Mr Chabrier's office," a bright female voice said.

"Bernice, this is Meyer Meyer up at the 87th. I hear Rollie called me a little while ago."

"That's right," Bernice said.

"Would you put him on, please?"

"He's gone for the day," Bernice said.

"Gone for the day? It's only a little after ten."

"Well," Bernice said, "nobody likes to work on Saturday."

The black lunch pail containing approximately fifty thousand scraps of newspaper was placed in the centre of the third bench on the Clinton Street footpath into Grover Park by Detective

Cotton Hawes, who was wearing thermal underwear and two sweaters and a business suit and an overcoat and ear muffs. Hawes was an expert ski-er, and he had ski-ed on days when the temperature at the base was four below zero and the temperature at the summit was thirty below, had ski-ed on the days when his feet went and his hands went and he boomed the mountain non-stop not for fun or sport but just to get near the fire in the base lodge before he shattered into a hundred brittle pieces. But he had never been this cold before. It was bad enough to be working on Saturday, but it was indecent to be working when the weather threatened to gelatinize a man's blood.

Among the other people who were braving the unseasonable winds and temperatures that Saturday were:

(1) A pretzel salesman at the entrance to Clinton Street footpath.

(2) Two nuns saying their beads on the second bench into the park.

(3) A passionate couple necking in a sleeping bag on the grass behind the third bench.

(4) A blind man sitting on the fourth bench, patting his seeing-eye German shepherd and scattering bread crumbs to the pigeons.

The pretzel salesman was a detective named Stanley Faulk, recruited from the 88th across the park, a man of fifty-eight who wore a grey handlebar moustache as his trademark. The moustache made it quite simple to identify him when he was working in his own territory, thereby diminishing his value on plants. But it also served to strike terror into the hearts of hoods near and wide, in much the same way that the green-and-white colour combination of a radio motor patrol car is supposed to frighten criminals and serve as a deterrent. Faulk wasn't too happy about being called into service for the 87th on a day like this one, but he was bundled up warmly in several sweaters over which was a black cardigan-type candy store-owner sweater over which he had put on a white apron. He was standing behind a cart that displayed pretzels stacked on long round sticks. A walkie-talkie was set into the top of the cart.

The two nuns saying their beads were Detectives Meyer Meyer and Bert Kling, and they were really saying what a son of a bitch Byrnes had been to bawl them out that way in front of Hawes and Willis, embarrassing them and making them feel very foolish.

"I feel very foolish right now," Meyer whispered.

"How come?" Kling whispered.

"I feel like I'm in drag," Meyer whispered.

The passionate couple assignment had ben the choice assignment, and Hawes and Willis had drawn straws for it. The reason it was so choice was that the other half of the passionate couple was herself quite choice, a police-woman named Eileen Burke, with whom Willis had worked on a mugging case many years back. Eileen had red hair and green eyes, Eileen had long legs, sleek and clean, full-calved, tapering to slender ankles, Eileen had very good breasts, and whereas Eileen was much taller than Willis (who only barely scraped past the five-foot-eight height requirement), he did not mind at all because big girls always seemed attracted to him, and vice versa.

"We're supposed to be kidding," he said to Eileen, and held her close in the warm sleeping bag.

"My lips are getting chapped," she said.

"Your lips are very nice," he said.

"We're supposed to be here on business," Eileen said.

"Mmm," he answered.

"Get your hand off my behind," she said.

"Oh, is that your behind?" he asked.

"Listen," she said.

"I hear it," he said. "Somebody's coming. You'd better kiss me."

She kissed him. Willis kept one eye on the bench. The person passing was a governess wheeling a baby carriage. God knew who would send an infant out on a day when the glacier was moving south. The woman and the carriage passed. Willis kept kissing Detective 2nd/Grade Eileen Burke.

"Mm frick sheb bron," Eileen mumbled.

"Mmm?" Willis mumbled.

Eileen pulled her mouth away and caught her breath. "I *said* I think she's gone."

"What's that?" Willis asked suddenly.

"Do not be afraid, *guapa*, it is only my pistol," Eileen said, and laughed.

"I meant on the path. Listen."

They listened.

Someone else was approaching the bench.

From where Patrolman Richard Genero sat in plainclothes on the fourth bench, wearing dark glasses and patting the head of the German shepherd at his feet, tossing crumbs to the pigeons, wishing for summer, he could clearly see the young man who walked rapidly to the third bench, picked up the lunch pail, looked swiftly over his shoulder, and began walking not *out* of the park, but deeper *into* it.

Genero didn't know quite what to do at first.

He had been pressed into duty only because there was a shortage of available men that afternoon (crime prevention being an arduous and difficult task on any given day, but especially on Saturday), and he had been placed in the position thought least vulnerable, it being assumed the man who picked up the lunch pail would immediately reverse direction and head out of the park again, on to Grover Avenue, where Faulk the pretzel man and Hawes, parked in his own car at the curb, would immediately collar him. But the suspect was coming into the park instead, heading for Genero's bench, and Genero was a fellow who didn't care very much for violence, so he sat there wishing he was home in bed with his mother serving him hot minestrone and singing old Italian arias.

The dog at his feet had been trained for police work, and Genero had been taught a few hand signals and voice signals in the squadroom before heading out for his vigil on the fourth bench, but he was also afraid of dogs, especially big dogs, and the idea of giving this animal a kill command that might possibly be misunderstood filled Genero with fear and trembling. Suppose he gave the command and the dog leaped for his *own* jugular rather than for the throat of the young man who was perhaps three feet away now and walking quite rapidly, glancing over his shoulder every now and again? Suppose he did that and this beast tore him to shreds, what would his mother say to that? *che bella cosa*, you hadda to become a police, hah?

Willis, in the meantime, had slid his walkie-talkie up between Eileen Burke's breasts and flashed the news to Hawes, parked in his own car on Grover Avenue, good place to be when your man is going the other way. Willis was now desperately trying to lower the zipper on the bag, which zipper seemed to have become somehow stuck. Willis didn't mind being stuck in a sleeping bag with someone like Eileen Burke, who wiggled and wriggled along with him as they attempted to extricate themselves, but he suddenly fantasised the lieutenant chewing him out the way he had chewed out Kling and Meyer this morning and so he really *was* trying to lower that damn zipper while entertaining the further fantasy that Eileen Burke was beginning to enjoy all this adolescent tumbling. Genero, of course, didn't know that Hawes had been alerted, he only knew that the suspect was abreast of him now, and passing the bench now, and moving swiftly beyond the bench now, so he got up and first took off the sun-glasses, and then unbuttoned the third button of his coat the way he had seen detectives do on television, and then reached in for his revolver and then shot himself in the leg.

The suspect began running.

Genero fell to the ground and the dog licked his face.

Willis got out of the sleeping bag and Eileen Burke buttoned her blouse and her coat and then adjusted her garters, and Hawes came running into the park and slipped on a patch of ice near the third bench and almost broke his neck.

"Stop, police!" Willis shouted.

And, miracle of miracles, the suspect stopped dead in his tracks and waited for Willis to approach him with his gun in his hand and lipstick all over his face.

The suspect's name was Alan Parry.

They advised him of his rights and he agreed to talk to them without a lawyer, even though a lawyer was present and waiting for him in case he demanded one.

"Where do you live, Alan?" Willis asked.

"Right around the corner. I know you guys. I see you guys around all the time. Don't you know me? I live right around the corner.

"You make him?" Willis asked the other detectives.

They all shook their heads. They were standing around him in a loose circle, the pretzel man, two nuns, the pair of lovers, and the big redhead with a white streak in his hair and a throbbing ankle in his thermal underwear.

"Why'd you run, Alan?" Willis asked.

"I heard a shot. In this neighbourhood, when you hear shooting, you run."

"Who's your partner?"

"What partner?"

"The guy who's in this with you."

"In *what* with me?"

"The murder plot."

"The *what*?"

"Come on, Alan, you play ball with us, we'll play ball with you."

"Hey, man, you got the wrong customer," Parry said.

"How were you going to split the loot, Alan?"

"What loot?"

"The loot in that lunch pail."

"Listen, I never seen that lunch pail before in my life."

"There's thirty thousand dollars in that lunch pail," Willis said, "now come on, Alan, you know that, stop playing it cosy."

Parry either avoided the trap, or else did not know there was supposed to be *fifty* thousand dollars in the black pail he had lifted from the bench. He shook his head and said, "I don't know nothing about no loot, I was asked to pick up the pail, and I done it."

"Who asked you?"

"A big blond guy wearing a hearing aid."

"Do you expect me to believe that?" Willis said.

The cue was one the detectives of the 87th had used many times before in interrogating suspects, and it was immediately seized upon by Meyer, who said, "Take it easy, Hal," the proper response, the response that told Willis they were once again ready to assume antagonistic roles. In the charade that would follow, Willis would play the tough bastard out to hang a phoney rap on poor little Alan Parry, while Meyer would play the sympathetic father figure. The other detectives (including Faulk of the 88th, who was familiar with the ploy and had used it often enough himself in his own squadroom) would serve as a sort of nodding Greek chorus, impartial and objective.

Without even so much as a glance at Meyer, Willis said, "What do you mean, take it easy? This little punk has been lying from the minute we got him up here."

"Maybe there really *was* a tall blond guy with a hearing aid," Meyer said. "Give him a chance to tell us, will you?"

"Sure, and maybe there was a striped elephant with pink polka dots," Willis said. "Who's your partner, you little punk?"

"I don't *have* no partner!" Parry said. Plaintively, he said to Meyer, "Will you please tell this guy I ain't *got* a partner?"

"Calm down, Hal, will you?" Meyer said. "Let's hear it, Alan."

"I was on my way home when . . ."

"From where?" Willis snapped.

"Huh?"

"Where were you coming from?"

"From my girl's house."

"Where?"

"Around the corner. Right across the street from my house."

"What were you doing there?"

"Well, you know," Parry said.

"No, we *don't* know," Willis said.

"For God's sake, Hal," Meyer said, "leave the man a little something personal and private, will you please?"

"Thanks," Parry said.

"You went to see your girl-friend," Meyer said. "What time was that, Alan?"

"I went up there around nine thirty. Her mother goes to work at nine. So I went up around nine thirty."

"You unemployed?" Willis snapped.

"Yes, sir," Parry said.

"When's the last time you worked?"

"Well, you see . . ."

"Answer the question!"

"Give him a chance, Hal!"

"He's stalling!"

"He's trying to answer you." Gently, Meyer said, "What happened, Alan?"

"I had this job, and I dropped the eggs."

"What?"

"At the grocery store on Eightieth. I was working in the back and one day we got all these crates of eggs, and I was taking them to the refrigerator, and I dropped two crates. So I got fired."

"How long did you work there?"

"From when I got out of high school."

"When was that?" Willis asked.

"Last June."

"Did you graduate?"

"Yes, sir, I have a diploma," Parry said.

"So what have you been doing since you lost the job at the grocery?"

Parry shrugged. "Nothing," he said.

"How old are you?" Willis asked.

"I'll be nineteen . . . what's today?"

"Today's the ninth."

"I'll be nineteen next week. The fifteenth of March."

"You're liable to be spending your birthday in jail," Willis said.

"Now cut it out," Meyer said, "I won't have you threatening this man. What happened when you left your girl-friend's house, Alan?"

"I met this guy."

"Where?"

"Outside the Corona."

"The what?"

"The Corona. You know the movie house that's all boarded up about three blocks from here, you know the one?"

"We know it," Willis said.

"Well, there."

"What was he doing there?"

"Just standing. Like as if he was waiting for somebody."

"So what happened?"

"He stopped me and said was I busy? So I said it depended.

So he said would I like to make five bucks? So I asked him doing what? He said there was a lunch pail in the park and if I picked it up for him, he'd give me five bucks. So I asked him why he couldn't go for it himself, and he said he was waiting there for somebody, and he was afraid if he left the guy might show up and think he'd gone. So he said I should get the lunch pail for him and bring it back to him there outside the theatre so he wouldn't miss his friend. He was supposed to meet him outside the Corona, you see. You know the place? A cop got shot outside there once."

"I told you we know it," Willis said.

"So I asked him what was in the lunch pail, and he said just his lunch, but he said he also had a few other things in there with his sandwiches, so I asked him like what and he said do you want this five bucks or not? So I took the five and went to get the pail for him."

"He gave you the five dollars?"

"Yeah."

"*Before* you went for the pail?"

"Yeah."

"Go on."

"He's lying," Willis said.

"That is the truth, I swear to God."

"What'd you think was in that pail?"

Parry shrugged. "Lunch. And some other little things. Like he said."

"Come on," Willis said. "Do you expect us to buy that?"

"Kid what'd you *really* think was in that pail?" Meyer asked gently.

"Well . . . look . . . you can't do nothing to me for what I *thought* was in there, right?"

"That's right," Meyer said. "If you could lock up a man for what he's thinking, we'd *all* be in jail, right?"

"Right," Parry said, and laughed.

Meyer laughed with him. The Greek chorus laughed too. Everybody laughed except Willis, who kept staring stone-faced at Parry. "So what'd you *think* was in that pail?" Meyer said.

"Junk," Parry said.

"You a junkie?" Willis asked.

"No, sir, never touch the stuff."

"Roll up your sleeve."

"I'm not a junkie, sir."

"Let's see your arm."

Parry rolled up his sleeve.

"OK," Willis said.

"I told you," Parry said.

"OK, you told us. What'd you plan to do with that lunch pail?"

"What do you mean?"

"The Corona is three blocks *east* of here. You picked up that pail and started heading *west*. What were you planning?"

"Nothing."

"Then why were you heading *away* from where the deaf man was waiting?"

"I wasn't heading anyplace."

"You were heading *west*."

"No, I musta got mixed up."

"You got so mixed up you forgot how you came into the park, right? You forgot that the entrance was *behind* you, right?"

"No, I didn't forget where the entrance was."

"Then why'd you head deeper into the park?"

"I told you. I musta got mixed up."

"He's a lying little bastard," Willis said. "I'm going to book him, Meyer, no matter *what* you say."

"Now hold it, just hold it a minute," Meyer said. "You know you're in pretty serious trouble if there's junk in that pail, don't you, Alan?" Meyer said.

"Why? Even if there *is* junk in there, it ain't mine."

"Well, *I* know that, Alan, *I* believe you, but the law is pretty specific about possession of narcotics. I'm sure you must realize that every pusher we pick up claims somebody must have planted the stuff on him, he doesn't know how it got there, it isn't his, and so on. They all give the same excuses, even when we've got them dead to rights."

"Yeah, I guess they must," Parry said.

"So you see, I won't be able to help you much if there really *is* junk in that pail."

"Yeah, I see," Parry said.

"He knows there's no junk in that pail. His partner sent him to pick up the money," Willis said.

"No, no," Parry said, shaking his head.

"You didn't know anything about the thirty thousand dollars, is that right?" Meyer asked gently.

"Nothing," Parry said, shaking his head. "I'm telling you, I met this guy outside the Corona and he gave me five bucks to get his pail."

"Which you decided to steal," Willis said.

"Huh?"

"Were you going to bring that pail back to him?"

"Well . . ." Parry hesitated. He glanced at Meyer. Meyer nodded encouragingly. "Well, no," Parry said. "I figured if there was junk in it, maybe I could turn a quick buck, you know. There's lots of guys in this neighbourhood'll pay for stuff like that."

"Like what's in the pail," Parry said.

"Open the pail, kid," Willis said.

"No." Parry shook his head. "No, I don't want to."

"Why not?"

"If it's junk, I don't know nothing about it. And if it's thirty Gs, I got nothing to do with it. I don't know nothing. I don't want to answer no more questions, that's it."

"That's it."

"That's it, Hal," Meyer said.

"Go on home, kid," Willis said.

"I can go?"

"Yeah, yeah, you can go," Willis said wearily.

Parry stood up quickly, and without looking back headed straight for the gate in the slatted railing that divided the squad-room from the corridor outside. He was down the hallway in a wink. His footfalls clattered noisily on the iron-runged steps leading to the street floor below.

"What do you think?" Willis said.

"I think we did it arse-backwards," Hawes said. "I think we should have followed him out of the park instead of nailing him. He would have led us straight to the deaf man."

"The lieutenant didn't think so. The lieutenant figured nobody would be crazy enough to send a stranger after fifty thousand dollars. The lieutenant figured the guy who made the pick-up *had* to be a member of the gang."

"Yeah, well the lieutenant was wrong," Hawes said.

"You know what I think?" Kling said.

"What?"

"I think the deaf man *knew* there'd be nothing in that lunch pail. That's why he could risk sending a stranger for it. He *knew* the money wouldn't be there, and he *knew* we'd pick up whoever he sent."

"If that's the case . . ." Willis started.

"He *wants* to kill Scanlon," Kling said.

The detectives all looked at each other. Faulk scratched his head and said, "Well, I better be getting back across the park, unless you need me some more."

"No, thanks a lot, Stan," Meyer said.

"Don't mention it," Faulk said, and went out.

"I enjoyed the plant," Eileen Burke said, and glanced archly at Willis, and then swivelled towards the gate and out of the squadroom.

"Can it be the breeze . . ." Meyer sang.

"That fills the trees . . ." Kling joined in.

"Go to hell," Willis said, and then genuflected and piously added, "Sisters."

If nobody in the entire world likes working on Saturdays, even less people like working on Saturday night.

Saturday night, baby, is the night to howl. Saturday night is the night to get out there and hang ten. Saturday night is when you slip into your satin slippers and your Pucci dress, put on your shirt with the monogram on the cuff, spray your navel with cologne, and laugh too loud.

The bitch city is something different on Saturday night, sophisticated in black, scented and powdered, but somehow not as unassailable, shiveringly beautiful in a dazzle of blinking lights. Reds and oranges, electric blues and vibrant greens assault the eye incessantly, and the resultant turn-on is as sweet as a quick fix in the penthouse pad, a liquid cool that conjures dreams of towering glass spires and enamelled minarets. There is excitement in this city on Saturday night, but it is tempered by romantic expectancy. She is not a bitch, this city. Not on Saturday night.

Not if you will love her.

Nobody likes to work on Saturday night, and so the detectives of the 87th Squad should have been pleased when the police commissioner called Byrnes to say that he was asking the DA's Squad to assume the responsibility of protecting Deputy Mayor Scanlon from harm. If they'd had any sense at all, the detectives of the 87th would have considered themselves fortunate.

But the commissioner's cut was deeply felt, first by Byrnes, and then by every man on the squad when he related the news to them. They went their separate ways that Saturday night, some into the streets to work, others home to rest, but each of them felt a corporate sense of failure. Not one of them realized how fortunate he was.

The two detectives from the DA's Squad were experienced men who had handled special assignments before. When the deputy mayor's personal chauffeur arrived to pick them up that night, they were waiting on the sidewalk outside the Criminal Courts Building, just around the corner from the District Attorney's office. It was exactly 8 PM. The deputy mayor's chauffeur had picked up the Cadillac sedan at the municipal garage a half-hour earlier. He had gone over the upholstery with a whisk broom, passed a dust rag over the hood, wiped the windows with a chamois cloth, and emptied all the ashtrays. He was now ready for action, and he was pleased to note that the detectives were right on time; he could not abide tardy individuals.

They drove up to Smoke Rise, which was where the deputy mayor lived, and one of the detectives got out of the car and walked to the front door, and rang the bell, and was ushered into the huge brick house by a maid in a black uniform. The deputy mayor came down the long white staircase leading to the centre hall, shook hands with the detective from the DA's Squad, apologized for taking up his time this way on a Saturday night, made some comment about the "damn foolishness of it all", and then called up to his wife to tell her the car was waiting. His wife came down the steps, and the deputy mayor

115

introduced her to the detective from the DA's Squad, and then they all went to the front door.

The detective stepped outside first, scanned the bushes lining the driveway, and then led the deputy mayor and his wife to the car. He opened the door and allowed them to precede him into the automobile. The other detective was stationed on the opposite side of the car, and as soon as the deputy mayor and his wife were seated, both detectives got into the automobile and took positions facing them on the jump seats.

The dashboard clock read 8.30 PM.

The deputy mayor's personal chauffeur set the car in motion, and the deputy mayor made a few jokes with the detectives as they drove along the gently winding roads of exclusive Smoke Rise on the edge of the city's northern river, and then on to the service road leading to the River Highway. It had been announced in the newspapers the week before that the deputy mayor would speak at a meeting of the B'nai Brith in the city's largest synagogue at nine o'clock that night. The deputy mayor's home in Smoke Rise was only fifteen minutes away from the synagogue, and so the chauffeur drove slowly and carefully while the two detectives from the DA's Squad eyed the automobiles that moved past on either side of the Cadillac.

The Cadillac exploded when the dashboard clock read 8.45 PM.

The bomb was a powerful one.

It erupted from somewhere under the hood, sending flying steel into the car, tearing off the roof like paper, blowing the doors into the highway. The car screeched out of control, lurched across two lanes, rolled on to its side like a ruptured metal beast and was suddenly ablaze.

A passing convertible tried to swerve around the flaming Cadillac. There was a second explosion. The convertible veered wildly and crashed into the river barrier.

When the police arrived on the scene, the only person alive in either car was a bleeding seventeen-year-old girl who had gone through the windshield of the convertible.

8

On Sunday morning the visiting hours at Buena Vista Hospital were from ten to twelve. It was a busy day, busier than Wednesday, for example, because Saturday night encourages broken arms and legs, bloody pates and shattered sternums. There is nothing quite so hectic as the Emergency Room of a big city hospital on a Saturday night. And on Sunday morning it's only natural for people to visit the friends and relatives who were unfortunate enough to have met with assorted mayhem the night before.

Steve Carella had met with assorted mayhem on Thursday night, and here it was Sunday morning, and he sat propped up in bed expecting Teddy's arrival and feeling gaunt and pale and unshaven even though he had shaved himself not ten minutes ago. He had lost seven pounds since his admission to the hospital (it being singularly difficult to eat and breathe at the same time when your nose is taped and bandaged) and he still ached everywhere, seemed in fact to discover new bruises every time he moved, which can make a man feel very unshaven.

He had had a lot of time to do some thinking since Thursday night, and as soon as he had got over feeling, in sequence, foolish, angry, and murderously vengeful, he had decided that the deaf man was responsible for what had happened to him. That was a good way to feel, he thought, because it took the blame away from two young punks (for Christ's sake, how could an experienced detective get smeared that way by two young punks?) and put it squarely on to a master criminal

117

instead. Master criminals are very handy scapegoats, Carella reasoned, because they allow you to dismiss your own inadequacies. There was an old Jewish joke Meyer had once told him, about the mother who says to her son, "*Trombenik*, go get a job," and the son answers, "I can't, I'm a *trombenik*." The situation now was similar, he supposed, with the question being altered to read, "How can you let a master criminal do this to you?" and the logical answer being, "It's easy, he's a master criminal."

Whether or not the deaf man was a master criminal was perhaps a subject for debate. Carella would have to query his colleagues on the possibility of holding a seminar once he got back to the office. This, according to the interns who'd been examining his skull like phrenologists, should be by Thursday, it being their considered opinion that unconsciousness always meant concussion and concussion always carried with it the possibility of internal haemorrhage with at least a week's period of observation being *de rigueur* in such cases, go argue with doctors.

Perhaps the deaf man wasn't a master criminal at all. Perhaps he was simply smarter than any of the policemen he was dealing with, which encouraged some pretty frightening conjecture. Given a superior intelligence at work, was it even *possible* for inferior intelligences to second-guess whatever diabolical scheme was afoot? Oh, come on now, Carella thought, diabolical indeed! Well, *yeah*, he thought, diabolical. It is diabolical to demand five thousand dollars and then knock off the parks commissioner, and it *is* diabolical to demand fifty thousand dollars and then knock off the deputy mayor, and it is staggering to imagine what the next demand might be, or who the next victim would be. There most certainly would be another demand which, if not met, would doubtless lead to yet another victim. Or would it? How can you second-guess a master criminal? You can't, he's a master criminal.

No, Carella thought, he's only a human being, and he's counting on several human certainties. He's hoping to establish a pattern of warning and reprisal, he's hoping we'll attempt to stop him each time, but only so that we'll fail, forcing him to carry out his threat. Which means that the two early extortion tries were only preparation for the big caper. And since he seems to be climbing the municipal government ladder, and since he multiplied his first demand by ten, I'm willing to bet his next declared victim will be James Martin Vale, the mayor himself, and that he'll ask for ten times what he asked for the last time: five hundred thousand dollars. This is a lot of strawberries.

Or am I only second-guessing a master criminal?

Am I *supposed* to be second-guessing him?

Is he really preparing the ground for a big killing, or is there quite another diabolical (there we go again) plan in his mind?

Teddy Carella walked into the room at that moment.

The only thing Carella had to second-guess was whether he would kiss her first or vice versa. Since his nose was in plaster, he decided to let her choose the target, which she did with practised ease, causing him to consider some wildly diabolical schemes of his own, which if executed would have resulted in his never again being permitted inside Buena Vista Hospital.

Not even in a private room.

Patrolman Richard Genero was in the same hospital that Sunday morning, but his thoughts were less erotic than they were ambitious.

Despite a rather tight official security lid on the murders, an enterprising newspaperman had only this morning speculated on a possible connection between Genero's leg wound and the subsequent killing of Scanlon the night before. The police and the city officials had managed to keep all mention of the extortion calls and notes out of the newspapers thus far, but the reporter for the city's leading metropolitan daily wondered in print whether or not the detectives of "an uptown precinct bordering the park" hadn't in reality possessed foreknowledge of an attempt to be made on the deputy mayor's life, hadn't in fact set up an elaborate trap that very afternoon, "a trap in which a courageous patrolman was destined to suffer a bullet wound in the leg while attempting to capture the suspected killer." Wherever the reporter had dug up his information, he had neglected to mention that Genero had inflicted the wound upon himself, due to a fear of dogs and criminals, and due to a certain lack of familiarity with shooting at fleeing suspects.

119

Genero's father, who was a civil service employee himself, having worked for the Department of Sanitation for some twenty years now, was not aware that his son had accidentally shot himself in the leg. All he knew was that his son was a hero. As befitted a hero, he had brought a white carton of *cannoli* to the hospital, and now he and his wife and his son sat in the semi-private stillness of a fourth-floor room and demolished the pastry while discussing Genero's almost certain promotion to Detective 3rd/Grade.

The idea of a promotion had not occurred to Genero before this, but as his father outlined the heroic action in the park the day before, Genero began to visualize himself as the man who had made the capture possible. Without him, without the warning shot he had fired into his own leg, the fleeing Alan Parry might never have stopped. The fact that Parry had turned out to be a wet fuse didn't matter at all to Genero. It was all well and good to realize a man wasn't dangerous *after* the fact, but where were all those detectives when Parry was running straight for Genero with a whole lunch pail full of God-knew-what under his arm, where were they *then*, huh? And how could they have known *then*, while Genero was courageously drawing his pistol, that Parry would turn out to be only another innocent dupe, nossir, it had been impossible to tell.

"You were brave," Genero's father said, licking pot cheese from his lips. "It was *you* who tried to stop him."

"That's true," Genero said, because it *was* true.

"It was *you* who risked your life."

"That's right," Genero said, because it *was* right.

"They should promote you."

"They should," Genero said.

"I will call your boss," Genero's mother said.

"No, I don't think you should, Mama."

"*Pèrchè no?*"

"*Pèrchè* . . . Mama, please don't talk Italian, you know I don't understand Italian so well."

"*Vergogna*," his mother said, "an Italian doesn't understand his own tongue. I will call your boss."

"No, Mama, that isn't the way it's done."

"Then how *is* it done?" his father asked.

"Well, you've got to hint around."

"Hint? To who?"

"Well, to people."

"Which people?"

"Well, Carella's upstairs in this same hospital, maybe . . ."

"*Ma chi è questa Carella?*" his mother said.

"Mama, please."

"Who is this Carella?"

"A detective on the squad."

"Where you work, *si?*"

"*Si*. Please, Mama."

"He is your boss?"

"No, he just works up there."

"He was shot, too?"

"No, he was beat up."

"By the same man who shot you?"

"No, not by the same man who shot me," Genero said, which was also the truth.

"So what does he have to do with this?"

"Well, he's got influence."

"With the boss?"

"Well, no. You see, Captain Frick runs the entire precinct, he's actually the boss. But Lieutenant Byrnes is in charge of the detective squad, and Carella is a detective/2nd, and him and the lieutenant are like this, so maybe if I talk to Carella he'll see how I helped them grab that guy yesterday, and put in a good word for me."

"Let her call the boss," Genero's father said.

"No, it's better this way," Genero said.

"How much does a detective make?" Genero's mother asked.

"A fortune," Genero said.

Gadgets fascinated Detective-Lieutenant Sam Grossman, even when they were bombs. Or perhaps especially when they were bombs. There was no question in anyone's mind (how much question *could* there have been, considering the evidence of the demolished automobile and its five occupants?) that some-one had put a bomb in the deputy mayor's car. Moreover, it was mandatory to assume that someone had set the bomb to

121

go off at a specific time, rather than using the ignition wiring of the car as an immediate triggering device. This aspect of the puzzle pleased Grossman enormously because he considered ignition-trigger bombs to be rather crude devices capable of being wired by any gangland ape. *This* bomb was a time bomb. But it was a very special time bomb. It was a time bomb that had not been wired to the automobile clock.

How did Grossman know this?

Ah-ha, the police laboratory never sleeps, not even on Sunday. And besides, his technicians had found two clock faces in the rubble of the automobile.

One of the faces had been part of the Cadillac's dashboard clock. The other had come from a nationally advertised, popular-priced electric alarum clock. There was one other item of importance found in the rubble: a portion of the front panel of a DC-to-AC inverter, part of its brand name still showing where it was stamped into the metal.

These three parts lay on the counter in Grossman's laboratory like three key pieces to a jigsaw puzzle. All he had to do was fit them together and come up with a brilliant solution. He was feeling particularly brilliant this Sunday morning because his son had brought home a 92 on a high-school chemistry exam only two days ago; it always made Grossman feel brilliant when his son achieved anything. Well, let's see, he thought brilliantly. I've got three parts of a time bomb, or rather *two* parts because I think I can safely eliminate the car's clock except as a reference point. Whoever wired the bomb undoubtedly refused to trust his own wrist watch since a difference of a minute or two in timing might have proved critical – in a minute, the deputy mayor could have been out of the car already and on his way into the synagogue. So he had set the electric clock with the time showing on the dashboard clock. Why an *electric* clock? Simple. He did not want a clock that *ticked*. Ticking might have attracted attention, especially if it came from under the hood of a purring Cadillac. OK, so let's see what we've got. We've got an electric alarum clock, and we've got a DC-to-AC inverter, which means someone wanted to translate direct current to alternating current. The battery in a Cadillac would *have* to be 12-volts DC, and the electric clock would doubtless be wired for alternating current. So perhaps we can reasonably assume that someone wanted to wire the clock to the battery and needed an inverter to make this feasible. Let's see.

He'd have had to run a positive lead to the battery and a negative lead to any metal part of the automobile, since the car itself would have served as a ground, right? So now we've got a power source to the clock, and the clock is running. OK, right, the rest is simple, he'd have had to use an electric blasting cap, sure, there'd have been enough power to set one off, most commercial electric detonators can be fired by passing a continuous current of 0.3 to 0.4 amperes through the bridge wire. OK, let's see, hold it now, let's look at it.

The battery provides our source of power . . .

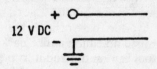

. . . to the inverter . . .

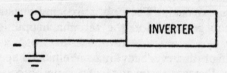

. . . and runs the electric clock . . .

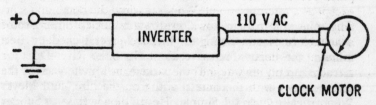

. . . which is in turn set for a specific time, about eight, wasn't it? He'd have had to monkey around with the clock so that instead of the alarum ringing, a switch would close. That would complete the circuit, let's see, he'd have needed a lead running back to the battery, another lead running to the blasting cap, and a lead from the blasting cap to any metal part of the car. So that would look like . . .

123

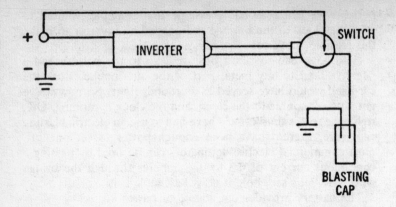

And that's it.

He could have assembled the entire package at home, taken it with him in a tool box, and wired it to the car in a very short time – making certain, of course, that all his wires were properly insulated, to guard against a stray current touching off a premature explosion. The only remaining question is how he managed to get access to the car, but happily that's not my problem.

Whistling brilliantly, Sam Grossman picked up the telephone and called Detective Meyer Meyer at the 87th.

The municipal garage was downtown on Dock Street, some seven blocks from City Hall. Meyer Meyer picked up Bert Kling at ten thirty. The drive down along the River Dix took perhaps twenty minutes. They parked on a meter across the street from the big concrete and tile structure, and Meyer automatically threw the visor sign, even though this was Sunday and parking regulations were not in force.

The foreman of the garage was a man named Spencer Coyle.

He was reading Dick Tracy and seemed less impressed by the two detectives in his midst than by the fictional exploits of his favourite comic strip sleuth. It was only with a great effort of will that he managed to tear himself away from the newspaper at all. He did not rise from his chair, though. The chair was tilted back against the tiled wall of the garage. The tiles, a vomitous shade of yellow, decorated too many government buildings all over the city, and it was Meyer's guess that a hefty hunk of graft had influenced some purchasing agent back in the thirties, either that or the poor bastard had been colour-blind. Spencer Coyle leaned back in his chair against the tiles, his face long and grey and grizzled, his long legs stretched out in front of him, the comic section still dangling from his right hand, as though he were reluctant to let go of it completely even though he had stopped lip-reading it. He was wearing the greenish-brown overalls of a Transportation Division employee, his peaked hat sitting on his head with all the rakish authority of a major in the Air Force. His attitude clearly told the detectives that he did not wish to be disturbed at *any* time, but especially on Sunday.

The detectives found him challenging.

"Mr Coyle," Meyer said, "I've just had a telephone call from the police laboratory to the effect that the bomb . . ."

"What bomb?" Coyle asked, and spat on the floor, narrowly missing Meyer's polished shoe.

"The bomb that was put in the deputy mayor's Cadillac," Kling said, and hoped Coyle would spit again, but Coyle didn't.

"Oh, *that* bomb," Coyle said, as if bombs were put in every one of the city's Cadillacs regularly, making it difficult to keep track of all the bombs around. "What *about* that bomb?"

"The lab says it was a pretty complicated bomb, but that it couldn't have taken too long to wire to the car's battery, provided it had been assembled beforehand. Now, what we'd like to know . . ."

"Yeah, I'll bet it was complicated," Coyle said. He did not look into the faces of the detectives, but instead seemed to direct his blue-eyed gaze at a spot somewhere across the garage. Kling turned to see what he was staring at, but the only thing he noticed was another yellow tile wall.

"Would you have any idea who installed that bomb, Mr Coyle?"

"*I* didn't," Coyle said flatly.

"Nobody suggested that you did," Meyer said.

"Just so we understand each other," Coyle said. "All I do is run this garage, make sure the cars are in working order, make sure they're ready to roll when ever somebody up there wants one, that's all I'm in charge of."

"How many cars do you have here?" Meyer asked.

"We got two dozen Caddys, twelve used on a regular basis, and the rest when ever we get visiting dignitaries. We also got fourteen buses and eight motorcycles. And there's also some vehicles that are kept here by the Department of Parks, but that's a courtesy because we got the space."

"Who services the cars?"

"Which ones?"

"The Caddys."

"Which one of the Caddys?" Coyle said, and spat again.

"Did you know, Mr Coyle," Kling said, "that spitting on the sidewalk is a misdemeanour?"

"This ain't a sidewalk, this is my garage," Coyle said.

"This is city property," Kling said, "the equivalent of a sidewalk. In fact, since the ramp comes in directly from the street outside there, it could almost be considered an extension of the sidewalk."

"Sure," Coyle said. "You going to arrest me for it, or what?"

"You going to keep giving us a hard time?" Kling asked.

"Who's giving you a hard time?"

"We'd like to be home reading the funnies too," Kling said, "instead of out busting our arses on a bombing. Now how about it?"

"None of our mechanics put a bomb in that car," Coyle said flatly.

"How do you know?"

"Because I know all the men who work for me, and none of them put a bomb in that car, that's how I know."

"Who was here yesterday?" Meyer asked.

"I was."

"You were here alone?"

"No, the men were here too."

"Which men?"

"The mechanics."

"How many mechanics?"

"Two."

"Is that how many you usually have on duty?"

"We usually have six, but yesterday was Saturday, and we were working with a skeleton crew."

"Anybody else here?"

"Yeah, some of the chauffeurs were either picking up cars or bringing them back, they're in and out all the time. Also, there was supposed to be an outdoor fishing thing up in Grover Park, so we had a lot of bus drivers in. They were supposed to pick up these slum kids and take them to the park where they were going to fish through the ice on the lake. It got called off."

"Why?"

"Too cold."

"When were the bus drivers here?"

"They reported early in the morning, and they hung around till we got word it was called off."

"You see any of them fooling around near that Cad?"

"Nope. Listen, you're barking up the wrong tree. All those cars got checked out yesterday, and they were in A-number-One shape. That bomb must've been put in there *after* the car left the garage."

"No, that's impossible, Mr Coyle."

"Well, it wasn't attached here."

"You're sure of that, are you?"

"I just told you the cars were inspected, didn't I?"

"Did you inspect them personally, Mr Coyle?"

"No, I got other things to do besides inspecting two dozen Caddys and fourteen buses and eight motorcycles."

"Then who *did* inspect them, Mr Coyle? One of your mechanics?"

"No, we had an inspector down from the Bureau of Motor Vehicles."

"And he said the cars were all right?"

"He went over them from top to bottom, every vehicle in the place. He gave us a clean bill of health."

"Did he look under the hoods?"

"Inside, outside, transmission, suspension, everything. He was here almost six hours."

"So he would have found a bomb if one was there, is that right?"

"That's right."

"Mr Coyle, did he give you anything in writing to the effect that the cars were inspected and found in good condition?"

"Why?" Coyle asked. "You trying to get off the hook?"

"No, we're . . ."

"You trying to pass the buck to Motor Vehicles?"

"We're trying to find out how he could have missed the bomb that was undoubtedly under the hood of the car, that's what we're trying to do."

"It *wasn't*, that's your answer."

"Mr Coyle, our lab reported . . ."

"I don't care what your lab reported or didn't report. I'm telling you all these cars were gone over with a fine-tooth comb yesterday, and there couldn't have been a bomb in the deputy mayor's car when it left this garage. Now that's *that*," Coyle said, and spat on the floor again, emphatically.

"Mr Coyle," Kling said, "did you personally see the deputy mayor's car being inspected?"

"I personally saw it being inspected."

"You personally saw the hood being raised?"

"I did."

"And you'd be willing to swear that a thorough inspection was made of the area under the hood?"

"What do you mean?"

"Did you actually *see* the inspector checking the area under the hood?"

"Well, I didn't stand around looking over his shoulder, if that's what you mean."

"Where were you, actually, when the deputy mayor's car was being inspected?"

"I was right here."

"On this exact spot?"

"No, I was inside the office there. But I could see out into the garage. There's a glass panel in there."

"And you saw the inspector lifting the hood of the deputy mayor's car?"

"That's right."

"There are two dozen Caddys here. How'd you know that one was the deputy mayor's car?"

"By the licence plate. It has DMA on it, and then the

number. Same as Mayor Vale's car has MA on it for 'mayor', and then the number. Same as the . . ."

"All right, it was clearly his car, and you definitely saw . . ."

"Look, that guy spent a good half-hour on each car, now don't tell *me* it wasn't a thorough inspection."

"Did he spend a half-hour on the deputy mayor's car?"

"Easily."

Meyer sighed. "I guess we'll have to talk to him personally," he said to Kling. He turned again to Coyle. "What was his name, Mr Coyle?"

"Who?"

"The inspector. The man from Motor Vehicles."

"I don't know."

"He didn't give his name?" Kling asked.

"He showed me his credentials, and he said he was here to inspect the cars, and that was that."

"What kind of credentials?"

"Oh, printed papers. You know."

"Mr Coyle," Kling asked, "when was the last time a man from Motor Vehicles came to inspect?"

"This was the first time," Coyle said.

"They've never sent an inspector down before?"

"Never."

Slowly, wearily, Meyer said, "What did this man look like, Mr Coyle?"

"He was a tall blond guy wearing a hearing aid," Coyle answered.

Fats Donner was a mountainous stool pigeon with a penchant for warm climates and the complexion of an Irish virgin. The complexion, in fact, over-reached the boundaries of common definition to extend to every part of Donner's body; he was white all over, so sickly pale that sometimes Willis suspected him of being a junkie. Willis couldn't have cared less. On any given Sunday, a conscientious cop could collar seventy-nine junkies in a half-hour, seventy-eight of whom would be holding narcotics in some quantity. It was hard to come by a good informer, though, and Donner was one of the best around, *when* he was around. The difficulty with Donner was that he was likely to be found in Vegas or Miami Beach or Puerto Rico during the winter months, lying in the shade with his Buddha-like form protected against even a possible reflection of the sun's rays, quivering with delight as the sweat poured from his body.

Willis was surprised to find him in the city during the coldest March on record. He was not surprised to find him in a room that was suffocatingly hot, with three electric heaters adding their output to the two banging radiators. In the midst of this thermal onslaught, Donner sat in overcoat and gloves wedged into a stuffed armchair. He was wearing two pairs of woollen socks, and his feet were propped up on the radiator. There was a girl in the room with him. She was perhaps fifteen years old, and she was wearing a flowered bra and bikini panties over which she had put on a silk wrapper. The wrapper was unbelted. The girl's near-naked body showed when ever she moved, but she seemed not to mind the presence of a strange man. She barely glanced at Willis when he came in, and then went about the room straightening up, never looking at either of the men as they whispered together near the window streaming wintry sunlight.

"Who's the girl?" Willis asked.

"My daughter," Donner said, and grinned.

He was not a nice man, Fats Donner, but he was a good stoolie, and criminal detection sometimes made strange bed-fellows. It was Willis' guess that the girl was hooking for Donner, a respectable stoolie sometimes being in need of additional income which he can realize, for example, by picking up a little girl straight from Ohio and teaching her what it's all about and then putting her on the street, there are more things in heaven and earth, Horatio. Willis was not interested in Donner's possible drug habit, nor was Willis interested in hanging a prostitution rap on the girl, nor in busting Donner as a "male person living on the proceeds of prostitution", Section 1148 of the Penal Law. Willis was interested in taking off his coat and hat and finding out whether or not Donner could give him a line on a man named Dom.

"Dom who?" Donner asked.

"That's all we've got."

"How many Doms you suppose are in this city?" Donner

asked. He turned to the girl, who was puttering around rearranging food in the refrigerator, and said, "Mercy, how many Doms you suppose are in this city?"

"I don't know," Mercy replied without looking at him,

"How many Doms you know personally?" Donner asked her.

"I don't know any Doms," the girl said. She had a tiny voice, tinged with an unmistakable Southern accent. Scratch Ohio, Willis thought, substitute Arkansas or Tennessee.

"She don't know any Doms," Donner said, and chuckled.

"How about you, Fats? You know any?"

"That's all you're giving me?" Donner asked. "Man, you're really generous."

"He lost a lot of money on the championship fight two weeks ago."

"Everybody I *know* lost a lot of money on the championship fight two weeks ago."

"He's broke right now. He's trying to promote some scratch," Willis said.

"Dom, huh?"

"Yeah."

"From this part of the city?"

"A friend of his lives in Riverhead," Willis said.

"What's the friend's name?"

"La Bresca. Tony La Bresca."

"What about *him*?"

"No record."

"You think this Dom done time?"

"I've got no idea. He seems to have tipped to a caper that's coming off."

"Is that what you're interested in? The caper?"

"Yes. According to him, the buzz is all over town."

"There's always some buzz or other that's all over town," Donner said. "What the hell are you doing there, Mercy?"

"Just fixing things," Mercy said.

"Get the hell away from there, you make me nervous.'

"I was just fixing things in the fridge," Mercy said.

"I hate that Southern accent," Donner said. "Don't you hate Southern accents?" he asked Willis.

"I don't mind them," Willis said.

"Can't even understand her half the time. Sounds as if she's got marbles in her mouth."

The girl closed the refrigerator door and went to the closet. She opened the door and began moving around empty hangers.

"*Now* what're you doing?" Donner asked.

"Just straightening things," she said.

"You want me to kick you out in the street bare-arsed?" Donner asked.

"No," she said softly.

"Then cut it out."

"All right."

"Anyway, it's time you got dressed."

"All right."

"Go on, go get dressed. What time is it?" he asked Willis.

"Almost noon," Willis said.

"Sure, go get dressed," Donner said.

"All right," the girl said, and went into the other room.

"Damn little bitch," Donner said, "hardly worth keeping around."

"I thought she was your daughter," Willis said.

"Oh, is that what you thought?" Donner asked, and again he grinned.

Willis restrained a sudden impulse. He sighed and said, "So what do you think?"

"I don't think nothing yet, man. Zero so far."

"Well, you want some time on it?"

"How much of a sweat are you in?"

"We need whatever we can get as soon as we can get it."

"What's the caper sound like?"

"Maybe extortion."

"Dom, huh?"

"Dom," Willis repeated.

"That'd be for Dominick, right?"

"Yes."

"Well, let me listen around, who knows?"

The girl came out of the other room. She was wearing a mini-skirt and white mesh stockings, a low-cut purple blouse. There was a smear of bright red lipstick on her mouth, green eyeshadow on her eyelids.

"You going down now?" Donner asked.

"Yes," she answered.

"Put on your coat."

"All right," she said.

"And take your bag."

"I will."

"Don't come back empty, baby," Donner said.

"I won't," she said, and moved towards the door.

"I'm going too," Willis said.

"I'll give you a buzz."

"OK, but try to move fast, will you?" Willis said.

"It's I hate to go out when it's so fucking cold," Donner answered.

The girl was on the hallway steps, below Willis, walking down without any sense of haste, buttoning her coat, slinging her bag over her shoulder. Willis caught up with her and said, "Where are you from, Mercy?"

"Ask Fats," she answered.

"I'm asking *you*."

"You fuzz?"

"That's right."

"Georgia," she said.

"When'd you get up here?"

"Two months ago."

"How old are you?"

"Sixteen."

"What the hell are you doing with a man like Fats Donner?" Willis asked.

"I don't know," she said. She would not look into his face. She kept her head bent as they went down the steps to the street. As Willis opened the door leading outside, a blast of frigid air rushed into the hallway.

"Why don't you get out?" he said.

The girl looked up at him.

"Where would I go?" she asked, and then left him on the stoop, walking up the street with a practised swing, the bag dangling from her shoulder, her high heels clicking along the pavement.

At two o'clock that afternoon, the seventeen-year-old girl who

133

had been in the convertible that crashed the river barrier died without gaining consciousness.

The Buena Vista Hospital record read simply: Death secondary to head injury.

9

The squadroom phone began jangling early Monday morning.

The first call was from a reporter on the city's austere morning daily. He asked to speak to whoever was in charge of the squad and, when told that Lieutenant Byrnes was not in at the moment, asked to speak to whoever was in command.

"This is Detective 2nd/Grade Meyer Meyer," he was told. "I suppose I'm in command at the moment."

"Detective Meyer," the reporter said, "this is Carlyle Butterford, I wanted to check out a possible story."

At first, Meyer thought the call was a put-on, nobody had a name like Carlyle Butterford. Then he remembered that *everybody* on this particular morning newspaper had names like Preston Fingerlaver, or Clyde Masterfield, or Aylmer Coopermere. "Yes, Mr Butterford," he said, "what can I do for you?"

"We received a telephone call early this morning . . ."

"From whom, sir?"

"An anonymous caller," Butterford said.

"Yes?"

"Yes, and he suggested that we contact the 87th Precinct regarding certain extortion calls and notes that were received before the deaths of Parks Commissioner Cowper and Deputy Mayor Scanlon."

There was a long silence on the line.

"Detective Meyer, is there any truth in this allegation?"

"I suggest that you call the Public Relations Officer of the

Police Department," Meyer said, "his name is Detective Glenn, and he's downtown at Headquarters. The number is Centre 6–0800."

"Would he have any knowledge of these alleged extortion calls and notes?" Butterford asked.

"I guess you'd have to ask him," Meyer said.

"Do *you* have any knowledge of these alleged . . . ?"

"As I told you," Meyer said, "the lieutenant is out at the moment, and he's the only one who generally supplies information to the press."

"But would *you*, personally, have any information . . . ?"

"I have information on a great many things," Meyer said. "Homicides, muggings, burglaries, robberies, rapes, extortion attempts, all sorts of things. But, as I'm sure you know, detectives are public servants and it has been the department's policy to discourage us from seeking personal aggrandizement. If you wish to talk to the lieutenant, I suggest you call back around ten o'clock. He should be in by then."

"Come on," Butterford said, "give me a break."

"I'm sorry, pal, I can't help you."

"I'm a working stiff, just like you."

"So's the lieutenant," Meyer said, and hung up.

The second call came at nine thirty. Sergeant Murchison, at the switchboard, took the call and immediately put it through to Meyer.

"This is Cliff Savage," the voice said. "Remember me?"

"Only too well," Meyer said. "What do you want, Savage?"

"Carella around?"

"Nope."

"Where is he?"

"Out," Meyer said.

"I wanted to talk to him."

"He doesn't want to talk to you," Meyer said. "You almost got his wife killed once with your goddamn yellow journalism. You want my advice, keep out of his sight."

"I guess I'll have to talk to you, then," Savage said.

"I'm not too fond of you myself, if you want the truth."

"Well, thank you," Savage said, "but that's not the truth I'm after."

"What *are* you after?"

"I got a phone call this morning from a man who refused to identify himself. He gave me a very interesting piece of information." Savage paused. "Know anything about it?"

Meyer's heart was pounding, but he very calmly said, "I'm not a mind reader, Savage."

"I thought you might know something about it."

"Savage, I've given you the courtesy of five minutes of valuable time already. Now if you've got something to say . . ."

"OK, OK. The man I spoke to said the 87th Precinct had received several threatening telephone calls preceding the death of Parks Commissioner Cowper, and three extortion notes preceding the death of Deputy Mayor Scanlon. Know anything about it?"

"Telephone company'd probably be able to help you on any phone calls you want to check, and I guess the Documents Section of the Public Library . . ."

"Come on, Meyer, don't stall me."

"We're not permitted to give information to reporters," Meyer said. "You know that."

"How much?" Savage asked.

"Huh?"

"How much do you want, Meyer?"

"How much can you afford?" Meyer asked.

"How does a hundred bucks sound?"

"Not so good."

"How about two hundred?"

"I get more than that just for protecting our friendly neighbourhood pusher."

"Three hundred is my top offer," Savage said.

"Would you mind repeating the offer for the benefit of the tape recorder?" Meyer said. "I want to have evidence when I charge you with attempting to bribe a police officer."

"I was merely offering you a loan," Savage said.

"Neither a borrower nor a lender be," Meyer said, and hung up.

This was not good. This was, in fact, bad. He was about to dial the lieutenant's home number, hoping to catch him before he left for the office, when the telephone on his desk rang again.

"87th Squad," he said, "Detective Meyer."

The caller was from one of the two afternoon papers. He repeated essentially what Meyer had already heard from his two previous callers, and then asked if Meyer knew anything about it. Meyer, loath to lie lest the story eventually broke and tangentially mentioned that there had been a police credibility gap, suggested that the man try the lieutenant later on in the day. When he hung up, he looked at the clock and decided to wait for the next call before trying to contact the lieutenant. Fortunately, there were now only four daily newspapers in the city, the leaders of the various newspaper guilds and unions having decided that the best way to ensure higher wages and lifetime employment was to make demands that would kill off the newspapers one by one, leaving behind only scattered goose feathers and broken golden egg shells. Meyer did not have to wait long. The representative of the fourth newspaper called within five minutes. He had a bright chirpy voice and an ingratiating style. He got nothing from Meyer, and he finally hung up in cheerful rage.

It was now five minutes to ten, too late to catch Byrnes at home.

While he waited for the lieutenant to arrive, Meyer doodled a picture of a man in a fedora shooting a Colt .45 automatic. The man looked very much like Meyer, except that he possessed a full head of hair. Meyer had once possessed a full head of hair. He tried to remember when. It was probably when he was ten years old. He was smiling painfully over his own joke when Byrnes came into the squadroom. The lieutenant looked dyspeptic this morning. Meyer surmised that he missed the painters. Everyone on the squad missed the painters. They had added humanity to the joint, and richness, a spirit of gregarious joy, a certain *je ne sais quoi*.

"We got trouble," Meyer said, but before he could relate the trouble to the lieutenant, the phone rang again. Meyer lifted the receiver, identified himself, and then looked at Byrnes.

"It's the Chief of Detectives," he said, and Byrnes sighed and went into his office to take the call privately.

Thirty-three telephone calls were exchanged that morning as

police and city government officials kept the wires hot between their own offices and Lieutenant Byrnes', trying to decide what to do about this latest revolting development. The one thing they did not need on this case was publicity that would make them all appear foolish. And yet, if there really *had* been a leak about the extortion attempts, it seemed likely that the full story might come to light at any moment, in which case it might be best to level with the papers *before* they broke the news. At the same time, the anonymous caller might only have been speculating, without any real evidence to back up his claim of extortion, in which case a premature release to the newspapers would only serve to breach a danger that was not truly threatening. What to do, oh, what to do?

The telephones rang, and the possibilities multiplied. Heads swam and tempers flared. The mayor, James Martin Vale himself, postponed a walking trip from City Hall to Grover Park and personally called Lieutenant Byrnes to ask his opinion on the 'peril of the situation'. Lieutenant Byrnes passed the buck to the Chief of Detectives, who in turn passed it back to Captain Frick of the 87th, who referred JMV's secretary to the police commissioner, who for reasons unknown said he must first consult with the traffic commissioner, who in turn referred the police commissioner to the Bridge Authority who somehow got on to the city comptroller, who in turn called JMV himself to ask what this was all about.

At the end of two hours of dodging and wrangling, it was decided to take the bull by the horns and release transcripts of the telephone conversations, as well as photocopies of the three notes, to all four city newspapers. The city's liberal blue-headline newspaper (which was that week running an exposé on the growth of the numbers racket as evidenced by the prevalence of nickel and dime betters in kindergarten classes) was the first paper to break the story, running photos of the three notes side by side on its front page. The city's other afternoon newspaper, recently renamed the *Pierce-Arrow-Universal-International-Bugle-Chronicle-Clarion* or something, was next to feature the notes on its front page together with transcripts of the calls in 24-point Cheltenham Bold.

That night, the early editions of the two morning newspapers

139

carried the story as well. This meant that a combined total of four million readers now knew all about the extortion threats.

The next move was anybody's.

Anthony La Bresca and his pool hall buddy, Peter Vincent Calucci (alias Calooch, Cooch, or Kook) met in a burlesque house on a side street off The Stem at seven o'clock that Monday night.

La Bresca had been tailed from his place of employment, a demolition site in the city's downtown financial district, by three detectives using the ABC method of surveillance. Mindful of the earlier unsuccessful attempts to keep track of him, nobody was taking chances any more – the ABC method was surefire and foolproof.

Detective Bob O'Brien was 'A', following La Bresca while Detective Andy Parker, who was 'B', walked behind O'Brien and kept him constantly in view. Detective Carl Kapek was 'C', and he moved parallel with La Bresca, on the opposite side of the street. This meant that if La Bresca suddenly went into a coffee shop or ducked around the corner, Kapek could instantly swap places with O'Brien, taking the lead 'A' position while O'Brien caught up, crossed the street, and manoeuvred into the 'C' position. It also meant that the men could use camouflaging tactics at their own discretion, changing positions so that the combination became BCA or CBA or CAB or whatever they chose, a scheme that guaranteed La Bresca would not recognize any one man following him over an extended period of time.

Wherever he went, La Bresca was effectively contained. Even in parts of the city where the crowds were unusually thick, there was no danger of losing him. Kapek would merely cross over on to La Bresca's side of the street and begin walking some fifteen feet *ahead* of him, so that the pattern read C, La Bresca, A, and B. In police jargon, they were 'sticking like a dirty shirt', and they did their job well and unobtrusively, despite the cold weather and despite the fact that La Bresca seemed to be a serendipitous type who led them on a jolly excursion halfway across the city, apparently trying to kill time before his seven-o'clock meeting with Calucci.

The two men took seats in the tenth row of the theatre. The show was in progress, two baggy-pants comics relating a traffic accident one of them had had with a car driven by a voluptuous blonde.

"You mean she crashed right into your tail pipe?" one of the comics asked.

"Hit me with her headlights," the second one said.

"Hit your tail pipe with her headlights?" the first one asked.

"Almost broke it off for me," the second one said.

Kapek, taking a seat across the aisle from Calucci and La Bresca, was suddenly reminded of the squadroom painters and realized how sorely he missed their presence. O'Brien had moved into the row behind the pair, and was sitting directly back of them now. Andy Parker was in the same row, two seats to the left of Calucci.

"Any trouble getting here?" Calucci whispered.

"No," La Bresca whispered back.

"What's with Dom?"

"He wants in."

"I thought he just wanted a couple of bills."

"That was last week."

"What's he want now?"

"A three-way split."

"Tell him to go screw," Calucci said.

"No. He's hip to the whole thing."

"How'd he find out?"

"I don't know. But he's hip, that's for sure."

There was a blast from the trumpet section of the four-piece band in the pit. The overhead leikos came up purple, and a brilliant follow spot hit the curtain stage left. The reed section followed the heraldic trumpet with a saxophone obbligato designed to evoke memory or desire or both. A gloved hand snaked its way around the curtain. "And now," a voice said over the loudspeaker system while one half of the rhythm section started a snare drum roll, "and *now*, for the first time in America, direct from Brest, which is where the little lady comes from . . . exhibiting her titillating terpsichoreal skills for your pleasure, we are happy to present Miss . . . Freida Panzer!"

A leg appeared from behind the curtain.

It floated disembodied on the air. A black high-heeled pump pointed, wiggled, a calf muscle tightened, the knee bent, and then the toe pointed again. There was more of the leg visible now, the black nylon stocking shimmered in the glow of the lights, ribbed at the top where a vulnerable white thigh lay exposed, black garter biting into the flesh, fetishists all over the theatre thrilled to the sight, not to mention a few detectives who weren't fetishists at all. Frieda Panzer undulated on to the stage bathed in the glow of the overhead purple leikos, wearing a long purple gown slit up each leg to the waist, the black stockings and taut black garters revealed each time she took another long-legged step across the stage.

"Look at them legs," Calucci whispered.

"Yeah," La Bresca said.

O'Brien sitting behind them, looking at the legs. They were extraordinary legs.

"I hate to cut anybody else in on this," Calucci whispered.

"Me neither," La Bresca said, "but what else can we do? He'll run screaming to the cops if we don't play ball."

"Is that what he said?"

"Not in so many words. He just hinted."

"Yeah, the son of a bitch."

"So what do you think?" La Bresca asked.

"Man, there's big money involved here," Calucci said.

"You think I don't know?"

"Why cut him in after we done all the planning?"

"What else can we do?"

"We can wash him," Calucci whispered.

The girl was taking off her clothes.

The four-piece ensemble in the orchestra pit rose to heights of musical expression, a heavy bass drum beat accentuating each solid bump as purple clothing fell like aster petals, a triple-tongued trumpet winding up with each pelvic grind, a saxophone wail climbing the girl's flanks in accompaniment with her sliding hands, a steady piano beat banging out the rhythm of each long-legged stride, each tassel-twirling, fixed-grin, sexy-eyed, contrived and calculated erotic move. "She's got some tits," Calucci whispered, and La Bresca whispered back, "Yeah."

The men fell silent.

The music rose in earsplitting crescendo. The bass drum beat was more insistent now, the trumpet shrieked higher and higher, a C above high C reached for and missed, the saxophone trilled impatiently, the piano pounded in the upper register, a tinny insistent honky-tonk rhythm, cymbals clashed, the trumpet reached for the screech note again, and again missed. The lights were swirling now, the stage was inundated in colour and sound. There was the stink of perspiration and lust in that theatre as the girl ground out her coded message in a cipher broken long ago on too many similar stages, pounded out her promises of ecstasy and sin, Come and get it, baby, Come and get it, Come and come and come and come.

The stage went black.

In the darkness, Calucci whispered. "What do you think?"

One of the baggy-pants comics came on again to do a bit in a doctor's office accompanied by a pert little blonde with enormous breasts who explained that she thought she was stagnant because she hadn't fenestrated in two months.

"I hate the idea of knocking somebody off," La Bresca whispered.

"If it's necessary, it's necessary."

"Still."

"There's lots of money involved here, don't forget it."

"Yeah, but at the same time, there's enough to split three ways, ain't there?" La Bresca said.

"Why should we split it three ways when we can split it down the middle?"

"Because Dom'll spill the whole works if we don't cut him in. Look, what's the sense going over this a hundred times? We *got* to cut him in."

"I want to think about it."

"You ain't got that much time to think about it. We're set for the fifteenth. Dom wants to know right away."

"OK, so tell him he's in. Then we'll decide whether he's in or out. And I mean *really* out, the little son of a bitch."

"And now, ladies and gentlemen," the loudspeaker voice said, "it gives us great pleasure to present the rage of San Francisco, a young lady who thrilled the residents of that city by the Golden Gate, a young lady whose exotic dancing caused the pious officials of Hong Kong to see Red . . . it is with

bursting pride that we turn our stage over to Miss . . .
Anna . . . May . . . Zong!"

The house lights dimmed. The band struck up a sinuous
version of *Limehouse Blues*. A swish cymbal echoed on the
air, and a sloe-eyed girl wearing mandarin garb came into the
spotlight with mincing steps, hands together in an attitude of
prayer, head bent.

"I dig these Chinks," Calucci said.

"You guys want to stop talking?" a bald-headed man in the
row ahead said. "I can't see the girls with all that gabbing
behind me."

"Fuck off, Baldy," La Bresca said.

But both men fell silent. O'Brien leaned forward in his seat.
Parker bent sideways over the armrest. There was nothing
further to hear. Kapek, across the aisle, could not have heard
anything anyway, so he merely watched the Chinese girl as she
took off her clothes.

At the end of the act, La Bresca and Calucci rose quietly
from their seats and went out of the theatre. They split up
outside. Parker followed Calucci to his house, and Kapek followed La Bresca to his. O'Brien went back to the squadroom
to type up a report.

The detectives did not get together again until eleven o'clock
that night, by which time La Bresca and Calucci were both
hopefully asleep. They met in a diner some five blocks from
the squadroom. Over coffee and crullers, they all agreed that
the only thing they'd learned from the eavesdropping was the
date of the job La Bresca and Calucci were planning: March
the fifteenth. They also agreed that Freida Panzer had much
larger breasts than Anna May Zong.

In the living-room of a luxurious apartment on Harbourside
Oval, overlooking the river, a good three miles from where
Detectives O'Brien, Parker, and Kapek were speculating on
the comparative dimensions of the two strippers, the deaf man
sat on a sofa facing sliding glass doors, and happily sipped at
a glass of scotch and soda. The drapes were open, and the view
of warm and glowing lights strung on the bridge's cables, the
distant muted reds and ambers blinking on the distant shore

gave the night a deceptively springtime appearance; the thermometer on the terrace outside read ten degrees above zero.

Two bottles of expensive scotch, one already dead, were on the coffee table before the sofa upholstered in rich black leather. On the wall opposite the sofa, there hung an original Rouault, only a gouache to be sure, but none the less quite valuable. A grand piano turned its wide curve into the room, and a petite brunette, wearing a miniskirt and a white crocheted blouse, sat at the piano playing *Heart and Soul* over and over again.

The girl was perhaps twenty-three years old, with a nose that had been recently bobbed, large brown eyes, long black hair that fell to a point halfway between her waist and her shoulder-blades. She was wearing false eyelashes. They fluttered whenever she hit a sour note, which was often. The deaf man seemed not to mind the discord that rose from the piano. Perhaps he really *was* deaf, or perhaps he had consumed enough scotch to have dimmed his perception. The two other men in the room didn't mind the cacophony either. One of them even tried singing along with the girl's treacherous rendition – until she hit another sour note and began again from the top.

"I can't seem to get it," she said, pouting.

"You'll get it, honey," the deaf man said. "Just keep at it."

One of the men was short and slender, with the dust-coloured complexion of an Indian. He wore narrow black tapered trousers and a white shirt over which was an open black vest. He was sitting at a drop-leaf desk, typing. The other man was tall and burly, with blue eyes, red hair, and a red moustache. There were freckles spattered over his cheeks and his forehead, and his voice, as he began singing along with the girl again, was deep and resonant. He was wearing tight jeans and a blue turtleneck sweater.

As the girl continued to play *Heart and Soul*, a feeling of lassitude spread through the deaf man. Sitting on the couch, watching the second phase of his scheme as it became a reality, he mused again on the beauty of the plan, and then glanced at the girl, and then smiled when she hit the same sour note (an E flat where it should have been a natural E) and then looked again to where Ahmad was typing.

145

"The beauty of this phase," he said aloud, "is that none of them will believe us."

"They will believe," Ahmad offered, and smiled thinly.

"Yes, but not at this phase."

"No, only later," Ahmad said, and sipped at his scotch, and glanced at the girl's thighs, and went back to his typing.

"How much is this mailing going to cost us?" the other man asked.

"Well, Buck," the deaf man said, "we're sending out a hundred pieces of first-class mail at five cents postage per envelope, so that comes to a grand total of five dollars – if my arithmetic is correct."

"Your arithmetic is *always* correct," Ahmad said, and smiled.

"*This* is the damn part I can't get," the girl said, and struck the same note over and over again, as though trying to pound it into her memory.

"Keep at it, Rochelle," the deaf man said. "You'll get it."

Buck lifted his glass, discovered it was empty, and went to the coffee table to refill it, moving with the economy of an athlete, back ramrod stiff, hands dangling loosely at his sides, as though he were going back for the huddle after having executed a successful line plunge.

"Here, let me help you," the deaf man said.

"Not too heavy," Buck said.

The deaf man poured a liberal shot into Buck's extended glass. "Drink," he said. "You deserve it."

"Well, I don't want to get crocked."

"Why not? You're among friends," the deaf man said, and smiled.

He was feeling particularly appreciative of Buck's talent tonight, because without it this phase of the scheme would never have become a reality. Oh yes, a primitive bomb *could* have been assembled and hastily wired to the ignition switch, but such sloppiness, such dependency on chance, had never appealed to the deaf man. The seriousness with which Buck had approached the problem had been truly heart-warming. His development of a compact package (the inverter had weighed a mere twenty-two pounds and measured only ten by ten by five) that could be easily transported and wired in a relatively short period of time, his specific demand for an inverter with a regulated sine-wave output (costing a bit more, yes, $64.95, but a negligible output in terms of the hoped-for financial realization), his insistence on a briefing session to explain the proper handling of the dynamite and the electric blasting cap, all were admirable, admirable. He was a good man, Buck, a demolition expert who had worked on countless legitimate blasting jobs, a background essential to the deaf man's plan; in this state, you were not allowed to buy explosives without a permit and insurance, both of which Buck possessed. The deaf man was very pleased indeed to have him in his employ.

Ahmad, too, was indispensible. He had been working as a draughtsman at Metropolitan Power & Light, earning $150 a week in the Bureau of Maps and Records, when the deaf man first contacted him. He had readily appreciated the huge rewards to be reaped from the scheme, and had enthusiastically supplied all of the information so necessary to its final phase. In addition, he was a meticulous little man who had insisted that all of these letters be typed on high-quality bond paper, with each of the hundred men receiving an original rather than a carbon or photocopy, a touch designed to allay any suspicion that the letter was a practical joke. The deaf man knew that the difference between success and failure very often depended on such small details, and he smiled at Ahmad in appreciation now, and sipped a little more of his scotch, and said, "How many have you typed so far?"

"Fifty-two."

"We'll be toiling long into the night, I'm afraid."

"When are we going to mail these?"

"I had hoped by Wednesday."

"I will finish them long before then," Ahmad promised.

"Will you really be working here all night?" Rochelle asked, pouting again.

"You can go to bed if you like, dear," the deaf man said.

"What good's bed without you?" Rochelle said, and Buck and Ahmad exchanged glances.

"Go on, I'll join you later."

"I'm not sleepy."

"Then have a drink, and play us another song."

"I don't know any other songs."

"Read a book then," the deaf man suggested.

Rochelle looked at him blankly.

"Or go into the den and watch some television."

"There's nothing on but old movies."

"Some of those old films are very instructive," the deaf man said.

"Some of them are very crappy, too," Rochelle replied.

The deaf man smiled. "Do you feel like licking a hundred envelopes?" he asked.

"No, I don't feel like licking envelopes," she answered.

"I didn't think so," the deaf man said.

"So what should I do?" Rochelle asked.

"Go get into your nightgown, darling," the deaf man said.

"Mmm?" she said, and looked at him archly.

"Mmm," he replied.

"OK," she said, and rose from the piano stool. "Well, good-night, fellas," she said.

"Goodnight," Buck said.

"Goodnight, miss," Ahmad said.

Rochelle looked at the deaf man again, and then went into the other room.

"Empty-headed little bitch," he said.

"I think she's dangerous to have around," Buck said.

"On the contrary," the deaf man said, "she soothes the nerves and eases the daily pressures. Besides, she thinks we're respectable businessmen promoting some sort of harebrained scheme. She hasn't the vaguest notion of what we're up to."

"Sometimes *I* don't have the vaguest notion either," Buck said, and pulled a face.

"It's really very simple," the deaf man said. "We're making a direct-mail appeal, a tried-and-true method of solicitation pioneered by businessmen all over this bountiful nation. *Our* mailing, of course, is a limited one. We're only sending out a hundred letters. But it's my hope that we'll get a highly favourable response."

"And what if we don't?"

"Well, Buck, let's assume the worst. Let's assume we get a one-per-cent return, which is the generally expected return on a direct-mail piece. Our entire outlay thus far has been $86.95 for a lever-action carbine; $3.75 for a box of cartridges; $64.95

for your inverter; $7.00 for the electric clock; $9.60 for a dozen sticks of dynamite at eighty cents a stick; sixty cents for the blasting cap; $10.00 for the stationery; and $5.00 for the postage. If my addition is correct . . ." (He paused here to smile at Ahmad.) ". . . that comes to $187.85. Our future expenses – for the volt-ohm meter, the pressure-sensitive letters, the uniform, and so on – should be negligible. Now, if we get only one-per cent return on our mailing, if only *one* person out of the hundred comes through, we'll *still* be reaping a large profit on our initial investment."

"Five thousand dollars seems like pretty small change for two murders," Buck said.

"*Three* murders," the deaf man corrected.

"Even better," Buck said, and pulled a face.

"I assure you I'm expecting much more than a one-per-cent return. On Friday, we execute – if you'll pardon the pun – the final phase of our plan. By Saturday morning, there'll be no disbelievers."

"How many of them do you think'll come through?"

"Most of them. If not all of them."

"And what about the fuzz?"

"What about them? They *still* don't know who we are, and they'll never find out."

"I hope you're right."

"I *know* I'm right."

"I worry about fuzz," Buck said. "I can't help it. I've been conditioned to worry about them."

"There's nothing to worry about. Don't you realize *why* they're called fuzz?"

"No. Why?"

"Because they're fuzzy and fussy and antiquated and incompetent. Their investigatory technique is established and routine, designed for effectiveness in an age that no longer exists. The police in this city are like wind-up toys with keys sticking out of their backs, capable of performing only in terms of their own limited design, tiny mechanical men clattering along the sidewalk stiff-legged, scurrying about in aimless circles. But put an obstacle in their path, a brick wall or an orange crate, and they unwind helplessly in the same spot, arms and legs thrashing but taking them nowhere." The deaf man grinned, "I, my friend, am the brick wall."

"Or the orange crate," Buck said.

"No," Ahmad said intensely. "He is the brick wall."

10

The first break in the case came at ten o'clock the next morning, when Fats Donner called the squadroom.

Until that time, there were still perhaps two thousand imponderables to whatever La Bresca and Calucci were planning. But aside from such minor considerations as *where* the job would take place, or at exactly what *time* on March fifteenth, there were several unknown identities to contend with as well, such as Dom (who so far had no last name) and the long-haired blonde girl who had given La Bresca a lift last Friday night. It was the police supposition that if either of these two people could be located, the nature of the impending job might be wrung from one or the other of them. Whether or not the job was in any way connected with the recent murders would then become a matter for further speculation, as would the possibility that La Bresca was in some way involved with the deaf man. There were a lot of questions to be asked if only they could find somebody to ask them to.

Donner was put through immediately.

"I think I got your Dom," he said to Willis.

"Good," Willis said. "What's his last name?"

"Di Fillippi. Dominick Di Fillippi. Lives in Riverhead near the old Coliseum, you know the neighbourhood?"

"Yeah. What've you got on him?"

"He's with The Coaxial Cable."

"Yeah?" Willis said.

"Yeah."

"Well what's that?" Willis said.

"What's *what*?"

"What's it supposed to *mean*?"

"What's *what* supposed to mean?"

"What you just said. Is it some kind of code or something?"

"Is what some kind of code?" Donner asked.

"The coaxial cable."

"No, it's a group."

"A group of *what*?"

"A group. Musicians," Donner said.

"A band, you mean?"

"That's right, only today they call them groups."

"Well, what's the coaxial cable got to do with it?"

"That's the name of the group. The Coaxial Cable."

"You're putting me on," Willis said.

"No, that's the name, I mean it."

"What does Di Fillippi play?"

"Rhythm guitar."

"Where do I find him?"

"His address is 365 North Anderson."

"That's in Riverhead?"

"Yeah."

"How do you know he's our man?"

"Well, it seems he's a big bullshit artist, you know?" Donner said. "He's been going around the past few weeks saying he dropped a huge bundle on the championship fight, made it sound like two, three Gs. It turns out all he lost was fifty bucks, that's some big bundle, huh?"

"Yeah, go ahead."

"But he's also been saying recently that he knows about a big caper coming off."

"Who'd he say this to?"

"Well, one of the guys in the group is a big hophead from back even before it got stylish. That's how I got my lead on to Di Fillippi. And the guy said they were busting some joints together maybe three, four days ago, and Di Fillippi came on about this big caper he knew about."

"Did he say what the caper was?"

"No."

"And they were smoking pot?"

"Yeah, busting a few joints, you know, social."

"Maybe Di Fillippi was out of his skull."

"He probably was. What's that got to do with it?"

"He might have dreamt up the whole thing."

"I don't think so."

"Did he mention La Bresca at all?"

"Nope."

"Did he say when the job would be coming off?"

"Nope."

"Well, it's not much, Fats."

"It's worth half a century, don't you think?"

"It's worth ten bucks," Willis said.

"Hey, come on, man, I had to do some real hustling to get this for you."

"Which reminds me," Willis said.

"Huh?"

"Get rid of your playmate."

"Huh?"

"The girl. Next time I see you, I want her out of there."

"Why?"

"Because I thought it over, and I don't like the idea."

"I kicked her out twice already," Donner said. "She always comes back."

"Then maybe you ought to use this ten bucks to buy her a ticket back to Georgia."

"Sure. Maybe I ought to contribute another ten besides to the Salvation Army," Donner said.

"Just get her out of there," Willis said.

"When'd you get so righteous?" Donner asked.

"Just this minute."

"I thought you were a businessman."

"I am. Here's my deal. Let the girl go, and I forget whatever else I know about you, and whatever I might learn in the future."

"Nobody learns nothing about me," Donner said. "I'm The Shadow."

"No," Willis said. "Only Lamont Cranston is The Shadow."

"You serious about this?"

"I want the girl out of there. If she's still around next time I see you, I throw the book."

"And lose a valuable man."

"Maybe," Willis said. "In which case, we'll have to manage without you somehow."

"Sometimes I wonder why I bother helping you guys at all," Donner said.

"I'll *tell* you why sometime, if you have a minute," Willis said.

"Never mind."

"Will you get the girl out of there?"

"Yeah, yeah. You're going to send me fifty, right?"

"I said ten."

"Make it twenty."

"For the birdseed you just gave me?"

"It's a lead, ain't it?"

"That's all it is."

"So? A lead is worth at least twenty-five."

"I'll send you fifteen." Willis said, and hung up.

The phone rang again almost the instant he replaced it on the cradle. He lifted the receiver and said, "87th, Willis speaking."

"Hal, this is Artie over at the school."

"Yep."

"I've been waiting for Murchison to put me through. I think I've got something."

"Shoot."

"La Bresca talked to his mother on the phone about five minutes ago."

"In English or Italian?"

"English. He told her he was expecting a call from Dom Di Fillippi. That could be our man, no?"

"Yeah, it looks like he is," Willis said.

"He told his mother to say he'd meet Di Fillippi in his lunch hour at the corner of Cathedral and Seventh."

"Has Di Fillippi called yet?"

"Not yet. This was just five minutes ago, Hal."

"Right. What time did he say they'd meet?"

"Twelve thirty."

"Twelve thirty, corner of Cathedral and Seventh."

"Right," Brown said.

"We'll have somebody there."

"I'll call you back," Brown said. "I've got another customer."

In five minutes, Brown rang the squadroom again. "That was Di Fillippi," he said. "Mrs La Bresca gave him the message. Looks like pay dirt at last, huh?"

"Maybe," Willis said.

From where Meyer and Kling sat in the Chrysler sedan parked on Cathedral Street, they could clearly see Tony La Bresca waiting on the corner near the bus stop sign. The clock on top of the Catholic church dominating the intersection read twelve twenty. La Bresca was early and apparently impatient. He paced the pavement anxiously, lighting three cigarettes in succession, looking up at the church clock every few minutes, checking the time against his own wrist watch.

"This has got to be it," Kling said.

"The payoff of the burley joint summit meeting," Meyer said.

"Right. La Bresca's going to tell old Dom he's in for a three-way split. Then Calooch'll decide whether or not they're going to dump him in the river."

"Six-to-five old Dom gets the cement block."

"I'm not a gambling man," Kling said.

The church clock began tolling the half-hour. The chimes rang out over the intersection. Some of the lunch-hour pedestrians glanced up at the bell tower. Most of them hurried past with their heads ducked against the cold.

"Old Dom seems to be late," Meyer said.

"Look at old Tony," Kling said. "He's about ready to take a fit."

"Yeah," Meyer said, and chuckled. The car heater was on, and he was snug and cosy and drowsy. He did not envy La Bresca standing outside on the windy corner.

"What's the plan?" Kling said.

"As soon as the meeting's over, we move in on old Dom."

"We ought to pick up *both* of them," Kling said.

"Tell me what'll stick."

"We heard La Bresca planning a job, didn't we? That's Conspiracy to Commit, Section 580."

"Big deal. I'd rather find out what he's up to and then catch him in the act."

"If he's in with the deaf man, he's *already* committed two crimes," Kling said. "And very big ones at that."

"*If* he's in with the deaf man."

"You think he is?"

"No."

"I'm not sure," Kling said.

"Maybe old Dom'll be able to tell us."

"If he shows."

"What time is it?"

"Twenty to," Kling said.

"Mmm," Meyer said.

They kept watching La Bresca. He was pacing more nervously now, slapping his gloved hands against his sides to ward off the cold. He was wearing the same beige car coat he had worn the day he'd picked up the lunch pail in the park, the same green muffler wrapped around his throat, the same thick-soled workman's shoes.

"Look," Meyer said suddenly.

"What is it?"

"Across the street. Pulling up to the kerb."

"Huh?"

"It's the blonde girl, Bert. In the same black Buick!"

"How'd *she* get into the act?"

Meyer started the car. La Bresca had spotted the Buick and was walking towards it rapidly. From where they sat, the detectives could see the girl toss her long blonde hair and then lean over to open the front door for him. La Bresca got into the car. In a moment, it gunned away from the kerb.

"What do we do now?" Kling asked.

"We follow."

"What about Dom?"

"Maybe the girl's taking La Bresca to see him."

"And maybe not."

"What can we lose?" Meyer asked.

"We can lose Dom," Kling said.

"Just thank God they're not walking," Meyer said, and pulled the Chrysler out into traffic.

This was the oldest part of the city. The streets were narrow, the buildings crowded the sidewalks and gutters, pedestrians crossed at random, ignoring the lights, ducking around moving vehicles with practised ease, nonchalant to possible danger.

"Like to give them all tickets for jaywalking," Meyer mumbled.

"Don't lose that Buick," Kling cautioned.

"You think I'm new in this business, Sonny?"

"You lost that same car only last week," Kling said.

"I was on *foot* last week."

"They're making a left turn," Kling said.

"I see them."

The Buick had indeed made a left turn, coming out on to the wide tree-lined esplanade bordering the River Dix. The river was icebound shore to shore, a phenomenon that had happened only twice before in the city's history. Devoid of its usual busy harbour traffic, it stretched towards Calm's Point like a flat Kansas plain, a thick cover of snow uniformly hiding the ice below. The naked trees along the esplanade bent in the strong wind that raced across the river. Even the heavy Buick seemed struggling to move through the gusts, its nose swerving every now and again as the blonde fought the wheel. At last, she pulled the car to the kerb and killed the engine. The esplanade was silent except for the roaring of the wind. Newspapers flapped into the air like giant headless birds. An empty wicker-wire trash barrel came rolling down the centre of the street.

A block behind the parked Buick, Meyer and Kling sat and looked through the windshield of the unmarked police sedan. The wind howled around the automobile, drowning out the calls that came from the radio. Kling turned up the volume.

"What now?" he asked.

"We wait," Meyer said.

"Do we pick up the girl when they're finished talking?" Kling asked.

"Yep."

"You think she'll know anything?"

"I hope so. She must be in on it, don't you think?"

"I don't know. Calucci was talking about splitting the take up the middle. It there're three people in it already . . ."

"Well, then maybe she's old Dom's girl."

"Substituting for him, you mean?"

"Sure. Maybe old Dom suspects they're going to dump him. So he sends his girl to the meeting while he's safe and sound somewhere, strumming his old rhythm guitar."

"That's possible," Kling said.

"Sure, it's possible," Meyer said.

"But then, *anything's* possible."

"That's a very mature observation," Meyer said.

"Look," Kling said. "La Bresca's getting out of the car."

"Short meeting," Meyer said. "Let's hit the girl."

As La Bresca went up the street in the opposite direction, Meyer and Kling stepped out of the parked Chrysler. The wind almost knocked them off their feet. They ducked their heads against it and began running, not wanting the girl to start the car and take off before they reached her, hoping to prevent a prolonged automobile chase through the city. Up ahead, Meyer heard the Buick's engine spring to life.

"Let's *go!*" he shouted to Kling, and they sprinted the last five yards to the car, Meyer fanning out into the gutter, Kling pulling open the door on the kerb side.

The blonde sitting behind the wheel was wearing slacks and a short grey coat. She turned to look at Kling as he pulled open the door, and Kling was surprised to discover that she wasn't wearing make-up and that her features were rather heavy and gross. As he blinked at her in amazement, he further learned that she was sporting what looked like three-day-old beard stubble on her chin and on her cheeks.

The door on the driver's side snapped open.

Meyer took one surprised look at the 'girl' behind the wheel and then immediately said, "Mr Dominick Di Fillippi, I presume?"

Dominick Di Fillippi was very proud of his long blond hair.

In the comparative privacy of the squadroom, he combed it often and explained to the detectives that guys belonging to a group had to have an image, you dig? Like all the guys in his group, they all looked different, you dig? Like the drummer wore these Ben Franklin eyeglasses, and the lead guitar player combed his hair down in bangs over his eyes, and the organist wore red shirts and red socks, you dig, all the guys had a different image. The long blond hair wasn't exactly his own idea, there were lots of guys in other groups who had long hair, which is why he was growing the beard to go with it. His beard was a sort of reddish-blond, he explained, he figured it would look real tough once it grew in, give him his own distinct image, you dig?

"Like what's the beef," he asked, "what am I doing inside a police station?"

"You're a musician, huh?" Meyer asked.

"You got it, man."

"That's what you do for a living, huh?"

"Well, like we only recently formed the group."

"How recently?"

"Three months."

"Play any jobs yet?"

"Yeah. Sure."

"When?"

"Well, we had like auditions."

"Have you ever actually been *paid* for playing anywhere?"

"Well, no, man, not yet. Not actually. I mean, man, even The Beatles had to start *some place*, you know."

"Yeah."

"Like, man, they were playing these crumby little cellar joints in Liverpool, man, they were getting maybe a farthing a night."

"What the hell do you know about farthings?"

"Like it's a saying."

"OK, Dom, let's get away from the music business for a little while, OK? Let's talk about *other* kinds of business, OK?"

"Yeah, let's talk about why I'm in here, OK?"

"You'd better read him the law," Kling said.

"Yeah," Meyer said, and went through the Miranda-Escobedo bit. Di Fillippi listened intently. When Meyer was finished, he nodded his blond locks and said, "I can get a lawyer if I want one, huh?"

"Yes."

"I want one," Di Fillippi said.

"Have you got anyone special in mind, or do you want us to get one for you?"

"I got somebody in mind," Di Fillippi said.

While the detectives back at the squadroom fuzzily and fussily waited for Di Fillippi's lawyer to arrive, Steve Carella, now ambulatory, decided to go down to the fourth floor to visit Patrolman Genero.

Genero was sitting up in bed, his wounded leg bandaged and rapidly healing. He seemed surprised to see Carella.

"Hey," he said, "this is a real honour, I mean it. I'm really grateful to you for coming down here like this."

"How's it going, Genero?" Carella asked.

"Oh, so-so. It still hurts. I never thought getting shot could hurt. In the movies, you see these guys get shot all the time, and they just fall down, but you never get the impression it hurts."

"It hurts, all right," Carella said, and smiled. He sat on the edge of Genero's bed. "I see you've got a television in here," he said.

"Yeah, it's the guy's over in the next bed." Genero's voice fell to a whisper. "He never watches it. He's pretty sick, I think. He's either sleeping all the time or else moaning. I don't think he's going to make it, I'll tell you the truth."

"What's wrong with him?"

"I don't know. He just sleeps and moans. The nurses are in here day and night, giving him things, sticking him with needles, it's a regular railroad station, I'm telling you."

"Well, that's not so bad," Carella said.

"What do you mean?"

"Nurses coming in and out."

"Oh, no, that's *great!*" Genero said. "Some of them are pretty good-looking."

"How'd this happen?" Carella asked, and nodded towards Genero's leg.

"Oh, you don't know, huh?"

"I only heard you were shot."

"Yeah," Genero said, and hesitated. "We were chasing this suspect, you see. So as he went past me, I pulled my revolver to fire a warning shot." Genero hesitated again. "That was when I got it."

"Tough break," Carella said.

"Well, you got to expect things like that, I suppose. If you

160

expect to make police work your life's work, you got to expect things like that in your work," Genero said.

"I suppose so."

"Well, sure, look what happened to you," Genero said.

"Mmm," Carella said.

"Of course you're a detective," Genero said.

"Mmm," Carella said.

"Which is sort of understandable."

"What do you mean?"

"Well, you expect detectives to get in trouble more than ordinary patrolmen, don't you? I mean, the ordinary patrolman, the run-of-the-mill patrolman who doesn't expect to make police work his life's work, well, you don't *expect* him to risk his life trying to apprehend a suspect, do you?"

"Well," Carella said, and smiled.

"Do you?" Genero persisted.

"Everybody starts out as a patrolman," Carella said gently.

"Oh, sure. It's just you think of a patrolman as a guy directing traffic or helping kids cross the street or taking information when there's been an accident, things like that, you know? You never figure he's going to risk his life, the run-of-the-mill patrolman, anyway."

"Lots of patrolmen get killed in the line of duty," Carella said.

"Oh, sure, I'm sure. I'm just saying you don't *expect* it to happen."

"To your*self*, you mean."

"Yeah."

The room was silent.

"It sure hurts," Genero said. "I hope they let me out of here soon, though. I'm anxious to get back to duty."

"Well, don't rush it," Carella said.

"When are *you* getting out?"

"Tomorrow, I think."

"You feel OK?"

"Oh yeah, I feel fine."

"Broke your ribs, huh?"

"Yeah, three of them."

"Your nose, too."

"Yeah."

"That's rough," Genero said. "But, of course, you're a detective."

"Mmm," Carella said.

"I was up the squadroom the other day," Genero said, "filling in for the guys when they came here to visit you. This was before the shooting. Before I got it."

"How'd you like that madhouse up there?" Carella said, and smiled.

"Oh, I handled it OK, I guess," Genero said. "Of course, there's a lot to learn, but I suppose that comes with actual practice."

"Oh, sure," Carella said.

"I had a nice long talk with Sam Grossman . . ."

"Nice fellow, Sam."

". . . yeah, at the lab. We went over those suspect notes together. Nice fellow, Sam." Genero said.

"Yeah."

"And then some kid came in with another one of those notes, and I held him there till the guys got back. I guess I handled it OK."

"I'm sure you did," Carella said.

"Well, you've got to be conscientious about it if you expect to make it your life's work," Genero said.

"Oh, sure," Carella said. He rose, winced slightly as he planted his weight, and then said, "Well, I just wanted to see how you were getting along."

"I'm fine, thanks. I appreciate your coming down."

"Oh, well," Carella said, and smiled, and started for the door.

"When you get back," Genero said, "give my regards, huh?" Carella looked at him curiously. "To all the guys," Genero said. "Cotton, and Hal, and Meyer and Bert. All of us who were on the plant together."

"Oh, sure."

"And thanks again for coming up . . ."

"Don't mention it."

". . . Steve," Genero ventured as Carella went out.

Di Fillippi's lawyer was a man named Irving Baum.

He arrived at the squadroom somewhat out of breath and the first thing he asked was whether the detectives had advised his client of his rights. When assured that Di Fillippi had been constitutionally protected, he nodded briefly, took off his brown Homburg and heavy brown overcoat, placed both neatly across Meyer's desk, and then asked the detectives what it was all about. He was a pleasant-looking man, Baum, with white hair and moustache, sympathetic brown eyes, and an encouraging manner of nodding when anyone spoke, short little nods that seemed to be signs of agreement. Meyer quickly told him that it was not the police intention to book Di Fillippi for anything, but merely to solicit information from him. Baum could see no reason why his client should not cooperate to the fullest extent. He nodded to Di Fillippi and then said, "Go ahead, Dominick, answer their questions."

"OK, Mr Baum," Di Fillippi said.

"Can we get your full name and address?" Meyer said.

"Dominick Americo Di Fillippi, 365 North Anderson Street, Riverhead."

"Occupation."

"I already told you. I'm a musician."

"I beg your pardon," Baum said. "Were you questioning him *before* I arrived?"

"Steady, counsellor," Meyer said. "All we asked him was what he did for a living."

"Well," Baum said, and tilted his head to one side as though considering whether there had been a miscarriage of justice. "Well," he said, "go on, please."

"Age?" Meyer asked.

"Twenty-eight."

"Single? Married?"

"Single."

"Who's your nearest living relative?"

"I beg your pardon," Baum said, "but if you merely intend to solicit information, why do you need these statistics?"

"Mr Baum," Willis said, "you're a lawyer, and you're here with him, so stop worrying. He hasn't said anything that'll send him to jail. Not yet."

"This is routine, counsellor," Meyer said. "I think you're aware of that."

"All right, all right, go on," Baum said.

"Nearest living relative?" Meyer repeated.

"My father. Angelo Di Fillippi."

"What's he do?"

"He's a stonemason."

"Hard to find good stonemasons today," Meyer said.

"Yeah."

"Dom," Willis said. "What's your connection with Tony La Bresca?"

"He's a friend of mine."

"Why'd you meet with him today?"

"Just friendly."

"It was a very short meeting," Willis said.

"Yeah, I guess it was."

"Do you always go all the way downtown just to talk to someone for five minutes?"

"Well, he's a friend of mine."

"What'd you talk about?"

"Uh music," Di Fillippi said.

"What about music?"

"Well uh he's got a cousin who's gonna get married soon, so he wanted to know about our group."

"What'd you tell him?"

"I told him we were available."

"When's this wedding coming off?"

"The uh sometime in June."

"When in June?"

"I forget the exact date."

"Then how do you know you'll be available?"

"Well, we ain't got no jobs for June, so I know we'll be available."

"Are you the group's business manager?"

"No."

"Then why'd La Bresca come to you?"

"Because we're friends, and he heard about the group."

"So that's what you talked about. His cousin's wedding."

"Yes, that's right."

"How much did you tell him it would cost?"

"I said uh it uh seventy dollars."

"How many musicians are there in the group?"

"Five."

"How much is that a man?" Meyer asked.

"It's uh seventy uh divided by five."

"Which is how much?"

"That's uh well five into seven is one and carry the two, five into twenty is uh four, so that comes to fourteen dollars a man."

"But you didn't know that when you asked for the seventy, did you?"

"Yes, sure I knew it."

"Then why'd you have to do the division just now?"

"Just to check it, that's all."

"So you told La Bresca you'd be available, and you told him it would cost seventy dollars, and then what?"

"He said he'd ask his cousin, and he got out of the car."

"That was the extent of your conversation with him?"

"That was the extent of it, yes."

"Couldn't you have discussed this on the telephone?"

"Sure, I guess so."

"Then why didn't you?"

"Well, I like to see Tony every now and then, he's a good friend of mine."

"So you drove all the way downtown to see him."

"That's right."

"How much did you lose on that championship fight?"

"Oh, not much."

"*How* much?"

"Ten bucks or so. How do *you* know about that?"

"Wasn't it more like fifty?"

"Well, maybe, I don't remember. How do you know this?" He turned to Baum. "How do they know this?" he asked the lawyer.

"How do you know this?" Baum asked.

"Well, counsellor, if it's all right with you," Meyer said, "*we'll* ask the questions, unless you find something objectionable."

"No, I think everything's been proper so far, but I *would* like to know where you're going."

"I think that'll become clear," Meyer said.

"Well, Detective Meyer, I think I'd like to know right *now* what this is all about, or I shall feel compelled to advise my client to remain silent."

Meyer took a deep breath. Willis shrugged in resignation.

"We feel your client possesses knowledge of an impending crime," Meyer said.

"What crime?"

"Well, if you'll permit us to question him . . ."

"No, not until you answer me," Baum said.

"Mr Baum," Willis said, "we can book him for Compounding, Section 570 of the Penal Law, or we can book him for . . ."

"Just a moment, young man," Baum said. "Would you mind explaining that?"

"Yes, sir, we have reason to believe that your client has been promised money or other property to conceal a crime. Now that's either a felony or a misdemeanour, sir, depending on what the crime is he's agreed to conceal. I think you know that, sir."

"And what's this crime he's agreed to conceal?"

"We might also be able to book him for Conspiracy, Section 580, if he's actually *involved* in this planned crime."

"Do you have definite knowledge that a crime is to take place?" Baum asked.

"We have reasonable knowledge, sir, yes, sir."

"You realize, do you not, that no agreement amounts to a conspiracy unless some act *beside* such agreement is done to effect the object thereof?"

"Look, Mr Baum," Meyer said, "this isn't a court of law, so let's not argue the case right here and now, OK? We're not going to book your client for anything provided he cooperates a little and answers . . ."

"I hope I didn't detect a threat in that statement," Baum said.

"Oh, for Christ's sake," Meyer said, "we know that a man named Anthony La Bresca and another man named Peter Calucci are planning to commit a crime, misdemeanour or felony we don't know which, on March fifteenth. We also have very good reason to believe that your client here knows *exactly* what they're up to and has demanded money from them to keep such knowledge or information from reaching the police. Now, Mr Baum, we don't want to pull in La Bresca and Calucci for conspiracy because (*a*) it wouldn't stick without that 'act' you were talking about, and (*b*) we might end up with only a misdemeanour, depending on what they've cooked up. As I'm sure you know, if they've planned the crime of murder, kidnapping, robbery One, selling narcotics, arson, or extortion, and if they've committed some act other than their agreement to pull the job, each of them is guilty of a felony. And as I'm sure you also know, some very big officials in this city were recently murdered, and the possibility exists that La Bresca and Calucci are somehow involved and that this crime they've planned may have to do with extortion or murder, or both, which would automatically make the conspiracy a felony. As you can see, therefore, we're not after your client *per se*, we're merely trying to prevent a crime. So we can cut all the legal bullshit and get a little cooperation from you, and especially from him?"

"It seems to me he's been cooperating splendidly," Baum said.

"It seems to me he's been lying splendidly," Meyer said.

"Considering what's involved here . . ." Baum started.

"Mr Baum, could we please . . . ?"

". . . I think you had better charge Mr Di Fillippi with whatever it is you have in mind. We'll let the courts settle the matter of his guilt or innocence."

"While two hoods pull off their job, right?"

"I'm not interested in the entrapment of two hoodlums," Baum said. "I'm advising my client to say nothing further, in accordance with the rights granted to him under . . ."

"Thanks a lot, Mr Baum."

"Are you going to book him, or not?"

"We're going to book him," Meyer said.

"For what?"

"Compounding a crime, Section 570 of the Penal Law."

"Very well, I suggest you do that with reasonable dispatch," Baum said. "It seems to me he's been held in custody an extremely long time as it is. I know you're aware . . ."

"Mr Baum, we're aware of it inside out and backwards. Take him down, Hal. Charge him as specified."

"Hey, wait a minute," Di Fillippi said.

"I suggest that you go with them," Baum said. "Don't worry

about a thing. Before you're even arraigned, I'll have contacted a bail bondsman. You'll be back on the street . . ."

"Hey, wait one goddamn minute," Di Fillippi said. "What if those two guys go ahead with . . ."

"Dominick, I advise you to remain silent."

"Yeah? What can I get for this 'compounding', whatever the hell it is?"

"Depends on what they do," Meyer said.

"Dominick . . ."

"If they commit a crime punishable by death or by life imprisonment, you can get five years. If they commit . . ."

"What about a hold-up?" Di Fillippi asked.

"Dominick, as your attorney, I must again strongly advise you . . ."

"What about a hold-up?" Di Fillippi said again.

"Is that what they've planned?" Meyer said.

"You didn't answer me."

"If they commit a robbery, and you take money from them to conceal the crime, you can get three years in prison."

"Mmm," Di Fillippi said.

"Will you answer some questions for us?"

"Will you let me go if I do?"

"Dominick, you don't have to . . ."

"Do *you* want to go to prison for three years?" Di Fillippi asked.

"They have no case, they're . . ."

"No? Then how do they know the job's coming off on March fifteenth? Where'd they get *that*? Some little birdie whisper it in their ear?"

"We've levelled with you, Dominick," Willis said, "and believe me, we wouldn't have brought any of this out in the open if we didn't have plenty to go on. Now you can either help us or we can book you and take you down for arraignment and you'll have an arrest record following you for the rest of your life. What do you want to do?"

"That's coercion!" Baum shouted.

"It may be coercion, but it's also fact," Willis said.

"I'll tell you everything I know," Di Fillippi said.

He knew a lot, and he told it all.

He told them that the hold-up was set for eight o'clock on

Friday night, and that the victim was to be the owner of a tailor shop on Culver Avenue. The reason the hit had been scheduled for that particular night and time was that the tailor, a man named John Mario Vicenzo, usually packed up his week's earnings then and took them home with him in a small metal box, which box his wife Laura carried to the Fiduciary Trust early Saturday morning. The Fiduciary Trust, as it happened, was the only bank in the neighbourhood that was open till noon on Saturday, bank employees being among those who did not like to work on weekends.

John Mario Vicenzo (or John the Tailor as he was known to the people along Culver Avenue) was a man in his early seventies, an easy mark. The take would be enormous, Di Fillippi explained, with more than enough for everyone concerned even if split three ways. The plan was to go into the shop at ten minutes to eight, just before John the Tailor drew the blinds on the plate glass window fronting the street. La Bresca was to perform that task instead, and then he was to lock the front door while Calucci forced John the Tailor at gun point into the back room, where he would tie him and leave him bound and helpless on the floor near the pressing machine. They would then empty the cash register of the money that had been piling up there all week long, and take off. John the Tailor would be left dead or alive depending on how cooperative he was.

Di Fillippi explained that he'd overheard all this one night in the pizzeria on South Third, La Bresca and Calucci sitting in a booth behind him and not realizing they were whispering a little too loud. At first he'd been annoyed by the idea of two Italians knocking over a place owned by another Italian, but then he figured What the hell, it was none of his business; the one thing he'd never done in his life was rat on anybody. But that was before the fight, and the bet that had left him broke. Desperate for a little cash, he remembered what he'd heard them discussing and figured he'd try to cut himself in. He didn't think there'd be too much static from them because the take, after all, was a huge one, and he figured they'd be willing to share it.

"Just how much money is involved here?" Willis asked.

"Oh, man," Di Fillippi said, rolling his eyes, "there's at least four hundred bucks involved here, maybe even more."

11

A lot of things happened on Wednesday.

It was discovered on Wednesday, for example, that somebody had stolen the following items from the squadroom:

A typewriter.
Six ballpoint pens.
An electric fan.
A thermos jug.
A can of pipe tobacco, and
Four bars of soap.

Nobody could figure out who had done it.

Not even Steve Carella, who had been released from the hospital and who was very delicately walking around with his ribs taped, could figure out who had done it. Some of the squadroom wits suggested that Carella, being an invalid and all, should be assigned to the Great Squadroom Mystery, but Lieutenant Byrnes decided it would be better to assign him to the tailor shop stakeout instead, together with Hal Willis. At twelve noon that Wednesday, the pair headed crosstown to John the Tailor's shop.

But before then a lot of other things happened, it was certainly a busy Wednesday.

At 8 AM, for example, a patrolman walking his beat called in to report that he had found a stiff in a doorway and that it looked to him as if the guy had been burned to death. Which meant that the two fire bugs had struck again sometime during the night, and that something was going to have to be done about them pretty soon before they doused every bum in the city with petrol. Kling, who took the call, advised the patrolman to stay with the body until he could get a meat wagon over, and the patrolman complained that the doorway and the entire street stank to high heaven and Kling told him that was tough, he should take the complaint to Captain Frick.

At 9.15 AM, Sadie the Nut came up to tell Willis about the rapist who had tried to steal her virginity the night before. Sadie the Nut was seventy-eight years old, a wrinkled toothless crone who had been protecting her virginity for close to fourscore years now, and who unfailingly reported to the squadroom every Wednesday morning, either in person or by phone, that a man had broken into her tenement flat the night before and tried to tear off her nightgown and rape her. The first time she'd reported this crime some four years back, the police had believed her, figuring they had another Boston Strangler on their hands, only this time right on their own back yard. They immediately initiated an investigation, going as far as to plant Detective Andy Parker in the old lady's apartment. But the following Wednesday morning, Sadie came to the squadroom again to report a second rape attempt – even though Parker had spent an uneventful Tuesday night alert and awake in her kitchen. The squadroom comedians speculated that perhaps Parker himself was the rape artist, a premise Parker found somewhat less than amusing. They all realized by then, of course, that Sadie was a nut, and that they could expect frequent visits or calls from her. They did not realize that the visits or calls would come like clockwork every Wednesday morning, nor that Sadie's fantasy was as fixed and as unvaried as the squadroom itself. Her rapist was always a tall swarthy man who somewhat resembled Rudolph Valentino. He was always wearing a black cape over a tuxedo, white dress shirt, black bow tie, black satin dancing slippers. His pants had buttons on the fly. Five buttons. He always unbuttoned his fly slowly and teasingly, warning Sadie not to scream, he was not going to hurt her, he was (in Sadie's own words) "only going to rapage her". Sadie invariably waited until he had unbuttoned each of the five buttons and taken out his "thing" before she screamed. The rapist would then flee from the apartment, leaping on to the fire escape like Douglas Fairbanks, and swinging down into the back yard.

Her story this Wednesday was the same story she had been telling every Wednesday for the past four years. Willis took down the information and promised they would do everything in their power to bring this insane womanizer to justice. Sadie the Nut left the squadroom pleased and excited, doubtless anticipating next week's nocturnal visit.

At a quarter to ten that morning, a woman came in to report that her husband was missing. The woman was perhaps thirty-five years old, an attractive brunette wearing a green overcoat that matched her Irish eyes. Her face was spanking pink from the cold outside, and she exuded health and vitality even though she seemed quite upset by her husband's disappearance. Upon questioning her, though, Meyer learned that the missing man wasn't her husband at all, he was really the husband of her very best friend who lived in the apartment next door to her on Ainsley Avenue. And upon further questioning, the green-eyed lady explained to Meyer that she and her very best friend's husband had been having "a relationship" (as she put it) for three years and four months, with never a harsh word between them, they were that fond of each other. But last night, when the green-eyed lady's best friend went to play Bingo at the church, the green-eyed lady and the husband had had a violent argument because he had wanted to "do it" (as she again put it) right there in his own apartment on the living-room couch with his four children asleep in the other room, and she had refused, feeling it would not be decent, and he had put on his hat and coat and gone out into the cold. He had not yet returned, and whereas the green-eyed lady's best friend figured he was out having himself a toot, the husband apparently being something of a drinking man, the green-eyed lady missed him sorely and truly believed he had vanished just to spite her, had she known he would do something like that she certainly would have let him have his way, you know how men are.

Yes, Meyer said.

So whereas the wife felt it would not be necessary to report him missing and thereby drag policemen into the situation, the

172

green-eyed lady feared he might do something desperate, having been denied her favours, and was therefore asking the law's assistance in locating him and returning him to the bosom of his family and loved ones, you know how men are.

Yes, Meyer said again.

So he took down the information, wondering when it was that he'd last attempted to lay Sarah on the living-room couch with his own children asleep in their respective rooms, and realized that he had *never* tried to lay Sarah on the living-room couch. He decided that he would try to do it tonight when he got home, and then he assured the green-eyed lady that they would do everything in their power to locate her best friend's husband, but that probably there was nothing to worry about, he had probably gone to spend the night with a friend.

Yes, that's *just* what I'm worried about, the green-eyed lady said.

Oh, Meyer said.

When the green-eyed lady left, Meyer filed the information away for future use, not wanting to bug the Bureau of Missing Persons prematurely. He was beginning to type up a report on a burglary when Detective Andy Parker came into the squad-room with Lewis the Pickpocket. Parker was laughing uncontrollably, but Lewis did not seem too terribly amused. He was a tall slender man with a bluish cast to his jowls, small sharp penetrating blue eyes, thinning sandy-coloured hair. He was wearing a beige trench coat and brown leather gloves, and he carried an umbrella in the crook of his arm and scowled at everyone in the squadroom as Parker continued laughing uproariously.

"Look who I got!" Parker said, and burst into a choking gasping fit.

"What's so special?" Meyer said. "Hello, Lewis, how's business?"

Lewis scowled at Meyer. Meyer shrugged.

"Best pickpocket in the precinct!" Parker howled. "Guess what happened?"

"What happened?" Carella asked.

"I'm standing at the counter in Jerry's, you know? The luncheonette?"

"Yeah?"

"Yeah, with my back to the door, you know? So guess what?"

"What?"

"I feel somebody's hand in my pocket, fishing around for my wallet. So I grab the hand by the wrist, and I whip around with my gun in my other hand, and guess who it is?"

"Who is it?"

"It's Lewis!" Parker said, and began laughing again. "The best pickpocket in the precinct, he chooses a *detective* for a mark!"

"I made a mistake," Lewis said, and scowled.

"Oh, man, you made a *big* mistake!" Parker bellowed.

"You had your back to me," Lewis said.

"Lewis, my friend, you are going to prison," Parker said gleefully, and then said, "Come on down, we're going to book you before you try to pick Meyer's pocket there."

"I don't think it's funny," Lewis said, and followed Parker out of the squadroom, still scowling.

"*I* think it's pretty funny," Meyer said.

A man appeared at the slatted rail divider just then, and asked in hesitant English whether any of the policemen spoke Italian. Carella said that he did, and invited the man to sit at his desk. The man thanked him in Italian and took off his hat, and perched it on his knees when he sat, and then began telling Carella his story. It seemed that somebody was putting garbage in his car.

"*Rifiuti?*" Carella asked.

"*Si, rifiuti,*" the man said.

For the past week now, the man went on, someone had been opening his car at night and dumping garbage all over the front seat. All sorts of garbage. Empty tin cans and dinner leftovers and apple cores and coffee grounds, everything. All over the front seat of the car.

"*Perchè non lo chiude a chiave?*" Carella asked.

Well, the man explained, he *did* lock his car every night, but it didn't do any good. Because the way the garbage was left in it the first time was that *quello porco* broke the side vent and opened the door that way in order to do his dirty work. So it didn't matter if he continued to lock the car, the befouler continued to open the door by sticking his hand in through the

174

broken flap window, and then he dumped all his garbage on the front seat, the car was beginning to stink very badly.

Well, Carella said, do you know of anyone who might want to put garbage on your front seat?

No, I do not know of anyone who would do such a filthy thing, the man said.

Is there anyone who has a grudge against you? Carella asked.

No, I am loved and respected everywhere in the world, the man said.

Well, Carella said, we'll send a man over to check it out.

"*Per piacere*," the man said, and put on his hat, and shook hands with Carella, and left the squadroom.

The time was 10.33 AM.

At 10.35 AM, Meyer called Raoul Chabrier down at the district attorney's office, spent a delightful three minutes chatting with Bernice, and was finally put through to Chabrier himself.

"Hello, Rollie," Meyer said, "What'd you find out?"

"About what?"

"About the book I called to . . ."

"Oh."

"You forgot," Meyer said flatly.

"Listen," Chabrier said, "have *you* ever tried handling two cases at the same time?"

"Never in my life," Meyer said.

"Well, it isn't easy, believe me. I'm reading law on one of them and trying to get a brief ready on the other. You expect me to worry about some goddamn novel at the same time?"

"Well . . ." Meyer said.

"I know, I know, I know," Chabrier said, "I promised."

"Well . . ."

"I'll get to it. I promise you again, Meyer. I'm a man who never breaks his word. Never. I promised you, and now I'm promising you again. What was the title of the book?"

"*Meyer Meyer*," Meyer said.

"Of course, *Meyer Meyer*, I'll look into it immediately. I'll get back to you, I promise. Bernice," he shouted, "make a note to get back to Meyer!"

"When?" Meyer said.

That was at 10.39.

At five minutes to eleven, a tall blond man wearing a hearing aid and carrying a cardboard carton walked into the Hale Street Post Office downtown. He went directly to the counter, hefted the carton on to it, and shoved it across to the mail clerk. There were a hundred sealed and stamped envelopes in the carton.

"These all going to the city?" the clerk asked.

"Yes," the deaf man replied.

"First class?"

"Yes."

"All got stamps?"

"Every one of them."

"Right," the clerk said, and turned the carton over, dumping the envelopes on to the long table behind him. The deaf man waited. At 11 AM, the mail clerk began running the envelopes through the cancellation machine.

The deaf man went back to the apartment, where Rochelle met him at the door.

"Did you mail off your crap?" she asked.

"I mailed it," the deaf man said, and grinned.

John the Tailor wasn't having any of it.

"I no wanna cops in my shop," he said flatly and unequivocally and in somewhat fractured English.

Carella patiently explained, in English, that the police had definite knowledge of a planned hold-up to take place on Friday night at eight o'clock but that it was the lieutenant's idea to plant two men in the rear of the shop starting tonight in case the thieves changed their minds and decided to strike earlier. He assured John the Tailor that they would unobtrusively take up positions behind the hanging curtain that divided the front of the shop from the rear, out of his way, quiet as mice, and would move into action only if and when the thieves struck.

"*Lei è pazzo!*" John the Tailor said in Italian, meaning he thought Carella was crazy. Whereupon Carella switched to speaking Italian, which he had learned as a boy and which he didn't get much chance to practise these days except when he was dealing with people like the man who had come in to complain about the garbage in his car, or people like John the

Tailor, who was suddenly very impressed with the fact that Carella, like himself, was Italian.

John the Tailor had once written a letter to a very popular television show, complaining that too many of the Italians on that show were crooks. He had seventy-four people in his immediate family, all of them living here in the United States, in this city, for most of their lives, and none of them were criminals, all of them were honest, hard-working people. So why should the television make it seem that all Italians were thieves? He had received a letter written by some programming assistant, explaining that not all the criminals on the show were Italians, some of them were Jews and Irish, too. This had not mollified John the Tailor, since he was quite intelligent and capable of understanding the basic difference between the two statements *Not all Italians are criminals* and *Not all criminals are Italians*. So it was very pleasant to have an Italian cop in his shop, even if it meant having to put up with strangers in the back behind the curtain. John the Tailor did not like strangers, even if they were Italian cops. Besides, the other stranger, the short one, definitely was *not* Italian, God knew what *he* was!

The tailor shop did a very thriving business, though Carella doubted it brought in anything near four hundred dollars a week, which was apparently La Bresca's and Calucci's estimate of the take. He wondered why either of the two men would be willing to risk a minimum of ten and a maximum of thirty years in prison, the penalty for first-degree robbery, when all they could hope to gain for their efforts was four hundred dollars. Even granting them the minimum sentence, and assuming they'd be out on parole in three-and-a-half, that came to about a hundred and fifteen dollars a year, meagre wages for *any* occupation.

He would never understand the criminal mind.

He could not, for example, understand the deaf man at all.

There seemed to be something absolutely lunatic about the enormous risk he had taken, a gamble pitting fifty thousand dollars against possible life imprisonment. Now surely a man of his intelligence and capabilities must have known that the city wasn't going to reach into its treasury and plunk down fifty thousand dollars solely because someone threatened murder.

177

The odds against such a payoff were staggering, and any shrewd manipulator of odds would have realized this. The deaf man, then, had not *expected* to be paid, he had *wanted* to kill the deputy mayor, as he had earlier killed the parks commissioner. But why? Whatever else the deaf man happened to be, Carella did not figure him for a thrill killer. No, he was a hardheaded businessman taking a calculated risk. And businessmen don't take risks unless there's at least some hope of a payoff. The deaf man had asked for five grand at first, and been refused, and committed murder. He had next asked for fifty grand, knowing full well he'd be refused again, and had again committed murder. He had then advised the newspapers of his unsuccessful extortion attempts and had since remained silent.

So where was the payoff?

It was coming, baby, of that Carella was sure.

In the meantime, he sat in the back of John the Tailor's shop and wondered how much a good pressing-machine operator earned.

12

Mr. Carl Wahler
1121 Marshall Avenue
Isola

Dear Mr. Wahler:

If you treat this letter as a joke, you will die.
These are the facts. Read them carefully. They can
save your life.
1) Parks Commissioner Cowper ignored a warning and
   was killed.
2) Deputy Mayor Scanlon ignored a warning and was
   killed.
3) JMV is next. He will be killed this Friday night.

What does all this have to do with you?
1) This is your warning. It is your only warning.
   There will be no further warnings. Remember that.
2) You are to withdraw five thousand dollars in small,
   unmarked bills from your account.
3) You will be contacted by telephone sometime within
   the next week. The man you speak to will tell you
   how and when and where the money is to be delivered.
4) If you fail to meet this demand, you too will be
   killed. Without warning.

Do not entertain false hopes!

The police could not save Cowper or Scanlon, although
sufficiently forewarned. They will not be able to save

JMV, either. What chance·will <u>you</u> have unless you pay?
What chance will you have when we strike <u>without warning</u>?

Get the money. You will hear from us again. Soon.

The letters were delivered to a hundred homes on Thursday.
The deaf man was very cheerful that morning. He went
whistling about his apartment, contemplating his scheme again
and again, savouring its more refined aspects, relishing the
thought that one hundred very wealthy individuals would suddenly be struck with panic come Saturday morning.

By five o'clock tonight, he could reasonably assume that
most of the men receiving his letter would have read it and
formed at least some tentative opinion about it. He fully
expected some of them to glance cursorily at it, crumple it into
a ball, and immediately throw it into the garbage. He also
expected a handful, the paranoid fringe, to call the police at
once, or perhaps even visit their local precinct, letter in hand,
indignantly demanding protection. *That* part of his plan was
particularly beautiful, he felt. The mayor was being warned,
yes, but oh so indirectly. He would learn about the threat on
his life only because some frightened citizen would notify the
police.

And tomorrow night, forewarned, the mayor would none the
less die.

Six months ago when the deaf man had begun the preliminary
work on his scheme, several rather interesting pieces of information had come to light. To begin with, he had learned that
anyone desiring to know the exact location of the city's underground water pipes need only apply to the Department of
Water Supply in Room 1720 of the Municipal Building, where
the maps were available for public scrutiny. Similarly, maps of
the city's underground sewer system were obtainable at the
Department of Public Works in the main office of that same
building. The deaf man, unfortunately, was not interested in
either water pipes or sewers. He was interested in electricity.
And he quickly learned that detailed maps of the underground
power lines were *not*, for obvious reasons, open to the public
for inspection. Those maps were kept in the Maps and Records

180

Bureau of the Metropolitan Light & Power Company, worked on by an office staffed largely by draughtsmen. Ahmad had been one of those draughtsmen.

The first map he delivered to the deaf man was titled "60 Cycle Network Area Designations and Boundaries Lower Isola", and it showed the locations of all the area substations in that section of the city. The area that specifically interested the deaf man was the one labelled "Cameron Flats". The mayor's house was on the corner of South Meridian and Vanderhof, in Cameron Flats. The substation serving South Meridian and Vanderhof was marked with a cross in a circle, and was designated "No. 3 South Meridian". Into this substation ran high-voltage supply cables ("They're called feeders," Ahmad said) from a switching station elsewhere on the transmission system. It would be necessary to destroy those supply cables if the mayor's house was to be thrown into darkness on the night of his murder.

The second map Ahmad delivered was titled "System Ties" and was a detailed enlargement of the feeder systems supplying any given substation. The substation on the first map had been labelled "No. 3 South Meridian". By locating this on the more detailed map, the deaf man was able to identify the number designation of the feeder: 65CA3. Which brought him to the third pilfered map, simply and modestly titled "65CA3", and subtitled "Location South Meridian Substation". This was a rather long, narrow diagram of the route the feeder travelled below the city's streets, with numbers indicating the manholes that provided access to the cables. 65CA3 passed through eleven manholes on its meandering underground travels from the switching station to the substation. The deaf man chose a manhole approximately a half-mile from the mayor's house and wrote down its number: M3860–120'SSC-CENT.

The last map, the crucial one, was titled "Composite Feeder Plate" and it pinpointed the manhole exactly. M3860 was located on Faxon Drive, a hundred and twenty feet south of the southern curb of Harris, in the centre of the street – hence the 120'SSC-CENT. The high-voltage cables passing through that concrete manhole were five feet below the surface of the street protected by a three-hundred pound manhole cover.

Tomorrow night, Ahmad, Buck, and the deaf man would lift

that cover, and one of Buck's bombs would effectively take care of the cables.

And then . . .

Ahhh, then . . .

The really beautiful part was still ahead, and the deaf man smiled as he contemplated it.

He could visualize the mayor's house at 10 PM tomorrow night, surrounded by policemen and detectives on special assignment, all there to protect the honourable JMV from harm. He could see himself driving a black sedan directly to the curb in front of the darkened brick structure, a police flashlight picking out the gold lettering on the front door, Metropolitan Light & Power Company (pressure-sensitive letters expertly applied by Ahmad to both front doors of the car, cost eight cents per letter at Studio Art Supply, total expenditure $4.80). He could see the car doors opening. Three men step out of it. Two of them are wearing workmen's overalls (Sears, Roebuck, $6.95 a pair). The third is wearing the uniform of a police sergeant, complete with a citation ribbon pinned over the shield on the left breast (Theatrical Arts Rental, $10.00 per day, plus a $75.00 deposit) and the yellow sleeve patch of the Police Department's Emergency Service ($1.25 at the Civic Equipment Company, across the street from Headquarters).

"Who's there?" the policeman on duty asks. His flashlight scans the trio. Buck, in the sergeant's uniform, steps forward.

"It's all right," Buck says. "I'm Sergeant Pierce, Emergency Service. These men are from the electric company. They're trying to locate that power break."

"OK, Sergeant," the cop answers.

"Everything quiet in there?" Buck asks.

"So far, Sarge."

"Better check out their equipment," Buck says. "I don't want any static on this later."

"Good idea," the cop says. He swings his flashlight around. Ahmad opens the tool box. There is nothing in it but electrician's tools: a test light, a six foot rule, a brace, four screwdrivers, a Stillson wrench, a compass saw, a hacksaw, a hammer, a fuse puller, wire skinners, wire cutters, gas pliers,

Allen wrenches, friction tape, rubber tape . . . "OK," the cop says, and turns to the deaf man. "What's that you're carrying?"

"A volt-ohm meter," the deaf man answers.

"Want to open it for me?"

"Sure," the deaf man says.

The testing equipment is nothing more than a black leather case perhaps twelve inches long by eight inches wide by five inches deep. When the deaf man unclasps and raises the lid, the flashlight illuminates an instrument panel set into the lower half of the case, level with the rim. Two large dials dominate the panel, one marked "Volt-Ohm Meter", the other marked "Ammeter". There are three knobs spaced below the dials. Factory-stamped lettering indicates their use: the two end knobs are marked "Adjuster", and the one in the middle is marked "Function". Running vertically down the left-hand side of the panel are a series of jacks respectively marked 600V, 300V, 150V, 75V, 30V, and Common. Flanking the dials on the right-hand side of the plate there are similar jacks marked 60 Amps, 30 Amps, 15 Amps, 7.5 Amps, 3 Amps, and Common. Another jack and a small bulb are below the second adjuster knob, and they are collectively marked "Leakage Indicator". In bold factory-stamped lettering across the length of the tester are the words "Industrial Analyser".

"OK," the cop says, "you can close it."

The deaf man snaps the lid of the case shut, fastens the clasp again.

"I'll taken them inside," Buck says.

"Right, Sarge," the cop says, and the trio go up the walk to the house, where they are stopped by a detective at the front door.

"Sergeant Pierce, Emergency Service," Buck says. "These men are from the electric company, here to check that power failure."

"Right," the detective says.

"I'll stick with them," Buck says, "but I don't want no other responsibility."

"What do you mean?"

"Well, if the mayor trips and breaks his ankle while they're on the premises, I don't want no static from my captain."

"We'll keep the mayor far away from you," the detective says, and smiles.

"OK, where you guys want to start?" Buck asks. "The basement?"

They go into the house. There are battery-powered lights set up, but for the most part the house is dim, the figures moving through it are uncertainly defined. The three men start in the basement, going through the motions of checking out circuits. They go through every room in the house, never once seeing the mayor in the course of their inspection. In the master bedroom, the deaf man shoves the testing equipment under the huge double bed, ostensibly searching for a leak at the electrical outlet. When he walks out of the room, he is no longer carrying anything. The "Industrial Analyser" is on the floor under the mayor's bed.

That analyser, with its factory-sleek assortment of dials, knobs, jacks, and electrical terminology is real – but none the less fake. There *is* no testing equipment behind those meters, the interior of the box has been stripped bare. Hidden below the instrument panel, set to go off at 2 AM, there is only another of Buck's bombs.

Tomorrow night, the mayor would die.

And on Saturday morning, the uncommitted would commit. They would open their newspapers and read the headlines, and they would know the letter was for real, no opportunist could have accurately predicted the murder without having engineered it and executed it himself. They would take the letter from where they had casually put it, and they would read it once again, and they would fully comprehend its menace now, fully realize the absolute terror inherent in its words. When one was faced with the promise of unexpected death, was five thousand dollars really so much to invest? Not a man on that list of one hundred earned less than $200,000 a year. They had all been carefully researched, the original list of four hundred and twenty names being cut and revised and narrowed down to only those who seemed the most likely victims, those to whom losing five thousand dollars at a Las Vegas crap table meant nothing, those who were known to have invested in speculative stocks or incoming Broadway plays – those, in short, who would be willing to gamble five thousand dollars in hope of salvation.

They will pay us, the deaf man thought.

Oh, not all of them, certainly not all of them. But enough of them. Perhaps a few more murders are in order, perhaps some of those sleek fat cats on the list will have to be eliminated before the rest are convinced, but they *will* be convinced, and they *will* pay.

After the murder tomorrow night, after that, when they know we're not fooling, they will pay.

The deaf man suddenly smiled.

There should be a very large crowd around City Hall starting perhaps right this minute, he thought.

It will be an interesting weekend.

"You hit the nail right on the head," Lieutenant Byrnes said to Steve Carella. "He's going for the mayor next."

"He'll never get away with it," Hawes said.

"He'd better *not* get away with it," Byrnes said. "If he succeeds in knocking off the mayor, he'll be picking up cash like its growing in the park. How many of these letters do you suppose he's mailed?"

"Well, let's try to figure it," Carella said. "First he warned the parks commissioner and demanded five thousand dollars. Next the deputy mayor, and a demand for fifty thousand. Now he tells us he'll kill the mayor this Friday night. So if the escalation carries through, he should be bucking for ten times fifty thousand, which is five hundred thousand. If we divide that by—"

"Forget it," Byrnes said.

"I'm only trying to figure out the mathematics."

"What's mathematics got to do with JMV getting killed?"

"I don't know," Carella said, and shrugged. "But it seems to me if we can figure out the progression, we can also figure out what's *wrong* with the progression."

Byrnes stared at him.

"I'm just trying to say it just isn't enough for this guy to knock off the mayor," Carella said.

"It isn't, huh? Knocking off the mayor seems like *more* than enough to me."

"Yeah, but not for somebody like the deaf man. He's too proud of his own cleverness." Carella looked at the letter again. "Who's this man Carl Wahler?" he asked.

"A dress manufacturer, lives downtown in Stewart City, 17th Precinct. He brought the letter in there this morning. Captain Bundy thought we'd want to see it. Because of our involvement with the previous murders."

"It seems to fit right in with the pattern, doesn't it?" Hawes said. "He announced the other murders, too."

"Yes, but there's something missing," Carella said.

"What?"

"The personal angle. He started this in the 87th, a little vendetta for fouling him up years ago, when he was planting bombs all over the goddamn city to divert attention from his bank job. So why's he taking it *out* of the 87th all at once? If he knocks off the mayor, nobody looks foolish but the special police assigned to his protection. *We're* off the hook, home free. And that's what I can't understand. That's what's wrong with the pattern."

"The pattern seems pretty clear to me," Byrnes said. "If he can get to JMV after advertising it, what chance will anybody have *without* warning? Look at how many times he says that in his letter. Without warning, without warning."

"It still bothers me," Carella said.

"It shouldn't," Byrnes said. "He's spelled it out in black and white. The man's a goddamn *fiend*."

The instant reaction of both Hawes and Carella was to laugh. You don't as a general rule hear cops referring to criminals as "fiends", even when they're child molesters and mass murderers. That's the sort of language reserved to judges or politicians. Nor did Byrnes usually express himself in such colourful expletives. But whereas both men felt a definite impulse to laugh out loud, one look at Byrne's face stifled any such urge. The lieutenant was at his wit's end. He suddenly looked very old and very tired. He sighed heavily, and said, "How do we stop him, guys?" and he sounded for all the world like a freshman quarterback up against a varsity team with a three-hundred-pound line.

"We pray," Carella said.

Although James Martin Vale, the mayor himself, was a devout Episcopalian, he decided that afternoon that he'd best do a lot more than pray if his family was to stay together.

So he called a top-level meeting in his office at City hall (a meeting to which Lieutenant Byrnes was not invited), and it was decided that every precaution would be taken starting right then to keep "the deaf man" (as the men of the 87th insisted on calling him) from carrying out his threat. JMV was a man with a charming manner and a ready wit, and he managed to convince everyone in the office that he was more concerned about the people of his city than he was about his own safety. "We've got to save my life only so that this man won't milk hard-earned dollars from the people of this great city," he said. "If he gets away with this, they'll allow themselves to be extorted. That's why I want protection."

"Your Honour," the district attorney said, "if I may suggest, I think we should extend protection beyond the Friday night deadline. I think if this man succeeds in killing you any time in the near future, the people of this city'll think he's made good his threat."

"Yes, I think you're right," JMV said.

"Your Honour," the city comptroller said, "I'd like to suggest that you cancel all personal appearances at least through April."

"Well, I don't think I should go into complete seclusion, do you?" JMV asked, mindful of the fact that this was an election year.

"Or at least *curtail* your personal appearances," the comptroller said, remembering that indeed this was an election year, and remembering, too, that he was on the same ticket as His Honour the Mayor JMV.

"What do you think, Slim?" JMV asked the police commissioner.

The police commissioner, a man who was six feet four inches tall and weighed two hundred and twenty-five pounds, shifted his buttocks in the padded leather chair opposite His Honour's desk, and said, "I'll cover you with cops like fleas," a not particularly delicate simile, but one which made its point none the less.

"You can count on however many men you need from my squad," the district attorney said, mindful that two of his most trusted detectives had been blown to that big Police Academy in the sky only days before.

"I would like to suggest," the city's medical examiner said, "that you undergo a complete physical examination as soon as this meeting is concluded."

"Why?" JMV asked.

"Because the possibility exists, Your Honour, that you've already been poisoned."

"Well," JMV said, "that sounds a bit far-fetched."

"Your Honour," the medical examiner said, "an accumulation of small doses of poison administered over a period of time can result in death. Since we're dealing with a man who has obviously evolved a long-term plan . . ."

"Yes, of course," JMV said, "I'll submit to examination as soon as you wish. Maybe you can clear up my cold at the same time," he said charmingly, and grinned charmingly.

"Your Honour," the president of the city council said, "I suggest we have each of the city's vehicles inspected thoroughly and at once. I am remembering, sir, the bomb placed in . . ."

"Yes, we'll have that done at once," the district attorney said hastily.

"Your Honour," the mayor's press secretary said, "I'd like to suggest that we suppress all news announcements concerning your whereabouts, your speaking engagements, and so on, until this thing blows over."

"Yes, that's a good idea," JMV said, "but of course I won't be venturing too far from home in any case, will I, Stan?" he said, and grinned charmingly at the district attorney.

"No, sir, I'd advise your becoming a homebody for the next month or so," the district attorney said.

"Of course, there may be a bomb in this office right this minute," the police commissioner said tactlessly, causing everyone to fall suddenly silent. Into the silence came the loud ticking of the wall clock, which was a little unnerving.

"Well," JMV said charmingly, "perhaps we ought to have

the premises searched, as well as my home. If we're to do this right, we'll have to take every precaution."

"Yes, sir," the district attorney said.

"And, of course, we'll have to do everything in our power meanwhile to locate this man, this deaf man."

"Yes, sir, we're doing everything in our power right now," the police commissioner said.

"Which is what?" JMV asked, charmingly.

"He's got to make a mistake," the police commissioner said.

"And if he doesn't?"

"He's *got* to."

"But in the meantime," JMV asked, "do you have any leads?"

"Police work," the commissioner said, "is a combination of many seemingly unconnected facets that suddenly jell," and frowned, suspecting that his metaphor hadn't quite come off. "There are a great many accidents involved in police work, and we consider these accidents a definite contributing factor in the apprehension of criminals. We will, for example, arrest a man on a burglary charge, oh, six or seven months from now, and discover in questioning him that he committed a homicide during the commission of another crime, oh, four or five months ago."

"Well," JMV said charmingly, "I hope we're not going to have to wait six or seven months for our man to make a mistake while committing another crime."

"I didn't mean to sound so pessimistic," the commissioner said. "I was merely trying to explain, Your Honour, that a lot of police work dovetails past and present and future. I have every confidence that we'll apprehend this man within a reasonable length of time."

"Hopefully before he kills me," JMV said, and grinned charmingly. "Well," he said, "if there's nothing further to discuss, perhaps we can set all these precautionary measures into motion. I'll be happy to see your doctor, Herb, whenever you want to send him in."

"Meanwhile, I'll get in touch with the Bomb Squad," the police commissioner said, rising.

"Yes, that's probably the first thing to do," JMV said, rising.

"Gentlemen, thank you for your time and your valuable suggestions. I'm sure everything will work out fine."

"You'll have men here in the next two or three minutes," the district attorney promised.

"Thank you, Stan," the mayor said, "I certainly appreciate your concern."

The men filed out of the mayor's office, each of them assuring him once again that he would be amply protected. The mayor thanked each of them charmingly and individually, and then sat in the big padded leather chair behind his desk and stared at the ticking wall clock.

Outside, it was beginning to snow.

The snow was very light at first.

It drifted from the sky lazily and uncertainly, dusting the streets and sidewalks with a thin fluffy powder. By 8 PM that night, when Patrolman Richard Genero was discharged from Buena Vista Hospital, the snow was beginning to fall a bit more heavily, but it presented no major traffic problems as yet, especially if – like Genero's father – one had snow tyres on one's automobile. Their ride home was noisy but uneventful. Genero's mother kept urging her son to talk to the captain, and Genero's father kept telling her to shut up. Genero himself felt healthy and strong and was anxious to get back to work, even though he'd learned he would start his tour of duty on the four-to-midnight tomorrow. He had also learned, however, that Captain Frick, in consideration for his recent wound, was not asking him to walk a beat for the next week or so. Instead, he would be riding shotgun in one of the RMP cars. Genero considered this a promotion.

Of sorts.

The snow continued to fall.

13

Friday.

The city was a regular tundra, you never saw so much snow in your life unless you happened to have been born and raised in Alaska, and then probably not. There was snow on everything. There was snow on roofs and walls and sidewalks and streets and garbage cans and automobiles and flowerpots, and even on people. Boy, what a snowfall. It was worse than the Blizzard of '88, people who didn't remember the Blizzard of '88 were saying. His Honour the Mayor JMV, as if he didn't have enough headaches, had to arrange with the Sanitation Department for the hiring of 1,200 additional temporary employees to shovel and load and dump the snow into the River Dix, a job estimated to cost five hundred and eight thousand four hundred dollars and to consume the better part of a full week – if it didn't snow again.

The men began working as soon as the snow stopped. It did not stop until 3.30 PM, fifteen minutes before Genero began riding the RMP car, an hour and a half before Willis and Carella took their posts in the rear of the tailor shop. The city had figured on working their snow people in three continuous shifts, but they hadn't figured on the numbing cold that followed the storm and lowered the rate of efficiency, a biting frigid wave that had come down from Canada or some place. Actually, nobody cared *where* it had come from, they merely wished it would continue going, preferably out to sea, or down to Bermuda, or even all the way to Florida; do it to *Julia*, everyone was thinking.

There was no doing it to Julia that day.

The cold gripped the city and froze it solid. Emergency snow regulations had gone into effect at noon, and by 4 PM the city seemed deserted. Most large business offices were closed, with traffic stalled to a standstill and buses running only infrequently. Alternate-side-of-the-street parking had been suspended, but stranded automobiles blocked intersections, humped with snow like igloos on an arctic plain. The temporary snowmen fought the cold and the drifted snow, huddled around coal fires built in empty petrol drums, and then manned their shovels again while waiting dump trucks idled, exhaust pipes throwing giant white plumes into the bitter dusk. The lamp-post lights came on at 5 PM, casting isolated amber circles on the dead white landscape. A fierce relentless wind howled across the avenue and street as the leaden sky turned dark and darker and black.

Sitting cosy and warm in the back room of John the Tailor's shop, playing checkers with Hal Willis (and losing seven games in a row since it turned out that Willis had belonged to the checkers club in high school, an elite group calling itself *The Red and The Black*), Carella wondered how he would get home after La Bresca and Calucci hit the shop.

He was beginning to doubt that they would hit at all. If there was one thing he did not understand, of course, it was the criminal mind, but he was willing to venture a guess that no self-respecting crook would brave the snow and the cold outside on a night like this. It would be different if the job involved a factor that might change in a day or so, like say ten million dollars of gold bullion to be delivered at a precise moment on a specific day, making it necessary to combine pinpoint timing with insane daring, but no such variable was involved in this penny-ante stick-up. The men had cased the shop and learned that John the Tailor carried his week's earnings home in a metal box every Friday night after closing. He had doubtless been performing this same chore every Friday night for the past seven thousand years and would continue to do it without variation for the next thousand. So, if not *this* Friday night, what are you doing *next* Friday, John? Or, better yet, why not wait until May, when the trees are budding and the birds are singing, and a man can pull off a little felony without the attendant danger of frostbite?

But assuming they did hit tonight, Carella thought as he watched Willis double-jump two of his kings, assuming they *did* hit, and assuming he and Willis behaved as expected, made the capture and then called in for a squad car with chains, how would he get home to his wife and children after La Bresca and Calucci were booked and put away for the night? His own car had snow tyres, but not chains, and he doubted if the best snow tyres made would mean a damn on that glacier out there. A possibility, of course, was that Captain Frick would allow one of the RMPs to drive him home to Riverhead, but using city property for transporting city employees was a practice heavily frowned upon especially in these days of strife when deaf people were running around killing city officials.

"King me," Willis said.

Carella snorted and kinged him. He looked at his watch. It was seven twenty. If La Bresca and Calucci hit as expected, there was little more than a half-hour to go.

In Pete Calucci's rented room on North Sixteenth, he and La Bresca armed themselves. John the Tailor was seventy years old, a slight stooped man with greying hair and failing eyes, but they were not taking any chances with him that night. Calucci's gun was a Colt Government Model .45, weighing thirty-nine ounces and having a firing capacity of seven, plus one in the chamber. La Bresca was carrying a Walther P–38, which he had bought from a fence on Dream Street, with eight slugs in the magazine and another in the chamber. Both guns were automatics. The Walther was classified as a medium-powered pistol whereas the Colt, of course, was a heavy gun with greater power. Each was quite capable of leaving John the Tailor enormously dead if he gave them any trouble. Neither man owned a holster. Calucci put his pistol into the right-hand pocket of his heavy overcoat. La Bresca tucked his into the waistband of his trousers.

They had agreed between them that they would not use the guns unless John the Tailor began yelling. It was their plan to reach the shop by ten minutes to eight, surprise the old man, leave him bound and gagged in the back room, and then return to Calucci's place. The shop was only five minutes away, but because of the heavy snow, and because neither man owned an automobile, they set out at seven twenty-five.

They both looked very menacing, and they both felt quite powerful with their big guns. It was a shame nobody was around to see how menacing and powerful they looked and felt.

In the warm snug comfort of the radio motor patrol car, Patrolman Richard Genero studied the bleak and windswept streets outside, listening to the clink of the chains on the rear wheel tyres, hearing the two-way short-wave radio spewing its incessant dialogue. The man driving the RMP was a hair bag named Phillips, who had been complaining constantly from the moment they'd begun their shift at 3.45 PM. It was now seven thirty, and Phillips was still complaining, telling Genero he'd done a Dan O'Leary this whole past week, not a minute's breather, man had to be crazy to become a cop, while to his right the radio continued its oblivious spiel, Car Twenty-one, Signal thirteen, This is Twenty-one, Wilco, Car Twenty-eight, signal . . .

"This reminds me of Christmas," Genero said.

"Yeah, some Christmas," Phillips said. "I *worked* on Christmas day, you know that?"

"I meant, everything white."

"Yeah, everything white," Phillips said. "Who needs it?"

Genero folded his arms across his chest and tucked his gloved hands into his armpits. Phillips kept talking. The radio buzzed and crackled. The skid chains clinked like sleigh bells.

Genero felt drowsy.

Something was bothering the deaf man.

No, it was not the heavy snow which had undoubtedly covered manhole number M3860, a hundred and twenty feet south of the southern curb of Harris, in the centre of Faxon Drive, no, it was not that. He had prepared for the eventuality of inclement weather, and there were snow shovels in the trunk of the black sedan idling at the kerb downstairs. The snow would merely entail some digging to get at the manhole, and he was allowing himself an extra hour for that task, no, it was not the snow, it was definitely not the snow.

"What is it?" Buck whispered. He was wearing his rented police sergeant's uniform, and he felt strange and nervous inside the blue garment.

"I don't know," Ahmad answered. "Look at the way he's pacing."

The deaf man was indeed pacing. Wearing electrician's coveralls, he walked back and forth past the desk in one corner of the room, not quite muttering, but certainly wagging his head like an old man contemplating the sorry state of the world. Buck, perhaps emboldened by the bravery citation on his chest, finally approached him and said, "What's bothering you?"

"The 87th," the deaf man replied at once.

"What?"

"The 87th, the 87th," he repeated impatiently. "What difference will it make if we kill the mayor? Don't you see?"

"No."

"They get away clean," the deaf man said. "We kill JMV, and *who* suffers, will you tell me that?"

"Who?" Buck asked.

"*Not* the 87th, that's for sure."

"Look," Buck said gently, "we'd better get started. We've got to dig down to that manhole, we've got to . . ."

"So JMV dies, so what?" the deaf man asked. "Is money everything in life? Where's the pleasure?"

Buck looked at him.

"Where's the *pleasure*?" the deaf man repeated. "If JMV—" He suddenly stopped, his eyes widening. "JMV," he said again, his voice a whisper. "JMV!" he shouted excitedly, and went to the desk, and opened the middle drawer, and pulled out the Isola telephone directory. Quickly, he flipped to the rear section of the book.

"What's he doing?" Ahmad whispered.

"I don't know," Buck whispered.

"*Look* at this!" the deaf man shouted. "There must be hundreds of them, *thousands* of them!"

"Thousands of what?" Buck asked.

The deaf man did not reply. Hunched over the directory, he kept turning pages, studying them, turning more pages. "Here we are," he mumbled, "no, that's no good . . . let's see . . . here's another one . . . no, no . . . just a second . . . ahhh, good . . . no that's all the way down-town . . . let's see, let's see . . . here . . . no . . ." mumbling to himself as he continued to turn pages, and finally shouting "Culver Avenue, *that's* it, that'll do it!" He picked up a pencil, hastily scribbled on to the desk pad, tore the page loose, and stuffed it into the pocket of his coveralls. "Let's go!" he said.

"You ready?" Buck asked.

"I'm ready," the deaf man said, and picked up the volt-ohm meter. "We promised to get JMV, didn't we?" he asked.

"We sure did."

"Okay," he said, grinning. "We're going to get *two* JMV's – and one of them's in the 87th Precinct!"

Exuberantly, he led them out of the apartment.

The two young men had been prowling the streets since dinner-time. They had eaten in a delicatessen off Ainsley and then had stopped to buy a half-gallon of petrol in the service station on the corner of Ainsley and Fifth. The taller of the two young men, the one carrying the open can of petrol, was cold. He kept telling the shorter one how cold he was. The shorter one said *everybody* was cold on a night like this, what the hell did he expect on a night like this?

The taller one said he wanted to go home. He said they wouldn't find nobody out on a night like this, anyway, so what was the use walking around like this in the cold? His feet were freezing, he said. His hands were cold too. Why don't *you* carry this fuckin' gas a while? he said.

The shorter one told him to shut up.

The shorter one said this was a perfect night for what they had to do because they could probably find maybe two guys curled up together in the same hallway, didn't that make sense?

The taller one said he wished *he* was curled up in a hallway someplace.

They stood on the street corner arguing for a few minutes, each of them yelling in turn, and finally the taller one agreed to give it another ten minutes, but that was all. The shorter one said Let's try it for another half-hour, we bound to hit pay dirt, and the taller one said No, ten minutes and that's it, and the shorter one said You fuckin' idiot, I'm telling you this is a good night for it, and the taller one saw what was in his eyes, and became afraid again and said, OK, OK, but only a half-hour, I mean it, Jimmy, I'm really cold, really.

You look like you're about to start crying, Jimmy said.

I'm cold, the other one said, that's all.

Well, come on, Jimmy said, we'll find somebody and make a nice fire, huh? A nice warm fire.

The two young men grinned at each other.

Then they turned the corner and walked up the street towards Culver Avenue as Car Seventeen, bearing Phillips and Genero, clinked by on its chained tyres sounding like sleigh bells.

It was difficult to tell who was more surprised, the cops or the robbers.

The police commissioner had told His Honour the Mayor JMV that "a lot of police work dovetails past and present and future", but it was fairly safe to assume he had nothing too terribly philosophical in mind. That is, he probably wasn't speculating on the difference between illusion and reality, or the overlap of the dream state and the workaday world. That is, he probably wasn't explaining time continua or warps, or parallel universes, or coexisting systems. He was merely trying to say that there are a lot of accidents involved in police work, and that too many cases would never get solved if it weren't for those very accidents. He was trying to tell His Honour the Mayor JMV that sometimes cops get lucky.

Carella and Willis got very lucky on that night of March fifteenth at exactly ten minutes to eight.

They were watching the front of the shop because Dominick Di Fillippi (who had never ratted on anybody in his life) had told them the plan was to go into the shop at ten minutes to eight, just before John the Tailor drew the blinds on the plate glass window fronting the street. La Bresca was to perform that task instead, Di Fillippi had further said, and then he was to lock the front door while Calucci forced John the Tailor at gun point into the back room. In Di Fillippi's ardent recital, there had been a lot of emphasis real or imagined, on the *front* of the shop. So everyone had merely assumed (as who wouldn't?) that La Bresca and Calucci would come in through the front door, open the door, ting-a-ling would go the bell, shove their guns into John the Tailor's face, and then go about their dirty business. It is doubtful that the police even *knew* there was a back door to the shop.

La Bresca and Calucci knew there was a back door.

They kicked that door in at precisely seven fifty, right on schedule, kicked it in noisily and effectively, not caring whether or not they scared John the Tailor out of ten years' growth, knowing he would rush to the back of the shop to see what the hell was happening, knowing he would run directly into two very large pistols.

The first thing they saw was two guys playing checkers.

The first thing La Bresca said was, "Fuzz!"

He knew the short guy was fuzz because he had been questioned by him often enough. He didn't know who the other guy was, but he reasoned that if you saw *one* mouse you probably had fifty, and if you saw one *cop* you probably had a thousand, so the place was probably crawling with cops, they had stepped into a very sweet little trap here – and that was when the curtain shot back and the front door of the shop burst open.

It was also when all the overlapping confusion started, the past, present, and future jazz getting all mixed up so that it seemed for a tense ten seconds as if seven movies were being projected simultaneously on the same tiny screen. Even later, much later, Carella couldn't quite put all the pieces together; everything happened too fast and too luckily, and he and Willis had very little to do with any of it.

The first obvious fact that crackled up Carella's spine and into his head was that he and Willis had been caught cold. Even as he rose from his chair, knocking it over backwards, even as he shouted, "Hal, behind you!" and reached for his revolver, he knew they'd been caught cold, they were staring into the open muzzles of two high calibre guns and they would be shot dead on the spot. He heard one of the men shout, "Fuzz!" and then he saw both guns come up level at the same time, and too many last thoughts crowded into his head in the tick of a second. Willis whirled, knocking checkerboard and checkers to the floor, drawing his gun, and suddenly John the Tailor threw back the curtain separating the rear of the shop from the front, and the front door of the shop burst open in the same instant.

John the Tailor later said he had run back to see what the noise was, throwing the curtain between the two rooms, and then whirling to see what Carella only later saw, three men standing in the front doorway of his shop, all of them holding pistols.

This was what La Bresca and Calucci must have seen as well, looking through the now open curtain directly to the front door. And whereas they must have instantly known they had caught the back-room cops cold, they now recognized the threat of the three other cops standing in the front door, all of them with pistols in their fists and kill looks on their faces. The three men weren't cops, but La Bresca and Calucci didn't know that. The sergeant standing in the doorway shouted, "Fuzz!" meaning he thought La Bresca and Calucci were fuzz, but La Bresca and Calucci merely thought he was announcing his own arrival. So they began shooting. The three men in the door, facing what they too thought was a police trap, opened fire at the same time. John the Tailor threw himself to the floor. Carella and Willis, recognizing a good healthy crossfire when they saw one, tried to flatten themselves against the wall. In the flattening process, Willis slipped on one of the fallen checkers and went tumbling to the floor, bullets spraying over his head.

Carella's gun was in his hand now. He levelled it at the front door because he had taken a good look at one of the men standing there firing into the back room, and whereas the man was not wearing his hearing aid, he was tall and blond and Carella recognized him at once. He aimed carefully and deliberately. The gun bucked in his hand when he pulled off the shot. He saw the deaf man clutch for his shoulder and then half-stumble, half-turn towards the open doorway. Someone screamed behind Carella, and he turned to see La Bresca falling over the pressing machine, spilling blood on to the white padding, and then four more shots exploded in the tiny shop and someone grunted, and there were more shots, Willis was up and firing, and then there was only smoke, heavy smoke that hung on the air in layers, the terrible nostril-burning stink of cordite, and the sound of John the Tailor on the floor, praying softly in Italian.

"Outside!" Carella shouted, and leaped the counter dividing the shop, slipping in a pool of blood near the sewing machine, but regaining his footing and running coatless into the snow.

There was no one in sight.

The cold was numbing.

It hit his naked gun hand immediately, seemed to wed flesh to steel.

A trail of blood ran from the shop door across the white snow stretching endlessly into the city.

Carella began following it.

The deaf man ran as fast as he could, but the pain in his shoulder was intolerable.

He could not understand what had happened.

Was it possible they had figured it out? But no, they couldn't have. And yet, they'd been there, waiting. How *could* they have known? How could they *possibly* have known when he *himself* hadn't known until fifteen minutes ago?

There had been at least twenty-five pages of "V" listings in the Isola directory, with about 500 names to a page, for a combined total of some 12,500 names. He had not counted the number of first names beginning with the letter "J", but there seemed to be at least twenty or thirty on every page, and he had actually gone through *eleven* names with the initials "JMV", the same initials as His Honour the Mayor James Martin Vale, before coming to the one on Culver Avenue.

How could they have known? How could they have pinpointed the tailor shop of John Mario Vicenzo, the final twist of the knife, a JMV located within the very confines of the 87th? It's impossible, he thought. I left nothing to chance, it should have worked, I should have got them both, there were no wild cards in the deck, it should have worked.

There were *still* some wild cards in the deck.

"Look," Jimmy said.

The taller boy, the one carrying the petrol can, lifted his head, squinted against the wind, and then ducked it immediately as a fiercer gust attacked his face. He had seen a tall blond man staggering off the pavement and into the centre of the snow-bound street.

"Drunk as a pig," Jimmy said beside him. "Let's get him, Baby."

The one called Baby nodded bleakly. Swiftly, they ran towards the corner. The wind was stronger there, it struck them with gale force as they turned on to the wide avenue. The vag was nowhere in sight.

"We lost him," Baby said. His teeth were chattering, and he wanted to go home.

"He's got to be in one of these hallways," Jimmy said. "Come on, Baby, it's fire time."

From where Genero sat in the RMP car, he could see the empty windswept avenue through a frost-free spot on the windshield, snow devils ascending with each fresh gust of wind, hanging signs clanging and flapping, an eerie graveyard sound rasping at the windows of the automobile. The avenue was deserted, the snow locked the street from sidewalk to sidewalk, lights burned behind apartment windows like warming fires in a primeval night.

"What's that?" he said suddenly.

"What's what?" Phillips asked.

"Up ahead. Those two guys."

"Huh?" Phillips said.

"They're trying doors," Genero said. "Pull over."

"Huh?"

"Pull over and cut your engine!"

He could hear them talking on the sidewalk outside, he could hear their voices coming closer and closer. He lay in the hallway with his shoulder oozing blood, knowing he had to climb those steps and get to the roof, get from this building to the next one, jump rooftops all night long if he had to, but first rest,

201

just rest, just rest a little, rest before they opened the door and found him, how had they got to him so fast? Were there policemen all over this damn city?

There were too many things he did not understand.

He listened as the voices came closer, and then he saw the doorknob turning.

"Hold it right there!" Genero shouted.

The boys turned immediately.

"Fuzz!" Baby shouted, and dropped the petrol can, and began running. Genero fired a warning shot over his head, and then belatedly yelled, "Police! Stop or I'll shoot!" and then fired another warning shot. Up the street, where he had parked the RMP at the kerb, Phillips was opening the door on the driver's side and unholstering his revolver. Genero fired again, surprised when he saw the running boy drop to the snow. I *got* him! he thought, and then whirled to see the second boy running in the opposite direction, Holy Jesus, he thought, I'm busting up a *robbery* or something! "Halt!" he shouted. "Stop!" and fired into the air, and saw the boy rounding the corner, and immediately ran after him.

He chased Jimmy for three blocks in the snow, pushing through knee-deep drifts, slipping on icy patches, the wind a constant adversary, and finally caught up with him as he was scaling a back-alley fence.

"Hold it right there, Sonny," Genero said, "or I'll put one right up your ass."

Jimmy hesitated astride the fence, debating whether to swing his legs up and over it, or get down before this trigger-happy bastard really carried out his threat.

Sighing, he dropped to the ground at Genero's feet.

"What seems to be the trouble, Officer?" he asked.

"*Trouble* is right," Genero said. "Get your hands up."

Phillips came puffing into the alley just then. He walked up to Genero like the hair bag he was, shoved him aside, and then pushed Jimmy against the fence while he frisked him. Genero was smart enough to make certain *his* handcuffs were the one they put on the kid, though there was a moment when it seemed like a touch-and-go race with Phillips.

By the time they got the kid back to the squad car, by the time they went up the street to ascertain that the other kid was still alive, though barely, by the time they located the hallway door the kids were about to open, by the time they opened that door themselves and flashed their lights into the foyer, all they saw was a puddle of blood on the floor.

The blood continued up the steps.

They followed the spatters to the top floor, directly to the open door of the roof. Genero stepped outside and threw the beam of his flash across the snow.

Bloodstains and footprints led in an erratic trail to the edge of the roof, and from there to the roof beyond, and from there to the rest of the city, or perhaps the rest of the world.

Two blocks away, they found Steve Carella wandering coatless in the snow like Dr Zhivago or somebody.

14

The clean up in the tailor shop was a gruesome job.

La Bresca and Calucci were both dead. The big red-headed man named Buck was also dead. Ahmad was alive and breathing when they carted him off in the meat wagon, but he had taken two slugs in the chest from Calucci's .45, and another in the stomach from La Bresca's Walther. He was gushing blood, and spitting blood, and shivering and mumbling, and they doubted very much if he'd make it to the hospital alive.

Carella was shivering a little himself.

He stood near the radiator in the tailor shop, wrapped in his overcoat, his teeth chattering, and asked John the Tailor how much money there was in the metal box he was taking home.

"*Due cento tre dollari*," John the Tailor said.

Two hundred and three dollars.

Ahmad knew the deaf man's name.

"Orecchio," he said, and the nurse wiped blood from his lips. "Mort Orecchio."

"That's not his real name," Willis told him. "Do you know him by any other name?"

"Orecchio," Ahmad repeated. "Mort Orecchio."

"Is there anyone who *might* know his real name?"

"Orecchio," Ahmad repeated.

"Was there anyone else in this with you?"

"The girl," Ahmad said.

"What girl?"

"Rochelle," he said.

"Rochelle what?"

Ahmad shook his head.

"Where can we find her?"

"Three . . . three . . . eight . . . Ha . . . Ha . . . Ha . . ." he said, and died.

He had not died laughing.

He was trying to say 338 Harbourside.

They found in Buck's pants a letter addressed to him at 338 Harbourside Oval. His full name was Andrew Buckley, and the letter was addressed to him c/o Mr Mort Orecchio. Carella and Willis hit the apartment and found a pretty brunette girl in lounging pyjamas, sitting at a piano playing *Heart and Soul*. They waited while she got dressed and then took her to the squadroom, where they questioned her for a half-hour in the presence of a lawyer. The girl told them her name was Rochelle Newell and that she had known the deaf man for only a short time, two or three months. She insisted his name was Mort Orecchio.

"That's not his name," Carella said.

"Yes, that's his name."

"What'd *you* call him?"

"Mort," the girl said.

"What'd you call him in *bed*?" Willis asked suddenly, hoping to surprise her.

"Sweetie," the girl answered.

Jimmy could not stop giggling.

They had just told him that his friend Baby was dead, and yet he could not stop giggling.

"You know the kind of trouble you're in, son?" Meyer asked.

"No, what kind?" Jimmy said, and giggled.

"We're going to book you for homicide."

"It won't stick," Jimmy said, and giggled.

"It'll stick, son," Meyer said. "We got a dying confession

from your pal, and it was taken in the presence of a lawyer, and we've got a cop outside who you tried to kill and who'll make a positive identification of both of you. It'll stick, believe me."

"Naw, it won't stick," Jimmy said, and kept giggling.

Meyer figured he was crazy.

Meyer figured Rollie Chabrier was crazy too.

He called at close to midnight.

"This is kind of late, isn't it?" Meyer said. "I was just about to head home."

"Well, I'm still working here at the goddamn office," Chabrier said. "You guys have it easy."

"Well, what is it?" Meyer said.

"About this book," Chabrier said.

"Yeah?"

"You want my advice?"

"Sure, I want your advice. Why do you think I contacted you?"

"My advice is forget it."

"That's some advice."

"Has Steve Carella ever had a book named after him?"

"No, but . . ."

"Has Bert Kling?"

"No."

"Or Cotton Hawes? Or Hal Willis? Or Arthur Brown? Or . . ."

"Look, Rollie . . ."

"You should be flattered," Chabrier said. "Even *I* have never had a book named after me."

"Yeah, but . . ."

"You know how many people go their entire lives and never have books named after them?"

"How many?"

"Millions! You should be flattered."

"I should?"

"Sure. Somebody named a book after you! You're famous!"

"I am?"

"Absolutely. From now on to the very end of time, people

will be able to go into libraries all over the world and see your name on a book, Meyer, think of it. On a *book*. Meyer Meyer," he said grandly, and Meyer could almost visualize him spreading his hands as though conjuring marquee lights. "God, Meyer, you should be thrilled to death."

"Yeah?" Meyer said.

"I envy you, Meyer. I truly and honestly envy you."

"Gee," Meyer said. "Thanks. Thanks a lot, Rollie. Really. Thanks a lot."

"Don't mention it," Chabrier said, and hung up.

Meyer went into the men's room to look at himself in the mirror.

Andy Parker brought the morning papers into the squadroom at 2 A.M.

"You want to read how smart we are?" he said, and dropped the papers on Kling's desk.

Kling glanced at the headlines.

"Sure," Parker said, "we busted the whole thing wide open. Nobody can lick *this* team, pal."

Kling nodded, preoccupied.

"Everybody can rest easy now," Parker said. "The papers tell all about the scheme, and how the ring is busted, and how none of those hundred marks have to worry any more. And all because of the brilliant bulls of the 87th." He paused and then said, "I bet Genero gets a promotion out of this. His name's all over the paper."

Kling nodded and said nothing.

He was pondering the latest development in the Great Squadroom Mystery. The stolen electric fan, it seemed, had turned up in a hockshop downtown. There had been an apple green fingerprint on its base.

"Now who do you suppose . . ." he started, but Parker had already stretched out in the swivel chair behind his desk, with one of the newspapers over his face.

DOWNTOWN

*This is for
Jan and Roy Dean*

1

Michael was telling the blonde he'd never been in this part of the city. In fact, he'd been to New York only twice before in his entire life. Hadn't strayed out of the midtown area either time.

"But here you are now," the blonde said, and smiled. "All the way downtown."

She was wearing a smart tailored suit, gray, a white silk blouse with a stock tie. Briefcase sitting on the empty stool to her right. He figured her for someone who worked on Wall Street. Late business meeting – it was now seven o'clock – she'd stopped off at the bar here before heading home. That's what he figured.

She was drinking Corona and lime.

He was drinking scotch with a splash.

The place looked like an old saloon, but it probably wasn't. Etched mirrors, polished mahogany and burnished brass, large green-shaded lamps over the bar, smaller versions on all the tables. There was a warm, cozy feel to the place. Nice buzz of conversation, too. Through the big plate-glass window facing the street, he could see gently falling snowflakes. This was Christmas Eve, a Saturday night. It would be a white Christmas.

"What brings you to New York this time?" the blonde asked.

"Same thing that brought me here the last two times," he said.

"And what's that?"

"My ad agency's here."

"You're in advertising, is that it?"

"No, I'm in oranges."

The blonde nodded.

"Golden Oranges?" Michael said, and looked at her expectantly.

"Uh-huh," she said.

"You've heard of them?"

"No," she said.

"That's my brand name. Golden Oranges."

"Sorry, I don't know them."

"But you know Sunkist, right?"

"Sure."

"Well, I'm just a small independent trying to get big. Which is why I've got a New York agency handling my advertising."

The blonde nodded again.

"So what do you do?" she asked. "*Grow* the oranges and everything?"

"Yep. Grow them and everything."

"Where?"

"In Florida."

"Ask a stupid question," she said, and smiled, and extended her hand. "I'm Helen Parrish," she said.

"Michael Barnes," he said, and took her hand. "Nice to meet you."

"So when do you go back to Florida?" she asked.

"Well, not till the twenty-sixth, actually. Monday morning. I'm flying up to Boston tonight. Spend Christmas with my mother."

"Your mother's up there in Boston, huh?"

"Yeah. Be good seeing her again."

"Business all finished here?"

"Finished it this afternoon."

He realized that her hand was still in his. To the casual passerby, they must have looked like a man and a woman holding hands. Good-looking blonde woman with flashing blue eyes, sun-tanned man wearing rimless eyeglasses. Dark brown hair. Brown eyes. Average height, he guessed. Well, five-ten, he guessed that was average these days. In the army, he'd felt short. The army had a way of making you feel short. Come to think of it, he felt short nowadays, too. Jenny had done that to him. Made him feel short all over again.

"Do you work down here in this area?" he asked.

"I do," she said.

Still holding his hand.

"I figured you were with one of the brokerage firms," he said.

"No, I'm a lawyer."

"Really? What kind of law?"

"Criminal."

"No kidding?"

"Everybody says that. No kidding, or wow, or gee, or how about that, or words to that effect."

"Because it's so unusual. A woman, I mean. Being a criminal lawyer."

"Actually, there are three in our office."

"That many."

"Yes."

"Criminal lawyers. Women."

"Yes. Trial lawyers, in fact."

"Then you're a trial lawyer."

"Yes."

"Do you like the work?"

"Oh, sure."

She retrieved her hand gently, drained her glass, looked at the clock over the bar, smiled, and said, "Well, I think I'll . . ."

"No, don't go yet," he said.

She looked at him.

"Have another drink," he said. "Then maybe we can go someplace for dinner together," he said. "I've got a rented car outside, we can go anyplace in the city you like. I don't have to start for the airport till nine-thirty or so. Unless you've got other plans."

"I don't have any *plans* as such, but . . ."

"Then what's the hurry?"

"Well, I'll have another drink, but . . ."

"Good," he said, and signaled to the bartender for another round. The bartender nodded.

"This doesn't mean we're having dinner together," she said. "I hardly know you."

"Ask me anything," he said.

"Well . . . are you married?"

"Divorced."

"How long?"

"Nine months. More or less."

"And on the loose in the big, bad city, huh?"

"Well, my plane leaves at eleven-oh-five. It's the last one out tonight. I was lucky to get anything at *all*. It's Christmas Eve, you know."

"Yes, I know," she said. She was looking at him steadily now. Penetrating blue eyes. "How long were you married?" she asked.

"Thirteen years."

"Unlucky number."

"Yes."

"Do you have any children?"

"No."

"How old are you?"

"Thirty-eight," he said. "How old are you?"

"Thirty-two," she said at once.

He liked that. No coy nonsense like Gee, a woman's not supposed to tell her age. Just straight out thirty-two.

"Are *you* married?" he asked.

"Corona and lime, Dewar's with a splash," the bartender said, and put the drinks down in front of them. "Shall I keep this tab running?"

"Please," Michael said.

He lifted his glass. She lifted hers.

"To a nice evening together," he said. "Till plane time."

She seemed to be looking through him, or at least past him, toward the other end of the bar, almost dreamily. She nodded at last, as if in response to a secret decision she had made, and smiled, and said, "That sounds safe enough," and clinked her glass against his and began sipping at her beer.

"But you didn't answer my question," he said.

"What was your question?" she said.

"Are *you* married?"

"Would it matter?"

"Yes."

She waggled the fingers on her left hand.

"See any wedding band?"

"That doesn't mean anything."

"I'm not married," she said.

"Divorced?" he said.

"Nope. Just single."

"Beautiful woman like you?"

"Ha."

"I mean it."

"Thank you."

"So what I'd like to do," he said, "you must know a lot of good restaurants . . ."

"Slow down," she said, smiling. "You didn't ask me if I'm engaged, or involved with anyone, or . . ."

"Are you?"

"No, but . . ."

"Good. Do you like Italian food?"

"Uh-huh," she said, and put down her glass, and slid her handbag over in front of her, and reached into it for a package of cigarettes.

"Well, if you know a good Italian restaurant, I'd like to . . ."

"All right," she said suddenly and coldly and somewhat harshly, "you want to give it back to me?"

He looked at her.

Her eyes had turned hard, there was no longer a smile on her face.

"The ring," she said.

She was whispering now.

"Just give it back to me, okay?"

She held out her right hand. Nothing on any of the fingers.

"The ring," she said. "Please, I don't want any trouble."

"What ring?" he said.

"The ring that was right here on this finger before we started holding hands. A star sapphire ring that was a gift from my father. I want it back, mister. Right now."

"But I don't have it," he said. He realized there was a foolish grin on his face. As if she were in the middle of a joke and he was smiling in anticipation of the punch line.

She looked at him. Eyes as blue and as hard as the star sapphire she claimed was missing from her hand. Eyes somewhat incredulous, too. She'd told him she was a lawyer, a *criminal* lawyer, no less; was he some kind of idiot to have stolen her ring? This was in her eyes.

"Listen," she said, her voice rising, "just give me the goddamn ring, and we'll forget . . ."

"I don't *have* your . . ."

"What's going on here?"

Michael turned on the stool.

Big, burly guy standing there at his right shoulder, between the two stools. Tweed overcoat. Shoulders looked damp. Crew-cut hair looked damp, too. As if he'd just come in from outside. Beard stubble on his face. Hard blue eyes. Tonight was a night for hard blue eyes. If you had brown eyes tonight, you were out of luck.

"Detective Daniel Cahill," he said, and opened a small leather case and flashed a blue-enameled gold shield. He snapped the case shut. "This man bothering you?" he asked Helen.

"It's all right, officer," she said.

"I'd like to know what's happening here," Cahill said.

"I don't want to make any trouble for him," she said.

"Why? What'd he do?"

It occurred to Michael that they were both talking about him as if he were no longer there. Somehow this sounded ominous.

"If he'll just give it back to me," Helen said.

"Give *what* back, miss?"

"Look, officer," Michael said.

"Shut up, please," Cahill said. "Give *what* back?"

"The ring."

"What ring?"

"Officer . . ."

"I asked you please to shut up," Cahill said, and suddenly looked around, as if aware for the first time that there were other people in the bar. "Let's step outside a minute, please," he said. "You, too, miss."

"Really, I don't want to make any trouble for him," Helen said.

"Please," Cahill said, and gestured slightly with his chin and his raised eyebrows, which seemed to indicate he had some concern for the owner of the place and did not want to make trouble for him, either. Which Michael considered a good sign. Helen got off her stool and put on her overcoat and picked up her briefcase, and Michael followed her and Cahill to where he'd hung his coat on the rack to the left of the entrance door. He was digging for the coat under the pile of other coats on top of it, when Cahill said, "You won't need it, this won't take a minute."

Together the three of them went outside, Helen first, then Michael, and then Cahill. It was still snowing. Bigger flakes now. Floating gently and lazily out of the sky. The temperature was in the low thirties, Michael guessed, perhaps the high twenties. He hoped this little conference out here in front of the bar really would be a short one.

"Okay, now what is it?" Cahill said.

Sounding very reasonable.

"He has my ring," Helen said.

Also sounding very reasonable.

"Officer," Michael said, "I never even *saw* this woman's . . ."

"Over here," Cahill said, and indicated the brick wall to the right of the bar's plate-glass front window. "Hands flat against the wall, lean on 'em," Cahill said.

"Hey, listen," Michael said.

"No, *you* listen," Cahill said. "The lady says you've got her ring . . . what kind of ring, lady?"

"A star sapphire."

"So you just put your hands on the wall here, and lean on them, and spread your legs, and if you ain't got her ring, you got nothin' to worry about."

"You've got no right to . . ."

"Then you want to go down the precinct? Okay, fine, we'll go down the precinct, we'll talk there. Let's go, my car's up the street."

"Why don't you just give me the ring, mister?" Helen said. "Save yourself a lot of trouble."

"I don't *have* your goddamn . . ."

"Okay, fine, let's go down the precinct," Cahill said.

"All right, all *right*," Michael said angrily, and leaned against the wall, his arms spread, his legs spread, his fingers spread, "let's get this over with, okay? I don't have the ring, you can search me from now to . . ."

"Fine, we'll just *see* what you got," Cahill said.

Michael's immediate impulse was to attack; the army had taught him that. But the army had also taught him never to start up with an M.P. Indignantly, angrily, he endured the frisk. Cahill ran his hands up and down Michael's legs, and then tossed up Michael's jacket and reached into the right hip pocket of his trousers, and took out his wallet. Behind him, Michael could hear him rummaging through the wallet.

"This you?" Cahill asked. "Michael Barnes?"

"Yes."

"This your driver's license?"

"Yes."

"You from Florida?"

"Yes."

"These your credit cards?"

"Yes, everything in the wallet is mine."

"Okay, fine," Cahill said, and put the wallet back into Michael's hip pocket and then began patting down the pockets of his jacket.

"If you don't mind," Michael said, "it's goddamn cold out here. I wish you'd . . ."

"Well, well, well," Cahill said, and his hands stopped. Michael felt a sudden chill that had nothing to do with the weather. Cahill was reaching into the right-hand pocket of Michael's jacket. "What have we here?" he said.

Michael held his breath.

"Off the wall," Cahill said, "*off* it! Turn around!"

Michael shoved himself off the wall. He turned. Cahill was holding a star sapphire ring between the thumb and forefinger of his right hand.

"This your ring, miss?" he asked Helen.

"Yes," she said.

"Officer," Michael said, "I don't know how that got in my pocket, but . . ."

"Let's go," Cahill said, "we all three of us got some work to do down the precinct."

"Could I have my ring, please?" Helen said.

"This is evidence, miss," Cahill said.

"No, it isn't *evidence*, it's a gift from my father, and I'd like it back, please."

"Miss, when we get down the precinct . . ."

"I'm not *going* down the precinct . . ."

"Miss . . ."

". . . or *up* the precinct or *around* the . . ."

"Miss, this individual here stole your ring . . ."

"Yes, but now we've got it back, so let me have it."

"Miss . . ."

"I told you I don't want to make any trouble for him."

"This individual is a *thief*, miss."

"I don't care what he is, just let me have the ring," Helen said.

Cahill looked at her.

"I do not wish to press charges, okay?" she said. "Do you understand that?"

"That's how criminals go free in this city," Cahill said. "Because people are afraid to . . ."

"Just give me the goddamn *ring*!" Helen said.

"Here's the goddamn ring," Cahill said sourly, and handed it to her.

"Thank you."

She put the ring on her finger.

"Good night," she said, and walked off.

"You're a very lucky thief," Cahill said, and walked off in the opposite direction.

"I'm not a goddamn *thief*!" Michael shouted to the empty air.

The words plumed out of his mouth, carried away on the wind, the vapor dissipating into the lazy swirl of snowflakes. His dark brown hair was covered with snow, the shoulders of his brown jacket were covered with snow, he had not been in a snowstorm for a good long time now – since before his mother sold the hardware business in Boston and loaned Michael the money for the groves in Florida – but now he was up to his ass in snow. Well, not quite. Not yet. Only up to the insteps of his shoes so far. He realized all at once that he was shivering. He shoved open the door to the bar.

Mahogany and brass, green-shaded lamps, the gentle *chink* of ice in glasses, the buzz of conversation, the friendly sound of laughter. Everything just as it had been before the blonde accused him of stealing her ring. Shaking his head, still amazed by what had happened, he went back to where he'd left his glass on the bar. He downed what was left of the scotch in two swallows and signaled to the bartender for another one.

The bartender scooped ice into a glass, began pouring from the bottle of Dewar's.

"What was *that* all about?" he asked.

"Don't ask," Michael said.

"Was that guy a cop?"

"Yeah."

"What was it? The girl hit on you?"

"What do you mean?"

"Was he Vice?"

"No, no, nothing like that."

"'Cause I thought maybe she was a hooker . . ."

"No, she was a lawyer."

"So what was it then?"

"She said I stole her . . . look, I don't want to discuss it," Michael said. "It's over and done with, I don't even want to *think* about it anymore."

Shaking his head again, he picked up the fresh drink and took a long swallow.

A man sitting three stools down the bar said, "I was watching the whole thing."

"With the hooker, you mean?" the bartender said, turning to him.

"She was a lawyer," Michael said.

"Hookers will often claim to be lawyers, bankers, university professors, what have you," the man down the bar said. He was tall and lanky, with a Lincolnesque face, a pronounced cleft in his chin, and a thick mane of white hair brushed back from a widow's peak. He was in his early to mid-fifties, Michael guessed, wearing a dark gray suit with a red-and-black silk rep tie. Brown eyes. Long-fingered hands. A deep, stentorian voice. "I've been chatted up by hookers who claimed to be investment counselors, architects, delegates to the U.N. and even children's book editors. They are all nonetheless hookers."

"It's hard to tell a hooker, this day and age," the bartender said, nodding in agreement.

"Until they name their price," the tall, thin man said, and then got off his stool and came up the bar to where Michael was sitting. Taking the stool the blonde had vacated, he said, "Arthur Crandall," and took from his vest pocket a business card made of very thin black plastic. The lettering on the card was in white, and it read:

CRANDALL FILMS, LTD.
Arthur Crandall, Director

In the lower left-hand corner of the card, there was a New York address and telephone number. In the lower right-hand corner, there was a Beverly Hills address and telephone number. The card looked and felt like a strip of movie film. Which Michael now realized was its intent.

"Michael Barnes," he said, and took a little leather card case from the right-hand pocket of his jacket, and slipped a card free, and handed it to Crandall. The card was illustrated with an orange tree that grew out of the lower right-hand corner, its branches and leaves spreading upward and leftward across the top of the card, its oranges overhanging green lettering that read:

GOLDEN ORANGE GROVES
16554 Fruitville Road
Sarasota, FL 34240

In the lower right-hand corner was Michael's name, followed by the word "President," and below that his telephone number.

"Pleased to meet you," Crandall said. "You grow oranges, I see."

"That's what I do," Michael said.

"I grow ideas, so to speak," Crandall said. "A writer comes to me with an idea, and I nurture it along until we have, *voilà, un film!*"

"Would I know any of your movies?" Michael asked.

"*War and Solitude?*" Crandall said, and looked at him expectantly.

"Uh-huh," Michael said.

"You've heard of it?"

"No."

"That was my most recent film. *War and Solitude.*"

"I'm sorry, but I don't know it," Michael said. "I think I've seen almost every movie ever made . . ."

"I see," Crandall said.

"Either in an actual theater or else on cable or on video-cassette . . ."

"I see," Crandall said again.

". . . but *War and Solitude* doesn't ring a . . ."

"But you know *Platoon*, right?"

"Oh, sure."

"*War and Solitude* was about the U.S. intervention in Nicaragua in 1926."

"Uh-huh," Michael said.

"It played art houses mostly," Crandall said.

"That must be why I missed it," Michael said. "We don't have too many art houses in Sarasota."

"It was meant to be a parable of sorts," Crandall said. "The film. But, of course, *Platoon* picked up all the marbles."

"It was a pretty realistic movie, I thought," Michael said. "*Platoon*. I was only over there for a little while, but . . ."

"Vietnam?"

"Yes. But I thought . . ."

"In combat?"

"Yes. I thought he really caught the feel of it. What it was like being there."

"You should see *my* movie," Crandall said. "You want the feel of war . . ."

"I'll look for it. Maybe it'll come to Sarasota someday."

"I doubt it," Crandall said.

"Well, you never know."

"Well, I *do* know, as a matter of fact," Crandall said somewhat heatedly. "Since the film was made eight years ago, and it didn't make a nickel then, it sure as hell isn't going to be re-released *now* after *Platoon* got the girl, the gold watch, and everything. Which, by the way, the reason I was so fascinated by the conversation between you and the girl was that it read like a movie script. A classic Hooker–John scene. Until she accused you of stealing her ring. That threw me. I found myself thinking if this hooker is trying to *land* this guy, why is she all at once accusing him of stealing her ring?"

"Yeah, well."

"Very puzzling," Crandall said.

"Anyway, she got the ring back, so I guess . . ."

"What do you mean?"

"It was in my pocket."

"It was?"

"Yeah."

"How did it get in your pocket?"

"I guess she put it there. At least, that's what I thought until she refused to press charges."

"Then why'd she put it in your pocket to begin with?"

"That's just it. Listen, who the hell cares? She got her ring back, the cop let me go . . ."

"Well, aren't you curious?"

"No."

"I guess that's why you grow oranges and I make movies," Crandall said.

"I hate to interrupt this discussion," the bartender said, "but do you want me to keep your tab running?"

"No, I better be on my way," Michael said. "What do I owe you?"

The bartender handed him the bill.

Michael glanced at it, took out his wallet, opened it, and reached into the bill compartment.

There was no money in the bill compartment.

There were no credit cards in the various little slots on either side of the wallet.

His driver's license was gone, too.

So was his card for the Sarasota Public Library.

"Shit," he said.

2

"Be that as it may," the bartender said, "who's going to pay for these drinks here?"

"*I'll* pay for the drinks," Crandall said, somewhat testily. "Is that all you can think of is who's going to pay for the drinks? This man has just had his money and his credit cards stolen and all you can think of . . ."

"All right, all right," the bartender said.

"Is it any wonder that this city has a reputation for insensitivity? Here's a man visiting from Florida, on Christmas *Eve*, no less . . ."

"All right, all right . . ."

"He has his credit cards and his money and his driver's license stolen, and all *you* can think of . . ."

"I said all *right* already!"

"We've got to report this to the police," Crandall said, taking out his own wallet, looking at the check, and then putting a twenty-dollar bill on the bar. "What precinct are we in?"

"The First," the bartender said.

"Where is that?"

"On Ericsson Place."

"*Where?*"

"Ericsson Place. You gotta go all the way over the West Side from here. It's just off Varick and Canal."

"Do you know how to get there?" Crandall asked Michael.

"No," Michael said. "This is the first time I've been down in this part of the city."

"Last time, too, I'll bet," the bartender said.

"I'll show you the way," Crandall said.

"Well, look, I have to catch an eleven-oh-five plane to Boston. What I thought . . ."

"That gives you over three hours," Crandall said.

"Well, I thought I'd leave the city by . . ."

"Even so. You don't want these people . . ."

"I thought I'd call from Boston, report it . . ."

"No, no, you can't do that," Crandall said. "You have to go to the police in person. That's the way it works. Otherwise nothing'll get done. Don't worry, I'll go with you. I have a photographic memory, I can give them a good description of that fake cop."

"Well, thanks but . . ."

"Where'd you park your car?"

"But you see, I thought it might be simpler . . ."

"Come on, this won't take a minute," Crandall said. "It's your duty as a citizen."

"He's right," the bartender said.

Michael looked at him.

"Really," the bartender said.

"Well, okay," Michael said, and nodded.

"So where's the car?" Crandall asked.

"Right around the corner."

"Probably be a parking ticket on it," the bartender said.

Crandall gave him a look.

"Sorry," he said, and went to the cash register.

"Do you remember what name he gave you?" Crandall asked.

"Yes. Detective Daniel Cahill."

"Good. Although the name was probably as phony as he was."

"Here's your change," the bartender said.

"Thank you," Crandall said. He looked at the check again, left a tip on the bar, and then said, "Let's go."

They walked out of the bar into a raging snowstorm.

What had earlier been a Charles Dickens sort of *Christmas Carol*-ish snowfall – with fat, gentle flakes swirling and dipping on the air, and little puffy white hats on the street lamps, and people hurrying by with long mufflers trailing, their footsteps hushed on sidewalks and streets covered with a thin dusting of white – had now turned into a blustery blizzard blowing wind and

15

tiny sharp snowflakes into every crack and crevice, covering the entire city with a fine, glistening, slippery coat of white already an inch thick.

"This we definitely do not need," Crandall said. "Where'd you say the car was?"

"Around the corner," Michael said.

They walked together to the corner, their heads ducked against the needle-sharp flakes driven by the wind, turned right, and then walked to the middle of the street where the rented car was parked under a street lamp. Michael unlocked the car on the driver's side, got in, and started it.

"If you'll flick open the trunk," Crandall said, "I'll see if we've got a scraper."

Michael reached for the trunk-release lever, close to the floor, and pulled on it.

"That's got it," Crandall said.

"Anything in there?" Michael called.

"Just a valise."

"Yes, that's mine."

"Nothing we can use," Crandall said, and slammed the trunk shut and came around the car to where Michael was sitting behind the wheel, the door open.

"One of those nights, huh?" he said.

"At least the defroster's working," Michael said.

"Good thing I wore gloves," Crandall said, and went around to the back of the car again, and began scraping at the rear window with the flat of his hand. It took them about five minutes to clear the windshield, the side windows, and the rear window. The car was toasty warm by then. Michael took off his glasses, wiped the lenses clear of condensation, and put them on again.

"You don't plan to drive, do you?" Crandall asked.

"What do you mean?"

"Well . . . he stole your license, didn't he?"

Michael said nothing.

He sat with his hands on the steering wheel, staring forlornly through the windshield, nodding.

At last he sighed and said, "Do you know how to drive?"

"Well, sure."

"Do you have a license?"

"Sure, but . . ."

"Would you please drive?"

"If you want me to, sure."

"I'd appreciate it," Michael said.

"I'll come around," Crandall said.

Both men got out of the car and walked around the front of it, through the snow, changing places. Behind the wheel now, Crandall familiarized himself with the dashboard instrumentation . . .

"Is this the headlight switch?"

"No, the one above it."

. . . and the gear-shift lever . . .

"Automatic transmission, huh?"

"Yes."

. . . and the brake and accelerator pedals.

"Shall I give it a whirl?" he asked.

"I'm ready when you are."

"I'll take it real slow," Crandall said, "make sure we don't get into any accidents."

He eased the car out of its space and into the street. The digital dashboard clock read 8:01, still early for a Saturday night. But this was Christmas Eve, and there was not much traffic in the streets. Besides, news of the impending storm had probably driven everyone home even earlier than usual.

"How does the road feel?" Michael asked.

"Not too bad."

Crandall drove knowledgeably through the narrow twisting streets of downtown Manhattan, a mysterious maze to Michael, inching the car along until finally they came to Canal Street, where Crandall waited out a red light and then made a left turn.

"They usually clear the main thoroughfares first," he said. "Here comes a snowplow now. We should have pretty clear sailing over to Varick. Why don't you put on the radio, see if we can get a forecast?"

Michael fiddled with the radio dial.

"Ten-ten is all news, all the time," Crandall said.

He was still driving slowly, although the road ahead was clear of snow. Wet but clear.

". . . Arab leaders maintaining that the proposed oil hikes were more than adequately . . ."

"Pain in the ass, the Arab leaders," Crandall said.

". . . justified by recent . . ."

"What the hell is *that*?" Crandall said.

". . . developments in the Persian Gulf. Should OPEC decide . . ."

"Turn that off," Crandall said.

Michael turned off the radio.

"Did you feel that?" Crandall said.

"No. Feel what?"

"Listen."

Michael listened.

"I think we've got a flat," Crandall said.

"You're kidding."

"I wish I were, my friend."

He glanced into the rearview mirror, rolled down the window on his side, and hand-signaled that he was pulling over to the curb. He double-parked alongside a laundry truck, looked into the rearview mirror again, and sighed deeply. "It's a horror movie, am I right?" he said, and shook his head. "You want to check that right rear tire?"

Michael opened the door on the passenger side and stepped out into *Nanook of the North*. He closed the door behind him and sidled back between the laundry truck and the car, his coat flapping around his knees, his hair dancing wildly on top of his head, snow beginning to cake on his eyeglasses. He stopped before the right rear tire, kicked at it perfunctorily, and was kneeling to study it more closely when the car pulled away.

He threw himself back against the laundry truck, thinking in that split second that Crandall had accidentally stepped on the accelerator, and then realizing in the next split second that Crandall hadn't made any damn mistake, the car was speeding away, swerving a little as it sought purchase on the wet roadway, and then shooting off as straight as an—

"Hey!" he shouted.

The car kept speeding away into the distance.

"You son of a bitch!" he shouted, and began running after the car.

He ran up the middle of Canal Street, waving his arms and shouting, his coat flapping, horns honking behind him, headlights coming at him from the other side of the road, blinding him. A fearful blast immediately at his back caused him to leap to his right just as the sound of air brakes filled the snow-laden air, and then another blast of the horn, and a voice shouting, "You dumb fuck!" and the rush of the trailer as it came by him like a locomotive on the way to Albuquerque, wherever that was, and then the truck was gone as certainly as was Crandall in the rented car.

Sucking in great gulps of air, trying to catch his breath, Michael leaned against a red Cadillac parked at the curb. The window on the driver's side slid down suddenly and electrically. He jumped away from the car, turned, saw a girl on the passenger side with her blouse wide open and her breasts bulging out of her brassiere, and alongside her, behind the wheel, a teenage Puerto Rican with a scraggly moustache and a lipstick-smeared face.

"You mine not leanin' on dee wagon?" the boy said.

A sign in Spanish on the wall behind the muster desk advised Michael of his rights. To the right of the sign was the same warning in English – which was considerate, Michael thought. The sergeant sitting behind the desk and before both signs was a very fat man wearing a long-sleeved blue sweater over his blue uniform shirt. He looked up and said, "Help you, sir?"

"I want to report a few crimes," Michael said.

"Let me hear 'em," the sergeant said.

"A fake detective stole all my money and my . . ."

"How do you know he was a *fake* detective?" the sergeant asked.

"Well, if he *robbed* me, I have to assume . . ."

"Oh, yeah, right," the sergeant said. "What did he get from you?" he asked, and picked up the phone receiver.

"My money, my credit cards, and my driver's license."

Into the phone, the sergeant said, "Tony, there's a man here had his money and his credit cards and his license stolen from him by a fake detective.

"My car, too," Michael said.

"His car, too," the sergeant said. "You want to talk to him?"

"By a different person," Michael said. "The car."

"Right, I'll send him up," the sergeant said, and hung up. "Sir," he said, "if you'll go right up those steps outside there to the second floor and follow the signs that say Detectives, you'll ask for Detective Anthony Orso, that means 'bear' in Italian, he'll take good care of you."

"Thank you," Michael said.

"Don't mention it," the sergeant said, and picked up a ringing telephone. "First Precinct, Mulready," he said.

Michael walked up the iron-runged steps to the second floor, followed the signs with the word DETECTIVES and a pointing arrow on them, and at last came to a blue door with a glass panel. Painted onto the panel was a large facsimile of a gold and blue-enameled shield like the one Cahill had flashed in the bar. Under that was a sign that read:

1st Precinct
Detectives
Room # 210

Michael guessed this was the detective squadroom. He opened the door and stepped into the room and the first thing he saw was a little man sitting on a blue upholstered chair behind one of the desks. He was badly in need of a shave and he looked like a street hoodlum.

"Detective Orso?" Michael asked.

"Tony the Bear, that's me," Orso said. "You the one Gallagher ripped off?"

Michael blinked.

"Come in, come in," Orso said, and got up, and ushered Michael in. The squadroom was small but freshly painted in a blue the same color as the door. Electric IBM typewriters sat on all the desktops. There were five or six desks in the room, but the room did not look crowded. A WANTED FOR MURDER poster with twelve photographs was taped to the wall over a small cabinet with fingerprinting equipment on it. A height chart was on the wall alongside the cabinet. Sitting on another blue-upholstered chair beside Orso's desk was a little man who looked remarkably like Orso's twin brother, except that his right hand was handcuffed to one of the chair rungs.

"We ain't got a detention cage," Orso explained.

"Some dump," the other man said.

"You shut up!" Orso said, pointing a finger at him.

"I know my rights," the man said.

"They all know their rights," Orso said sourly, and held out a chair for Michael. "Please, sir," he said.

20

From where Michael sat he could see both Orso and his look-alike in the other chair. The resemblance was uncanny. Michael wondered if Orso realized the man looked like him. And vice versa.

"So," Orso said. "Tell me what happened."

Michael told him what had happened. Orso listened. So did his twin brother.

"That's Gallagher, all right," Orso said.

"No, his name was Cahill," Michael said. "Detective Daniel Cahill."

"Are you sure? Was he working with a redhead calls herself Nikki Cooper, or sometimes Mickey Hooper, or sometimes Dorothy Callahan?"

"That don't rhyme," the other man said.

"Who asked you?" Orso said.

"Dorothy Callahan don't rhyme with the other two, that's all."

"I *know* it don't rhyme," Orso said. "Who says it has to rhyme?"

"She picks two names that rhyme, you figure the third one's gonna rhyme, too. But it don't."

"Do all *your* names rhyme?" Orso said.

"I got three names, too, and they all rhyme," the other man said, somewhat offended. "Charlie Bonano, Louie Romano, and Nicky Napolitano."

"What name were you using tonight when you stuck up the liquor store?" Orso asked.

"Charlie Bonano, and I didn't stick up no liquor store."

"No? Then who was it holding the gun on the proprietor?" Orso asked. "Musta been one of them two *other* guys, huh? Romano or Napolitano."

"Which ain't the point," Bonano said. "The point is a person chooses names that rhyme, then the names should rhyme. You don't go throwing in a Dorothy Calabrese."

"Callahan."

"Whatever."

"Shakespeare we got here in the squadroom," Orso said. "Worryin' about his iambic parameter."

"The point is . . ."

"The point is shut up. The point is we got this phony cop calls himself Gallagher runnin' all over the precinct workin' with a female redhead and rippin' off honest citizens like this gentleman here. Also, if you want to know somethin', Bonano, it's wops like you give Italians a bad name."

"*Three* bad names," Bonano said.

"And you're ugly besides," Orso said.

"So are you," Bonano said.

"Maybe so, but I ain't going to jail," Orso said, and turned back to Michael. "We'll have to fill out some papers, sir," he said, "but I can tell you right now we ain't got a chance in hell of getting back the cash, and we'll be lucky Gallagher don't clean out Tiffany's tomorrow with your credit cards. First thing you better do is advise all the companies that your cards were stolen – do you know the numbers on the cards?"

"Nobody knows the numbers on their cards," Bonano said.

"Who asked you?"

"*You* asked *him*."

"But nobody asked you, did they?"

"What's the point askin' the man an impossible question to answer? Excuse me, sir, but do you know the numbers on your credit cards?"

"No," Michael said.

"There you are," Bonano said.

"It so *happens*," Orso said, "I happen to *know* nobody knows the numbers on their credit cards. But it don't hurt to ask because one chance in a million, the person will know. It don't matter whether he knows or not, *anyway*, 'cause the credit card company has all this shit on a computer, and all you have to do, sir," he said, turning again to Michael, "is give them your name and address, and tell them your cards were stolen, and they'll make sure the word goes out. Otherwise, Gallagher's gonna buy himself a ticket on the Concorde to Paris and charge it to your Master-Card."

"*Two* tickets," Bonano said. "One for his girlfriend Dotty."

"You'll have to inform all your credit card companies," Orso said solemnly. "Now, sir," he said, and rolled some forms and some sheets of carbon into his typewriter. "Can you tell me your name, please?"

"Michael J. Barnes."

"What does the J stand for, sir?"

"Just J. Just the letter J."

"Yes, sir, and your address, sir? In case we catch Gallagher in the next hour or so."

"Ha!" Bonano said.

Orso gave him a look. Bonano shrugged.

"I *was* staying at the Hilton," Michael said. "But I've already checked out. In fact, my valise was in the . . ."

"On Fifty-fourth and Sixth?"

"Yes."

"I stayed at the Hilton once," Bonano said.

"What is it with you, huh?" Orso said. "Don't you know how to keep your mouth shut?"

"It's a very nice hotel, sir," Bonano said, as though complimenting its owner.

Orso rolled his eyes. "Your home address, please," he said.

"16554 Fruitville Road," Michael said. "Sarasota, Florida."

"Ah-ha," Orso said. "Something told me you were from Florida."

"Like maybe his suntan," Bonano said. "Are you near Hollywood Park? I go to Hollywood Park for the races."

"That's on the east coast," Michael said.

"So," Orso said, "from what the desk sergeant told me on the phone, Gallagher stole not only your money, your credit cards, and your driver's license, but also your car. What kind of . . ."

"No, it wasn't Cahill who stole the car," Michael said.

"Gallagher, you mean."

"Neither one."

"Then who was it?"

"Arthur Crandall."

"Who?" Bonano said.

"Arthur Crandall," Michael said. "He's a movie director. Here's his card."

"He stole your car and gave you his *card*?" Orso said, astonished.

"That is *some* classy thief," Bonano said.

Orso looked at the card.

"This looks like a piece of film," he said.

"It's his business card," Michael said.

"I can't get over it. A guy steals your car and hands you his card."

"He gave me the card first," Michael said.

"And *then* stole your car?" Bonano said.

"One thing I know for sure," Orso said, "a guy planning to steal your car hands you a business card with a name and two addresses on it, the name and the addresses are phony."

"For sure," Bonano said.

"So what we got here," Orso said, "is two unrelated cases. We got a phony cop and his copy editor girlfriend . . . did she tell you she was a copy editor?"

"No, a lawyer."

"Not a copy editor?"

"A criminal lawyer."

"Hmm," Orso said, and shook his head. "Well, what we got here nonetheless is this phony pair who stole your money and your credit cards and your driver's license . . ."

"My library card, too," Michael said.

"Do you read a lot?" Bonano asked.

"Yes," Michael said.

"I do, too. I developed the habit in the slammer."

"Sir, are you paying attention here?" Orso said.

"Yes, I'm sorry," Michael said.

"That's perfectly all right, sir. And we also got this phony movie director who stole your car . . ."

"It was a rented car," Michael said.

"Good thing," Bonano said.

"Which in no way diminishes the fact of Grand Theft, Auto," Orso said. "The point being we now got *two* cases here instead of one. Which now makes it *twice* as hard." He sighed heavily, and then said, "When did you plan on leaving the city, sir? In case we hear anything."

"I'm catching an eleven-oh-five plane out of Kennedy," Michael said, and looked at his watch.

"Do you have your plane ticket already?"

"Yes, I do."

"All paid for and everything?"

"Yes."

"That's very good, sir. How did you plan on getting to the airport, sir?"

"Well, I haven't given that any thought, actually."

"Since all your money was stolen, you see."

"Yes, that's true."

"In fact, sir, how did you plan on getting to Chambers Street?"

"Why would I want to go to Chambers Street?" Michael asked.

"Because that's where you can catch an express train to Kennedy."

"Oh."

"Are you familiar with our subway system, sir?"

"No."

"I will give you a subway map, sir, which will acquaint you with all the lines in the city."

"How's he gonna ride the subway if he ain't got no money?" Bonano asked.

"Well, I have some change," Michael said, and reached into his right-hand pocket. "What's the fare, something like a quarter?"

"A quarter!" Orso said.

"A quarter!" Bonano said.

Both men burst out laughing.

"The fare hasn't been a quarter since the *Dutch* were here!" Orso said, laughing.

"The *Indians*!" Bonano said, laughing.

"Well, I've got . . ." Michael quickly counted the coins on his palm. "Sixty cents," he said.

"Sixty cents!" Orso said, and burst into new gales of laughter.

"Sixty cents!" Bonano said. "I'm gonna wet my pants!"

"Sir," Orso said, "the fare has been a dollar since Hector was a pup, sir. That is the subway fare in the city of New York. For *now*, anyway."

"How much does it cost in Sarasota?" Bonano asked.

"We don't have a subway," Michael said, and looked at the coins on his palm again. "Mr Orso," he said, "do you think I can . . . ?"

"No, don't, sir," Orso said.

Michael looked at him.

"Please, sir."

Michael kept looking at him.

"Please don't ask me for a loan, sir. Please. I know that all you need is forty cents to make up the difference between the subway fare and what you've got. But, sir, perhaps you don't know how many victims we get in here all the time, day and night, this city never sleeps, sir, victims who have had every penny taken from them and who need bus fare or subway fare to get them back home again. Sir, I can tell you that if I gave every one of those victims forty cents, or even a quarter, or a dime, sir, even a thin dime, why, sir, I'd be giving away my entire salary to these people and I'd have nothing left to put clothes on my children's backs or food in their bellies. So, please, sir. As much as I'd like to . . ."

"You're breaking my heart," Bonano said, reaching into his pocket with his free hand. "Here's ten bucks," he said to Michael, and with some difficulty extracted two five-dollar bills from his wallet. "This'll get you to Kennedy."

"That is probably tainted money, sir," Orso said. "But do as you see fit."

Michael looked at the bills.

"Money from the proceeds of prostitution or drugs," Orso said. "But let your conscience be your guide."

Michael took the money.

"Thank you," he said to Bonano. "I'll pay you back."

"You can send your check to Sing Sing," Orso said.

"My luck, I'll get Attica," Bonano said.

"Write it out to any one of his names," Orso said. "And, sir, I hope there are no hard feelings. It's just that if I lend money to . . ."

"Where are the violins?" Bonano asked.

"Actually," Michael said, "I wasn't about to ask for a loan."

"You weren't?" Orso said.

"You wasted a whole speech," Bonano said.

"I only wanted to use your toilet."

"Oh. Well, it's just down the hall."

"Thank you."

"But they have very nice toilets at the airport," Bonano said.

"You don't want my subway map?" Orso said, sounding hurt.

"I *do*," Michael said. "Yes, thank you for reminding me."

"Here's what you do," Orso said, opening the map. "You go outside, you make an immediate right the minute you come down the steps, and the first street you hit is Varick. Okay, you make another right on Varick, and you walk past Moore, which there's a place called Walker's on the corner, and the next cross street you come to is Franklin. But you don't want to go all the way to Franklin . . ."

"I don't?"

"No, because just before you get to Franklin, what you'll see is a subway kiosk, that's the one right here," he said, and put his finger on the map. "Okay, you go downstairs, and you buy a token for a dollar, and you go to the downtown platform, make sure it's the *downtown* platform, and you get on the A-train. The first stop after Franklin is Chambers Street, that's right here," he said, and put his finger on the map again. "You get off at Chambers, and you wait for the JFK Express it's called, which'll cost you five and a half bucks direct to the airport. There'll be directions when you get off the train," Orso said, and nodded in conclusion, and folded the map, and handed it to Michael.

"Thank you," Michael said.

"I hope you understand about the money and all. It's just that with all the victims in this city . . ."

"Bring on the Philharmonic," Bonano said.

"Will you let me know if you hear anything?"

"They *never* hear anything," Bonano said. "You'll get old and gray waiting for them to catch that phony cop and his girl. Or the phony movie guy, either."

"We caught *you*, didn't we?"

"Only 'cause my pants fell down when I pulled the gun," Bonano said.

"You're even uglier with your pants down," Orso said, and both men burst out laughing.

They were still laughing when Michael left the squadroom.

He went down the hall to use the toilet, and then came down the iron-runged steps, waving the subway map in farewell to a uniformed cop going up, and then opened one of the blue wooden doors leading to the street, and stepped outside into *Fang, Son of Claw*. The wind almost blew him off the front steps of the station house. It was snowing even more heavily now, the flakes swirling dizzily around the green globes on the station house wall, the lights casting an eerie glow onto the thick carpet of snow on the steps and the sidewalk below. He pulled up the collar of his coat, walked to the corner, turned right on Varick, walked past Moore, and was just approaching the lighted subway kiosk ahead when a huge man wearing blue jeans, a leather jacket, black gloves, and a ski mask stepped out of a doorway and stuck a gun in his face.

3

One good thing Michael had learned in Vietnam was that a bad situation could only get worse. Either you reacted immediately or you never got a chance to react at all. Only three words came from the man's mouth, cutting through the wind and the slashing snow, but those words meant trouble. "Hands up, man!" and Michael moved at once, inside the gun hand, knee coming up into the man's groin, head rising swiftly to butt the ski-masked chin as the man doubled over in pain. There was the click of teeth hitting teeth. The man lurched, his hands flailing the air as he twisted partly away from Michael, who reached out for the collar of the leather jacket, caught it, twisted his hand into it, and yanked back on it.

He might have been in the jungle again, this could have been Vietnam again. But there was snow underfoot and not the damp rot of vegetation, and the man was wearing black leather instead of black pajamas. Nor was this a slight and slender Oriental who you sometimes felt you could break in half with your bare hands, this was a giant who measured perhaps six-feet two-inches tall and weighed two hundred pounds, and he wasn't about to be yanked over on his back by someone who was shorter by four inches and lighter by thirty pounds. Michael hadn't done this kind of work for a long time now. You got fat living in Florida. Eating oranges and watching the sun go down. You forgot there were such things as people wanting to hurt you. You forgot there were such things as sometimes getting killed.

In the old days, there'd have been a knife in his hands and he'd have gone for the throat. But that was then, and this was now, and Michael was working very hard and breathing very hard as the man turned and swung the gun at the same time, slamming the butt into the side of Michael's head, knocking the subway map out of his hand and knocking Michael himself to the sidewalk. He immediately rolled away in the snow, because jungle fighting had taught him yet another thing: if one man is holding a gun and the other man is on the ground and the first man doesn't fire, then the gun is empty and the next thing that's coming is a kick.

Michael didn't know how the gun could be empty since not a single shot had been fired, but the kick came right on schedule, aimed straight for the spot on his head where the gun had already hit him. His head wasn't there anymore, though. His head was perhaps six inches from where the kick sliced the air, eight inches now because he was still rolling away from the kick, a foot away now, rolling, rolling, and then scrambling to his knees and bracing himself because the man was coming at him again, bellowing in what seemed to be genuine rage although Michael hadn't done a damn thing to him but kick him in the balls and butt him under the chin a little.

"Freeze!" a woman's voice shouted, but nobody froze anything. Michael kept coming up off his knees because being on your knees was a bad position when a gorilla was charging you, and the gorilla kept right on charging and bellowing but not firing the gun, which caused Michael to think yet another time that the gun was empty.

"I said, freeze, *police*!" the woman shouted again, which wasn't at all what she'd said the first time, and which this time caused the gorilla to hesitate for just the slightest bit of an instant, but that was all the time Michael needed. He feinted at the masked man's head with a right jab, and then kicked sideways and hard at his ankles, hoping the snow underfoot would help the maneuver, which it did. The man's feet slid out from under him and he went crashing down in the opposite direction, the gun flying out of his hand. This time Michael was on him in a wink, straddling him, and chopping the flat of his hand across the bridge of where the nose should have been under the mask. The man screamed. Michael hoped he'd broken the nose. The woman screamed, too.

"Police, police, break it *up*, goddamn it!"

She was standing at the top of the steps leading down to the subway.

She didn't look like any cop Michael had ever seen in his life.

She was, in fact, a very fat woman in her late thirties, he guessed, wearing a short black monkey-fur jacket over a red garter belt, red panties, red seamed silk stockings, and red high-heeled boots.

At first, Michael thought she was a mirage.

Coming up out of the subway that way. Half-naked. In a snowstorm no less.

Flaming red hair to match the lingerie and boots. Blazing green eyes, five-feet four-inches tall and weighing at least a hundred and fifty pounds.

Michael picked up the gun and pointed it at the man in the snow.

"Up!" he said. "On your feet!"

"Drop the gun," the fat redhead said.

Michael had no intention of dropping the gun. Not while the man sitting in the snow was still breathing.

"You hurt me," the man said.

High, piping, frightened voice.

"No kidding?" Michael said, and reached down for the ski mask, pulling it off his head, wanting to see just how *much* he'd hurt him.

The man was Chinese.

Or Japanese.

Or, for all Michael knew, Vietnamese.

Everything seemed suddenly like a dream. He was back in the jungle again, where everyone had slanted eyes, and where day and night he dreamed of naked redheaded women materializing in the mist, though not as short or as fat as this one was. Back then the women who materialized were very slender, but they were all carrying hand grenades in their armpits. The bad guys were slender, too. And very small. This bad guy was very large.

"You son of a bitch," he said.

In perfect English.

"Nice talk," the fat redhead said. "You," she said to Michael. "I told you to drop the gun."

"Where's your badge?" Michael said.

"Here's my badge," she said, and took from her handbag a shield that looked very much like the one Cahill had flashed in the bar, gold with blue enameling. "Detective O'Brien," she said, "First Squad."

"Officer," the Oriental man said at once, "this person broke my nose."

"No, I don't think so," Michael said.

"Get up," Detective O'Brien said.

"I think he broke some of my *teeth*, too."

He was on his feet now, tongue searching his teeth for chips, hand rubbing his nose at the same time. Michael knew the nose wasn't broken. He'd have jumped out of his skin just touching it. The teeth were another matter. He'd butted the man pretty hard.

"What are you doing sticking up people?" he asked.

He had the idea that Chinese guys – if he was Chinese – didn't go around sticking up people. Japanese guys, neither. He wasn't so sure about Vietnamese.

"What are *you* doing trying to *kill* people?" the man said.

"I was defending myself," Michael said.

"From what? A fake gun?"

Michael looked at the gun in his hand. It had the weight and heft of a real gun, but it was nonetheless plastic. By now, the man had decided that nothing was broken. Teeth all okay, nose still intact. Which put Michael in a dangerous position in that the gun in his hand was plastic and the man standing before him was beginning to look bigger and bigger every minute. Michael had never seen such a large Oriental in his life. He wondered if perhaps the man was a fake Oriental, the way Cahill had been a fake detective and the way the plastic gun in his hand was a fake Colt .45 automatic.

The gun Detective O'Brien pulled out of her handbag looked very real.

"I'll shoot the first one of you fucks who moves," she said.

Which sounded like authentic cop talk, too.

"You," she said. "What's your name?"

"Charlie Wong."

"Chinese, huh?" she asked.

"No, Jewish," Wong said sarcastically, which Michael figured was the wrong way to sound when a fat lady in only her underwear and a monkey-fur jacket was standing in the shivering cold with a pistol in her hand.

"And you?" she said to Michael.

"Presbyterian," he said.

"Your *name*," she said impatiently, and wagged the gun at him.

"A cop," Wong said, shaking his head, "I can't believe it. I thought you were a hooker."

"Why, thank you," Detective O'Brien said.

"That's the way the hookers dress down here," Wong explained to Michael. "Even in cold weather like this. All year round, in fact."

"If you two *gentlemen* don't mind," Detective O'Brien said, sounding as sarcastic as Wong had earlier sounded, "what we're gonna do now is march to the station house, 'cause quite frankly I don't appreciate disorderly conduct on my . . ."

Wong shoved out at Michael, who in turn lost his footing and crashed into Detective O'Brien, who fell over backward onto her almost-naked behind, her silk-stockinged legs flying into the air, her gun going off. Michael figured that what he had here was a fat lady who was a real cop with a real badge and a real gun, but who thought he was a two-bit brawler instead of a two-bit victim. He decided he did not want to spend the rest of the night explaining that Wong had tried to hold him up. Especially since Detective O'Brien was now sitting up in the snow at the top of the steps leading down to the subway, her elbows on her knees, the pistol in both hands, taking very careful aim at him.

He had learned another thing in Vietnam.

"Aiiii-eeeeeee!" he yelled.

When you heard this in the jungle, your blood ran cold.

It worked here in downtown Manhattan, too.

Detective O'Brien screamed back at him in terror. Her gun went off wildly, and so did Michael, in the same direction Wong had gone, running back toward Moore, and crossing the street, and seeing Wong up ahead going a hundred miles an hour.

Michael took a quick look at his watch.

8:45.

His plane would be leaving in two hours and twenty minutes.

He could not go down into the subway to catch his A-train to Chambers because Detective O'Brien was behind him, sitting between him and his transportation. There was not a taxi anywhere in sight, and besides the ten dollars Bonano had loaned him was not enough for cab fare to Kennedy. He did not know this goddamn city where everyone seemed to be either a cop or a crook and all of them seemed to be crazy. He did not know where there might be *another* subway station where he could catch an express train to the airport, because his map was behind him, too, there on the sidewalk between him and O'Brien. He knew only that when you were lost in the jungle, you followed a native guide.

Behind him, Detective O'Brien fired her gun. Into the air, he hoped.

He ran like hell after Wong.

They ran for what seemed like miles.

Wong was a good runner. Michael was out of shape and out of breath. His shoes were sodden and his socks were wet and his feet were cold and his eyeglasses kept caking with snow, which he repeatedly cleared as he followed Wong, both of them padding silently over fields of white, the curbs gone now, no difference now between sidewalk and street, just block after block of white after white after white in a part of the city that was totally alien to him. But at last he turned a corner behind Wong and saw him ducking into a doorway with Chinese lettering over it. Michael looked at his watch again. 8:57. Wong disappeared into the doorway. Michael followed him.

He wiped off his glasses and put them back on again.

He was inside a Chinese fortune-cookie factory.

A Chinese man in white pants, a white shirt, a long white apron, and a white chef's hat stood behind a stainless steel counter stuffing fortune cookies with little slips of paper.

"Which way did he go?" Michael asked.

"True ecstasy is a golden lute on a purple night," the fortune-cookie stuffer said.

There was a door at the far end of the room. Michael pointed to it.

"Did he go in there?" he asked.

"He who rages at fate rages at barking dogs," the man said, and stuffed another cookie.

"Thank you," Michael said, and went immediately toward the door.

Behind him, the fortune-cookie stuffer said, "Dancers have wings but pigs cannot fly."

33

Michael opened the door.

He was suddenly in a downtown-Saigon gambling den.

In Saigon, there were only three things to do: get drunk, get laid, or get lucky. There were a great many gambling dens lining the teeming side streets of Saigon, and he had gambled in most of them and had never got lucky in any of them. Nor had he ever seen anyone playing Russian roulette in any of them. That was for the movies. He had told Arthur Crandall – or whatever his real name was – that *Platoon* was a pretty realistic movie but the operative word in that observation was "movie." Because however realistic it might have been, it was still only and merely a movie, and everyone sitting in that theater knew that he was watching flickering images on a beaded screen and that the guns going off and the blood spurting were fake. In the jungle, the guns going off and the blood spurting were real.

You could never show in a movie the *feel* of a friend's hot blood spilling onto your hands when he took a hit from a frag grenade. Never. You could never explain in the most realistic of war films that you had shit your pants the first time a mortar shell exploded six feet from where you were lying on your belly in the jungle mud. In war movies, nobody ever shit his pants. You could never explain the terror and revulsion you'd felt the first time you saw a dead soldier lying on his back with his cock cut off and stuffed into his mouth. In war movies, guys compensated for their terror and revulsion by playing Russian roulette in Saigon gambling dens. In real life, what you did in Saigon gambling dens was you bet on the roll of the dice, the turn of the card, or – occasionally – the courage and skill of a rooster. Cockfights in Saigon were as common as severed cocks in the jungle, but you never saw a cockfight in the same building where people were shooting crap or playing poker.

Here and now, in this section of the fortune-cookie factory, there were no cockfights. There were stainless steel ovens, and there were two crap games on blankets against one of the walls, and two poker games at tables, and a mah-jongg game at yet another table. The mah-jongg table was occupied entirely by Chinese men who looked as if they had stepped full blown out of the Ming Dynasty. This was by far the noisiest table in the room, the Chinese men slamming down tiles and shouting what sounded like orders to behead someone, and the men standing around the table shouting either encouragement or disparagement, it was difficult to tell. There was some noise, but not as much, coming from the two crap games on the blankets, where – as had been the case in Saigon – there were Orientals playing with white guys, black guys, and Hispanics. A television set on a shelf high on the wall was turned up to its full volume, and Andy Williams had just come on in a Christmas special that contributed mightily to the overall din. In contrast to the television jubilance, the poker players were virtually solemn. A pall of smoke hung over the entire room. Charlie Wong was nowhere in sight.

Michael looked at his watch. 9:05. He had to get out of here and find a way to get to Kennedy by subway. His plane would be leaving in exactly two hours, the last plane to Boston tonight. He wandered over to one of the crap games, thinking he'd ask one of the players how to get to a subway stop that would connect with the Kennedy train. A short Hispanic – who looked remarkably like the young man who'd asked him not to lean on his car – picked up the dice, blew on them, said, "*Mama necesita un par de zapatos nuevos!*" and promptly rolled snake eyes. "*Mierda!*" he shouted, and immediately walked away from the blanket. On the television screen, Andy Williams was singing "Jingle Bells."

Michael stepped into the space the little Hispanic had vacated.

Taxi fare would be nice, he thought.

There were five players in the game now: two blacks, two Chinese, and a white man. One of the black men was named Harry. Michael discerned this when the dice were handed to him and one of the Chinese men said, "Come on, Hally, ketchum up hot," sounding like the cook in an old movie about the Gold Rush. At the mah-jongg table, one of the Chinese men there shouted something that sounded fierce and warlike, but everyone at the table laughed. Here at the blanket, Harry laughed, too. Michael figured he was laughing not because he spoke or understood Chinese but because it was now his turn to roll the dice, and a man holding a pair of dice in his hand is – for the moment, at least – in control of his own destiny.

Harry did indeed look like a man with the world on a string. Tall and wiry and chocolate-colored, he possessed in addition to his good looks a dirty Eddie Murphy laugh, a mischievous Bill Cosby twinkle, and the calm, confident air of a man about to make a fortune. Michael would have bet all the oranges on every tree in his groves on the roll of the dice this man held in his hand. But he had only the ten dollars Charlie Bonano had loaned him.

"Bet a hundred," Harry said, and put five twenty-dollar bills on the blanket. The hundred was covered in thirty seconds flat; apparently most of these players had seen Harry roll before and the air of confidence he exuded impressed them not a bit. The only man at the blanket who seemed to have any faith in him at all was the Chinese man who'd earlier urged him to ketchem up hot. He now said, "Twenny say Hally light."

"Ten says he's wrong," the other black man at the blanket said.

"Me, too, hassa ten long," the other Chinese man said, sounding like a stoker on an American gunboat during the Boxer Rebellion.

"Ten more says he's right," Michael said, and tossed onto the blanket all the money he had in the world.

The white guy – a burly man wearing a blue sweater and a blue watch cap, and looking like a seaman off a cargo ship – said, "Ten says he's wrong," and tossed his money onto the blanket.

On the television screen, Andy Williams and what appeared to be the entire Mormon Tabernacle Choir began bellowing "God Rest Ye Merry, Gentlemen."

"Come on, sugah," Harry whispered, and shook the dice gently, and let them roll easily off the pink palm of his hand and onto the blanket. The dice rolled and rolled and rolled, and hit the wall, and bounced off the wall, and one of them flew to the right and came up with a six-spot, and the other one flew to the left and came up with a five-spot, for a total of eleven, which was a winner.

Michael now had twenty dollars.

Was twenty enough for a taxi to Kennedy?

He looked at his watch.

9:15.

His heart almost stopped.

The girl walking toward the blanket was tall.

Five-nine, he supposed.

Much taller than the girls who'd worked the Saigon bars.

But every bit as beautiful. So achingly beautiful, those Vietnamese girls. Girls, yes, some of them were barely in their teens. That long glossy black hair and the slanted loam-colored eyes, the complexion as pale as a dipper of cream, a faint tint to it, not

36

yellow, you could not call any Oriental on earth yellow, any more than you could call anyone black, or red for that matter, or even white, it was pointless to try to identify people by color because the colors simply didn't match. Here and now she came gliding sleekly out of the din and the smoke, a sinuous glide unique to Orientals, a green silk dress slit high on her right thigh, a red rose in her black hair, green satin high-heeled pumps, the colors of Christmas, fa-la-la-la-la, Andy Williams sang, and Michael wondered how many Saigon hookers he had fallen in love with. And later killed their sisters in the jungle.

"Hello, Harry," she said, "are you winning?"

"Jus' rolled me a 'leven," Harry said.

Michael smiled at her. She did not smile back.

An hour and fifty minutes to plane time.

"Let the twenty ride," he said, and realized he was showing off for her, big spender betting all his money without batting an eyelash.

Harry picked up the dice, winked at him, and said, "Man knows a winner. Bet the two hunnerd."

"I'll take it all," the other black man said.

"You facin' disaster, Slam," Harry told him and laughed his dirty Eddie Murphy laugh.

"I'm facin' a man got lucky one time," Slam said.

"Oh, my my my," Harry said to the dice, "you hear this man runnin' his mouth?"

"Who wanna fiffy more?" the first Chinese man asked.

"I'll take thirty of that," the seaman with the watch cap said.

"I hassa twenny," the second Chinese man said.

Harry brought the dice up close to his mouth.

"Sugah," he whispered, "we don't wanna disappoint our friends here, now do we?"

He was talking to the dice as if he were talking to a woman. How could they possibly fail a man who speaks so gently and persuasively? Michael thought, and realized he was smiling. The girl thought he was smiling at her. Maybe he was. But she still did not smile back. Oh well, he thought.

"You know jus' what we need," Harry told the dice, "so I'm jus' goan let you do yo' own thing," and he shook the dice gently, and opened his hand again, and the dice rolled off his palm and strutted across the blanket, and kissed the wall, and skidded off the wall to land with a five-spot and a six-spot showing for a total of eleven again, which was another winner.

Michael now had forty dollars, certainly enough to get him to Kennedy by cab.

"How's that, James?" Harry asked.

"Good," the first Chinese man said, beaming.

"*No* good," the second Chinese man said sourly.

"Bet the four hundred," Harry said.

Michael looked at the girl one last time. She seemed not to know he existed. He pocketed his forty bucks and started moving away from the blanket.

"Don't go, man," Harry said softly.

Michael looked at him.

"You my luck, man."

In Vietnam – ah, Jesus, in Nam – too many young men had said those words to too many other young men. Over there, you needed something to believe in other than yourself, you needed a charm, a rabbit's foot, a buddy to stand beside you, to be your luck when it looked as though your luck might run out at any moment.

Michael looked at his watch.

9:30.

If he could get out of the city in the next half hour or so, he'd be okay. The roads to Kennedy would surely be clear of snow by now, it would be a quick half-hour run by taxi, walk directly to the gate, no luggage – thanks to Crandall – and off he'd go.

"You with me or not?" Harry asked.

There was something almost desperate in his eyes. "I've got forty says you're good," Michael said, and tossed the money onto the blanket and smiled at the girl. This time, she smiled back.

"What's your name?" she asked.

"Michael," he said.

"How do you do?" she said.

"We shootin' dice here?" Slam asked, "or we chattin' up Miss Shanghai?"

"Miss Mott Street, you mean," the seaman with the watch cap said.

"Miss China Doll," the second Chinese man said.

"Are you really all those things?" Michael asked.

"No, I'm Connie," she said.

"Willya please *roll* 'em?" Slam said.

Grinning from ear to ear, Harry picked up the dice.

He was good for the next pass, and three more passes after that, by which time Michael's initial ten bucks had grown to six hundred and forty dollars. He looked at his watch again – 9:45 – and decided to let all of it ride on Harry's phenomenal luck. He wondered if he was risking the money just so he could stay here by Connie's side. All at once, the plane to Boston didn't seem too very important. Missing a plane to Boston wasn't the end of the world. On the television screen, Andy Williams began singing "Silent Night."

Harry rolled a ten, a tough point to make.

Then Harry rolled a four . . .

And a nine . . .

And a six . . .

And an eight . . .

And Michael began wondering how many numbers he could roll before a seven came up and killed them both dead. Michael had never in his life won a nickel in a Saigon gambling house, but he'd kept rolling number after number out there in the jungle, never sevening out while everywhere around him brief good friends were dying.

"Tough point," he said.

"Very," Connie said, and smiled.

He smiled back.

Harry was whispering to the dice again.

This time I buy the farm, Michael thought.

"Sugah, we need a six and a four," Harry whispered.

It was almost ten o'clock.

On the television set, Andy Williams was saying good night to everyone, wishing everyone in America a Merry Christmas. Michael paid no attention to him. His eyes were on Connie and his six hundred and forty bucks were on the blanket.

"Two fives, baby," Harry whispered to the dice, and shook them gently in his fist, and opened his hand and said, "Ten the hard way, sugah," and the dice rolled out and away toward the wall.

On the television screen, the news came on. The headline story was a bombing in Dublin, but no one was listening to it.

One of the dice bounced off the wall.

A three.

The second die hit the wall.

Bounced off it.

A four.

Shit, Michael thought, there goes my taxi.

"In downtown Manhattan tonight," the male anchor said, "motion-picture director Arthur Crandall . . ."

Michael looked up at the screen.

". . . was found shot to death in a rented automobile. Police report finding a wallet in the car, possibly dropped by Crandall's murderer. It contained . . ."

Everyone around the blanket was looking up at the screen.

". . . sixty-three dollars in cash, several credit cards, and a driver's license identifying . . ."

"Good night," Michael said, "thank you," and began walking toward the door across the room.

". . . a man named Michael Barnes, who the Hertz company confirms rented the car at Kennedy this past Mon . . ."

Michael closed the door behind him.

The same man was still behind the stainless-steel table, stuffing fortune cookies.

"Have a nice holiday," Michael said.

"The down of white geese shall float upon your dreams," the man said.

The door opened again.

"Wait for me," Connie said.

4

It had stopped snowing.

She was wearing a short black coat over the green dress. The red rose was still in her hair. Black coat, black hair, green dress and shoes, red rose – all against a background of white on white. The silent night Andy Williams had promised. Still and white, except for the flatness of the black and the sheen of the green and the shriek of the red in her hair.

"You've got trouble, huh?" she said.

He debated lying.

"Yes," he said, "I've got trouble."

Their breaths pluming on the frosty air.

"Come on," she said, "I've got a limo around the corner."

He thought that was pretty fortunate, a rich Chinese girl with a chauffeured limo to take her hither and yon in the city. He didn't want to go anywhere in this city but *out* of it. Straight to Kennedy, where he would catch his plane to Boston and Mama, or else try to get a plane to Florida. Get out of this rotten apple as soon as possible, call his lawyer the minute he landed someplace. Dave, they are saying I murdered somebody in New York, Dave. What should I do?

Hushed footfalls on the fresh snow.

Everything looking so goddamn beautiful.

But they were saying he'd killed somebody.

The limousine was parked outside a Chinese restaurant on Elizabeth Street. Long and black and sleek, it looked like a Russian submarine that had surfaced somewhere on an Arctic glacier. There were Christmas decorations in both front windows of the restaurant, all red and green and tinselly. The building up the street seemed decorated for Christmas, too, with green globes flanking the –

"Hey," Michael said, "that's a . . ."

"I know," Connie said, "the Fifth Precinct. Don't worry about it. Just get in the back of the car the minute I unlock it."

She hurried ahead of him on the sidewalk, struggling through the thick snow in her high-heeled pumps while up the street a Salvation Army band played "Adeste Fideles," and a man with a microphone pleaded with passersby to be generous. It was a little past ten-fifteen by Michael's watch, but the streets here in Chinatown were still crowded with Christmas Eve shoppers. He watched Connie as she stepped off the curb, walked around to the driver's side of the car, and inserted a key in the lock. She opened the door, nodded to him, and immediately got into the car. He came up the street swiftly, stopped at the back door on the curb side, opened it. He got in at once, closed the door behind him, and said, "Where's the chauffeur?"

"I'm the chauffeur," she said.

"This is your car?"

"No, it's a China Doll car." She turned on the seat, looking back at him. "China Doll Executive Limousine Service," she explained. "I'm one of the drivers." To emphasize the point, she settled a little peaked chauffeur's hat on her head. The rose seemed suddenly incongruous. She handed him a card. Everyone in this city had a card. The card read:

CHINA DOLL
EXECUTIVE LIMOUSINE SERVICE
Charles Wong, President

"Charlie Wong!" he said.

"You know him?"

"He tried to hold me up!"

"Charlie? No. He's a respectable businessman. He has twelve limos."

"I don't care if he has a *hundred* limos. He stuck a gun in my face."

"Charlie?"

42

"Well, a plastic gun. Yes, *Charlie*! A big Chinese guy with . . ."

"No, you must be thinking of another Charlie Wong. Wong is a very common Chinese name. Sixty-two percent of all the people in China are named Wong."

"Is that true?"

"I think so. My name isn't that common. Kee. That's my family name. Connie is my given name."

"That's a very nice name," he said. "Connie Kee."

"Yes, it's illiterate."

"Alliterative."

"Yes. Although actually, it's Kee Connie. The same as it's really Wong Charlie. In China, they put the family name first."

"Then what should I call you?"

"Connie Kee. Because this isn't China, you know. This is America, you know."

"Right now I'd rather be in China," he said. "Would you like to drive me to Kennedy?"

"If you're going to China, you'll need a visa," she said.

"In that case, I'll go to Boston."

"I've never been to Boston, so I don't know. But when my Uncle Benny went to Hong Kong – this wasn't even mainland China – I know he needed a visa. Anyway, you don't want to go to Kennedy," she said, shaking her head.

"How about La Guardia?"

"No good, either. They'll be watching all the bus stations, railroad terminals, and airports."

"Then how would you like to drive me to Sarasota?" he asked.

"I'd love to," she said, "but I have a twelve-thirty pickup. Why'd you kill that movie director?"

"I didn't kill any goddamn movie director," he said.

"The police think you did."

"The police are wrong."

"Right or wrong, everyone in this city knows what you look like."

"How can they know what I . . . ?"

"Because they showed your picture on television."

"My *picture*? Where'd . . . ?"

"Right on the screen, just as you were running out."

"Where'd they get . . . ?"

"On your driver's license. Nice big close-up of your face."

"Oh shit."

"Actually, it wasn't *that* bad a picture."

"Then they *will* be watching the airports."

"Is what I said."

"Because if they have my license . . ."

"Oh, they have it, all right."

"Then they know I'm from Florida . . ."

"Oh, they know, all right."

"And they have to be figuring I'll be heading down there."

"Is what anyone would figure."

"So I *can't* head down there."

"Not if you killed this guy Randall."

"Crandall," Michael said.

"I'm sure they said Randall."

"It was Arthur *Crandall*," Michael said.

"Well, I won't argue with you. I guess you know who you killed."

"I *didn't* kill him. And it was *Crandall*, damn it, I have his card right here."

He fished into his jacket pocket.

"See?" he said, and showed her the card that looked like a strip of film. "Arthur Crandall, there's his name in black and white."

"There's his address, too," Connie said.

The entrance to the building on Bowery was a door with a plate-glass upper portion upon which the words CRANDALL FILMS, LTD. were lettered in big black block letters. Michael wondered what kind of film company would have its New York office here in this bedraggled part of the city; he guessed that *War and Solitude* had been a flop of even vaster dimensions than Crandall had described. He tried the doorknob. The door was locked. A dim light inside showed a steeply angled flight of steps leading upstairs. To the right of the door was a store selling plumbing appliances. To the left was a hotel that called itself the Bowery Palace. Michael stepped back and away from the door. He looked up at the second-story windows, where the name of Crandall's company was positioned in yet larger block letters. Not a light was showing up there. Apparently, the police hadn't got here yet. Either that, or they'd already come and gone.

44

A traffic signal was on the corner, and several enterprising Christmas Eve businessmen had set up shop there with buckets and chamois cloths, pouncing on the windshield of any car unfortunate enough to get caught by a red light. There was even less traffic in the streets now; the storm had frightened off all but a few hearty adventurers, and the rest were already home for Christmas. The windshield-washers on the corner kept looking up the avenue for signs of fresh customers. Meanwhile, they kept passing around a pint bottle of something that looked very dark and very poisonous. When one of them spotted the black limo, he started for it at once, bucket in his left hand, chamois cloth in his right. Connie waved him off. He kept coming.

"My windshield's clean," she said.

"I'm Freddie," he said. "Clean your windshield?"

"I just told you it's clean."

"Clean your windshield for a dollar?"

"A dollar!" Connie said. "That's outrageous!"

"So make it half a buck," Freddie said, and shrugged.

"Now you're talking," Connie said, and Freddie dipped the chamois into the bucket and slapped the cloth onto the windshield. A greasy film of ice immediately formed on the glass.

"Terrific," Connie said sourly.

"I want to find the backyard," Michael whispered.

"Why?" Connie asked.

"See if there's a fire escape."

"I'll come with you," she said.

"Are you a movie star?" Freddie asked Michael.

"No."

"'Cause you look familiar," he said. "You wouldn't happen to have a scraper, would you?" he asked Connie.

"In the trunk," Connie said, and went around to the back of the car.

"Haven't I seen you on television?" Freddie asked.

"No," Michael said.

"In a series about Florida?"

"No."

"You sure look familiar."

"I have a very common face," Michael said.

"Ah, thank you," Freddie said, and accepted the scraper from Connie. "This should do the trick."

She was no longer wearing the green satin, high-heeled pumps she'd had on a few minutes ago. Black galoshes were on her feet now, the tops unbuckled. She looked like pictures Michael had seen of flappers in the Twenties, except that she was Chinese. She saw him looking down at the galoshes.

"I changed my shoes," she said.

He looked up into her face. So goddamn beautiful.

"I bought these in a thrift shop," she said, "to keep in the trunk. For inclement weather." On her lips, the word "inclement" sounded Chinese. She shrugged, and turned to where Freddie was already scraping the windshield. "You want to watch the car for me?" she asked.

"No, ma'am, I don't wash entire cars," he said, "I only do windshields."

"You keep an eye on the car for me, I'll give you that dollar you wanted."

"Make it two dollars."

"Two dollars, okay," she said, and locked the car and then turned back to Michael and said, "Let's go."

Michael looked at the Bowery Palace Hotel. He nodded, and then started toward its entrance door. Connie followed immediately behind him.

"Ask for room five-oh-five," Freddie called after them. "It has a mattress."

The hotel lobby was done in what one might have called Beirut Nouveau. Plaster was crumbling from the walls, electrical outlets hung suspended by dangling wires, the bloated ceiling bulged with what was certainly a water leak, wooden posts and beams seemed on the imminent edge of collapse, wallpaper was peeling, framed prints of pastoral scenes hung askew, and ancient upholstered furniture exposed its springs and stuffing. Altogether, the place looked as if it had recently been attacked by terrorists with pipe bombs. The clerk behind the scarred and tottering desk looked like a graying, wrinkled Oliver North who had just made his last covert deal with the Iranians.

"Good evening, Merry Christmas," Michael said to the clerk, and walked past the desk, and then past a hissing, clanging radiator that seemed about to explode and then past two men in long overcoats who were flipping playing cards at a brass spittoon against one of the flaking walls. It took Michael a moment to realize the spittoon wasn't empty. Behind him, he heard Connie clanking along in her unbuckled galoshes. "Merry Christmas," she said to the clerk, and he replied "Merry Christmas," sounding somewhat bewildered, and then – as Michael approached a door under a red-and-white EXIT sign – "Excuse me, sir, may I ask what you think you're . . . ?"

"Building inspector," Michael said gruffly, and would have flashed his driver's license or something if he'd still had it in his possession.

"Merry Christmas," the clerk said at once, "I'm sure you'll find everything in order."

"We'll see about that," Michael said, and opened the exit door, and stepped out into the backyard. Telephone poles grew from the snow-covered ground, their sagging wires wearing narrow threads of white. Fences capped with snow spread raggedly north, south, east, and west. Where tenements rose to the starry night, there were clotheslines stiff with frozen clothes. Not a breeze stirred now. Moonlight tinted the backyard world a soft silvery white.

"It's beautiful," Connie said beside him.

"Yes," he said.

He sighed then, and looked up at the back of the hotel, getting his geographical bearings, and then turned his scrutiny to the building on its left. A fire escape zigzagged up the snow-dusted, red-brick wall.

"You'd better wait for me here," he said.

"I'll go with you," Connie said.

He looked at her.

"There's no reward, you know," he said, and was sorry the instant the words left his mouth.

"Is that what you think?" she asked.

"I don't know what I . . ."

"I mean, is *that* what you think?"

"All I know is that a very beautiful girl . . ."

"Yes, I know."

". . . has latched onto a stranger . . ."

"Yes."

". . . who she thinks *killed* someone, which by the way I *didn't*. Not tonight, anyway."

"Then when?" she said at once.

"A long time ago. I've been living a very quiet life since I . . ."

"Are you married?" she asked.

"Divorced."

"Then what's wrong with my latching onto you?"

"I find it peculiar, that's all."

"You have a very low opinion of yourself, don't you?"

"No, I happen to have a very healthy ego, in fact."

"What happened? Did they break your spirit in jail?"

"Jail? Why would I . . . ?"

"For killing somebody."

"It was my *job* to kill those people."

"More than one?" she asked, astonished.

"Yes, but . . ."

"How many?"

"Eleven or twelve."

"Which? I mean, a person gives you a contract, you ought to know whether it's for eleven people or . . ."

"A contract? What con . . . ?"

"For eleven, twelve, fourteen, however many people you killed."

"It certainly wasn't fourteen."

"Then how many?"

"The figure was disputed."

"Who disputed it? The defense attorney?"

"No, the RTO."

"The what?"

"The company radioman. He claimed *he* was the one who got the . . ."

"Listen, do you have a tattoo?" she asked.

"No, I . . ."

"Because forty-three percent of all convicts have tattoos, you know."

"I'm not a convict."

"Well, an *ex*-con."

"I've never been in jail in my life."

"You beat the rap, huh?"

"What rap? I was in the . . ."

"Listen, if a jury found you innocent, that's good enough for me."

"Connie, I never . . ."

48

"Do you have any children?"

"No."

"Do you think our lips would freeze together if you kissed me?"

He looked at her again.

"I know you didn't kill anyone," she said.

He kept looking at her.

"I knew it long ago," she said. "Because you stayed for Harry. A man who killed somebody doesn't hang around like that. Not to bring another person luck. That's a kind and gentle person who does something like that. Not a murderer. Anyway, I like your cute little face," she said, and raised her arms and then draped them on his shoulders, and stepped in closer to him. "So let's try it," she said.

And kissed him.

He had not kissed anyone this way since the divorce, which was exactly nine months and six days ago, the eighteenth of March, in fact, a very blustery Friday in Sarasota, Florida, he knew because he'd taken the boat out into the Gulf the moment the papers were signed, sailing off into a four-foot chop and drinking himself into oblivion the way he very often had in Vietnam, a wonder he'd got back to shore alive. Hadn't kissed anyone this way since the last time he'd kissed Jenny – well, no, that wasn't true.

The whole reason for the divorce, in fact, was that Jenny *hadn't* been kissing this way anymore, or at least not kissing *him* this way. It turned out that she'd been kissing the man who was the branch manager at the bank where she worked as a teller, kissed him a lot, in fact, fucked him a lot, too, in fact. Told Michael she was madly in love with the man – whose name was James Owington, the fat bastard – married him a month after the divorce became final, easy come, easy go, right?

No, Michael thought, they didn't break my spirit in jail.

The V.C. did a pretty good job of breaking it in Vietnam, and Jenny finished the job later.

Kissing Connie Kee like this, he felt like weeping. Not the bitter tears he'd wept in Vietnam when his closest friend, Andrew, died in his arms, nor the kind of angry tears he'd wept that day on the boat with the waters of the Gulf threatening the gunwales. He did not know whether there were any kind of tears that could express what he was feeling here and now with this beautiful girl in his arms. Were there really tears of happiness? He had read a lot about them, but he had never shed such tears in his life. He knew only that kissing Connie Kee like this, he wished their lips *would* freeze together out here in the cold and the dark. He wanted to go on kissing Connie Kee forever. Or even Kee Connie.

He remembered, however, that the police in this winter wonderland of a city thought he had killed Arthur Crandall. He supposed he could go visit his old friend Tony the Bear Orso at the First Precinct, explain to him that the man who'd stolen the car was now the man who'd turned up dead in it – remember we were talking about all this, Tony, old pal, remember I showed you his card? Arthur Crandall, remember? You said it looked like a piece of film, remember? His card. Well, that's the man who turned up dead. In the car he stole from me. So you see, Tony, I can't be the one who killed him. He stole my car, you see. And the other ones – the phony cop and his phony lawyer girlfriend – stole my credit cards and my license, so maybe it's the other ones who killed Crandall, but it wasn't me, it couldn't have been me. In fact, I was probably sitting right there chatting with you while Crandall was getting himself killed. That's a definite possibility and something you may wish to investigate. Meanwhile, I'll be running on back to Sarasota. Tony, give me a call when you break the case, I'll send you a crate of oranges.

So, yes, maybe he should drop in on the First, it wasn't everyone in this city who had Police Department connections. On the other hand, if he could not convince Tony the Bear that he'd had nothing whatever to do with the murder of Arthur Crandall, he might find himself sharing a cell with Charlie Bonano – why were so many people in this city named Charlie? Except for Charlie's News, which was a store selling books, and magazines, and cards, and newspapers, Michael did not know a single Charlie in Sarasota. Did not know any other Charlies in the entire state of *Florida*, for that matter. But here in New York, three of them in the same night, and two of them named Charlie *Wong*. Remarkable. The very same night. Two Charlie Wongs. He wondered if Charlie was as common a name as Wong, and he thought of asking Connie – once they were finished with all this kissing – what the statistics on the frequency of Charlies in any given location might be. She showed no indication of wanting to stop the kissing, however, until a light snapped on overhead and someone shouted, "Hey! What the hell are you doing down there?"

They broke apart at once and looked immediately heavenward because this sounded like a demand from a vengeful God instead of a person shouting from the fourth-floor window of the tenement to the right of the hotel – which, they now discovered, was where the shout had come from: a light was showing in the fourth-floor window, silhouetting the person doing all the yelling.

"I'm gonna call the police!" the person – man or woman, it was difficult to tell – shouted.

"No, don't do that!" Michael yelled, and he yanked Connie out of the glare of the moonshine and ran over the snow and into the shadows created by the rear of Crandall's building. They both listened. They could sense but not see the person up there straining to catch a glimpse of them in the dark.

"I know you're still there!" the voice shouted.

They said nothing.

A window slammed shut.

They waited.

Silence.

The light upstairs went out. The backyard was dark and still again. She grinned at him. He grinned back.

And then he leaped up like Superman for the fire-escape ladder, caught the bottom rung on the first try, and yanked it down.

There was a small Christmas tree on one of the filing cabinets, decorated with Christmas ornaments and lights that Michael now turned on to add a bit more illumination than was flowing in from the street lamp outside. The lights had a blinker on them. In fits and starts – on again, off again, yellow, green, red, and blue – Michael and Connie took in the rest of the office.

From the looks of the place, there'd been one hell of a party here. Someone had decorated the single large room with red and green streamers strung from wall to wall, crisscrossing the office like the rows and rows of protective barbed wire around the base camp at Cu Chi. Dangling from the streamers were cardboard cutouts of Santa Claus and Rudolph the Red-Nosed Reindeer and Frosty the Snowman, all of whom – together with the Easter Bunny and the Great Pumpkin and St Valentine's Day, especially

St Valentine's Day – Michael had learned to distrust in Vietnam during the Tet Offensive in February of 1968, when Jenny (then) Aldershot forgot to send him a card asking him to be her valentine. And when, too, what with all that hardware flying around, he'd begun to doubt he'd ever get back home again to Jenny or anyone else, ever get back to shore again. He should have known then and there that one day she'd start up with a fat bastard bank branch manager, oh well, live and learn.

In addition to the streamers and the dangling reminders of Christmases past, there was a huge wreath hanging in the front window, which Michael hadn't noticed when he was looking up at the window from the street outside. There were also a great many ashtrays with dead cigarette butts in them, and a great many plastic glasses with the residue of booze in them, and a folding table covered with a red paper cloth upon which rested the tired remnants of a baked ham, a round of cheese, a crock of chopped liver, a tureen of orange caviar dip, a basket of crumbling crackers, several depleted bottles of gin, scotch, vodka, and bourbon, and a partridge in a pear tree. Or at least what appeared to be a partridge in a pear tree, but which was actually the tattered remains of a roast turkey on a wooden platter with a carving knife and fork alongside it. There were red paper napkins and green paper plates and white plastic knives and forks in evidence on every flat surface in the room. What at first appeared to be another red napkin lying on top of a large desk otherwise covered with plates and such – blink ON, blink OFF, went the Christmas tree lights – actually turned out to be a pair of red silk panties someone had inadvertently left behind. It must have been one hell of a party.

"Did you ever do it on a desktop?" Connie whispered.

"Never," Michael whispered back.

He wondered if she was propositioning him.

He also wondered if she was wearing red silk panties under her green silk dress.

"What are we looking for?" she whispered.

"I don't know," he said.

He did not, in truth, know what the hell they were looking for. He did not like this entire business of having been accused of murdering someone, did not like the sort of hospitality New York City extended to a visitor from the South, did not in fact like

52

anything that had happened to him tonight with the exception of Connie Kee. He knew for certain – or, rather, *felt* for certain – that if he went to the police, he would find himself in deeper shit than was already up to his knees. He resented this. He was a goddamn taxpayer, and the police should have been working *for* him instead of *against* him. Why should he have to be doing *their* goddamn job? Well, a taxpayer in Sarasota, anyway.

He supposed he would have to learn how to do their job.

He hadn't wanted to learn how to avoid the punji sticks planted on a jungle trail, either, but he had learned. Had learned because if you stepped on one of those sharpened bamboo stakes it went clear through the sole of your boot and since Charlie had dipped the stakes in his own excrement –

Charlie.

Even in Vietnam, it had been Charlie.

For the Vietcong.

The V.C.

Victor Charlie.

And then just Charlie for short.

Good old Charlie.

Who had taught him to dance the light fandango along those jungle paths, live and learn. Or rather, learn and live. The way he had to learn now. Here in this city of New York, downtown here in this rotten city, his problem was a dead man. Arthur Crandall. And this was the dead man's office, as good a place to start learning as any Michael could think of.

"Cahill and Parrish," he whispered to Connie.

"Who?"

"We're looking for anything that might tie them to Crandall."

"Who are they?" Connie asked, sitting on the edge of the desk and crossing her long legs.

He explained who they were.

She listened intently.

She was so goddamn beautiful.

He kept wondering if she was wearing red silk panties.

Or any panties at all.

They began searching. The first thing they found in this office in holiday disarray, the first thing they found in this two-bit Sodom and Gomorrah show-biz office was a framed newspaper article on the wall alongside the blinking Christmas tree.

The article was written in French.

"Do you speak French?" he whispered.

"Chinese," she whispered back. "And English, of course. Cantonese dialect. The Chinese. Do *you* speak French?"

"A little. The Vietnamese spoke French. And my mother, too, every now and then."

The article was from a newspaper called the *Nice Matin*. In translation, the headline read:

DIRECTOR SHOWS WAR FILM

The article told about the showing of the film *War and Solitude* at the International Film Festival in Cannes. The article also summarized the critical reaction to it. Apparently, the reaction had been excellent. Everyone had thought, in fact, that *War and Solitude* could walk away with all the honors. Michael suddenly wondered if Oliver Stone, the director of *Platoon*, had killed Crandall and left him in Michael's car. The article had appeared in May, eight years ago. Someone, probably Crandall himself, had inked in the newspaper's date in the margin on the right-hand side of the article. The caption under the accompanying photograph read: *Arthur Crandall before the showing of his film* War and Solitude *yesterday afternoon*.

The man in the photograph was not Arthur Crandall.

Or at least not the Arthur Crandall who'd been so helpful to Michael before stealing his car.

This Arthur Crandall – the one in the photograph – had a little round pig face with a pug nose and plump little cheeks. He was short and stout and he looked more like Oliver Hardy than Abraham Lincoln.

"This is not Arthur Crandall," Michael said. "I mean, this *says* he's Arthur Crandall, but he's not the man I met earlier tonight."

"Who later got himself killed."

"This isn't that man."

"Then who is he?"

"I don't know who he is."

"Let's see what's in his desk."

Together they went through the desk drawers. The red silk panties sat like a fallen poinsettia leaf not a foot from where they worked. He noticed that Connie smelled of oolong tea and soap, and he wondered if she knew she smelled so exotically seductive.

"I think we should take that picture with us," she said. "In case we need it later. Whoever he is. Because sailors who measure the tide sail with the wisdom of seers, you know."

He looked at her.

"Have you ever stuffed fortune cookies?" he said.

"No. Why do you ask?"

"Just wondered. You smell of oolong tea and soap, did you know that?"

"Did you know that the word 'oolong' is from *wu' lung*, which means black dragon in Mandarin Chinese?"

"No, I didn't know that," Michael said.

"Yes," she said. "Because oolong tea is so dark."

"I see."

"Yes."

He was getting dizzy on the scent of her.

"Here's his appointment calendar," Connie said, taking it from the top drawer of Crandall's desk.

"Do you think it's safe to turn on this lamp?" Michael asked, and snapped on the gooseneck desk lamp. Connie sat in the swivel chair behind the desk, and he dragged over another chair and sat beside her. Their knees touched. The calendar was of the Day At-A-Glance type. She flipped it open to the page for Saturday, December 24, and then automatically looked at her watch.

"*Still* the twenty-fourth," she said.

"Ten minutes to midnight," he said.

"Ten minutes to Christmas," she said.

There were several handwritten reminders on the page:

Call Mama

"Dutiful son," Michael said.

Send roses to Albetha

"Who's Albetha?" he asked.

"Who knows?" Connie said.

Mama @ Benny's
8:00 PM

"Mama again," Michael said. "But who's Benny?"

"Who knows?" Connie said, and flipped the calendar back to the page for Friday, December 23.

There were three entries for that date:

Bank @ 2:30

"Deposit?" Connie asked. "Withdrawal?"

Charlie @ 3:30

"Another Charlie," Michael said.

"Huh?" Connie said.

"There are a lot of Charlies in this city."

"Yes," Connie said. "Now that you mention it."

"But not too many Albethas, I'll bet."

Christmas party
4:00–7:00 PM

"Let's find out why he went to the bank," Connie said.

"How?"

"His checkbook. If we can find it."

They began searching through the desk drawers again. In the bottom drawer, Michael found two large, ledger-type checkbooks, one with a blue cover, the other with a black one. The blue checkbook had yellow checks in it. Each check was headed with the names ALBETHA AND ARTHUR CRANDALL and an address on West Tenth Street.

"There's Albetha," Connie said.

"His wife."

"The roses."

"Nice."

"Yes."

"I wonder if she knows he's dead."

The black checkbook had pink checks in it. Each check was headed with the name CRANDALL PRODUCTIONS, LTD. and the address here on Bowery. Michael flipped through the business checkbook and found the stubs for the last several checks written, all dated December 23. There was a check to Sylvia Horowitz for a $200 Christmas bonus . . .

"His secretary?" Connie asked.

"Could be."

And a check to Celebrity Catering for $1,217.21 . . .

"The party, must be," Michael said.

"Some party," Connie said.

And a check to Mission Liquors for $314.78.

56

"More party," Connie said.

"Some party," Michael said.

No checks beyond the twenty-third. They leafed backward through the stubs. The last payroll checks had been made out on December 16, the ones before that on December 2. The firm paid its employees – apparently only Crandall and the woman named Sylvia Horowitz – on a biweekly basis.

"Let's try the personal checkbook," Connie said.

In the personal book, they found only one stub for a check written on Friday, December 23.

It was made out to cash.

For $9,000.

They both fell silent.

Outside, there was only the keening of the wind. Snow broke off from the telephone wires, fell soundlessly to the backyards below.

"It's almost Christmas, you know," Connie whispered.

Michael looked at his watch.

"Two minutes to Christmas," Connie whispered.

His digital watch blinked away time, tossed time into the past.

"I want to give you a present," she whispered.

It was one minute and twenty-two seconds to Christmas.

"Because you really do have a very nice face," she whispered. "And also, I like kissing you." She cupped his face in her hands. "You don't have anything communicable, do you?" she asked.

"No, I . . ."

"I don't mean like a common cold," she said. "I mean like anything dread."

"Nothing dread at all," he said.

"Good," she said.

He told himself that when this was all over and done with, if ever it was over and done with, he would remember this last minute before Christmas more than anything that could possibly happen afterward. Because in that slow-motion moment, Connie kissed him and murmured, "Merry Christmas, Michael," and moved in so close to him that he could feel her heart beating, or at least his own, and then he heard bells going off and he thought he'd died and gone to heaven until he realized it was only the telephone.

5

The telephone kept ringing into the otherwise blinking stillness of the room.

Michael picked up the receiver.

"Crandall Productions, Limited," he said.

"Arthur?" a woman's voice said.

"Who's this?" he said.

"Is that you, Arthur?" the woman asked.

"Yes," he said.

"You sound funny," she said.

"Who's this?" he said again.

"This is Albetha," the woman said.

"Uh-huh," he said.

"Arthur?"

"Uh-huh."

"Arthur, your children are waiting for Santa Claus, what are you doing at the office? It's Christmas morning already, do you know that? It's already five minutes past Christmas, do you know that? Now when do you plan on coming home, Arthur?"

Michael gathered she did not know he was dead.

"Did you get the roses?" he asked.

"Yes, I got the roses," she said. "Thank you very much for the roses, Arthur, but I'm *still* getting a divorce."

"Now, now, Albetha," he said.

"Arthur, the only reason I want you to come here tonight is because it's Christmas and the children expect you to be here, that's the only reason. Tomorrow I'll explain to them how their daddy is a no-good philanderer, but this is Christmas right now, and you'd better come home here and get in your Santa Claus suit and be Santa eating the cookies and drinking the milk for your goddamn children, do you hear me?"

"I hear you," he said.

"Or is *she* there with you?" Albetha asked.

"Is who here?" he said.

"Jessica," she said.

"I don't know who that is," he said.

"Your blonde bimbo with her red panties," she said.

"Oh, her," Michael said.

"Come on home to your children, you *louse!*" Albetha said, and hung up.

"Albetha?" he said. He jiggled the rest bar. "Albetha?"

"His wife, huh?" Connie said.

"Maybe I ought to call her back," Michael said.

"No, I think we'd better get out of here," Connie said. "Because I think I heard a police siren."

Michael listened.

"I don't hear anything," he said.

"Not now," she said. "While we were kissing. I thought it was a siren, but maybe it was just a cat."

They both listened.

Nothing.

"It was probably just a cat," she said.

"Let's see if he's got an address book," Michael said, and went to the desk and began rummaging through the drawers again. "I want to call her back."

"Although it sounded very much like a siren," Connie said.

"Here we go. Do you think his home number might be in it?"

"I don't know anyone who lists his own number in his address book. Did you just see a light in the backyard?"

"No."

"I thought I saw a light," Connie said, and went to the window. "Yep," she said, "there's a light moving around down there. You know what? I think that *was* a siren I heard. Because those are two cops with a flashlight down there."

Michael went to the window.

"Shit," he said.

"Yes," she said. "Heading for the fire escape."

"Let's get the hell out of here," he said.

"Don't forget Crandall's picture."

"I've got it."

". . . and his address book," she said, "the tall one's starting up the ladder."

He pulled her away from the window and together they hurried to the front door. He turned the thumb knob on the lock, opened the door, and then followed her down the steep flight of steps to the street-level door. Through the thick plate-glass panel on the door, they could see a police car parked at the curb in front of the limousine, its dome lights flashing. Freddie was sitting on the limo's fender, looking innocent. The lock on the street-level door was a deadbolt. No way to unlock it on either side without a key. Michael backed off, raised his leg –

"Don't cut yourself!" Connie warned.

– and kicked out flat-footed at the glass panel.

A shower of splinters and shards exploded onto the sidewalk. Freddie, startled, jumped off the fender of the car. From the office upstairs, one of the cops yelled,"Downstairs, Sam!"

Michael was busy kicking out loose shards.

Cold air rushed through the open panel.

He helped Connie climb through, her long legs flashing, green panties winking at him for only an instant as she jumped clear. He climbed through after her and began running toward the limo. Connie slapped a five-dollar bill into Freddie's hand, ran around the limo's nose, and began unlocking the door on the driver's side. Behind him, Michael heard one of the cops yell, "You! Hey *you*! Hold it right there!" The electric lock on his side of the car clicked open. He yanked open the door, climbed in, and slammed the door shut just as Connie stepped on the starter. There were gunshots now. He pulled his head instinctively into his shoulders, but the cops were only shooting at the deadbolt on the door to Crandall Productions, Ltd. The engine caught just as they kicked open the door and came running out of the building.

"Police!" one of them yelled. "Stop!"

Connie rammed her foot down on the accelerator. The car's tires began spinning on ice, its rear end skidding toward the curb, and then the tires began smoking, and suddenly they grabbed bare asphalt, and the car lurched away squealing from the curb and into the night.

Behind them, Freddie said to the cops, "Clean your windshield, officers?"

The house on West Tenth Street was a three-story brownstone just off Fifth Avenue. The address on the checks in Crandall's personal checkbook. Presumably the house he shared with Albetha and the kiddies.

"Every light in the house is burning," Connie said. "The lady's waiting up for you."

"For Crandall."

"Too bad he's dead," Connie said, and looked at her watch. "My twelve-thirty pickup is in the Village," she said. "Here's a China Doll card, call me when you're done here. If I'm free, I'll come get you. Otherwise, here's my home address. And here's twenty dollars."

"I don't want to take any money from you," he said.

"Then how are you going to get anyplace? If I can't come pick you up? Take it."

"Really, Connie . . ."

"It's a loan," she said.

He nodded, accepted the card and the money, and put both in his wallet. He now owed Charlie Bonano ten bucks and Connie Kee twenty. He was running up a big debt in this city.

"You sure you want to go see this lady?" Connie asked. "Might be cops in there, for all you know."

"I don't see any police cars, do you?"

"Detectives drive unmarked sedans."

Michael shrugged.

"Pretty brave all of a sudden," Connie said.

Michael was thinking that sometimes you could sense things. You could smell the enemy. Sniff the trail and you knew whether it was clear ahead or loaded. He did not think he would find any policemen in Crandall's house. If he was wrong—

He shrugged again.

"I'll see you later," he said.

"Yes," she said, and waited till he walked to the front stoop of the building and up the steps before she eased the limo away from the curb. He watched the tail lights disappearing up the street, the red staining the snow. There was a sudden hush on the night. He looked up at the sky, expecting to see a star in the east. Disappointed, he looked at his watch instead. Twenty minutes past twelve. He rang the doorbell.

The woman who answered the door was perhaps thirty-four years old. She was almost as tall as Michael, her eyes brown, her mouth full, her hair done in the style Bo Derek had popularized in the movie *10*, more beautiful and natural on this woman in that her skin was the color of bittersweet chocolate.

"Yes?" she said.

"Is Mrs Crandall home?" he asked.

"I'm Mrs Crandall," she said.

"Oh," he said, and tried to hide his surprise. The newspaper photograph had shown Arthur Crandall as a white man.

"Yes?" she said.

"Well . . . we spoke on the phone a little while ago," he said. "You told me . . ."

"No, we didn't," she said, and started to close the door.

"Mrs Crandall," he said quickly, "you called your husband's office . . ."

She looked at him.

"I answered the phone . . ."

Kept looking at him.

"You told me your kids were waiting for Santa . . ."

"What were you doing in my husband's . . ."

"Long story," he said.

Behind her, a small, excited voice said, "Mommy, come quick! Daddy's on television!"

"Who are you?" she asked Michael.

"My name is Michael Barnes," he said.

"Mommy, hurry *up*!"

Another voice. Two of them in the hallway now. And then a third voice from someplace else in the house.

"Annie? Are you *getting* her?"

Albetha Crandall looked him up and down. Sniffing the trail. Trying to catch the whiff of danger. She decided he was safe. "Come in," she said.

Two little girls in granny nightgowns were already running down the hall ahead of her. She let Michael into the house, closed and locked the door behind him, and then said, "You're not an ax murderer, are you?" and smiled in such marvelous contradiction that he was forced to give the only possible answer.

"Yes, I am," he said.

Albetha laughed.

"Mommmmmmmy! For Chriiiiiist's sake, come *on*!"

He followed her down the hall. It occurred to him that the police were showing pictures of the dead man on television. Arthur Crandall. His daughters were watching photographs of their dead father. And soon Albetha would be seeing those same photos. And they would undoubtedly be followed in logical sequence by the driver's license picture of the man alleged to have killed him, Michael Barnes the notorious ax murderer.

An eight-year-old girl in a granny nightgown sat on a couch facing the television set. The other two little girls – one of them six, the other four, Michael guessed – had just come into the room and were standing transfixed in the doorway, watching the screen. This was a newsbreak special. The words trailed incessantly across the bottom of the screen. NEWSBREAK SPECIAL NEWSBREAK SPECIAL NEWSBREAK SPECIAL. A very blond television newscaster was talking to the man whose picture had been hanging on the wall in Crandall's office. He was short and stout and almost bald, and he was wearing a three-piece suit with a Phi Beta Kappa key hanging on a gold chain across the vest.

He looked very much alive.

"I am very much alive," he said to the blond man. "As you can plainly see."

"Yes, I see that," the blond man said.

"What does he mean?" the eight-year-old on the couch said.

"Of *course* he's alive," the six-year-old said.

"Boy oh boy," the four-year-old said.

They all looked like different sizes of the little girl who played Bill Cosby's youngest daughter.

Albetha was watching the screen, an enormously puzzled look on her face.

"So what do you make of all this, Mr Crandall?" the blond man asked.

"Well, if it weren't for the fact that there *is* a dead man . . ."

"Indeed there is," the blond man said, putting on a television newscaster's solemnly grieving face.

63

"Yes. But if it weren't for that, I'd think this was some kind of hoax."

"Ah, yes. But there *is* a real corpse, Mr Crandall. And the police found your identification on him."

"Yes."

"Yes."

"Extraordinary."

"Really. So what do you make of it?"

"I can only believe that this Michael J. Barnes person is responsible."

Albetha gave Michael a sharp look.

"Yes, the man whose car . . ."

"Yes, the body . . ."

"Found in the . . ."

"Yes."

"For those of you who missed our newscast earlier tonight, I should mention that the body of a man carrying Mr Crandall's identification . . ."

"Yes."

". . . was found in an automobile rented by a visitor to New York . . ."

"Is this a series?" the four-year-old asked.

"No, Glory, it's a newsbreak special," Albetha said.

". . . a man named Michael Barnes, whose wallet was also found . . ."

"Yes," Crandall said.

"In the automobile."

"Yes."

"So it would appear at least *possible* that the man the police are now actively seeking . . ."

"Are you *sure* this isn't a series?" Glory asked suspiciously.

"Positive," Albetha said, and gave Michael another sharp look.

". . . *is*, in fact, the man responsible for the murder. But *why* – and this is the big question, isn't it, Mr Crandall – why would he have put *your* identification in the dead man's pocket?"

"I have no idea," Crandall said.

"Nor does anyone else at this moment," the blond man said hurriedly, obviously having received an off-camera signal to wrap. "Believe me when I say, however, that we're happy one of our most talented screen directors is still with us. Mr Crandall . . ."

His face taking on a sincere and solemnly heartfelt look, his voice lowering . . .

"Thank you so much . . . *literally* . . . for being here with us tonight."

"After the false reports of my death," Crandall said, smiling, "I'm happy I was *able* to be here."

"He's so full of shit," Albetha muttered.

"What?" the eight-year-old said.

"I said it'll be a while before Daddy gets home, so I want you all to go to bed now. If I hear Santa coming to drink his milk and eat the cookies you left by the tree, I'll come wake you. But you mustn't frighten him off or he won't leave any presents. All right now?"

"Who's this?" the four-year-old said, looking at Michael.

"One of Daddy's friends," Albetha said. "I'm sure."

Michael smiled.

"What's your name?" the six-year-old asked.

"Michael," he said.

"Come on, kids, bed," Albetha said, and shooed them off down the hallway.

Michael watched them go.

He debated running.

He decided not to.

When Albetha came back some five minutes later, she said, "You still here? I thought you'd be in Alaska by now."

"No," he said.

"A ploy, right? Murderer sticks around, lady thinks, Gee, he can't be the murderer."

"No, not a ploy."

"You going to slay my children in their beds?"

"No, ma'am."

"You better not. And don't call me ma'am. I'm at least five years younger than you are. What size suit do you wear?"

"Thirty-eight long."

"Arthur's a forty-six regular. Come along with me."

"Where are we going?"

"Put you in a Santa suit."

He followed her up the stairs.

"Why do they think you killed somebody?" she asked.

"I don't know."

"But you didn't, huh?"

"I didn't. It wasn't even my wallet. All they stole from me were my credit cards and my driver's license. And my library card."

They were in the master bedroom now. Four-poster bed covered with a gauzy canopy. Imitation Tiffany lamp in one corner. Plush velvet easy chair. Old mahogany dresser.

"What are you doing here?" Albetha asked.

"I thought you might be able to help me."

"How?"

"This was before I knew your husband was still alive."

"Yeah, well, that's a pity," she said. "Him still being alive."

"You're divorcing him, right?" Michael said.

"Right."

"Because of Jessica."

"Right."

"Jessica who?"

"Here, put this on," she said, and handed him a Santa Claus suit on a hanger. "I'll get some pillows."

"Jessica who?" he asked again.

Albetha went to the closet. He began taking off his trousers.

"Wales," she said. "Why do you want to know?"

"What does she look like?"

"She looks like a bimbo," Albetha said. Her back was to Michael. She was reaching up for a pair of pillows on the closet shelf. The trousers were much too large for him. He suspected they'd be too large even with pillows in them.

"What color hair does she have?"

"The same color hair *all* bimbos have," Albetha said. "Blonde. Even *black* bimbos have blonde hair."

"Is she black then?"

"No," Albetha said. "Here. Stuff these in your pants."

He accepted the pillows.

"She's white?"

"Yes. Even as the driven snow."

"I need something to fasten these pillows with," he said.

"I'll get one of Arthur's straps."

She went to the closet again.

"Are her eyes blue?" he asked.

"No. Brown."

Which eliminated the woman in the bar. Whose star sapphire

ring he hadn't stolen. And who'd called herself Helen Parrish.

"How does your husband happen to know her?" he asked.

"Intimately," Albetha said, and came back with a very large brown belt.

He took the belt, wrapped it around the pillows, and buckled it. He fastened the trousers at the waist. They felt good and snug now.

"How do you know she wears red panties?" he asked.

"Don't ask me about her goddamn panties. Goddamn blonde bimbo with her red panties. God knows what I may have caught from her panties."

"What do you mean?"

"I had her panties on once."

"How'd that happen?"

"They were in my dresser drawer. Can you imagine that? He hides his bimbo's panties in my dresser drawer, mixed in with all my own panties. So I go to put on a pair of red panties, I put on *her* panties instead. I got out of them the second I realized I'd made a mistake. But who knows what I may have caught from them?"

"Well, you only had them on for a second."

"Even so. That's why they won't let you return panties, you know. Department stores. I wanted to call her and ask who she'd been intimate with lately. Besides my husband. You can get trichinosis from just eating the gravy," she said.

"You can?"

"Sure. From the pork. So don't tell me about only a second. Who *knows* what was in her panties?"

"Well, there's no sense worrying about it now," Michael said.

"Sure, *you* don't have to worry, you're not the one who was in her panties. Do you think I can get them analyzed? Put them in a paper bag and take them to a lab and get them analyzed?"

"For what?"

"For whatever she may have. I really *would* like to call her, I mean it. Hey, Jessie, how are you? Listen, do you remember those red silk panties Arthur left in my dresser drawer? They're walking across the room all by themselves, who've you been with lately, Jess?"

"I'm sure she wouldn't tell a perfect stranger who . . ."

"I'm not such a perfect stranger. I had her panties on. Also, she's no stranger to my husband, believe me."

"Does she work for him or something?"

"She's an actress," Albetha said. "She's in his new movie."

"I didn't know there *was* a new movie."

"How would you know there was any movie at *all*?" Albetha asked, and looked at him suspiciously.

"A person who said he was your husband told me all about *War and Solitude*."

"When was this?"

"Earlier tonight. In a bar. Before he stole my car," Michael said, and put on the Santa Claus jacket.

"Was this person five-feet eight-inches tall, chunky, going bald, with brown eyes, a pot belly, and a Phi Beta Kappa key on his vest? From Wisconsin U?"

"No, he was . . ."

"Then he wasn't Arthur."

"I know he wasn't. *Now* I know. But he was very credible at the time. Told me all about your husband's work, gave me his business card . . ."

"Arthur's business card?"

"Yes."

"Well, anyone could have that. Arthur hands them out all over the place."

"Does the name Helen Parrish mean anything to you?"

"No."

"She's not an actress or . . . ?"

"No."

"Or anyone with whom your husband may have worked?"

"My husband has worked with a lot of women over the years, but I don't remember anyone named Helen Parrish. He was in television before he made *Solly's War*, and in television . . ."

"I'm sorry, what was that?"

"We called it *Solly's War*. Because the man who put up the money was named Solomon Gruber, and he was always yelling about budget, and about frittering away time, that was his favorite expression, 'Arthur, you're frittering away time.' Arthur hated him."

"What does *he* look like?"

"Gruber? An Orthodox rabbi."

"He wouldn't be a big, burly guy with a crew cut and a beard stubble, and hard blue eyes, would he?"

"No, he's tall and thin and hairy."

"Solomon Gruber."

"Yes."

"Who put up the money for *War and Solitude*."

"Yes. And lost it all. Or most of it."

"How much, would you say?"

"Did the film cost? Cheap by today's standards. Cheap even by the standards nine years ago, when it was shot."

"How much?"

"Twelve million."

"That's cheap?"

"Here's the beard," Albetha said.

He put on the beard.

"And the hat," she said.

He put on the hat.

She studied him.

"The kids think *Arthur* is Santa Claus, but you'll have to do," she said. "Come on downstairs and drink your milk and eat your cookies. If you keep your back to them . . ."

"Tell me about your husband's new picture."

"Strictly commercial," she said. "Solly *hopes*. He financed this one, too."

"What's it called?"

"*Winter's Chill*. It's a suspense film. What the British call a thriller."

"I don't think I've seen it."

"It doesn't open till the fifth."

"Here in New York?"

"*Everywhere*. As we say in the trade, it is opening *wide* – which does not have sexual connotations, by the way. The expression refers to opening on thousands of screens simultaneously, as opposed to two or three dozen. The ads should break in Tuesday's papers. Arthur's giving it nine days' lead time. He's hoping to make a killing, you see. Which may be the way to do it, who knows?"

Albetha shrugged.

"His last film was a class act. This is crap. But maybe the public wants crap. I find it ironic. In television, Arthur was doing crap.

He left television to do a really fantastic film that didn't make a nickel. Now he's back to doing crap again."

He looked at her for a moment. She seemed to be searching his eyes for answers, but he had none for her.

"How do I find your husband's mother?" he said.

"You don't," she said.

"He was supposed to call her yesterday. Maybe if I can learn what they talked about . . ."

"He didn't call her yesterday."

"It was on his calendar. Call Mama."

"His mother's been dead for seven years."

"Oh."

"May she rest in peace, the old bitch."

"Do you have Jessica Wales's address?"

"Yes. Why do you want it?"

"I want to talk to her."

"How do you know I won't call the police the minute you leave here?"

"I don't think you will."

"Why not? You're wanted for murder?"

"Yes, but I'm Santa Claus," he said, and smiled behind the beard.

Albetha smiled with him.

"Have you ever been Santa before?" she asked.

"No. But I was Joseph a long time ago. In elementary school in Boston."

"When the world was still holy and silent," Albetha said.

He looked at her.

Tears were suddenly brimming in her eyes.

"Come," she said softly. "Be Santa for my little girls."

6

It was bitterly cold when he left the Crandall apartment. He had changed out of the Santa Claus suit and back into the clothes he'd been wearing to Bos . . . oh my God, he still hadn't called his mother!

She was probably suspecting the worst by now. His plane had crashed over Hartford, Connecticut. He was lying in a heap of wreckage, her Christmas gift smoldering beside him. If he knew his mother at all, and he thought he did, she'd be more concerned about her smoldering gift than his smoldering body. When he'd got back from the war, she'd seemed enormously surprised to see him. As if she'd already chalked him off. Later, when he began having the nightmares, an analyst told him this had probably been his mother's defense mechanism. Telling herself he was already dead, so that she'd be prepared for it when she found out he really *was* dead.

"But I was *alive*," Michael told the shrink. "I came home alive."

"Yes, but she didn't know you would."

"But there I was. Hi, Mom, it's *me*!"

"She must have been surprised."

"That's just what I've been telling you."

"You're lucky she didn't have a heart attack."

"She gave away all my clothes while I was gone. My civilian clothes."

"Yes, her defense mechanism."

"My blue jacket," Michael said.

"What?"

"My best blue jacket."

"Poor woman," the analyst said.

Well, maybe so. Poor woman had grieved for years after his father died. Poor woman had sold the hardware store and loaned Michael the money to buy the groves in Florida. A *loan*, she'd said, stressing the word. Paid her back every nickel, plus interest. He'd asked her to come live down there in Florida with him, she'd said, No, she wanted to keep living right there in Boston, even if the neighborhood *was* going to the dogs. She meant it was turning black. Michael's best friend in Vietnam had been black. Andrew. Died in his arms. Blood bubbling up onto his lips. Michael had held him close. First and only time he'd ever cried in Vietnam. He wondered later if Andrew's mother had given away *his* clothes while he was gone. He wondered if Andrew's mother had told herself he was dead in preparation for the Defense Department telegram that would confirm her worst fears. Michael wished he could forgive his mother for looking so surprised to see him alive. Surprised and perhaps a trifle disappointed. He wished he could forgive the poor woman for giving away his blue jacket.

He turned up the collar on his coat.

He had twenty dollars in his pocket, the money Connie had given him.

"A loan," she'd said.

Albetha Crandall had given him Jessica Wales's address, but he did not know this city's public transportation system and there did not seem to be any taxicabs on the street. It didn't seem to him that one-thirty was very late for Christmas morning; there were probably taxis on the street even in *Sarasota* at this hour. He began walking. He knew that the address Albetha had given him was downtown because she'd mentioned that it was. After he'd come only a block, he knew he was headed in the right direction because the streets were still numbered up here and the one following West Tenth was West Ninth. He told himself that after tonight he would never again go downtown in this city, maybe in any city, he would forever after stay *uptown*, where it was safe and well-lighted and patrolled by conscientious policemen. Meanwhile, he had to get to Jessica Wales's apartment because there were things he had to find out. Like, for example, why

Crandall was now saying that Michael was the person responsible for the murder of the person who *wasn't* Crandall.

On television just a little while ago, Crandall had told the blond newscaster, "I can only believe that this Michael J. Barnes person is responsible."

Exactly what he'd said.

Go check it.

Rerun the tape, Blondie.

Michael J. Barnes.

His dear mother in Boston had given him the middle name Jellicle, after the Jellicle Cats in T. S. Eliot's *Old Possum's Book of Practical Cats*, which she'd read long before Andrew Lloyd Webber was even a glimmer in an Englishman's eye. Michael Jellicle Barnes, a name his schoolmates had found enormously amusing, reciting over and over again as they beat him up, "Yellow Belly Jellicle, Yellow Belly Jellicle," he could have killed his mother. He had tried unsuccessfully to hide the name from the girls he met in high school and later in college, all of whom naturally found out mysteriously and at once, and who dubbed him "Jellybean Barnes," which was better, but not much, than getting beat up, he supposed. In the army, he had become "Jelly-ass Barnes" because of the slight accident he'd had the first time the squad went into battle, a name everyone had called him . . . except Andrew.

Dear, dead Andrew.

Easy come, easy go, right?

The moment Michael got out of the army, he'd become plain old Michael J. Barnes, and that was the name he'd used when he'd applied for his driver's license and his library card in Florida. And later on, his credit cards. Michael J. Barnes. No middle name, just the initial. And that's what he'd been ever since, Michael J. Barnes, no Jellicle, just plain old Michael J. Barnes.

This Michael J. Barnes person.

Was what Crandall had said.

This Michael J. Barnes person is responsible.

For murder.

He was suddenly lost.

Lost in thoughts as tangled as the Vietnam underbrush. Lost in time, because the Jellicle was out of his past and the present was an unknown man he had not killed. Lost in space as well, because the streets had run out of numbers and now there were only names and he did not know where in hell he was. Why was he all at once on Bleecker and then Houston and then King and Charlton and . . . where the hell was he? He looked at the slip of paper upon which Albetha had scribbled the address for him.

He looked up at the street sign on the corner.

He was on Vandam and Avenue of the Americas.

So where was St Luke's Place?

Downtown, Albetha had told him. Between Hudson and Seventh. But where was Hudson? Or, for that matter, Seventh? He studied the empty avenue ahead as he would have studied a suspect trail, and then he looked to his right and looked to his left and decided it was six of one, half a dozen of the other, and began heading east, never once realizing that St Luke's Place was to the north and west.

He walked for what seemed like miles.

Not a numbered street anywhere in this downtown maze. Sullivan and West Broadway and Wooster and Greene and Mercer and now Broadway itself though it did not seem like the Great White Way down here in lower Manhattan except for the snow in the streets. Kept walking east, although he did not have a compass and did not in fact *know* he was heading east. No sun up there in the sky. Just a cold, dead moon and stars that told him nothing. He turned corners, seemed at times to be doubling back on his own tracks, coming to the same street sign again and again, thoroughly lost now. He studied the sign on the corner. Mulberry and Grand. He looked up Mulberry. It was festively hung with welcoming arches of Christmas lights. Blinking. Beckoning. Surely there was a telephone somewhere on this beautifully decorated street.

He began walking.

Italian restaurants, all of them already closed for Christmas. Hand-lettered signs in some of the windows, advising that they would not be open again till the fourth of January, which, come to think of it, was when Michael had planned to head back to Sarasota. If he'd ever made it to Boston. He decided that if he found an open restaurant or an open *anything*, he would first call his mother to let her know he wasn't dead even though she didn't have any of his clothes she could give away prematurely, and then he would call China Doll Limo to see if Connie Kee was yet free to take him to St Luke's Place, wherever the hell *that* was.

The awning over the restaurant read:

RISTORANTE BLUE MADONNA

The sign in the door read:

CLOSED

But there were lights blazing inside, and the sound of music – the Supremes singing "Stop in the Name of Love." The early Sixties came back in a rush. Boston before he was drafted. Sixteen-year-old Jenny Aldershot sitting on a wall overlooking the Charles River, her blonde hair blowing in the wind. He tried the door. It was unlocked. He opened it a crack. The music was louder now. He opened the door fully and stepped inside, and then he almost ran right out into the street again because the place was full of cops!

Beautiful young women wearing garter belts, panties, seamed silk stockings, and high heels – which was just what Detective O'Brien had been wearing earlier tonight. Dancing with men in business suits. As he started for the door again, someone clapped a hand on his shoulder. He turned to see a short roly-poly man who looked a lot like both Tony the Bear Orso and Charlie Bonano.

"Help ya?" the man said.

"I'm looking for a telephone," Michael said.

"This is a private party," the man said.

"I'm sorry," Michael said. "I thought this was a restaurant."

"It *is* a restaurant, but it's also a private party. Dinn you see the sign in the door? The sign says 'Closed.'"

"I'm sorry, I didn't see it."

"It says 'Closed' whether you seen it or not."

"All I want to do is make a phone call, it won't take a . . ."

"Are you a cop?" the man asked.

"No," Michael said.

The man looked at him.

"What are you then?"

"An orange-grower."

"My grandfather grew grapes," the man said. "I'm Frankie Zeppelin." He extended his hand to Michael. "What's your name?"

"Donald Trump," Michael said.

"Nice to meet you, Mr Trump," Frankie said, and shook hands with him. "Come on, I'll get you a drink. What do you drink, Mr Trump?"

"You can call me Don," Michael said.

"Well, that's very nice of you, Don. And you can call me Mr Zepparino. What do you drink, Don?"

"If you have a little scotch . . ."

"We have a little everything," Frankie said, and grinned as if he'd made a terrific joke. Putting his arm around Michael's shoulders, he led him toward the bar. "You look familiar," he said. "Do I know you?"

"I don't think so."

"Are you from the neighborhood?"

"I'm from Minnesota," Michael said at once, just in case Frankie had seen the earlier news broadcast.

"A lot of the girls here come from Minnesota," Frankie said. "These very dumb blonde girls with blue eyes, they must drink a lot of milk out there in Minnesota."

"Yes, it's called the Land of the Lakes," Michael said.

"I thought it musta been," Frankie said. "Kid," he said to the bartender, "pour Donny here some scotch."

The bartender picked up a bottle of Dewar's Black Label, and poured generously into a tall glass.

"Anything with that?" he asked.

"Just a little soda," Michael said.

"Hello?" a voice said over the loudspeaker system. "Hello? Can you hear me? Hello? One, two, three, testing, can you hear me? Hello, hello, hello, hell . . ."

"We can *hear* you already!" Frankie shouted.

Michael looked over to where a man wearing brown shoes and what looked like his blue confirmation suit was standing behind a microphone set up near a big copper espresso machine.

"Ladies and gentlemen," he said, "I want to wish you first, one and all, a very merry . . . is this thing on?"

"It's *on* already!" Frankie yelled.

"Hello?" the man at the speaker said. "Can you hear me?" He began tapping the microphone. "Hello? If you can hear me, please raise your hands please. Hello? Can you hear me?" Frankie threw up both his hands. All around the hall, people were putting their hands up. "Looks like a police raid in here," the man at the microphone said, which not too many people found funny, including Michael.

A redheaded woman wearing a black negligee over a black teddy and black garters and black silk stockings and black high-heeled patent leather shoes came over to the bar, said, "Hello, Frankie," and extended her glass to the bartender. "Just vodka," she said.

"I think I can safely say, at this our annual Christmas party here," the man at the microphone said, "that this year was a better year than any year preceding it. And I think I can say without fear of contradiction that next year is going to be an even better one!"

There were cries of "Tell us about it, Al!" and "Attaway, Al!" and "Let's hear the figures, Al!"

"Hi," the redhead said. "I'm Hannah."

"How do you do?" Michael said.

"You look familiar," she said. "Have I ever seen you on television?"

"No," he said at once.

"Aren't you the one who does the Carvel commercials?"

"Yes," he said, "come to think of it."

"No kidding? I *love* your Cookie Puss cakes."

"As an example," Al said, "in hotel encounters in the midtown area of Manhattan alone, revenues were up seven percent from last year for a total of . . ."

"Who's this?" a voice at Michael's elbow said.

He turned. He was looking at a very large man wearing a brown tweed suit, a yellow button-down shirt, a green knit tie, and an angry scowl.

"Jimmy, this is the man does the Carvel ice cream commercials," Hannah said.

"No kidding?" Jimmy said, immediately disarmed. He took Michael's hand, began pumping it vigorously. "I love your Black Bear cakes," he said. "I'm Jimmy Fingers."

"How do you do, Mr Fingers?" Michael said.

"It's Finnegan, actually. But that's okay, everybody knows me as Jimmy Fingers."

"Especially the cops," Hannah said.

"Yeah, *them*," Jimmy said.

"Mobile encounters," Al said into the microphone, "by which I'm referring only to passenger automobiles and not vans or pickup trucks – and, mind you, I'm not even including figures for the Holland Tunnel or the George Washington Bridge – were up a full fifteen percent over last year."

"That's very good," Jimmy said appreciatively.

"Good? That's sensational," Frankie said.

"But it can give you backaches," Hannah said.

"Does anyone know where I can find a telephone?" Michael asked.

"Why you need a telephone?" Frankie said.

"I want to call a friend of mine. She may be able to take me to St Luke's Place."

"Why you wanna go to St Luke's? What's the matter with here?"

"Here is very nice, but . . ."

". . . know I speak for all of us," Al said at the microphone, "when I extend our sincere appreciation and gratitude to our fine mayor, Ed Koch, and our excellent police commissioner, Benjamin Ward, and also the good Lord above us, thank you one and all!"

"Hear, hear," Jimmy Fingers said.

"And now, ladies and gentlemen, I am going to ask you to please enjoy the food and the beverage and the music and to stay as long as you like, although some of us may have made previous arrangements. To one and to all, to those of us in management, and to you – the rank and file in the front lines – I wish you a merry Christmas and a new year even more financially and spiritually rewarding than this one has been. Enjoy!" he shouted, and extended both arms in the V gesture Richard Nixon had made famous.

"You wanna go to St Luke's, I'll take you to St Luke's," Frankie said. "It's Christmas, I feel like Santa Claus. Anyway, it's on my way home."

"Well, thank you, that's very kind of you," Michael said.

"I got the car right outside," Frankie said.

At the microphone, four women began singing, "Deck the whores with boughs of holly, fa-la-la-la-la, la-la-la-la. Lookin' for a good-time Charlie, fa-la-la . . ."

The moment they were seated in Frankie's red Buick Regal, he turned to Michael and said, "So they want you for murder, huh?"

Michael's hand shot out for the door handle.

"Relax, relax, maybe I can help you."

"I think you have the wrong party," Michael said.

"I seen you on television, I ain't got the wrong party. Relax."

"It's the kind of face I have, I'm often mistaken for . . ."

"Relax, willya please? I'm only tryin'a help here."

"Well, thanks, but how can you possibly. . . ?"

"I can hide you out for a coupla days," Frankie said.

"But I didn't kill anybody," Michael said.

"Well, of *course* you didn't, nobody *ever* killed anybody. But this is *me* you're talking to."

"Well . . ."

"So you want to go under or not?" Frankie asked. "You surface again sometime next week, the cops'll forget you even existed."

"Excuse me," Michael said, "but I don't think that's the way to go."

"Then what *is* the way to go?" Frankie said, sounding a bit irritated. "I mean, no offense meant, but you're the fuckin' guy *murdered* somebody, not me."

"I think I've got to find out who got killed."

"Who got killed is this guy Crandall."

"No, it wasn't Crandall."

"On television, they said he was the dead guy. And they said *you* killed him. Which, by the way, your name ain't Donald Trump."

"That's right, it isn't."

"I mean, nobody in this whole fuckin' *world* could be named Donald *Trump*. I mean, if you had to pick a phony name . . ."

"It's Michael Barnes," Michael said.

"Which also sounds phony. I'm tryin'a help you here, and you keep layin' this bullshit on me. Is it that you don't trust me? I mean, I spent all my life in this fuckin' downtown community, tryin'a build a reputation for honesty and trust, so if there's one thing you can do, it's trust me."

"I do trust you," Michael said.

"Good," Frankie said, and pulled a gun from a holster under his jacket and stuck it in Michael's face. "You know what this is?" he asked Michael.

Michael knew what it was. It was a Colt .45 automatic. He had handled many guns exactly like it while he was in the army.

"Yes," he said, "I know what it is."

"Good," Frankie said. "You know how to use it?"

"Yes."

"Good. 'Cause I want you to use it."

Michael looked at him.

"There is a person I would like you to kill," Frankie said.

Michael kept looking at him.

"Because I understand you're very good at that," Frankie said.

Everyone in this city is crazy, Michael thought.

"You already killed this movie guy," Frankie said, "so it . . ."

"No, I *didn't* kill this movie . . ."

"Hey," Frankie said, "*listen*, okay?" and put the gun to his ear as if it were a finger. "This is *me*, okay?" he said, and winked. "Never mind what you tell nobody else, this is me. Now. If you already killed one guy and the cops are lookin' for you . . ."

Michael sighed.

". . . then it won't make no difference you kill another guy, 'cause the cops'll *still* be looking for you, am I right?"

"No, you're wrong," Michael said. "Because killing *two* people is a lot more serious than killing *one* person."

"Well, you certainly should know," Frankie said.

"And besides, I *didn't* . . . look, do me a favor, okay? It was nice meeting you, really, and I enjoyed being there at your union meeting . . ."

"We're not a union," Frankie said. "We're a social and athletic club."

"Whatever, it was very nice. I'm glad business was so good, I'm very happy for you. And I appreciate your offer to drive me to St Luke's Place . . ."

"So then take the gun and help me out," Frankie said. "I mean, that's the fuckin' *least* you can do."

"You make it sound as if I *owe* you something," Michael said.

"I'm not turnin' you in, am I?"

"Goddamn it, I didn't *kill* anybody!"

"If you can't do the time, don't do the crime," Frankie said.

"Mr Zepparino," Michael said, "I'm going to get out of this car now."

"Please take the gun," Frankie said, "or I'll blow your fuckin' brains out."

"All right, give me the gun," Michael said.

"Now you're talkin' sense," Frankie said, and handed him the gun.

"Thank you," Michael said, and pointed the gun at him. "And now I'm going to bid you a fond . . ."

"That won't do no good," Frankie said.

Michael looked at him.

"The gun ain't loaded," he said.

"What?"

"The clip's here in my pocket."

"What? What?"

"Also, if a person asks you nice to kill somebody for him, why don't you just *do* it?"

"Because I . . ."

"Instead of threatening that person with an empty pistol?"

Michael was thinking first Charlie Wong with his fake gun, and now Frankie Zeppelin with an empty one. He was thinking he had to get out of this city. He was thinking that he had to get out of here before he himself went crazy.

"The person I want you to kill is Isadore Onions," Frankie said.

"I'm not about to kill Mr Onions or anyone else," Michael said wearily.

"There's a deli on Greenwich Avenue," Frankie said, "which is where he hangs out all the time. He should be there now, this is still very early in the day for Isadore, even if it's Christmas. What I'm going to do, I'm going to drive to that deli, it's called the Mazeltov All-Nite Deli. When we get there, Donny, I'll give you . . ."

"Michael," Michael said.

"Michael, sure," Frankie said, and rolled his eyes. "What I'll do when we *get* there, *Michael*, I'll give you the clip to put in the gun, and then I want you to go in and blow him away. Does my calling you Michael make you feel better, *Michael*?"

"I am not going to kill anyone," Michael said.

"I admire a man who sticks to his guns," Frankie said, "but you don't understand. Isadore Onions *needs* killing."

"But not by me," Michael said.

"Then by who?" Frankie said. "Me? And then *I'll* get in trouble with the law, right? When you're *already* in trouble with the law. Does that make sense? Try to make sense, willya please?"

"Mr Zepparino, have you ever . . . ?"

"Isadore Onions is a very fat man with a Hitler moustache," Frankie said. "He usually dresses very conservative except he wears red socks. If you aim for the moustache you will probably kill him."

"Probably, but . . ."

"Just don't let the socks distract you."

"Look, Mr Zepparino . . ."

"You can call me Frankie. Now that we're doing business together. Did I mention that there is five bills in this for you? If you do a good job? Five big ones, Donny."

"Mr Zepparino, have you ever heard of a Mexican standoff?"

"No. What is a Mexican standoff?"

"A Mexican standoff is where *I* have the empty gun and *you* have the clip to put in it, and neither one of us can force the other one to do a goddamn thing. That is a Mexican standoff."

"Have you ever heard of a Russian hard-on?" Frankie asked. "A Russian hard-on is where *you* have the empty gun and *I* have the clip to put in it, but I also have *this*," he said, and pulled another gun from inside his coat. "This is a .38 caliber Detective Special, and it is loaded. Which means that you are going to get out of this car outside the Mazeltov All-Nite Deli on Greenwich Avenue, and you are going to go inside and shoot Isadore Onions in the moustache or I will have to shoot you instead and throw you out on the sidewalk. On a very cold night."

The car was suddenly very still.

"Which they will prolly give me a medal for shooting a cold-blooded murderer," Frankie said.

"Where's Greenwich Avenue?" Michael asked.

7

In Vietnam, one of the first things Sergeant Mendelsohnn told him was, "When the going gets tough, the tough get going." This did not mean going home. Or going back. It meant going forward. Advancing. Blowing apart the whole fucking jungle as you moved *toward* the enemy. Leaves flying, mounds of earth exploding, whole trees coming down as you trashed the countryside, rat-tat-tat, pow, zowie, boom, bang, Rambo for sure, only you didn't have glistening muscles you bought in a Hollywood gym.

You were a lean, somewhat scruffy-looking nineteen-year-old kid from Boston, and you wore eyeglasses, and you just wished your glasses wouldn't get shattered in all that noise and confusion while you were bringing down the countryside hoping you'd get some of the bad guys. But you never refused to advance. And you never pulled back unless you were ordered to. This had nothing to do with patriotism. It had to do with the fact that Mendelsohnn or somebody even higher up would shoot you in the back if you either refused to advance or turned tail and ran back to safety when the shit began flying.

As Michael got out of that red Buick on Greenwich Avenue, he knew that Frankie Zeppelin was sitting there behind him with a .38 Detective Special trained on his back, and he knew that if he did not advance into the Mazeltov All-Nite Deli as ordered, he would be shot in the back. *Plus ça change, plus c'est la même chose*, as his mother had been fond of saying back in Boston each time winter howled in off the Common. His mother's ancestry was French. His father's was English. An odd match, considering that the English and the French had been traditional enemies even before Agincourt. Sometimes their house resembled a battlefield. Well, not really. Nothing but a battlefield even remotely resembled a battlefield. This empty, windblown, bitterly cold street was not a battlefield, either, even though Michael had one pistol in the pocket of his coat and another pistol trained on his back, and there was a man sitting inside whom he was expected to kill.

Like fun.

This was not a battlefield, and Frankie Zeppelin was not a sergeant.

Michael opened the door to the deli.

For a little past two o'clock on Christmas morning, the place was thronged. Men in suits or sports jackets or tuxedos; women in slacks or dresses or evening gowns. Radiators clanging and steaming. Wooden tables, no tablecloths on them, paper-napkin holders, salt and pepper shakers. Waiters in black jackets and unmatching black trousers, white shirts, no ties, running frantically back and forth, to and from a counter behind which a steam table added yet more warmth to the place. The sudden aroma of food reminded Michael that he hadn't had anything to eat since lunch with Jonah today – yesterday actually, although his mind-clock always considered it the same day until the sun came up in the morning, no matter *what* time it really was.

Jonah Hillerman of the Hillerman-Ruggiero Advertising Agency. Who had proposed a scenario for the upcoming Golden Oranges television campaign. Beautiful suntanned blonde girl doing the commercial, okay? Wearing nothing but a bikini. Sun shining. Eating an orange in the first scene, juice spilling onto her chin. "Eat 'em," she whispers, and wipes away the juice with the back of her hand. In the next scene, she's squeezing an orange. Frothy, foaming juice bubbles up over the rim of the glass. "Squeeze 'em," she whispers. "Mmmm, good," she whispers. "Mmmm, sweet. Mmmm, Golden. Mmmm, *Oranges!*"

"Subliminal sex," Jonah said. "The viewer thinks we're asking him to eat the blonde's pussy and squeeze her tits. We're telling him the blonde is good, she's sweet, she's golden. Eat her, squeeze her! What do you think?"

"What about women?" Michael asked. "They're the ones who go shopping for the oranges."

"That's a sexist attitude," Jonah said.

Michael was almost faint with hunger. He went to the counter and ordered two hot dogs with sauerkraut and mustard, a side of French fries, a Coca-Cola, and a slice of chocolate cake. Isadore Onions – wearing a dark suit, red socks, a Hitler moustache, and the worst hairpiece Michael had ever seen in his life – was sitting at a table with a blonde wearing a very tight fluffy white sweater and a narrow black leather mini-skirt. Michael figured she could make a fortune doing orange-juice commercials. Or even working for Frankie Zeppelin.

"Two dogs," the man behind the counter said. "Fries, a Coke, and a slice a chocolate. Pay the cashier."

Michael picked up his tray and went to the cash register.

The cashier tallied the bill.

"Seven-forty," she said.

Michael reached into his pocket for his wallet.

His wallet was gone.

Not again, he thought.

He patted down all his other pockets. No wallet. He wondered if Frankie Zeppelin had stolen his wallet. The cashier was looking at him.

"Seven-forty," she said.

"Just a second," Michael said.

He left the tray at the cash register, walked over to Isadore Onions's table, pulled out a chair, sat, and said, "Mr Onions?"

"Mr Ornstein," the man said. "No relation."

"To who, honey?" the blonde asked.

"Nick Ornstein, the gangster who was Fanny Brice's husband."

"That was Nick *Arn*stein," the blonde said.

"Exactly," Ornstein said. "So who are *you*?" he asked Michael.

"Mr Ornstein," Michael said, "there's a contract out on you."

"Thank you for telling me," Ornstein said, "but what else is new?"

"What else is new is that I'm the one who's supposed to shoot you," Michael said.

"Don't make me laugh," Ornstein said.

"But you won't have to worry about that if you give me seven dollars and forty cents to pay for my food over there."

"Who is this person?" Ornstein asked the blonde.

"Michael Barnes, sir."

"You look familiar," the blonde said.

"You've probably seen me on television," Michael said. "I'm already wanted for a murder I committed earlier tonight. So another one won't matter at all to me. I work cheap, Mr Ornstein. All I want is seven dollars and forty cents to forget the whole matter."

"Get lost," Ornstein said.

"Mr Ornstein, I'm a desperate man."

"Who isn't?"

"I'm starving to death . . ."

"So starve."

"If I don't get something to eat soon, I'll fall down on the floor here."

"So fall."

"I think it was nice of him to tell you," the blonde said, and shrugged.

"Sure, very nice," Ornstein said. "He comes in, he sits down, he tells me he's supposed to shoot me, this is a nice thing to say to a person? And then ask him for a loan besides? This is nice by you?"

"He only asked for seven dollars," the blonde said.

"And forty cents, don't forget," Ornstein said. "On my block, seven dollars and forty cents don't grow on trees."

"Come on, Izzie, it's Christmas."

"Too bad I'm Jewish."

"If this man falls down on the floor . . ."

"Let him, who cares?"

"If there's a commotion, there'll be cops in here."

"I hope not," Michael said.

"Me, too," Ornstein said. "Here," he said, immediately taking out his wallet and reaching into it and handing Michael a ten-dollar bill. "Get lost."

"Thank you, Mr Ornstein," Michael said, "thank you very much, sir," and got up at once and went to the counter to pay for his order and to pick up his tray. He looked around the room. The only vacant chair was at Ornstein's table. He went to it, said, "Hello, again," sat, and began eating.

"I thought I told you to get lost," Ornstein said.

"No, it's better he came back," the blonde said.

"Why?"

"Because now he can tell us who put out the contract on you."

"Yeah, who?" Ornstein asked Michael.

Michael was busy eating.

"I never seen such a fresser in my life," Ornstein said.

"He's cute when he eats," the blonde said, and smiled at him.

Michael had the distinct impression that she had just put her hand on his knee.

"Who sent you to kill me?" Ornstein asked.

In the army, they had told Michael that if he was ever captured by the enemy, he should tell them nothing but his name, rank, and serial number. He was not to tell them where the Fifth Division was, or the Twelfth, or the Ninth, he was not even to tell them where the nearest latrine was.

"Frankie Zeppelin," he said.

"Of course," Ornstein said, and nodded to the blonde.

"Of course," she said, and her hand moved up onto Michael's thigh.

"Excuse me," he said, "but I don't believe we've met."

"Irene," she said, and smiled.

"You know why he wants me killed?" Ornstein asked Michael.

"No, why?"

"Because of *her*," Ornstein said.

"Really?" Michael said.

"He's insanely jealous," Ornstein said. "So am I."

"I think I'd better go," Michael said. "If you'll let me have your name and address, I'll . . ."

"Finish your meal," Irene said, and smiled again.

Her hand was still on his thigh.

"What I was going to say . . ."

"Yes?" Irene said.

". . . was I'll send Mr Ornstein a check. When I get home."

"Frankie Zeppelin will kill anyone so much as *looks* at this girl," Ornstein said.

"That's true," Irene said, and smiled again at Michael.

Michael was very careful not to look at her.

"So you can imagine how he feels about us sleeping together," Ornstein said.

"I can imagine," Michael said.

"But who can blame him?"

"Not me," Irene said.

"Not me, neither," Ornstein said, and belched. His hairpiece almost fell off his head. He adjusted it with both hands, looked across the table at Michael as if wondering if he'd noticed either the belch or the adventurous wig, and then said, "I myself would kill anyone got funny with her."

"Oh my," Irene said.

"I would," Ornstein said.

Michael kept eating. He wondered if Ornstein knew he had a terrible wig. He wondered if Ornstein knew that Irene's hand was on his thigh. He wondered if Frankie Zeppelin was still outside in the Buick, counting the money in Michael's wallet and waiting to shoot him. He was beginning to think he had a better chance of getting killed here in this city than he'd ever had in Vietnam.

"So, Michael," Ornstein said, "this is what I . . . it *is* Michael, isn't it?"

"Yes."

"Is what I thought it was, what a dumb name. Michael, I want you to go back to that goniff . . ."

"Which means thief," Irene said, and smiled.

". . . and tell him if he ever sends anybody *else* around here to shoot me . . ."

"Oh my," Irene said.

". . . I'll send him back in a box," Ornstein said. "You think you can remember that, Michael?"

"I think I can remember it," Michael said.

"So go tell him," Ornstein said.

Michael stood up, pulling his coat around him like a cloak.

"Thank you," he said.

"Don't mention it," Irene said.

"For the loan," he said.

"Of *course* for the loan," Ornstein said. "What else?"

He almost started for the front door, and then remembered that Frankie Zeppelin was sitting out there in the red Buick with a .38 caliber Detective Special in his fist. He turned abruptly, almost knocking over a woman carrying a tray of what appeared to be four bowls of soup, incurring her wrath and a question he assumed to be strictly New York: "Whattsamatter you're cockeyed?"

The men's room was at the rear of the deli, in a corridor that dead-ended at a door marked EMERGENCY EXIT. A sign warned that this was to be used only in an emergency, and advised that a bell would sound if anyone opened the door. Michael went into the men's room, washed his hands at one of the sinks, tried the window over the toilet bowl, discovered it was painted shut, and then went out into the corridor again.

The sign was still there on the door.

A push bar was set on the door about waist-high.

Michael read the sign yet another time.

Then he shoved out at the bar.

The door flew open.

Sergeant Mendelsohnn had told him that the war in Vietnam was merely a piss-ant war compared to the one in Korea, in which noble war he had been proud to serve because it had been a *true* test of manhood. In Nam, the way Charlie scared you shitless was he crept around the jungle in his black pajamas and you never *saw* him. It was a phantom army out there. That's what was so terrifying. You *imagined* Charlie to be something worse than he really was. But in Korea . . . ah, Korea. Mendelsohnn waxed entirely ecstatic about Korea. In Korea, the Chinese lit up the whole battlefield at night! Could you imagine that? You were advancing in the dark and *whappo*, all of a sudden these floodlights would light up the whole place, it was like having your ass hanging on the washline in broad daylight. And *also* in Korea – man, what a war that had been – there were Chinese cavalry charges! Could you imagine *that*? Cavalry charges! With bugles and gongs! Unlike the gooks in Nam, the ones in Korea made all the noise they possibly could. They terrified you with their noise. You were ready to die just from the noise alone.

Like now.

The minute Michael shoved open the door, the instant the door opened just the tiniest little crack, the bells went off. Not *a* bell, as had been promised on the warning sign, *A Bell Will Sound*. These were *bells*. Bells in the plural, bells in the multiple, bells that would have deafened the hunchback of Notre Dame, bells that would have sent the entire American Army in Korea fleeing in terror with or without gongs or horses or floodlights, bells that if Hitler had mounted them instead of whistles on his Stuka dive-bombers, there would now be his picture on American hundred-dollar bills.

Michael reeled back as if he'd been struck in the face with a hammer.

And then he remembered that when the going got tough the tough got going, and he pushed the door open wider and hurled himself out into the night, the cold air joining with the bells to assault his ears in fierce combination as he stepped onto and into the unshoveled snow behind the diner. The bells would not stop. Or perhaps they had stopped and he was now hearing only their echo. Perhaps –

And suddenly there were lights!

And horns!

The goddamn Chinese were coming!

This was Korea, and this was the test of his manhood!

Standing there trapped in the glaring lights, with the gongs still echoing in his ears and the horns blowing, Michael knew they would come riding out of the night on their Mongolian ponies and slash him to ribbons with their sabers. And then . . .

Oh Jesus . . .

The first Chinese soldier came out of the glare of the lights and moved toward him slowly as if in a dream, white snow underfoot, white covering the world, white and green and long black hair and . . .

"Michael!" she shouted.

"Connie!" he shouted back.

"This way! Quick!"

She grabbed his hand in hers, and together they crashed through the fans of brilliant illumination coming from the limo's headlights. Snow thick underfoot. Shoes sodden. Socks wet. They reached the car. She ran around to the driver's side. He opened the door on the passenger side. No bells went off. The bells were still ringing in his head, though. He got in.

"You okay?" she asked. "I've been searching all over for you."

"Yes," he said.

Her voice reverberated inside his head.

He pulled the door shut. The good solid sound of a luxury car's door settling snugly and securely into its frame. And then a small, expensive electric-lock click that miraculously cleared his ringing ears.

Behind them, he heard someone shouting.

He didn't know who and he didn't care why.

"Where to now?" Connie asked, and eased the limo into the night again.

*

St Luke's Place was a tree-shaded street with a public park on one side of it, and a row of brownstones on the other. It was exactly one block long, a narrow oasis between the wider thoroughfares that flanked it. At three in the morning, the only house with lights showing was in the middle of the block. Michael looked up at the third-floor window, located the name Wales in the directory set in a panel beside the door, rang the bell, identified himself as the man who'd telephoned not five minutes ago, and was immediately buzzed in.

The woman who answered the door to the third-floor apartment was perhaps thirty-three years old, a Marilyn Monroe look-alike with a Carly Simon mouth. She had short blonde hair ("The same color hair *all* bimbos have") and wide brown eyes, and she was wearing high-heeled silver slippers and a long silver robe belted at the waist. Michael did not think either the robe or the slippers were *real* silver, but they certainly did look authentic. Like the gun in Detective O'Brien's hand had looked authentic. All those many years ago, it seemed. Was it still only Christmas morning? Had it been only three hours since he'd first learned from Albetha Crandall on the telephone that there was a bimbo with red silk panties in her husband's life? He wondered if Jessica Wales was wearing red silk panties now.

"Please come in," she said.

Little tiny breathless Marilyn Monroe voice.

Carly Simon smile.

She stepped back and away from the door, the robe parting over very long, very shapely Cher legs. It suddenly occurred to Michael that Jessica Wales was not wearing red silk panties or anything else under that robe. There was nothing and nobody but Jessica Wales under there. Here I am with a famous movie star who's wearing nothing under her robe, he thought.

A Christmas tree was in one corner of the large living room festively decorated with ornaments that looked expensively German in origin, and minuscule white lights and angel's hair spun into tunnels that seemed to recede into a distant childhood where sugarplum fairies danced in everyone's head. Wrapped Christmas packages in different sizes and colors were spread under the tree and a pair of bulging red stockings with white cuffs were hanging over a fireplace in which cannel coal was burning. The record player, or the radio, Michael couldn't tell which, was playing what

91

sounded like Old English carols. He stepped past Jessica, the scent of Poison wafting up from her, and heard the door clicking shut behind him. She turned the lock, put on the safety chain.

"So," she said, "how can I help you?"

"Well, as I told you on the phone . . ."

"Yes. But I don't know where he is."

"I thought he might be here."

"No. In fact, until you called, I still thought he was dead."

"No, he's alive."

"You're sure?"

"Yes. I saw him on television."

"I'm so happy to hear that," she said, "would you like a drink?"

"No, thank you, Miss Wales, it's urgent that I find Mr Crandall."

"Yes, so you told me. Are you sure? A little cognac?"

"Well, just a little, thank you."

Jessica moved like molten silver to a built-in bar on the wall alongside a unit containing a television set, a VCR, a turntable, a tuner, a tape deck and a compact disc player. Michael still didn't know whether he was listening to a recording or to the radio. He looked around as Jessica began pouring the cognac. The living room adjoined the dining room, an open swinging door between them. Beyond the dining room, he could see only a portion of a kitchen with sand-colored cabinets. On the other side of the room there was an open door with a small library beyond it, and a closed door leading to what Michael guessed was the bedroom. The place was luxuriously furnished. He wondered how long Jessica had been a famous movie star he'd never heard of.

On the radio – it was the radio, he now discovered – an announcer was telling the world or at least the tri-state area that this was WQXR and that an uninterrupted program of Christmas music would continue immediately after the three A.M. news. Michael moved closer to one of the speakers. Jessica handed him a snifter half full of cognac.

"Roll it around in your hands," she said. "Like this."

She was holding her own snifter in both hands, close to her abundant breasts, rolling it gently between her palms. Michael was suddenly reminded of the commercial Jonah Hillerman had pitched at lunch yesterday, Eat 'em. Squeeze 'em. Mmmm, good. Mmmm, sweet.

"To bring out the bouquet," Jessica said.

On the radio, a newscaster was giving the latest on the continuing conflict in the Middle East.

Jessica kept rolling the snifter between the palms of her hands.

The newscaster said that a large American corporation had sold one of its divisions to the Japanese for a billion dollars.

"Mmmm, good," Jessica said, and brought the snifter to her nose.

The newscaster said that a United States senator had been indicted for violating the law against . . .

Jessica was sniffing the bouquet.

. . . said in a televised news conference that he would be exonerated once the true and complete story was : . .

"Mmmm, sweet," Jessica said.

The newscaster said that the dollar had fallen against most major currencies in U.S. trading.

"Taste it," Jessica said.

The newscaster said that a new cold front was moving in from the Canadian Rockies.

It seemed to Michael that he might have been listening to this very same newscast yesterday or two weeks ago or two months ago. Some American corporation was always selling off something to the Japanese, elected senators were always being indicted for breaking one law or another and then assuring the public that they would be proven innocent once the true facts were known, the American dollar was always weaker against most major currencies, there was always a cold front moving in from the Canadian Rockies, even in the summertime, and there was always and forever a continuing conflict in the Middle East. Even at Christmastime. Peace on earth, the man had said, but where was it? Meanwhile, Jessica was sipping her cognac.

The newscaster started giving the weather forecast for New York City and vicinity. Continued cold . . .

"Mmmm," Jessica said.

. . . temperatures in the single digits . . .

"This is sooo good," she said.

. . . possibility of more snow before morning.

"Terrific," Michael said.

"But you haven't tasted it yet," she said.

"I meant the weather."

The newscaster was now telling everyone to stay tuned for an uninterrupted program of Christmas music. No mention of the dead body found in the rented automobile. No mention of Michael Barnes, the wanted desperado. Another voice came on, saying there would now be uninterrupted music until the next news report at four A.M. Something medieval flooded from the speakers.

Michael took a sip of the cognac.

"Yes," he said, "delicious. Who's Mama?"

"Mama?"

"In Crandall's appointment calendar, it said 'Call Mama.' And he was also supposed to meet her at eight o'clock last night. So who's Mama?"

"Arthur's mama is dead."

"I know. So whose mama was he calling and meeting?"

"Maybe Albetha's."

"No, they don't get along."

"Well, certainly not *my* mama. She's on vacation in London, England."

"Then whose?"

"I have no idea. How'd you see Arthur's calen . . . ?"

"Do you know why he went to the bank on Friday?"

"I think he goes to the bank every Friday," Jessica said, and shrugged.

"He wouldn't have gone there to cash a check, would he?"

"How would I know?"

"For nine thousand dollars?"

"I really couldn't say."

"Which is exactly a thousand dollars less than has to be reported to the IRS."

"Really? Gee."

"Who else was at that Christmas party?"

"What Christmas party? How do you know about the Christmas party?"

"I was in Crandall's office earlier tonight. Do you know anyone who lost a pair of red silk panties?"

"Gee," she said, "no."

"Okay, who's Charlie?"

"Which Charlie? There are a lot of Charlies in this city, you know."

"Yes, I know. Which Charlie did *Crandall* know?"

"Well, there's Charlie Nichols, no relation to Jack Nichols the big movie star."

"You mean Jack Nicholson, don't you?"

"Exactly. Charlie Nichols used to be on *Mister Ed* years ago. Arthur used him in *Winter's Chill*. To do one of the voices."

"A horse's voice?"

"No, a ghost's voice. There are a lot of ghosts in the picture. Or at least I'm supposed to *think* they're ghosts. The character I play. She thinks they're ghosts. They're trying to drive her crazy, you see. The character I play."

"Like Ingrid Bergman in *Gaslight*?"

"No!" she said sharply. "Not at *all* like *Gaslight*. Don't even *breathe* the word *Gaslight*. This is a very scary picture."

"So was *Gaslight*."

"Will you please stop with *Gaslight*? This is a much better picture than *Gaslight*, you'll see when it opens."

"When will that be?"

"On the fifth. That's a Thursday. So we'll catch the *Weekend* section of the *Times*. When they review all the new movies. The Friday paper."

"What does Charlie Nichols look like?"

"What difference does it make? He's only a voice."

"Yes, but what does he look like?"

"I never met him. I just told you, he's a voice."

"Have you met any Charlies who are *more* than voices?"

"Everybody has met a Charlie who is more than a voice."

"I mean, who is also a Charlie that Crandall knows."

"I can't think of any other Charlies he knows."

"You said he knows a *lot* of Charlies."

"No, I said there are a lot of Charlies in this *city* is what I said."

"But Charlie Nichols is the only Charlie that Crandall knows."

"He's the only Charlie that *I* know Arthur knows. For all I know, Arthur may know a *hundred* Charlies, maybe even a *thousand* Charlies, there are probably *millions* of Charlies in this city. All I'm saying is that Charles R. Nichols is the only Charlie . . ."

"Okay, I've got it. Do you know where he lives?"

"No."

"But I do."

The voice came from behind him.

A man's voice.

He turned at once.

Arthur Crandall was standing in the doorway to the bedroom. Fat and short and bald and wearing the same three-piece suit he'd worn on television, a Phi Beta Kappa key hanging on a gold chain across the front of his vest.

"Merry Christmas, Mr Barnes," he said.

"Who's the dead man?" Michael asked. "And why are you running around town telling people *I* killed him?"

"Which of course you didn't do," Crandall said, and looked at his watch.

"And why are you looking at your watch?" Michael asked.

"I was wondering when the police would get here," Crandall said. "I called them the moment you arrived. They should be . . ."

"Thank you for the warning," Michael said, and started for the door. "It was nice meeting you both, there certainly are some charming and delightful people here in downtown New . . ."

"No," Crandall said, and reached into his pocket.

His hand came out with a gun in it.

Everybody in this city has a gun, Michael thought.

And took a step toward him.

"No, please don't," Crandall said. "This is a gun, you know."

"So is this," Michael said.

8

You usually knew in that first split second whether the other guy was serious.

In Vietnam, lots of guys had to prove they were big macho killers, had to keep telling this to themselves over and over again because otherwise they'd go weak with terror whenever a leaf rattled out there in the jungle. So one way they tried to prove it was to lean on anybody they thought would back down. Come to think of it, this may have been the origin of all that Russian roulette stuff in *The Deer Hunter*. Because lots of times out there, weapons came into play during the showdown process.

Now if you were going to lean on somebody, it was usually better not to choose some guy who weighed three hundred pounds and was built like the Chesapeake and Ohio. Because this man would chew up both you *and* your rifle and then spit out railroad spikes. So you didn't go bumping on him, you didn't go waving your weapon around in his face unless you felt it would be patriotic to get killed by a fellow American instead of a gook.

What you tried to do, if you were looking to bolster your own courage and make yourself feel like a great big macho killer, was you tried to pick on somebody who wore eyeglasses and who looked sort of scrawny and whose middle name was Jellicle, was what you tried to do. Shove your rifle in *his* face, man. See if you could get *him* to back down. And usually you knew in that first split second whether you had him or not.

And vice versa, if you were the one who was looking into the barrel of the rifle – as had so often been the case with Michael –

you knew immediately whether the guy threatening you would really paint the jungle with your blood if you didn't back off *toot sweet*, as they all used to say in their bastardized, learned-from-the-gooks French.

Michael had never backed off.

Even when he knew the other guy was dead serious.

The ones who were all bluff and bravado, you dismissed with a wave of the hand, boldly turned your back on them, went back into the hooch to smoke a joint.

But the red-eyed ones . . .

The ones who'd had too much of the jungle and were no longer capable of telling friend from foe . . .

The ones who had murder scribbled crookedly on their mouths . . .

These were the ones it was essential to stare down.

Because if you backed off from them now, if you let the barrel of that automatic rifle force you to turn away, why then one day they would shoot you as soon as look at you. No warning next time. Just *pow* when the jam was on, in the back, in the face, in the chest, it didn't matter, they knew you were nothing but dog shit and they could waste you whenever they wanted to, and wasting you would give them the magical power to kill all the gooks in the jungle. It was like eating your testicles or your heart or whatever Long Foot Howell had told him the Indians used to eat after they'd scalped you.

What you did, you said, "Fuck off, okay?"

And if he didn't choose to do that, you walked right up to him, and you slapped the muzzle of the rifle aside with the palm of your hand.

And if the muzzle refused to be slapped aside, if those little red pig eyes in the man's head were telling you that he was going to blow you away in the next count of three, why then what you had to do was kick him in the balls the way Michael had kicked Charlie Wong in the balls only several hours ago. And while the man was writhing on the ground in pain, you stepped on his face hard, which Michael guessed he'd have done to Charlie Wong if Detective O'Brien hadn't shown up in her sexy underwear, braving the cold and all. And once you'd stolen the man's face, why then you could turn your back on him the way you did with the other kind, just saunter away into the hooch for a little smoke. Maybe ask him to join you if you were feeling generous. And maybe he'd shoot you anyway one fine day, but chances were he wouldn't.

The situation here was identical to all those showdowns Michael had survived in Vietnam, where he'd sometimes thought he'd rather face a whole platoon of gooks rather than another red-eyed American trying to show he wasn't scared. Crandall wasn't doing such a good job of showing he wasn't scared. It was Michael's guess that the man had never held a gun in his hand before this very moment and that the sight of the larger weapon in Michael's hand was causing him to have some second thoughts about keeping him here until the police showed. Panic was in his eyes. He definitely did not want a gunfight here at the old OK Corral.

So Michael did what he would have done in Vietnam when facing a bluff. He dismissed Crandall with a wave of his free hand, turned his back on him, and started for the door.

Which should have worked.

But didn't.

Because apparently Michael hadn't learned a lesson he should have learned many, many years ago, and the lesson was Watch Out For That Harmless Little Vietnamese Woman With Her Gentle Smile And Her Innocent Eyes Because She Is Deadlier Than A Crack Male Regiment.

It was Jessica Wales who hit him.

She hit him very hard on the back of his head with something that sent him staggering forward toward the front door, in which direction he'd been heading anyway. He knew better than to let go of the gun. He also knew enough to roll away, the way he'd rolled away into the snow when Charlie Wong was trying to kick his brains into New Jersey. This time the foot that came at him was wearing an ankle-strapped shoe with a stiletto heel that looked like silver or perhaps stainless steel as it came flashing toward—

The woman was trying to stomp him.

He had seen many black soldiers in Vietnam stomping other soldiers. They had learned this art while growing up in lovely ghettos here and there across the United States.

Where lovely Jessica had learned it was anyone's guess.

But she definitely was trying to stomp him.

Not kick him.

Stomp him.

Kicking and stomping were two different things, although often used in conjunction. When you kicked someone, you were trying to send his head sailing through the goal posts. When you stomped someone, you were trying to break open his head like a melon. Squash it flat into the pavement. The pressure point in the stomping process was the heel. In Vietnam, the heel had been flat and attached to a combat boot. Here in the living room of Jessica Wales's apartment, it was four inches long and tapered to a narrow point. If that heel connected with his head—

Michael kept rolling away.

There were here-again gone-again glimpses of long legs flashing, white thighs winking, the silver robe parting and flapping as Jessica tracked him across the floor, searching for an opportunity to step on him good. He rolled, rolled, rolled blindly into the wall, came to a frightening dead stop, and was scrambling to his feet when he saw Jessica bending her right leg and reaching down for the shoe. Tired of stepping and stomping, she had undoubtedly decided it would be better to wield the shoe like a hammer. And was now in the process of getting the shoe off her foot and into her hot little hand.

Fascinated, he watched her little balancing act.

Blonde Jessica standing on one foot, opposite leg bent backward at the knee, right hand sliding the heel of the shoe off the heel of her foot –

He would never have a better shot.

He lunged forward, ramming his shoulder hard against the leg she was standing on, knocking her off balance. The shoe flew off her foot and out of her hand. As she tumbled over backward, legs splayed, the robe opened disappointingly over a triangular patch of very black hair.

Michael leaped to his feet.

"I warned you!" Crandall shouted.

And fired.

At first, Michael thought he'd made a terrible and perhaps fatal mistake. For the first time in his life, he'd wrongly identified a genuine shooter as a bluffer. But then he saw that Crandall was looking at the smoking gun in his hand as if it had suddenly developed fangs and claws. This thing here in his hand had actually gone off! That's what his astonished face said. He had pulled the trigger and this thing had exploded in his hand and a bullet had come out of it and had in fact whistled across the room to shatter a mirror on the wall above where Jessica was already getting up off the floor in a tangle of legs and open robe and mons veneris and one silver shoe.

Michael wondered if he should walk over to Crandall, push the muzzle of the gun aside, tell him to fuck off, and then go back into the hooch for a smoke. He figured it just might work. While he was doing all this calculation, he forgot about Jessica for the second time that night, and remembered too late that once may be oversight but twice is stupidity.

The way he remembered was that Jessica hit him on the head again with the same object she'd used earlier, which he now realized was a metal tray of some sort, this time connecting more solidly and causing him to stagger forward almost into Crandall's arms. Crandall backed away as if being attacked. He certainly did not want this thing in his hand to go off again. Nor did he want to catch Michael in his arms, which he would have to do if Michael kept stumbling toward him. But Michael suddenly brought himself up short because even in his dizziness he had clearly and finally perceived that Jessica and not Crandall was the real danger.

Where? he thought.

And turned, hoping he would not get shot in the back, after all, because getting shot in the back would be a first for him. On Christmas Day, no less. Which would not be such a terrific surprise since he seemed to be experiencing a great many firsts here in festive New York City, the least of which was being attacked by a ferocious movie star who now looked not like Marilyn Monroe but that lady, whatever her name was, in *Fatal Attraction* with the frizzed hair and the long knife in her hand.

Jessica did not have a knife in her hand.

Jessica had a poker in it.

Which she had grabbed from a little stand alongside the fireplace, leaving a shovel and a brush still hanging from it. She came limping at Michael, one shoe on, one shoe off, her lips skinned back, her capped movie-star teeth glistening with spit, her eyes blazing. He figured she was angry because he'd knocked her on her ass.

But then Crandall put a very clear perspective on the entire situation.

"Careful!" he shouted. "He's a killer!"

And Michael realized in a dazzling epiphany that Crandall either really believed he had murdered someone, or else was putting on a damn good show of believing it. Convincing Jessica – who did not seem to need very much convincing – that Michael was an armed and dangerous murderer, and this was a simple matter of survival. Which explained the desperate look in Jessica's eyes and the headlong rush at him with the poker. But which did not explain why Crandall stood there with a weapon in his hand and his thumb up his ass.

Michael had never hit a woman in his life.

When he'd learned about Jenny and her branch manager, he'd wanted to hit her, but then he'd wondered what good that would do. He'd already lost her. James Owington had already taken her from him, so what was the sense of hitting her? Wouldn't that be more punishing to him than it would be to her? The eternal knowledge that he had hit a woman who was only five-feet six-inches tall and weighed a hundred and twenty pounds? Who wasn't even working for the Viet Cong?

Jessica wasn't working for the Viet Cong, either.

She was merely a sensible woman trying to save her own life. She had a good cheering section, too. As she came at Michael, the poker swinging back into position, Crandall whispered little words of encouragement like "*Hit* him, *kill* him!" From the look on her face, she needed no urging. Crandall had warned her that Michael was a killer; unless she took him out, he would kill again. The thing to do now was knock off his head. Before he knocked off hers.

Which Michael did.

He hit her very hard.

There was nothing satisfying about the collision of his fist with her jaw. He hit her virtually automatically, bringing his fist up from his knees as if he were throwing an uppercut at a sailor in a Saigon bar, repeating an emotionless action he had gone through at least a dozen times before, unsurprised when he heard the click of teeth against teeth, unsurprised when he saw her eyes roll back into her head. He watched as she collapsed. One moment she was standing, the poker back and poised to swing, and the next moment she folded to the floor as if someone had stolen her spine.

Michael walked to where Crandall was standing with the gun in his hand.

"Fuck off, okay?" he said, and took the gun from him and went to the door.

He now had two guns.

Like a Wild West cowboy.

One in each pocket of his coat.

He was happy that the two uniformed cops who came up the steps as he was going down did not stop and frisk him.

"Are you looking for the guy beating his wife?" he asked.

"No, we're looking for Wales," one of the cops said.

"That's near England, I think," Michael said, and continued on down.

Connie was waiting outside in the limo, the engine running.

"I think it's time we went home," she said.

She drove the limo to the garage China Doll used on Canal Street, and they began walking from there to her apartment on Pell. As promised, the temperature was already starting to drop. Michael guessed it was now somewhere in the low twenties or high teens. They walked very rapidly despite the packed snow underfoot and the occasional patches of ice on sidewalks that had been shoveled, their heads ducked against the wind, Connie's arm looped through his. Under the other arm, she carried the green satin high-heeled shoes she'd retrieved from the limo's trunk. The streets were deserted. This was four o'clock on Christmas morning, and everyone was home in bed waiting for Santa Claus. But Michael was brimming with ideas.

"What we have to do is find out where Charlie Nichols lives," he said.

"Okay, but not now," Connie said. "Aren't you cold?"

"Yes."

"I mean, aren't you *freezing*?"

"Yes, I am. But this is important."

"It's also important not to die in the street of frostbite."

"You can't die of frostbite."

"For your information, frostbite is freezing to death."

"No, it's not."

"Can you die of freezing to death?"

"Yes."

"All right then," she said.

"Connie, the point is we've got to talk to Nichols. Because if he's the Charlie in Crandall's calendar . . ."

"Please hurry."

"Then maybe he can tell us who Mama is, or why Crandall drew nine thousand dollars from the bank, *if* he did, or what he did with that money, or what his connection is with the two people who took all that stuff from my wallet and the one who stole my car."

The words came out of his mouth in small white bursts of vapor. He looked as if he were sending smoke signals. The clasps on Connie's galoshes clattered and rattled as she led him through yet another labyrinth, this goddamn downtown section of the city was impossible to understand. None of the streets down here were laid out in any sensible sort of grid pattern, they just crisscrossed and zigzagged and wound around each other and back again, and they didn't have any numbers, they only had names, and you couldn't get anywhere without a native guide, which he supposed Connie was. A very fast one, too. She walked at a breakneck pace, Michael puffing hard to keep up, both of them sending smoke signals with their mouths. He hoped there weren't any hostile Sioux on ponies in the immediate neighborhood. He would not have been surprised, though. Nothing that happened in this city could ever surprise him again.

They came at last to a Chinese restaurant named Shi Kai, just off the corner of Mott and Pell. The restaurant was closed, but a sign in the front window advised:

**OPEN FOR BREAKFAST
AS USUAL
CHRISTMAS DAY**

Connie took a key from her handbag, unlocked a door to the left of the restaurant, closed and locked it behind her, opened another door that led to a flight of stairs, and began climbing. There were Chinese cooking-smells in the hallway. There were dim, naked light bulbs on each landing. She kept climbing. Behind her, he watched her legs. Her galoshes rattled away. He hoped they wouldn't wake up anyone in the building. On the third floor, she stopped outside a door marked 33, searched in the dim light for another key on her ring, inserted it into the latch, unlocked the door, threw it open, snapped on a light from a switch just inside it, and said what sounded like "Wahn yee" or "Wong ying," Michael couldn't tell which.

"That means 'Welcome' in Chinese," she said, and smiled.

"Thank you," he said, and followed her into the apartment.

He supposed he'd expected something out of *The Last Emperor*. Sandalwood screens. Red silk cloth. Gold gilt trappings. Incense burning. A small jade Buddha on an ivory pedestal.

Instead, against a wall painted a pale lavender, there was a long low sofa done in a white nubby fabric and heaped with pillows the same color as the wall, and there was an easy chair and a footstool upholstered in black leather and there was a coffee table with a glass top, and a bar unit hanging on the right-angle wall, and several large framed abstract prints on the wall opposite the sofa.

Connie sat, took off her galoshes, and then padded in her stockinged feet to the bar unit.

"This has been *some* night," she said, and rolled her eyes, and lowered the drop-leaf front of the bar. "I had a man vomit all over the backseat, did you notice?"

"No, I didn't."

"I mean that the limo I picked you up in outside the deli wasn't the same one I dropped you off in when you went to see Crandall's wife?"

"No, I couldn't tell any difference."

"Charlie was very upset. Charlie Wong. *My* Charlie Wong. About the stink in the car."

"I can imagine."

"Do you know how to make martinis?" she asked.

"Yes, I do," he said.

"Why don't you mix us some very nice, very dry martinis while I go take my shower, and then you can take your shower, and then we can sip our martinis in bed, would you like that?"

"Yes," he said.

His voice caught a little.

Because he was thinking about what she'd just said.

Not about mixing the martinis or taking the showers.

But about sipping the martinis.

In bed.

That part.

"A twist, please," she said.

You came through the bedroom doorway and the first thing you saw was the bed facing the door, its headboard against the far wall, a window on each side of it, a night table under each window. It was neither a king nor a queen, just a normal double bed. With a paisley-patterned quilt on it. There was a dresser on the wall to the right of the bed, and bookcases on the wall to the left, and a door to the closet on that same wall, and on the entrance-door wall, which he didn't really see until they got into bed together, there was an easy chair with a lamp behind it to the left of the door, and a full-length mirror to the right of it.

They left the quilt on the bed because it was so damn cold.

Every few minutes, they poked out from under the quilt to take a quick sip of their drinks, and then they hurriedly put the glasses back on the night tables on either side of the bed. They did this until the glasses were empty. Then they pulled the quilt up over their shoulders and settled in close together.

"He turns the heat off at eleven o'clock every night," Connie said. "There's nobody cheaper in the world than a Chinaman."

Under the quilt, the whole world was cozy and warm and safe.

Under the quilt, with Connie in his arms, he felt the way he'd felt long long ago in Boston, when his father was still alive and there to take care of him, and when the house was full of the smells of his mother's good French cooking and when at night she wrapped him in a big white fluffy towel after his bath, and patted him dry, and then tucked him into bed and pulled the covers to his chin, and told him Good Night, Sleep Tight, Don't Let The Bedbugs Bite, and kissed him on the cheek. In the darkness, he would smile. And fall asleep almost instantly.

After Boston, he hadn't slept too well for a long time. That was because the Cong's main job was keeping the Americans awake all night, never mind killing them. If the Cong could keep the Americans awake, why then they'd have to go home eventually in order to get a good night's sleep. He was sure that had been the strategy. It worked, too. Even when you knew they couldn't possibly be out there, even when intelligence reports told you they were fifty miles away, a hundred miles away, *retreating* even, you still imagined them out there creeping up on you while you slept. So you never really slept. Never completely. You closed your eyes, yes, and occasionally you caught ten minutes here, ten minutes there, even a half hour's deep sleep sometimes until your own snoring startled you into frightened wakefulness, and you jumped up in a cold sweat, your rifle fanning the jungle even before your eyes were fully open.

When he'd got back home . . .

Boston.

Home.

Jenny told him he'd filled out a lot.

She had learned how to soul-kiss.

From *Cosmopolitan* magazine, she told him.

His mother had given away all his clothes.

And his father was sick and dying.

He'd come back to where it was safe – the Boston he remembered, the Boston he'd longed for all those months, the Boston that was the reality as opposed to the jungle nightmare – but his father was sick and dying and his mother, who was only forty-two, looked suddenly old, and the nightmare was here, too, here in Boston where it was supposed to be safe.

They buried his father on a cold November morning.

It was raining.

He remembered thinking he would never be safe again.

He told his mother one night that his dream was to marry Jenny and take her someplace where it was warm all year round. He almost said warm and *safe* all year round. His mother had looked at him with that sad, grieving expression she wore all the time now, and then she'd merely nodded. He wondered what she was thinking. Was she thinking it did not pay to dream because eventually all dreams die? His father's dream had been to own a chain of hardware stores all across New England. But cancer had cut him down when he was forty-four, and all he'd left behind him was the big old house and the one store. Good Night, Sleep Tight, Don't Let The Bedbugs Bite, and don't let the Cong creep up on you in your sleep, either. How can you dream if they won't let you sleep?

It took his mother two years to get over his father's being dead. At the end of that time, she told Michael she'd had a good offer for the store and was going to sell it. Said she could lend him the money for his dream. At prevailing interest rates. Told him to go find his Someplace Warm, take his Jenny there with him. He'd never known whether she was trying to get rid of him or trying to help him. He'd had the feeling that maybe . . .

Well, he'd discussed this with the shrink.

That somehow his mother blamed *him* for his father's death.

That because she'd prayed so hard for Michael to come home safe and sound, the gods had somehow taken payment for his survival. Had spared his life and taken his father's instead.

That she hated him for this.

The shrink wondered out loud if she'd given away Michael's clothes the day she'd learned his father had cancer.

Michael said he didn't know.

In Vietnam, Sergeant Mendelsohnn had told him to shoot first and think it over later. Michael took the money, asked Jenny to marry him, and moved down to Florida with her.

Where he'd felt safe for a while.

Until Jenny started up with James Owington at the bank.

And after that, you know, a man began to think there wasn't much sense to *anything* anymore. You go fight a dumb fucking war where nobody will let you sleep and everybody including the people on your own side are trying to kill you, and you get through it by the skin of your teeth and you come home to find your father dying and your mother blaming you for it and your girlfriend soul-kissing her way through Boston and its suburbs, you begin to think, Hey, *sheeee*-it, as Andrew would have put it. And when even the sweet Florida dream turns sour, when the enemy creeping up on your sleep now is a fat fucking branch manager who's getting in your wife's pants, hey, man, what was the sense of *anything*?

Part of his dream . . .

Well, he'd wanted to start a family down there.

Little girl, little boy. Two kids, that would've been nice.

Name the girl Lise, after his mother.

Well, maybe not.

But *shit*, Mom, it really wasn't my fault he died.

Name the boy Andrew for sure.

But if you can't sleep you can't dream, and anyway all the dreams died forever – or so he'd thought – nine months and six days ago, *seven* days ago now, but who was counting? All the dreams had drowned in the Gulf of Mexico on that blustery March day, drowned together with his sorrows.

But tonight . . .

He could see snow beginning to fall again outside the window on his side of the bed. Fat fluffy flakes drifting down in the light of the lamp post.

He held Connie in his arms.

She felt so small and delicate.

He held her close and watched the snow coming down.

And almost instantly, he fell deeply asleep.

And for the first time in years, he dreamed again.

9

It was Christmas Day.

Cooking smells from the restaurant downstairs drifted up the stairwell and seeped under the door and wafted across the apartment into the bedroom where he lay with Connie Kee in his arms. It was still snowing. He guessed there had to be eight feet of snow out there by now. Maybe ten feet. It had to be Minnesota out there by now.

He had fallen asleep instantly, but now he was wide awake and a bit leary of waking up Connie, who might discover there was a stranger here in bed with her and go running out into the snow naked. The last time he'd been to bed with anyone was with a woman named Zara with a Z Kaufman in Miami, where he'd gone to an orange-growers' convention. That was in September, it was still hurricane season down there in Florida and the Keys. He had not been to bed with anyone since the divorce in March, but there he was with the palms rattling outside his motel window and the wind blowing at forty miles an hour and a fifty-year-old woman who grew oranges in Winter Haven teaching him a few tricks he hadn't learned in Saigon.

Zara with a Z Kaufman.

A very lovely person.

He had never seen her again after that night.

So here he was now with a Chinese girl dead asleep in his arms, afraid to wake her up because whereas last night there had been only two of them here in this bed, this morning there were three of them if you counted his hard-on, which Connie suddenly seized

110

in her right hand, leading him to believe she hadn't been asleep after all.

They kissed.

It was like their kiss last night under the stars in that snow-bound backyard where telephone poles grew from an endless field of white and snow-capped fences ran forever. Except better. Because although last night there had been the attendant if remote possibility that their lips might in fact freeze together – she always seemed to be worried about freezing, he now realized – the bed today was quite warm under the quilt, thank you, and there was in fact steam banging in the radiators, and no one was about to freeze, not today when Christmas was upon the world.

And whereas last night someone up there in a fourth-floor window had asked them what the hell they were doing and had threatened to call the police, which he or she had in fact later done, the bastard, there was now no one here in this radiator-clanging, steam-hissing room to hurl a challenge or to dial 911 to report a dire emergency. There was no dire emergency in this room. Unless the urgency of their mutual need could be considered an emergency of sorts, and a dire one at that. He could not recall ever wanting a woman as much as he wanted this one. Nor could he recall any woman ever wanting him as much as Connie seemed to want him.

They could not stop touching each other.

They could not stop kissing.

Her murmuring little sounds hummed under his lips.

His hands were wet with her.

When at last he entered her—

"Oh, Jesus," they whispered together.

It was Christmas Day.

There were four Charles Nicholses listed in the Manhattan telephone directory, but none of them had an *R* for a middle initial.

Which meant that none of them was the Charles R. Nichols who was no relation to Jack Nichols the big movie star.

Charles R. Nichols, who had been on *Mister Ed* years ago, and who had played a ghost's voice in Crandall's latest, as-yet-unreleased film, *Winter's Chill*.

Connie suggested that perhaps the Nichols they wanted was

listed in the Bronx, Brooklyn, Queens, or Staten Island directories instead. In which case, she and Michael could run over to Penn Station and check out the phone books there.

"The police will be watching the railroad stations," Michael said.

"Then I'll go alone."

"The police know what you look like, they saw you driving me away from Crandall's office," he said. "Connie . . . maybe I . . .'

"No," she said.

"What I'm trying to say . . ."

"You're trying to say you love me."

"Well . . ."

"And you're worried about me. That's so nice, Michael. You say the sweetest things, really."

"Connie, the point . . ."

"But I'm not afraid," she said. "So you don't have to . . ."

"I *am*," he said.

She looked at him.

"Afraid," he said.

She kept looking at him.

"The time to be afraid," he said, "is when you don't know what's happening. And when you feel helpless to stop whatever *is* happening."

"Then what we have to do is find *out* what's happening. And *stop* it from happening. Then you won't be afraid anymore and we can just make love all the time."

He took her in his arms. He hugged her close. He shook his head. He sighed. He hugged her again.

"What was that other man's name?" she asked.

"What man?"

"The one Crandall's wife told you about. The one who put up all the money for his war movie."

"Oh. Yes."

"She told you he looked like a rabbi . . ."

"Yes, tall and thin and hairy . . . "

"Magruder!" Connie said.

"No."

"Magruder, yes!"

"Connie, there are no rabbis named Magruder."

"Then whose name is Magruder?"

"I have no idea. But that's not *his* name."

"Then what *is* his name?"

"I don't remember. It had something to do with the movie."

"Yes, he put up the money for . . ."

"Yes, but not that. Something about *War and – Solly's* War! His first name is Solly! No, Solomon! *Solomon* something!"

"Magruder!"

"No!"

"I'm telling you it's Solomon Magruder!"

"And I'm telling you no!"

"Then what?"

"I don't know."

"Gruber!" she shouted.

"Yes!"

"Solomon Gruber!"

"Yes!"

"The phone book!" she said.

"Be there," he said. "Please be there."

There were no Solomon Grubers listed in the Manhattan directory. There were a lot of S. Grubers, but no way of knowing which of them, if any, might be Solomon. There was, however, a listing for a Gruber Financial Group, and another listing for a Gruber International, and yet another for a Gruber Foundation, all of which sounded like companies that might have had twelve million dollars to invest in a flop movie eight years ago. Michael tried each of the three numbers. No answer. This was Christmas Day. But in studying the S. Gruber listings a second time –

"Look!" Connie said.

"I see it."

"*This* S. Gruber has the same address . . ."

"Yes."

". . . as the Gruber Financial Group."

"But a different phone number," Michael said. "Let's call him."

"Let's eat first," Connie said.

The S. Gruber whose address was identical to that of the Gruber Financial Group lived in Washington Mews, which was a gated little lane that ran eastward from number 10 Fifth Avenue to

113

University Place. Connie explained that they were still in what she considered downtown Manhattan.

"As far as I'm concerned," she said, "it's all downtown till you get up to Forty-second Street. Then it starts to be *mid*town. This is the Sixth Precinct here. Driving a limo, I like to know where all the precincts are, in case I get some weirdo in the back. The precincts are funny in this city. For example, the First starts at Houston Street on the north and ends at Battery Park on the south. Which means if you get killed, for example, on Fulton Street, you have to run all the way uptown and crosstown to Ericsson Place to report it. Anyway, this is the Sixth, which is mostly silk stocking."

They were walking up what could have been a little cobblestoned lane in a Welsh village. Doors that only appeared to be freshly painted flanked the pathway, their brass knockers and knobs gleaming in the noonday light. The cobblestones had been shoveled clean of snow. There were wreaths in the windows, electrified candles in them. The twinkling multicolored glow of illuminated Christmas trees behind diaphanous lace curtains. Classical music wafting through a street-level window opened just a crack. Swelling violins. And now a clarinet. Or maybe a flute. Dying with a dying fall on a Christmas Day already half gone. Michael wished he could identify the composition. Or even its composer. There were so many things he wished. Down in Sarasota he read *The New York Times* all the time, and he listened to WUSF 89.7, which was the public radio station, but he never could tell one piece of classical music from another. To him, they all sounded like somebody practicing.

"A penny for your thoughts," Connie said.

"I was just vamping till ready," Michael said.

"I hope you're ready now," she said, "because here it is."

A black door.

A brass escutcheon on it.

Solomon Gruber, engraved in script lettering.

To the right of the door, set into the doorjamb, a heavy brass bell button.

Michael pressed his forefinger against it.

Inside, chimes began playing a tune you didn't have to be Harold Schoenberg or even Newgate Callendar to recognize.

The tune was "Mary Had a Little Lamb."

They listened to it. It sounded nice on the frosty Christmas air. When the chimes reached "fleece as white," the door opened.

The man standing there in the doorframe was not tall and thin and hairy, and he did not look like a rabbi, either. The man standing there was wearing a red turtleneck sweater with a black velvet smoking jacket over it. He had a very bushy handlebar moustache, which may have been why Albetha Crandall had thought he was hairy. Otherwise, he wore his hair in a crew cut that made him look like a German U-boat commander. Why she'd thought he was tall and thin was anyone's guess. Perhaps she'd meant in comparison to her husband, who was short and chubby. Solomon Gruber, if that's who this man turned out to be, was of medium height and build. Compact, one might say. Chunky, like a bulldog.

"Yes?" he said.

He looked as if he expected them to start singing Christmas carols. He looked as if he would close the door in their faces if they did. Or run up to the roof to pour boiling oil on them.

"Mr Gruber?" Michael asked.

"Yes?" he said again.

"My name is Michael Bond, I'm with *The New York Times*, I wanted to talk to you about *Winter's Chill*. This is Constance Keene, my assistant."

Gruber blinked.

"Come in," he said at once, and stepped aside to allow them entrance. "*Mary!*" he shouted. "Come quick, it's *The New York Times*! Come in, come in, please," he said.

Michael wondered if it was a crime to impersonate a person from *The New York Times*.

Gruber's townhouse was furnished the way Michael hoped one day to furnish the house in Sarasota, now that Jenny was out of it and living with her fucking branch manager. In recent months, he had browsed through enough home furnishing magazines to know that the extremely modern furniture here in Gruber's living room was either Herman Miller or Knoll, all leather and glass and chrome and wood. The house in Sarasota was at the end of a dirt road that ran alongside the groves. Behind the house was a manmade lake that had been dug by the former owner of the groves. Sliding glass doors opened onto the lake. Modern furniture would look good in that house. He knew Connie liked modern because of the way her apartment was furnished. Now he wondered if she'd like the Sarasota house.

The walls in the Gruber living room were done in rough white plaster, except for the fireplace wall, which was done in black marble, with a chrome surround for the hearth. A painting that looked like a genuine Matisse hung on one of the white walls. Another that looked like a real Van Gogh hung on the wall adjacent to it. A Christmas tree was in the far corner of the room, near the windows facing the lane outside. A woman came in through a rosewood swinging door that led to the kitchen. She was wearing a long red gown that matched Gruber's red turtleneck sweater. She was taller than Gruber, and she had blonde hair – but she was not the woman who'd conned Michael in the bar last night. It occurred to Michael that there were a lot of blondes in the city of New York. Just as there seemed to be a lot of Charlies. Which was why he was here.

"Mr Gruber," he said, "I . . ."

"Mary, this is Michael Bond," Gruber said, "and his assistant, Constance Keene."

"How do you do?" Mary said.

Which was why the doorbell played "Mary Had a Little Lamb," Michael guessed.

"Can I get you something to drink, Mr Bond?" Gruber said.

"Some hot toddy?" Mary said.

She was smiling like one of the women in *The Stepford Wives*. Michael wondered if she had wires and tapes inside her.

"Mary makes a great hot toddy," Gruber said.

He was smiling like a shark approaching a Sarasota beach at the height of the season. Probably because *The New York Times* was in his living room.

"I'd like to try a hot toddy," Connie said. "I've never had one."

"One hot toddy coming up," Mary said. "Mr Bond, what will you have?"

"A Diet Coke, if you've got one."

"Will a Diet Pepsi do?"

"Yes, thank you."

"One hot toddy and one Diet Pepsi coming up," she said, and went out into the kitchen.

"From what I understand," Michael said, "the Gruber Group put up all the financing for Arthur Crandall's new film."

116

"Boy oh boy oh boy, *The New York Times*," Gruber said, shaking his head. "On Christmas *Day*, no less. You guys have sources not to be believed."

"That's true, though, isn't it?"

"Yes, the Gruber *Financial* Group – it's Gruber *Financial* Group, not Gruber *Group*."

"Yes, sir, Gruber *Financial* Group."

"Maybe you ought to jot that down," Gruber said.

"Yes, sir, have you got a pencil and some paper?"

"I've got some," Connie said, and reached into her shoulder bag and took from it a bill pad with the lettering CHINA DOLL LIMOUSINE across its top. She handed this to Michael together with a ballpoint pen that had tobacco shreds clinging to its tip.

"Gruber Financial Group, yes, sir," Michael said, and wrote it onto the pad.

Mary came out of the kitchen. She was carrying a tray with a mug and a glass on it. The mug had a cinnamon stick poking up out of it like the periscope on a miniature submarine.

"Here you are," she said, and extended the tray.

Connie picked up the mug.

Michael picked up the glass.

Mary put down the tray and said, "We were in Japan last year, Miss Keene. It's a lovely country."

"Thank you, I've never been there," Connie said, and sipped at the toddy. "This is very good," she said. "Would you like to taste this, Michael?"

"No, thank you," Michael said. "Mr Gruber, do you know a man named Charles Nichols?"

"Huh?" Gruber said.

"Charles R. Nichols."

"What part of Japan do your people come from?" Mary asked.

"I'm Chinese," Connie said.

"Oh, dear," Mary said.

Gruber shot her a look that said *Now* look what you've done, you've offended a Chink on the fucking *New York Times*! Mary started to shrink, as if he'd thrown water on a witch. Michael hoped she wouldn't melt right down into the carpet, leaving only her red gown behind. Gruber turned back to Michael.

"Are you doing a piece on *Charlie*?" he asked. There was a look on his face that said there was no understanding the ways of

The New York Times. Charlie Nichols, who had been on *Mister Ed* years ago, and who now played the voice of a ghost in *Winter's Chill*? Of all the actors in the film, *this* was who *The New York Times* had singled out for a piece? Incredible.

"Do you know where we can reach him?" Michael asked.

"Is this for the Arts and Leisure section?" Gruber asked.

"Yes," Michael said.

"That's the approach you're taking, huh?"

"We thought we'd like to talk to him."

"I mean . . . look, I certainly don't want to tell *The New York Times* what approach it should take. Far be it from me. But what *is* the approach you're taking? I mean . . . why *Charlie*, of all people?"

"Because of his *Mister Ed* affiliations," Michael said.

"He wasn't the horse or anything," Mary said.

"That's right, thank you, Mary," Gruber said.

"I mean, he didn't do the *horse's* voice, you know. He was just a regular actor."

"He had a bit part, in fact," Gruber said.

"This is all very good stuff," Michael said, writing.

"It is?" Mary said, looking astonished.

"This begins to hit you after a while, doesn't it?" Connie said, and took another sip of the toddy.

"You're supposed to stir it,' Mary said. "With the cinnamon stick."

"Oh," Connie said, and began stirring it.

"All he does is play one of the ghosts in *Chill*," Gruber said.

"One of the voices," Mary said.

"There are ghost voices," Gruber said.

"Trying to make her crazy."

"The character."

"The woman Jessica plays."

"Jessica Wales," Gruber explained.

"They're trying to make her crazy," Mary said.

"Like in *Gaslight*," Michael said, nodding.

"Oh *no*!" Gruber said at once.

"No, no, no," Mary said. "Not at *all* like *Gaslight*."

"This is a highly suspenseful film about a woman on the cutting edge of terror and deceit," Gruber said, sounding like the headline of an ad for the movie.

"Is she mad or is she only too sane?" Mary said, sounding like another headline.

"This makes your fingers sticky, doesn't it?" Connie said.

"A true departure for Arthur," Gruber said. "I don't know if you saw *War and Solitude*, but . . ."

"No, I didn't."

"A beautiful film," Mary said, looking soulful.

"Wonderful, the man's a genius," Gruber said. "We lost a fortune, of course, but does this take away from the man's genius? Does *Jaws* take away from the genius of Steven Spielberg?"

"But *Jaws* didn't *lose* money, did it?" Michael said.

"Exactly," Gruber said. "This beautiful film went down the tubes . . ."

"Not *Jaws*."

"No, *Solitude*. Because of Vincent Canby's lousy . . . excuse me, I bear no ill will toward the *Times*, believe me. I lost twelve million dollars plus another two million in advertising and promotion, but Canby is entitled to his opinion, would I deprive a man of his right to free speech? I notice, of course, that eight years later he thinks *Platoon* is a masterpiece, but listen, bygones are bygones, we're talking about *Winter's Chill* now, am I right? Despite the fact, by the way, that in Cannes *Solitude* almost walked off with all the marbles and *Cahiers* called it the best war film ever made. This was eight years *before* Mr Canby decided to fall in love with *Platoon*, a genius before his time, Arthur Crandall, mark my words. And *Chill* is an even better film."

"There are murmurings, however," Michael said, and he saw panic flash suddenly in Gruber's eyes, "that whereas Crandall's last film was a class act" – quoting Albetha now – "this new one is crap, you'll pardon the . . ."

"Nonsense!" Gruber said.

"Why, he's being compared to *Hitchcock*!" Mary said.

"That's right, thank you, Mary," Gruber said.

"At the peak of his career! Hitchcock!"

"His *Psycho* days!"

"His *Birds* days!"

"Why, when people in the motion-picture community thought Arthur was *dead* last night . . ."

"Then you'd heard about that," Michael said, suddenly alarmed.

"Yes, of course, it was all over television."

"We were *so* relieved when he called," Mary said.

"To say he was alive."

"We couldn't believe it was him calling. He was supposed to be dead. But there he was on the *phone*! It was a miracle!"

"Believe me," Gruber said, "there was universal mourning in the motion-picture community when . . ."

"MGM, too," Mary said.

"When his murder . . ."

"United Artists, Columbia, Disney. Not only Universal," she said.

"When his murder was erroneously reported. Genuine and universal *grief* for this *genius* cut down in his prime, this new master of . . . excuse me, what did you say your name was?"

"Bond," Michael said. "Michael Bond. No relation."

"Because you look familiar."

"I'm sure I don't."

"Have I seen you in anything?" Mary asked.

"No, I'm just with *The New York Times*."

"Exactly my point," Gruber said. "Mr Bond, I think you understand what I'm saying. I'm saying there is greed and malice everywhere in this world, but honesty and truth will prevail as surely as the cry of a newborn babe."

"Do you write fortune cookies?" Connie asked.

"Do you understand me, Mr Bond? Whoever told you that Arthur Crandall's new film is . . . *what* did you say you'd heard?"

"I heard it was crap."

"Crap, I can't believe it," Gruber said.

"The man's a fucking *genius*," Mary said.

"Crap," Gruber said again, shaking his head. "Who told you this?" Gruber asked.

"His wife, actually," Michael said.

"*That* bitch!" Mary said, and her husband gave her a look that said, This is *The New York Times* here, so watch your fucking language.

"What she said, actually," Michael said, "was that in television he'd been doing crap . . ."

"Absolutely," Gruber said.

". . . and he left television to do a really fantastic film . . ."

"*Truly* fantastic!"

". . . that didn't make a nickel . . ."

"Not a dime," Gruber said.

". . . but now he was back doing crap again."

"False," Gruber said. "Do you know how much this movie cost to make?"

"How much?" Michael asked.

"Three times what *Solitude* cost."

"Thirty-six million dollars," Connie said at once. "This is very good, this toddy. Why do they call it a toddy?"

"Thirty-six million, correct," Gruber said, "plus I have to figure at least another five, six million for prints and advertising, and it'll come to forty, forty-five million before all is said and done. Now tell me something, Mr Bond, how can a forty-five-million-dollar picture be crap? Can you tell me that, please? You don't plan to *print* that, do you? His wife's remark?"

"I mean, she *is* a bitch," Mary said, shaking her head.

"What we planned to do," Michael said, "was leave the review to the daily reviewer . . ."

"Who?" Gruber said at once. "Canby? Or Maslin? Don't say Canby or I'll have a heart attack."

"I don't think it's been assigned yet."

"It hasn't been *assigned* yet? It's opening on the fifth, we had screenings all last week, it hasn't been *assigned* yet?"

"Not that I know of. But the Sunday section's approach would be . . ."

"I'll bet it's Canby," Gruber said to his wife.

"*That* prick," she said.

"We thought we'd talk to Charlie Nichols, take an oblique approach to . . ."

"Why don't you talk to Jessica Wales? She's the *star* of the fucking thing," Gruber said, "why don't you talk to her?"

"Well, we wanted a unique approach . . ."

"I thought you said oblique."

"*And* unique."

"We've got some great stills of Jessica, you could use those with the story."

"The scene where they're coming at her with the knife, ooooooo," Mary said, and shuddered.

"The ghosts," Gruber said.

"What she *thinks* are ghosts."

"Don't give it away, for Christ's sake," Gruber said.

"They aren't *really* ghosts, don't worry," Mary said to Michael, as if trying to still the fears of a very small child.

"That's right, tell him," Gruber said, shaking his head. "Give away the whole fucking plot."

"Are you really a rabbi?" Connie asked him.

"What?" he said.

"Because I didn't know rabbis talked that way."

Gruber blinked.

Mary rolled her eyes and said, "*Whatever* you do, don't mention *Gaslight*."

"Very good, tell him not to mention *Gaslight*," Gruber said. "That's like telling somebody not to stare at somebody's big nose. Did you see that picture?"

"No," Michael said.

"The Martin picture."

"Sheen?"

"Steve. Anyway, this isn't *Gaslight* we did, this is an entirely new and original approach to psychological suspense. Jessica Wales gives the performance of her career and Arthur Crandall has never been . . ."

"I wonder, Mr Gruber, do you think you could let me have Charlie Nichols's address, please?"

"You're determined to do this interview with Charlie, huh?"

"That's my assignment, sir."

"Who thinks up these crazy assignments? Gussow?"

"I'll bet it's Canby," Mary said.

"Do we even *have* his address?" Gruber said. "I mean, he's a bit player. Why the hell do you want to interview *him*?"

"I just take orders," Michael said.

"Oh, sure, everybody just takes orders," Gruber said. "The Nazis just took orders, Canby just takes orders, *you* just take orders, where's the address book?" he asked Mary.

"I'll get it," she said, "don't get excited. He gets so excited," she said to Michael.

"Maybe I oughta just call Arthur, he's probably got the address right at his finger . . ."

"No, I don't think you should do that," Michael said.

"Why not? You said you want to talk to Charlie . . ."

"We'd like to surprise Mr Crandall."

"Oh, he'll be surprised, all right, don't worry. An interview with Charlie Nichols? Oh, he'll wet his pants, believe me. When's this thing gonna be in the paper?"

"Next Sunday."

"You work a week ahead, huh?"

"Yes."

"Here it is," Mary said, and handed the address book to her husband.

The chimes suddenly began playing "Mary Had a Little Lamb."

"I love this song," Mary said.

Gruber waited until the entire little song had played.

Then he said, "Who is it?"

And a man answered, "Police."

10

It was as if someone in the platoon had yelled "Charlie!"

His heart stopped.

He almost threw himself flat on the ground. But the ground was a thick white carpet, across which Gruber was now walking to the front door. Michael glanced quickly at Connie. Connie smiled back mysteriously. It occurred to him that Mary's little hot rum toddy had done a real number on her.

Gruber opened the door.

There were two men standing there.

They were both wearing blue jackets with yellow ribbed cuffs and waistbands.

"Mr Gruber?" one of the men asked.

He was about Gruber's height and weight. He had curly red hair and blue eyes that matched his jacket.

"Yes?" Gruber said.

"Detective Harold Nelson, Seventh Precinct," he said, and immediately turned his back to Gruber. Across the back of the blue jacket, in yellow script lettering, were the words SEVENTH PRECINCT BOWLING TEAM. He turned to face Gruber again. "I called a little while ago," he said. "This is my partner, Detective Marvin Leibowitz."

"How do you do?" Leibowitz said. He was taller than Nelson, with black hair and brown eyes. Together they looked like *Car 54, Where Are You?* In bowling jackets.

"Marvin is our captain," Nelson said.

"An honor to meet you," Gruber said.

"Not of the precinct," Nelson said. "The team."

"Still an honor," Gruber said. "Come in, please."

The way he was treating them, Michael figured Gruber had paid off a great many cops on the streets of New York while filming this or that wonderful motion picture. When he was still living in Boston, they had shot a movie titled *Fuzz* up there, which was about cops. Burt Reynolds had played the detective in it. Raquel Welch was in it, too, though they never got to kiss because Reynolds was already married to a woman who couldn't hear or speak. Michael went to see it later, it turned out to be a lousy movie. But while they were shooting this movie, there were so many *real* cops hanging around that Michael was sure the entire Boston P.D. was on the take. He suddenly wondered if *Winter's Chill*, the new Arthur Crandall masterpiece, had been shot right here in New York City.

"The reason we're here, sir," Nelson said, "as I mentioned on the telephone, is we're the detectives investigating this homicide which we caught in our precinct . . ."

"Yes, I realize that," Gruber said.

"Although you wouldn't know it from the jackets, would you?" Leibowitz said.

"We're playing later tonight," Nelson explained.

"The Ninth," Leibowitz explained.

"Who's conducting?" Connie asked.

Both Nelson and Leibowitz looked at her. Michael wished they weren't looking at her that way. She still had the mysterious smile on her face, which made her look somehow insulting. To cops, anyone smiling that way was either mentally retarded or trying to be a wise guy. He could sense both cops bristling at the way she was smiling. It never occurred to either of them that she might have had too much toddy. They merely saw this Oriental smiling in a superior manner, and they figured her for somebody challenging authority. In Vietnam, sometimes you got an American soldier questioning a native who either lowered his eyes or looked away, and the soldier figured he had something to hide. Couldn't look you straight in the eye, then he had to be lying or something. Didn't realize this was a sign of respect, not looking a superior directly in the eye. It caused a lot of trouble in Vietnam. In Vietnam, a lot of innocent people had got themselves shot because they wouldn't look an American soldier in the eye when he was

125

asking them questions. He wished Connie would stop smiling.

"Is there something comical, miss?" Nelson asked.

"Yes," she said.

"May I ask *what*?"

"No," she said, and kept smiling.

Nelson looked at her as if trying to freeze her solid with his icy blue stare. Leibowitz, standing behind him and to his left, was scowling now. Suddenly, they no longer looked like *Car 54*. Instead, they looked like two mean detectives who would kick Connie's ass around the block as soon as look at her.

"At *any* rate," Nelson said, dismissing her and turning to Gruber again, "we thought that since you are an associate, so to speak, of Mr Crandall . . ."

"Yes, I am."

"Who at first we thought was the dead man, but who isn't . . ."

"Oh, thank God," Mary said, "such a genius."

Nelson looked at her.

"I don't believe I have met these other people, sir," he said to Gruber.

"My wife, Mary," Gruber said.

"How do you do?" Nelson said.

"Ma'am," Leibowitz said, and almost touched the bill of a cap he was no longer wearing, a holdover from his days as a uniformed cop.

"Mr Bond and Miss Keene of *The New York Times*," Gruber said.

Michael said, "Nice to meet you."

Connie smiled mysteriously.

"What're you gonna do?" Nelson asked her. "Write about how *incompetent* the cops in this city are?"

"Because we ain't got the killer yet?" Leibowitz said.

"You look familiar," Nelson said to Michael.

"I don't think so," Michael said.

"You ever done a story up the Seventh Precinct?"

"No, sir, I'm sure I haven't."

"Me, neither," Connie said.

"I could swear I know you," Nelson said. "How about the Two-Six uptown? You ever write about the Two-Six?"

"Never."

"'Cause I used to work up the Two-Six."

"I've never been there."

"Up in Harlem? On a Hun' Twenny-sixth Street?"

"No, sir, I'm sorry."

"Five-twenny West a Hun' Twenny-sixth?"

"No."

"Boy, I could swear I seen you someplace."

"Me, too," Leibowitz said, staring at him.

"Mr Gruber," Michael said, extending his hand for the book Gruber was clutching like a hymnal, "if you'll just let me have that address . . ."

"When *do* you expect to catch him?" Gruber asked.

"Barnes? Who knows? The man's from Florida, for all we know he's already back there by now."

"Well, as a matter of *fact*," Michael said, bristling somewhat, "for all you know, he may not have killed that person at *all*. Whoever that person may be."

"Oh, so *that's* gonna be the *Times*'s approach, huh?" Nelson said, and nodded knowingly to his partner.

"Of course," Leibowitz said. "The police in this city don't know if Michael Barnes *really* done it . . ."

". . . and we *also* don't know who got killed."

"Who *did* get killed?" Michael asked.

"We don't know," Nelson said.

"But that doesn't mean . . ."

"That doesn't mean *Barnes* didn't kill him," Nelson said.

"Well, I'm sure you'll work it out," Michael said. "Connie, let's go. Mr Gruber, if you'll . . ."

"Okay, Michael," Connie said.

". . . let me have . . ."

"*Michael*, did you say?" Leibowitz asked.

Michael thought Uh-oh.

Leibowitz was looking at him.

"Mr *Who*, did you say?" Nelson asked.

Nelson was looking at him, too.

Both of them trying to remember if this was the man they'd seen on television.

The picture on the license.

Not a very good likeness, but—

"Bond," Michael said.

It wasn't going to wash.

"Mr Bond," Nelson said, reaching under his jacket for the gun holstered to his belt, "I wonder if you'd . . ."

Michael did two things almost simultaneously.

Three things, actually.

In such rapid succession that he might just as well have been doing them all at the same time.

He grabbed Connie's hand; he yanked the address book out of Gruber's hand; and he hit Nelson with his shoulder.

"Oh my *God*!" Mary yelled.

"Stop or I'll shoot!" Nelson yelled.

"Don't!" Gruber yelled. "The paintings!"

The door seemed so very far away.

Moving through the jungle with Andrew in his arms, his life leaking away. The medical choppers so very far away. The jungle path a long, dark tunnel through overhanging leaves of green, vines of green, everything dripping green except Andrew, who kept spilling red. Behind Michael, someone called, "We no wanna hurt you, no run, Yank, we wanna help you," and he wondered why every fucking ARVN soldier in this country sounded like a Jap in a World War II—

Nelson fired.

He didn't hit any pictures.

What he hit was Michael.

In the left arm.

He dropped the address book.

He said, "Oh, shit."

Which sobered Connie at once. Or maybe the sudden sight of blood sobered her. She yanked open the door, picked up the book, grabbed the hand on Michael's good arm, and pulled him through the doorway after her. Behind them, Nelson – or perhaps Leibowitz – fired a shot that sent splinters flying out of the jamb.

Here we are again on the streets of Fabulous Downtown New York, Michael thought, with the fun just about to begin, folks, because my arm is bleeding very badly, and there are two cops chasing us with guns in their hands, and I can't shoot at either one of them because I'm as innocent as the day is long, which so far happens to be the longest day in my life.

He told himself he could not afford to pass out, even though his arm was killing him – where was the address book, had Connie picked up the address book? Charlie Nichols was in that book

128

and Charlie just might know what the hell was going on here. If this were a War Movie, which with all this shooting it was beginning to resemble a lot, he'd have told the Chinese girl guiding him through enemy lines to go on without him, he was hurt too bad and he wasn't going to make it. Or if this were a Show Biz Movie, he'd have told his Chinese dancing partner to accept the job Ziegfeld had offered because he himself was only a second-rate hoofer who didn't want to stand in her way. But this wasn't a movie at all, this was real life, and so he clung to Connie's hand as if he were hanging outside a tenth-story window with nothing but her support between him and the pavement below. Behind him, he heard Nelson yelling like a fucking ARVN Jap, "We don't wanna hurt you, Barnes," although he'd already hurt Michael pretty badly.

They had almost reached the sidewalk now.

"Police!" someone yelled. "Freeze!"

They both stopped dead in their tracks.

A blue-and-white car was at the curb.

The lettering on it read SIXTH PRECINCT.

Two uniformed cops in what looked like padded blue parkas with fake-fur collars were running toward them.

"Freeze!" one of them shouted again.

"Police!" the other one shouted.

Still running toward them.

"Drop those guns!" one of them yelled.

What? Michael thought.

And then he realized that these nice police officers had heard gunfire, and had pulled their car to the curb and had seen a bleeding man and a nice Chinese woman running out of this nice little Welsh lane here, and chasing them were a menacing tall guy and an equally menacing short guy in bowling jackets, both of them screaming, and each of them with a gun in his hand.

Michael wondered if Nelson and Leibowitz would turn to flash the yellow SEVENTH PRECINCT BOWLING TEAM lettering on their jackets.

But Connie was rushing him away from the alley.

This was some city, this city.

Here was a man bleeding from a bullet wound in his left arm, the blood staining the sleeve of his overcoat – though admittedly the coat was a dark blue and the blood merely showed on it as a darker purplish stain – being rushed into a taxi by a gorgeous Chinese girl, and nobody on the street batted an eyelash. Michael found this amazing. In Sarasota, if you belched in public, you got a standing ovation.

The cab driver said, "What is that there? Is that blood there?"

"Yes, my husband just got shot," Connie said.

"Sure, ha-ha," the cabbie said.

Michael realized she had called him her husband.

He tried the name for size: Mrs Michael Barnes.

Constance Barnes.

Connie Barnes.

"So what *really* happened?" the cabbie wanted to know.

"We were walking down the street minding our own business," Connie said, "when this man came along from the opposite direction with a tiger on a leash."

"Boy oh boy," the cabbie said, shaking his head, watching her in the rearview mirror.

"So my husband told him he thought that was against the law, having a tiger on a leash . . ."

Again.

She'd said it again.

". . . and the man said, 'Sic him!'"

"To the tiger?"

"Yes."

"Sheeesh," the cabbie said. "What a city, huh?"

"You said it," Connie said.

"So what'd the tiger do? This musta been a trained tiger, huh?"

"Oh, yes. He jumped on my husband."

"An attack tiger, huh?"

"Oh, yes."

"Mauled him, I'll bet. Your husband."

"Exactly what happened."

"Sheeesh," the cabbie said again. "What was his name?"

"I don't know. He was a tall, dark man wearing . . ."

"No, I mean the tiger."

"Why do I have to know the tiger's name?"

"So you can report this to the police."

"I don't think I heard his name."

"Then how you gonna identify him? All tigers look alike, you know."

"I know, but . . ."

"So you have to know his name. If the police should ask you his name."

"Well, why would they do that? I mean, I don't think there are too many tigers on leashes in this city, do you?"

"Who knows? There could be."

"I mean, have *you* ever seen a tiger on a leash in this city?"

"I'm just now hearing about one, ain't I?" the cabbie said.

"His name was Stripe," Connie said.

Michael was thinking that everybody in this city was crazy.

"That's a good name for a tiger," the cabbie said. "So what's this address on Pell Street? A doctor?"

"No, it's where I live," Connie said.

"'Cause don't you think you ought to see a doctor?"

"I want to look at it first."

"Are *you* perhaps a doctor, lady?"

"No, but . . ."

"Then what good is it gonna do, *you* looking at it?"

"Because if it looks bad, *then* I can call a doctor."

"On Christmas Day? This is Christmas Day, lady."

"I'll call a Chinese doctor."

"Do *they* work on Christmas Day?"

"Yes, if they're Buddhists."

"Look, suit yourself, lady," the cabbie said. "You want a Buddhist doctor, go get a Buddhist doctor."

He was silent for the rest of the trip to her apartment. Michael guessed he was offended. When they got to Connie's building, he pocketed the fare and her generous tip, and then said, "Also, they got rabies, you know. Them attack tigers." Michael himself was beginning to believe he'd really been attacked by a tiger. As he got out of the cab, he looked up and down the street in both directions, to make sure there weren't any more of them around. He also looked up toward the roof to make sure one of them wasn't going to jump down into the street from up there. He got a little dizzy looking up. He swayed against Connie, suddenly feeling very weak. But he did not pass out until they were safe inside the apartment.

*

"Ah, ah, ah," the doctor said.

He looked like Fu Manchu.

A scarecrow of a man with a long, straggly beard and little rimless eyeglasses. He wasn't wearing silken robes or anything, he was in fact wearing a dark suit and a white shirt and a tie with mustard stains on it, but there was something about his manner that seemed dynastic. He was bent over Michael, his stethoscope to Michael's heart. Michael's shirt was open. He had bled through the bandage Connie had put on his arm before calling the doctor. The sheet under him was stained with blood. The doctor moved the stethoscope. He listened to Michael's lungs.

"Very good," he said.

"Yes?" Connie said.

"Yes, the bullet did not go through his lungs."

"Perhaps because he was shot in the arm," Connie said respectfully.

"Ah, ah, ah," the doctor said.

His name was Ling.

He took the bandage off Michael's arm.

"Mmm, mmm, mmm," he said.

"Is it bad?" Connie asked.

"Someone shot him in the arm," Ling said.

"Is the bullet still in there?" Connie asked.

"No, no," Ling said, "it's a nice clean wound."

Good, Michael thought.

"Good," Connie said.

"You'll be able to play tennis in a week or so," Ling said, and chuckled. "Are you left-handed?"

"No."

"Then you'll be able to play tennis tomorrow," he said, and chuckled again.

Michael watched as Ling worked on his arm. He was wondering if he planned on reporting this to the police. He felt certain that reporting gunshot wounds was mandatory.

"How did this happen?" Ling asked.

He was sprinkling what Michael guessed was some kind of sulfa drug on the wound. In the field, you stripped a sulfapak and slapped it on the wound immediately. In the field, people were spitting blood on you while you worked. In the field, everyone got to be a doctor. You lost a lot of patients in the field.

"We were walking down the street minding our own business," Connie said, "when this man came along from the opposite direction with a gun in his hand."

"Ah, ah, ah," Ling said.

"So Michael said to the man . . ."

"Excuse me, but is this your husband?" Ling asked.

"Not yet," Michael said.

Connie looked at him.

Ling looked at them both.

"You must be cautious," Ling said. "There are many problems in East–West marriages."

"Like what?" Michael asked.

"Like food, for example," Ling said.

"But I like Chinese food," Michael said.

"Exactly," Ling said.

"I see," Michael said.

"So what did you say to this man?"

"Which man?"

"The one who shot you."

"Oh."

"What he said," Connie said, "is that he thought it was against the law to be walking down the street with a gun in your hand."

Not in Florida, Michael thought.

Florida was the Wild West these days.

Though not as much as New York seemed to be.

"So the man shot him," Connie said.

"Tch, tch, tch," Ling said.

"Are you going to report this?" Connie asked flatly.

Ling looked at her.

"Are we both Chinese?" he asked.

"I'm only walking wounded," Michael said. "And walking wounded are allowed to walk."

Dr Ling had bandaged his arm neatly and tightly, and it was no longer bleeding and certainly in no danger of becoming infected unless Michael went rolling around in the dirt someplace. Moreover, it hardly hurt at all now, so what he wanted to do . . .

"No," Connie said. "What we're going to do is I'll go down for some food and we'll eat here in the apartment and I'll call Charlie Wong and tell him I'm not feeling good and won't be able to work tonight. Then you'll go to bed and get some . . ."

"No," Michael said.

"Dr Ling said you have to rest."

"Dr Ling isn't wanted for murder. What I want to do is go see this Charlie Nichols person . . ."

"No. You can call him on the phone if you like, but I won't let . . ."

"I don't *want* to call him on the phone. Every time I talk to somebody on the phone, the police show up in the next ten minutes. I am wanted for *murder*, Connie! Can't you. . . ?"

"You're yelling at me," she said.

"Yes. Because you're behaving like a . . ."

"We're having our first argument," she said, grinning.

"Let's go see Charlie Nichols," he said.

She did not want to ask Charlie Wong for the use of a limousine because she had already called to tell him she was sick. She did not want to go to a car rental place because she suspected the police would have contacted all such places and asked them to be on the lookout for the wanted desperado Michael Barnes. So she went to Shi Kai, who ran the restaurant downstairs.

Mr Shi had a car he only drove during the summer months. The rest of the time, it sat idle in a garage he rented on Canal. That was because the car was a 1954 Oldsmobile convertible with a mechanism that had broken while the top was in the down position. Mr Shi handed the keys over to Connie and told her not to freeze to death. Michael was beginning to understand that Connie had a great many friends in New York City's Chinese community, all of whom seemed willing to perform all sorts of favors for her. This may have been only because she was Chinese, but he suspected it was because she was extraordinarily beautiful as well.

He loved the way she wore her beauty.

His former wife, Jenny, was beautiful, too, if you considered long blonde hair and green eyes and a spectacular figure beautiful, which apparently not only Michael had considered beautiful but all of Harvard's football team while he was in Vietnam, and most recently the branch manager and God knew who else at Suncoast

134

Federal. But Jenny *flaunted* her beauty, wearing it like a Miss America who was certain her smile would bring her fame, fortune, and a good seat at Van Wezel Hall, which was Sarasota's big contribution to Florida culture, such as it was. It had sickened Michael every time Jenny gently placed her hand on someone's arm and leaned in close to flash that incandescent smile of hers, and the person – male *or* female – melted into a gushing pool of gratitude and awe. Jenny knew without question that wherever she and Michael went, she was the most beautiful woman in the room. This was true. An indisputable fact. You could no more doubt that than you could doubt the certainty of the sun rising in the morning or the tides going in and out. Jenny was gorgeous. That she knew this and used this was not a particularly admirable trait.

Connie seemed not to know that she was extravagantly beautiful.

She wore her beauty like Reeboks.

Or galoshes.

It never occurred to her that Mr Shi would feel honored when she asked to borrow his convertible with a top that could not be put up. She went to him as a supplicant, politely asking for the use of the car, eyes respectfully lowered when talking to this person who was older than she was, and Mr Shi – recognizing the beauty and the grace and the modesty of this young woman who came to him as a dutiful daughter might have – handed her the keys and accepted her gratitude with a tut-tut-tut, and then cautioned her paternally against freezing to death.

Connie smiled so radiantly, it almost broke Michael's heart.

He guessed he was beginning to love her a whole lot.

"One of the nice things about a convertible," Connie said, "is you can see all the buildings."

Michael was thinking that in this city you could drive a convertible with the top down in the dead of winter and nobody paid any attention to you. That was one of the nice things about this city, the way everyone respected everyone else's privacy. Indifference, it was called.

He was beginning to learn the downtown area.

For example, he now knew that if you wanted to get out of

Chinatown, you didn't have to go very far until you were in Little Italy. And if you wanted to get out of Little Italy . . .

"This is all the Fifth Precinct," Connie said.

"Thank you," he said.

. . . you either drove east toward the East River or west toward the Hudson River. On the other hand, if you wanted to get to Charlie Nichols's apartment in Knickerbocker Village, you first drove east on Canal, and then you made a left on Bowery and drove past the Confucius Plaza apartments and P.S. 124 all the way to Catherine, where you made another left that took you past P.S. 1 on your right and then a Catholic church and school on your left – there were certainly a great many educational opportunities in this fine city – and then you made another left onto Monroe, which was a one-way street, and you looked for a parking space.

You could fit all of downtown Sarasota in Knickerbocker Village. That was another thing about this city. You could drive all over the downtown area, which was really just an infinitesimal part of New York, and you'd see more buildings and more restaurants and more movie theaters and more people than you would driving through the entire state of Florida. Michael found this amazing. He suddenly wondered if Connie planned to stay in New York for the rest of her life. He hoped not.

They were surrounded now by tall brick buildings.

They walked on paths shoveled clear of snow.

The evening was cold and brisk. Connie was wearing jeans and leg warmers and boots and the short black coat she'd had on last night when she'd followed him out of the fortune-cookie factory. Michael was wearing a brown leather bomber jacket he'd bought from a friend of Connie's named Louis Klein who ran an Army & Navy store on Delancey Street, which he opened for Connie even though this was Christmas and he was leaving for Puerto Rico in the morning. Michael had also bought from him – with money borrowed from Connie – a pair of Levi jeans, a blue wool sweater reduced from sixty-four dollars to twenty-three ninety-five, and a pair of white woolen socks "to keep your feet warm," Klein said paternally. It was amazing how Connie brought out the paternal instinct in all these fifty-, sixty-year-old men. When Klein clucked his tongue and asked Connie how her boyfriend had hurt his arm, Connie told him simply and honestly that he'd been shot. Klein said, "This city, I'm not surprised," and threw in an extra pair of woolen socks free.

She clung to his right arm now as they wandered through the development, following signs that told them which building was which. Somehow there was no sense of urgency here in this cloistered enclave. It was close to five o'clock now. There was a hush on the city. The street lamps, already lighted, cast a warm glow on the snow banked along the paths. Window rectangles glowed with the warmth of rooms beyond. Christmas tree lights blinking red and blue and green and white. Strings of lights outlined windows and balconies. One window was decorated with a huge white star. It was still Christmas.

They found Nichols's building, located his name in the lobby directory downstairs, and took the elevator up to the sixth floor. The corridor smelled of Christmas. Birds and beef that had been roasted, pies that had been baked. There was laughter behind one of the closed doors. Music behind another. They walked to the door for Nichols's apartment and Michael pressed the bell button set into the jamb. He listened. Nothing. He looked at Connie. She shrugged. He rang the bell again. No answer.

"He's out," he said.

"Knock," she said.

He knocked.

No answer.

He knocked again.

He shook his head.

"Damn it," he said.

"What do we do now?"

"I'd like to get in there," he said.

"Do you know how to do something like that?" she asked.

"Something like what?"

"Opening a door with a credit card?"

"No. Anyway, they *stole* my credit cards."

He was beginning to get angry all over again. Just thinking about what had happened to him since seven o'clock last night made him angry. Not knowing *why* these things were happening to him made him angry. Not knowing *who* was doing these things to him made him angry. And now Nichols not being here made him even angrier.

"Do *you* have a credit card?" he asked.

137

"Yes, but you just said . . ."

"I can learn."

She dug in her shoulder bag, found her wallet, and took from it an American Express card. He looked at the card, looked at the place in the jamb where the door fit snugly into it, grabbed the knob in his hand, slid the card between door and jamb, twisted the knob – and the door opened.

He looked at the door.

He looked at the credit card.

"Boy," Connie said, "you're *some* fast learner."

He eased the door open the rest of the way. There were lights on in the living room. A lighted Christmas wreath in the living-room window as well. He motioned Connie in, closed the door behind them. There was a deadbolt lock on the door. In the open position. Which meant he hadn't worked any magic with the credit card, the door had been unlocked already. He turned the thumb bolt now. The tumblers fell with a small oiled click that sounded like a rifle shot in the silent apartment.

"This is breaking and entry, you know," Connie said.

They stood just inside the entrance door.

There were two lamps on end tables in the living room, casting warm pools of illumination on a sofa and a pair of easy chairs. The wreath in the window glowed red and green. There was not a sound anywhere in the apartment.

"Let's see if we can find a desk someplace," Michael whispered.

"Why a desk?"

"See what's in it."

They moved out past the kitchen, and discovered off the hallway just beyond it a room that was furnished as a study. Big window on the wall across from the door. Bookcases on the wall to the right, an easy chair and a reading lamp in front of them. A desk and a chair on the opposite wall. Michael went to the desk and snapped on the desk lamp. The wall above the desk was decorated with framed pictures, most of them in black and white, all of them showing the same man in various costumes and in various poses. But in whichever costume and whatever pose, he was definitely the man who'd stolen Michael's car, and presumably the man whose apartment this was: Charles R. Nichols. It looked as if Nichols had once played Sherlock Holmes, if the deerstalker hat and pipe meant anything. Julius Caesar, too, judging from the toga and the laurel wreath. And either Napoleon or Hercule Poirot, it was difficult to tell from the photo. There were also photographs of him playing what appeared to be the leading man to various leading women. Holding the ladies' hands, gazing into their eyes, grinning in a goofy juvenile manner. It was always embarrassing to see photographs of an essentially unattractive man who thought he was handsome and who posed like a lady-killer. Michael thought of himself as merely okay in a world populated by spectacularly handsome men. He sometimes wished he had the kind of nerve it took to pose for pictures like the ones here on Charlie's wall.

"We're looking for anything about Crandall," he said. "Or Parrish or Cahill."

"Okay," Connie said.

She pulled out the bottom desk drawer and sat on the floor beside it, legs crossed Indian style. Michael sat in the chair and began looking through the drawer over the kneehole.

"Have you got enough light?" he asked.

"Yes," she said.

It occurred to him that he liked the way they worked together. They were getting good at working together.

Last night in Crandall's office had been the very first time they'd ransacked any place together. Now, working as a team, they . . .

"The check," Michael said.

"What check?"

"The one Crandall wrote on Friday. For nine thousand dollars."

"What about it?"

"He went to the bank at two-thirty. If that's when he cashed it . . ."

"Uh-huh."

". . . then maybe he gave the cash to Charlie . . ."

"Uh-huh."

". . . when he came to the office at three-thirty. That's all on Crandall's calendar, Connie. The bank, and Charlie coming to the office."

"Okay, so what are we looking for?" she asked. "Nine thousand dollars in cash?"

"Well, I guess so."

"And if we find it? What will that mean?"

"I don't know," Michael said, and sighed heavily.

They did not find nine thousand dollars in cash in any of the drawers in Charlie's desk.

They found instead a tarnished penny in a tray containing rubber bands, paper clips, a roll of Scotch tape, and a pair of scissors. That was all the cash they found.

They did, however, find an address book and an appointment calendar.

And for Friday, the twenty-third of December, Charlie had listed his three-thirty meeting at Crandall's office.

And for Saturday, the twenty-fourth of December . . .

Last night . . .

The night this whole damn thing had started . . .

Charlie had written onto his calendar:

Call Mama

"Mama again," Michael said.

"Let's check his address book."

There was a listing for Arthur Crandall in Charlie's address book.

For both his office and his home.

So *that* connection, at least, was clearly established.

There was no listing for either a Parrish or a Cahill.

"Is his mother listed?" Connie asked.

"Why his mother?" he asked.

"Mama," Connie said, and shrugged.

"Why would Crandall have called *Charlie's* mother 'Mama'?"

"I don't know. Maybe she's a big, fat woman. People call big, fat women 'Mama' even if they're somebody else's mother."

"I don't even call my *own* mother 'Mama,'" Michael said.

"Sophie Tucker was big and fat and she was the last of the Red Hot Mamas," Connie said.

"Who's Sophie Tucker?" Michael asked.

"I don't know. I drove somebody to see a play about her."

Michael looked under Nichols.

He found a listing for a Sarah Nichols in New Jersey.

"Try her," Connie said.

He debated this.

"Wish her a merry Christmas, ask her if she's talked to her son lately."

Michael still hesitated.

"Go ahead," Connie said.

He was thinking that the last time he'd talked to a strange woman on the telephone – Albetha Crandall, last night – the police had come up the fire escape the very next minute. Maybe talking to strange women on the telephone had a jinx attached. In Vietnam, you did all sorts of things to avoid jinxes. Jinxes could get you killed. You wrote all sorts of magic slogans on your helmet, you hung little amulets and charms from your flak jacket, anything to ward off a jinx, anything to stay alive. He did not want any more cops coming up the fire escape. He did not want to get shot by anyone else in this city, good guy or bad guy. But if the Mama in both Crandall's *and* Charlie's appointment calendars *was* in fact Charlie's mother, then maybe she could tell him something about what was going on here. If he played his cards right. If he crossed his fingers and mumbled a bit of voodoo jive to keep away the jinx. In Vietnam, Andrew had taught him some voodoo jive. Andrew was from New Orleans, where they sometimes did that kind of shit.

He dialed the number.

"Hello?"

A woman's voice.

"Sarah Nichols?" he said.

"Yes?"

"Merry Christmas," Michael said.

"Who's this, please?" Sarah said.

"A friend of Charlie's."

"Is anything wrong?" she asked at once.

"No, no. I've been trying to locate him, I wonder if you've talked to him lately."

"Not since this morning," she said. "He was supposed to come here for an early dinner, I told him I was having some friends in, but he never showed. Well, you know how Charlie is."

"Oh, yeah, Charlie," Michael said, and chuckled. "What time this morning?"

"Oh, around eleven, it must have been. The minute Charlie hears I want him to meet some girl, he runs for the hills."

"That's Charlie, all right," Michael said. "And you haven't talked to him since, huh?"

"No. Would you like to leave your name? In case he *does* pop in? Though it's really quite late, I doubt if even my brother would walk in at nine-thirty."

"Your brother, uh-huh," Michael said. "You don't think he might be with Benny, do you?"

"Who's Benny?"

"I don't know. I thought you might know."

"No, I'm sorry, I don't."

"Do you think your mother might know Benny? Do you have a mother?"

"Everyone has a mother."

"I mean, she isn't dead or anything, is she?"

"Not that I know of."

"What do you call her?"

"I call her . . . who did you say this was?"

"Do you call her Mama?"

"Sometimes."

"Is she spry? Does she get around?"

"Yes, she's very spry. Excuse me, but . . ."

"Would you know if someone named Arthur Crandall took her to meet someone named Benny last night?"

"I have no idea. Can you tell me who this is, please?"

"Michael."

"Michael who?" she asked.

"Bond," he said. "No relation. Please tell Charlie I called."

"I will," she said. "Good night, Mr Bond."

"Good night," Michael said.

He put the receiver back on the cradle.

He was beginning to like that name.

Maybe he'd take it on as a middle name.

It was certainly a hell of a lot better than Jellicle.

"His sister," he said.

"I gathered," Connie said.

"Let's see if there's anything in the bedroom," he said.

Charlie Nichols was in the bedroom.

On the bed.

All bloody.

11

Michael had seen a lot of dead bodies in his short lifetime, but none quite so messily dispatched as this one. Whoever had shot and killed Charlie seemed to have had a difficult time *finding* him. There were bullet holes in the headboard, bullet holes in the wall behind the bed, and several bullet holes in Charlie himself. If there were awards for sloppy murders, whoever had shot Charlie should start preparing an acceptance speech.

Connie looked as if she was about to throw up.

"You okay?" Michael asked.

She nodded.

He looked at the body again, went to the bed, and was leaning over the corpse when Connie yelled, "No!"

"What's the matter?" he said.

"Don't touch him," she said.

"Why not? Is that a Chinese superstition?"

"No, it's not a Chinese superstition."

"Then what is it?"

"It's disgusting."

"I just want to see if he's carrying a wallet," Michael said, and tried the right-hand pocket in his pants, and found what appeared to be several white rock crystals in a little plastic vial.

"Must collect these, huh?" he said, showing the vial to Connie.

Connie looked at him.

"Rocks, I mean," Michael said.

"Crack, you mean," Connie said.

"What?"

143

"That's crack."

"It is?" Michael said, and looked at the vial more closely. "I thought crystallography was perhaps his hobby."

"Smoking cocaine is perhaps his hobby."

"I'll tell you something," Michael said, "if this turns out to be another goddamn *dope* plot . . ."

"A single vial of cocaine doesn't necessarily . . ."

"I've had dope plots up to here, I mean it. You can't go to a movie nowadays, you can't turn on television . . ."

"There is no reason to believe that this is linked to a *dope* plot."

"Then what's this?" he asked, and showed her the vial again.

"That's crack."

"And is crack dope?"

"Crack is dope."

"And is this man dead?"

"He appears to be dead."

"There you are," Michael said, and rolled him over.

"Irrrgh," Connie said, and covered her eyes with her hands.

Michael was patting down the right hip pocket. "Here it is," he said, and reached into the pocket and yanked out a wallet.

Connie still had her hands over her eyes.

"You can look now," he said, and opened the wallet.

The first thing he saw was a driver's license with a picture of the man on the bed. The name on the license was Charles Robert Nichols.

"Well, it's him," Michael said.

"Good, give him back his wallet."

"Let's see what else is in it."

There were three credit cards in the wallet.

And an Actors Equity card.

And a Screen Actors Guild card.

And an AFTRA card.

And three postage stamps in twenty-two-cent denominations, no longer any good for first-class mail.

And this year's calendar, small and plastic and soon to expire.

And a TWA Frequent Flight Bonus Program card.

And a slip of paper with what looked like a handwritten telephone number on it.

"Here we go," he said.

"Good idea," Connie said. "Let's."

"What's the matter with you?"

"I don't like being here with that person on the bed."

"Is this a New York exchange?" he asked, and showed her the telephone number.

"Yes."

"Let's try it."

"No. Let's leave."

"Connie . . ."

"Michael, that person on the bed is dead."

"I know."

"You're *already* wanted for one murder . . ."

"I know."

"You've already been *shot* . . ."

"I know."

"So let's get out of here, okay? Before . . ."

"Let's try this number first."

"Michael, every time you try a number . . ."

"Maybe this time we'll get lucky," he said, and winked.

Connie did not wink back.

Instead, she followed him sullenly down the hallway and into the study again. He sat at the desk with the wall of black-and-white photographs in front of him, and he dialed the telephone number scrawled in a spidery handwriting on the slip of paper, and he waited, waited, waited . . .

"Hello?"

A woman's voice.

"Yes, hello, I'm calling for Charlie Nichols," he said.

"Sorry, he's not here," the woman said.

"I know he isn't, I'm calling *for* him. Who's this, please?"

"Judy Jordan," she said. "Who's this?"

"Hello?" he said.

"Hello?" she said.

"Hello, Miss Jordan?"

"Yes, I'm here."

"Hello?" he said.

"I can hear you," she said.

"I'll have to call back," he said, and hung up.

"Did you get cut off?" Connie asked.

"No," he said.

He was already looking through Charlie's address book again. He flipped rapidly through E, F, H . . .

"Here it is," he said. "Jordan, Judy."

Connie looked at the address. "The Seventh Precinct," she said. "Where they found the body in your car."

"Then we'd better go see her," he said.

"Why?" Connie asked.

He looked at her.

And felt suddenly foolish.

She was right, of course.

He'd found a telephone number in a dead man's wallet, and he'd called that number, and the woman who'd answered the phone was named Judy Jordan.

So?

Why go see her?

He was tired. And beginning to feel that perhaps the best thing to do, after all, was run on over to the police station and tell them he was the man they were looking for and could he please make a call to his lawyer, Mr David Lang in Sarasota, Florida? Connie knew where all the precincts were, they could drive over to the nearest one in Shi Kai's broken convertible. Or perhaps he should call Dave first, ask him to take the next plane up to New York, hole up in Connie's apartment until he got here, and *then* go to the police togeth –

"Judy *who*, did you say?"

This from Connie.

Who not five minutes ago had been urging him to please get the hell out of here. But who now seemed to have a note of renewed interest in her voice.

"Jordan,' he said, and turned to look up at her.

Connie was looking at the wall.

Specifically, she was looking at a photograph of Charlie Nichols and a teenage girl. Charlie was a much younger man in the photograph; Michael guessed the picture had been taken at least fifteen years ago. The girl couldn't have been older than sixteen or seventeen. She was wearing a white sweater and a dark skirt and she was grinning up into Charlie's face. Charlie was holding both her hands between his own.

Written in blue ink across the girl's sweatered breasts were the words *To My Dear Daddy, With Love* and beneath that the signature *Judy Jordan*.

Michael leaned in closer to the picture.

The young girl had long, dark hair.

But aside from that, she was a dead ringer for Helen Parrish.

"Also," Connie said, "does Benny have to be a *person*?"

"What?" Michael said.

"Because there's a place called Benny's in SoHo, and maybe that's where Crandall went to meet Charlie's mother, in which case we should take Crandall's picture there in case somebody might remember him from last night, don't you think?"

Michael kissed her.

The bartender's name was Charlie O'Hare.

"There are lots of Charlies in this city, you know," he said.

"Yes, I know," Michael said.

They were sitting at the bar. The place was unusually crowded for Christmas night, but then again Michael had never been in a bar on Christmas night, and maybe they were all this crowded. It was a very Irish bar. No frills. A utilitarian saloon designed for drinkers. Sawdust on the floor. No cut-glass mirrors, no green-shaded lamps like in the place last night where they'd set Michael up for theft and accusation. A nice friendly neighborhood saloon with a handful of people sitting in the booths or at the tables or here at the bar, all of them wearing caps and looking like nice friendly IRA terrorists.

"Here's his picture," Michael said, and showed him the eight-year-old clipping from the Nice newspaper. He had taken it out of its frame. The back of the clipping was a story about a Frenchman who'd leaped into the Mediterranean to save a German tourist who should have known better than to be swimming in the sea in May. Crandall smiled out from his photograph.

"He's even fatter now," Michael said.

"No, I don't know him," O'Hare said. "Is this French here?"

"Yes."

"What's it say here under the picture?"

"Arthur Crandall before the showing of his film *War and Solitude* yesterday afternoon."

"So what is he, an actor?"

147

"No, he's a director."

"Sheesh," O'Hare said. "And this is a new movie?"

"No, it's an old one."

"Then how come they showed it yesterday afternoon?"

"They showed it eight years ago."

"I musta missed it."

"Do you recognize him?"

"No."

"Take a look at the picture again. He would've been here last night at eight o'clock."

"I don't remember seeing him."

"Were you working last night?"

"Yeah, but I don't remember seeing this guy."

"He would've been meeting somebody's mother."

"Well, we get a lot of mothers in here, but I don't remember this guy sitting with anybody's mother," O'Hare said.

"Were you working the bar alone?"

"All alone."

"So he couldn't have been sitting at the bar."

"Not without my noticing him." O'Hare looked at the newspaper clipping again. "This is a French movie?" he asked.

"No, it's American."

"Then why is this written in French?"

"Because that's where they showed it."

"I can understand why they never showed it here. That sounds real shitty, don't it, *War and Solitude*. Would you go see a movie called *War and Solitude*?"

"They did show it here."

"Here? In New York?"

"I think so."

"I never heard of it. *War and Solitude*. I never heard of it. It sounds shitty."

"A lot of people agreed with you," Michael said.

"Don't she speak English?" O'Hare asked, jerking his head toward Connie.

"I speak English," she said.

"'Cause I thought maybe you spoke only Chinese, sitting there like a dummy."

"I don't have anything to say," Connie said.

"You're a very pretty lady," O'Hare said.

"Thank you," Connie said.

"She's very pretty," O'Hare said to Michael.

"Thank you," Michael said. "Who would've been working the booths last night? And the tables."

"Molly."

Michael looked around. He didn't see any waitresses in the place.

"Is she here now?"

"She was here a minute ago," O'Hare said.

He craned his neck, looking.

The door to the ladies' room opened. A woman who looked like Detective O'Brien, except that she was fully clothed, came out and walked directly toward where someone signaled to her from one of the booths. She had flaming red hair like O'Brien's and she was short and stout like O'Brien, and she waddled toward the bar now with a sort of cop swagger that made Michael think maybe she *was* O'Brien in another disguise.

"Two Red Eyes," she said. "Water chasers."

O'Hare took from the shelf behind him a bottle of what looked like house whiskey, the label unfamiliar to Michael. He poured liberally into two glasses, filled two taller glasses with water, and put everything onto Molly's tray.

"When you got a minute," he said, "this gentleman would like a few words with you."

Molly looked Michael up and down.

"Sure," she said, and swaggered over to the booth.

"Molly used to wrestle in Jersey," O'Hare said.

"Really?"

"They called her the Red Menace."

"I see."

"Because of the red hair."

"Yes."

"Which is real, by the way," O'Hare said, and winked.

Molly came back to the bar.

"So," she said. "What now?"

Michael showed her the newspaper clipping.

"Ever see this man in here?" he asked.

"You a cop?" Molly asked.

"No," Michael said.

"You sure?"

"Positive."

"'Cause I was thinking of calling the cops."

"No, I don't think we need . . ."

"Last night, I mean. When I heard what the two of them were talking about."

"Who do you mean?"

"Mr Crandall. And the Spanish guy with him."

"You mean you know him?"

"No, I don't *know* him. I only recognize him."

"Arthur Crandall?"

"I don't know his first name. I only know he's Mr Crandall."

"How do you happen to know that?"

"Because of the phone call."

"What phone call?"

"The phone call that came in the phone booth over there. For Mr Crandall."

"Who turned out to be the man in this picture, am I right?"

"Yes."

"Arthur Crandall."

"If that's his first name."

"That's his first name."

"Then that's who it was."

"What about this phone call?"

"Don't rush me. That was later. Earlier, they were sitting at that table over there," she said, and gestured vaguely, "which is when I heard them talking."

"What time was this?"

"Around eight-fifteen."

"And you're sure this is the man?" Michael asked, and showed her the clipping again.

"Yeah, that's him all right. Though he's fatter now."

"But you say he was with another *man*? Not a woman?"

"Not unless she had a thick black moustache," Molly said.

"Why'd you want to call the cops?" Connie asked.

"Who's this?" Molly said, and looked her up and down.

"Connie Kee," Michael said.

"Is she Chinese?"

"Yes."

"I thought so," Molly said. "Is it okay to talk in front of her?"

"Yes, absolutely."

150

"Because Chinese people are funny, you know," Molly said.

"Funny how?" Connie asked, truly interested.

"They're always yelling," Molly said.

"That's true," Connie said. "But that's because they're not sure of the language. If they yell, they think you'll understand them better."

"Well, I wish they wouldn't yell all the time."

"Me, too," Connie said.

"It makes me feel like I did something wrong."

"Japanese people never yell, did you notice that?" O'Hare said.

"Excuse me," Michael said, "but why *did* you . . . ?"

"Yes, they're very quiet and polite," Molly said.

"Why did you want to . . . ?"

"Well, they're two very different cultures," Connie said.

"Oh, certainly," Molly said. "The Koreans, too. And also the Vietna . . ."

"Excuse me," Michael said, "but why did you want to call the police?"

"What?"

"Last night."

"Oh. Well, because of what they were *talking* about, why do you think?"

"What were they talking about?"

"A *body*," Molly said, lowering her voice. "A dead *body*."

"Who?" Michael asked.

"The two of them in the booth. Mr Crandall and the Spanish guy with the moustache."

"I mean, the body. Who was it?"

"They didn't say."

"Well, what did you hear them . . . ?"

"The Spanish guy was saying he already had the corpse. That's when I almost called the police."

"But you didn't."

"No. Because I figured the man had to be an undertaker."

"Uh-huh."

"Or one of those people who does autopsies at the hospital."

"Uh-huh."

"But then Mr Crandall said if Charlie could de . . ."

"Charlie!" Michael shouted and almost leaped off the stool.

"Jesus, you scared the *shit* out of me," Molly said, backing away.

"Did you say *Charlie*?"

"What the hell's wrong with you?"

"What *about* Charlie?"

"I think this guy's crazy," Molly said to O'Hare.

"Nah, he's okay," O'Hare said, indicating with a shrug that in his lifetime as a bartender he had served many, many nutcases picking at the coverlet.

"Tell me about Charlie," Michael said.

Molly sighed and rolled her eyes.

"He said if Charlie could deliver what they needed . . ."

"Crandall said?"

"Yes. Said if Charlie could deliver what they needed, then they could plant the stiff before midnight."

"Plant the stiff."

"He meant the corpse."

"Uh-huh."

"He meant they could bury the corpse before midnight."

"That's what *you* think," Connie said knowingly.

"Which is when I almost called the cops again," Molly said. "Because even if the man *was* an undertaker, why would he be burying anybody at midnight? On Christmas Eve, no less."

"*Before* midnight," O'Hare corrected.

"Right," Molly said, "on Christmas *Eve*. But then the Spanish guy told Mr Crandall there wasn't any hurry, the body would keep, it was on ice, so I guessed he was a legitimate undertaker, after all."

"Did you happen to catch his name?"

"No."

"What this was," O'Hare said, "this Spanish undertaker was waiting for Charlie to bring the dead man's suit and underwear or whatever, his *stuff*, you know, so they could dress him all up before they buried him."

"That's what *you* think," Connie said again.

"Which is another thing I don't like about Chinese people," Molly said.

"What's that?" Connie asked, truly interested again.

"They think they're so fucking smart," Molly said.

"Yes, that's true," Connie said.

"That's 'cause they *are* so fucking smart," O'Hare said.

"That's true, too," Connie said.

"Excuse me," Michael said, "but did either of them say what Charlie was supposed to deliver?"

"Your I.D., of course," Connie said.

"So when they planted the corpse with *Crandall's* I.D. on it . . ."

"They could *also* drop . . ."

"Do you know what these two are talking about?" Molly asked O'Hare.

"Sure," O'Hare said.

"What?"

"The stiff's dog tags."

"What dog tags?"

"To put in his mouth. The stiff's."

"I think *you're* crazy, too," Molly said, shaking her head.

"What else did they say?" Michael asked.

"Mr Crandall said he wanted to get moving on it, and he wished Charlie would hurry up and do what he had to do."

"Did he mention Charlie's last name?" Michael asked.

"No."

"He didn't say Charlie Nichols?"

"I just told you he didn't mention his last name, so why are you asking me Charlie this or Charlie that? What's the *matter* with this guy?" she asked O'Hare.

"He's okay," O'Hare said, indicating with a shrug that in his many, many years as a bartender he had encountered many a fruitcake who had escaped from this or that mental institution.

"It goes right back to Charlie again," Michael said to Connie. "And the pair working with him. The phony cop and . . ."

"*All* cops are phonies, you want to know," O'Hare said.

"Tell me about the phone call," Michael said.

"The phone in the booth rang, I went to answer it, and a woman on the other end . . ."

"A *woman*!" Michael shouted.

"Listen, if you're gonna keep yelling like that . . ."

"I'm sorry. Did she give you her name?"

"No."

"Helen Parrish," Michael said to Connie.

"I just told you she didn't give me her name," Molly said.

"Or Judy Jordan," Connie said.

"Who's Judy Jordan?" Molly asked.

"Tell me exactly what she said," Michael said.

"She asked to talk to Mr Crandall. So I yelled out was there a Mr Crandall here, and the guy in your picture gets up and goes to the phone booth."

"Then what?"

"Then the Spanish guy ordered another beer."

"And then what?"

"Then Mr Crandall comes back to the table all smiles and tells the Spanish guy everything's okay, they got it."

"Got *what*?" Michael asked.

"Your license and your credit cards," Connie said.

"What time was this?" Michael asked.

"Around eight-thirty," Molly said.

"Right after Crandall stole my car," Michael said.

"She probably told him that, too. That they also had your car."

"So now the Spanish guy could plant the corpse in my car . . ."

"With Crandall's I.D. on it . . ."

"And my stuff alongside the body . . ."

"And set the whole thing in motion."

"What whole thing?" O'Hare asked.

"This is giving me a headache," Molly said, and walked off.

The real headache began at eight o'clock that night, as they were approaching Connie's building.

That was when the shots came.

Michael had developed a sixth sense in Vietnam, you didn't survive unless you did. You learned to know when something was coming your way, you heard that tiny oiled click somewhere out there in the jungle, and you knew someone had squeezed a trigger and a round was right then speeding out of a rifle barrel, or a dozen rounds, you didn't wait to find out, you threw yourself flat on the ground. They said in Vietnam that the only grunts who survived were the ones who got good at humping mud. Michael had survived.

There was no mud to hump on Pell Street that Sunday night, there was only a lot of virgin white snow heaped against the curbs on either side of the street. The plows had been through, and the banks they'd left were three, four feet high. In the bright moonlight, Connie and Michael came walking up the middle of the street, which was clearer than the sidewalks, and were about to climb over the bank in front of her building when Michael heard the click.

The same oiled click he'd come to know and love in dear old Vietnam, a click only a trained bird dog might have heard, so soft and so tiny was it, but he knew at once what that click meant.

In Vietnam, he'd have thought only of his own skin.

Hear the click, hump the mud.

Here, there was Connie.

He threw himself at her sideways, knocking her off her feet and *down*, man, out of the path of that bullet or bullets that would be coming their way in about one-one-hundredth of a—

There!

A sharp crack on the air.

And another one.

First the click, and then the crack.

If you hadn't heard the click, you never heard the crack, because by then you were stone-cold dead in the market.

For a tall, slender girl, Connie went down like a sack of iron rivets. Whammo, on her back in the snow, legs flying. "Hey!" she yelled, getting angry. Another crack, and then another, little spurts of snow erupting on the ridge of snow above their heads, better *snow* spurts than *blood* spurts, Charlie.

"Keep down!" he yelled.

She was struggling to get up, cursing in Chinese.

He kept her pinned.

Listened.

Nothing.

But wait . . . wait . . . wait . . .

"Are you crazy?" she said.

"Yes," he said.

Wait . . . wait . . .

He knew the shooter was still up there. Sensed it with every fiber in his being.

"Stay here," he said. "And stay down. There's someone up there trying to kill us."

"What?"

"On the roof. Don't even lift your head. I'll be right back."

"Michael," she said. Softly.

"Yes?" he said.

"I love you, Michael, but you *are* crazy."

It was the first time she'd said that.

The loving him part.

He smiled.

"I love you, too," he said.

The street ran like a wide trench between the banks of moonlit snow on either side of it. Connie lay huddled close to the bank on the northern side of the street, hidden from the roof. Up there was where the shooter was. Michael began wiggling his way up the street, on his belly, using his elbows, dragging his legs. Working his way toward the corner of Pell and Mott, where he planned to make a right turn, out of the shooter's line of fire. Then he would get up to those rooftops up there, and see what there was to see.

It was such a beautiful night.

Long Foot Howell, the only Indian guy in the platoon – an *American* Indian whose great-great-grandfather' had ridden the Plains with Sitting Bull – always used to say, "It's a good day for dying."

His people lived on a reservation out West someplace. Arizona, maybe, Michael couldn't remember.

Long Foot told him that his people used to say that before they rode into battle.

It's a good day for dying.

Meaning God alone knew what.

Maybe that if you were going to die, you might as well do it on a nice day instead of a shitty one.

Or maybe it referred to the enemy. A good day for killing the *enemy*. A good day for the *enemy* to die.

Or maybe it was a reverse sort of charm. The Indian's way of wishing himself good luck. If he said it was a good day for dying, then maybe he wouldn't get killed. Maybe whichever god or gods the Indian prayed to would hear what he'd said and spare him. If that was it, the charm hadn't worked too well for Long Foot.

On a very good day in Vietnam, with the sun shining bright on his shiny black hair, Long Foot took a full mortar hit and went to join his ancestors in a hundred little pieces.

This was a beautiful night.

But not for dying.

Not here and not now.

However much whoever was on the roof might have wished it.

Michael had reached the corner now, the two narrow streets intersecting the way he imagined country roads did in England, where he'd never been. The hedgerows here, however, were made of snow, high enough to keep Michael hidden from the sniper on the roof, who was still up there silent and waiting.

On his hands and knees, Michael came around the corner.

The building immediately on his right had the inevitable Chinese restaurant on the ground floor, a blue door to the right of it. The door had a sign on it reading TAIWAN NOODLE FACTORY. Michael figured the door to a business would be locked shut on Christmas Day. He could not afford fiddling with a locked door after he climbed over the snowbank and onto the sidewalk where he would be seen if the sniper was roaming around up there.

He crawled to a spot paralleling the next building in line.

Lifted his head quickly.

Saw a door painted green.

Ducked his head.

Waited.

Lifted it again. Saw numerals over the door, nothing else, no sign, no anything. An apartment building. Meaning steps going up to the roof. He hoped.

Ducked again.

Waited.

He crawled several buildings down the street, staying close to the snowbank, and then he took a deep breath, counted to three, and scrambled over the side of the bank as if it were a suspect hill in Vietnam except that over there he'd have had a hand grenade in his fist. He landed on his feet and on the run, sprinting for the green door, which he now saw was slightly ajar, flattening himself against the side of the building to the right of the door. He shot a quick, almost unconscious glance upward toward the roof, saw nothing in the moonlight, and shoved the door fully open.

The entrance vestibule was dark and cold.

He closed the door behind him.

Or, at least, tried to close it. There was something wrong with the hinge, the door would not fully seat itself in the jamb. He gave it up for a lost cause, went to the closed inner door just past the doorbells and mailboxes, and tried the knob. The door was locked. He backed away from it at once, raised his knee, and kicked out flatfooted at a point just above the knob.

"Ow!" he yelled. "You son of a *bitch*!"

The door hadn't budged an inch.

Still swearing, he moved over to where the doorbells were set under the mailboxes. At random, he selected the doorbell for apartment 2A, rang the doorbell, waited, waited, waited and got nothing. The sole of his foot was sending out flashing signals of pain. He wondered if it was possible to break the sole of your foot. He rang another doorbell. A voice came instantly from a speaker on the wall. The voice said something in Chinese. Michael said, "Police, open the door, please." An answering buzz sounded at once. Pleased with himself, Michael opened the door and was starting toward the steps when another door opened at the end of the little cul de sac to the right of the staircase. A short, very fat Chinese man wearing a tank-top undershirt, black trousers, and black slippers, stepped out into the hallway, squinted toward where Michael was standing, and yelled, "Wassa motta?"

"Nothing," Michael said.

"You police?" the man yelled.

"Yes."

"Me supahtennin."

"Go back to sleep," Michael said. "This is routine."

"Where you badge?"

"I'm undercover," Michael said.

The man blinked.

"Wah you wann here?" he asked.

"There's a sniper on the roof," Michael said.

"I go get key," the man said, nodding.

"What key?"

"For loof," the man said, and went back into his apartment.

Michael waited. He did not want a partner. On the other hand, his foot still hurt and he didn't want to have to try kicking in another door. He suddenly wondered if in real life it was possible to kick in a door the way detectives did in the movies and on television. He knew it wasn't possible in real life to slam a car into another car and just go on your merry way. Teenagers saw a car chase in a movie, they thought, Hey terrific, I can run into el pillars and concrete mixers and I'll just bounce right off them like a rubber ball, that should be great fun. That same teenager got a drink or two in him, he decided he was a big-city detective in a car chase. He rammed his car into a bus, expecting either the bus

158

would roll over on its back or else his car would bounce off it like in the movies and the next thing you knew a real-life steering wheel was crushing his chest, or his head was going through a real-life windshield. Michael suddenly wondered if Sylvester Stallone had ever been to Vietnam.

"Okay, I gotta key," the man said, and came out into the hallway, and pulled the door to his apartment shut behind him. To Michael's dismay, the man had taken off his slippers and put on socks and high-topped boots that looked like combat boots. He had also put on a shirt and a heavy Mackinaw and a woolen stocking cap.

They climbed the steps to the fourth floor and then up another short flight of steps to a metal door. Nodding, flapping his hands, turning the key on the air, shaping his other hand into a gun, Michael's guide and new partner indicated that this was indeed the door to the roof and that he was now going to open the door to the roof, so if Michael was a real cop and there was a real sniper out there maybe he should take out a gun or something. Obligingly, Michael took out a gun. The one he had taken from Crandall, which upon inspection had turned out to be a .32 caliber Harrington & Richardson Model 4, double-action revolver.

"Ahhhhhh," the man said, and nodded. He liked the gun. He showed Michael the key again, and then inserted it into the padlock that hung from a hinge and hasp on the metal door, and as if performing a magic trick, he turned the key and opened the padlock, and grinned and nodded at Michael. Michael nodded back. The Chinese man took the padlock off the hasp, and then moved aside. If there really was a sniper out there, he wasn't going to be the first one to step out onto the roof. He almost bowed Michael out ahead of him.

"You stay here," Michael said.

"More cops," the man said, and nodded. "I call more cops."

"No!" Michael said. "No more cops. This is undercover."

The man looked at him.

"What's your name?" Michael asked.

"Peter Chen," the man said.

"Mr Chen, thank you very much," Michael said, "the city is proud of you. But you can go back down, thank you," Michael said. "Good-bye, Mr Chen, thank you."

"I come with you," Chen said.

Michael looked at him.

Chen smiled.

Michael sighed in resignation, opened the door, and stepped quickly out onto the roof. He paused for a moment, getting his new bearings, trying to work out where he was in relationship to Connie's building, where the sniper was. Because once he did that, the rest would be simple. The buildings here were all joined side by side, there were no airshafts to leap, it would merely be a matter of climbing the parapets that separated one rooftop from the next. So if the cross street was *here*, then Connie's street was *there*, and he'd have to go over this rooftop and then the next one to the corner—

"What you do?" Chen asked.

"I'm thinking."

"Ahhhhh."

– and then make a left turn and continue on over the rooftops till he came to the middle of the block somewhere. Long before then, on a clear moonlit night like tonight, he'd have seen the sniper. The trick was to make sure the sniper didn't see *him*. Or his new friend, Chen, who was now behind him and staying very close as he made his way across the roof toward—

"I see nobody," Chen said.

"Give it time," Michael whispered. "And keep it down."

The snow had drifted some four feet high in places. It was almost impossible to tell where one rooftop ended and the next began. He discovered the first parapet only by banging into it. He climbed over it, Chen close behind him, and was working his way laboriously through the snow toward the corner where the buildings joined at a right angle when he saw up ahead—

He signaled with his hand, palm down and patting the air.

Chen got the meaning at once, and dropped immediately flat to the snow.

Michael raised his head.

There.

He squinted into the distance. Someone in black. Crouching behind the parapet facing the street. Rifle in his hands.

"Stay here," he whispered to Chen.

Chen nodded.

Michael began creeping forward.

He did not want to kill anyone. He had Crandall's .32 in his right hand and Frankie Zeppelin's .45 in the left-hand pocket of his bomber jacket, but he did not want to use either of those guns to kill anyone. He'd already been accused of killing *one* person, and he did not want to add to that list the *actual* murder of yet another person. It was too bad, of course, that the person lying on the roof up ahead was armed with a rifle he'd already fired at Michael. Because if that person wanted to kill him, as seemed to be the case, then he certainly wasn't going to put down his rifle and come along like a nice little boy. In which case Michael might very well have to shoot him. Perhaps kill him. The way he'd killed people in Vietnam, where it hadn't seemed to matter much. Kill or be killed. Like tonight. Maybe.

He suddenly wondered why this person wanted him dead.

Crawling across the snow – closer and closer, keeping his eyes on the man as he advanced steadily toward him, ready to fire if he had to, if he was spotted, if the man turned that rifle on him – the question assumed paramount importance in his mind.

Why does this person want to kill me?

And then another question followed on its heels, so fierce in its intensity that it stopped Michael dead in his tracks.

Who is the person they've already killed?

The corpse wasn't Crandall's, that was for sure, even though Crandall's identification had been found on it.

But there *was* a corpse, there was no mistake about that, the police of the Seventh Precinct had found a dead man in the car Michael had rented, so who was that man?

Maybe the man in black over there would have the answers to *both* questions.

Michael began moving toward him again.

He could see the man clearly in the moonlight now. Forty yards away from him now. Black watch cap. Black leather jacket. Black jeans. Black boots. Black gloves. Crouched behind the parapet facing the street, hunched over a rifle, Michael couldn't tell what kind at this distance. Telescopic sight on it.

The man suddenly got to his feet.

Michael froze.

In an instant, the man would spot him, and turn the rifle on him.

In an instant, Michael would have to shoot him.

But no, the man—

Huh?

The man was taking the telescopic sight off the rifle. He was putting the rifle and the scope into a gun case. He was snapping the case shut. He was, for Christ's sake, quitting! Giving the whole thing up as a botched job!

He rested the gun case against the parapet. Angled it against the parapet so that the wider butt end of the case was on the snow, the muzzle end up. He reached into his jacket pocket. Took out a pack of cigarettes. Lighted one. Nice moonlit night, might as well enjoy a cigarette here on the rooftops overlooking downtown New York. His back to Michael. Looking out over the lights of the city. Enjoying his little smoke. So he'd bungled the job, so what? Plenty of time to get the dumb orange-grower later on.

Unless the dumb orange-grower had something to say about it.

It was not easy moving across the snow-covered roof. Silence was the only advantage the snow gave Michael. He glanced behind him once to make sure Chen was still glued in place and out of sight. He saw no sign of the fat little Chinese. At the parapet, the man in black was still enjoying his moonlight smoke, his back to Michael, one foot on the parapet, knee bent, elbow on the knee. Not five feet separated them now. Michael hoped the cigarette was a king-sized one.

The man suddenly flipped the cigarette over the edge of the roof.

And reached for the gun case.

And was starting to turn when Michael leaped on him.

He caught the man from behind, yanking at the collar of his jacket, trying to pull him over backward onto the snow, but he was too fast and too slippery for Michael. He turned, saw the gun in Michael's hand, knew that his own weapon was already cased and essentially useless, and used his knee instead, exactly the way Michael had used his knee on Charlie Wong last night, going for the money but coming up a little short, catching Michael on the upper thigh instead of the groin, and then looking utterly surprised when Michael threw a punch at him instead of firing his gun.

Michael went straight for the nose, the way he'd gone for Charlie Wong's nose yesterday, because a hit on the nose hurt more than a hit anyplace else, even sharks didn't like to get hit on their noses, ask any shark. The man all in black looked like a sixteen-year-old kid up close, but Michael had killed fourteen-year-old Vietnamese soldiers and this kid's age didn't mean a damn to him, the only thing that mattered was that he'd tried to kill Michael not twenty minutes ago. Peachfuzz oval face, slitted blue eyes, a very delicate Michael Jackson nose, which Michael figured wouldn't look so delicate after he made it bleed, which was another nice thing about going for the nose. Noses bled easily, whereas if you hit a guy on the jaw, for example, with the same power behind the punch, he wouldn't bleed at all.

The kid slipped the punch.

Ducked low and to the side and slipped it.

Michael's momentum almost caused him to fall.

He grabbed for the kid, trying to keep his balance, clutched for the kid's shoulders, and that was when the kid got him good, right in the balls this time, square on. Michael dropped the .32. Caught his breath in pain. The kid was turning, the kid was starting to run for the door of the roof. Michael reached out for him, clutched for his jacket, his head, anything, caught the black watch cap instead, felt it pulling free in his hands, and the kid was off and loping through the thick snow like an antelope.

Michael fell to his knees in pain.

Grabbed for his balls.

Moaned.

Did not even try to find the .32 where it had sunk below the snow some two feet away from him.

Did not even try to reach for the .45 in his jacket pocket.

The person running away from him across the rooftop was not Helen Parrish.

Nor was she Jessica Wales.

But she was a tall, long-legged, slender woman with blonde hair that glistened like gold in the silvery moonlight now that it was no longer contained by the black watch cap Michael still clutched in his hands close to his balls.

Maybe he didn't try shooting her because he was in such pain himself.

Or maybe he'd shot and killed too many women.

In Vietnam.

Where anyone in black pajamas was Charlie.

The roof door slammed shut behind her.

And he was alone in pain in the moonlight.

12

"Are you sure she was blonde?" Connie asked.

She was asking about Helen Parrish.

"Yes, she was blonde," Michael said.

"But Charlie's daughter has *dark* hair."

"She's the same person, believe me."

They were driving toward the address in Charlie Nichols's book. Judy Jordan's address. Judy Jordan who was also Helen Parrish whose dear dead daddy was Charlie Nichols. In the bar last night, Helen Parrish had told him she was thirty-two years old. Which was about right if the picture in Charlie's study had been taken fifteen years ago and if she'd been seventeen at the time.

It was very cold outside, driving alfresco this way. The dash-board clock wasn't working, which came as no surprise in a convertible with a broken top-mechanism. Michael waited to look at his watch until they stopped for a traffic light on a corner under a street lamp. It was almost ten o'clock.

He was very eager to see Miss Helen Parrish again.

The *fake* Miss Parrish, who was in reality—

Well, that wasn't necessarily true.

It was possible that Judy Jordan was now married, although in that bar last night Helen Parrish had told him she wasn't married, wasn't divorced, she was just single. Well, she'd told him a lot of things. But if she *was* married, and if Helen Parrish was indeed her real name now, which she'd have been crazy to have given him, then her maiden name *could* have been Judy Jordan, the girl with the long brown—

But no.

Charlie Nichols was her father.

Isn't that what she'd written on the photo?

To My Dear Daddy.

Then why had she signed her name Judy Jordan?

"What I'd like to know," Connie said, "is if Judy Jordan is Helen Parrish then how come she's not Judy Nichols if Charlie Nichols is or was her father?"

"I love you," Michael said, and kissed her fiercely.

The Amalgamated Dwellings, Inc., were cooperative apartments at 504 Grand Street, but the entrance to the complex was around the corner on a street called Abraham Kazan, no relation. You went down a series of low brick steps and into an interior courtyard that might have been a castle keep in England, with arches and what looked like turrets and a snow-covered little park with shrubs and trees and a fountain frozen silent by the cold. The lettered buildings – A, B, C, and so on – were clustered around this secret enclave. Judy Jordan lived in E. The name on the mailbox downstairs was J. Jordan.

"Women who do that are dumb," Connie said. "Using an initial instead of a name. You do that, and a rapist knows right off it's a woman living alone. You can bet I don't have C. Kee on *my* mailbox."

"What *do* you have?"

"Charlie Kee."

"That's a very common name in this city," Michael said. "Charlie."

"Which is why I put it on my mailbox," Connie said, and nodded.

"Why?"

"So a rapist would think it was a common man named Charlie Kee up there."

"How about the postman?"

"Mr Di Angelo? A rapist? Don't be ridiculous!"

"I mean, how will he know where to deliver mail addressed to Connie Kee?"

"That's *his* worry," Connie said.

Michael looked at the name on the mailbox again.

J. Jordan.

"I'll go up alone," he said. "You go back to the car."

"If this blonde is as beautiful as you say she is . . ."

"She may also be dangerous."

"I'll bet."

"Connie, please go wait in the car for me, okay?"

"I'll give you ten minutes," she said. "If you're not back by then, I'm coming up after you."

"Okay. Good."

He kissed her swiftly.

"I still think I ought to go with you," she said.

But she was already walking out of the courtyard.

Michael pressed the button for Judy Jordan's apartment.

"Yes?" a woman's voice said.

He could not tell whether the voice was Helen Parrish's or not. As a matter of fact, he'd completely forgotten what Helen Parrish had sounded like.

"Miss Jordan?" he said.

"Yes?"

"Charlie Nichols sent me," he said.

"Look," she said, "this is an inconvenient time. I was just dressing to . . ."

"I'd like to talk to you, Miss Jordan, if . . ."

"Oh, well, all right, come on up," she said, and buzzed him in.

He climbed to the third floor, found her apartment just to the left of the stairwell, and was about to ring the bell set in the doorjamb when he hesitated.

If Judy Jordan did, in fact, turn out to be Helen Parrish, or vice versa, then the woman inside this apartment was the person who'd set the whole scheme in motion, the MacGuffin as she might be called in an Alfred Hitchcock film. Was he going to simply knock on the door and wait for the MacGuffin to answer it, perhaps to do him more harm than she'd already done? Michael did not think that was such a good idea. He reached into the right-hand pocket of his new bomber jacket, and took out the .32 he had appropriated from Arthur Crandall. He flipped the gun butt-side up, and rapped it against the door. Twice. Rap. Rap. And listened.

"Who is it?" a woman said. Same voice that had come from the speaker downstairs.

"Me," he said.

"Who's me?"

"I told you. Charlie sent me."

"If it's about the money, I still haven't got it," the woman said from somewhere just inside the door now. There was a peephole set in the door at eye level. She was probably looking out at him. He still couldn't tell whether the voice was Helen Parrish's.

"I'd like to talk to you, if I may," he said, ducking his chin, trying to hide his face so that if this *was* Helen Parrish looking out at him, she wouldn't get such a good look.

"Just a minute," she said, "I'm still half-naked."

He wondered if this really was Helen Parrish, half-naked inside there. He thought back to the beginning of their relationship together, their gentle, easy conversation, the way they'd held hands, the way they'd looked deep into each other's eyes. He thought what a shame it was that she'd turned out to be a MacGuffin but maybe all beautiful women turned into MacGuffins sooner or later. He certainly hoped that wouldn't be the case with Connie.

He looked at his watch.

What the hell was taking her so long in there?

He rapped on the door with the gun butt again.

Three times.

Rap. Rap. Rap.

"Miss Jordan?" he called.

No answer.

"Miss . . ."

"Put your hands up, Mr Barnes."

A man's voice.

Behind him.

"Up!" the man said. "Now!"

The thing in Michael's back felt very much like the muzzle of a gun.

Michael raised his hands over his head, the .32 in his right hand. The bandaged left arm hurt when he raised it. He almost said Ouch.

"Just let the gun fall out of your hand," the man said. "Just open your hand and drop the gun."

He opened his hand. The gun fell out of it. Dropped to the floor. Hit the floor with a solid *thwunk*.

"Thank you," the man said. "Now stand still, please."

Kneeling to pick up the gun now, Michael supposed. There was a small scraping sound as it came up off the tile floor. A hand began patting him down. All his pants pockets. Then the right-hand pocket of the jacket, and then –

"Well, well, another one," the man said.

Frankie Zeppelin's .45 came out of Michael's pocket.

"Mr Barnes?" the man said.

And hit him on the back of the head with at least one of the guns.

He heard voices.

A man's voice. A woman's voice.

". . . blow the whole thing," the man said.

". . . other choice, do you?"

He opened his eyes.

A tin ceiling.

The shrink he had gone to in Boston had an office with a tin ceiling. Michael used to lie on his couch and look up at all the curlicues in his tin ceiling. He was not on a couch now. He was on a bed. An unmade bed. The bed smelled as if someone had peed in it. He wondered if it was a child's bed. The bed had a metal footboard, which he could see by lifting his head. Wrought iron painted white. He was spread-eagled on the bed with his ankles tied to the footboard and his arms up over his head and tied to the headboard, which was also wrought iron painted white.

He had never seen this room in his life.

The room looked like the sort he imagined you'd find in any cheap hotel that catered to hookers and dope dealers. He figured this had to be a drug plot. Otherwise why would a man who'd known he was Michael Barnes – or at least *Mr* Barnes – have hit him on the head with his own gun and then tied him to a bed in what was truly a very shitty room? A drug plot for sure. Paint peeling off the walls. A pile of dirty laundry in one corner of the room. No curtain or shade on the window leading to the fire escape. And – hanging crookedly on the wall beside the window – a framed and faded print of an Indian sitting on a spotted pony. Michael was really very surprised and disappointed by this totally shitty drug-plot room because the building itself had looked so nice from the street and the hallways had been so neat and clean, which proved you couldn't always judge a book by its cover.

He lifted his head again.

A closed door. The voices beyond it.

". . . in a garbage can someplace," the woman said.

". . . like behind a McDonald's."

". . . drive the cops nuts."

Three people in that other room. Two men and a woman. None of them sounded like anyone he'd ever met. All three of them were laughing now. They thought this would be comical. Driving the cops nuts.

"Or kill him and just leave him *here*," one of the men said. "In Ju Ju's bed."

They all thought this would be even more comical. Killing him and leaving him here in Ju Ju's bed. Was Ju Ju's bed the one he was tied to? The one that stank of piss? Was Ju Ju a cutesy-poo name for Judy Jordan? Was this, in fact, Judy Jordan's bedroom? Was Judy Jordan a bed-wetter? There was hysterical laughter in the other room now. It was contagious. Michael almost laughed himself. He had to stifle his laughter.

Michael wondered who Ju Ju was.

He hated movies with casts of thousands.

"We'd better wait till Mama gets here," the woman said.

Mama again.

The *woman's* mother?

Or did *everybody* call her Mama?

Maybe Connie was right. Maybe Mama was a big, fat lady who everyone—

Connie!

She'd told him if he wasn't back in ten minutes she'd come up and get him. How much time had gone by since he'd left her down there on the ground floor? Five minutes to climb to the third floor, another three minutes while he'd waited in the hallway for the naked woman to put on her—

The doorbell rang.

Oh, Jesus, he thought. Connie!

Or maybe Mama.

Either way, that ringing doorbell could only mean more trouble.

Because if the person doing the ringing was Connie, they would hit her on the head and then tie her up alongside him on the bed.

And then when Mama finally arrived, it would be so long to

169

both of them. Shoot them both and leave them in Ju Ju's bed, ha ha. Or else shoot them and drop them in a garbage can behind McDonald's, which would be almost as amusing. Michael found neither choice acceptable. Because if they were going to shoot anyone at all, he much preferred it to be himself alone, leave Connie out of this entirely. The doorbell kept ringing. He began actively wishing that one of them would go answer the door and it would be big, fat Mama standing there, Hi, kids, it's me.

"Who is it?" one of the men yelled.

"Abruzzi Pizzeria," someone yelled back.

Michael listened.

Someone was coming into the apartment.

"You order a large pizza?"

A delivery boy.

"That's right."

The woman. Obviously the one who'd placed the order.

"Half anchovies, half pepperoni?"

"Right."

"Three Cokes?"

"Three Cokes, right."

"Here's the napkins, that comes to thirteen dollars and twenty-one cents."

"That sounds like a lot," one of the men said.

"How do you figure it's a lot?" the delivery boy asked.

"For a pizza and three lousy Cokes? Thirteen bucks and change?"

"Yeah, but it's a large anchovies and pepperoni."

"Only *half* anchovies and *half* pepperoni."

"Which costs nine dollars and ninety-five cents. For the large with the anchovies and pepperoni."

"So how much are the Cokes?"

"Seventy-five cents each."

"That sounds high, too."

Cheap bastard, Michael thought.

"How do you figure that's high?" the delivery boy asked.

"For a lousy Coke? Seventy-five cents?"

"Yeah, but these are twelve-ounce Cokes."

"That's still high. That's six cents and change for an *ounce*!"

"Yeah, but that's what it *costs* an ounce," the delivery boy said.

"That's very high for an ounce of Coke."

"Yeah, but that's what it costs. Seventy-five cents for twelve ounces."

"So how do you get thirteen dollars and twenty-one cents?"

"There's an eight and a quarter percent tax. See it here on the bill? A dollar is the tax. So if you add a dollar to the nine ninety-five for the pizza and the two and a quarter for the Cokes, you get thirteen twenty-one. See it here?"

"Who added this?"

"The cashier."

"What's her name?"

"Marie. Why?"

"She's a penny off."

"What do you mean?"

"You see this here? Add it yourself. Nine ninety-five for the pizza, two twenty-five for the Cokes, and a dollar for the tax is thirteen dollars and *twenty* cents, not thirteen dollars and twenty-*one* cents."

"Gee," the delivery boy said.

"Tell Marie."

"I will."

Cheap bastard, Michael thought again.

"Here's fifty bucks," the man said. "Keep the change."

Michael heard the door opening and closing again.

The sudden aroma of cheese and garlic and tomatoes and pepperoni and anchovies wafted into the room where he was tied to the bed.

In that moment, he wanted nothing more from life than a slice of pizza.

If they told him they would kill him the moment Mama got here, his last request would be a slice of pizza.

"This is very good pizza," the woman said.

A rap sounded at the window.

He turned his head sharply.

A man wearing a black silk handkerchief over his nose and down to his chin was standing on the fire escape. He put his forefinger to where his lips would have been under the handkerchief, signaling Michael to keep quiet.

Michael looked at him.

The man was wearing a black cap to match the black handkerchief. And a black jacket bristling with little chrome studs. In keeping with his attire, the man himself was black, or at least what was nowadays *called* black even though his exposed hands were certainly not the color of his clothing. His hands were, in fact, the color of Colombian coffee.

The man hefted something onto the windowsill.

A black satchel.

He opened the satchel and took out some kind of black tool.

Terrific, Michael thought. A burglar.

In the other room, they began talking about pizza.

One of the men maintained that pizza with a thin crust was the best kind. The woman said she preferred her pizza with a thick crust. The other man said extra cheese was the secret. They all agreed that extra cheese was desirable on a pizza.

Michael was dying of hunger.

The black man was working on the window with the black tool, which Michael surmised was a jimmy.

"When we finish this pizza here," one of the men said, "I think we ought to go do him. Whether Mama's here or not."

Michael guessed they were talking about him.

About doing *him*.

"Anchovies I don't find too terrific on a pizza," the woman said.

"Me, neither, Alice," the other man said.

Alice.

The woman's name was Alice.

"They're too salty," she said.

"They overpower all the other ingredients," the man said, agreeing.

"Because the longer this man stays alive, the bigger the threat he is," the first man said, making a reasonable case.

"I think we should wait for Mama," Alice said.

"It was Mama sent you after him the first time," the other man said.

"I know that, Larry."

Larry. Another county heard from.

"So if Mama wanted him dead at eight o'clock tonight," he said, "why should it be any different now?"

"Because now is ten-thirty and not eight o'clock," Alice said.

"Which, by the way, you fucked up," the first man said. "On the roof there."

"No, by the way, I *didn't* fuck up, I was *ambushed*, Silvio."

So Alice was the blonde who'd been firing from the roof.

"Which it don't matter," Silvio said, "so long as we do the job right *this* time."

"That's *still* saying I did it wrong *last* time," Alice said.

"All I know is what Mama told me. Barnes was down Benny's asking questions about Arthur Crandall. So Barnes had to go. So you got sent to do him and you *didn't* do him, which is why he's tied to the bed in there now and you're telling me we should wait for Mama, which I don't know why."

"Because I say so," Alice said flatly.

"And I say we do him and leave him here in Ju Ju's bed," Silvio said, and they all burst out laughing again.

They were silent for the next few minutes or so.

Eating.

"As far as I'm concerned," Alice said, "the best combination is sausage and peppers."

"On a pizza, you mean?" Larry asked.

"No, on a piano," Alice said. "*Certainly* on a pizza. We're *talking* about pizza, aren't we?"

"I thought you were talking about a sandwich," Larry said.

"If you don't mind," Silvio said, "*I'm* talking about let's finish the goddamn *pizza* here and *do* the man, okay?"

"A grinder, I thought you meant," Larry said. "A sausage and pepper grinder."

"No, a pizza," Alice said. "Half sausage, half pepper."

Michael was hoping the burglar would hurry up and open the window. Then maybe he could talk the man into untying the ropes. Before they finished their pizza and came in here to do him. But the burglar seemed pretty new at the job. He had put the first tool back into the satchel and had taken out another one, but he didn't seem to be having any better luck with the new one. Meanwhile, in the other room, the pizza seemed to be dwindling. Michael was happy it had been a large one to begin with.

"Who wants this last slice?" Alice asked.

"Go ahead, take it," Larry said.

"Hey, *wait* a minute," Silvio said, "don't be so fucking generous with *my* pizza, if you don't mind."

"If you want it, take it," Alice said.

"Go ahead, Silvio, take it," Larry said.

"If Alice wants it, she can have it," Silvio said.

"No, this slice is all anchovies," Alice said.

"That's why I don't want it," Silvio said.

"I thought you *did* want it," Alice said.

"No, I only said he shouldn't be giving it away so fast in *case* I wanted it."

"Well, I don't want it," Alice said. "It's all anchovies."

"I don't want it, either," Larry said.

"Then the hell with it," Silvio said. "Throw it in the garbage, and let's go do him."

No, Michael thought. *Somebody* eat it. Please.

"Well, if nobody wants it," Alice said, "I'll take it."

"In fact, let's split it," Larry said.

"Three ways," Silvio said.

The window opened a crack. Cold air rushed into the room. And what smelled like fish. The black man all in black pushed the window up higher, letting in more cold air and the very definite stink of fish. He climbed over the sill and came into the room. Came directly to the bed. Pulled the handkerchief off his face, leaned in close to Michael's ear, and whispered, "Connie sent me."

"Untie me," Michael whispered.

In the other room, Silvio said, "It's a sin to let good food go to waste."

"This is very hard to cut," Larry said.

"Hold it with the fork," Alice said.

The black man began untying the ropes. He was no better at untying than he was at jimmying. In the other room, they were silent now. Michael figured they were concentrating on slicing the slice of pizza into three even slices, which was probably more difficult than untying a man tied to a bed. He hoped. He wished they would say something in there. The silence was somehow ominous. Maybe they had *already* sliced the slice of pizza and already eaten it. Maybe they were at this very moment loading pistols instead of slicing—

"Listen," he whispered, "don't you have a *knife* in that satchel?"

"This'll only take a minute," the black man whispered.

He had finally untied the first wrist.

That left two ankles and a wrist to go.

"Get the ankles," Michael said. "I'll try the other wrist."

"Did you hear something just then?" Larry asked.

Silence.

Oh, Jesus, Michael thought.

"No," Silvio said. "What did you hear?"

"Like somebody talking," Larry said.

"Where?"

"I don't know. Like next door."

They all listened again.

The black man had untied Michael's left ankle and was now working on the right one. Michael was plucking at the knots in the rope holding his left wrist to the headboard. He figured that in about two minutes he would be a dead man.

"I *still* don't hear anything," Silvio said.

"Are you going to finish these Cokes, or what?" Alice asked.

"I'm done," Larry said.

"Me, too," Silvio said.

"Me, too," the black man whispered.

So was Michael.

He yanked his left hand free of the rope, swung his legs over the side of the bed, and went immediately to the window. The black man was right behind him. As they went out onto the fire escape, Michael heard Silvio saying, "Let's go do him."

The black man's name was Gregory Washington.

The name of the club was the Green Garter.

Gregory told him that this was where Connie had said she would meet them. He also told Michael that the club was sometimes known as the Green *Farter* because it attracted a very old clientele. Michael looked around the place and did not see anyone who looked older than thirty. But Gregory was only nineteen.

A lot of the women standing at the bar, or sitting in the booths or at the tables, seemed to be wearing only lingerie. Garter belts and panties and seamed silk stockings and teddies and negligees and stiletto-heeled shoes that made them look a lot like either the redheaded detective named O'Brien, who'd mistaken him for a cheap hold-up artist, or the redheaded hooker named Hannah, who'd mistaken him for the man in the Carvel commercials. Michael wondered if Frankie Zeppelin had yet found someone to

175

kill Isadore Onions. He wondered whose thigh Isadore's girlfriend had her hand on now. He wondered if all the women in New York City walked around in their underwear at Christmastime.

"You have adorable buns," Gregory said. "Has anyone ever told you that?"

Which was when Michael began to suspect that both Gregory and the Green Garter were what you might call gay, and that all these underdressed women were in actuality men.

One of them winked at him.

"Oh, look," Gregory said. "Phyllis has her eye on you."

He sounded like Eddie Murphy doing his gay bit in *Beverly Hills Cop*. In fact, he even looked a little like a younger Eddie Murphy, if there *was* such a thing as a younger Eddie Murphy. It seemed to Michael that nowadays there were no male movie stars who were his age. All the male movie stars up there on the screen were twenty years old. Making love to stark-naked women who had to be at least in their thirties. The only twenty-year-old movie stars Michael believed were the ones in war movies because in Vietnam almost everybody was twenty years old or younger. Even the lieutenants were twenty years old. The only people who weren't twenty years old were sergeants.

Phyllis winked at him again.

Phyllis was wearing a blonde wig, a red silk blouse, and a green silk skirt with high-heeled pumps to match. Most of the people in the room, Michael noticed, were dressed in either red or green in honor of the yuletide season, except for the ones who were wearing swastikas and chains and jeans and black leather jackets bristling with metal spikes and studs. They looked tougher and meaner than any man Michael had ever seen in his life, but he guessed they were gay, too, otherwise what were they doing here?

Which was probably what Phyllis, who needed a shave, was wondering about him.

"What time did Connie say she'd be here?" he asked.

"Soon as she does what she has to do," Gregory said.

"What is it she has to do?" Michael asked.

"Find out who the corpse is."

"And how does she plan to do that?"

"At the Gouverneur Hospital morgue," Gregory said. "On Henry Street. 'Cause the corpse was found in the Seventh Precinct, and that's the only hospital in the Seventh, so she figured that's where they must've took it. She knows a man there works with the stiffs."

"So that's where she is now," Michael said.

"Lucky her," Gregory said, and grinned.

"Excuse me," Michael said, "but how do *you* fit into all this?"

"Oh, very comfortably," Gregory said, and looked around the room. "I been comin' here since it opened."

"I meant, how did you happen to get the job of rescuing me?"

"Oh, Connie asked me to climb on up there."

"Why you? Are you a burglar?"

"No, I'm a dancer."

"I still don't understand how Connie knew I was in trouble."

"Well, from what she told *me*, she was waiting outside the Amalgamated when she saw this man carrying you out of the building. Unconscious. You, not the man. So she followed his car to this warehouse near the Fulton Market. The *fish* market. On Fulton Street. And that's how come you're sitting here with me now, doll."

"Connie just ran into you, is that it? And asked you to . . ."

"No, she called me on the telephone."

"And you ran on over with your satchel . . ."

"I borrowed the satchel from my brother-in-law."

"Is he a dancer, too?"

"No, *he's* a burglar. But he's white, you wouldn't *'spect* him to have no rhythm."

"So Connie called you . . ."

"Right, and asked me to meet her at this warehouse, where she was waiting outside."

"How'd she know what apartment I was in?"

"It isn't an apartment building, it's a warehouse. She watched the elevator needle. And I went up the fire escape to the fifth floor, where I found you, aren't you glad?"

"You mean to tell me Connie just picked up the telephone, and you ran on down to meet her?"

"I owe her," Gregory said, and left it at that.

"Well, I'm grateful to you."

"*How* grateful?" Gregory said, and was putting his hand on Michael's thigh when Phyllis walked over.

"Won't you introduce me, Greg?" she said.

"Michael, this is Phyllis," Gregory said, and squeezed Michael just above the knee.

"Care to dance, Michael?"

Michael figured he could do worse.

"Do you come here often?" Phyllis asked.

She was a very good dancer.

The jukebox was playing "It Happened in Monterey." Frank Sinatra was singing.

"My first time," Michael said.

"You have adorable buns," Phyllis said. "Has anyone ever told you that?"

"Yes, as a matter of fact," Michael said.

"Oh my, she's modest as well," Phyllis said.

Her beard was scratching against Michael's cheek.

"Are you married?" Phyllis asked.

"Divorced," he said.

"Oh, good," Phyllis said.

"But very serious about someone," Michael said quickly.

"Oh, drat," Phyllis said.

"May I cut in, please?" someone asked.

The someone was Connie.

"I said the Green *Garden*," she said.

13

The three of them sat in a booth.

Connie was irritated because Gregory had taken Michael to the Green Garter instead of the Green Garden, which was a health food place on Orchard Street, and a hell of a lot closer to Gouverneur Hospital than Greenwich Avenue was.

"It all gets down to a matter of precincts," she said. "The Sixth Precinct is *not* the Seventh Precinct. If I'd wanted the Green *Garter* in the *Sixth* Precinct, I wouldn't have picked the Green *Garden* in the *Seventh* Precinct."

"I'm contrite," Gregory said.

He wasn't being sarcastic, he really did sound enormously sorry for his error. Moreover, as Michael now reminded Connie, he was the one who'd charged to the rescue when –

"Well, not exactly *charged*," Gregory said modestly.

"But Michael's right," Connie said. "I'm sorry I yelled at you."

"It's the stink of the morgue," Gregory said. "Have you ever been inside a morgue?" he asked Michael.

"Never."

"About two years ago," Gregory said, "a friend of mine OD'd on heroin, and I had to go to the morgue to identify him. It truly does stink in there. It can give you a headache in there. It can also make you very anxious. All those dead people stacked up on drawers that slide out."

"Don't remind me," Connie said.

Michael was thinking that at times the stench in Vietnam had been unbearable. He could not imagine any morgue in the world

179

stinking more than a jungle clearing littered with three-day-old bodies.

"He didn't even *look* like Crandall," Connie said.

"You saw him?" Michael asked.

"Yes. A tall, thin man. Pockmarked face. Tattoo on his arm."

"White?"

"Yes. But that's the only resemblance."

"How old was he?"

"My friend at the morgue guessed maybe forty, forty-five."

"What's his name?"

"Max Feinstein. I know him from when he was driving an ambulance for . . ."

"No, I mean the corpse."

"Oh. Julian Rainey. They finally identified him from his finger-prints. He has a record that goes back forever."

"Yes, he's a dealer," Gregory said, nodding.

"*Was* a dealer," Connie corrected. "You mean you *know* him?"

"Oh, yes, he works this entire downtown area."

"*Used* to work," Connie corrected.

A drug plot, Michael thought. I knew it.

"A red heart, am I right?" Gregory said. "The tattoo?"

"Yes," Connie said.

"On his left arm."

"The left arm, yes."

"And in the heart it says Ju Ju, am I right?"

"I don't know what it said in the heart."

"Ju Ju. That's his nickname."

"*Was* his nickname," Connie corrected.

Michael was looking at both of them.

"I think we have to go back to that warehouse," he said.

"Without me," Gregory said.

It was close to midnight when they got there.

Christmas was almost gone.

Not a light showed in the entire building.

"That's because nobody lives here," Connie explained. "This is a *real* warehouse, it's not like the buildings they're renting for lofts all over town. People actually store things here."

"What do you suppose Ju Ju was storing here?" Michael asked.

"Take a wild guess," Connie said.

Michael looked up at the front of the building. It was seven stories high, with five evenly spaced windows on each floor. From the fifth floor down, huge white letters below the windows announced the building's original intent, stating its past like a huge poster that faced the East River:

WAREHOUSE
Wholesale–Retail
OFFICE FURNITURE
Broad Street Showrooms
NEW YORK–MIAMI–LOS ANGELES

The entire area smelled of fish.

"We're just a few blocks from the market," Connie said.

The metal entrance door was locked.

"It was open earlier tonight," she said. "It's on the fifth floor. I watched the needle."

They were both getting very good at using fire escapes. Michael figured that if ever they were trapped in a burning building together, they'd know how to get out of it in a minute. He supposed it was good to know such things. On the fifth floor, they found the window Gregory had earlier jimmied open. It was closed now. Michael guessed the three pizza-eaters had closed it after they'd come into the room and found only Ju Ju's bed with no one in it. He hoped the pizza-eaters were not still here. He did not think they were: not a light was burning anywhere inside. But you never could tell; in Vietnam, Charlie could see in the dark.

He eased the window open.

Listened.

Not a sound.

He climbed in over the sill, and then helped Connie into the room.

They waited, eyes adjusting to the darkness, moonlight slowly giving shapes to objects . . .

First the bed with its white wrought-iron headboard and foot-board . . .

Then the bundle of clothes in the corner . . .

And then the Indian sitting his spotted pony.

181

Nothing else.

"I think somebody peed in this room," Connie whispered.

It was not truly a *room*, Michael now realized, but merely a space defined by a partition. The door to the other side of the partition was slightly ajar. No light beyond it. He went to the door and listened. He heard nothing. He nodded to Connie and opened the door wider. Together they moved into the space beyond the partition. And waited again while their eyes adjusted to what seemed a deeper blackness but only because of its vastness. When Michael felt certain they were alone, he groped along the wall for a switch, found one, and turned on the lights.

If he'd expected a cocaine factory, he was disappointed.

From the evidence here on this side of the partition, you would never have guessed that Ju Ju Rainey was a drug dealer. For here was a department store of the first order, stocked with television sets and cameras, record players and home computers, typewriters and silverware, fur coats and jewelry, cellular telephones—

"A fence," Connie said. "Lots of dealers accept goods in exchange for dope."

A drug plot after all, Michael thought.

There were windows on the wall facing the street. Distant traffic lights below tinted the glass alternately red and green. It was still Christmas, but just barely. The wall opposite the windows was lined with clocks. They ticked in concert like a conglomerate time bomb about to explode. Grandfather clocks ticking and tocking and swinging their pendulums, smaller clocks on shelves whispering their ticks into the vast silent room.

On a table near the metal entrance door on the right-angled wall, there was a tomato-stained and empty pizza carton and three empty Coke bottles. A green metal file cabinet was on the wall near an open door that led to the toilet. On the other side of the door, there was a huge black safe with the word MOSLER stamped on its front.

Michael went to the file cabinet and pulled open the top drawer. A glance at one of the folders told him that this was where Ju Ju Rainey kept his inventory records. A methodical receiver of stolen goods. The bottom drawer was locked.

"Do you know how to do something like that?" Connie asked.

"Like what?"

"Like pick a lock?"

"No," Michael said.

"Let's see if anybody brought in a set of tools," Connie said.

They began rummaging through the stolen goods as if they were at a tag sale. It was sort of nice. Shopping this way, you could forget that dead bodies were involved. Like that day in the jungle. With the baby. Not a thought of danger, Charlie was miles and miles away. Just strolling in the jungle. Birds twittering in the treetops. Andrew smoking a cigarette, the baby suddenly—

He turned off all thoughts of the baby.

Click.

Snapped them off.

Connie had stopped at a pipe rack from which hung at least a hundred fur coats.

The baby crying.

Click.

"This is gorgeous," Connie said.

She was looking at a long red fox coat.

Michael moved away from her, deeper into what looked like a smaller version of the *Citizen Kane* storehouse. There was a makeshift counter – sawhorses and planks – covered entirely with Walkman radios. There had to be at least a thousand Walkman radios on that counter. All sizes and all colors. Michael wondered if all those radios had come from a single industrious thief. Or had a thousand less ambitious thieves each stolen one radio? Another counter was covered entirely with books. It looked like a counter in a bookshop. Very big and important books like *Warday* and *Women's Work* and *Whirlwind* were piled high on the counter. Michael could easily understand why someone would want to steal these precious books and why Ju Ju had been willing to take them in trade for dope. He'd probably planned to resell them later to a bookseller who had a blanket on the sidewalk outside Saks Fifth Avenue.

Connie was lingering at the fur-coat rack. In fact she was now trying *on* one of the coats, which he hoped she didn't plan to steal. The temptation to steal something from a thief was, in fact, overwhelming. The goods, after all, were not the thief's. The thief, therefore, could not rightfully or even righteously claim that anything of his had been stolen, since the stolen goods had already been stolen from someone else. Moreover, the transaction by which the thief had come into possession of the property was in itself an illegal one, the barter of stolen goods for controlled substances, and the thief could expect no mercy on that count. Especially if he was dead, which Ju Ju Rainey happened to be. On the other hand, if it was okay to steal stolen goods from a dead thief, then maybe it was also okay to have *caused* that thief's death, and to have put another man's identification on his corpse, and to have laid the blame on a third person entirely, which third person happened to be Michael himself. It was all a matter of morality, he guessed.

The coat Connie was trying on happened to be a very dark and luxuriant ankle-length sable.

The coat was screaming, "Steal Me, Steal Me!"

He hoped she wouldn't.

The baby screaming.

Click.

"I would love a coat like this," Connie said.

Michael was at a counter covered with musical instruments now. There were violins and violas and cellos and bass fiddles and even lyres. There were piccolos and oboes and saxophones and clarinets and English horns and bassoons and flutes. There was an organ. There were acoustic guitars and electric guitars and banjos and mandolins and a pedal steel guitar and a synthesizer and a sitar and an Appalachian dulcimer. There was a set of drums. And three bagpipes. And fourteen harmonicas and a book called *How to Play Jazz Harp*, which had wandered over from the book display across the room. There were trumpets and sousaphones and tubas and French horns and cornets and bugles and seventy-six trombones. Michael guessed it was profitable to steal musical instruments.

The next counter was covered with tools. More tools than he had ever seen in one place in his entire lifetime. He guessed it was profitable to steal tools, too. On the other hand, maybe it was profitable to steal *anything*. There were hammers and hatchets and mallets and mauls. There were pliers and wrenches and handsaws and drills. There were planes and rasps and chisels and files. There were circular saws and scroll saws and electric sanders and electric chain saws. Michael picked up one of the electric hand drills and a small plastic case with bits in it, and carried them to where Connie was now standing at a table covered with weapons.

"Look at all these guns," she said.

"Yes," he said.

There were revolvers and automatic pistols of every size and caliber and make. Smith & Wesson, Colt, Browning, Walther, Ruger, Harrington & Richardson, Hi-Standard, Iver Johnson, you name it, you had it. There were rifles and shotguns, too – Remington, and Winchester, and Mossberg, and Marlin, and Savage, Stevens & Fox. And there were several military weapons as well, guns Michael recognized as AK-47 assault rifles and AR-15 semi-automatics. Rambo would have felt right at home at this counter. Rambo could have picked up an entire attack arsenal at this counter.

"I think we can drill out the lock with this," Michael said.

"Is it a crime to steal stolen goods?" Connie asked.

"Yes," he said.

"Is what I thought," she said.

He walked past her to where the filing cabinet stood against the wall. He opened the little plastic case, and was searching for a bit he hoped would tear through the metal lock on the cabinet, when Connie joined him, her hands in the pockets of the short black car coat. Michael chose his bit, fitted it into the chuck collar, tightened the collar with a chuck key, found a wall outlet near the cabinet, knelt to plug in the drill, tested it to see if he had power, and then went back to the cabinet. Connie was still standing there with her hands in her pockets. He studied the lock for a moment, and got to work.

The bit snarled into the metal.

There was a high whining sound.

Baby over there, Andrew was saying.

Where?

Over there. Crying.

Curls of metal spun out from behind the bit.

The lock disintegrated.

Michael yanked open the drawer.

They were looking in at an open shoe box containing two little plastic vials of crack.

"Must've used all his dope to pay for the merchandise in here," Michael said.

"Either that, or there's *more* dope someplace else."

"Like where?"

"Like where would *you* keep a whole bunch of crack?"

Michael looked at the safe.

"Do you know how to do something like that?" Connie asked.

"No," Michael said.

"I didn't think so."

"But I have a question."

"Yes?"

"Would you lock a file drawer that had nothing but two vials of crack in it?"

Connie looked at him.

"Neither would I," he said.

He knelt down beside the file cabinet, lifted the shoe box, turned it upside down, and looked at it. Nothing. He ran his hands along the bottom and back of the drawer, and then moved them forward along each side of the drawer to the front of it, and then felt along the back of the front panel and—

"Here it is," he said.

He bent over the drawer and looked into it.

Scotch-taped to the back of the panel was a slip of paper. It was fastened upside down, so that the writing on it could be read easily from above. It read:

> 4 L 28
> 3 R 73
> 2 L 35
> Slow R Open

"You're so smart," Connie said. "Do you know it's almost midnight?"

"Is it?"

"Only a minute left."

He looked at his watch.

"Yes," he said.

"And then Christmas will be gone. Forty seconds, actually."

"Yes."

"Do you remember what we did last night at this time?"

"I remember."

"I think we should do it again, don't you?" she said, and put her arms around his neck. "Make it a tradition."

Their lips met.

And even as bells had sounded when they'd kissed last night in

Crandall's office, and even as bells had sounded when Michael left the Mazeltov All-Nite Deli, so did bells sound now. This time, however, the bells were not on a ringing telephone, and they weren't attached to a trip mechanism on an emergency door, they were instead the bells and gongs and chimes on the multitude of stolen clocks that lined the wall opposite the windows. This was a symphony of bells. This was bells pealing out into the vastness of the warehouse, floating out over the rows and rows of stolen items, reverberating on the dust-laden air, enveloping Connie and Michael in layers and layers of shimmering sound where they stood in embrace alongside a stolen Apple IIe computer, their lips locked, bong bong went the bells, tinkle tinkle went the chimes, bing bang bong went every clock in the place, announcing the end of Christmas Day, heralding the twenty-sixth day of December, a bright new Monday morning in a world of abundant riches, witness all the shiny new merchandise here in the late Ju Ju Rainey's storeroom. And suddenly the bells stopped. Not all at once since the clocks weren't in absolute synchronization, but trailing off instead, a bong clanking heavily, a chime chinging tinnily, a dissonant bing here, a reluctant tink there, and then stillness.

"It's Boxing Day, you know," she said.

"I didn't know," he said.

"Yes," she said. "The day after Christmas. It's called Boxing Day."

"I see."

"I know because it's celebrated in Hong Kong, which is still a British colony."

"Why is it called Boxing Day?"

"Because they have prizefights on that day. Throughout the entire British Empire."

"I see," he said.

They were still standing very close to each other. He wondered if anyone had ever made love to Connie on a counter bearing stolen Cuisinarts.

"Listen," she said.

He remembered that she had terrific ears.

"The elevator," she said. "Someone's using the elevator."

He listened.

He could hear the elevator whining up the shaft.

The baby sitting just off the trail.

Crying.

The elevator stopped.

He heard its doors opening.

Footsteps in the corridor now.

Voices just outside the metal entrance door to Ju Ju's bargain bazaar.

When you were outnumbered, you headed for the high ground. The highest ground here was the rack holding all those expensive fur coats. He took Connie's hand, and led her silently and swiftly across the room, moving past a table bearing a sextant, an outboard engine, an anchor, a compass, and a paddle, and then past another table upon which there were . . .

A key turning in the door lock.

. . . seven baseball bats, three gloves, a catcher's mitt and mask, a lacrosse stick, and a pair of running shoes . . .

Tumblers falling with a small, oiled click.

. . . and reached the end of the rack where a seal coat with a raccoon collar was hanging.

The door opened.

"Who left these lights on?" a woman said.

Michael knew that voice.

He could not see her from where he was hunched over behind what looked like a lynx jacket, but this was Alice the Pizza Maven, who was also the lady who owned the Mannlicher-Schoenauer carbine with its Kahle scope, which she'd fired from the rooftop at them earlier today – or yesterday, as it now was officially – which gun was now snug in its case in Connie's bedroom closet, which was where Michael now wished *he* was. Because the next voice he heard belonged to Silvio, who had earlier thought it would be hilarious to kill Michael and leave him either in Ju Ju's piss-stinking bed or else in a garbage can behind McDonald's. And the voice after that was Larry's, both men now vigorously denying that either of them had left the lights on.

"In which case," Alice wanted to know, "how come the lights *are* on?"

There was dead silence.

Michael wondered if he and Connie should have gone to hide in the bathroom.

"Check out the toilet," Alice said.

He guessed it was good they hadn't gone to hide in the bathroom.

Silence.

The sound of metal rings scraping along a shower rod as the curtain was thrown back.

More silence.

"So?" Alice asked.

"Nobody in there."

"Check out the whole floor," Alice said.

And suddenly there were more voices.

A man said, "All this stuff has to go, huh?"

"All of it," Alice said.

"The piano, too?" a second man said. "'Cause we ain't piano movers, you know."

"That's good," Silvio said, "'cause it ain't a piano."

"Then what is it, it ain't a piano?"

"It's an organ."

"Take *this* organ," the man said.

"If you don't mind," Larry said, "there's a lady present here."

"So?"

"So stop grabbing your balls and telling us what's an organ."

"I'm telling you we ain't piano movers."

"And I'm telling you it's an organ."

"And I'm telling you take *this* organ."

"Just shoot him in the balls," Alice said calmly.

"Some lady," the man said, but presumably he let go of his balls.

A third man said, "Okay, where's all this stuff has to go?"

A fourth man said, "Look at this joint, willya? What's this, a discount store?"

A fifth man said, "You want this stuff boxed?"

"What's breakable," Alice said. "And wrapped, too."

"What's that?" the third man asked. "A *piano*?"

"I already told them," the second man said.

"'Cause we don't move pianos," the third man said.

"It's an organ," Silvio said, "and don't reach for your balls."

"My father used to play drums," the fifth man said.

The first man said, "Why don't Mama move in the daytime, like a normal human being?"

Larry said, "Whyn't you go take that up with Mama, okay?"

"No, thank you," the man said.

"Then get to work," Larry said.

"Where's that combo?" Alice asked somebody.

"I got it," Silvio said.

"If he was gonna give you the combo, anyway," Larry said, "why you suppose he wet the bed?"

They all began laughing.

Even the moving men.

"'Cause if you wet the bed," Silvio said, laughing, "then a person won't shoot you."

"It's a magic charm," Alice said, laughing. "You wet the bed, the bad guys'll go away."

"First time I ever had a man wet the bed before I shot him," Silvio said, still laughing.

"Give me the combo," Alice said.

"I tell you," one of the moving men said, "this wasn't Mama, I wouldn't go near that piano."

"You could get a hernia from that piano," another one of the men said.

"It's an *organ*," Silvio said, but his voice was muffled and Michael guessed he was standing at the safe with his back turned. From where Michael crouched behind the furs with Connie, he felt like Cary Grant in *Gunga Din*, the scene where the three of them are hiding in the temple and all the lunatics are yelling "Kali!"

"Read it to me," Alice said.

"Four left to twenty-eight," Silvio said.

"Look at this, willya?" one of the moving men said. "Roller skates, ice skates, dart boards, a pool table . . ."

"I ain't lifting that pool table, I can tell you that."

"That's heavier than the piano."

"It's an organ," Silvio said over his shoulder. "Three right to seventy-three."

"What's *this* thing?"

"A toboggan."

"What do you do with it?"

"Two left to thirty-five," Silvio said.

"I never seen so much stuff in my life."

"And this is what's left *after* Christmas, don't forget."

"Slowly to the right till it opens," Silvio said.

Silence.

Then:

"Holy shit!"

This from Larry.

More silence.

"That's got to be at least a million dollars' worth of dope," Alice said.

Yep, Michael thought. A dope plot.

"I thought Mama said Ju Ju was only small-time," Silvio said.

"Mama was wrong," Larry said.

"Or lying," Alice said, and there was another silence.

A longer one this time. A contemplative one. A pregnant one. The silence of thieves considering whether another thief had screwed them. It was an interesting silence, laden with possibilities. Michael waited. Connie squeezed his hand. She had understood the silence, too.

"Maybe Mama didn't know there'd be so much stuff in the box," Larry said.

"Maybe," Alice said.

She did not sound convinced.

Silence again.

All three of them were trying to figure it out.

"Listen, we ain't touching that pool table," one of the moving men said. "There's slate in that table, it weighs a ton."

"Fine," Alice said.

"Damn straight," the moving man said.

Silence except for the sound of newspapers being crumpled, cartons being snapped open, work shoes moving across the floor, men grunting as they lifted heavy objects.

"We got paid," Larry said.

A shrug in his voice.

"But did we get paid *enough*?"

This from Alice.

"The deal was to deliver Ju Ju," Larry said. "That's what we done."

Trying to make peace.

But he was standing with the rest of them at that safe, and he was looking in at what Alice had described as at least a million dollars' worth of dope.

"That was the *original* deal," Larry said.

"The deal changed yesterday," Alice said.

"The deal changed to doing Barnes, too."

"And cleaning out Ju Ju's store."

"Was what the deal changed to."

"But did Mama know there'd be all this stuff in Ju Ju's box?"

They were all silent again.

"The answer is no," Alice said.

Silence.

"Because I'll tell you why."

Michael was extremely interested in hearing why.

"Because if *you* were Mama," Alice said, "would *you* trust the three of *us* with a million dollars' worth of dope?"

They all began laughing.

Michael nodded in agreement.

"Sure, laugh," one of the moving men said. "It ain't you three gonna get the hernia."

"What I think," Alice said, "I think the trucks can deliver all this fine merchandise to Mama . . ."

"As agreed," Silvio said.

"But *us* three will take what's in the box here, how does that sound to you?"

"It sounds only fair to me," Silvio said.

"More than," Larry said.

"But who left on the lights?" Alice asked.

14

Michael thought it was a bad idea to be standing here behind all these dead animal skins. He should have been standing at the table with the weapons instead. Because Alice and her two chums were now fanning out over the warehouse floor, earnestly trying to determine who had left the lights on.

He guessed this was going to be a process of elimination.

This was going to be Gee, it wasn't *us* who left the lights on, and it couldn't have been the moving men, so it had to have been someone else. And maybe the someone else is still in here. Like maybe hiding behind the counter over there, upon which were displayed six Tandberg FM tuners, three Nakamichi cassette decks, and a Denon direct-drive turntable.

A woman came around that counter now.

Alice.

For sure.

The same woman who'd been firing at them from the rooftop.

The long blonde hair and slitted blue eyes, the delicate Michael Jackson nose, the pale ivory oval of her face. In her hand, a gun that looked foreign. She could have been playing a Russian assassin in a James Bond movie. It was bad enough, however, that she was an American assassin in a real-life drama starring Michael Barnes and Connie—

It occurred to him that Connie was no longer at his side.

Before he had time to wonder how or when she'd disappeared, he saw a short, thickset man coming around the sleeve of a chinchilla coat hanging at the far end of the rack. Except for his broken nose, the man looked a lot like Tony the Bear Orso or Charlie Bonano, both of whom looked like Rocky's brother-in-law. He had a gun in his hand. Michael guessed this was Silvio.

"Hey!" Silvio yelled, if that's who he was, and Michael immediately slipped between a Siberian yellow weasel coat and a Persian lamb, brushing past the furs and through the rack to emerge on the opposite side where a tall, angular, craggy-faced blondish man who looked like Sterling Hayden in *The Godfather* was coming around the end of a table upon which was displayed an open coffin with no one in it.

Michael figured he himself would soon be displayed in that coffin, which was made of fine mahogany and lined with white silk and hung with bronze handles.

If the other one was Silvio, then this one was Larry.

So there was Silvio coming through the rack of furs farther up the line now, emerging between a Mexican ocelot and a Mongolian marmot, and here was Larry spotting Michael now and also shouting "Hey!" and here, too, was Alice coming around the home entertainment center display and seeing Michael, and grinning like an African lioness contemplating a warthog dinner. Michael figured this was it. The full deck had been dealt at last and there were no more aces in it.

"Freeze!" a voice said.

It sounded like Detective O'Brien.

But it was Connie.

Standing with a gun in each hand.

Behind Alice and Larry, who had probably heard that word a great many times in their separate careers and who did not move a muscle when they heard it now. Coming through the rack swathed in furs left and right, Silvio froze, too. Connie looked like the Dragon Lady. Cool and beautiful and deadly. Ready to blow away anyone who did not take her by overnight junk to Shanghai. The guns were only .22 caliber revolvers, but in her delicate hands they looked like big mother-loving cannons.

"Help us here!" Alice shouted to the moving men, but they, too, had seen the guns in Connie's hands and the look in her eyes, and they had heard the word "Freeze!" thundering like a Chinese curse into that echoing space, and when they'd realized that they themselves were not the ones being asked to freeze, they decided

194

this might be a good time to get the hell out of here before someone asked them to move a piano. There was a rush toward the metal entrance door, now an exit door too narrow to accommodate the sudden traffic. The moving men piled into the doorway like Keystone Kops, wedging themselves there for an impossibly tangled moment, unraveling themselves, and then hurling themselves headlong into the corridor outside.

Larry shook his head in dismay when he heard the elevator starting. Still shaking his head, he dropped his gun to the floor and looked at his watch, probably wondering if Johnny Carson was still on. Silvio raised his hands over his head. He looked like a man who did not have to be told that Chinese people stuck bamboo under your fingernails. Especially Chinese women. Or maybe it was the Japanese who did that. Either way, he wanted nothing further to do with this entire enterprise.

Only Alice seemed undecided.

Michael had his doubts as well.

Which was why he was moving so swiftly toward Connie.

Because it was one thing to have a look on your face that said handling a gun was second nature to you and you'd as soon shoot a person as treat him to an ice cream cone, but it was another thing to be *holding* a gun as if you'd never had one in your hand before. Connie was holding those pistols the way Crandall had held the .32 last night. They were both amateurs. Michael recognized this because when it came to oranges or guns, he was a pro. But so was Alice. And in thirty seconds flat, she was going to recognize that Connie didn't know a trigger from a click sight. In fact, the knowledge was seeping into her eyes that very instant, and Michael knew he had to reach Connie and grab one of those guns from her before Alice made her play.

She moved sooner than he'd expected.

Didn't say a word.

Merely fired at Connie.

And missed.

And was sighting along the gun barrel to fire again when Michael realized that this was not a time for dueling in the sun, this was a time for definitive action – like throwing himself at her. He flung himself sideways, hoping to knock her off balance and realizing an instant too late that he was rushing her with his bad side, rushing her with the bandaged shoulder and arm that had been injured by one of those *Car 54*, Seventh Precinct cops – where were they now, when he needed them? He let out a horrible yell, similar to the "Aiiii–eeeeee!" he'd screamed at Detective O'Brien all those years ago on Christmas Eve, but this one was involuntary in that the body contact with Alice sent arrows of pain shooting from his arm clear up into his skull. There was another gunshot, and he thought, *Oh, Jesus, no!* and then Alice screamed and he thought it was because his own scream had frightened her the way it had earlier frightened O'Brien. But his hands where he grabbed for Alice were suddenly sticky and wet, and he realized all at once that Connie had actually *fired* one of those guns, Connie had actually *shot* Alice, who was stumbling backward now as Michael stumbled forward. He said something like "Watch it," or "What shit," and Alice very *definitely* said, "What shit," and then both of them collapsed to the floor in a hurt and bewildered heap.

Connie was on them in an instant.

Legs widespread.

Both guns angled down at Alice's head.

"One move," she said.

"Don't get dramatic," Alice said, and tossed her gun onto the floor.

She was bleeding from the shoulder.

"It went off," Connie explained.

"I see that," Michael said.

"Remember when I asked you if it was a crime to steal stolen goods? That's when I stole them. From the table. Because he who gathers up his nuts need never leave his hole."

"If you don't mind," Larry said, "there's a lady present here."

"Get me a doctor," Alice said.

Michael wondered if Dr Ling would make a house call all the way over here in the First Precinct.

"Who's Mama?" he asked.

"Go fuck yourself," Alice said.

"Tch," Larry said, and rolled his eyes.

Silvio still had his hands up in the air.

"Can I put my hands down, lady?" he asked. "Or shall *I* go fuck myself, too?"

"You can put them down," Connie said.

"First promise me no bamboo shoots," Silvio said.

"What?" Connie said.

"And no MSG," Larry said. "It's the MSG gives you headaches."

"Keep your hands up," Michael said. "Who's Mama?"

"*Quien sabe?*" Silvio said.

"Are you Spanish?" Michael asked.

"No, I'm Italian. But everybody knows what *quien sabe* means."

"Sure," Larry said. "It's what Tonto calls the Lone Ranger."

"Anyway," Alice said testily, "we don't know who Mama is, and please get me a goddamn doctor."

"Why are you trying to kill us?" Michael asked.

"*We're* trying to kill *you*?" Alice said. "This Asian person almost takes off my arm with that *weapon* in her hand, and *we're* trying to kill *you*?"

"That's certainly comical, all right," Larry said, shaking his head in wonder.

"Can I put my hands down?" Silvio asked.

"No," Michael said. "Who's Mama?"

"Call a doctor," Alice said.

"No. Who is she?"

"Call the police, too. I want to press charges against this illegal alien."

"I'm legal," Connie said.

"Sure. So's Mama."

"Go ahead, tell them," Larry said, shaking his head again.

"I didn't tell them anything."

"You told them Mama's an illegal alien."

"No, *you* just told them."

"*I* said Mama's illegal?"

"An illegal alien, is *exactly* what you said."

"Did I say that?" Larry asked, turning to Silvio.

"How come everybody can put their hands down but me?" Silvio asked.

"If I bleed to death here, they'll deport you," Alice said to Connie.

"Let's talk a deal," Michael said. "If you had one wish in the whole world, and you could get that wish by telling us who Mama is, what would that wish be?"

"Could I please put my hands down?" Silvio said.

"Yes," Michael said.

"You just blew your wish, dummy," Larry said.

"That wasn't my wish," Silvio said, shaking his hands out from the wrists. "That was just a polite request."

"Just get me a doctor," Alice said.

"Is that your wish?"

"I wish my mother would go back to Palermo," Silvio said.

"I wish she'd take *my* mother with her," Larry said, and both men burst out laughing.

Alice laughed, too.

Blood was trickling from her left shoulder, but she suddenly began laughing along with her buddies. Michael was thinking it would be fun to work with these three if only they weren't killers. He tried to remember if any of it had been fun in Vietnam. Working with the killers there. He guessed maybe some of it had been fun. Before the baby.

Hell she doing out here? Andrew asked.

The baby crying.

Must've crawled out from the village, the RTO said.

"Who's Mama?" Michael said.

"You want to get us all killed?" Larry asked.

"I'll tell you what I'm going to do," Michael said. "I'm going to make the wish *for* you, okay? I'm going to wish that I don't go to that phone on the wall there, and call the police, and tell them to come up here and get you, that's what I'm going to wish."

"First Precinct," Connie said. "I have the number in my book."

"Go ahead, call them," Alice said.

"I keep all the precinct numbers handy," Connie said. "In case I get a weirdo. I know all the desk sergeants down here."

"Do you know Tony Orso?" Michael asked.

"No. Is he a desk sergeant?"

"No."

"Then I don't know him."

"Tony the Bear Orso."

"No."

"I know him," Silvio said.

"So do I," Larry said.

"Do you know Detective Daniel Cahill?" Michael asked.

"Go call all these cops, why don't you?" Alice said. "Tell them your Chink girlfriend tried to kill me."

"How would you like a punch in the mouth?" Connie asked pleasantly.

"Go ahead, hit me. That'll look good on your record, too."

"Detective Cahill?" Michael said. "Ring a bell?"

"There was a cop up Sing Sing named Cahill," Larry said.

"No, that was Cromwell," Silvio said.

"Oh, yeah," Larry said, and nodded and smiled, as though fondly remembering Sing Sing.

"How about you, Alice?" Michael asked.

"How about me, what? I'm bleeding to death here, that's how about me."

"Do you know anybody named Cahill?"

"No."

"How about Helen Parrish?"

"No."

"Charlie Nichols?"

"No."

"Did you kill Charlie Nichols?"

"How could I kill somebody I don't even know?"

"Charlie Nichols. Mama sent you to kill him, didn't she?"

"This man is deaf," Alice said to the air. "I'm telling you I don't *know* anybody by that name."

"Charlie Nichols. An actor."

"Is he related to Charlie Belafonte?"

"You mean *Harry* Belafonte," Larry said. "I know because his name is almost like mine."

"Can you sing 'Day-O'?" Silvio asked him.

"Charlie Nichols?" Michael said. "Nice little apartment in Knickerbocker Village?"

"Where's that? Westchester County?"

"The Fifth Precinct," Connie said.

"Go ahead, call the cops," Alice said.

"How about Judy Jordan?" Michael asked.

"Call her, too."

"Do you know her?"

"I don't know *any* of these people. Go call the goddamn cops. Just for spite, I'll be dead when they get here."

"Good," Connie said.

"You don't know any of them, huh?" Michael asked.

"You're deaf, am I right?" she said, and turned to Larry. "He's deaf."

"My uncle in Chicago is deaf, too," Larry said sympathetically.

"And I suppose you don't know anything about what happened to me on Christmas Eve, either," Michael said.

"The first time I laid eyes on you was through a telescopic sight. I was told to put you away because you'd been snooping around Benny's downtown, and that's all I know. Mama likes things clean and neat."

"She's a neat, clean illegal alien, huh?" Michael said.

Alice said nothing.

"Why would killing *me* make things clean and neat?" he asked.

"Go ask Mama."

"I will. Where do I find her?"

Alice shook her head.

"Where is she?"

Alice shook her head again.

"You're that scared of her, huh?"

Alice said nothing.

"Tell me where to find her."

She just kept staring at him.

"Then it's the cops, right?" he said. "You want me to call the cops, right?"

"Sure," she said. "Call them."

The last time Michael had stood in this hallway outside the door to Judy Jordan's apartment, he'd been alone. And someone, either Larry or Silvio, had come up behind him and hit him on the head with one of his own guns. Or rather, guns that had previously belonged to Frankie Zeppelin and Arthur Crandall. This time, Connie was by his side. With Connie by his side, he figured he would not get hit on the head again. The only thing that happened to him when Connie was by his side was that he got shot. Or, at best, shot *at*.

He wondered if the police had ever before walked into a warehouse full of stolen goods to discover a safe full of a million dollars' worth of crack, and three thieves swathed in furs and trussed with the electric cords from sundry household appliances.

He did not think Alice – despite her dire warnings or perhaps promises – could possibly have bled to death by the time the police arrived. An axiom of the killing and maiming profession was that if a person was feeling good enough to laugh he wasn't about to die in the next ten minutes. He wished, however, that Alice had chosen to tell him who Mama was.

It was a little unsettling to know that somewhere out there in this wonderful city there was a woman who wielded enough power to order Ju Ju Rainey's murder first and next to order Michael's own, a woman who could generate such fear that three grown thieves had chosen to face the police rather than reveal who or where she was. Michael wasn't sure he *ever* wanted to meet Mama. He knew intuitively, however, that before this was over he would have to look her in the face and demand to know all the whys and wherefores. He tried to visualize her.

She would be fat, he knew that. As Connie had suggested, a woman named Mama *had* to be fat. Bloated and fat and as pale as a slug, a female with a breath that reeked of gunpowder and piss. She would have breasts like dugs, and she would obscenely expose them to Michael, threatening to suckle him if he did not do as she commanded. Standing before Mama, he would search her slightly crossed eyes for some sign that here was reason, here was cause, here was sanity, but there would be none. The .22 caliber pistols he was now carrying in the pockets of the bomber jacket would be of no use to him. He would be staring into the darkest part of evil, and he would be doomed. He did not want to find Mama, did not want to face what he knew was inescapable if this ever was to be resolved – but he knew that he had to. Mama was fate. If you had an appointment in Samarra, you did not drive instead to Newark, New Jersey.

But in the beginning, there'd been Judy Jordan.

Or Helen Parrish, if you preferred.

And to get to the end, you went to the beginning.

And prayed that somewhere along the way—

The village looked abandoned at first. Not a soul in sight.

Michael knocked on the door to the apartment.

"Cops listen first," Connie said.

Belatedly, he put his ear to the door and listened.

He did not hear anything.

"Nobody home," he said.

Charlie musta flew the coop, Sergeant Mendelsohnn said.

Michael knocked on the door again. And waited. No answer. He studied the locks. Four of them. One under the other. To get into this apartment, you would need a battering ram. He wondered if they should try the fire escape again. But how many fire escapes could you climb before someone yelled fire?

Careful, Andrew said.

An old man had appeared in the doorway to one of the thatched huts. Nodding. Smiling. Scared shitless. Six automatic rifles suddenly trained on him.

"We'd better go," Michael said.

Cover me, Mendelsohnn said.

Rain coming down. A light rain. Everything looking so green. So fresh. Waiting in the rain. The whisper of the rain. Mendelsohnn talking quietly to the old man. Scraps of Vietnamese, snippets of French, bits and pieces of English. Other gooks peering around doorways now. Women mostly. Some other old men. Watching solemnly. Looking scared. Big American liberators standing in the rain with their guns. All but one of them no older than twenty, scaring women and old men to death.

Says Charlie went through about three days ago, Mendelsohnn said.

All of them listening.

Took all their rice, Mendelsohnn said. Got to be miles away by now.

"Maybe you ought to knock again," Connie said.

"No," Michael said. "Let's go."

Looka the one in the blue over there, the RTO said.

Yeah, Andrew said.

Givin' us the eye.

Give her some big Indian cock, Long Foot said.

Let's move it out, Mendelsohnn said.

The rain still falling lightly.

A breeze coming up over the rice paddies.

They were coming down the steps when Michael heard the footsteps below. Coming up. Moving up toward them. Another tenant, he thought. Or maybe – but no, that would be too lucky. But why not? Judy Jordan coming home. By her own admission, she'd been naked the last time he was here, probably dressing to go out, it had been only ten o'clock. So she'd put on a robe and peeked out into the hallway to find nobody there, this city was full of mysteries, and she'd finished dressing, and had gone out on the town. But the night had vanished all at once, and this was now one o'clock in the morning on Boxing Day, and here she was, folks, home sweet home again, coming up the steps to the second floor, reaching the second-floor landing just as Michael and Connie came down from the third floor, hand on the banister, hello there, Judy, long time no—

But it wasn't Judy Jordan.

Or even Helen Parrish.

Instead, it was—

"You!" Michael shouted.

The man looked at him. His mouth fell open, his eyes opened wide in his head.

"You!" Michael shouted again.

And the man turned and started running downstairs.

Michael took off after him.

The streets were deserted. It would have been impossible to lose him, anyway, because he was wearing a yellow ski parka that served as a beacon, which Michael thought was extremely considerate of him. He was fast for a big man, but Michael was faster; he'd had practice chasing Charlie Wong all the way from the subway kiosk on Franklin to the fortune-cookie factory someplace in Chinatown only two nights ago, and it seemed to him he'd been running ever since. He wanted very badly to get his hands on this son of a bitch in the yellow ski parka, and so he ran faster than he'd ever run in his life, arms and legs pumping, eyeglasses steaming up a bit, but not so much so that he couldn't see the yellow parka ahead, the distance closing between them now, ten feet, eight feet, six feet, three feet, and Michael hurled himself into the air like a circus flier, leaping off into space without a net, arms outstretched, reaching not for a trapeze coming his way from the opposite direction, but instead for the shoulders of Detective Daniel Cahill, who had called him a thief after stealing his money, his driver's license, his credit cards, and his library card to boot.

His hands clamped down fiercely on either side of Cahill's neck, the weight and momentum of his body sending the man staggering forward, hands clawing the air for balance. They fell to the sidewalk together, Michael on Cahill's back, the big man trying to shake Michael off. Michael was tired of being jerked around in this fabulous city, tired of being shaken up and shaken off. He allowed himself to be shaken off now, but only for an instant. Rolling clear, he got to his feet at once, and then immediately reached down for Cahill and heaved him up off the sidewalk. His hands clutched into the zippered front of the yellow parka, he slammed Cahill against the wall of the building, and then pulled him off the wall and slammed him back again, methodically battering him against the bricks over and over again.

"Cut it out," Cahill said.

"I'll cut it out, you son of a bitch!"

"Are you crazy or something?"

"Yes!" Michael shouted.

"Ow!" Cahill shouted.

"Detective Daniel Cahill, huh?"

"Damn it, you're hurting me!"

"Let's go down the precinct, huh?"

"Ow! Damn it, that's my *head*!"

Michael pulled him off the wall.

"Speak," he said.

"You're a very violent person," Cahill said.

"Yes. What's your name?"

"Felix. And I don't have your money, if *that's* why you're behaving like a lunatic. Or anything *else* that belongs to you."

Felix. Big burly man with hard blue eyes and a Marine sergeant's haircut. On Christmas Eve, he'd sported a *Miami Vice* beard stubble, but now – at a little past one A.M. on Boxing Day – he was clean-shaven. On Christmas Eve, he'd been wearing a tweed overcoat and he'd been carrying a detective's blue-enameled gold shield, and he'd sounded very much like a tough New York cop. Tonight he was wearing a yellow ski parka over a brown turtleneck sweater, and he sounded like a frightened man protesting too loudly that he did not have Michael's—

But didn't he know that Michael's identification had been planted alongside the dead body of Ju Ju Rainey?

"Felix what?" Michael asked.

"Hooper. And I'm telling you the truth. I gave everything to Judy. And she still hasn't paid me, by the way. I mean, I think it's demeaning for a person to have to come to another person's apartment at one in the morning to ask for his money, don't you?"

"I assume you mean Judy Jordan."

"Yes, of *course* Judy Jordan. Your friend Judy Jordan who owes me a thousand bucks."

"How do you happen to know her?"

"We've worked together in the past."

"Stealing things from people?"

"Ha-ha," Felix said.

Michael looked at him.

"I am an *actor*, sir," Felix said, proudly and a trifle indignantly. In fact, he tried to pull himself up to his full height, but this was a little difficult because Michael still had his hands twisted into the throat and collar of the parka. "I was asked to play a police detective," Felix said. "I'd never played one before. I thought the role would be challenging."

"You thought stealing my . . ."

"Oh, come on, that was for a good purpose."

"A good . . ."

"In fact, you should have been delighted."

"Delighted? Do you know what Judy *did* with those things? My credit cards and my license and my . . . ?"

"Yes, she had them blown up as posters."

"She *what*?"

"For your birthday party."

"My *what*?"

"How terrible it must be," Felix said.

"What?"

"To be born on Christmas Day, do you think you could let go of my collar now?"

"Born on . . . ?"

"It's like being upstaged by Christ, isn't it?" Felix said. "I really think you're closing off an artery or something. I'm beginning to feel a bit faint."

Michael let go of the collar.

"Thank you," Felix said.

"So that's what she told you. Judy."

"Yes."

"That my birthday was on Christmas Day . . ."

"Well, her friend's birthday. She didn't tell me your name."

"And she was going to have my credit cards blown up as posters."

"Yes, and your driver's license, too. To hang on the walls. For the party."

"Which is why you went to this bar with her . . ."

"Yes. And waited for her signal."

"Her signal."

"She said she would signal when she wanted me to move in."

"I see."

"She would hold out her hand to you, palm up."

Asking for the ring back, Michael thought.

The ring. Please, I don't want any trouble.

"And that was when you were supposed to come over and do your Detective Cahill act."

"Yes."

"Where'd you get the badge?"

"A shield. We call it a shield. I bought it in an antiques shop on Third Avenue."

"You were very convincing."

"Thank you. I thought so, too. Did you like it when I said, 'This individual is a thief'? That's the way policemen talk, you know. They will never call a person a *person*, he is always an individual."

"Yes, that was very good."

"Thank you."

"But why'd you steal my money? If Judy wanted the . . ."

"I don't know why she wanted the money. She said your money and all your identification. Which is all I took."

"Which was only everything in my wallet."

"Well, that was the job."

"Which you did for a thousand dollars."

"Yes, but I'm between engagements just now. How was the party?"

"Mr Hooper, do you know where all that stuff ended up?"

"No. All I know is that I still haven't got my thousand dollars."

"That stuff ended up alongside a dead man."

"That's a shame," Felix said. "But I'm sure it had nothing to do with my performance."

"Do you know who Mama is?"

"No. Is that a riddle?"

"Did Judy Jordan ever mention a woman named Mama?"

"No. Mama who?"

"She didn't say, did she, that it was *Mama* who wanted that stuff taken from my wallet?"

"No."

"Did she ever mention a man named Arthur Crandall?"

"Arthur Crandall? The *director*? The man who did *War and Solitude*? What are you saying?"

"Did she tell you it was Crandall who wanted my . . . ?"

"Oh my God, was I auditioning for *Crandall*?"

"No, that's not what I'm saying. I'm trying to find out if . . ."

"Crandall, oh, *God*, I'm going to faint."

"Would you know if . . . ?"

"Why didn't you *tell* me? I mean, I hardly even *prepared*! I mean, I went on cold! If I'd known I was doing it for *Crandall* . . ."

"Well, that's what I'm trying to . . ."

"I'll kill her, I swear to God! Why'd she give me that story about a birthday party? *Crandall*, I'm going to cry."

"No, don't cry, just . . ."

"I'm going to die, I'm going to kill her, I'll go kill her right this minute."

"You can't, she isn't home."

"Then where is she?"

"I don't know where she . . ."

"The *theater*!" Felix shouted.

15

The theater was on Thirteenth Street off Seventh Avenue, a ninety-nine-seat house in what had once been the rectory of a Catholic church. The church was still functional, although the theater – according to Felix – barely scraped by. All of the street lamps on either side of the block had been smashed by vandals, and the only illumination at one-forty in the morning was a floodlight bathing the facade of the church and causing it to look like a sanctuary for Quasimodo. A hand-lettered sign affixed to a stone buttress on the northwest side of the church advised that the Cornerstone Players could be found in the direction of the pointing arrow at the bottom of the sign.

"They're rehearsing a medieval play," Felix said, "an allegory of sorts."

Michael thought it odd that a group of players would be rehearsing at this hour of the morning. Then again, he did not know anything at all about allegories. Perhaps an allegory had to be rehearsed in the empty hours of the night.

"They were supposed to open just before Christmas," Felix said, "but the director's wife ran off with another woman, and they had to bring in a replacement. They'll be lucky if they make it before the end of the year. Even *with* all these crash rehearsals."

He was leading them familiarly up the lighted alleyway on the side of the church, feeling very chipper now that Michael had stopped banging him against the wall and had released his grip on the parka. On the way downtown in the open convertible, he'd told them he was really looking forward to killing Judy Jordan.

Michael doubted he would actually kill her, even though he sounded simultaneously serious and cheerfully optimistic about the prospect. Apparently, an audition with Arthur Crandall was an important thing. Working in an Arthur Crandall film, even if the movie didn't make any money, could help an actor's career enormously. Which was why Felix was so incensed that Judy hadn't told him the detective role was an audition. Michael assured Felix it had been nothing of the sort, but Felix thought he was just mollifying him, Judy Jordan being a good friend of his and all, who'd even thrown a surprise birthday party for him. Michael was thinking that in his own way Felix was crazier than any of the people he'd met in the past few days. But Felix was an actor; perhaps he was only *acting* crazy.

There was an arched doorway near the rear of the church, which Felix explained was the entrance to the theater, but he walked right past it and around to the back of the church, where a metal door was set in a smaller arch. A sign advised that this was the stage door and asked all visitors to announce themselves. Felix pressed a button under a speaker. A woman's voice said, "Yes?"

"Felix Hooper," he said.

"Minute," the woman said.

There was a buzz. Felix grasped the doorknob, twisted it, and led them into a space that looked like a one-room schoolhouse, with students' desks and a teacher's desk and a piano in one corner, and an American flag in another corner. A dark-haired woman wearing a wide, flower-patterned skirt over a black leotard and tights came into the room, carrying a clipboard.

"Hi, Felix," she said.

"Hi. Is Judy here?"

"Onstage," she said.

Michael noticed that she was barefoot.

"I'm Anne Summers, the stage manager," she said.

"I'm Connie Kee, the chauffeur," Connie said.

Michael did not introduce himself because he was still wanted for murder, albeit the murder of a dope dealer fence.

"You look familiar," Anne said.

"Everybody tells me that," Michael said.

"Okay to go in?" Felix asked.

"Sure."

"'Cause I want to kill Judy," Felix said, and smiled.

"So does Kenny," Anne said, and turned to Michael. "Kenny Stein, the director," she explained.

Michael figured that in the theater, everyone had a title. He wondered if he was supposed to recognize Kenny Stein's name. Anne was looking at him expectantly.

"Gee," Michael said.

"You'd better sit way in the back," she said to Felix. "Kenny likes a lot of space around him. Are you sure I don't know you?" she asked Michael.

"Positive," Michael said, and followed Felix across the room to a doorframe hung with a black curtain. Felix pushed the curtain aside, whispered, "Stay close behind me," and stepped through the doorframe. Connie went out after him. Anne was watching Michael. He smiled at her. She smiled back.

There was darkness beyond the curtain.

And a man's voice.

"Let's take it from Judy's entrance again."

And then a voice Michael remembered well.

"Kenny, could you please refer to me as the Queen?"

Judy Jordan speaking. The woman who'd called herself Helen Parrish on Christmas Eve. Wishing to be called the Queen on Boxing Day.

"Because if I'm going to stay in character . . ."

"Yes, yes," the man said patiently.

". . . and you keep referring to me as *Judy* . . ."

"Which, by the way, is your name."

"Not in this *play*," Judy said. "In this *play*, I am the *Queen*, and I wish you'd refer to me as that."

"Yes, Your Majesty," the man said. "Can we take it from the Queen's entrance, please?"

"Thank you," Judy said.

Michael was following Felix and Connie up the side aisle of the small theater, turning his head every now and then for a glimpse of the lighted stage, where Judy Jordan was standing with three men. Michael stumbled, caught his balance, and then concentrated entirely on following Felix, who was now at the last row in the theater, moving into the seats there.

"What's the problem?"

The man's voice again. Kenny Stein, the director.

"Some problem, Your Majesty?"

"Did you want this from the top of the act, or from my entrance?" Judy asked.

"I said from your entrance, didn't I?"

"That's so close to the top, I thought . . ."

"From your entrance, please."

Seated now, Michael turned his full attention to the stage. The set seemed to be an ultramodern apartment in Manhattan, judging from the skyline beyond the open French doors leading onto a terrace. But the people in the set – Judy and the three men – were dressed in medieval costumes. Judy was wearing a crown and an ankle-length, scoop-necked gown. One of the men was wearing a black helmet that completely covered his head and his face. Another of the men was holding what looked like a real sword in his right hand. The third man, younger than the other two, was wearing leggings wrapped with leather thongs, and a funny hat with a feather in it; he looked like a peasant.

"They're rehearsing in the set for a play that's already in performance," Felix whispered, leaning over Connie, who was sitting between them.

"It's only two A.M.," Kenny said patiently, "just take all the time you need."

"We just want to make sure we've got the right place," the man with the sword said.

"The right place is Judy's entrance," Kenny said.

"From my line?"

"Yes, your line would be fine."

"The White Knight? At your service, fair maiden?"

"Yes, that is your line," Kenny said. "Can we do it now, please?"

"Thank you," the man with the sword said. "Judy, are you ready?"

"Please don't call me Judy," she said.

"Well, I'm not supposed to know you're the Queen yet. You haven't come in yet."

"Yes, please do come in," Kenny said. "Just say your line, Hal, and Judy will come in."

"The play is called *Stalemate*," Felix explained.

On the stage, the man with the sword said, "The White Knight. At your service, fair maiden."

"I'm not a maiden," Judy said. "I'm a queen."

The White Knight knelt at once. "Your Majesty," he said. "Forgive me."

Judy turned to the man who looked like a peasant. "Who are *you*?" she asked.

"I am the White Knight's squire," he said, "a mere pawn, Your Majesty."

"And this poor creature?" she asked, indicating the man in the black helmet.

"A helpless servant of the Queen, Your Majesty, tell him to put up his sword!"

"Release him," Judy said.

"He's a dangerous man, Your Majesty."

"Release him, I say."

The White Knight and his squire immediately let go of the man wearing the black helmet.

"Take off your helmet," Judy said. "I want to see your face."

"No," the man in the helmet said.

"I'm a *queen*!" Judy said. "Do as I say!"

"You're not *my* queen, lady," the man in the helmet said, and immediately turned to look out into the theater. "Kenny," he said, "I don't get this, I really don't. A minute ago, I'm calling her 'Your Majesty,' and now I'm telling her she's not my queen."

"That's because this is the first time you can really see her," Kenny said patiently.

"Why can't I see her before this?"

"Because she's standing in the dark. This is when she moves toward the fire. On 'I'm a *queen*,' she moves toward the fire. And you can see her face in the firelight, and that's when you say 'You're not *my* queen, lady.'"

"Then whose queen is she?" the man in the helmet asked.

"That's not the point, Jason. The point is . . ."

"You know, I think Judy's right, you shouldn't call us by our real names when we're supposed to be other people."

"It would be clumsy to call you 'Black Knight,'" Kenny said.

"Then call me 'Sire,'" the Black Knight said.

"Me, too," the White Knight said.

"And what would *you* like to be called, Jimmy?"

"I'm the Pawn," the young man in the peasant outfit said, looking stunned.

"Yes, that's what the playwright has chosen to call you, the Pawn, that is part of the metaphor. The chess metaphor. But shall *I* call you 'Pawn' when I address you?"

"Yes, that would be fine, Kenny," the young man said.

"Very well, then. Sire, would you please take it from your denial line?"

"Me?" the White Knight asked.

"No, the *other* sire, please."

"My *what* line?" the Black Knight asked.

"The line where you deny the Queen. If you please."

"Oh."

"Thank you," Kenny said.

Michael wondered if allegory and metaphor were one and the same thing. Whichever, it was certainly a very confusing play, at least the part of it they were rehearsing. At one point, he thought he was beginning to catch on to the idea that the Black Knight represented black men everywhere, but then the play swerved off in another direction and he figured he was wrong. Puzzled, he began to lose interest, until—

"I can still remember the day Arthur died," the Black Knight said.

"Oh, yes, of course," the Queen said, "the whole *world* remembers."

"I'd been in the woods with a friend of mine," the Black Knight said. "It was a bright, clear November day, the forest was alive with sound, we walked on crackling leaves, and breathed needles into our lungs. And when we came out of the forest, there was a beggar woman sitting by the side of the road, wringing her hands and weeping, and we said to her, 'Why do you weep, old woman?' and she answered, 'Arthur is dead.' And we didn't believe her. Arthur could not be dead. But as we walked further along the road, we came upon more and more people, all of them saying, 'Arthur is dead,' until at last there was a multitude of people, all of them weeping and saying the same words, 'Arthur is dead, Arthur is dead,' and then we believed it. And the sun went out, and a wind rose up, and there was no longer the sound of life in this land of ours, there was only the sound of muffled drums."

He's talking about John F. Kennedy, Michael thought.

The Queen shuddered and said, "You're a very morbid person."

"He was a good king," the Black Knight said.

"Yes, but we've all got to go sometime, you know."

"Things would be different if he were still alive," the Black Knight said. "He had a vision, that man, you could see it flashing in his eyes, you just knew he had a *dream* clenched tight in those hands of his. And when a man can dream that strong, it makes you want to join him, it makes you want to move right in and say, 'Yes, Daddy, take me where you're going, I'm *with* you, Daddy, let's yell it out together.' There was no bullshit about that man. I loved him."

Now he's talking about Martin Luther King, Jr., Michael thought.

"You talk too much," the Queen said, "and not about the right things. Also, I don't like profanity. And if you want to know something, I'm beginning to find you enormously boring and a trifle sinister."

This is *Alice in Wonderland*, Michael thought.

"Besides, I don't trust masked men," the Queen said. "Nobody does."

Everything in this city is *Alice in Wonderland*, Michael thought.

"This isn't a mask!" the Black Knight shouted.

"Then what is it?"

"My *head* is inside this black cage," the Black Knight shouted. "My *brain* is in here, I *think* in here, I *feel* in here, it is not a goddamn *mask*!"

"You're frightening me," the Queen said. "Look, the fire's going out."

"The fire went out the day Arthur died," the Black Knight whispered.

"Very good," Kenny said, "very nice indeed. Let's take a ten-minute break, and then I want to do the dragon scene, the H-bomb scene."

"Oh, God, is *that* it?" the White Knight said.

"Sire?"

"Is the dragon supposed to be the *H*-bomb?"

"Yes, Sire, that is the metaphor," Kenny said.

"I'm glad to know that. Because, actually, I was wondering why I was so afraid of a little dragon. I'm supposed to be an experienced knight, but I'm afraid of a little dragon. It didn't make sense to me. Now that you tell me it's the H-bomb . . ."

"That's the metaphor, yes."

"Well, that's an enormous relief, I can tell you. Did you know it was the H-bomb, Jason?"

"Oh, sure," the Black Knight said, and both men walked off the stage. The Pawn, looking somewhat bewildered, followed them. "Ten minutes, please," Kenny called after them, and left the theater through the curtained doorway that led to the one-room schoolhouse.

Judy Jordan sat alone on the stage.

Sat on a wooden plank stretched across several stacked cinder blocks.

Head bent, studying her script.

Looking blonde and beautiful and serene and quite regal.

"I want her first," Felix said, and stood up.

"No," Michael said.

He said it quite softly.

Almost whispered it, in fact.

There was no reason for Felix to have obeyed him.

But he sat down at once.

Michael walked up the aisle to the front of the theater. He climbed the steps onto the stage. Judy was absorbed in the script, probably trying to dope out all its inherent metaphors and allegories. He walked directly to her.

"I'm looking for a good criminal lawyer," he said.

Her head jerked up.

"Because I've been accused of murder," he said.

She started to rise.

He put his hands on her shoulders and slammed her back down onto the makeshift plank and cinder-block seat, which was undoubtedly a metaphor for a medieval bench.

"Remember me?" he said.

"Yes," she said. "Hello."

She was playing a woman in a movie about the French Resistance. She was really a Nazi spy and he was the wounded American soldier who had fallen in love with her and been betrayed by her. It was now his painful duty to turn her over to the authorities. He had come to take her away. She still loved him. She was looking up at him wistfully, her blue eyes wide.

"How have you been?" she asked.

"*Comme ci, comme ça,*" he said, in the French he had learned in Vietnam. "*Et toi?*"

"Not very good," she said. "I saw it on television."

"Oh. And what did you see, Miss Parrish?"

"My name is Judy Jordan," she said.

"I know."

"I'm sorry," she said. "That's not what I thought would happen."

"What did you think would happen?"

"Charlie said he was playing a joke on a friend of his."

"By Charlie . . ."

"Charlie Nichols."

"You call your father by his first name, do you?"

"My father?"

"Yes, Charlie. You call your father 'Charlie'?"

"No, I call my father 'Frank.'"

Michael looked at her.

"Isn't it true that you call Charlie 'Daddy'?" he asked.

"No, I call Charlie '*Charlie.*'"

"Look, Miss Jordan, I happen to *know* that Charlie Nichols is your goddamn *father*. So please don't . . ."

"No, Frank Giordano is my goddamn father, which is where I got the name Jordan, from Giordano, and I really don't know *what* you're talking about!"

"I am talking about a photograph of you and Charlie Nichols . . ."

"Oh."

"Yes, oh, inscribed 'To My Dear Daddy, With Love,' and signed Judy Jordan, who is *you*, Miss Jordan, Miss Parrish, Miss Giordano, who*ever* the hell you are!"

Nodding, Judy said what sounded exactly like, "I remember Mama."

"Good," Michael said at once. "Who is she?"

"*Who?*" Judy said. "*I Remember Mama* is a play. I was Christine in a revival. Charlie was Papa."

"What?"

"Yes. In the play. My father."

"In a play?"

"Yes. *I Remember Mama*. And at the end of the run, I signed a photograph . . ."

"To My Dear Daddy . . ."

"Yes, With Love."

"Referring to . . ."

"Yes, the characters in the play. Also, it was an inside joke, in that Charlie and I were sleeping together at the time."

"I see."

"Yes. Charlie was my first lover."

"I see."

"Yes. I was seventeen. I was a virgin at the time."

"So he wasn't your father."

"No, that would have been incest. Also, my own father would have shot him dead if he'd found out."

Michael wondered if her own father had now belatedly if messily shot Charlie dead. He also wondered if Judy even *knew* that Charlie was dead. He decided not to mention it. From seeing a lot of cop movies, he knew that this was an old cop trick. You did not mention that someone was dead. You waited for the suspect to trap himself by mentioning that the last time he'd seen So-and-So alive was Thursday, and then you yelled, "Ah-ha, how did you know he was *dead*?"

"I am really sorry," Judy said. "When I saw on television that they'd accused you of murdering Arthur Crandall . . ."

"Oh, you saw that, did you?"

"Oh, yes. I was *shocked*!"

"But I *didn't* murder Crandall, you know."

"Well, of *course* you didn't."

"In fact, I didn't murder *anyone*."

"Well, I'm not too sure about *that*."

"You can take my word for it. And please don't change the subject. The reason the police *think* I killed Rainey . . ."

"Who?"

". . . is that you and Felix Hooper stole my goddamn identification and . . ."

"Yes, but that was for a joke."

"What joke? What do you mean?"

"The joke Charlie was going to play on his friend."

"What friend?"

"He didn't say."

"What *did* he say?"

"He said he needed someone's identification to play a joke on a friend of his. He said it wouldn't really be stealing . . ."

"Oh, it *wouldn't*, huh?"

"In that he would return the stuff to its rightful owner the moment he was through with it."

"And just how did he plan to do that?"

"He said he would mail it all back."

"And you believed him, huh?"

"Not entirely. But a thousand dollars is a lot of money."

"What do you mean?"

"Charlie paid each of us a thousand for the job."

"You and Felix."

"Yes."

Which accounted for two thousand dollars of the check Crandall had cashed on Friday. But where had the other seven thousand gone?

"I was the one who picked Felix for the part," Judy said. "He was very good, didn't you think?"

"Yes, excellent," Michael said.

"Yes, he's a very good actor. I still owe him the thousand, but Charlie hasn't paid me yet."

Nor is he likely to, Michael thought.

"So as I understand this," he said, "you were supposed to steal my identification . . ."

"Well, borrow it, yes. And your money, too."

"Why the money? If all you needed was my . . ."

"In case you went to the police. So it wouldn't look as if we'd been after your I.D. Actually, it was the best improv Felix and I ever did together."

"The best what?"

"Improvisation. Picking up a stranger in a bar, and then . . ."

"You mean I was chosen at *random*?"

"Well, not entirely. Charlie gave me the nod."

"What nod?"

"To go ahead."

"Go ahead?"

"Yes. He was sitting at the bar, listening to everything we said . . ."

"Yes, I know that."

"And he gave me the okay, just this little nod, you know – do you remember when I looked down the bar?"

"No."

"Well, I did. To get his okay. The nod."

"To get his permission, you mean, to *steal* my goddamn . . ."

"Well, it was only for a joke, you know."

"A *murder* was committed!"

"Well, I'm sorry about that, but Felix and I had nothing to do with it."

"Where does Crandall fit in?" he asked.

"I have no idea, but he's a very good director and I'm glad it wasn't him you killed."

"I didn't kill *anyone*, goddamn it!"

"I don't like profanity," she said at once. "And if you want to know something, I'm beginning to find you enormously boring and a trifle sinister. If the police made a mistake, you should go to *them* and correct it, instead of breaking the concentration of someone who's trying to master a very complex role."

"That was very good," he said sincerely. "You sounded absolutely royal."

"Do you really think so?" she asked.

"Positively majestic. Better than Bette Davis in *Elizabeth and Essex* . . ."

"Honestly?"

"Even better than Hepburn in *The Lion in Winter*."

"Oh dear," she said.

"But would you happen to know a bar called Benny's?"

"No. I'm not being *too* forceful, am I? Maybe I should temper the steel with a touch of lace."

"No, I think you've got exactly the proper balance, really. On Christmas Eve, Crandall went to Benny's to meet a man sent there by someone named Mama. Would you happen to know who Mama is?"

"Well, of course."

"You do?"

"Mady Christians, am I right?"

"Who?" he said.

"That was in the original 1944 production, of course. When *we* did it fifteen years ago, a woman named . . ."

"Yes, but *this* Mama is an illegal alien. Would you know anyone . . . ?"

"Oh," she said. "*That* Mama."

He held his breath.

"Charlie's crack dealer," she said. "I've never met her, but he talks about her all the time."

"Do you know where she lives?" Michael asked.

Only her last name was on the mailbox.

Rodriguez.

The match Michael was holding went out.

The hallway was very dark again.

"Somebody peed in here," Connie said.

Michael was thinking it would be very dangerous to ring Mama's bell and then go up there to see her. He wondered if they should go up the fire escape again. Apartment 2C. Was what it said under the name Rodriguez on the mailbox.

Michael rang the bell for apartment 3B.

There was no answering buzz.

He tried 4D.

No answer.

"Is this an abandoned building?" he asked Connie.

"Not that I noticed," she said. "Why don't you just kick the door in?"

He did not want to hurt the sole of his foot again by trying to kick in yet another door. And he didn't want to throw his shoulder against the door, either, because his arm still hurt from getting shot and then hurling himself at Alice. He wondered if there were any medics here in this almost abandoned building.

What's the matter, honey? Andrew asked.

Cute little baby girl, eight months old, not a day older. Crying her eyes out. Sitting the way the Orientals did. Squatting really. Legs folded under her, feet turned back. Bawling. Birds twittering in the jungle. The village not six hundred yards behind them. Friendlies. Charlie had left three days ago, the old man had told Mendelsohnn. Took all the rice, moved out. Had to be miles and miles away by now. The baby crying.

Come to Papa, sweetie.

Andrew reached for her.

Michael kicked out at the doorjamb, just above the lock. The door sprang open, surprising him, catching him off balance. He stumbled forward, following the opening door into a small

220

ground-floor rectangle directly in front of a flight of steps. Connie was immediately behind him.

"2C," he said.

She nodded.

They began climbing the steps.

Four apartments on the second floor. 2A, B, C, and D. They stopped outside the door to 2C. He put his ear to the wood, listened the way Connie had told him cops did. He couldn't hear a thing. He took the .22 out of the right-hand pocket of the bomber jacket. He wondered if he would need both pistols. Suppose Mama Rodriguez was sleeping inside there with a .357 Magnum under her pillow? In Vietnam, you slept – *when* you slept, *if* you slept – with your rifle in your hands. But sometimes . . .

Andrew's rifle was slung.

His arms extended to the baby.

Come on, darlin'.

The baby blinking at him.

It had stopped raining.

A fan of sunlight touched the baby like a religious miracle.

"I don't hear anything in there," Michael said.

Birds twittering in the jungle. The leaves still wet. Water dripping onto the jungle floor. The baby had stopped crying. Fat tear-stained cheeks. Looking at Andrew wide-eyed as his hands closed on either side of her body, fingers widespread, lifting her, lifting her—

Michael was suddenly covered with sweat.

Terrified again.

Terrified the way he'd been that day in Vietnam when Andrew picked up the baby.

Afraid of what might be beyond that door. Afraid to enter the apartment beyond that door. Because beyond that door was the unknown. Mama. A woman named Mama who had ordered him murdered. Fat Mama Rodriguez inside there. Waiting and deadly. Like the baby.

Here we go, darlin', Andrew said.

The baby in Andrew's widespread hands, coming up off the jungle mat, the birds going suddenly still as—

Michael did not want to know what was behind this closed door.

Behind this door was something unspeakably horrible, something that went beyond fright to reach into the darkest corners of the unconscious, the baby going off in a hundred flying fragments, her arms and legs spinning away on the air, eyeballs bursting, bone fragments, tissue, blood spattering onto Andrew as the bomb exploded. A moment too late, Long Foot yelled, "She's *wired*!" and a surprised look crossed Andrew's face as the metal shards ripped through his body and blood spurted out of his chest. A piece of the dead baby was still in Andrew's hands. The hands holding what had been the baby's rib cage. But the hands were no longer attached to Andrew's arms. The hands were on the trail some twelve feet away from him. And the stumps where his wrists ended were spurting blood. And a hundred smoking wounds in his jacket were spurting blood. "Oh, dear God," Michael said, and dropped to his knees beside Andrew, and the RTO said, "Barnes, they're . . ." and the jungle erupted with noise and confusion. They were flanked by Charlie left and right. Charlie had wired the baby, had stolen a baby from the village and wired it, and left it just off the trail for the dumb Americans to find, Come on, darlin', here we go, and the baby exploding was the signal to spring the trap, Andrew hoisting her off the jungle mat and tripping the wire.

And in that instant, the true horror of the war struck home. The truly senseless horror of it, they had wired a baby. And recognizing the horror, they had wired a *baby*, Michael was suddenly terrified. Running through the jungle with Andrew in his arms, and the Cong assuring him in their sing-song pidgin English that they did not want to hurt him, and the baby's gristle and blood on Andrew's face, and Andrew's own blood bubbling up onto his lips, oh dear God his *hands* were gone, they had wired a *baby*, Michael knew only blind panic. Suddenly there was no logic and no sense there was only a wired baby exploding between the hands of a good dear friend and the friend was dying the friend's blood was pumping out of his body in weaker spurts the friend was oh God dear God dear Andrew *please*, and he began crying. In terror and in sorrow. A sorrow he had never before known. A sorrow for Andrew and himself and for every American here in this place where he did not wish to be or choose to be and a sorrow, too, for a people that would use a baby that way because no cause on earth was worth doing something as terrible as that but behind him Charlie kept saying it was okay Yank no need to worry Yank nobody's gonna hurt you Yank.

Andrew was already dead for half an hour when Michael found the medical chopper.

He would not let them take the body out of his arms.

He kept holding the handless body close, rocking it.

"Come on, man," the black medic said. "Get a grip."

Michael turned to him and snarled at him.

Like a dog.

Lips skinned back over his teeth.

Growling deep in his throat.

The medic backed off.

A colonel came over to him later.

"Let's go, soldier," he said, "we've got work to do."

"Fuck you, sir," Michael said.

And growled at him, too.

Click.

A sound to his right. He whirled, terrified.

The door to apartment 2B was opening. A girl the color of cinnamon toast was standing in the doorway. She was wearing only a half-slip. Nothing else. Naked from the waist up. She stared blankly into the hall.

"You lookin' for Mama?" she asked.

"Yes," Connie said.

"Try the club," the girl said.

Michael felt a tremendous rush of relief.

Mama was at the club.

She was not behind this closed door.

She would not have to be faced just yet.

He put the pistol back into his pocket.

"What club?" he asked.

He did not want to know.

He hoped the girl would not tell him.

Stoned out of her mind, she would not be able to remember the name of the club. No older than sixteen, stoned beyond remembrance. He had seen that same glazed look in Vietnam. Young Americans going into battle stoned. To face the faceless enemy and the nameless horror in the jungle. For Michael, here and now, inexplicably here in this hallway in downtown Manhattan, the horror was an unseen, unknown woman named Mama,

223

and he did not wish to face that horror again. Because this time it would destroy him. This time, the horror would explode in *his* hands, and he would run weeping all the way to Boston, his stumps spurting blood, only to learn that *his* Mama had given away even his best blue jacket. No cause, he thought. No cause on earth.

"Oz," the girl said.

"All the way downtown," Connie said. "Over near the river."

No cause, Michael kept thinking.

"Are you all right?" she asked him.

"Yes," he said. "I'm fine."

16

Oz was a disco on a peninsula that hugged the exit to the Battery Tunnel. Located on Greenwich Street, as opposed to Greenwich *Avenue* farther uptown, it seemed undecided as to whether it wished to be closer to Edgar or to Morris, which were streets and not people. In any event, the club was so far downtown that in the blink of an eye the West Side could suddenly and surprisingly become the East Side. Or rather, and more accurately, the West Side could become the *South* Side, for it was here at the lowest tip of the island that West Street looped around Battery Park to become South Street.

"It's all very confusing," Connie explained, "but not as confusing as the borough of Brooklyn."

They had parked the open convertible in an all-night garage on Broadway, and had walked two blocks south and one block west to the disco, passing several young girls shivering in the cold in short fake-fur jackets, high-heeled shoes, and lacy lingerie. Michael wondered if any of these girls had earlier been at the Christmas party where he'd met Frankie Zeppelin. He did not think he recognized Detective O'Brien among them.

At three o'clock in the morning on Boxing Day, there were at least a hundred people standing on the yellow brick sidewalk outside Oz. Not a single one of them appeared to be over the age of twenty, and most of them were dressed like characters from *The Wizard of Oz*. Standing on line in the shivering cold were a dozen or more Tin Men, half again that number of Scarecrows, six Cowardly Lions, eight Wicked Witches of the West, a handful of Glendas, three or four Wizards, a great many people wearing monkey masks on their faces and wings on their backs, some shorter folk chattering in high voices and pretending to be Munchkins, and a multitude of Dorothys wearing short skirts, red shoes, and braids. Michael felt a bit out of place in his jeans and bomber jacket.

The sidewalk outside the disco was not merely *painted* a yellow brick, it actually *was* yellow brick. The building itself had once been a parking garage, shaped like a flatiron to conform to the peninsulalike dimensions of the plot. Its old brick facade was now covered with thick plastic panels cut and fitted and lighted from within to resemble the many facets of a sparkling green emerald rising from the sidewalk. The name of the club was repeatedly spelled out in brighter green neon wrapped around the front and sides of the building, just below the roof. There were no visible entrance doors. There was only the yellow brick leading to this huge green multifaceted crystal growing out of the sidewalk.

The girls and boys standing on line outside were talking noisily among themselves, trying to look supremely confident about their chances of getting into the place. The man in charge of granting admission was about six and a half feet tall, and Michael guessed he weighed at least three hundred pounds. He had bushy black eyebrows, curly black hair, wide shoulders, a narrow waist, and hands like hamhocks. Despite the cold, he was wearing only a black jacket over a white turtleneck shirt, black loafers, white socks, and gray trousers that were too short. Michael heard one of the kids on the line referring to him as Curly.

There was a sudden buzz of excitement when what earlier had appeared to be part of the building's seamless facade now parted to reveal two green panels that served as entrance doors. An intense green light spilled out onto the sidewalk. There was the blare of heavy metal rock. Two youngsters walked out – the girl dressed as a somewhat precocious Dorothy in a pleated skirt that showed white panties and half her ass, the boy wearing a gray suit and a funnel on his head. Both were wearing grins that indicated they'd been allowed to meet the Wizard and all their wishes had been granted.

On the line, all faces turned expectantly toward Curly, who was now parading the sidewalk like a judge at a dog show. He chose two people at random, pressed a button that snapped the doors

226

open again, and, with a surly nod, admitted the couple. The girl was dressed as a Munchkin with a frizzed blonde hairdo. The boy was wearing blue jeans and a long cavalry officer's overcoat. Apparently, then, admission to the club was not premised on fidelity to the film. The doors swung shut again. The sound of music was replaced by the keening of the wind blowing in fiercely off the Hudson. Nobody on the line complained, not even the kids standing at the head of it. This was simply the way it was. Curly decided who would go in, Curly decided who would stand out here in the cold. Nor was there any way of knowing upon which criteria he premised his choice. Either you waited for his approving nod or you went home with your dreams. That was it, and this was Oz, take it or leave it.

Michael walked over to where Curly was disdainfully glaring out over the crowd.

"Mama's expecting me," he said.

Curly looked him over.

"Expecting *who*?" he said.

"Silvio," Michael said.

"Silvio who?"

"Just say Silvio."

"Mama ain't here yet."

"I'll wait. Inside."

Curly hesitated.

"Push your button," Michael said.

Curly shrugged. But he pushed the button.

The panels sprang open. Connie and Michael stepped together into the interior of the jewel, and were immediately inundated by a mortar explosion of battering sound and emerald-green light. The place was thronged with Tin Men, Cowardly Lions, Flying Monkeys, Dorothys, Wicked Witches, Munchkins, Wizards, Glendas, Scarecrows, and even ordinary folk. Green smoke swirled on the air. Bodies twisted on the small dance floor. On the bandstand, five blond men wearing black leather trousers, pink tank-top shirts, and long gold chains played guitar and electric-keyboard backup to a young black woman standing at the microphone and belting out a song that seemed to consist only of the words "Do me, baby, do me good" repeated over and over again. She had a big, brassy gospel singer's voice. She was wearing brown high-heeled boots and what appeared to be draped animal skins. The thudding of the bass guitars sounded like enemy troops shelling the perimeter. The room reverberated with noise, skidded with dazzling light. Out of the deafening din of the music and the refracted green glare of the lights and the dense hanging fog of smoke, a young man in a red jacket materialized.

"Sir?" he asked. "Did John admit you?"

He looked extremely puzzled. Had the system somehow broken down?

"Mama's expecting me," Michael said.

"Who's Mama?" the young man asked.

Michael winked.

"John knows," he said.

"It's just that I haven't got a table," the young man said.

He seemed on the edge of tears.

"We'll wait at the bar," Michael said.

"But how will I *know* her?" he asked.

"Don't worry about it," Michael said, and winked again.

He took Connie's elbow and led her toward a bar hung with rotating green floodlights that restlessly swept the room like the eyes of Martians, striking the tables around the dance floor, exploding upon them like summer watermelons and then moving on swiftly as if there'd been a prison break, Michael's motion-picture associations recklessly mixing similes and metaphors, the probing green searchlights in a London air raid, the sky-washing green klieg lights outside Graumann's Chinese, green tracer shells on a disputed green killing field – but in reality the shells had been yellow and red and the world of Oz was green and loud and somewhat frightening in its insistence on colorization. They sat on high-backed stools alongside a young man dressed as a Cowardly Lion whose mane, awash in the overhead light, looked as green as wilted asparagus.

He turned to Michael and said, "You're in the wrong movie."

Ever since Christmas Eve, Michael had been thinking exactly the same thing.

"What are you, *Twelve O'Clock High*?" the lion asked.

"*A Guy Named Joe*," Michael said.

"She's *The World of Suzie Wong*, am I right?"

"*Shanghai Gesture*," Connie said.

"What'll it be?" the bartender asked.

"*Lost Weekend*," the lion said, and nudged Michael with his elbow.

Michael figured that in this splendidly green place a person should order either crème de menthe or chartreuse.

"Do you know how to make a hot rum toddy?" Connie asked.

"Come on, lady," the bartender said.

"A Beefeater martini then," she said, "on the rocks, two olives. Green."

"Tonic with a lime," Michael said. "Green."

"Hard or soft, the minimum's the same," the bartender said.

"That's okay," Michael said.

"And besides, the tonic costs three bucks."

"Fine," Michael said.

"Hello, darling," a voice behind him said. "You're out of costume."

He turned.

Glenda the Good Witch of the East was standing there in a diaphanous blue gown, wings on her shoulders, waving a wand. Wings on *his* shoulders, actually, since Glenda was in reality Phyllis from the Green Garter, with whom Michael had danced earlier tonight, oh what a small world Oz was turning out to be, not to mention the city of New York itself. Phyllis was with a Scarecrow who under all that straw turned out to be Gregory who had rescued Michael from the bad guys and then admired his buns, curiouser and curiouser it was getting to be.

"A Pink Lady please," Glenda, or Phyllis, or both, said to the bartender.

"And a Whisper, please," Gregory said.

The room was stultifyingly hot. Michael took off the bomber jacket and draped it over the high back of the bar stool. The music was still deafening, but the beat was slower now, designed for dirty dancing, the bass guitar chords jangling insistently into the room like the bone-jarring sound of bedsprings in a cheap hotel, the black girl's gospel-singer voice soaring to the roof where the air was thin and clear, high above the poisonous green smoke, setting the rafters atremble the way it had back home in Mississippi, where Michael imagined she used to sing with the Sunday choir.

"Dance with me," Connie said.

There was – for him in the next several moments, and perhaps

229

for Connie as well – the certain knowledge that they were the two most beautiful people in the joint, perhaps in the entire city, glowing with an inner light that shattered the emerald-green myth and illuminated them as sharply as if a follow-spot were leading them out to the dance floor. In the movies, this would have been Ginger and Fred, he in elegant tails rather than Levi's and a sweater, she in a long pale gown rather than jeans and leg warmers and a long-sleeved blouse. And in the movies, they would glide out onto a crowded dance floor – just as the dance floor here was crowded with people pressed against each other, sweating against each other, pumping against each other, dry-humping to the thud of the guitars and the angelic voice – and the crowd would part as Fred stepped out and Ginger followed, those first graceful steps indicating to the mere dancers on the floor that here were italicized *dancers*, here were goddamn capitalized DANCERS to be reckoned with! And the floor would clear at once, and they would be alone at last, a heavenly mist rising from beneath their feet, and they would dance divinely on clouds, oh so easy, oh so beautifully airy and light and incredibly easy, the way Michael and Connie were dancing now.

The black singer from Mississippi was caressing the dirty lyrics of the song as if the devil had entered her little church and corrupted not only the minister but the entire congregation. The song's double meaning was as subtle as a rubber body bag, designed to be understood by the dullest adolescent. With a forked tongue, the song spoke of "breaking and entry" and "shaking and trembling" and "taking so gently," the rhymes so slanted they were bent, the stumbling lyrics pounded home in a tune as simple as the village idiot. But transformed by Ginger and Fred, this crudest of melodies with its thinly disguised pornographic patter became a Cole Porter accompaniment to a dance of unimaginable sensitivity and skill.

Oh how they floated on that sea-green dance floor, oh how they drifted airborne on wafted winds of invention, oh how they wove intricate Terpsichoreal patterns around and among the stunned bystanders who watched them in envy and awe, openmouthed and wide-eyed, here a black teenager wearing a modified Afro and a Scarecrow's stuffed suit, here a stunning brunette in a green micro-mini and braids and red stiletto-heeled shoes, here a lanky, loose-limbed fellow who strongly resembled a young Ray Bolger, and here a beautiful, long-legged woman with short blonde hair and wide brown eyes that opened even wider as he and Connie glided – holy Jesus!

It was Jessica Wales.

Dressed as the Wicked Witch, wearing a skintight black gown, and sparkly red high-heeled shoes, and pale white makeup and blood-red lipstick, and dancing with—

Arthur Crandall.

Who looked portly and pompous and pleased as Punch, which was probably the way most fat men looked when they had slender gorgeous blondes in their arms.

"Long time no see," Michael said.

The self-satisfied smile vanished. Perhaps Crandall had expected Michael to be in handcuffs by now, in a holding cell at one or another of the city's lovely police stations. Or perhaps he'd expected him to be in a garbage can behind one of the city's many beautiful little McDonald's locations, which was where Alice might have left him, given her wont. But wherever he'd expected him to be, it was certainly not here in a smoke-filled disco called Oz at twenty minutes past three on Boxing Day.

He went immediately pale.

But not because he thought Michael was a murderer.

Oh no.

That would have been good enough reason to have gone pale, oh yes, a wanton killer here inside this nice noisy club, a cold-blooded murderer here inside this jewel of a joint, good enough cause for Crandall's eyes to have grown round with fear. But whereas Michael had bought Crandall's little act in the Spring Street apartment on Christmas morning – *"Careful! He's a killer!"* – he now knew far too much to accept it all over again. Green lights blinking on his round, sweaty face, Crandall was realizing that somehow Michael had tracked Mama here. Which meant that he had also tracked Mama to Crandall himself.

"May I cut in, please?" a voice said, and suddenly Michael was in the arms of a short, thin, mean-looking man with a thick black moustache, wearing a shiny silk gray suit that was supposed to make him look like the Tin Man.

"This is a knife," he said, and Michael suddenly detected the faint Spanish accent, and realized at once that this was the illegal alien Mama had sent to meet Crandall on Christmas Eve. The knife was in the man's left hand. The point of the knife was against Michael's ribs. The man's right arm was around Michael's back, pulling him in tight against the knife. The man danced them away from Connie, who stood looking puzzled as a swirl of Dorothys and Cowardly Lions and Wicked Witches flowed everywhere around her in the dense green fog. Michael suddenly remembered that his bomber jacket was draped over the back of the bar stool. All the way over there, the pistols were of no use to him. The man smiled under his moustache.

"I'm Mario Mateo Rodriguez," he said.

"You dance divinely," Michael said.

"Thank you."

"But I wonder if . . ."

"Mama for short," the man said.

Michael looked at him.

"Mama," the man said. "For Mario Mateo."

"You're a *man*?" Michael said.

"Nobody's perfect," Mama said.

Michael winced. Not because Mama had just quoted the best closing line of any movie Michael had ever seen in his life, but only because he accompanied the line with a quick little jab of the knife. Michael was suddenly covered with sweat. He did not know whether Mama planned to kill him here on the dance floor under all these swirling green lights or whether he planned to dance him out of here at knife point, onto the yellow brick road, and over to the Hudson River, where once stabbed he could be disposed of quite easily, but either way was a losing proposition. Crandall and his Wicked Bimbo of the West had vanished into the green fog. So had Connie. There was only Michael now, and Mama, and the knife, and the pounding music and the swirling green lights and the enveloping smoke, and all of it added up to being in death's embrace for no damn reason, no damn cause.

"May I?" a voice asked.

The voice belonged to Phyllis in his blue Glenda gown and his diaphanous wings. He held his magic wand in his left hand, and his right hand was gently urging Mama back and away from Michael. He was attempting to cut in, the dear boy, which Michael considered infinitely preferable to getting cut up.

There was a sweaty, uncertain, awkward moment.

Mama naturally resisting any intrusion at such an intense juncture.

Phyllis naturally intent on dancing the light fantastic.

Michael naturally wishing to stay alive.

The scream shattered the hesitant moment. High and shrill and strident, it cut through the din as sharply as the word that defined it.

"*Knife!*"

Someone had seen the knife.

"He has a knife!"

Mama froze.

Suddenly the center of attention, unprepared for such concentrated focus, he smiled in what seemed abject apology, made a courtly Old World bow, his arm sweeping across his waist, and then immediately straightened up and turned to run. Phyllis was directly in his path. Mama hit him with his shoulder, knocking him over backward, his wings crushing as he hit the floor, his head banging against the waxed parquet, his legs flying up to reveal gartered blue stockings under his Glenda skirt. Mama pushed his way through a gaggle of chittering midgets dressed as Tin Men instead of Munchkins, all of them squealing indignantly as he shoved them aside. More people had seen the knife now. Someone shouted at Mama as he pushed his way off the dance floor, knocking over chairs and tables on his way to the exit doors, cursing in Spanish when he banged his knee against a busboy's cart, angrily slashing at the air with his knife. Michael was right behind him.

He wondered why he was doing this.

Chasing death this way.

He knew only that to find his way again, he had to follow Mama, follow him out of the green smoke and through the green exit doors that swung out onto the sidewalk, follow him into the cold night air past Curly and the waiting hopefuls, onto the yellow brick sidewalk on Greenwich Street, follow that to where it ended as abruptly as a shattered dream, pound along after Mama on a plain gray sidewalk now, past Rector and a girl in her underwear standing under a red-and-green neon sign that read GEORGE'S LUNCH, and then Carlisle where an armless man stood under an elegant white canopy lettered in black with the words HARRY'S AT THE AMERICAN EXCHANGE, and then Albany on the left, the street, not the city, and Thames on the right, the street, not the river, and another canopy stretching to the sidewalk, tan and brown this time, PAPOO'S ITALIAN CUISINE & BAR, and then O'HARA'S PUB on the corner of Cedar and Greenwich, the place names blurring with the street names until at last Greenwich dead-ended at Liberty and the World Trade Center loomed high into the night on the left. Michael was breathing hard, sweating in what was no longer fear but what had become certainty instead: he would follow Mama to his death. That was what this was all about. Michael dying.

There.

Up ahead there.

A black Cadillac limousine.

A China Doll car, he thought.

Connie, he thought.

But no, it was only Arthur Crandall stepping out of the car with a gun in his hand. And suddenly the limo resembled a hearse.

"Join us," Crandall said.

Michael figured he *still* didn't know how to use a gun. But as he moved toward him, Mama suddenly appeared again out of the night, and the knife was still in his hand, and besides, Michael could now see that Connie was inside the car.

Mama grinned.

"Yes?" he said.

Michael nodded.

The limo was quite cozy.

Mama and Michael on jump seats facing Connie on the left, Crandall in the middle, and Jessica on the right. Crandall still had the gun in his hand. Mama had the knife pressed into Michael's side between the third and fourth ribs on the left. About where his heart was, he guessed. Jessica looked somewhat bewildered. He wondered if she knew what was going on here. Did she still think he'd murdered someone? How big a story had Crandall sold her? Her eyes kept snapping from the gun in Crandall's hand to the knife in Mama's.

"This is Mama Rodriguez," Crandall said.

"Yes, we've had the pleasure," Michael said, and then realized that Crandall was introducing him to Jessica. Which meant she'd never met him before tonight. Again, he wondered how much she knew about what was going on. He also wondered how much he *himself* knew about what was going on.

"How do you do?" Jessica said.

She seemed even more bewildered now that she knew this man's name was Mama. A man with a thick black moustache? Mama? Her eyes now snapped from the knife in his hand to the moustache under his nose. Michael was more worried about the knife than he was about the moustache.

"You *did* say Mama?" Jessica said.

"For Mario Mateo," Mama said, and smiled at her like one of the banditos in *Treasure of the Sierra Madre*.

"I see," she said.

She did not look as if she saw anything at all. She looked as confused as Goldie Hawn in a hot air balloon over the city of Pittsburgh, Pennsylvania. Mama's fingers were dancing all over the handle of the knife, as if he simply could not wait to use it. This was a good movie back here in the backseat of the limousine. Beautiful Chinese girl looking gorgeous and alert. Beautiful blonde girl looking like a dumb bimbo, which she probably was, Albetha had been right. Fat motion-picture director with a Phi Beta Kappa key across his belly and a gun that looked like a Luger in his hand. Little Mexican bandito holding an open switchblade knife in *his* hand, coveting either Humphrey Bogart's high-topped shoes or the blonde's sparkly red ones. And sitting on one of the jump seats, the hayseed from Sarasota, Florida, the death-defying orange-grower who after the Tet Offensive in the year 1968, when he was but a mere eighteen years old—

"Let me tell you what I think happened," he said.

"No, let me tell you what's *going* to happen," Crandall said. "Jessica and I are going to get out of this car on St Luke's Place, and then Mama is going to take you and your lovely little friend . . ."

"I'm five-nine," Connie said.

". . . out to Long Island someplace . . ."

"And I don't want to go to Long Island," she said.

"The ocean breezes are very nice at this time of the year," Mama said. "You'll enjoy Jones Beach."

"Why are you sending them to Long Island?" Jessica asked,

puzzled. "Why don't we take them to the police instead? This man's a murderer!"

"Don't worry," Crandall said.

"What does that mean, don't worry? This person *killed* a person!"

"There are police on Long Island," Crandall said. "Don't worry."

"Why did you do that, Mr Barnes?" she asked, turning to him. "I'm an actress, as you know . . ."

"Yes."

"So I keep wondering about your motivation. Are you a crazy person? Is that it?"

"Ask your director," Michael said. "Ask him why he went to Charlie Nichols and asked him to hire two other actors . . ."

"Are you casting another movie?" Jessica asked.

"No, this wasn't a movie," Michael said. "This was Christmas Eve in a bar on – why'd Nichols give me your card?" he asked, turning suddenly to Crandall, who sat smiling and shaking his head as if Michael were certifiable.

Jessica, however, was not smiling.

Jessica was trying to understand what the hell was happening here.

Maybe she wasn't such a dumb bimbo after all.

"You *expected* me to go to the police, didn't you?" Michael said.

"He already knows the whole fucking thing," Mama said suddenly.

Jessica looked at him.

Michael did, in fact, think he already knew the whole fucking thing.

But this wasn't a movie. This wasn't the scene where the bad guys said, All right, Charlie, since we're going to kill you in the next five minutes, anyway, it won't do any harm telling you all about the terrible things we did. Nor was this the scene where the hero was playing for time waiting for the police to kick in the door, during which suspenseful moments he could explain to the bad guys exactly why they had committed all those gruesome murders. This was real life, such as it was, here in the backseat of this limousine, and the way Michael figured it, Mama was ready to make his move.

236

Dumb blonde bimbo notwithstanding, Mama was ready. Even if it meant throwing away the blonde with the bathwater. The blonde meant nothing to Mama. Mama wanted home free. Mama had gone into this to kill two birds with one stone. Get paid for ridding himself of a competitor and take over his business besides. Now he had both stones in his back pocket and a switchblade knife in his hand and the only thing standing between him and prosperity was a dumb fuck from Sarasota, Florida. And his Chink girlfriend. So naturally, they both had to go. That was the way Rodriguez thought. That was the way to become successful in America. And if the blonde accidentally happened to become a witness to something she shouldn't have seen, why then the blonde would have to go, too, and Mama would later give her red shoes to his *own* mama. The way Michael figured it, Mama was a businessman. And business was business. And 'twas the season to be jolly.

On the other hand, Crandall was now in over his head. Michael guessed that Mama was supposed to have done his job and then disappear into the woodwork again. Supply Crandall with a body, that was all. Charlie Nichols must have told him that he knew someone who could pick up a body for them. His crack dealer. A man named Mario Mateo Rodriguez, familiarly called Mama. No questions asked. Six thousand big ones and he'd deliver a corpse. Crandall was the sort of man who wouldn't want to know where the corpse was coming from. This was commerce. He needed a dead body. Period. He did not want to know about murder. He preferred believing that Mama would find a dead derelict in a Bowery hallway. Or in a garbage can behind McDonald's. No great loss to the city. Here's the money Charlie promised you, six thousand bucks out of the nine I safely drew from the bank, no questions asked, the other three already gone to Charlie and his fellow thespians for their contribution to the scheme. It was nice not knowing you, Mama, good-bye and good luck.

"Mr Crandall?"

The chauffeur's voice, coming over the loudspeaker.

Crandall threw a switch.

"Yes?"

"We're approaching Houston, sir. Will you and the lady still be getting out on St Luke's?"

"Yes, please," Crandall said.

In Vietnam, Michael had simply quit. He had told that colonel to go fuck himself, sir, and he had meant it. He had quit. Because after the way Andrew died, there was no sense pursuing this dumb fucking war any further. This war was all about people doing unspeakably horrible things to themselves and to other people. If he had been the one who'd picked up that baby, if he had been the one who'd reached for that little girl a second before Andrew did, then *his* hands would have been blown off, *his* chest would have blossomed with blood, Andrew would have carried *him* through the jungle, and *he* would have been the one who was loaded onto that chopper in a body bag, dead. The obscenity had been as much in the randomness of death as in the singularly callous act that had preceded it, the wiring of a baby, yet *another* random victim. The whole fucking thing was a lottery, and Michael had wanted nothing more to do with it.

He wanted nothing more to do with *this*, either.

But on Christmas Eve, for no reason and no cause, he had been chosen at random to take part in yet another obscenity.

The promotion of a goddamn *movie*.

So he went for Mama's knife.

17

A lot of people got hurt in that limousine. Including the driver. Who'd been nowhere near that slashing knife. A couple of people got hurt *outside* the limousine, too. What happened was that he had her up against this brick wall in this sort of little alleyway between two buildings on Houston Street and he had his hand up under her skirt and they were both breathing very hard and all of a sudden there was a screeching sound and lights flashing and he thought at first that perhaps he'd had an orgasm since he was only thirteen years old or perhaps *she'd* had one since she was only twelve or perhaps *both* of them'd had one together because that was when the earth was supposed to move. But instead it was only a big mother of a black Cadillac jumping the curb and coming up onto the sidewalk and almost into the mouth of the alley, forcing him to fall down on top of her with his hand still up under her skirt, causing him to break his wrist and causing her to lose her virginity, for which dire injuries their separate attorneys said they could collect big money for damages.

This was what Tony the Bear Orso told Michael in his room at St Vincent's Hospital. It was still Boxing Day. Eight o'clock in the morning. From the window of his room, Michael could see a rooftop Christmas tree, its branches tossing wildly in the fierce wind.

"It was a terrible accident, sir," Orso said. "The driver told me everybody was screaming and kicking in the backseat and yelling in Spanish and Chinese and grabbing for guns and knives and kicking at the window separating them from where he was sitting,

239

so naturally he lost control, just like you and me would've."

"Naturally," Michael said.

"When a person is wielding a sharp instrument," Orso said, "the backseat of a limousine can become a very small place."

The instrument had indeed been sharp.

In the Operating Room, when Michael came out of the anesthesia, the doctor told him he'd been slashed and stabbed eighteen times. He said it was a miracle that Michael was still alive, since one of the slash wounds was dangerously close to the jugular and another had almost severed his windpipe.

"Is Connie all right?" Michael asked him.

The doctor did not know who Connie was. He thought Michael was hallucinating, and asked the nurse to give him a sedative.

"Is Connie all right?" Michael asked Orso.

"Yes, she is a brave Chinese person," Orso said. "When she saw Mama carving you up like a Christmas turkey, she right away jumped on him. She got cut herself, too, on the hand, but she's okay."

"Where is she?"

"I don't know where she is now, sir. I talked to her in the Emergency Room."

"Does she know where I am?"

"I don't know if she knows where you are or not. The last she saw of you was when they were wheeling you upstairs to the O.R. She herself was bleeding, and they were bandaging Crandall's head, and the blonde was still yelling at him. There was a good deal of confusion, sir."

"Yes," Michael said.

"Yes. But everybody's okay now, including Mama. Who, if you'd have killed him, sir, the city would have given you a ticker-tape parade on Fifth Avenue. Which, as you may know, sir, is *up*town."

"Where is he now?"

"Mama? Down the hall, with a police officer outside his door. Not that he is going anyplace. He went through the window."

"What window?"

"That separated the back of the limo from the driver. Crashed through it headfirst when the car jumped the curb and almost hit them two kids in the alley. You should see him, sir. He looks like the Invisible Man all bandaged up."

240

"Good," Michael said.

"Yeah, fuck him," Orso agreed.

On the rooftop, the Christmas tree danced in the wind.

"Why were they bandaging Crandall's head?" Michael asked.

"Because the blonde hit him with one of her sparkly red shoes."

"She's good at that," Michael said.

"Yes, very good. She put two holes in his head like she was wielding a balpeen hammer instead of a high-heeled shoe."

"Did she say why?"

"Because she suddenly realized," Orso said.

"Realized what?"

"That something was fishy, but she didn't know what. All she knew was Crandall had a gun in his hand and Mama was cutting you to ribbons and blood was flying all over the car and the Chinese girl was throwing herself on Mama and yelling what sounded like orders to the kitchen, so she figured she might as well take off her shoe and hit Crandall on the head with it. She ain't very bright, you know."

Michael nodded.

"What I got here," Orso said, "which I will probably forget and leave on your bed and have to come back for later, is a transcript of the Q and A we done with Crandall after they bandaged his head and we got him up the squadroom. That little cockroach Mama wouldn't tell us nothing, he's a pro, the son of a bitch, he knows his rights. In fact, he threatened to sue us for false arrest, the little bastard. But Crandall spilled his guts. Without out a lawyer present, no less. *He* thought he was being slick as baby shit, but he gave us enough to hang him. I was thinking that if I should leave this here on your bed, sir, because I'm so absentminded, and if you should happen to glance through it, I know you won't mention it to Crandall because then his lawyers'll say his rights were violated. Every lawyer in this city is lookin' for a rights loophole. You get a guy he shot his grandmother, his grandfather, his twin sisters, his mother, his uncle, and his pet goldfish, the lawyer looks for a rights loophole. Which, by the way, sir, Charlie Bonano sends his regards."

"Where is he now?"

"Out on bail, of course. He read all about you killing Crandall in the newspaper, and he called me up to say if we caught you I should tell you never mind the ten bucks. He also said you couldn'ta done it, which I already knew."

"How'd you know?"

"Because nobody's so dumb he's gonna kill a person and then take the person's business card to the police, no offense, sir. Not even somebody from Florida. But Crandall was figuring . . . well, it's all in the transcript here, if I should absentmindedly leave it behind and if you should happen to read through it before I remember and come back for it in about ten, fifteen minutes."

"Thank you," Michael said.

"I'll ask around outside about Connie, case she's wandering the hospital lookin' for you. It's a big hospital."

"Thank you," Michael said again.

"Oops, I'll bet I'm gonna forget this fuckin' Q and A," Orso said, and tossed a blue binder onto the bed, and walked out of the room.

Michael reached for the binder.

His right wrist was bandaged. He wondered if there were stitches under the bandage. He wondered if he'd been stitched together like Frankenstein's monster. He wondered what his face looked like. He wondered if Mama had got to his face. If so, he wondered if Connie would think he looked okay. He hoped that she would.

He opened the blue binder.

There was a sheaf of photocopied typewritten pages inside it. Michael began reading. The Q & A had taken place earlier this morning, at precisely twelve minutes to six, in the office of someone named Lieutenant James Curran at the First Precinct. Present were the lieutenant, Detective/Second Grade Anthony Robert Orso, Detective/Third Grade Mary Agnes O'Brien, and an Assistant District Attorney named Leila Moscowitz. The lieutenant advised Crandall of his rights under Miranda-Escobedo, and then turned the questioning over to the A.D.A.

Q: Mr Crandall, I'd like to clarify some of these points you've already discussed with the two detectives who responded at the scene of the accident, namely . . . uh . . . Detectives . . . uh . . .

A: (from Detective Orso) Orso. Anthony Orso.

Q: Yes, and Ms O'Brien.

A: (from Detective O'Brien) *Mrs* O'Brien.

Q: Mrs O'Brien, forgive me. May we proceed in that way, Mr Crandall? Would that be all right with you?

A: Yes, certainly.

Q: Very well then. As I understand it, when Detectives Orso and O'Brien arrived at the scene, you were in possession of a Walther P-38, nine-millimeter Parabellum automatic pistol, is that correct?

A: Not in possession of it.

Q: In your hand, though, wasn't it?

A: Well, yes. If you want to get technical.

Q: Is this the pistol you had in your hand?

A: Yes, it looks like the pistol.

Q: Is it your pistol?

A: It's a pistol I had in my hand at the time of the accident.

Q: Do you have a license for this pistol?

A: No, I do not.

Q: How did you come by this pistol, Mr Crandall?

A: I have no idea. I was getting hit on the head with a high-heeled shoe and there was a pistol in my hand.

Q: Are you saying you don't know how it got in your hand?

A: Mr Rodriguez must have put it there.

Q: Put the pistol in your hand.

A: Yes.

Q: By Mr Rodriguez, do you mean Mr Mario Mateo Rodriguez, alias Mama Rodriguez?

A: Well, I'm not sure he'd appreciate your using the word "alias."

Q: But Mama *is* his alias, isn't it?

A: A great many people choose names that they use for professional purposes, such as actors and writers and occasionally dentists. They do not call these names . . .

Q: Dentists?

A: Oh, yes.

Q: But Mr Rodriguez isn't an actor or a dentist, he's a gangster.

A: Oh, I don't know about that.

Q: He had a criminal record in his native Colombia, and he's been arrested twice in the United States for trafficking in controlled substances.

A: I wouldn't know about that, either.

Q: Well, when you hired him, didn't you . . . ?

A: *Hired* him? Ho ho ho, let's slow down a bit, shall we? *I* hired Rodriguez?

Q: Isn't that what you told Detectives Orso and O'Brien?

A: That was when I was still dizzy. That was just a few minutes after the accident.

Q: No, that was at a quarter past four this morning. Which was forty minutes *after* the accident.

A: That may be so, but . . .

Q: And it's now ten minutes to six.

A: My how the time does fly.

Q: Mr Crandall, I'm going to remind you that the conversation you had with Detectives Orso and O'Brien . . .

A: I might add, by the way, that I don't think it seemly for a police officer to be questioning a person while she's sitting in provocative underwear. I'd like to say that for the record, if you please.

Q: It is noted for the record. But I was saying that the conversation . . .

A: Especially an officer who could stand to lose a few pounds.

Q: I was saying that the conversation you had with them – and you were aware of this, Mr Crandall, you gave them your permission – the conversation was being taped. Just as *this* conversation is now being taped. Again, with your permission.

A: My, how very state-of-the-art we are.

Q: And I have the typewritten transcript taken from that tape, Mr Crandall, I am holding it right here in my hand. And on this transcript, you told the detectives that you had hired Mr Rodriguez to requisition – that is your exact language, Mr Crandall – to requisition a body for you. A dead body. A corpse. Isn't that what you told them?

A: Well, yes.

Q: Then you *did* hire him.

A: No, Charlie hired him. Listen, if we're going to get *this* technical here . . .

Q: Yes, we are.

A: Then maybe I *ought* to have a lawyer.

Q: If you'd like a lawyer . . .

A: Why do I need a lawyer? I can take care of myself just fine, thank you.

Q: If you want a lawyer, you're entitled to one. Just say the . . .

A: Dickens was right, we should first kill all the lawyers.

Q: It was Shakespeare. And the exact quote was "The first thing we do, let's kill all the lawyers." And I'm a lawyer, Mr Crandall.

A: I *still* don't want one.

Q: Fine. May we continue, please?

A: Please.

Q: Did you or did you not hire Mama Rodriguez to . . . ?

A: Charlie Nichols hired him.

Q: How did that come about, can you tell me?

A: It was all Charlie's idea. We were talking about how it would be nice if the picture got some column space . . .

Q: By the picture . . . ?

A: My new picture. *Winter's Chill*.

Q: Yes?

A: Some column space to counteract what we were afraid might be adverse critical reaction when it opened – the similarity to *Gaslight*, you know, what the critics might *perceive*, in their abysmal ignorance, as a similarity to *Gaslight*.

Q: Yes?

A: And Charlie recalled an incident that had taken place several years back when this woman fell from a roof and she had a copy of Meyer Levin's novel *Kiss of the Spider Woman* in her . . .

Q: It was *Ira* Levin. And the novel was *Kiss Me, Deadly*.

A: (from Detective O'Brien) Excuse me, please, but I think it was *A Kiss Before Dying* and Carole Landis was in the movie.

A: (from Detective Orso) You're thinking of *Farewell, My Lovely*, by Dashiell Hammond.

A: (from Lieutenant Curran) "It was easy." That's the last line of the book.

A: (from Detective O'Brien) Which book is that, Loot?

A: (from Lieutenant Curran) The one where he shoots the
broad in the belly.

A: (from Mr Crandall) You'll forgive me, but neither the title
nor the author has anything whatever to do with the
point of my story.

Q: What *is* the point of your story?

A: The point is that in the novel the woman is about to get
pushed off the roof, and in real life a woman actually *fell*
off the roof with a copy of the novel in her hand and it
made headlines all over the country. So Charlie said,
"Wouldn't it be terrific if something like that happened to
Winter's Chill?" and I said, "No such luck," and Charlie
said, "Why does it have to be *luck*?" and that's how the
whole thing came about.

Q: What whole thing?

A: Hiring Rodriguez. Who was Charlie's crack dealer and
who Charlie thought would know where to find a dead body.

Q: And did he find one?

A: Yes.

Q: Julian Rainey's body, isn't that so?

A: I have no idea whose body it was. Mama supplied the
body.

Q: And you supplied the identification to put on the body.

A: Well, that was the whole idea.

Q: Tell us what the whole idea was.

A: To make it appear that someone had murdered me. And
then for me to show up alive, contradicting the fact.
And to have the mystery continue through the opening of
the film on the fifth. To generate publicity for the film,
you see.

Q: But, of course, Mr Rodriguez didn't simply *find* a corpse,
did he?

A: I have no idea where he . . .

Q: He *caused* a corpse, didn't he?

A: I don't know where you got that idea.

Q: We got it from a woman named Alice Chaffee whom we
found in a red fox coat tied up with the cord from a General
Electric steam iron in a warehouse downtown.

A: Oh.

Q: Where there was something close to a million dollars' worth of crack in an open Mosler safe.

A: Oh.

Q: And something like five hundred thousand dollars' worth of stolen goods elsewhere on the floor.

A: I see.

Q: She told us that Mr Rodriguez hired her to kill Julian Rainey.

A: Well, that's not what *I* hired him to do.

Q: I thought Charlie Nichols hired him.

A: Well, yes. I mean indirectly. All *I* asked him to do was *find* a dead body.

Q: Where? On the street? In the park . . . ?

A: Wherever dead bodies *are*.

Q: In the trees? In a garbage can behind McDonald's?

A: I'm glad you find this so amusing, Ms Moscowitz.

Q: *Mrs* Moscowitz. And I find it quite serious. Whose idea was it to blame the murder on Michael Barnes?

A: Mine. But there was no harm in that. It was just a way to keep it going. To keep the headlines rolling. When he went to the police with his story about having been robbed – and showed them my *card*, no less – there'd be headlines all over again. And then while he was being investigated, there'd be more headlines. And when he was cleared, there'd be headlines again. And meanwhile the picture would have opened and it wouldn't matter *what* the critics said about it.

Q: So you chose Mr Barnes as your fall guy . . .

A: Oh, it didn't have to be him. It could have been *anyone*. He simply presented himself.

Q: Popped up, so to speak.

A: Well, yes.

Q: And refused to lie down again.

A: Well.

Q: Which is why Mr Rodriguez ordered *his* murder as well.

A: I don't know anything about that.

Q: Alice Chaffee *does*.

A: That's *her* problem. *And* Mama's, I would suppose.

Q: *Your* problem is that you ordered the *first* murder, Mr Crandall. You're the one who set the whole thing in . . .

A: I did not order a *murder*. I ordered a *corpse*! And anyway, it was Charlie's idea. He was the one who contacted Mama. I had nothing to do with it.

Q: Alice Chaffee says Mama paid her four thousand dollars for the job. Who gave Mama that money?

A: I have no idea.

Q: Did Charlie Nichols give him that money?

A: He must have.

Q: Why? It was *your* movie, why would Charlie . . . ?

A: I don't know anything about any of this. Charlie came up with a good idea. And he followed through on it. If someone got killed because of what Charlie did, I certainly am not re—

Q: All Charlie's idea, huh?

A: Yes. I had nothing to do with anyone getting killed! I was trying to save my movie. If Charlie was alive, he'd—

Q: Yes?

A: Nothing.

Q: He'd what?

A: Nothing.

Q: Is Charlie *dead*, Mr Crandall?

A: I don't know what Charlie is.

Q: Well, as a matter of fact, he *is* dead, Mr Crandall. But how did you know that?

A: I don't know anything at all about Charlie's condition, dead or alive.

Q: Then you don't know he was killed with a P-38 Walther nine-millimeter Parabellum automatic pistol.

A: I have nothing more to say.

Q: Ballistics will have something more to say, I'm sure.

A: It was all Charlie's idea. If Charlie's dead, that's too bad, but . . .

Q: I thought you had nothing more to say.

A: All I have to say is that it was Charlie's idea.

Q: Except for pinning the murder on Michael Barnes. *That* was *your* idea.

A: Yes.

Q: Why'd you change the script, Mr Crandall?

A: *Why?*

Q: Please tell us.

A: Because I'm a *director*!
Q: Oh.
A: Yes.

Michael sensed her presence before he looked up.

Knew she'd be there.

Standing in the doorway.

Her right wrist was bandaged where Mama had cut her. There was a smile on her face. She stepped into the room. Into a bar of sunshine lying in a crooked rectangle on the floor. The sunlight touched her hair, touched her face.

"They have you listed as dead," she said. "But Detective Orso told me you weren't."

"I'm glad I'm not," he said.

"Me, too," she said, and came to the bed.

He would have to call his mother, let her know he was still alive. Tell her he'd met a wonderful Chinese girl he wanted to marry. Mom? Are you there, Mom? Please take your head out of the oven, Mom.

"Let me see your cute little face," Connie said, and sat on the edge of the bed, and cupped his face between her hands, and turned it this way and that, searching it. "I was so afraid he'd cut your face," she said. "But you look beautiful. Could I kiss you?"

"We'll have to ask the nurse," he said.

"No, I don't think we have to," she said.

Mom? he would say. I'm alive, Mom.

I'm alive again.

A List of Ed McBain Titles Available from Mandarin

While every effort is made to keep prices low, it is sometimes necessary to increase prices at short notice. Mandarin Paperbacks reserves the right to show new retail prices on covers which may differ from those previously advertised in the text or elsewhere.

The prices shown below were correct at the time of going to press.

☐	7493 0882 6	**Doll**	£3.99
☐	7493 0289 5	**Downtown**	£3.99
☐	7493 0883 4	**Fuzz**	£3.99
☐	7493 0898 2	**Like Love**	£3.99
☐	7493 0901 6	**Sadie when she Died**	£3.99
☐	7493 0596 7	**Vespers**	£3.99
☐	7493 0774 9	**Widows**	£3.99

All these books are available at your bookshop or newsagent, or can be ordered direct from the publisher. Just tick the titles you want and fill in the form below.

Mandarin Paperbacks, Cash Sales Department, PO Box 11, Falmouth, Cornwall TR10 9EN.

Please send cheque or postal order, no currency, for purchase price quoted and allow the following for postage and packing:

UK including BFPO £1.00 for the first book, 50p for the second and 30p for each additional book ordered to a maximum charge of £3.00.

Overseas including Eire £2 for the first book, £1.00 for the second and 50p for each additional book thereafter.

NAME (Block letters) ....

ADDRESS ....

....

☐ I enclose my remittance for ....

☐ I wish to pay by Access/Visa Card Number

Expiry Date